Praise for the *Raining Thorns* series:

'This book is SO funny. It has a classic British fantasy-comedy feel in the style of Monty Python and the Holy Grail (a film that I adore), yet it's still modern and easy to read. The writing style feels so refreshing.' - *Jae Waller, author of the* Call of the Rift *series*

'Overall this book was a whole lot of fun to read. There is a fantastic humorous undertone throughout the story and I love how it is capable of pointing out the absurdism of a situation in which our characters find themselves in while never detracting from the events themselves... The story is so well written, that you dive in and just want to keep going. There were many twists and turns throughout that kept things fresh and interesting.' – *Elizabeth Daly, author of* Legacy Bound

'In short, if you like fantasy, you'll enjoy this. If you like British humor, you'll love it.' – *Cat Bowser, author of* The Second Star *trilogy*

'If you like comedy, fantasy, and political intrigue, definitely pick up this book, it will be well worth your time.' – *jamsworldofbooks, Goodreads reviewer*

'There is no better combination than high fantasy and comedy. If you're a fan of Terry Pratchett or Douglas Adams, then I highly recommend giving it a read.' – *Rhelna, Goodreads reviewer*

'100% it was fun, thrilling, hilarious and emotional. I've never read a novel so quickly. I was so gripped I couldn't put it down, and read the bulk of it within a week. Infectious humor and storytelling.' – *David B, Goodreads reviewer*

'Monty Python vibes?? Here for it. This story made me literally laugh out loud so many times. I love how this author made you care about each character early on but my favorite HAS to be Qattren. Read it and trust me you'll know why!' – *Stephanie, Goodreads reviewer*

Books by Donna Shannon:

The Raining Thorn Series

Rosethorn
Finding Retribution
Godly Enlightenment

Book 3
The Raining Thorns Series

Godly Enlightenment

Donna Shannon

Copyright © 2025 by Donna Shannon

Cover, Maps and Interior Illustrations by © 2025 Donna Shannon

Donna Shannon asserts the moral right to be identified as the author of this work.

All rights reserved. No part of this publication may be reproduced, distributed, or transmitted in any form or by any means, including photocopying, recording, or other electronic or mechanical methods, without the prior written permission of the publisher.

The story, names, characters, and incidents portrayed in this production are fictitious. Any resemblance to actual persons (living or deceased), places, buildings, and products is coincidental and should not be inferred as intentional.

Hardcover ISBN: 978-1-7394337-7-2
Paperback ISBN: 978-1-7394337-6-5

1st Edition 2025

For Ray, Esther and the rest of the Crüe crew, for putting up with my unwanted loitering in the comedians' VIP area.

For Dawn (may she heckle on in heaven).

And for fellow authors Elizabeth Daly and Chris Carton, who championed this series always, even though it isn't sexy enough for Bookstagram.

Truphoria

8

PROLOGUE

The Chapel of the Creys' Keep, the first week of summer, two weeks before the Night of Raining Thorns, 1345 YM

'Your Eminence!'

Abraham Furlong pivoted in his seat.

The sun left an echo of light behind, floating into the windows in a cobalt haze. It rebounded from wall to mahogany wall of His Eminence's office, illuminating enough layers of lacquer to cost the equivalent of an entire city's church donations.

Which it did. His Eminence knew how to put a donation bucket to good use. If it couldn't purchase world peace and love, then mahogany panelling would do just as well.

He turned his back to the matching writing desk by the back wall. An eight-year-old boy hovered across the room, a wraith cloaked in grey linen, his fingertips lingering on the doorframe – Joseph, his nephew.

'It's late,' His Eminence said in greeting.

The child bobbed up and down. His grey shift pooled at his feet for a moment, rippling atop the long floorboards.

'Eminence, I found something.' He displayed a bundle of paper to the balding priest.

Furlong rose, his crimson robes swishing around him. The priest flicked the makeshift book into one hand, extended it a foot away from his face, and started reading with a squint.

The paper scratched his palm, the edges roughly torn. He glowered at large pencilled letters, written by a heavy hand, over the top of what appeared to be gilded illumination – the leaves had been ripped from a copy of Salator's Texts, the priest discovered with horror, and bound with bootlaces after being written over with, with—

He scanned the awkward, crooked lines of text in bemusement.

A children's story, by the looks of it.

The pages wilted under his scrutiny. His rheumy gaze fell on Joseph. 'Where did you find this, child?'

'In the vestry, Father. I was brought there by Father Giery, but I found this by the windowsill and thought I ought to bring it to you immediately.'

Wise, thought His Eminence. Furlong would rather carry a fully-grown elephant across Serpus's diameter than be an eight-year-old novice alone with Father Giery. He wouldn't be surprised or at all ashamed if Joseph had vandalised the holy scripts himself just to get away from him.

Nothing to be done about the man, he sighed to himself. He was a cousin of the Creys, so he had to stay. Pity, really. The killing of the altar boys aside, Giery made a fine preacher. His fearsome baritone was matched only by that of His Eminence himself.

Furlong inspected the binding. Three tiny crosses ripped across the margin with the bootlace inserted into each, woven together to form a short book. It was painstaking work, if a bit haphazard.

The childlike pencilwork meandered clumsily atop the Text's pristine intricacy. The priest could see where the charcoal had been blunted and re-blunted across the pages, the author pressing down so hard it tore the paper. The story was frantic, as though relaying a precious piece of information in fear of it being forgotten. And yet it was left in the store cupboard.

His Eminence frowned at it in silence.

Joseph cleared his throat. 'Shall I go back to Father Giery?'

'Good lord, no,' Furlong said, aghast. He quickly remembered himself and cleared his throat. 'A boy needs his sleep,' he amended in a demure intone. 'Head to your bunk, I'll explain to Father Giery about your absence.'

And about the consequences should His Eminence's nephew be found near the vestry again, he added internally with venom.

Joseph swallowed and bowed, turning to leave.

The priest examined him a moment before turning back to the manuscript. It was the work of a child. It couldn't be anything but. No adult in the church of Serpus had spelling that bad.

And any story written so hurriedly and bound so carefully was a story worth paying attention to.

Something niggled in the depths of his memory. He squinted at the manuscript some more, trying to remember. There had been a rumour around the acolytes of late, something about a clairvoyant. But who? A monk? A nun? One of Giery's victims? His Eminence leaned a palm on either side of the mangled illumination, willing it to reveal its author somehow.

He finally heaved a great sigh. He'd never find this child. If it was written in the vestry, there was a high chance the author was in Father Giery's open grave by now. Unless…

His Eminence's eyes narrowed.

… it was one of Giery's special children. Those few who were too well-off or important to kill afterwards…

His gaze shot immediately to Joseph's wake.

~

Mortimer squirmed out of the narrow window beside his bed. His sandals crunched the gravel underfoot, causing him to wince.

Dusk reduced the bright flora of the castle grounds to a dull greyscale. The cool twilight wind lifted goose bumps along his arms. His shadow erupted from that of the chapel wall, protruding in a rotund lump from the sharp edge across the gravel path. Mortimer flattened himself against the concrete wall, the bulb of his shadow's head vanishing.

Don't be seen, he chanted to himself, *don't be seen*. The only candlelight came from His Eminence's office at the other side of the chapel, but he couldn't be too careful. The only indication of life in the grounds of the Creys' Keep chirped their harmlessness from the flowerbeds sprawled ahead of him, a light skitter on the outskirts of hearing. He kept a wary eye for human-shaped silhouettes. So far, there were none to be seen.

Mort shoved himself to his feet. Kicking the noisy sandals from his soles, he sprinted to the edge of the palace grounds.

Gravel stung his bare feet. Darkness blanketed the spiralling flowerbeds and verdant lawns. He squeezed his eyelids closer, straining to discern his path. Only the vague shapes of the fortress walls and a faint light from the back gate were apparent as the eight-year-old boy forced his eyes to adjust to the gloom. As he finally clutched the inner wall, Mort held his breath.

The distant sounds of celebration floated out of the keep an acre away from him – another party for Prince Seth's engagement. It was all the clergy could talk about for weeks. Even His Eminence had put up an appearance. Usually, he dwelled in the basilica in the centre of Serpus, but he came to the palace himself to bless the prince's betrothal personally. A pity nobody had let Father Giery know. The archpriest's presence was always a relief for Mort. Father Giery tended to be on his best behaviour when superiors visited.

Mort cast a lingering gaze at the keep. His entire family dwelled inside.

Mort couldn't go in there. Last time he ran away from the chapel, his father had had him beaten for telling lies about Father Giery. His Uncle Theo might have believed him if his horrid stepmother hadn't found Mort first.

A familiar, awful swelling began in his eyes and throat. He clenched them both shut. No. No tears for her.

His mother would have believed him. But the last time he saw her was when his father had given him to the church three years ago, and a year after that she was dead.

His chest swelled next, this time with a violent pinch. He punched the wall with one small fist. It burned and he gave a sharp gasp as blood dribbled down his wrist. Mort wiped it on the end of his grey shift. A small cut opened on his knuckle, weeping bulbous inky droplets. He sucked it, trying to stem the flow.

Ensuring that the serenity of the grounds remained, he took off for the gate at a sprint, the grass soft against his chapped soles.

Faint conversation hummed from the battlements above the open portcullis.

'Beer's gone to piss these days,' a guard commented.

Mort crept under the grating, keeping an eye out for horsemen. No doubt the gate awaited the return of late-evening hunters.

A *pfftrit* erupted overhead, shortly followed by a tiny plume of liquid. Mort ducked to the wall with a disgusted grimace. The guard flung a nonchalant glance in Mort's direction. The head pulled back a second later, indifferent.

Mort fled into the woods.

His toes sank into the mud underfoot, but he ran regardless. Undergrowth crackled and crunched with each step, but he paid no notice to the noise now. He listed to the left and shook his head, correcting himself. Spots crept in from the edges of his vision, obscuring the faint outlines of the foliage ahead. He'd been locked into the vestry after today's 'confession' with Father Giery – this time, he thought with faint satisfaction, for leaving a bible-shaped dent in Giery's forehead mid-coitus. Mort's supper had been thrown to the king's dogs and he'd only been released half an hour ago in time for lights-out. He was starving.

Blood caked his fingers now, the tips still stained with charcoal. He'd had another vision again – an important one. He hoped he would remember it later. Already the details began to taper away like ringlets from a scissor-edge, fluttering into oblivion.

His vision – of the un-prophetic kind – wavered. His foot caught a protruding root and he tilted face-first into the muck. As the white spots faded from behind his eyelids, he discovered his left temple was caked in blood too.

His pulse pounded in his ears and across his ribs. Panic began to join it, spidering through his limbs and into his ears.

He could see Father Giery finding him in the woods, *tsk, tsk, deary me, what are we doing out here, then? Snuck out for a stroll, have we? Must be time for confession…*

And then the door would close and the invasion would begin, over and over, all while Mort knelt perfectly still, his consciousness hovering slightly outside of his own body because the inside of an eight-year-old body wasn't a safe place to be when you were given to Father Giery… he could see it clearly, so very, very clearly…

He tucked his knees into his chest and squeezed his eyes shut, trying to block out the impending future, just for now—

Until a different future arrived with an immense *BANG*!

Mort's eyes burst open. His surroundings were no different: black branches and leaves dappled with a ghost of the day's light. All silent but for the slight rustling of foliage.

Inside his head however, a blaze had erupted.

Bricks scattered around him, soaring into the air. Men screamed in pain and fury, soldiers fought beasts between the trees, huge, black animals with massive teeth, all around a huge crater beside the ruins of a castle, the grounds littered with rose petals and clutches of blue flames…

Mort swallowed the terror rising in his chest. This was about to happen. He knew it. He was as sure about this as he was about the certainty of more 'confession' with Giery. Except…

Giery felt imminent. This new event felt somewhat distant. Mort couldn't explain how. A glance around confirmed his thoughts: there was no castle to be seen for miles, apart from the Creys' and he would have recognised that one anywhere, ruins or not.

If he was to be present at the events to come, he had a long way to travel. But there was no guarantee his father wouldn't send guards out after him before he got there.

Another vision appeared to disagree.

He was hiding inside the ruins. Mort cowered beneath a corner of cracked ceiling, his eyes squeezed shut as though not being able to see the horrible beasts would result in the vice versa…

And then King Theo burst through a knot of fighting men, axe raised high above one shoulder. His armour gleamed a bright blue, echoing the flames outside. It contrasted with his dark red beard – which swung towards him sharply with a bellow.

'BOY! TO ME! QUICKLY NOW!'

The vision melted away, swiftly replaced by another.

It was Arthur Stibbons' Street, brimming with throngs of citizens – in a scene of bustling interest rather than terror, thankfully. He recognised the cobbled lanes behind him, in the shape of a man lying down: the 'torso', 'legs', half an 'arm' veering off to the right, and in the head, a line of gallows.

An elderly Father Giery at the end of the noose, swinging in the breeze…

Mort glanced down at himself. He was taller, he realised, his shoulders slightly broader and his novice's robe replaced with trousers, a plain shirt and a jerkin. He was an adult – an *adult*, he thought in awe. He never thought the old bastard would let him live that long.

Clarity washed over him as the vision washed away. If he found the ruined castle and his uncle, King Theo would believe him. Giery would get away with it for a while, but he'd find the gallows eventually. Mort would be an adult. Giery would be caught in the end. The wait would be worth it, because King Theo would protect Mort. Mort would be safe.

These visions were different. They had been random before now – all true, it turned out, even the one about Sister India giving birth unexpectedly – but never anything directly involving Mort. This was something he could change, prevent. He was given a choice.

He could turn back to Father Giery and accept the punishment for running away. It would be horrifying, but at least he knew he could survive it.

Or he could throw himself into battle, find Uncle Theo, and escape the tyranny of the church to watch Father Giery hang for the horrors inflicted on Mort and the dozens of other children—

And Mort would live the rest of his days as a servant, happy, unmolested, useful to society – he'll own chickens, Mort saw in bewilderment, and change his name, and live in a cottage a mile into the woods, work for a man called Jimmy, maybe have a family one day—

Mort didn't know why he would want to do any of those things, but 'happy' and 'unmolested' sounded good. He wondered what he'd change his name to.

'Jon' sounded quite good.

He wondered where this battle was going to be. What castle did he see? Where was it? How was he going to get there?

He supposed there was only one way to find out.

In the morning, he told himself sleepily.

Jon rose to his feet and wandered around, looking for a place to sleep.

~

PART ONE: RETURNING

I

n a corridor, cold and frightened, the man, mid-thirties, squinted into the darkness.

Steady breathing echoed up from below him.

He strode down the corridor, his jaw tight. A level concrete floor clacked with each booted step. The fingers of his right hand tracing the bare bricks beside him, he treaded carefully, his eyes slowly focussing in the gloom. He wracked his brains. Nothing. He had no single idea how he came to be in this corridor. He didn't even remember where he had last been: his only memory was a twilit forest with a small fire in the centre of it, burning softly. He couldn't even remember his own name.

His free hand flailed in front of him as he manoeuvred blindly along the hallway.

One sole found the edge of a step during his careful pacing. He discovered a set of stairs at the end of the corridor, a banister lightly touching his right elbow. Slipping his fingers down the wall to meet it, he gripped the banister and descended with care into the darkness. As he felt his way down with the toe of one boot, faint music floated out from below, as though from a jewellery box…

His foot landed heavily on level flooring, looking for another step.

He started, looking around.

A handful of candles surrounding him revealed a large square room. This

16

room, too, appeared to be empty.

No breathing. No jewellery boxes. Nothing.

He wondered how long he had been wandering around this place. Was it an hour? An evening? A day? Weeks? Seasons? It felt like forever. He briefly entertained the idea that his entire life had been spent in this darkness, but he vaguely recalled having a wife and children somewhere.

He froze and opened his ears, listening for heavy breathing.

It was only as he stalked to the other end of the room in search for a door that he heard the music rise in volume and – he strained his ears to make sure – the laboured breathing back from the direction he came.

He slowly pivoted, blinking repeatedly in the gloom, searching vainly for an outline of a person who was not there. He approached the stairs, listening to his own footsteps clicking on the tiles and the music, and the breathing…

It came closer and closer with each footstep before, abruptly, stopping.

He glanced in all directions.

Hot breath landed on the back of his neck.

He gasped involuntarily and swung around, his eyes wide.

King Theo Crey stood before him, his clothes charred, his face burnt, his eyes bloodshot.

'You're in for it now, boy,' he said. The king smelled strongly of burnt pork.

The man trembled, his lungs working overtime, echoing the heavy breathing he had heard earlier. Was it the king's breathing he had heard earlier, or a premonition of his own?

King Theo's breath smelled foul, like he had drunk a gallon of sour milk.

The man whimpered, his voice getting ready for a scream.

'No point screaming, boy,' King Theo said, reading his thoughts. 'No one but you and I will be able to hear it.'

King Theo's entire form lunged forward. His thick hands grasped him by the throat, clutching the scream before it had the chance to come out.

He lurched upright in bed, his face veiled in sweat. His wife jolted awake beside him, peering at him from under their blanket. 'Seth?'

Seth, he remembered. *My name is Seth.*

~

Everything was marble now.

The granite pebble castle that had been named simply the Stonekeep had been upgraded since the day King Samuel Horne had been declared missing. It wasn't a castle anymore. It was a *palace*.

The immense entrance hall gleamed in gold-streaked white marble and every surface shone, despite the late autumn weather. Ridged pillars lined the edge of the hall, bearing braziers flickering cheerfully despite the afternoon sun beaming in from high above. The pillars yawned up the height of the chamber, curving into a peak at the apex of the vaulted ceiling to frame a long window on the back wall that was, to Howie's estimations, roughly the height of himself and Adrienne put together.

The only thing ruining the serenity was the inclusion of the deadpan expression of Gomez Emmett. He sat in the Stonethrone – the only survivor of the explosion, albeit a heavily charred one – atop a bright red cushion, while his sister Felicity stood beside him, holding her son's hand.

He was, Howie thought cynically, the perfect villain. His black hair glistened, pressed slick to the back of his head, and his eyes bored into him, the iris as black as the pupil. The contours of Emmett's face disturbed Howie. They appeared artificial somehow, as though the high cheekbones and fleshy lips disguised something more jagged. It was like some sort of demon had snuck amongst them in a human skin that was a size too small.

Felicity on the other hand looked like a doe-eyed teenager with a baby brother that slightly scared her. Compared to her older brother, she looked quite pretty, almost elf-like with her large, wide-set blue eyes and delicate features.

And Azrael… just looked like a pudgy brown-haired toddler, Howie thought. All four-year-olds looked like that. Though most of the ones he usually saw held their mother's hand when in the presence of strangers. Felicity appeared to be at pains to avoid it.

Howie ran a hand through his fair hair, noting it needed a trim again.

Emmett scrutinised him intently. He braced his elbows on the hard stone arms of the Stonethrone, lacing his fingers together in front of him. 'You requested an audience?' he said levelly, his voice particularly deep.

Howie cleared his throat politely. 'My name is Howard.'

'I'm sure everybody on the earth is aware of that,' said Emmett with the faintest glimmer of a smirk. 'What can I do for you?'

Words abruptly failed him. They caught on Howie's lips and hid behind them like frightened children. Howie flapped his mouth open and shut inanely, attempting to dislodge them.

'Well,' he managed. He laced his fingers, tapping them on his knuckles. He then turned to Adrienne at the door for moral support.

Howie's girlfriend stood tall in a burgundy work dress tied with a leather jerkin. Her pale skin gleamed with the marble around her, a contrast to the warm auburn of her shining braid - the image of radiance. Until she waved at him to hurry up with an impatient scowl.

'Right, um,' said Howie with a gulp, 'I've come to request—'

'*Demand*,' Adrienne corrected.

'Um, demand,' Howie amended, 'a tax exemption for my partner's apothecary.'

Adrienne glared up at Emmett from behind Howie. Howie felt the hatred emanating from her, a visceral wave. It really should have been him standing behind *her* in this meeting, but Archie's advice was, as ever, saddeningly prudent. Stoneguard hated women. If they had any chance of having a request—no, *demand* granted, it had to come from Howie.

The word *danger* kept coming up his throat, of its own accord. Howie swallowed it down again.

'As you are no doubt aware,' Emmett said, slowly as ever, 'the country is in some amount of disrepair since the fall of the Horne dynasty. Therefore, we cannot simply hand out exemptions willy-nilly.'

'Your *castle* certainly looks to be in "disrepair",' Adrienne drawled.

'Everyone is taxed,' he said. 'That is a fact of life wherever you go.'

'That is precisely my point,' Adrienne said coldly. 'Potions and rare plants cost money, and I can't ethically charge the earth to working class people and medical professionals simply to be able to pay off *your* taxes. I'm going to need a tax exemption. From you.'

'That is quite impossible. We're being very lenient with taxation as it is, we simply cannot afford—'

Adrienne snorted loudly. 'Lenient,' she said, her voice taking a jovial,

Archie-esque timbre, 'yes, we only have the window tax, the house made with bricks tax, the family-members-that-live-in-Adem-now tax—'

'It is all in the interests of the country,' he cut in.

'How is this helping the country? Where are the taxes going? As far as I can see, the only person around here getting any money is you! And look at what you're using it for!' She flung her hands at the vaulted ceiling.

'None of this makes any difference,' Emmett said, unapologetic. 'All non-essential businesses must pay a tax. That's just life.'

She blinked incredulously. 'Non-essential? It's *healthcare*. What's non-essential about living without illness, exactly?'

'The smallfolk are perfectly capable of gathering and making their own herbal remedies for illness,' he said flatly. 'Much of Stoneguard, you'll find, consist of farming communities. I'm sure they'll suss it out for themselves without being charged for it to keep the likes of you in luxury. As for medical professionals, they are professionals for a reason. I'm sure they'll do without the convenience of having *you* do their job for them.'

Adrienne's jaw hung open. 'So what am I supposed to do?'

'Perhaps a change of employment might suit you better,' he said dismissively. 'I hear the seamstresses are recruiting.'

Adrienne's eyes narrowed. She strode forward to push a worried-looking Howie out of the way.

Noooo, an imaginary echo of Archie trilled despairingly in the back of Howie's head.

'You're bankrupting the only apothecary in the city,' she snarled, 'to make me darn socks for a living?'

Howie winced.

Emmett simply looked at her with a blank expression. Her fury bounced from him like raindrops. He didn't trouble himself to acknowledge it.

Adrienne snorted and turned on her heel. 'I think our services would be better served elsewhere in the world. *You* can get on with it.'

'I hope you're aware there's currently a tax on emigrating?' Emmett said to her retreating form.

'Take my apothecary, then,' she said. 'God knows I've spent enough money on it.' She snatched Howie's elbow on her way out.

Howie's arm *jerked* backward. 'Yeeuurk,' he grunted involuntarily.

Boots slapping a furious tattoo on the shining floor, Adrienne strode out, Howie stumbling along as best he could. He flailed as she thrust him out ahead of her and attempted to slam the door behind them, only to be beaten to it by the doorman.

Howie righted himself, standing upright with a sigh. 'What now, then?'

They made their way through the needlessly elaborate gardens, morose. They seemed to be in competition with the triskele pattern of the Creys' castle, Howie mused, casting a cursory glance across the meandering rows of florals. He didn't like them as much as he had liked the Creys' work. The colours hurt his eyes and the patterns hurt his brain.

'You heard. We're emigrating.'

Howie blinked away echoes of the bright gravel. 'To where? We can't afford to go anywhere.'

'We can afford a horse – I haven't paid my taxes yet, so we can use that. We can go to Adem.'

Howie winced. 'Through the Wastelands?'

'Don't be a wuss. I've been through there and there's nothing to be afraid of.'

He grimaced. 'Well, fine, but… are you sure you want to go back to Adem? After everything that happened…'

Adrienne paused. 'I don't,' she admitted. The words came thickly, as words pertaining to the events of that year always did. 'But at least the Creys don't take advantage of their citizens. People are a lot… happier now that Seth is king. They're less scared.'

Howie snorted audibly. 'He hardly induces fear, does he? With his dodgy eye?' He pointed a finger in front of his left eye and twirled it in mocking circles.

Adrienne tactfully ignored this comment. 'Archie's there,' she pointed out instead. 'And I liked it there, despite… everything.'

Howie watched her pensively. 'I suppose we could live in a village or something,' he said. '*Far away* from Seth Crey.'

She gave him a small smile.

A tiny part of her wondered about Seth. *I wonder what he's doing now that he's king?*

~

Seth bolted upright, his fair hair threaded with leaves and grass.

'She's here,' he whispered.

White clouds bestowed the Forest with a light breeze, but the autumn rain still held out, for the moment. Which was lucky for Seth. He scrambled to his feet and hitched his trousers up. The sound of footsteps was close. He'd have to leave his jacket behind.

His fingers half-heartedly scrambled with his shirt laces and gave up. There was something to be said for having a manservant for these silly things – even if it did delay the mood a bit. He leapt into a run to the coach – not before reaching back to grab his lover's hand.

Leaves crunched behind them. Their pursuer approached, slowly and steadily.

Seth halted a yard from the coach and gestured to the door.

'Ladies first,' he said breathlessly, with a half-grin.

His companion lifted her skirts to step on.

The horses bolted two yards forward, yanking the coach from their grasp. They recoiled, the carriage door flapping out of Seth's hand.

'What a pleasant surprise,' Qattren said brightly.

Seth and Cienne froze sheepishly, still hand in hand.

Qattren folded her arms in quiet disapproval, standing just behind the spot where their coach had previously stood. Bright red hair tumbled in loose curls around her shoulders – she had grown it long since they had last met, the ends now brushing the long skirts of her elaborate gown, one of many. This season's garish ensemble featured a cacophony of colours rendered in feathers plucked from just about every avian this side of the Forest border, or so Seth thought. *Cacophony*, he added internally. *What a nice word*. He made a note to write that whole bit down to fling at her later.

'Hello Qattren,' Seth said coolly.

Qattren raised an eyebrow at him. She turned her gaze to Cienne. 'You should revise how you position yourself with your husband. As it is, I see more of him than you do.'

Cienne blushed deeply. Her cream skirts bore the marks of the Forest floor, darkening at the hem where the mud had scraped it with each step. The

22

bodice remained very much intact though, Seth noted, her own skilled embroidery delicately framing what he liked to call her 'upper assets'. Much subtler than Qattren's ridiculous fare. And still more attractive.

She hid her face in Seth's shoulder.

Seth grimaced at Qattren and, pointedly, looked her up and down.

'Three years without a word of greeting,' he said. 'Then you spy on me when we're making love.'

'You should try doing it in your bedchamber next time,' said Qattren, unabashed.

'There's no excitement in that.'

'Not my problem. Look what you did to my grass. You flattened it.'

'It's our anniversary,' he objected.

'You were married in the summer.'

'I'm sure it's an anniversary of *something.*'

Qattren lifted both eyebrows. He had a point, in an abstract way. 'Speaking of anniversaries,' she said, 'how are the preparations for your birthday soiree coming along?'

'My birthday was weeks ago,' said Seth. 'Rather disappointed you forgot it, actually. I thought our adventures together had bonded us. Apparently not.'

She gave him a cynical look. 'Nice try. The deception hurts me, it really does.'

He heaved a sigh. 'It's in three weeks' time,' he said sullenly. '*Do* come along.'

'I certainly will. I will bring Ronald.'

'Why not?' Seth said dully. 'We'll set up Pin the Tail on the Donkey.'

'He'll like that. I'll see you in three weeks.'

'Don't you want to know what day it's on?' Cienne asked.

Seth tutted. 'This is Qattren, silly mortal,' he intoned. 'Qattren knows what day *everything's* on.'

'Ah, you're learning,' Qattren said with a grin. 'Just revise our lesson on not using my Forest as a brothel and I will continue to tolerate your general existence.'

'I was an *inch* into your bloody Forest,' Seth hissed, holding his thumb and forefinger apart in demonstration. '*This...*' he sliced the air next to him with the side of his hand, 'is my bit.'

'Putting one hand on the line at all times doesn't count,' Qattren informed him. 'Your lower torsos were colliding on my side of the line, therefore—'

'And so ends another *scintillating* conversation with the pervy red-haired bitch in the Forest,' Seth cut in, shaking his head. He made a beeline for the coach, Cienne in tow.

'I would say we should do this again, but—'

'Let's not,' Seth said.

Cienne followed him into the coach, giggling.

They sat beside one another, watching Qattren stalk off.

'I wish she'd leave my poor horses alone,' said Seth. 'The driver could have had a heart attack.'

'I like your confidence,' Cienne said. 'Not so much as a red face from the fact that another woman just watched your love-making prowess.'

'With it being described as "prowess", it appears I have nothing to be red-faced about.' He shot her a roguish grin.

She met his gaze and smirked back.

Cienne picked leaves out of Seth's hair as he dropped a hand on her thigh. They sat in comfortable silence for a while.

'Where to now?' he asked, his thumb tracing her knee.

'The wheat field?'

He shot her a side glance.

She raised an eyebrow.

'The wheat field it is,' he agreed with a smile.

~

Qattren returned to their quarters just as Ron was starting his breakfast.

'Morning,' he greeted with his mouth full. He swallowed and gave her a bright smile through the wafting steam of poached eggs. 'Visitor arrived for you. Gave me a heart attack, as always.'

Qattren rolled her eyes. She sat across from Ron at their mahogany dining table and met his gaze with a sigh. 'I wish he'd change his face, just this once, to something that isn't for terrorising a bereaved family member.'

'That wouldn't be any fun,' Vladimir Horne's voice said playfully from behind her.

Ron shuddered at the sound. He let his next forkful of egg plummet back onto the plate.

Qattren pivoted to face the new Geldemar.

Given that he was a member of the duplicitous Seven Devils of Sal'plae, they weren't too surprised to find that Geldemar had changed his appearance to drastically resemble the late Vladimir Horne. Well, Qattren wasn't surprised – *Ron* had almost had a coronary when the Devil told him almost seriously that his brother had overthrown the Seven and reincarnated himself into a demi-god.

In actual fact, Vladimir was still very dead and currently chained to a wall in the Devil's Domain – where he was to stay, if Geldemar had anything to do with it. The God of Greed had taken a distinct liking to the late Crown Prince of Stoneguard – so much so that he'd decided to adopt Vladdy's facial features, silver tooth and voice, adding a white-blond shoulder-length cut for reasons known only to Geldemar, which made Qattren wonder when he was going to change the eyebrows to match.

'You're looking well, friend,' Qattren said. 'The new look is very becoming on you.'

'Ooh, thank you!' Geldemar trilled. He framed his new hairstyle around his face with a vain grin. 'I do get ever so many compliments on it. I'm thinking of introducing myself to young Mister Crey, exchange some fashion tips, you know…' He winked mischievously.

Qattren gave him a severe glance. 'Don't go scaring him,' she scolded. 'He means well.'

'I thought you had gone to give out to him?' Ron said.

'I did,' she said. 'I quite like him, despite his faults. But that's a secret.' She gave them a wink. 'We don't want him feeling too comfortable in his own skin.'

'My sentiment exactly,' Geldemar said with a grin with an extra *glint*. 'I dare say we'll meet at some stage.'

'Quite.' She eyed him suspiciously. 'So what brings you here?'

'Can't I visit a dear friend and—'

She glared at him.

'Oh, alright,' he said with a huff.

He circled the table to sit at Ron's side. Ron flinched away, out of habit more than anything else.

'I came to inform you that the Prophet has finally emerged. And to scare Ron again, obviously.'

'Didn't I get enough of a fright the first time?' Ron said with a scowl. 'You know, when you told me my mother was coming for me from beyond the grave?'

'Oh, it was only a joke,' Geldemar scoffed. He propped one foot on the table and crossed the other over it, toppling Ron's glass of juice in the process. 'She was obliterated. Ask Vladdy if you don't believe me, he saw the whole thing.'

'I'll bet he was happy about that,' Ron muttered.

'Prophet?' Qattren asked. '*The* Prophet?'

'Oh, yes,' Geldemar said brightly, folding his arms behind his white head. 'A friend of a friend spoke to him a couple years ago. Planning to make a home for himself in the Creys' palace, apparently. Although,' he said in the tones of a gossip, 'our Gale heard tell during one of his, you know, maternal meddlings, that he was making a home for himself within the ranks of religion. Or so the midwife was saying – you know, in between sets of triplets.'

'I highly doubt it,' Qattren said. 'Being privy to his childhood.'

'That's what I thought at first,' Geldemar said, lifting a brow. 'Speaking of religion by the way, there's a rumour going around that an old pastime is making a reappearance.' He grinned at Qattren.

Qattren drew a pained expression. 'Not again.'

'What not again?' Ron wondered.

Geldemar rubbed his hands together. 'Should be fun, shouldn't it?'

'Not for my dresses,' she said mournfully.

'I'm sure fashion can wait while you're getting to know the author of the Great Prophecy,' Geldemar said cheerfully.

'I already know him,' Qattren said. 'I gave him a home when he was eight, remember?'

'Who, though?' asked Ron.

'Yes, you already know the Prophet,' Geldemar said with glee. 'Just wait until you meet the new one.'

Qattren tilted her head to one side. 'The *new* one?'

Ron exhaled through his teeth and glowered at them. 'Mind telling me what's going on instead of talking in riddles all the time?'

'All in good time, little brother.' Geldemar patted Ron on the head, making him flinch away. 'All in good time.'

~

The afternoon clouds waned to a heavy blue. Five black ravens exited the White Tower of the Emmettfort and separated into the sky. Two circled around the coast of the Wastelands and flew over Seth's head in the distance.

He was, as ever, oblivious.

'Oh, God,' he breathed, landing on his back amidst the wheat stalks with a thump. 'I've been looking forward to this all day…'

Cienne grinned and adjusted her skirts to kneel between his knees.

The sky darkened incrementally on their journey back to Castlefoot. The royal farming grounds sprawled over the back of the castle hill, golden and serene. The warm air settled onto the syrupy golden wheat field, engulfing the two in its embrace.

There was some heavy breathing for a moment.

'Shall we?' Cienne said in a murmur. She ran her bottom lip down the front of Seth's shirt.

'Yes, please,' he said blissfully. He snaked his arms around his head, stroking the wheat stems as he went. The soft ends tickled his hands. Stretching both arms to their full length, his eyes fluttered shut.

Until his fingers connected with something squidgy. His eyes bolted open and a low, ululating wail escaped his lips.

Cienne glanced up with a frown. 'I haven't done anything yet.'

'No, no, no, not you,' Seth said with a grimace. He pulled his hands back to eye level.

His fingers were coated in a reddish-brown mud. Upon further examination, Seth and Cienne were horrified to discover that the red streaks were blood.

They met each other's gaze fearfully.

Slowly, in the terrified fascination of the proverbial cat in front of the fireplace, they tilted their heads back to peer between the wheat stalks, Seth's scalp grinding against the dirt on the way.

The crumpled body of a nobleman lay tangled in the grip of an uprooted tree, staring at them through a film of his own blood.

~

II

Ablyminded Street, Serpus.

Father Hope shuffled between the double doors of the chapel and eased them closed. The hinges creaked, straining to shift the heavy oak doors.

The sun shone on his balding pate, but despite the glorious weather, the priest was not cheerful. A cloaked bundle of darkness waited for him under the stained glass. It was giving him a nervous constipation.

Father Hope stuck a hand inside his own cloak to rub his abdomen and walked to the altar in as dignified a manner as possible.

The bundle in question had adopted the colour of the Seven Gods — a deep burgundy that hid his face in an all-encompassing black shadow. He was little more than a standing robe on the marble flooring of the dais, wreathed in a kaleidoscope of little rainbows from the panes at his back.

Father Hope halted five paces from him and cleared his throat. 'Good morning.'

The seemingly empty cloak bowed. 'Father, I am pleased you could meet me this fine day,' he said politely in a Truphorian accent so posh it made Seth Crey sound like an East Serpus orange seller.

'As am I, my son.' Hope hesitated. 'To what do I owe this pleasure?'

'You remember His Eminence, Father Furlong?'

Father Hope shuddered. 'How could I forget? The man was terrifying. His services could bring down the Devils themselves, just so they could pat his back for the favour.' He paused before lightly adding, 'He hasn't died, has he?'

'No, no…'

'Oh,' said Hope in disappointment.

'… in fact,' he added proudly, 'he has revolutionised the influence of religion forever, as it happens. Well,' he cut across himself, 'I have. He just helped a little bit.'

'Oh?' Hope asked, feeling wary. 'What did that entail?'

The cloak raised itself up to its full height. 'I have brought peace to the church… by joining the two faiths of Truphoria.'

Hope blinked. 'But… but we hate each other,' he said. 'We have done since… forever. Their Gods are devils. It's as much a fact as the sky being blue—'

'It was a lie invented by the villains who split apart our faith in the Gods!' He took a breath. 'That was merely the means to an end. A glorious end. This end.' He spread his arms wide, the sleeves of his robes sliding behind two bony elbows.

He's a flaming lunatic, Hope thought, arching an eyebrow.

'I really don't think joining the faiths is such a good idea,' said Hope.

He couldn't see from beneath the hood, but Hope felt the strange conviction that the man's eyes had narrowed maliciously.

'I do,' he said simply. 'And I think you should listen to me, because I'm much more important than you seem to realise.'

Father Hope held his breath. 'What do you mean? Who are you?'

The man lifted both hands to his cowl and gripped both sides to throw it back.

Father Hope flinched at an internal image of some hideous demon, but in reality, he saw merely a pale young man, his black hair cropped short and his beard cropped even shorter.

'I am Raphael Emmanuel III,' he announced dramatically. 'And I… am the Prophet.'

~

The rookery master handed Lilly-Anna Crey a missive and hurried off as the king's sister opened it. Lilly's eyes scanned the parchment, and she cracked a mischievous smile, tucking it into her belt.

The sun's descent marked the end of the weekend market. It bruised the sky from yellow to purple-grey over the busy thoroughfare. Lilly squeezed her way out of the throngs of evening shoppers and exited Castlefoot, stashing her earnings into her hip pouch.

Since being abruptly married to the half-prince of Portabella, Lilly had spent the last three years trying vainly to shake off her new husband. He insisted upon gifting her with fabulous jewels and gowns for each day he lived without her 'beauty and spirit'. Lilly had timely pawned each and every one of his gifts to pay Stan's wages and had all missives with the word 'visit' written on it destroyed, unread. Lilly had no single idea why the poor man bothered. Cienne had informed her that he preferred the company of men anyway.

Stan strode alongside her, hands tucked in the pockets of his jerkin, as they ascended the steep path to the keep. The crunch of their feet on the gravel gradually drowned out the noise from the late-evening market.

'How much did you make this week?'

Lilly jingled the full bag of coins with a smile. 'Twenty pounds of silver for eight pounds of tat,' she said proudly. 'Well-crafted tat, but tat nonetheless. No need to applaud: it's a talent that pays for itself.'

Stan grinned and followed her through the portcullis of the Serpent's Knot.

As the sun's rays weakened, the stained-glass windows of the keep's ground floor reflected their scenes onto the grass towards the east. Lilly didn't know what scenes they were depicting – the artwork was rendered quite poorly – but she admired them, nonetheless. They may not have been drawn well, but they brightened the place up.

'Let's see if my brother has come back yet, shall we?' Lilly said as they reached the keep porch.

'Why? What fresh torture have you devised for his return?'

Lilly halted halfway up the steps and lifted the missive into the air with a flourish. 'Devised itself, mate,' she said with a grin. 'From Seth's biggest fan.'

Stan was none the wiser as the footman opened the doors for them.

'Hello, Jon,' Lilly said fondly.

'Evening,' Jon said with a smile.

The doorman stood shoulder-height to Stan, despite his straight-backed stance. A vicious gust of wind rustled his black curls. He bounced on his toes in defence of it, his hands clasped behind his back.

What Stan noticed most about Jon was that he smiled too much – constantly, even, as though he knew something no one else did and was very pleased about it. It was the kind of smile, Stan thought, that someone who could see into the future might have.

Jon caught Stan's gaze and gave him a brisk nod, still wearing his knowing smile.

'No sign of the king on your travels?' Jon asked.

Lilly shuddered, not completely because of the chill wind. 'If he isn't back yet, he won't be until morning. And good riddance.'

'Nah, he'll be back soon,' Jon said, smiling down at the vacant portcullis.

Stan shivered. That knowing smile was giving him the creeps.

'Aw, you miss him?' Lilly teased.

'No, but Jimmy will.'

'Why's that?' Stan asked.

'*She's* tired, that's why.'

Lilly made a face. 'Ginny.'

Inside the keep, one massive throne room away from them and to the left, plumes of white steam billowed from the doors and windows, all gaping open to welcome the cooling weather. The dinner rush was in full swing, the kitchen brimming with the scents of various meats roasting in the ovens to the back. A series of cauldrons dangled on the long spit connecting them, each accompanied by a large cut of meat. The distant, quiet cursing to each end marked the labours of the two kitchen boys cranking the levers in slow rotations.

A long row of kitchen staff lined the counter facing the tall windows, scrubbing and rinsing the remains of the feast from their wares. The butler, head of the household – apparently, he often scathed – stood at the end of it. Isla was ill again – apparently. Jimmy didn't consider himself schooled in the knowledge of pregnancy, but he was half sure she was milking it.

He was being bombarded as usual by a miniature Crey, though, as ever, he couldn't tell exactly which miniature Crey it was.

'He won't be back until later,' he said curtly, scrubbing an oven pan. 'It's his and Mummy's special day out.'

'Why?' the small human demanded.

'Don't ask me,' Jimmy said tiredly. 'The question is why I don't get to have a special day out. I haven't had a holiday in fifteen years.'

"Cause Daddy doesn't like you,' the child said.

'Probably,' he said dully.

'Okay.' There was a brief pause – but only a brief one. 'Can I have a cake?'

Bingo, Jimmy thought. That was the sign he was looking for: Russell never went five minutes into a conversation without asking for a cake.

'Of course you can,' he said. *As long as you go away*, he added privately. He handed over a slice of apple pie he had prepared beforehand.

'Thanks!' Russell trilled, brushing his overly long flaxen hair off his face before accepting it.

Jimmy shook his head in amusement. Seth Crey had his faults, but somehow – probably to do with their nanny Despina – he had actually managed to produce a pair of inexplicably well-behaved children.

Well. 90% of the time, anyway.

The other 10% was entirely up to whether Russell was hungry or Ginny was tired. It baffled Jimmy as to how Ginny chucking food at people and running around like a lunatic was a sign that she was tired, but he was assured this was a baby thing.

Seth's son jogged away happily, plate in hand.

Ginny entered from the courtyard, quickly. *Very* quickly. Jimmy surmised from the evidence of her loose, messy hair that it had worked itself out of its neat, intricate plait during one of her energetic guard-tormenting episodes, which meant she was tired.

He hoped Seth would come home soon. Only the arms of her beloved father could set an exhausted Ginny to sleep. No one in the world could replicate the effect he had on that child. It was his only talent, Jimmy reflected.

'Jimmee!' Ginny trilled. 'I wanna go round and round!'

'Forget it,' Jimmy told her tiredly. 'If I touch as much as a hair on your head, I'll have the word "nonce" slapped on me faster than you can blink.'

'Come on!' she wailed. She grabbed his knee and shook it aggressively.

He leaned on the counter with a wince as the joint gave a dangerous creak.

'I wanna go up-up-up!'

Jimmy rolled his eyes and, for a quiet life, lifted the girl onto his shoulder.

A kitchen maid halted on her way to the well outside and watched the flurry of purple silk and white-blond hair. 'You're brilliant with her, you know.'

Jimmy staggered and righted himself, placing Ginny's feet back on the ground. He cleared his throat, regaining posture. 'I have to be. We've all seen his father with women.'

Emma giggled, a slender hand over her small mouth.

Jimmy smiled and gave her a wink.

Emma smirked back and turned to leave.

Ginny scrutinised the tightly wound golden bun on the back of her head. 'Is she your *girl*friend?' she said, inflecting the 'girl' part with a low voice.

'Not… yet.' He arched an eyebrow at the giggling toddler. 'Go and play, then, you're getting in the way.'

Ginny snickered, her fist pressed against her mouth.

Russell returned, empty plate in hand.

'I take it you haven't come simply to return the plate.'

'No, I wan' some more.' He paused for a moment, pondering which part of the sentence he had left out. 'P'ease?' he hazarded.

Jimmy handed him the whole three quarters of remaining apple pie and a spoon. He didn't bother to cut it up first. It seemed a pointless exercise.

'Thanks!' Russell said a lot more enthusiastically.

He jogged away, an affronted Ginny in tow.

'Gimme some!'

'No!' He ran as fast as his small legs could carry him.

Jimmy smiled fondly at them on their way out. Not because he was particularly fond of them, but because they were the biggest asset to his love life since Albert the Grinning Dog.

He was sure Albert the Grinning Dog had a bigger motive than helping him get a lady's attention, but he quickly shook that off. Silliness. Albie was just a slightly grizzly little dog Lilly had taken a liking to during one of her adventures and brought back to loiter in the kitchen for scraps. Jimmy wasn't sure if he could even grin properly.

Only humans had such things as an ulterior motive.

Or so Jimmy told himself, on nights when things like Jon being able to see into the future began to make sense to him.

Luckily for Jimmy, he was not the dog's target. The target was on his way up the path at a sprint and due to arrive in the throne room in half a minute, or so a happy Bastard surmised.

He wasn't entirely looking forward to being present in the events to ensue in the wheat field, but at the moment there was a small boy sharing an apple pie with him and you couldn't be unhappy in the face of the cook's famous apple pie.

Half a minute passed with the only sounds in the hall being Russell's lips smacking and Ginny grumbling, trying to take his spoon.

The double doors burst open.

'What do you mean, you found King Sam's body?'

The Bastard bolted to attention, sitting on his haunches.

'He's in the wheat field,' Seth said in a high voice, pacing to the throne. His hair stood on end, a single wheat stalk dangling from a tangled knot in the crown of his head. *Could have tidied himself up post-coitus*, the Bastard thought nastily. 'We found him, just lying there all tangled up in some sort of tree. Can you send a letter to Ronald Horne?'

'Ron? Yeah, but how am I supposed to explain what you were doing in the—'

'Without detail.'

Albie blinked, a picture of innocence.

Lilly tailed her brother to the dais, and then around it three times as Seth circled it in manic horror. 'Was there anyone else there?'

'No, no other bodies, and there was no one else around, that's why we were there in the first place.' Seth halted abruptly and squinted at the pie. *'Who gave him that?'*

Russell tried to look innocent. 'It's the doggy's.' He pushed the plate in front of Albie.

The Bastard whooped, burying his nose in the plate.

Seth's eyes rolled to the vaulted ceiling. 'They're going to make him rotund at this rate.'

Russell bowed his head, his lower lip sticking out. Though you couldn't see this through the matted curtain of blond hair that had flopped over his face.

'And he needs a haircut,' Seth added.

'Hello, Daddy,' Ginny said with a grin.

Seth gazed at her solemnly and knelt on the floor. She ran and threw herself into his arms.

Curious, the Bastard followed her.

'Where'd you go, Daddy?' she said in his ear.

'You don't want to know,' he said with a shiver. His gaze settled on that of the Bastard. 'What are *you* looking at?'

The Bastard pulled his head back, his upper lip lifted in an indignant grimace.

'That dog is a creep,' he muttered, lifting Ginny into his arms.

Lilly clicked her fingers. Albie scrambled to her side, obedient.

'Leave him alone,' Lilly scolded Seth. 'He's a sweet boy. There's nothing wrong with him.'

'Except that he keeps eyeballing me and doesn't age,' he pointed out. 'Kind of like Qattren.'

He kissed Ginny on the temple and flung her playfully over one shoulder, making her squeal.

The Bastard glared at him. 'And making love outside the house of a father of three isn't creepy at *all*.'

'I see bad father-son relationships still run in the family,' a voice taunted.

Panic erupted in his chest, but thankfully none of the Creys had understood him. The Bastard glanced around to make sure no one was looking at him and vanished in a flash of purple light. 'Who are you when you're at home?'

A young, white-haired man in evening dress stood before him in the purple-tinted Sal'plae. Air hurriedly left the Bastard's lungs which, contrary to most cases, he found a relief. Air wasn't something he needed as an undead poltergeist – it was mainly an inconvenience.

The Creys stood around them stoically, the Aspect's time drag slowing their movements to a halt.

'I am Geldemar,' the stranger said. 'I'm your new teacher.' He held out a hand.

The Bastard ignored it. He lacked the capacity to shake it in his dog form anyway. 'Where is He?'

'He?' Geldemar asked innocently.

The Bastard jerked his nose upwards.

'Oh, Him. He's busy – some difficulty upstairs only He can sort out. He sent me to help you instead.'

'Who said I needed a babysitter?'

'I'm not a babysitter as such. I'm more like a personal trainer. Like a dog trainer, for instance. Sorry, where are my manners? Would you like a biscuit?'

The Bastard rolled his eyes. There was no use trying to get a decent conversation in *this* form. He popped out of existence for a moment and re-emerged as Seth Crey's bodily double.

'Ah, so this is your true form,' Geldemar said with a grin.

'Only by default,' he said, 'It's a guilt trip. My father's image, my mother's eyes—'

'And the scars delivered by the two,' he finished. 'You can't say it hasn't got style.'

'I'd rather he hadn't,' the Bastard said sourly. 'Seth Crey isn't exactly a looker, is he?'

'True.' Geldemar paused for a moment. 'So you're a dog, then.'

The Bastard licked his teeth in annoyance. 'Part-time.'

'Part-time.' He paused again. 'What's that like?'

'You get the urge to lick your ass more than the average poltergeist. Look, is this conversation going anywhere?'

'Sorry. I digress.' He straightened up to his full height. 'I am one of the Seven. I assume you've heard of us?'

'Gods, demons,' the Bastard said. 'Clowns, more like it. Famous for meddling with people's feelings and orchestrating the world. Only I gather you're second fiddle these days.'

Geldemar scowled at the Bastard's smug expression.

'That's us,' he sang. 'Second fiddle to a part-time dog. So tell me, what's this big plan I've been told so much about?'

The Bastard cracked his knuckles. 'Well, that's a secret.'

'Can I guess?'

'Well, you could try, but you'll find its subtlety is rather—'

36

'You're getting Seth and Adrienne to have another affair so that Howard Rosethorn will kill him.'

The Bastard's eyes widened. 'How did you know that?'

'Secrets are my bread and butter. I make it my business to know these things – in addition to the meaning of the word "subtlety". What we are doing to make this happen is my question.'

The Bastard bristled at this – mainly the audible suggestion of the quotation marks. 'I'm already doing that – the body's in the cornfield, the whore is on her way here. Now we just have to wait for them to find each other.' He knitted his fingers together in demonstration.

Geldemar quirked an eyebrow. 'Suppose they *don't* just fall into each other's arms?'

'They will if I tell them to,' the Bastard said with venom.

'How are you going to tell them to? Piddle the words onto the floor?'

The Bastard scowled. 'I can manipulate dreams, if you must know.'

Geldemere sighed. 'And here we get to the heart of the problem.'

If the Bastard had had his hackles on his person, they would have risen in anger.

'The average dream is forgotten within the first five minutes of wakefulness,' Geldemar went on. 'You'll need to be more present than that.'

The Bastard made a face of potent discomfort. 'I can't rummage around in people's heads again.'

'Why not?'

'I'm rubbish at it.'

'That's what I'm here to remedy,' Geldemar reminded him.

'You'll have a job remedying me, I turned the Prophet into a gibbering idiot.'

'I am aware of what you did to the Prophet. I can show you how to do it *better*.'

The Bastard growled. 'I told you, I don't need a babysitter.'

'You won't budge her with a stupid dream. She's been deciding and changing her mind about the matter for three whole years. She isn't coming back.'

The Bastard's face twisted into a sullen grimace. 'What do you suggest, then? Put a collar around her neck and *drag* her here?'

Geldemere brightened. 'No need. She's on her way already with Howard Rosethorn.'

The Bastard's eyes bulged in disbelief. 'You just told me she wasn't coming back!'

'She wasn't,' Geldemar snapped back. 'Until *I* got to her. Because it took a lot more than just a dream to get her to up sticks and leave for the city where she lost her unborn child.

'It took, in fact, the collective effort of the Seven to bring the minds of Emmett and his council to the conclusion that Howard Rosethorn and his lovely girlfriend are not wanted in the kingdom of Stoneguard before we could even get *started* on young Adrienne – and don't even get me started on breaking the resolve of that hideous uncle of hers in order for him to move closer to the palace for your little trap, which *isn't* guaranteed to come to fruition, in case you weren't aware.'

Geldemar paused this torrent to breathe heavily, which said a lot for someone who didn't even need to breathe in the first place.

'All of that took three years,' he said, more slowly this time, 'and Adrienne hasn't even stepped into the kingdom yet. If you think this is a simple task that can be completed with the most basic level of dream sculpting, then perhaps making me "second fiddle" to you was an error on His part. You are an infant in this world, Bastard. And you're going to need a lot of training in order to walk.'

The Bastard scowled at him. 'What do you suggest, then?'

Geldemar circled the Bastard. 'Dreams are all very well and good, but at one point they wake up and realise it was just an image. A vivid one, if you're as good as you claim, but otherwise, just a glancing picture.'

He slowed to a halt behind the Bastard's left shoulder and followed his gaze to Seth, who still had Ginny hoisted onto one shoulder with a grin.

'What makes a dream resonate is its relationship to real life. A flashback of a quick fumble with the mistress back in the day isn't going to cut it. You need to play on his feelings, make them relevant to *today.*' He regarded the apparition solemnly. 'It's not just his new children he loves, you know.'

The Bastard snorted. 'He loves himself.'

'And you.' Geldemar watched the Bastard glare at his father. 'And so does she.'

'Never you mind my mother, she'll be dealt with later.'

Geldemar lifted an eyebrow. 'I dare say she will.' He clapped his hands behind the Bastard's head, making him flinch. 'But before you can deal with anyone, you need to learn the tricks of the trade.'

The Bastard tore his gaze from Seth Crey to look at the white-haired young man. 'What are we doing first?'

Feeling a Vladdy urge and deciding to embrace it, Geldemar grabbed the Bastard by the throat and pulled him forward until their noses touched. Echoes of Vladimir's temperamental demeanour had been erupting from Geldemar's new face with fervour over the past three years, and he was starting to enjoy them.

He eyed the dead boy's stricken expression and met his gaze, one royal-double to another.

'First,' he said in a low voice, tracing the Bastard's most prominent scar from his left eyebrow to the side of his nose, 'we're going to learn to never refer to me as "second fiddle". You're an infant in this world, Bastard. Never forget it.'

The Bastard met his gaze and, briefly, the fear gave way to some of the old Crey defiance.

He'll have to be weaned off that, Geldemar surmised.

'And before you can learn to walk,' Geldemar continued, 'you must learn to crawl.'

$\sim$

III

Felicity Emmett was not having a good day.

Her brother was too busy organising his upcoming Peace Tax meeting to talk to her, her father hadn't written to her in half a year and her three-year-old son was running rings around her, quite literally – he had a rope wound five times around her torso, binding her arms together.

Legs splayed across the marble flooring, Felicity sat dejected in the middle of her drawing room, Azrael waddling in wide circles around her. The rope dug into her elbows.

'Az?' she said mildly, squirming. 'Can you let Mummy go now? You'll make yourself dizzy if you're not careful.' *That and my arms have gone numb,* she added internally but didn't bother saying aloud. He wasn't likely to care.

'No!' he shouted, kicking her leg. She felt a bruise developing already. 'Uncle Gomez says prisoners shouldn't be given mercy.'

The little monster tied Felicity's wrists together and dragged her along the Great Hall by the remaining foot of rope. Servants wandered in and out of the hall. Each made a concerted effort to avoid their queen's gaze.

Queen in naught but name, Felicity thought sourly.

Felicity scooted along on the balls of her feet, striving to avoid a tantrum.

Azrael Horne was without a doubt the most monstrous thing to happen to Felicity in her entire life. To say that Azrael was his father in miniature would be a lie – Vladimir was prickly, but he never crossed her as inherently evil. Azrael was more like a miniature, male Aaliyaa Horne. Felicity had always gotten the impression that her mother-in-law could read minds, and she had a feeling her only child had inherited that gift more than any other.

Felicity heard the double doors being opened and reddened in humiliation.

Her brother entered.

As fond of him as she was, she forgot about his towering superiority complex: he was the tall, dark-eyed, intelligent new regent of Stoneguard, albeit one with a skull shaped like an arrowhead and a mouth that hadn't seen a smile since… ever. It wouldn't do to have a sister who was bullied by a toddler.

They would walk all over us, he told her one afternoon, and she assumed he was right because he was always, as a rule, correct about these things.

That wasn't to say she wasn't afraid of him.

A lingering memory stirred in her mind of a half-forgotten afternoon, when she was eight, when she had visited him in Stoneguard, when he was being fostered by the Hornes (whom he had never liked), when she had followed him outside, when her uncle Zephyr had stopped her a moment too late – when she had seen him in the flowerbed.

She shook off the memory quickly, as she always had. Her brother had always looked after her, she admonished herself. So long as she kept her guard up.

She wished he wasn't so stiff. She'd seen the way the Crey siblings were with each other – constantly telling jokes and making fun of each other. She wanted that, that genuine sibling nonsense.

Bizarrely, despite the events resulting in the destruction of the Stonekeep four years prior, she sometimes wished Seth Crey was her big brother. The reputation he had built in Stoneguard, of a negligent dragon owner at best and a murderer at worst, hadn't fazed Felicity at all. He seemed genial at every social event they had attended together. And he was *funny*. Felicity daydreamed at times of swapping him with her real brother – even if it meant she might get a kick up the bum occasionally, like Lilly-Anna got back at King Theo's tournaments where she couldn't sit down for the entire meal without wincing. She could never imagine Seth Crey intentionally killing her husband, despite what her brother thought. Her brother, who had always been Vladimir's real enemy…

Felicity eyed her own brother sheepishly, lifting her shoulders. 'Would you mind untying me?'

Gomez Emmett arched an eyebrow and clicked his fingers.

A servant emerged from a door behind Felicity and began to free her from her bonds.

Azrael bounded up to his uncle and dealt him a magnificent bow for a not-quite-four-year-old.

'Nephew,' he said in a stiff baritone – as ever refusing to acknowledge the name Aaliyaa Horne had forced upon the child via a threat of bastardization. 'Still practising, I see.'

'Yes, uncle,' he replied very formally. 'I tie her up just like the guards did with the goat lady.'

'Well done.'

Felicity rose to her feet, glowering.

'You're becoming quite the conqueror. However, we have servants for that kind of carry on. Your job requires you to attack with words rather than rope. I will educate you when you're older.'

Azrael bowed again and stalked outside, two armoured bodyguards in tow.

Felicity brushed dust from her skirts in disgruntlement. They had turned from sky blue to light brown in a matter of moments, she noticed in resignation. But this was always the case.

'Worry not, sister,' he said, almost kindly. 'He will grow out of it.'

'He won't if you don't scold him for attacking me,' Felicity seethed under her breath.

'Why should I scold him?' he asked, his hearing as stellar as ever. 'In the future, you might be glad of him detaining prisoners with rope rather than by other means.'

She felt a shiver go up her spine.

'I will arrange for him to be fostered for a few years, meet some boys closer to his own age. That will teach him some humility.'

It didn't teach you any, she thought irately. *It just got me married to Vladdy. Which is the real point, isn't it?*

She had been fair game ever since Vladimir died – and so had Azrael himself. She might have been slow on the uptake, but she was catching on quick. You didn't bring cows to the cattle market for them to make friends.

'If it's any consolation, there are rumours that Seth Crey's children are of much the same disposition,' he went on in what, had a different man said it, might have been amusement. 'If a couple of three-year-old children can walk all over him, there's no hope for the man. They should have left him rotting in his casket.'

'Be nice to him,' Felicity blurted, to her own surprise. 'He's always treated me kindly. As he has our cousin.'

Emmett snorted, almost imperceptibly. 'Queen Cienne had been suffering from depression for twenty years before that halfwit could impregnate her. And if she thinks she's happy now, she's deluding herself. She's nothing but a toy to him, and she knows it. Besides,' he added, passing his gaze around her private quarters, 'I have no great love for our cousin.'

'I don't think that's true,' said Felicity. She chose to ignore the last comment because if he didn't love his cousin, who's to say he loves his own sister either? 'I've seen them together, they're a fine couple—'

'They aren't in love, Felicity.' A definite note of amusement emerged at this statement. 'There's no such entity. Do you love your son?'

Felicity hesitated.

42

He smirked slightly. 'Exactly. He's a beast; who on this earth would feel attached to that? Similarly, you don't form a bond with some foreign woman shoved into your bed by your father's advisors. She's sufficient for now, but once his old toy returns, things will change – and she will change along with them.'

Felicity frowned. 'What toy?'

He walked past her to drop himself behind her desk, in an oak armchair cushioned with red velvet.

'A young lady called Adrienne,' he said smugly.

She blinked.

He nodded once.

'Who's she?' she said blankly.

He snorted once, mirthlessly. *At his sister's ignorance, most like,* she thought sourly. 'Seth Crey's former mistress,' he explained. 'And the mother of his illegitimate son.'

~

'My father wants me to attend in his place and report back.'

Seth frowned. Impatience rankled at him, sending his left foot into an impatient tapping.

The crowds of Castlefoot Market bustled around them – or around the bodyguards surrounding him, at any rate. A motley crew circled a tall pavilion in the centre of the market square – they had arrived to host a talent show in the centre of the market, with the royal family in front of the stage.

Not before the entirety of the royal guard, at Sir Marbrand's command, had checked each and every artist for criminal intent and inspected the premises and preparations for each performance first, most particularly as regards to the fire-eater, who Seth hoped would be worth the hassle. Common sense would have suggested that the guards be placed *aside* from the stage, but alas Seth still had to shout at them a total of thrice to get out of the bloody way.

Marbrand's paranoia dated back three years, to the incident in which some priests from Stoneguard had attempted to murder Seth's children. He had since been appointed as head of the sovereign guard. Armed soldiers had been posted left, right and centre ever since the incident, and every visit and public event was meticulously screened for malign intent. Petitioners to the king had ceased calling entirely due to the hassle of it all – the only positive outcome, Seth thought.

The aforementioned hassle meant that none of the performances had started yet, which left Seth and Cienne time to discuss the letter Lilly had given them from his old friend, Mister Emmett. It had contained a summons to Emmettfort, the apparent new name for the replacement Stonekeep. It didn't say what the meeting was for.

A glorified gloat-fest, most like, Seth mused with hatred. 'Why can't he go himself?' he asked Cienne, returning to the subject of her father.

'He's on his deathbed, apparently.' Cienne rolled her eyes. 'Means he has man flu. I don't think it's anything to worry about. At least it means we can go together.'

'That's good.' Seth's left ear throbbed. His coronet had slipped askew again. He fiddled with it as he spoke before simply lifting it off and throwing it on the floor in disgust. 'I don't think I could stick five weeks of celibacy on top of a summons from Lord Horseface.'

'Horsey,' Russell echoed. He leaned forward in Cienne's lap and grinned at something behind them.

'Anyway, I don't want you to be left on your own after that wheat field incident,' she added. 'Nobody's confirmed that it *is* King Samuel's body yet – it could be a member of our court. Someone could be after you next.'

'You don't need to worry about that,' Seth said in annoyance. 'This lot like to barge in when I'm taking a dump, just to make sure it doesn't jump back out and get me.'

'Just doing our job, sir,' one of them mumbled behind him.

'Yes, because it's a well-known fact that assassins always take a bathroom break in the middle of the job, isn't it?'

The guard decided not to comment. 'When's the fire-eater coming on?'

Seth unrolled a scroll given to him by the show's presenter. The guards shuffled closer to peer into it, their armour jangling. Seth clenched his jaw at the sound. 'First there's a musician, then an impressionist, *then* the fire-eater's coming on. Can't we bugger off for twenty minutes and come back?'

'No,' said Cienne. 'What kind of musician?'

'Who cares, I just came to see the fire-eater have a nasty accident.'

'Horsey,' Russell said happily.

Seth scanned the parchment. 'I don't see any horsey, love.'

'No, horsey!' He pointed with one pudgy finger.

A massive tongue licked Seth's right ear. For a terrifying moment, Seth thought it might be his Cousin Elyse. He shrieked, scrambling to the other side of the chair to lean against Cienne.

'Look, he likes you!' squealed a tiny voice.

Seth was alarmed to find his daughter on the back of the pony, beaming. 'Who put you up there?' He glared at a grinning idiot in red and yellow evening dress. 'I've warned you people for the last time, don't touch my children!'

A guard lifted Ginny from the horse and deposited her on the king's lap. She lifted her head to look straight up at Seth's face.

He wrinkled his nose playfully, making her giggle.

The sound of a trumpet made him look up. The talent contest was about to begin, and it was about to begin with a small man with a lute.

Seth groaned. 'Not another bastard *lute*. We have six million of these fuckers *inside*, can we not watch this shite *away* from the wind?'

The musician heard this comment and flung the instrument backstage with a bong. 'I will now sing the Fair Maidens of Sullenport, minus… the… instrumental,' he finished grudgingly. 'Right…' He cleared his throat twice and began to croon.

Seth's eyes rolled in annoyance regardless.

Cienne nudged him to prompt focus. 'He has a lovely voice, hasn't he?'

'Yes, dear,' he said patronisingly.

'It's boring,' Russell whispered.

'Yes, it is boring,' Seth said loudly, displaying the lack of common decency his son had somehow inherited. 'Why do we have to get up at the crack of dawn to hear the same boring song every week? I want to see the fire-eater and go back to bed.'

'You're worse than the children,' said Cienne. 'Just sit quietly and listen.'

He glared at the musician, who was shooting daggers at him while belting out the high notes. 'Don't glare at me! Sing something new for a change!'

'SETH!' Cienne exclaimed loudly. 'How old are you? Three?'

'I'm three,' Ginny said.

'I'm three too!' Russell piped up, in case being three warranted some kind of reward.

'That's lovely,' Cienne said tiredly, 'but Daddy is thirty-seven, and that means he has to start behaving like an adult in public.' *As if that will ever happen*, her eyes suggested, rising to the heavens.

Seth heaved a sigh and rolled his shoulders. He placed a hand on Cienne's elbow. 'I'm sorry. I'm just cold and sleepy and bored, and the guards are breathing down my neck and *jingling in my bloody ear.*'

They each took half a step back, sheepish.

The singer finished his song before time and bowed out, red faced. Another gust of wind raked through the hairs on the back of Seth's neck, making him shiver.

The impressionist next boarded the stage. He was quite evidently a comedian by the oversized leotard and comically huge crown that was half his height and caught the sunlight, blinding them.

'Good morning!' he bellowed, his clean-shaven face grinning under the rim of his oversized crown.

Seth flung him a withering glance. Another King Crey impression. He wondered which of his illustrious predecessors would be targeted today.

'It is I, King—AAH!!' He pointed theatrically at the pony the royal guard was still trying to shoo away. 'A horse! Get it AWAY!!'

The crowd burst into fits of laughter.

Seth frowned. 'Is that supposed to be me?' he said shrilly.

'SET THE DRAGON ON IT!' demanded 'King Seth', pointing at the animal.

A plume of yellow flame fired over their heads from backstage, sending a cloud of black smoke into the faces of the crowd. The pony bolted as the crowd applauded.

'YAY!' cheered 'King Seth', throwing his arms in the air.

The real Seth knuckled smoke from his eyes.

'King Seth' screamed again.

Seth whined, his fingers massaging his ears.

Wooden ravens propped on poles flew from side to side above a backdrop of some trees. 'King Seth' shrieked, cowering. Some people backstage started throwing stuffed ravens at him.

The audience roared with laughter.

Seth gawked in disbelief.

Cienne giggled treacherously.

'Stop laughing!' he snapped, glowering.

'AAAH! B-B-B-BIRDS!' the idiot shouted, flailing his arms in all directions. 'SET THE DRAGON ON THEM!'

Bright clothes of red and orange billowed out this time to surround the comedian. Seth decided real flame would have looked better on this occasion.

'He looks like Daddy,' Ginny said in amusement.

'No he does not!' Seth said, appalled. 'I thought this was a talent contest? The material is terrible! If it wasn't for the dirty great crown, you wouldn't even know it was—EEK!!'

A black raven landed on his knee and tumbled to the ground. Seth's feet flew up onto the seat and he clutched Ginny in terror.

The crowd roared with laughter at this involuntary addition to the act.

Seth scowled at everyone. He clapped both hands over Ginny's ears and told the performer to do something with his crown that made Cienne's ears turn red with embarrassment.

'I tried that once,' the comedian said to everyone's surprise. He made a small circle with his thumb and index finger. 'Doesn't quite fit.'

Seth licked his lips, hoisted Ginny onto Russell's lap and bolted to his feet to draw his guard's sword.

'And that's my cue to leave,' the comedian said hurriedly, skipping off stage. 'Goodbye, my friends!'

Cienne clicked her fingers repeatedly. Two bodyguards threw Seth back into his throne and confiscated his sword. Seth simmered in his seat, enraged.

'If this fire-eater isn't any good,' he sneered at no one in particular, 'I'm going to have everyone *killed*.'

'And here I was, wondering why they would *possibly* want to pick on *you*,' Cienne said flatly.

A man in formal robes of green peered out from the very edge of the stage and cleared his throat. He spoke quickly before anyone could instigate a riot.

'The fire-eater regrettably cannot perform today due to a horrible accident that occurred backstage during his side performance alongside King Howard.'

'Oh, *what?*' Seth fumed. In part due to the comedian's insinuation that he and Howard Rosethorn were the same person.

'Instead, we will move onto our next act, by the enigmatic…' he paused for effect, '… Raphael Emmanuel III.'

The man shuffled off, to be replaced by a slim man hidden in a burgundy cowl that hid his face entirely.

'Good afternoon, my people,' he intoned, in a deep, pompous voice.

A withering groan erupted from Seth, unbidden. He glared at him through his eyelashes.

'I, of course, have many talents,' he said knowingly.

Seth shifted in his seat, getting ready to leave.

Cienne shoved his shoulder back, scowling at him.

'But today, I will be displaying my artistic talents with the medium of the coloured oils.'

'He's painting?' Seth groaned in disbelief.

'I'm not sure that's what they meant by talent competition,' Cienne commented.

Seth flung his head back to groan at the clouds. 'We're going to be sat here for hours!'

'Not quite, my liege,' Raphael Emmanuel III said breezily. 'It is true that I am a painter, but I will not be displaying my talent here. When we arrive at my work's destination, all shall be perfectly clear.'

With that, he strode from the stage, walked between Seth and Cienne and the guards, and marched uphill towards the castle.

Seth and Cienne frowned at each other and rose to follow him.

With the entire audience in tow, Raphael Emmanuel III led the way imperiously up the road to the palace gates, nodding curtly to a pair of baffled guards manning the gates.

Seth waved for everyone to be let through.

The crowd formed an arrow through the castle grounds with Raphael at the head of it, heading between the armoury and the mortuary, past the sparring grounds until they all halted at the portcullis to the inner grounds, waiting for the guard to slowly winch it open.

The white-grey stone of the Serpent's Knot gleamed in the sunlight. The show's entire audience swarmed the path to the keep, the light gravel dark with sweeping cloaks and skirt hems. Jon swung open the doors and ducked to one side in bemusement. Half of Castlefoot Market filed into the fortress, led by the mysterious cloaked painter with the royal family close behind him.

They filed up the spiral staircase in single file, Seth and Cienne carrying a twin each, and finally arrived in the corridor of the third floor, where a guard planted both feet stubbornly in front of the entrance to the king and queen's private apartment.

'No entry, sir,' he said curtly.

'No, no,' Seth said, sidling into view, intrigued. 'Let him in.'

The guard shrugged, nonchalant, and slid out of the way.

The artist placed a hand on the doorknob.

'Ladies and gentlemen,' he announced, 'I present to you... the Confirmation of the Empire!'

Seth followed his gesture into the drawing room and stopped short, stunned.

Where once a blank, white stone wall had stood innocently behind the king's writing desk, a mural not unlike the style of that of the Seth Crey Shrine beamed brightly at them in shades of yellow and pink. The difference between that artwork and his mural was that this mural's subject matter depicted a very different interpretation of romance than Cienne's innocent little refuge – or so Seth saw as he eyed his and Cienne's likenesses with his head cocked to one side.

Cienne's ears burned bright red again.

'W-well,' she said, glancing at Seth, 'um...'

''S very,' Seth said, licking his lips, '... graphic.'

'Yes,' said Cienne. 'Very detailed...' She shuffled in front of Russell's line of sight.

'They're nakey,' Ginny said abruptly.

Seth nodded, his mouth opening and closing for words that did not come. '… yes. Avert your eyes, darling.'

'Interesting choice of subject matter,' a nobleman murmured in an attempt to critique.

'Yes, a very important moment in recent political history, albeit meekly overlooked,' Raphael Emmanuel said in earnest. 'Do you like it?'

Seth's mouth hung open. He patted the air around him until he found Ginny's face and covered her eyes. Noises squirmed out of him, frantically seeking words.

'Have you,' he said, mouthing the words before continuing, 'have you been following us to the fields to *paint* us?'

'Whatever happened to privacy?' Cienne wondered in a hollow voice.

'One could argue that the king's life belongs wholly to his subjects, hence being devoid of privacy…' The art critic trailed off under Cienne's steely gaze.

Seth's mouth opened and closed like a fish out of water before he finally caught his bearings.

'How did you get in *here*? We have a guard outside the door at all times…'

'Oh, I snuck in while you and the family were out,' Raphael Emmanuel III said.

'But I was *here*!' exclaimed the guard. 'I would have *seen*!'

'He nipped off to relieve himself,' the artist explained. 'I had plenty of time to create and leave before he returned.'

'A painting that size would have taken hours,' Seth said. 'No one paints a mural in the space of time needed to take a piddle.'

'I never said he went to take a *piddle*.'

The guard flushed under the royal couple's glares. 'I had the squirts.'

'So did she. Thoughts on the brushwork, anyone? Composition, realism? I had a bit of trouble with his majesty's nose, but I think I just about got an acceptable likeness…' Raphael Emmanuel III held a hand over the wall, splaying his fingers over Seth's facial likeness.

'I do like the wheat stalks,' one lady said in encouragement. 'Very artistically placed, I thought.'

'Well, we want it to be family friendly,' he said, gesturing to the twins.

Seth gaped at him. He turned to face Cienne, who was gazing up at the mural.

'I wish I really looked like that,' she said.

'So do I,' he agreed.

The stranger tilted back his head, admiring his handiwork. His hood slipped back just enough for Seth to see the man's short black beard.

'So,' the painter said with a grin. 'Do I get the prize?'

There was a pause as the crowd waited for an answer from Seth, who had suddenly become the contest's judge.

'Alright then,' he said.

'You're not thinking of keeping it?' Cienne asked in horror. 'Our children come in here!'

'It's educational,' he said, gazing up at it with sudden fondness. He quite liked it. It was a good likeness, despite the wonky nose. It showed off muscle definition Seth wasn't aware he had. 'And it's technically their very first portrait.'

'Well,' the green-clothed presenter announced, 'it appears we have our winner.'

'What?' snapped a blond man in the crowd. Seth recognised him gleefully as King Howard. 'There are seven more acts yet!!'

'But I'm home now,' Seth said, as though that excused everything. He shooed them away, flapping his hands. Not before giving King Howard a smug little smirk.

The comedian's upper lip curled.

Everyone filed out, the remaining performers grumbling.

Cienne ushered the twins out into the hall, where Despina lingered in wait at the doorframe.

'We're not keeping it,' she told Seth firmly.

Seth sighed heavily in disappointment and admired his biceps while he had the chance.

Ronald Horne appeared in the doorway at a sprint, panting.

'Lilly said to come straight through…' His eye caught the lewd painting. 'Seven Gods, that's a large… painting.'

Seth glanced at the hooded painter, ill at ease.

The Prophet stood in the centre of the drawing room, his hands folded behind his back.

'Enjoy your prize money,' Seth said politely.

The Prophet smiled and bowed.

'… somewhere else,' Seth added. He waved a bit as well in emphasis.

Raphael Emmanuel III looked slightly dejected. He exited through the doorway before turning back. 'Did you really like my paint—'

Seth shut the door in his face, with a grimace.

'Well?' Ron said. 'Where did you find my father?'

Seth gestured sheepishly at the painting.

$\sim$

IV

An hour later they had waded through the stalks to that exact spot, where a grotesque-looking King Sam lay, still tangled in branches and foliage.

Ron took a deep breath, laying a hand over his mouth. 'That's him, alright.'

Lilly placed a hand on his shoulder.

The sun's rays pelted down on the trio as they hovered over the late king. The stench of decay was palpable now – it rose from the corpse in the way the scent of spring wafted from freshly-cut grass, a faint but cuttingly distinct essence. A recent addition, Seth mused. It hadn't been noticeable the previous evening.

Seth shifted from foot to foot slightly, glancing down every so often at Lilly's dog, as though expecting it to jump him.

Ron crossed his arms over his chest, where a silver chain with a phoenix on the end glinted in the sun. 'So you and her highness found him when you were…'

'Yes,' Seth said, his cheeks a delicate shade of pink. 'On the bright side, at least he wasn't alive to remember the encounter.' He shivered violently and rubbed his palms on his front. 'Would have been nice to have met him under… better circumstances.'

'I think so too,' said Ron. 'He would have liked you.' His voice cracked with that last sentence.

Seth softened at that note, pity sweeping over his face.

Lilly put an arm around his ribs, giving him a squeeze.

Ron shook his head. 'He should look worse than this. After four years, he should look...'

'Skeletal,' Seth finished for him. He wrinkled his nose at the thought. 'It's like he's still... fresh. Like he died yesterday.'

'It must have made him travel through time or something,' Lilly pondered.

None of them needed an explanation as to what 'it' was.

Nearly four years ago, Qattren Meriangue had appeared in front of Seth and Cienne and revealed that Cienne's teenage request for a clone of her husband had brought forth an infant, named Howard Rosethorn.

This tale would have been strange enough were it not for the added fact that his mere arrival had brought forth an entity nicknamed the Hole, a rip in the very world itself that drew any- and everything into its depths until it found what it was looking for: the orphan of the Night of Raining Thorns – or an equivalent substitute.

Cue in Seth and Howie's joined love interest and the unborn bastard son of Seth Crey was sacrificed in Howie's place – leaving Adrienne the two's unlikely saviour and Seth a very unhappy man.

Lilly and Ron exchanged a look before giving Albie a furtive glance.

The Bastard gave her boot an innocent lick.

She, Stan and Ron had made a pact not to ever speak of the reincarnation of Seth's unborn son. The dog made Seth uncomfortable enough without him knowing that. It would only upset him. It didn't seem to make much difference anyway: the dog was little more than the average canine – albeit a runty one.

As far as she was aware.

Lilly cleared her throat and changed the subject. 'What do you want to do now, Ron?'

Ron looked up. 'Qattren suggested burying him in the Forest. There's a little meadow there, she offered to build a crypt...'

The Bastard zoned out of the conversation and looked up at Seth. Despite Lilly's efforts, his eyes looked distant. The Bastard bristled. As if he had the right...

The dog edged to the right and jumped claws first onto Lilly's calf.

'Ow, Albie, mind your nails!' Lilly exclaimed, interrupting Ron. 'Sorry, Ron, he's getting ratty because he wants food. Oh, give it a rest, will you?'

The Bastard scratched her leg once more and wandered away from them through the stalks, glancing back as if beckoning her to follow.

Lilly frowned and went after him.

'Ron,' Seth said suddenly as Lilly vanished. 'Have you seen or heard anything lately from…'

Ron waited a moment for him to continue, which he didn't, which didn't matter because he knew who he meant anyway. 'Not a word.'

Seth stared into space in silence after that.

Lilly pushed wheat stalks out of her way, her shoulders automatically tensed. Not because of the dead body – she was well accustomed to the sight of the dead ever since a covert militia of rebels attacked her father when she was four. King Theo butchered them mercilessly before his family's eyes. Her brother had screamed the house down and her mother had been catatonic for a week, but Lilly had been enraptured. She loved violence. Apparently, it was a Crey thing.

What was keeping her on edge was the thing she had met the last time she was in the cornfield – a venomous scorpion. Which, as soon as she thought of it, happened to be snoring gently right in front of her. Lilly froze as Albie stared at it.

'Careful, Albie,' she said in a low voice, 'one sting means hallucinations, two means paralysis, three means—'

Albie scooped it up in one mouthful. Lilly heard the creature crunch between his jaws and paused a moment to observe him. A minute later and Albie remained content, tail sweeping against the stalks in rapid tempo.

'Never mind, then,' she said after a moment.

She wondered what would have happened had her betrothed simply eaten it like that instead of getting stung. They wouldn't have had their first kiss, anyway. Maybe they wouldn't have kissed at all…

Orl had been killed only three years before, but Lilly was finding it easier to think about him. Not how his voice sounded or about their long talks on the various journeys to and from the Deadlands. Or the future they might have had together if their parents' wedding had gone well and Lilly's own had been to the man she loved instead of her current estranged spouse.

She didn't dare think of those, in case she started crying.

Lilly dragged herself back to the present to find that Albie was waiting for her to follow him again.

He led her on through the wheat, in a winding path that led her further away from Seth than she would have liked. She turned every so often to catch a glimpse of him, but instead of finding her brother, she found various items around her that looked entirely out of place.

Trees, much like the one King Samuel was entangled in, lay littered in every direction. As they meandered between pieces of debris from the Forest, Lilly saw an upturned cart to her right, crushed to a pulp of splintered wood. The Hole had dropped it from above, she guessed. Along with the rest of its plunder. The lush produce of the wheat field lay crumpled underneath it, crushed back into the soil.

Albie bounded ahead and Lilly had to jog to keep up. A few paces took her to where Albie needed her to go – a tiny enclosure in the stalks with a small crevice in the centre.

Lilly lowered herself to one knee, eyes focussed on the crevice in particular. Albie dropped to his belly beside it, resting his chin on the edge of it.

Her breath caught in her chest once she realised what was in it. She exhaled with a shudder.

'Seth!' she called, instantly regretting it.

She glimpsed the top of his head, rising over the wheat stalks in enquiry. A feeling of dread crept into her stomach as he approached.

'What's wrong?' Seth asked. He glared at Albie as usual. He frowned at the anomaly before him and stepped towards it. It took him a moment to register that the crevice housed a deceased infant.

Lilly saw the horror creep over his face. 'Get that thing away,' he said quietly, referring to the dog.

Lilly scooped Albie up in one fluid motion.

The baby's face came into view. He was in the same condition as the king almost – perfectly preserved, his wounds superficial but still open and red. Lilly examined his long lashes and puckered lips and a cold wave passed up her spine. He looked the same as the twins when they were born, his face near identical. He lay bare on the soil, flat on his back. It was as though he had been born and simply thrown there. But that wasn't what had happened at all...

Seth brushed against her shoulder. She was alarmed to see him kneel and reach for the corpse.

'Seth—' she began.

Seth paid her no notice. He lay his cloak across the ground adjacent to the crater and delicately lifted the child onto it, wrapping him delicately. He rose to his feet, the boy cradled in his arms. He walked back to the gate, where their coach and guard waited.

Albie wriggled free of Lilly's arms, landing harshly in the rushes to follow.

'Seth...'

He ignored her and just walked faster, the little dog in tow.

Outside the field, on a little dirt road parallel to the rusty gate, Russell Marbrand yawned and gazed at the slim figure approaching from within the wheat. 'Looks like they're ready to haul him out,' he observed. 'In you go, then.'

A pair of guards carrying a stretcher nodded and waited for Marbrand to open the gate before walking through.

Marbrand stuck his hands into his pockets and turned to three coaches: the royal carriage, patterned in garish green and gold, the guards' comparatively decrepit cart of plain timber, and the black funereal coach, for King Samuel Horne.

Marbrand was turning sixty next winter: a sobering thought when Samuel Horne's death was considered. King Sam was fifty-two when the Hole took him, and that was a ripe old age compared to his son Vladimir.

Marbrand didn't expect to die in a comfortable bed somewhere, unless it happened to be blood-soaked from a sword wound, but he reckoned he might well die of old age at this stage. If the gods were too busy making royalty suffer, he and his daughter might just outlive them all.

The figure arrived at the gate and Marbrand swung it open casually. 'Nice day for bringing out the dead, isn't it?'

The farmer nodded, his hands in his pockets and a large, empty basket in one elbow. 'Isn't it always?'

They looked out at the golden stalks.

'Terrible thing, that,' the man said in a low voice. 'Poor buggers… you know, I never trusted sorcery. The state of those two bodies shows completely why no one should—'

Marbrand held up a finger, silencing him. *Two* bodies?'

'Oh, yeah, no one mentioned?' the man said, shaking his head. 'Poor little mite.'

Marbrand felt a pang, deep in his ribs. 'A child?' he asked. 'How old?'

'Barely a day, I reckon.' He lifted the basket. 'Thought I'd better bring this out, collect the little boy to take to the church before his majesty finds him.'

On that note, the sounds of movement in the wheat diverted Marbrand's attention.

Seth Crey was returning, cradling something small in both arms.

'Looks like you spoke too soon,' Marbrand murmured. He scooped the basket from the man's grasp and headed into the field.

Seth Crey had never looked like a king – his boyish face and tendency towards shrill dialogue made 'charming prince' sound too kind. But the expression on that boyish face as he speed-walked through the field was close to how he had looked during the assassination attempt three years ago – drawn and grey with pure, absolute terror.

'Sir,' Marbrand said as they reached each other. 'Allow me to take the child. You return to the coach.'

Seth shook his head fervently. Marbrand saw his fingers pinch the cloth wrapping the child, emerald embroidered with gold. King Seth's own cloak.

'He's staying with me,' Seth said, his voice ringing with authority. 'Leave him be.'

Marbrand frowned. 'Who is this child?'

Seth gazed down at the boy. A tear squeezed out of one eye and rolled down his right cheek. 'I don't know,' he whispered.

Marbrand held up the basket.

Seth settled the child into it.

'I'll take him,' Seth whispered after, grasping the hand in both hands. He walked back to the gate with Marbrand in tow. Marbrand watched him climb into the coach, still cradling the basket.

'Make sure Lilly and Ron get back safely,' Seth told Marbrand, who nodded. 'I… have to sort this, and then…' he paused. 'Is the morgue empty?'

'Has been for three years, sir.'

'Good, good.'

Seth stared into space for a moment and knocked on the roof of the carriage.

Ron and Lilly emerged from the field as Seth's coach rolled away.

'Where's he going?' Lilly asked Marbrand. 'Is he okay?'

Marbrand stared after him, his brow furrowed.

'I don't know,' he said to both questions.

~

'First lesson,' Geldemar said, snapping his fingers in front of the Bastard's eyes. 'Don't lose yourself in the story.'

The Bastard blinked.

The coach rattled down a winding country road, little-used and lumpy. Seth bounced up and down inside as a tapestry of green rolled past the window, his eyes locked on the basket in which the infant's corpse lay.

The Bastard's ghost hovered on the seat beside him while his earthly dog form lay fast asleep on Seth's lap. Seth was so engrossed in his own thoughts he hadn't noticed that the dog had stopped breathing five minutes ago.

'How do I not lose myself in the story,' the Bastard seethed, 'when the story is all about how I died the other year?'

Geldemar similarly hovered on the seat across from them. He too was apparently a ghost, because Seth couldn't see him.

'I don't know, do I?' Geldemar snapped back. 'You'll have to find your own way around that, but I want you focussed, not blubbing into your handkerchief during your funeral.'

The Bastard scowled at him. 'What are you going to do, then? Make him just leave the dead baby in the coach so he can take off chasing skirt?'

'Oh, you won't be doing anything just yet,' Geldemar said firmly. 'I'll take care of Act One. You just pay close attention.'

'What's happening in Act One?'

'I'll show you when you're finished asking useless questions,'

Geldemar said. 'I need you to pay close attention. This is what we call *subtlety*. You'll see this in more detail in a moment.'

The Bastard glowered at him and leaned back against the edge of the seat. The inherent power of his own sense of being stopped him from falling through the coach by accident.

'I don't suppose buggering up my mother's life factors in Act One?' he asked hopefully. 'Subtlety's fine, but it sounds a bit boring.'

'As intelligent a woman as your mother is, she is quite capable of buggering her own life on her own,' Geldemar said. 'I say we leave her to her own devices for now. It's Seth's brain we have to figure out at the moment. And his is quite the conundrum.'

The Bastard arched an eyebrow and gazed out of the window as the village approached.

~

A man with a dog tapped a short, grey-haired woman on the shoulder. 'How much for the little bed?'

The woman glanced at it without facing him. 'Four silvers.'

'Can I owe you?'

She turned to tell him to naff off and her eyes widened. Her hands scrambled at her beige dress, smoothing it in frantic repetition.

'My liege, take it for free!' she exclaimed. 'What is this in aid of? Is there a new arrival on the way again?'

Seth plastered a fake grin on his face. 'Not for me. A lord at court.'

'Oh, lovely!' she trilled. 'My sister's husband's mother was a midwife for one of your lords, can't recall his name…'

Seth's attention quickly diverted from the details of the old midwife. His eye had caught a swaddling blanket with embroidered trim, and his hand immediately fell upon it.

The woman fell silent, upon registering that he wasn't paying attention to her.

Albie wandered across the marketplace.

'Would you like any assistance?' the lady asked Seth.

'Nope,' he said swiftly, tucking the blanket into the cot. 'I'll send you what I owe you. Thank you.'

'There's really no need, sir, I can cover the price of…'

He was already across the square, cot in hand.

Buttercup Village lay north of the castle, a small cluster of cottages circling an absurdly large market square, mostly empty. It was double the distance from the palace than Castlefoot Market, but Seth knew the undertaker was based here. The quiet village suited him at present. The less people around to gawk at him, the better.

He reached the carriage and shoved the cot inside, tucking it under the seat bearing the little basket. Seth's eyes lingered on it.

It wasn't his dead son. He didn't know why he ever thought it would have been. His child had died in the womb: it had barely come partway to term. This was someone else's stillborn baby, a child carried fully and born naturally. And yet… the facial features, the set of his eyelashes… he was an amalgamation of his twins when they were born. The resemblance was uncanny. He couldn't shake the feeling that he had an obligation towards this child – perhaps because he had shirked the responsibility of his own.

He turned and wandered around, pretending to browse while he scoured his memory for the location of the undertakers. The coach rolled into an alley and slid into the shadows, to Seth's approval.

He moved to the nearest clothes stall and mulled over the coats while he racked his brains.

When his father had died, he'd definitely been in the marketplace while he was waiting for the undertaker to return from a funeral, so whereabouts was the bloody undertaker's?

He chose a long navy coat, which this seller, too, refused payment for, and slung it on, pulling the hood up as drizzle started to fall.

He decided to head down the alley his coach had vanished down to ask directions.

The sound of hooves and trundling wheels turned him around.

Normally he would have ignored such an ordinary sound. Maybe it was because the village was so empty – coaches passed through the palace like air passed through his lungs and weren't unusual enough to warrant a glance.

Or perhaps he turned out of jumpy nervousness at the idea of someone finding out he had a dead child in his possession.

In any case, Seth turned at the very normal coach, contrary to ordinary circumstances, and caught a flash of auburn hair. And contrary to ordinary circumstances, he stared, despite not being able to see her face, or if her acquaintance had, like him, the blond hair and blue eyes that had compelled her to make a child with him.

As he saw what he thought was Adrienne's coach roll past, Seth suddenly wasn't so eager to find the undertaker anymore. He didn't want to organise a funeral, in a discreet corner of the grounds where only he could find it. He didn't want to talk to the man who had dressed his murder victim as best he could for his public funeral and spoken to Seth so kindly, as if he'd loved his father and hadn't ruptured his jugular out of pure hatred. He didn't want this innocent child to have a proper send-off. He didn't want to look at the child at all.

He wanted her to be in love with him… which was strange, because he wasn't in love with her anymore. She had broken something in him that day, four years ago – something deep and fundamental, and he'd forgotten about it. And seeing a reminder of the child he had lost had broken it all over again.

Seth didn't want to see him today. Or her. Or anyone.

'But he doesn't have a choice,' Geldemar finished to the Bastard, the two standing nearby as ghostly entities.

The Bastard sighed, digging his hands in his pockets. 'He'll kill himself at this rate.'

'No, he won't,' Geldemar said with a smile. 'Follow me.'

~

'Is he still awake?' Geldemar asked as they arrived. 'Good. Now, let's have a look.'

He padded across the emerald green floor, his velvet boots sinking pleasantly into the thick carpet with each step. An opulent drawing room had opened around them as they materialised, enveloping them in warm amber light from braziers hanging between floral tapestries. It echoed the royal chambers of the Creys' Keep, the rich emerald carpets contrasting the pastel patterning that could only have been influenced by Cienne. It had that sickly-sweet *poshness* about it.

How luxurious, the Bastard thought sourly. *How self-indulgent. Only the best for King Seth of Adem, eh?*

Seth Crey's brain, contrary to expectations, was not, in fact, empty. His mind had opened around them as Geldemar guided him inside, the décor indicating his social status and aesthetic preferences immediately. Every square foot of the emerald carpet contained a mahogany chest, each closed but with the golden latch lifted, unlocked. *His memories,* the Bastard surmised.

He happened to know courtesy of Geldemar that his own mind was a dingy dungeon, covered in a kind of debilitating fungus and littered with congealed memories. He'd grown so used to it that the clean opulence of Seth's self-assured mind made him squirm with discomfort.

'How's him being awake going to make any difference?'

Geldemar made a beeline for a row of trunks at the back wall. 'Do you know what dreams are? Ordinary dreams, I mean.' He swept over the lids of the trunks with the flat of his hand.

'No, not really,' the Bastard admitted. 'I've never had one. My mother put paid to that before they had begun.'

'Hmm. I could tell as much from the state of your mind. Remember me telling you about the memories going sour inside your head?'

The Bastard gave him a nod.

'That's because you haven't had a proper sleep in over four years,' he told him, meandering around the identical trunks with care. 'When you sleep, your mind organises all the information gathered throughout the day, files away everything important, throws out the rubbish, etc. Dreams are flashes of your thoughts and memories of the day as they're being sorted. It's essentially like having Jimmy De Vil enter your mind every evening and tidy it up for you.'

'Lovely,' the Bastard grimaced.

He'd listened in on Jimmy's mind in passing, during his periodic wanders through Sal'plae. It was a tidy mind, but it certainly wasn't a clean one.

'Because your ethereal self doesn't tire or need a break, you tend to just keep going – meaning your mind doesn't get time to sit down and organise itself. Your bad memories and bitter thoughts are left lying around the place for you to find, and you pick them up and handle them ten times more than the average human being, because there's nowhere else for them to go. Because of this, they decay.'

'I have a mouldy brain,' the Bastard mused. 'That explains a lot.'

'I can teach you how to train a part of your mind to clean up your memories as you go,' Geldemar offered. 'Like mine does. I don't sleep either, but my mind is as clean as a whistle. 'Course yours will need a deep clean first, which unfortunately means giving you a total memory wipe. So that will have to wait until after our plans come to fruition.'

He lifted the lid on a trunk to peer inside before closing it again.

'But anyway, back to Seth. It's handier to have him awake while we rifle through his precious memories. Otherwise the organising process will alert him to our presence. Awake, he's outside the house, so to speak. Asleep and he'll be in the room with us, watching us and listening to every word we say. So we need to be gone before he goes for another nap. Aha.'

He lifted the lid on another trunk and swung it open, kneeling in front of it.

The Bastard stepped forward, intrigued. 'What's in there?'

'Details of his and your mother's affair,' he said, rummaging inside with both hands. 'And pretty much every other dirty fantasy he'd ever had, as well. It's all symbolic items, really.'

The Bastard was about to ask what items they were when the sound of muttering interrupted him. 'Whose voice is that?'

Geldemar grinned at him. 'Don't you recognise it? It's your own voice. Seth's voice, actually. He's thinking.'

The Bastard paused to listen for a moment.

Bloody dog, shitting on my bed, bloody dog, why did she have to bring that thing home anyway, home anyway, bloody dog, dog, dragon not enough for her, going to have words with her about that bloody dog—

The Bastard grinned broadly. 'He's found the present I left for him.'

– of all the animals she brings home, it had to be that mongrel, it's like what they say, dog looks like its owner—

'Oi,' the Bastard said, hurt.

Seth's internal monologue repeated that line a couple times, with a clear note of fondness for it.

'He loves to repeat himself, doesn't he?'

'It's a human thing,' Geldemar said absently. 'Some of them often rehearse their lines in their head about seven times before saying it. Very annoying.'

Jon's nasally voice cut into Seth's inner monologue. A memory.

That's not dogs, that's cats.' Bloody does smother small children, I swear it tried to kill Ginny that day—

The Bastard scowled up at the ceiling.

'Don't take it personally, he loves you really,' Geldemar said, frowning into the trunk. 'My God, there are a surprising amount of phallic objects in here for a heterosexual male.'

'What's a phallic—and suddenly I know exactly what a phallic object it,' the Bastard said, his face morphing into a grimace.

'Absorbed a bit of Seth's knowledge, have you?' Geldemar said with a smile. 'He has a vivid imagination, that man.'

The Bastard shook his head, ridding himself of it as much as possible. 'What's in these other trunks?'

'Various collections of things, you know. Sceneries. Childhood memories. Politics, though that one's pretty empty, actually, probably from avoiding the council meetings. Painful memories. A whole three trunks dedicated to his father. I must have a root through those someday. Always been a personal interest of mine, your grandfather. Did you know he hid a embalmed snake in his crown so that Seth would be killed by the venom on his coronation?'

The Bastard blinked. 'No, I didn't know that. Why didn't it work?'

'Seth suddenly became allergic to gold. They had to make a new one for him out of silver or else he'd break out in lumps.'

The Bastard snorted. Oh yeah. He'd forgotten about that one.

'The original's in storage in the castle, snake still in place. No one's the wiser.'

'Oh.'

Geldemar pried open a trunk to the right of the one he was nosing in and lifted the lid a smidge. 'This one's about you, by the looks of it.'

The Bastard paused, then squeezed through the gaps between the trunks. Geldemar opened the trunk for him as the Bastard knelt at his side, peering in.

A basket lay inside and little else. The Bastard pinched the handle. It was what his corpse had lain in. Which meant it was only added recently.

'You're telling me it's been this empty all this time?'

'Stick your ear in there.'

The Bastard frowned, lowering the left side of his head into the trunk. Seth's voice whispered the same few sentences in a never-ending loop.

I'm sorry I'm sorry I'm sorry I love you I'm sorry I failed I failed you I'm a failure I'm sorry…

The Bastard winced. 'That's just sad.'

'Isn't it?' Geldemar said, shaking his head. He handled the latch of a nearby trunk and tugged. A padlock rattled against it. Locked. 'Hmm.' Geldemar glanced around, his brow furrowed.

'Who's this?' the Bastard demanded.

Geldemar shifted his attention to the Bastard. He held up a small, framed canvas roughly the size of his hand. Upon it was a painting of a little boy with a strong resemblance to Seth and a grin with gaps in it.

'That's you,' Geldemar said brightly. 'That's how he imagines you would look like now. It changes the older his other children get. He reckons you would have looked like them.' Geldemar gazed at the Bastard's expression, which was identical to Seth's when he was confused. 'He was right, in a way.'

The Bastard snorted with disgust. 'This is his other son, only a bit bigger.'

'Exactly,' Geldemar agreed. 'Except that in his vision of you, you love him and stand in his shadow in admiration. Russell couldn't care less for anything that hasn't got icing sugar sprinkled on top.'

The Bastard was about to throw it unceremoniously back into the trunk.

Geldemar stopped his hand.

'Keep it,' he told him. 'Could come in useful later.'

The Bastard glared at the image before sliding it into the inside pocket of his jerkin.

Geldemar's gaze returned to the trunk. He heaved a sigh. 'Shoot.'

'What?'

'Unbelievably, he's repressed his memories of your mother's

appearance,' Geldemar said, shaking his head. 'He's locked them in here. I was hoping we could use that to convince him to search her out.'

'In a dream, you mean,' the Bastard said.

'Yes, I figured if we remind him of her, he might—' He froze. 'Actually, that might still work.'

'What's that?'

He turned to the Bastard, a smile creeping over his face.

'We need your mother's face,' he said. 'It's been filed in here, locked away, where no amount of searching can accidentally lift it. To get it, we'll need to trigger him into opening it.'

He lifted an eyebrow.

'He's due a nap in the coach this morning. Think you can come up with something to get him to open that trunk?'

The Bastard laced his fingers together and cracked his knuckles with a smile.

~

V

Archie heard a knock on the door and dropped his hammer with a sigh. 'If you don't bog off, I'm calling the town guards. There are only so many chairs you can nick without me noticing!'

'I'm not here to nick anything, you mad old fart,' Adrienne said playfully.

Archie swung around.

'Adrienne!' he squealed in delight.

Adrienne grinned at him, the little dimples on either side of her smile taking him back twenty years. Her reddish-brown hair hung in a clumsy braid down her left shoulder. Apparently, her nimble needlework talents did not extend to plaiting hair. She'd taken to wearing dresses, he noticed, eyeing a slightly worn grey article.

Adrienne tiptoed into his workshop. The tiptoeing was mandatory – everyone remembered that harrowing afternoon when a hasty pair of crutches had to be fastened for Howie, who had impaled his own foot in one clumsy step. Howie had learned his lesson, but Archie hadn't. His workshop remained as it always was on a weekday, an obstacle course of discarded cuttings, semi-finished furniture and, to Adrienne's exasperation, clusters of jagged tools, many of them blade-up, somehow. And all coated with a liberal layer of sawdust. Of course.

They embraced warmly, Archie's arms tight around her neck as the taller girl stooped slightly to rest her chin on his shoulder.

'What are you doing here?' he asked happily. 'I thought you were never coming back here again. What happened to "I'd rather drink boiling oil and shit on hot coals"?'

Adrienne laughed. 'I changed my mind. I missed my Uncle Archie.'

'Oh!'

He smacked three big kisses on Adrienne's cheek, making her giggle.

'I missed you too. Where's He Who Must Not Be Named?' he asked playfully, releasing her. 'Still flogging the dead horse of his carpentry career?'

'He's not that bad at carpentry,' she said in amusement. 'Howie's fine, he's just doing up the new house.' A corner of Adrienne's mouth turned down slightly. '... he was getting annoyed, so I left him to it,' she said in a sheepish undertone. 'Why is he not to be named?'

Archie returned his attention to the day's project: the reconstruction of a cracked cabinet drawer. He stared at a section for a moment, picking up a chisel to shave a piece from the joining. 'Oh, that was a joke a client made about him being the Antichrist, when I told him he used to be my apprentice. He claimed he heard a rumour that every time a person speaks his name aloud, a ball of flame gets thrown at a small cat—'

Suddenly the words 'new house' settled on him. He pivoted to face her, wide-eyed. 'New house? You've *moved* here?'

'In a small village a few miles away, yes,' she said, grinning broadly.

'Why? Did something happen?' Archie asked, his joy taking on an anxious tone. 'It was those bloody taxes, wasn't it? Don't tell me he bankrupted you?'

'No! Well, yes,' she conceded, 'but we had enough money after selling up to travel here, and Howie did a few odd jobs along the way...'

Archie sniggered. Anyone following Howard Rosethorn would easily find him by following the trail of collapsed fences, furniture, sheds and house extensions from one end of the country to the other. He hoped the silly sod didn't leave a business card.

'… he's earning enough money to rent a small house on condition we do it up ourselves, so…' She lifted her shoulders happily. 'We're staying here.'

Archie pressed his lips together and pinched her chin. 'Good. How is the little oik, anyway? What's he up to, opening a shop? A stall? Making little apprentices for me, perhaps?'

Adrienne suddenly tensed. 'We aren't trying for a child, Archie.'

Archie pulled his head back with a frown. 'Why not?'

She exhaled and licked her lips. 'I don't think I want to have children,' she said. 'I'm not the… maternal type.'

He tutted. 'Course you are.' He tucked some loose strands of hair behind her ears. ''S why you started medicine. Babies are just like sick people, only in miniature and a little less green.'

She gave a little laugh, but to Archie it sounded insincere.

'Take your time,' he said firmly, laying a hand on her cheek. 'You've plenty of time for all that.' He rubbed her cheekbone with his thumb and tapped the underside of her chin. 'Come on, since you're here you can hold these parts up while I hammer this drawer back together. You always helped me with that when you were a kid.'

'I remember,' she said fondly, circling the workbench as the sounds of Serpus rush hour filtered in from the open door. 'It was mostly because Howie was too busy breaking them.'

Archie arched an eyebrow. 'Yes. He was a class-A twit, wasn't he?'

'He still is,' Adrienne said with a laugh.

Archie was glad to hear a bit more mirth in this one.

~

Seth awoke to find himself face down on a tiled floor.

He pulled himself up on two hands and frowned, glancing around.

He lay in a large room covered in white tiles. Although fully illuminated, Seth couldn't identify the light source – no windows were apparent on the tiled walls and the flat ceiling bore no chandelier or brazier. There was no way in. There was no way out.

'Lilly, what have you done now?' he demanded to the room at large. If in doubt, blame Lilly.

'Lilly isn't here.' A female voice. Quite young, and formal.

'Ginny, then?' he guessed. The diction was a bit advanced, but you never knew with toddlers.

'You know who I am.'

Seth lifted himself to his feet. 'Is that Qattren?'

And Qattren suddenly appeared, dressed uncharacteristically in Ron's clothing, and not his best clothing, either. Her copper ringlets were tied in a messy plait over her left shoulder, which Seth found inexplicably attractive.

'Is this going to be a sex dream?' he asked.

'No, dear, I'm afraid it isn't,' Qattren said dryly.

'Oh, good,' he said in relief. ''Cause I'm half sure I fell asleep next to my three-year-old and I don't really want him to see me, you know…'

'Erect,' she finished.

'Yes.' He frowned. 'We are still *asleep* on the coach, right?'

'Yes.'

'Not… dead or anything?'

'Not at present, no.'

'Oh, good,' he said, relaxing.

There was a silence for a moment.

'So why are we here?' Seth asked.

'I'm afraid I can't answer,' Qattren said, idly picking her nails. 'It's your mind, you know. For some reason, your mind has decided it necessary for you to see a red-haired young woman in men's clothing.'

'But you don't wear men's clothing,' he said, baffled. 'I've only ever seen you wear dresses. The only women I know who wear men's clothing are Lilly and Adrienne.' His eyes widened. 'Am I going to have an affair with Qattren in real life?'

'No, of course not. She finds you repulsive.'

His nose wrinkled. 'It isn't going to be Lilly, is it?' he asked in a low voice, squirming.

'This isn't about your trousers, Seth,' she said, 'and anyway, I'm not Qattren.'

He jerked his head backward. 'But you look like Qattren.'

She shook her head.

'Adrienne,' she said by way of explanation. She gestured at her trousers in confirmation.

His eyes narrowed. 'But you look like Qattren,' he repeated with emphasis.

'That's because you can't remember her face,' Qattren/Adrienne pointed out. 'Four years is a long time. The closest you can come to Adrienne...' she gestured to her appearance, '... is me.'

Seth paused. 'But you're Qattren,' he said stubbornly.

Qattren rolled her eyes.

'You're *old.*'

'I'm immortal,' she said, gritting her teeth a bit. 'That's not old at all. There's no such thing as "old" with me.'

'You used to sleep with my granddad.'

'I'm not old!' she snapped.

It was Seth's turn to roll his eyes. 'So why am I thinking of "Adrienne" then?'

She scowled at him for the 'old' remark. 'Because you miss her.'

'Bullshit,' he said. 'I miss her like I miss being drowned by my father.'

'You miss your father too, though,' she said. 'Deep down. And you suffer from repressed guilt, but that's an issue for another dream. This is a dream about love—'

He pointed at her gleefully. 'Ah! So it *is* a—'

'Not that kind of love!'

His face fell, crestfallen.

Qattren exhaled through her elegantly sculpted nose. She reassumed her dreamy expression.

'You have a choice to make,' she began in an ethereal voice.

Seth tapped an index finger on his chin. 'Hmm, let me think! Love of my life, mother of my children and the most beautiful woman in the world, or spotty teenager whose face I can't even remember? That's a *real* pickle, isn't it?'

Qattren threw her arms into the air. 'Are you going to listen to me or do you want to be confused for the rest of your life? *Listen.* Your happiness is coming to you. Will you ignore it? Or will you follow where your heart tugs you from day to day and meet with your true love at last?'

Seth pondered carefully, his eyes turned up to the ceiling. 'You know, it would be much easier to make a decision if you and I just—'

'Get your mind out of the gutter,' she said sharply. 'Think about it. Whose face makes your chest contract and your heart beat fast to look at? Whose voice renders your mind empty and devoid of intelligence? Whose breath on your neck sends heat to your heart and down to your—'

'Stop right there,' Seth said, his hands in the air. 'That's quite enough of that, thank you! I am a married man, a very happy one, with—'

'An obsession with dreams of an erotic nature.'

'Shut up!' Seth pointed a finger at her. 'That… person is not to be spoken of in my presence as anything other than a child murderer – even if she did set my spine on fire and render me a gibbering wreck in the night with visions of skin and legs and auburn hair…' he trailed off in a little squeak, his eyelids fluttering shut.

When he opened them again, inhaling wistfully into his nose, Adrienne's real image stood in place of Qattren's. Entering him along with that wistful gasp were floral notes – she was always around flowers and plants, inspecting them, creating some kind of sorcery only she knew of with them. That scent clung to the membranes in his nostrils, the way it had back in the mansion. *God, that week was amazing*, Seth thought with an ache.

She was smiling at him.

Before he knew it, he had broken out into a sweat, his abdomen tingled and his pulse throbbed in his ears.

'Don't come near me,' he half-begged.

'You don't mean that,' she purred, stepping forward. 'I've missed you, Seth…'

He groaned with a pained expression.

'Come find me, Seth,' she breathed, now an inch from his face.

Seth jolted awake as the coach hit a bump in the road.

Russell lay curled in a foetal position, using Seth's right thigh as a pillow.

Seth flushed prolifically, her breath still lingering on his face. It gave him shivers. He glowered at his trousers. *Don't even* think *about it.*

He jerked his head from side to side, expelling her from his mind.

He stroked Russell's hair idly, gazing out at the countryside. The little boy had been complaining of stomach pains this morning, so Cienne had sent

Seth out with him for a bit of fresh air. Seth was glad of it, if a bit wary. Russell with stomach pains meant he'd had one too many cream cakes, and one too many cream cakes equalled gastric explosion.

He figured gastric explosion wasn't the only reason Cienne wanted them out together. Seth had been falling into a pit of depression ever since finding… the boy. He never even had a name, Seth thought with a pang. Neither had Russell for the first week of his life – he seemed to have immense difficulty coming up with names for people.

He expelled the thought of him from his mind also, with difficulty.

Cienne popped into his mind again. He softened. She was too good for him, he realised. She had been more than sympathetic, despite the entire situation. She searched him out as soon as Lilly had told her what had happened and found him at the undertaker's, sidling up beside him to take his hand. She didn't owe him that, he thought.

His thoughts drove back to Adrienne, without warning. The smell of her, the colour of her hair, her voice… he blinked her image away. The dream had been so vivid. What had brought that to mind?

The boy, he thought with a pang of sadness.

He supposed he ought to tell her. Supposing it actually *was* her in that coach – it could have been anyone. It was probably someone else, he decided finally. He hoped it was, anyway.

He stroked his son's head again.

'Where are we going again?' he wondered aloud.

'Buttercup Village market, my liege,' the coachman said brightly over the rattling wheels. 'You wanted the best place to get a cake to bribe the prince with.'

Seth made a face. 'Oh.' He'd been in such a daze when they set off that he hadn't noticed their journey to Adrienne's home.

He examined his surroundings some more as the cottages of Buttercup Village began to file past. They must have only been travelling for little more than ten minutes. He thought the dream had lasted longer. The vision of Adrienne standing before him was still vivid.

I'd forgotten how pretty she was, he thought, enraptured.

Russell jerked awake on a bump in the road and rubbed his face into Seth's trousered knee. A disturbing moisture sank into the fabric.

'Excuse me,' Seth murmured, rapping on the top of his head gently with one knuckle. 'I'm not a handkerchief, you know.'

Russell wiggled around until they were face to face and gave him the sweetest smile he could muster.

Seth smirked at him. 'Don't try to be cute, you're still disgusting.'

He grabbed the boy's giggling face in one hand, turning it from side to side playfully.

The faint sounds of the village broke them from their exchange, and the coach ground to a halt. Seth hoisted Russell upright by the armpits and swung the door outward.

It was a busy day for the village, at least in comparison to Seth's last visit. There was a grand total of four coaches lingering on the skirts of the market, including Seth's, and the three stalls littering the wide expanse of flagstones were busy catering for three customers each. Seth found it a breath of fresh air to be able to walk through a village and, well, breathe fresh air.

He strolled past a clothing stall and made a beeline for the pastry merchant, Russell cradled in one elbow.

'Hello there,' he said to the middle-aged woman.

She curtsied until her knees grazed the gravel.

Seth rolled his eyes and waved his free hand up and down in the air. 'Get up, get up, I just want a cake for the little man. This one will do. No, the little one on the left. *No*, you piglet,' he said over his son's protestations, 'don't listen to him, he's having trouble with his bowel movements as it is…'

Oblivious to Seth, a small coach rolled past with Archie and Adrienne Hart inside. It halted in an alley between a greengrocer's and a delicatessen.

The pastry merchant shook her head frantically, refusing to accept Seth's money.

Seth set his jaw. 'Listen,' he said, mustering patience, 'I have a room at home in the basement, the same size as this entire market, full of gold coins. I won't miss two of them, so just take the money.'

'I couldn't, my liege. Have it on me, it can be a gift to the little prince from me—'

'But it's your money!' he exclaimed, handing her the entire purse. 'That's the whole point of you making cakes is to get money for them!'

'I don't need the money that much, sir,' she said feebly. 'I just want to show my patriotism and besides, that's far too much money.'

'Call it a tip, then. Half of Serpus would have bitten my arm off by now. Just take the damn money!'

'I couldn't, sir, it's on the house—'

'TAKE THE MONEY!' he exploded.

Over the road, Adrienne turned to see who was doing the yelling as Archie peered into the delicatessen in interest.

Her eyes widened as they found Seth's face, and a miniature version of the same alongside it, eating an iced slice.

The woman had started trembling. She looked as if she might shatter into a million pieces, like glass.

'Look, just take the money, it's fine,' Seth said softly, trying to retract his outburst.

This didn't stop the effect.

Seth sighed, stuffed the purse into her bosom and turned to walk away before the now crimson-faced woman could give it back.

Then his and Adrienne's eyes met.

Adrienne, looking astonished but otherwise exactly as she did in the dream, stared at him blankly, her eyes flitting from Seth's face to Russell's and back again. She raised her hand slowly to one side of her neck, self-consciously.

Seth simply stared at her with his mouth open a crack. He felt as though a hummingbird had gotten stuck between his lungs and his diaphragm. He swallowed hard and turned as red as the pastry merchant.

Adrienne's hand faltered and she hurried away, horror-stricken.

Seth swung a hundred and eighty degrees and stared at the gravel in front of him, a bemused Russell waving a hand in front of his face.

She was back. Adrienne was back. But what for? To see him?

The hummingbird in his ribs flapped a little harder at the thought.

A small finger prodded his right cheek. 'Aren't you gon' talk to the lady?'

Seth stared at him, dazed.

'Should I?' he asked him, as if Russell held the answers to the universe. 'What am I supposed to say? What do I do? I can hardly start flirting with her as if nothing happened, can I?'

'Woss flirting?' Russell asked, nonplussed.

'It's that way Jimmy is around pretty girls in the kitchens—why did I feel the need to tell you that?' Seth cut across himself, his face screwed up.

Russell shrugged.

'T's good a' helping Jimmy wi' pretty ladies,' he babbled, as though trying to help.

Seth considered this for a moment – mostly to discern the coherent words from Russell's toddler-speak, which was often the case when either he or his sister spoke more than three words together – before thinking better of it and carrying him back to the coach.

'You'd better stay here, with the horseys,' he said.

He deposited Russell atop the coach between the driver and their accompanying palace guard, who was picking apart a steak and kidney pie.

'Mind him for me?'

''Course, m'liege,' he said with his mouth full. He handed a very happy Russell a corner of his pie.

Seth smiled and gave him a wink before taking a deep breath and, the lucid dream still imprinted on the front of his mind, turning towards the marketplace after Adrienne.

He stalked across the market square, rolling his shoulders, trying to loosen up.

It will be fine, he told himself.

He strode over the cobblestones, each step calculated, one after another.

This doesn't have to be awkward. It could be Cousin Elyse. You managed to have a normal conversation with her the other year while she was undressing you with her eyes, how hard can this be? At least Adrienne won't try to grope you while Cienne gives the stink-eye in the background.

Although the possibility of Adrienne groping him did make him feel a little more *eager.*

He kept a casual pace down the alley Adrienne had bounded down and glimpsed her walking at a similar pace into a cluster of cottages, her basket of foodstuffs in hand.

This part of the village was considerably fuller, he noticed. Children skipped and chased each other right into Seth's way as he passed seemingly unnoticed through the throng, one eye on the auburn beauty in front of him and the other on the obstacles playing hopscotch under his feet.

She paused as an elderly neighbour harangued her into helping her carry a stack of curtains from one house to another.

Seth took this moment to catch up, cowering behind a cart of hay for cover.

Once her good deed was done, Adrienne sped off, rolling her eyes.

Seth followed exactly three yards behind, hands in pockets, unable to take his eyes away from her untidily braided hair and wrinkled grey dress and flowing grey-green overcoat. He watched her greet the neighbours, pet the local stray dogs, help and brush down a weepy little boy who had landed heavily at her feet, deposit said little boy to his mother two yards away and head towards an old little cottage with ease, pulling a dull black key from a pocket of her skirt.

Seth hid around a nearby house. Something in him told him there was something creepy about a thirty-seven-year-old man following a twenty-two-year-old woman home from the shops, but he quickly dismissed it. This was different. This was love. True love didn't follow the rules of civilised people. Love made its own rules.

Thatch fluttered gently in the breeze on the rooftop over her head. A window stood propped against the wall under its own sill – whether it fell out *because* of the rhombus-shaped window frame or before its installation, Seth wasn't quite sure. Adrienne glanced around, presumably looking for him. Satisfied that he was nowhere to be seen, she entered the house, leaving the door ajar behind her. She, at the moment at least, appeared to be alone.

Seth glanced around to ensure that he wasn't recognised. Then, straightening his jacket and licking his lips, he strode directly to the little cottage, adjusting his sleeves confidently and smoothing back his hair.

Whereupon he tripped on the step, stumbled into the right-hand corner of the cottage and flopped into the flowerbed adjacent.

'Shit!' he exclaimed shrilly.

He propped himself onto his elbows to pick pieces of gravel from his grazed palms. He was half-sure he could hear children laughing at him.

What he was completely sure of hearing was the sound of footsteps from his left.

'Archie?' Adrienne's voice called softly. 'Have you tripped or something?'

Her voice held the wobbly quality of one trying very hard not to laugh.

'No,' Seth said unconvincingly.

Adrienne twirled in confusion, trying to place where the voice was coming from.

Seth tried to lift himself into a standing position before realising his leg was tangled in a shrub. He wriggled it, trying to dislodge his ankle, before promptly losing his balance and skidding on the gravel to land his face in another shrub.

Establishing that both ends of him were now trapped in some kind of foliage, he gave up and cleared his throat. 'Ahem.'

Adrienne frowned, turning again.

'I'm stuck.' He twisted. His ear stung in warning.

'Where are you?' Adrienne asked. 'I can't see you.'

He tried to catch a glimpse of her. Her steps on the gravel began to fade.

'Wait, don't go!' he yelped, wriggling.

A thorn scraped the inside of his left ear, making him hiss.

He pulled his left arm from under him and managed to dislodge his ear – only to get his sleeve stuck instead. He shifted up onto his knees and peered over his shoulder to see Adrienne squinting over at next door's shrubbery, puzzled.

'Over here,' he called, reddening.

This is not the kind of reunion I had in mind, not by a long shot.

'To the right. No, your other right,' he said patiently as she turned left by mistake.

'The right of the house?' she asked, facing the house next door.

'No, not there, I'm here, in the shrubbery,' he said feebly.

She squinted and leaned sideways.

'*Your* shrubbery,' he said. He shook his trapped hand in exasperation.

Finally the message hit home. She followed the noise of flapping foliage around the corner of her cottage to see Seth crouched over the thorn bush. 'Seth?'

'Bingo,' he said, rising to his feet with his trapped foot still in the shrub.

He jerked his arm from the thorn bush with difficulty.

To his intense irritation, Adrienne simply stood and watched as he clambered upright via the pebbled wall. He pulled savagely at his trapped foot until it suddenly broke free, sending him staggering.

He righted himself quickly and drew himself to his full height.

'Adrienne,' he said, with as much integrity as possible despite having half a shrub still wrapped to his ankle. He licked his lips, brushing some stray leaves from his front.

Adrienne simply stared, baffled.

'Well, nice seeing you,' he said, speed-walking past her.

'Wait!' She grabbed the inside of his elbow.

His breath lurched at the physical contact.

'What are you doing here?' she demanded.

His eyes flitted from object to object, avoiding her gaze and pondering both what to say and why he was in fact outside her house in the first place. His thoughts flickered from the dream to their affair to Russell's offer to help in quick succession and he blurted out incoherently, 'My son wants me to have sex with you.'

Adrienne's eyes widened significantly.

Seth's face twisted in physical pain. He turned slowly away to face the neighbour's shrubbery.

The Bastard jerked his head around the corner of Adrienne's house. 'He's sussed me!'

Geldemar's head joined his. 'No, he hasn't,' he snapped. 'Stay focussed.'

Seth looked helplessly at her.

'Please ignore that, that's not what I meant,' he said quickly. 'I meant he wanted me to flirt with—*talk* to you, because he saw me staring at you and, no, ignore that, I wasn't staring, that's weird, ignore that, ignore *all* of that, er…'

He exhaled with a pained expression and started again.

'I came to see you because I saw you in the coach – well, I didn't see you, I saw your hair, but I thought it was you, so I came looking and it turns out it *was* you, so I came here to find you to see if it was actually you, which it is, and I just, just wanted to see how you were because of, of the stuff that happened, a, a, a-a-aah…'

Adrienne gaped at him, her mouth ajar.

He grimaced and wrung his hands. 'You look incredible, by the way. The dress is lovely. I found our son.' The confession slipped out at the end, unnoticed.

Adrienne patted her skirt down, looking as flustered as Seth felt. 'Um, thank you… it has pockets…'

The final sentence registered. She paused in the act of displaying the highly coveted skirt pockets, her eyes glazing over. 'What do you mean, you found our son?'

Seth looked vacant. Then he bolted back down the road, sprinting for the market as fast as his legs – plus half a shrub – could carry him.

Adrienne stared at his back as he meandered around the throng of children, so engrossed in the sight she didn't even see Archie return from the delicatessen, shopping in hand.

Archie halted at her side, following her gaze.

'Did he fall into the shrubbery?' he asked, oblivious to Adrienne's thoughts. 'What a tit.'

~

VI

'That went dismally,' Geldemar said in a flat voice.

'I got the woman's face, what more do you want?' the Bastard exclaimed.

They sat on a sofa in the middle of Geldemar's domain – the other Six were engrossed in some kind of card game at the circular table behind them, no doubt aligning it with the life of some poor disbeliever of the Seven.

Vladimir hovered behind Geldemar's seat, wielding a teapot and a look of deep hatred. Geldemar had dressed his servant in a pink leotard with silver flowers embroidered on it, to match the settee collection. Vladimir appeared distinctly irritated by it.

The Bastard held his mother's portrait in both hands, frowning at it.

'I have known Qattren my entire life,' Geldemar said, 'and that is by far the *worst* impression of her I have ever seen. More to the point, you were *supposed* to be imitating your mother anyway, *not* Qattren, meaning you've somehow failed to the power of two.'

'I was getting annoyed with him,' the Bastard muttered. 'One more comment of a sexual nature and I was about to make a quip about the phallic objects.'

Vladimir suppressed a smirk. The first he'd worn in a long time.

'Just as well you didn't,' Geldemar said with a scowl. 'There's no point in you starring in Seth's dreams if you're not going to get into character.'

'I *was* in character—'

'You looked like Qattren,' Geldemar interrupted. 'But you sounded like the Bastard.'

'He doesn't know the Bastard, so it doesn't matter—'

'Perhaps not,' Geldemar said. 'But my point is that your craft needs a bit more honing. Not to worry – I have something in mind for him. I just need a second pair of hands.'

'What for?'

'Same as before,' he said. 'Only you should find it easier this time – you'll be playing a small cameo part in this dream.'

'As?' the Bastard prompted.

'Yourself,' Geldemar said with a grin.

~

Jon smiled in content at the deserted castle entrance. He liked being the doorman very much. Apart from the occasional pie-chucking Crey twin, everyone was much easier to get along with once they realised that Jon's happiness was what would determine their entrance to the keep – in particular whether they would be admitted with an amiable smile or in chains.

The only reason Seth allowed this door-keeping dictatorship was because Jon was his first cousin – the fabled Cousin Mortimer, in fact; the nephew of King Theo that was so obscure not even King Theo knew for sure if he actually existed. Jon had packed in his claim for nobility, plus his much-loathed first name, and was now known simply as Jon the Doorman. And occasionally the Prophet.

Jon was beginning to certify that his successor might be insane.

The man wore a thick black ceremonial cowl in the middle of a bright summer's day for a start, which was a sure-fire recipe for sunstroke. It wasn't crazy per se, but added to the intense detail of his portrait of Seth Crey making love, it wasn't far off the scale.

Jon had also heard on the grapevine that Raphael Emmanuel III claimed to be the Prophet. No self-respecting prophet went around telling people he could see into the future. *Causes all sorts of problems, divulging information like that.*

Jon frowned at the approaching madman, his contented smile fixed in place to confirm the visitor's knowledge of his comfortable authority. 'Hello. Can I help you?'

'Indeed you can, my good man,' the stranger intoned. 'I wish to see the king.'

'Right you are.' Jon produced a little trumpet and blew a *toot*.

A window opened above them.

Jimmy's head protruded out in annoyance.

'Crazy person to see the king,' Jon called cheerfully.

'He's off out in a minute, he has to get dressed again,' said Jimmy, his tone sharp with irritation. 'Can't it wait?'

Raphael Emmanuel III shook his head.

Jon peered up at Jimmy. ''Parently not.'

Jimmy exhaled angrily. 'I'll have the king's sister receive you while I dress the little sod and pack his shit up.' The window slammed shut again.

'Someone got up on the wrong side of the fireplace today,' Jon commented, swinging the doors open.

Raphael Emmanuel entered with narrowed eyes, wondering if Jon was joking or not.

Lilly descended the spiral staircase a few moments after that, feeling elated. She was going to be queen regent – for a fortnight, but still. It was more than enough time to instil sufficient terror into the hearts of the people, she thought cheerfully. Just to keep them on their toes.

She was her father's daughter, the Bastard noted, watching her from Sal'plae in interest.

She was perfectly aware that one of her tasks as regent was to talk to crazy people, but she didn't quite anticipate being as wary of Raphael Emmanuel III as she was. She halted in front of the cloaked artist.

'Hello,' she said.

He bowed with a flourish.

She smiled and nodded, then gave him a little bow in return as an afterthought. 'Thank you.' She paused. 'Can I help you?'

'Would you like to talk about God, your grace?'

Lilly gave him a baffled blink at the 'your grace' bit before realising with a start that Seth had dubbed her Duchess of a new district called Squirm for her birthday – more as a joke than anything else. 'Your grace' was a term she had yet to get used to. Usually it was a shove to one side to make way for the real Lilly-Anna Crey. Or at least someone who didn't look like she belonged in the stables.

'Not really,' she said in response to his query. 'I'm not a fan of fairy tales.'

The Prophet's eyes narrowed. 'Hmm,' he said. 'When can I speak with your brother the king?'

'In a minute, he's just struggling to remove half a shrub from his ankle.' She frowned in amusement at him. 'What possessed you to paint that weird portrait of him?'

Raphael tried to eradicate the frown on his forehead, failing as he did so. 'I admire him very much.'

'Hmm,' Lilly said in amusement. 'He's an inspiration to under-achievers everywhere.'

'Having said that,' the Prophet cut in, 'some of his decisions of late have crucially threatened the positive effect of the prophecy, which is what I have come to speak to him about.'

Lilly looked at him blankly. 'The prophecy is a thing now? I thought it was just an excuse to get my old man murdered?'

'No, not at all. I wrote it myself,' he said proudly. 'I saw it in a dream one night, twenty-four years ago.'

She pulled a face. 'Where, in the womb?'

Raphael Emmanuel III flapped a hand in the air.

'You flatter me,' he giggled. 'No, in the dormitory of the monastery, of course. I was eight years old.'

'And remembered it long enough to write it all out the next morning?'

'Well,' he said, looking sheepish, '*some* of the material might be, you know, *filler—*'

The double doors swung open.

'I'll have you know, it took fifteen precognitive episodes to write that prophecy! I didn't make up any of it!'

Lilly rolled her eyes. 'Come off it, Jon, you haven't had a vision in your life and you know it.'

Jon growled under his breath.

'*You're* a heathen!' she retorted, pointing at him. 'Stop eavesdropping and shut the doors, you're letting a draft in.'

Jon's mouth twitched. He stepped back outside and slammed the doors.

'Don't listen to him, he's a nutter,' Lilly said by way of apology. 'Yesterday he was convinced my dog could do magic. Anyway, how is this still an issue? According to some wizard we met from the Forest, the end of the world was stopped.'

'By your brother,' Raphael Emmanuel III said. 'God, he's amazing, isn't he?'

Lilly looked at him, slightly terrified. Anyone with a crush on Seth was bad news. 'But that was an accident,' she said. 'Wasn't it?'

He shook his head slowly. 'Accidents are just events planned by something else. I should know, for I…'

And here he paused dramatically, tilting his face towards the ceiling to catch the sunlight.

'… am the Prophet.'

Lilly stared at him with her mouth ajar. 'Seeeth,' she called slowly.

Thankfully, Seth's footfalls landed on the staircase, swiftly followed as ever by his voice.

'I didn't fall over,' he said to Jimmy, 'I was… knocked over by a kid… a big kid. A man, in fact.'

'Of course, sir,' Jimmy said agreeably from behind him. 'He just happened to blend extremely well into the background while the shrubbery leapt out and grabbed you. A veritable lynch mob, to be sure.'

Lilly giggled.

'It was a very *pointy*,' Seth emphasised, '*prickly,* shrub, thank you. And it might have taken a *tiny* half hour to get off, but that was because it was vindictive. At least it's off now.'

Lilly pointed.

Seth frowned and looked down.

The shrub was back on his foot.

'You trod on it on your way out,' Jimmy said, his eyes fluttering to the heavens.

'I didn't,' Seth said, puzzled.

Lilly hesitated. 'Anyway, this... gent wants a word with you about... summink?'

Seth turned his gaze onto their visitor and his brow furrowed.

The young man with the cowl gazed back at Seth in complete adoration. His mouth hung slightly ajar. He looked like one of the acolytes in the frescos that used to reside in the palace chapel, before Seth let Marbrand gut it out.

'I'm a massive fan,' he said, enraptured.

Seth narrowed his eyes, his own jaw hanging open a bit. 'Great,' he said, smiling. He glanced around. 'You wanted to speak about...'

'Oh yeah,' he giggled nervously, 'um... sorry, I'm just so excited to meet you I completely forgot!' He grinned inanely.

Jimmy curled his upper lip. 'He's got a shrub stuck to his foot.'

'I am royalty, I hasten to remind you,' Seth said, haughtily.

'Half at best, going by the rumours,' Jimmy muttered under his breath.

'Nah, he's got my dad's height,' Lilly piped up. 'My nearly-father-in-law was a puny fucker.'

'Even so,' Jimmy went on, before Seth could register that exchange, 'he's not that fascinating. He doesn't even wear his crown.'

'That's because...' Seth paused, his index finger in the air. 'Never mind.'

'That's because?' Lilly enquired.

Seth made a face.

'Mllurgictwit,' he mumbled.

'You which?' Lilly pressed, cupping a hand around her ear.

'I'm allergic to it,' he growled.

'Again?'

'I'M ALLERGIC!!' he exploded, his face reddening. 'Every time I wear it, I break out in dirty great lumps! I'm allergic to it.' He glowered at his feet.

Jimmy looked puzzled. 'You're allergic to gold?' he asked incredulously. 'Is that what all that fuss was about during your coronation?'

'That's right, they had to make a new one for him,' Lilly said. 'We had to delay the thing for a year while they made a worthy replacement. I thought he'd dropped it or lost it or something, but no, they must have had to make it with a different metal—'

'I don't want to talk about it anymore,' Seth said sulkily.

'This is hilarious – the *king*,' Lilly said in amusement, 'is allergic to his own *crown*.'

'I said I don't want to talk about it anymore!' Seth snapped, flushing a deep purple.

'I prayed for a laugh when Dad died, but I didn't think anyone was listening.' Lilly pressed her palms together, in homage to the heavens. 'Thank you!'

Somewhere just outside of the world's physical atmosphere, the Bastard flicked Lilly a salute. 'Any time!'

Seth scowled at her.

'So you can't even wear it for a couple of hours?' Jimmy asked in interest.

'Nope,' he said grumpily.

'Talk about karma, eh?'

Seth glowered at him. 'What's that supposed to mean?'

Jimmy's eyes became slightly wider than usual.

Raphael Emmanuel III lifted a perceptive eyebrow.

'Nuffin, just a comment,' Jimmy said innocently.

Seth glared at him. 'I'm not that nasty to you.' He glanced at Lilly, who was engrossed in Seth's forehead. 'What are you staring at?' he asked his sister venomously.

'Your rash spells "twat".'

'You're a twat,' he said, poking her ribs.

She pressed her gold wedding ring into his face.

'Lilly, don't,' he yelped, twisting away.

Lilly cackled, chasing him.

Jimmy shook his head. 'Juveniles.' He turned to Raphael Emmanuel

III. 'Have you remembered what you wanted to talk about?'

He tore his gaze dreamily from the king. 'Oh, that. No, it doesn't matter.'

'Didn't sound like it,' said Lilly, having slipped her ring off to twiddle into Seth's ear. 'Apparently Seth's crucially affected the prophecy.'

'What, again?' Seth sneered. He slapped Lilly's ring out of her hand, sending it tumbling towards the left antechamber.

Lilly glanced at it a moment and said, 'meh,' deciding to leave it there.

Seth continued, 'What am I meant to have done now?'

'You mean apart from systematically expelling the clergy from Serpus?' Jimmy said.

'Jimmy,' Seth hissed.

Raphael Emmanuel III's jaw dropped. 'You've killed more of us?'

'A few,' Seth admitted. 'Only the guilty ones. It's harrowing, the amount of mass graves there are in the countryside. I'm doing the country a favour.'

The Prophet's mouth worked soundlessly, attempting to express thoughts too numerous to concisely express. 'Are they getting a fair trial?'

'It's children's remains in a big fuck off grave,' Jimmy said. 'How fair a trial is that?'

'This-this is discrimination, you know!' Raphael spluttered. 'You're getting taxes now, what more do you expect from us?'

'To stop getting cloaked visitors in the night trying to baptise my children,' Seth said, irate. 'They soak their beds enough on their own as it is.'

'They mean well,' Raphael argued.

'They bloody don't,' Lilly and Seth said together.

'Spend an hour alone with Jon and tell me if the priest meaning well did him any good,' Jimmy said.

'That was an isolated event,' he said with conviction.

'Not according to the mass grave, it isn't,' Jimmy said. 'Marbrand found no less than twenty skulls under his floorboards the other year. *Little ones.* Not the kind of buried treasure you hope to stumble on during a building renovation. And we all know what they did to poor Jon. Ever heard of the late Father Giery?'

Raphael Emmanuel III paled. *I'll take that as a yes,* Jimmy thought. The

Prophet didn't grace this with an audible answer. He hurriedly shook his head and scowled instead.

'Personally, I would take the word of this Jon fellow with a pinch of salt. I happened to have been taken in by the same clergy as him and can confirm that he is nothing but a heretic and a liar—'

The doors opened.

'Says you, your name isn't even Raphael whatever it is, it's Joe without the "E".'

'It is not,' said Jo, rather shrilly, 'Joe without the "E", my name is Raphael Emmanuel III, and I am the Prophet, for I have found *Godly Enlightenment*,' he finished in a high-pitched voice, his arms raised to the ceiling in a 'V'.

'And you lot call *me* a nutter,' Jon said, shaking his head.

The Prophet's arms flapped at his sides. 'And in actual fact, I was not referring to the priest-killing as regards to the Prophecy.'

'Why, what else have I done?' Seth asked, rolling his eyes.

To Seth's alarm, the religious zealot reached out and placed a hand on each of his shoulders.

'My liege,' he said urgently, 'you mustn't give in to temptation—'

'Jimmy, I'm being handled,' Seth said in a strained voice.

'—you must ignore the wants of the flesh, you are tempting fate—'

'*Jimmy*,' Seth said more urgently.

Jimmy timidly tapped the Prophet's shoulder. 'You really ought to let go now, he—'

'Shh!' he snapped.

Jimmy flinched backward.

'This is *very* important!'

Jimmy backed away, hands raised in surrender. 'Sorry, sir, I tried,' he said in a high voice.

'You mustn't give yourself to the pulling of your loins—' He pulled Seth's face away from Jimmy, his cold fingers pushing the king's cheeks together. 'You are tempting fate, my lord! Another child between you and the girl is sure to become the Antichrist! Whatever you do, you must not approach this woman! Stay away from Adrienne at all costs!'

'Adrienne?' Jimmy asked in surprise.

'What about Adrienne?' Lilly demanded.

Seth looked around guiltily, his mouth still pressed into a grotesque pout.

'Right, you,' Lilly spat at the Prophet. 'Unhand my brother and piss off.'

'Only if he promises me he won't touch that woman!'

Lilly dragged him off by the back of his robe.

'Come on, out you go,' Jimmy said kindly, ushering him out by one elbow.

'Promise me!' he squealed, hauled away by the two.

'Listen, you lot might enjoy being celibate,' Seth called out to him, 'but I am a red-blooded animal!'

Lilly's eyes rolled behind her lids. 'Sweet mother of Christ.'

She and Jimmy hauled the Prophet out of the door.

'I won't be told what to do by a robed maniac! I am a HOT-BLOODED MALE!!!' Seth howled, thumping his chest with the side of his fist.

Jon stuck his tongue out at the Prophet, pulling the doors in after him.

'You're a loony, is what you are,' Lilly said, shaking her head. 'Especially if you're seeing *her* again. What is wrong with you?'

Seth sighed, his gaze fixed to the doors as Jon closed them.

'I dunno,' he said feebly.

Cienne peered in from the courtyard before he could muse further. 'Once you've finished screaming at the clergy, we should probably leave,' she said. 'Emmett won't be impressed if we show up to this meeting late.'

'Dooooon't,' Russell crooned, close to tears.

Seth spied his son wrapped around her left ankle with every available limb. He gazed at him for a moment.

'Lemme get Ginny,' he said swiftly.

~

Despina felt a knock on the edge of her brain. She put her book upside down on her lap and sighed. 'It's you again, isn't it?'

Marbrand frowned at her inquisitively over his shoulder. He gave the pile of kindling a pat to stabilise it before planting both palms on the flagstone hearth, easing the pressure on his knees.

Shh, the Bastard hissed between her ears. *Don't catch his attention!*

'He knows who you are, I told him,' she said aloud in a conversational tone.

So I saw, the Bastard said reproachfully. *I have a job for you and he can't know about it, so unless you divert his attention—*

'You'll do horrible things to him and my mother, unpleasant situations, blah, blah, blah,' Despina droned. 'He can look after himself. What do you want?'

'Is this the Bastard you're talking to?' Marbrand demanded. 'Tell him to come out where I can see him.'

Tell your old man to butt out of other people's conversations! said the Bastard hotly.

'He says to butt out of other people's private conversations,' Despina obediently relayed.

It was implied, said the Bastard sourly, *for you to paraphrase that.*

Despina sighed, brushing her dark-brown hair behind her ears. 'Let me just see what he wants.' She marked her page with a slip of paper and snapped the covers shut, dissipating into a layer of dust around it.

'Now what do you want?' she said to the realm of Sal'plae in general.

Her home took on the usual violet tint as Sal'plae enveloped her. Her father's face froze in time mid-shudder as he knelt in front of the ornate fireplace in the centre of what, three years ago, used to be the royal chapel of Salator Crey.

Despina always smiled at the thought of what the executed priest's face would look like if he saw his church today. It currently had smoke billowing from the church spire, which had been converted into a very large, pointy chimney. Timber-panelled walls had also been raised throughout the hall, creating an ample five-room living space for the two of them, and a collection of modest sleeping quarters throughout the rest of the belltower housed the rest of the night watch. It was at Marbrand's insistence – their prior quarters had resided in the turret flanking the extremely *squeaky* portcullis, which until three years ago had suffered chronic damage from several brick-throwing incidents. The vestry had been thoroughly scrubbed with every cleaning agent available before ending up as a junk closet because of everyone's mutual discomfort of being in there.

What resulted from Marbrand's eager creativity was a rather luxurious home fitted out with old furniture and knick-knacks belonging to the palace that were a hundred years out of fashion but in perfect condition.

All that was missing was the Bastard – until two hands covered her eyes.

She turned irritably to see the king's double grinning at her. Age didn't appear to affect him – while her own hair had lengthened over the years and she had filled out around the hips and shoulders, he remained the same, always approximately thirty, his eyes lineless despite their frequent mischievous squint. His scar bit into the centre of his face, a long stripe parallel to his nose.

'Hello,' he said brightly. 'Long time no see.'

'Long time no threaten, you mean,' she said with a glower. 'Again: what do you want?'

'Cheerful as always,' he said with a smirk. 'I told you. I have a job for you.'

'Why, who's my old man trying to kill this time?' she asked. 'I think he's nearly running out of people to bunk off at this stage. And he *is* getting old.'

'No, nothing to do with him,' the Bastard brushed off. 'No, this concerns someone new. I don't know if you've met, but he's quite famous. Howard Rosethorn.'

'Never heard of him.'

The Bastard pulled his head back. 'Really?'

Despina curled her upper lip and shook her head.

He turned the corners of his mouth down. 'Oh. Makes a change.'

'What do you want done with him?'

'I don't want anything done with him,' he said simply.

She turned her head to give him a side-glance. 'Then what do you want me for?'

'I just want you to distract him. Using your… talents.'

Her nose wrinkled. 'I don't *have* any "talents". I'm not a trollop.'

'Not those talents.' He rolled his eyes. 'He's such a bloody prude he probably wouldn't put out anyway. I have a much neater plan all made up for

90

you, which I'll run by you in a minute. But I need to know if you'll do it first.'

'Depends. How am I being blackmailed this time?'

'You're not. I'm paying you.'

'In what?'

'Dog shit.' He shot her a look. 'Gold, obviously.'

'It had better be lots of gold if he's as famous as you say.'

He smiled. 'It is.'

'And what if I say no?'

He shrugged. 'I find someone else to do it.'

'Why do you want me for if you can get someone else? What's so special about me that someone with more experience in messing up people's lives can't do this "job" for you?'

He didn't answer at first.

Despina raised her eyebrows impatiently.

The Bastard put his hands in his pockets and gazed at her. If she hadn't known better, she would have sworn he was trying his best to look smoulderingly handsome at her.

'Well?' she pressed, annoyed. 'Why?'

'Because I like you,' he said quietly with a shrug.

Despina paused.

'Like or *like*-like?' she asked finally.

~

Marbrand looked up from the roaring fire as his daughter rematerialized on top of her book. 'Is everything alright?'

She pulled the book from underneath her and gazed at it, as though wondering how it got there in the first place. 'Yep,' she said finally.

He arched an eyebrow. 'What did he want?'

She shook her head. 'Just a job. It wasn't a threat this time: he offered me money to keep someone called Howard Rosethorn in his uncle's house.'

'He didn't say why?'

'Why what?' she said distractedly.

'Why he wanted Rosethorn kept away?'

She shook her head. 'He didn't say anything else.' She smiled faintly to herself.

Marbrand tilted his head to one side, still crouched in front of the fire. 'Is there something else?'

She stared into space for a moment.

'He's got a massive crush on me,' she said, with another smile.

~

PART TWO: THE DEAD BOY

I

wo fingers tapped Marbrand's shoulder. 'Sadie Marbrand?'

Marbrand turned both eyes to the heavens.

Despina giggled loudly.

'I knew I'd regret giving the king my birth name,' Marbrand muttered, pivoting to face the stranger. 'You're the undertaker, is it?'

The man nodded once, though he needn't have confirmed it. His long black overcoat and soft velvet boots confirmed his vocation as he stood in front of a lavishly decorated litter, his customary funereal hat perched over shoulder-length hair almost identical to Despina's. *Only the best for the dead*, Marbrand thought morosely, eyeing the coach. Even the king's vehicles were of less quality than this.

'The departed is inside,' the man supplied, as though the information was necessary.

Marbrand nodded and led the way. The undertakers carried the litter inside the palace grounds, to the mortuary in the outskirts of the inner wall. Marbrand extracted a large ring of keys from his belt and opened the large double doors one by one for the undertakers to simply carry the litter straight through.

Despina looked on sombrely. 'It

93

must be odd burying him so long after his death,' she said. 'It seems like forever since the Stonekeep exploded.'

'It was difficult for Prince Ronald, seeing his brother so soon after finding his father's body,' Marbrand said carefully, hating the lie, even though it was necessary. 'They'll need to make arrangements to lay the two to rest somewhere in the Forest, since the Emmetts have claimed the land the Hornes are traditionally buried in. They'll have to stay here until then.'

'I can't help wondering how he ended up in that cornfield,' Despina said.

'Abducted shortly beforehand, we think,' Marbrand lied again, avoiding her gaze. 'Of course, this is all between us two and the king. The Emmetts would claim all sorts of things to fill the gaps.'

'Of course.'

The undertakers lifted the body from the litter.

Marbrand quickly shut the door on them, before Despina could see the size of the corpse.

He hoped Despina was naïve enough to believe his lies. He knew she wasn't, but he hoped anyway. He couldn't have her sussing out the truth – her mind hadn't always been her own, he remembered.

An entity known as the Bastard had occupied her mind for a time, an entity with a particular focus on the preservation of Mister Emmett – which wouldn't bode well if he happened to pass on certain information.

The Bastard, he mused, strolling with Despina to the front portcullis. He wondered what his agenda was. Despina had agreed to seek out and distract Howard Rosethorn for him, but why? And who was this Bastard, anyway? Despina said he bore a very strong resemblance to Seth Crey, which was an impossibility.

Possibly a warlock under Emmett's employ, he decided, leaning on the wall outside the portcullis, spying on them in case he was helping Ronald reclaim his throne. Fat chance of that, he thought with a snort. Ron didn't have it in him. He had king's blood but he didn't have a king's brain.

They basked in the midday sun in silence, watching the guards practise as though the undertakers hadn't arrived. Two more fingers tapped his shoulder and Marbrand turned.

Adrienne Hart faced him, looking morose.

'I want to see Seth Crey.'

~

White and gold marble dulled to beige in the evening chandelier light. Even the meeting table was marble, Seth noticed with rage. Who did this twat think he was, King of Truphoria?

The deep navy sky in the windows overhead bore a striking contrast. The glint of light shining from each glossy surface irritated Seth to no end – no less because he was uncomfortable enough as it was.

'Thank you for coming,' Emmett said amiably, without any facial signs of amiability. 'I have requested your presence today to discuss two things: the lesser issue being the tax on public relations with our neighbours, the Creys…' He gestured to Seth and Cienne across the table from him. '… and the more pressing matter of the disappearance of our local Father of the Order, George Toffer, who may have been the victim of an attack by a recent cult that has emerged of late throughout the continent.' Emmett stared blankly at Seth. 'I think this discussion would be best operated away from the gentle ears of your young children.'

'Not on your nelly,' Seth growled.

His son sat in Seth's lap, strapped to his front with his daughter tucked into an identical pouch on his back.

Ginny combed her father's hair with her fingers.

Russell squinted at his Uncle Emmett from across the long table. 'You're funny-looking.'

Emmett gazed at him uneasily before clearing his throat slightly. 'So, has anyone any news as regards to this cult?'

Qattren cleared her throat from beside Cienne. Her usual menagerie flowed down the length of her cream silk skirts, the decorative feathers draped along the length of her knees and calves.

'There has been a worrying development on the outskirts of my Forest, just east of Serpus,' she announced. 'We hear that witch-burnings have been taking place.'

'You can guess why we find this worrying,' Ron added from his wife's left. His own attire, the light grey colours of the Hornes, appeared dull and lifeless beside the avian-themed gown to his right.

'Witch-burnings have been occurring in bouts for the past hundred years. I hardly find the development surprising,' Emmett said.

'If they were burning actual witches, this wouldn't be worrying,' Qattren said. 'As it is, they only appear to be targeting unpleasant neighbours and the occasional male. The fact that I have been left well alone demonstrates their failure. What I want to know is who they're really targeting and why.'

'Witch-hunting rarely produces a list purely consisting of actual witches. I hardly think we need to delve too much into human error. If we over-examined everyone, I would be wondering myself whether or not you really were left alone by these people, since you're impervious to flame in any case. Short of collecting sightings of each article of your clothing and searching your wardrobe for any missing or burnt pieces, there is no proof that you were left alone at all.'

'The only time I was burned alive was on a pirate ship between here and the Deadlands,' she said. 'How would you know anything about that?'

Emmett hesitated.

Seth suddenly felt a newfound respect for Qattren. 'That was like carpet burn, but with words.'

'They do call me the Queen of Fire,' Qattren said blithely.

Emmett cleared his throat, irked. 'Yes. Well, if what you say is correct, it would explain the rumours my council have surfaced about the targeting of certain noblewomen in the area.'

'Yes,' Cienne piped up. 'My father's letter mentioned a small group of Truphorian monks that had approached my stepmother, intending to arrest her in the name of Salator Crey and the Seven. You don't suppose they're targeting mistresses, do you?'

Seth felt a jolt of panic. *Adrienne,* he thought. Aloud he said, 'Lucky I haven't got one, then.'

'Are you sure, your highness?' Emmett said with a shadow of a smirk. 'I have one. Everyone likes to have another woman to play with, when the wife's away. Isn't that so, Prince Ronald?'

Qattren faced Ron, more out of interest than anything else.

Ron, who was asexual, shrugged. 'I play draughts with other people occasionally.'

Emmett paused for a fraction of a second.

'Yes,' he said slyly. 'Draughts.'

Qattren suppressed a smirk, bowing her head to allow a curtain of copper hair to mask it.

'I didn't know you had a wife to play away *from*,' Seth said.

'I have a betrothal pending,' Emmett said. 'I can't imagine her saying no.'

Seth's nose wrinkled.

'But it's customary for a lord to play "draughts" outside of the homestead, regardless of the match – isn't that so?'

'Not me,' Seth said, quirking an eyebrow. 'Some people grow out of it.'

Cienne smiled affectionately.

Emmett scowled, to Seth's relief. He knew he was trying to slip him up.

'What of the priest, then?' said Emmett sulkily.

'Father Tosser, was it? Never heard of him,' Seth said with an offhanded wave.

'Father George Toffer,' Emmett corrected. 'I'm told he was last seen loitering on your property shortly after the birth of your children. Your council were arranging a manhunt, to question him over an assassination attempt?'

Seth shrugged.

'They would have mentioned it in your council meetings?' Emmett pressed.

'He doesn't go to those meetings,' Cienne said dully. 'He says they're too early in the morning.'

Emmett's eyes narrowed.

'I like my lie-ins!' Seth protested shrilly.

'So you have absolutely no idea of your lord's progress with the Toffer manhunt?'

'No,' he said in a small voice.

A little fit of babbling erupted from behind Seth's back. Once Ginny had finished, everyone carefully translated it in their heads.

'I heard the Topper thing! He wen' onna boat and he's hiding in Potty

Bell. Uncle Ozzly said.'

Emmett arched an eyebrow.

Seth ran a hand through his hair sheepishly.

'What has the world come to,' Emmett said, 'when the king's three-year-old child knows more about his realm than the king himself?'

'She's very advanced for a three-year-old,' Seth said.

'That means good,' said Ginny.

'See?' Seth exclaimed, jerking a thumb back at her.

'Indeed,' he said with a hint of smugness. 'You'll need to sacrifice your lie-ins if you want to stay on top of your affairs. Mister Toffer won't be the only priest to make an attempt on your family's lives. You might not have a mistress for them to pray on, but I daresay the cult will find something to complain about.'

'He's right,' Qattren agreed.

Seth glared at her. 'Whose side are you on?'

'Your family's,' Qattren said icily. 'Each member of your family has been accused of being the Antichrist at this point, including the children. This cult Mister Emmett refers to is led by the apparent Prophet himself.'

'The Prophet?' Seth asked with a smirk. 'You mean Joe-without-the-"E" who likes to paint pictures of royalty in the thralls of pleasure? What's he going to do, embarrass me to death?'

'He might try to burn your wife,' Qattren pointed out. 'Those rumours about her love affair with Vladimir Horne didn't die with him.'

'You know that isn't true,' Cienne growled.

'I know, you know, everyone but he knows,' said Qattren, with a shrug. 'Unless Vladimir returns from the dead and tells him otherwise, he could quite possibly be after you. So I'd keep an eye on your walls from now on.'

Seth sulked, trying to disguise the anxiety he really felt underneath.

Cienne tried to wipe the scowl from her face, to no avail. 'What did you want to discuss regarding the tax?'

'Ah, the tax.' Emmett cleared his throat. 'The tax is due for review. As you all know, the peace tax ensures that all nasty rumours are kept between us to avoid possible conflicts. At the moment, this tax only applies to the Creys due to the matter of my departed brother-in-law, but you see, my nephew has gotten to that age where questions about his father have inevitably begun to arise. This is why I have decided to review your case and decide whether the fee needs to be increased or not—'

'Why would the fee need to be increased?' Qattren asked mildly. 'Surely the queries of a small child aren't that expensive?'

'If only that were the case,' Emmett said. 'Young Azrael we can handle. It's the queries from fellow members of court here at Stoneguard that the Peace Tax is muting. We might be a small country in comparison, but the lords are extremely powerful men – it is they who rallied with your husband's grandfather and financed his achievements. There would be no Stoneguard without them.'

'Stoneguard is hardly much of an adversary since the Battle in the Orchard ate it up,' Cienne remarked. 'If they were that powerful, we would not be sitting here talking to you.'

'Small isn't necessarily weak, your highness,' Emmett said. 'The Battle in the Orchard may have eaten their lands and people, but it gave them one thing in return: anger. Tears don't achieve anything. *Anger gets things done* – it gets alliances made, contracts signed, armies formed. Alliances equals land, land equals people, and people equals armies.'

He leaned back in his oak chair, elbow on each wooden arm, fingers linked between them.

'Fortunately, money rarely makes people angry. Unfortunately, it's currently in very short supply.' He spread his hands apart. 'You see my dilemma.'

'You're charging us more for your silence?' Seth demanded. He leaned forward, accidentally pressing Russell's collarbone against the edge of the table.

'It's your country,' Emmett said, reclining. 'I can always look after it for you if you don't want to protect yourself from future invasion.'

'You can't use their money to pay off your lords,' Seth said, pointing to Ron and Qattren.

'They don't give me any money.'

Seth blinked and met Qattren's gaze. 'You're not getting the Peace Tax anymore?'

'I never got the Peace Tax in the first place,' Qattren said slowly.

Seth frowned at her, then at Emmett, who remained nonchalant as ever.

'She was with me on the night Vladimir Horne died,' Seth said. 'She was with me from dusk to dawn!'

'That's no reason to humiliate your wife with the fact,' Emmett said.

Seth strangled the air briefly. 'That's not what I meant!' he snapped. 'If I'm suspected to be involved with his death, then so is she! If it was purposeful—'

'Which, as we established, it was not,' Qattren cut in.

'Exactly, yes,' Seth agreed, 'then she should get taxed as well!'

'She has been established as an innocent bystander, nay, potential victim,' Emmett informed him. 'For all I know, you could be buying her silence on the matter. It was your pet that destroyed the palace, therefore the perpetrator is you.'

'Be careful who you call perpetrator, Mister Emmett,' Seth said in a low voice, 'since I'm the one with hundreds of witnesses to a massacre led by a man claiming loudly to be working for *you*.'

Emmett blinked a few times, as though trying to dislodge an eyelash.

'So while we're discussing perpetrators, let's hear your thoughts on a few queries of our own.'

Seth shifted in his seat, piqued that he couldn't recline smugly like Emmett because Ginny was in the way.

'The men who killed the Ambassador and his wedding guests captained a ship. Our Lilly was a prisoner of theirs on this ship,' (he hurriedly skipped the part about her taking over the crew), 'and learned a little bit about it.'

'It was a ship belonging to the navy,' Ron recalled. 'It was built by sorcerers in order to travel through time—'

'Sal'plae,' Qattren corrected, 'but basically to manipulate time and space, yes.'

'Thank you,' Seth said, irked by the interruption. 'Lilly distinctly remembered the captain bragging that it was "state-of-the-art". Only a year before that, my father signed a contract ordering some ships of that description for our navy – except that the order arrived two years late due to one Mister Emmett ordering an entire fleet's worth at short notice as a *matter of urgency*. This leaves Stoneguard in the possession of lots of very expensive ships that no one else has *at the exact time* that one such ship happened to be crewed by the Ambassador's murderer.'

Emmett set his jaw.

'Now surely, having only just received brand new state-of-the-art ships, your navy would make a lot of fuss if one of them was stolen by pirates? And surely the pirates would have a hard time getting away with the crime what with a whole fleet of magical ships on their trail, armed with magical wizards to go with them? And I don't claim to be an expert in piracy, but why would a pirate crew abandon such a valuable vessel just to go into a strange nobleman's wedding and kill some of the guests? It just doesn't make a lot of sense.'

'I don't see what the antics of a pirate have to do with the Peace Tax,' Emmett said, peeved.

'Look at it from my point of view,' Seth said, leaning forward. 'My mother and sister are due to be married to noblemen, standing to inherit an army of trained dragons – except both men get assassinated *seconds* before it can happen, along with their *entire family*. Leaving my poor mother and sister empty-handed and the Desertlands to elect a *new* leader with no connections to my family *whatsoever*.'

Seth's hand made a fist, which landed on the tabletop, hard. 'That's a *damn* shame, isn't it? For me, that is. For anyone with their eye on the fair kingdom of Adem, not so much.'

Emmett blinked once, slowly.

Seth glared at him. 'Bit too big of a political move for a random pirate to make, isn't it?'

Emmett leaned forward in his chair to place his forearms along the edge of the tabletop. He turned his gaze to Qattren. 'Perhaps you might enlighten King Seth as to the identity of the aforementioned "random pirate".'

Qattren glared at him before turning to Seth. 'It's said that he is the bastard son of your mother.'

Cienne glowered at her, appalled. '*Bastard son?*'

Seth frowned. 'My *mother?*'

'Your mother. Making his actions personal, not political.' She glanced at Emmett. 'Having said that, the rumour of Queen Eleanor's bastard son says that he was sent into exile as an infant. Meaning he wouldn't have known his parentage… unless someone told him about it.' She turned her gaze to Emmett in unspoken query.

Emmett rolled his mouth. 'I have only ever been an ally of the Creys,' he stated woodenly.

'Allies don't charge for their help,' Seth seethed. 'And they don't single out one person over another.'

'As I say,' Emmett said coolly, giving Qattren a respectful nod, 'Queen Qattren was judged to be an innocent bystander.'

Seth lifted his eyebrows, his brow wrinkling. 'Oh, I see how it is. Because you're scared shitless of her, she gets no bastard tax.'

'I'm not scared shitless of anyone,' said Emmett quietly. 'You'll soon learn that.'

'Oh! Oh!' exclaimed Seth, pointing at him. 'Is that a threat? Is it, now? What are you going to do, tax me some more? Well, guess what? I'm not paying it!'

'Seth,' Cienne warned.

'No!' He rose to his feet, his children's feet dangling all around him. '*I'm* the only king on this continent, bar the little boy *you* work for, and if *he* feels the need to charge me for a misunderstanding, then *maybe* I'll consider it, but *you* aren't getting a *penny* of my people's money, so bloody *there.*'

He took a deep breath.

'And if you want your sodding priest,' he added as an afterthought, 'you can wait in line. Because I have two assassination attempts to account for.'

Emmett paused for a moment. 'Alright,' he said breezily.

Seth glared at him, his mouth still twisted in fury. 'What?' he hissed.

'Alright,' he said easily, his face unreadable.

Seth's eyes narrowed momentarily and he glanced at the other three in angry disbelief. 'I'm serious!' he shrilled. 'I'm not paying it!'

Emmett simply nodded once.

Seth scowled at everyone and everything in the room and made for the door.

'Your family's quarters are located in the north tower,' Emmett said helpfully.

'*I know*!' Seth shouted, throwing the door open and startling the guard outside.

'You also appear to have half a shrub attached to your boot.'

'I know that too!' The door slammed behind him.

Seth stood in the hall, fuming and alone except for Russell hanging from his chest and Ginny clinging to his back.

'Are you mad?' Ginny asked timidly.

'Not at you, lovey, Daddy's just a little bit annoyed at the horsey-looking bas—man in there,' Seth said through clenched teeth. He exhaled and unclenched them to glare down at the foliage around his foot.

Emmett's guard gave him a wary side-glance.

'WHERE'S THE NORTH TOWER?!' Seth howled at him.

The guard jingled a yard away from him in fright, his armour rattling.

~

II

Adrienne waited patiently outside the mortuary, her hands folded neatly in her lap.

The undertakers had left about an hour ago, which left Marbrand waiting impatiently for Lilly-Anna Crey to return from the market. The girl was slightly upset that Seth Crey wasn't there and demanded to be let in to see the child. Marbrand didn't dare without Lilly's approval.

Lilly finally arrived, her manservant Stan in tow. Both carried bulging purses of gold, from the pawning of her estranged husband's gifts, no doubt.

Marbrand strode to her side and put his head close to hers. 'Adrienne Hart has arrived to see the king,' he murmured.

Lilly closed her eyes and breathed in. 'Bring me to her, then,' she exhaled. She touched Stan's elbow. 'Put that in the vault.' She handed him her coin purse. 'My mother will show you the way, she knows I trust you.'

Stan nodded and inclined his head to Marbrand before leaving.

Lilly followed Marbrand to the entrance of the mortuary, where a chair had been placed by the door for Adrienne.

Tears trickled on Adrienne's cheeks. Lilly's shadow fell over her and Adrienne lifted her head, meeting her gaze.

'Your highness,' Adrienne greeted flatly.

Lilly glared down at her. 'You want to see the child, I take it?'

Adrienne's eyes fell slightly. She nodded at Lilly's shoulder. 'I... I suppose so—'

'Get a move on, then,' Lilly said briskly.

Adrienne rose from her seat and curtsied. 'Thank you, your—'

'Now,' Lilly snapped.

A flush crept in from the edges of Adrienne's face. She curtsied again and hurried into the mortuary.

Marbrand watched his exchange with a puzzled expression.

Lilly halted a step inside the door.

The room was free of the pomp and ceremony the priesthood had previously demanded of it – replacing the religious tapestries and multitudes of candles and statues were bare bricks and mortar. The emerald-coloured carpet beneath their feet was the only distinguishing feature in the room.

Adrienne hovered between two tables set into the middle of the room – one with King Samuel Horne's remains wrapped in silver cloth in the standard fashion, and one with a crib.

Lilly's gaze carefully avoided the crib.

Adrienne's mouth hung open, moving slightly, as if struggling to form words. 'It... he... do you think it might be him?'

Lilly gave a noncommittal shrug.

Adrienne inhaled, shuddering. 'I suppose,' she said to herself, 'with the Hole, it mightn't have... he might have grown before...'

Lilly's face remained stony.

Adrienne licked her lips. 'When can I bury him?' Her voice brushed the air softly. The din from outside had somehow faded since Lilly had entered the mortuary, leaving her question ring clearly.

'Seth paid for the undertaker's services,' Lilly said in a cold tone. 'I think he ought to decide when he can bury him.' She watched Adrienne's profile as the girl's lip quivered. Lilly had no sympathy for her.

Adrienne's hand rose to hover over the child's body. She thought better of it and lowered her hands to her sides again. 'I'll speak to the king about it when he returns.' She turned and fled, her skirts gathered in her fingers.

Lilly waited for her footsteps to pass. As they did, the noises of the yard rose to their previous volume, as though Adrienne's presence had been a buffer.

Lilly stepped up to the crib, her fingers brushing along the edge of the table. She rested a forearm on the far edge of the crib and peered inside.

The child lay in a sea of white silk. She stroked the boy's face with the back of one finger. His skin chilled her knuckle, depositing a sticky powder onto it. Her gaze travelled briefly to the lumpy scarring on either side of her hand, back from her time on the pirate ship with Orl.

One finger tentatively prodded a lumpy path down her nephew's face. Albie had that scar, she realised – a dog version, running all the way down his little snout under the fur. *It is him, then*, she thought, her heart sinking. *A* jagged slice marred the infant's face. They had done their best, but the undertakers couldn't disguise the damage. His waxy face lay still, too still, but she didn't flinch away. She had no fear of the dead.

A knock landed gently on the door. 'Lilly?' Stan's voice said softly.

She tore her gaze from the boy's face.

'The queen dowager needs you.'

She had another lumpy scar inside her, she realised. She had been too engrossed in distractions to notice, but it was there, she could feel it. Her nephew was in there, and her father too, and Orl. All those wounds that hadn't yet healed properly, coagulating into one.

She tucked the thought away for later inspection and gave Stan a nod, sliding from the child's side.

Lilly's mother met her halfway up the hill, skittering down the gravel drive with her skirts gathered in her fists. Her grey hair – she had abandoned the hideous yellow bleaching a couple of years ago, to Lilly's relief – fled free of the intricate braiding circling the crown of her head, large sections of it flapping behind her on her descent from the hilltop.

'What's wrong?' Lilly asked, frowning.

Eleanor skidded to a halt, grabbing her elbow with urgency. 'Do you know who's been in the vault?'

Lilly stared at the clouds in thought. 'Um, just Uncle Osney, as far as I know. He's been putting my rents from Squirm in there for me. Why?'

Eleanor heaved a sigh, glancing around.

'You'd better see for yourself,' she said, beckoning her to the keep.

~

Cienne lay in darkness with the blanket tucked under her armpits. Seth lay in a similar fashion, simmering quietly. Their arms folded identically, they lay in silence. For a little while.

'Who does he think he is?' Seth snarled at the ceiling. He kicked the end of the blanket into the air to cross his ankles. It billowed, sending a gust of cool air up the length of Cienne's shins. '"I have a betrothal pending, I can't *imagine* her saying *no*",' he mimicked in the smarmiest, haughtiest voice he could muster.

'Mmm,' she murmured.

'Who'd want to marry him, anyway?' he demanded to the world at large. 'I'm assuming she's blind because, well, look at the man. I bet he bribed her for good measure. Imagine bribing a blind woman.'

'I know,' Cienne drawled.

'And then making fun of me for not knowing what the bloody council were talking about.' He snorted mirthlessly. 'I swear I could bloody swing for—'

'Are you finished?' Cienne asked irately.

Seth's head flopped to the left, nostrils flaring. 'What? I'm outraged!'

She shifted herself onto her elbow, dropping her chin onto her palm. 'I thought you didn't want to be celibate for two weeks?'

Seth opened his mouth, then paused. 'As you command,' he said in delight, grinning.

Five minutes passed in which, in the next room, Russell bolted upright in his bed beside a sleeping guard, glanced around frantically and, upon realisation that the boogieman had been left at home, slowly settled down to drift back to sleep.

Behind the east wall, Seth slid back to his side of the bed and yawned, exhausted.

'Had enough already?' Cienne asked with a smirk.

He nodded with a small laugh and pressed his forehead into the pillow, trying to catch his breath.

Soon, the week's journey caught up with them. Fatigue, coupled with the heady warmth of the hearth at their feet, swept them up into a warm, deep contentment. Some moments passed in silence as Cienne dozed and Seth mused.

He found it a cruel fact of life that in such a moment of utter perfection, he couldn't help drifting back to them – his son and Adrienne. His imperfect other family.

He shook his head, derisive. She wasn't family. Family didn't sacrifice their own blood. Family ties ran deeper than anything. A fresh wave of anger rushed through his core. He didn't owe her anything. She took their child away from the world, not him.

The hypocrisy hit him. *Family ties ran deeper than anything*. Says the man who murdered his father and set him alight to destroy the evidence.

A gulf opened in him again, for the first time since the twins were born. He tugged his mind out of his own self-loathing and forced himself to render them instead, his only triumph. The only perfect creation, born of love and raised with it. With Cienne.

He gazed at her in the gloom, lit by a single candle too far from the bed for them to reach. An idea was forming in his head. *She would hate it, though*, he reminded himself. He traced the contours of her face, her delicate features, pictured her eyes, now closed but normally a piercing blue. And always full of affection. Unlike *hers*.

The thought swelled in him, becoming unbearable to hold in. Despite her peaceful rest, he reached over and gave Cienne's shoulder a poke.

She rolled her head around to squint at him. 'I thought you were tired?' she asked playfully.

He braced himself. 'I… would like us to have… another child.'

~

Jimmy squinted into the candlelight. 'I remember it being less… roomy.'

Lilly had only been inside the coin vault once as a child, and she'd had to be blindfolded on the way to stop her memorising the route and dipping into it when no one was looking. Her mother hadn't bothered to blind her and Jimmy on this occasion as she led them into the bowels of the castle cellars, past the boiler room and into the back of the family vault, where a secret door resided in the corner.

It was much the same as the last time she had been here: huge and cool, with dark grey brick walls, an echo and a soggy ceiling. All that was missing was the sodding *money*. The dozens of shelves lining the walls bore heavy oak trunks, usually filled with coin – now they lay empty.

Lilly swept down a row of shelves, lifting each lid in horror. 'Where did it all go?'

'You didn't let Russell in here, did you?' Jimmy asked in alarm. 'I thought he was getting heavy.'

'He's getting heavy because you're bribing him into being your miniature wingman,' Eleanor scolded. 'No, this is Emmett's doing.'

'What isn't Emmett's doing?' Lilly said with a sigh. She examined the dust coating the inside of a trunk, where gold had once gathered in abundance.

'You're saying the Peace Tax has bankrupted the royal family?' Jimmy asked in disbelief.

'Well, that and the palace council,' Eleanor scoffed, wiping some dust from the doorframe with the tip of her forefinger. 'I suspect they've squandered it amongst themselves while Seth's back was turned – which it always is. How else does a palace manage to go bankrupt in a time of peace? No one else has access to the vault except for Seth, and what would he use that much money for?'

Lilly and Jimmy exchanged glances. Lilly sighed. 'I hate to break it to you, Mum, but Seth isn't exactly the archangel, is he?'

'He hasn't bought another elephant, has he?' Eleanor groaned, her gaze gravitating to the ceiling.

'No, we're talking the purchase of gifts in exchange for, you know…' Jimmy supplied, twirling a hand outward.

'Meaning he has a mistress, then?' Eleanor said, catching on quick, which wasn't like her.

Jimmy had to stop himself from applauding. Lilly could sense the effort radiating from him.

'Is it Lady Elizabeth del Loux de Hae, the girl that used to be Cienne's handmaiden before she married the master of coin?' Eleanor suddenly asked in earnest. 'She's very pretty, they'd be very well suited, I think.'

'Mother, if Seth were having relations with her, the vault would be overflowing, not depleting,' Lilly said. 'Mister Tilloodle-ooh's been pimping her out for years.'

'Del Loux de Hae,' she corrected haughtily.

'Close enough,' Jimmy said. 'She hasn't the personality to warrant a name with a silent "X" in it.'

'I take that to mean you've had your way with her already?' Lilly said with a grin.

Jimmy tapped the side of his nose. 'Hundred per cent discount,' he said, and smoothed back his hair.

Lilly snorted loudly. She turned to face her mother. 'So anyway, when are you going to grass him up?'

Eleanor snorted. 'Why would I do that? You think I want Cienne to kill him? She doesn't need to know, it's not her place to meddle with the king's mistresses.'

'But you hang around her every minute of the day,' Lilly said with a frown. 'How do you expect to keep such a massive secret from her?'

Eleanor laughed softly at her daughter and tucked some stray strands of Lilly's hair behind her ear. 'If you think that's the biggest secret I've had to keep in this family, then it seems you have a lot to learn about your dear mother.'

Lilly watched her sweep out of the room, her skirts flapping behind her. 'What does she mean by that?'

'Nothing, probably,' Jimmy scoffed. 'She's been trying to make herself seem interesting for years. What we need to figure out is this money issue. Seth can't have spent this much on the secrecy of the coachman.'

'Think we ought to let Seth deal with this? He's due back in a day or so.'

'Ah, no,' Jimmy advised. 'He's a bit tactless with this sort of thing. And if Seth really is spending obscene amounts of money on Adrienne, we don't want another "shovel first, ask questions later" situation, which leaves us with no option but to not tell Cienne either. Unbelievably, the best person to sort this out right now is you.'

Lilly grimaced. 'Well, I suppose there's a first time for everything.' She heaved herself to her full height, which didn't happen often, and put on as best a regal tone as she could with the accent of an East Serpus street urchin.

'Summon the small council and tell them to get their paperwork together. I want them in my chambers on Monday. And if Seth gets back before then, find something to distract him.'

'Already got something,' Jimmy said with a rare grin.

'Really? What?'

'I'll tell you when it comes to fruition,' he said with a raised eyebrow.

He smoothed back his hair again.

~

A knock on the door startled Emmett from his afternoon paperwork. 'Yes?'

A manservant entered with a bow. 'Queen Qattren Meringue requests your audience, my lord.'

'Mar-ee-ange, not meringue,' Qattren corrected irritably. 'I'm not a cream cake.'

Emmett rose. 'Have a seat, your highness.'

Qattren met his gaze, sitting across from him over the width of the same table they had gathered around for their meeting a week before. This time, the afternoon sun bore down upon the surface and rebounded, causing everyone in the vicinity to squint. Apart from Emmett, whose eyes were constantly narrowed anyway.

'I hope you and your husband have made yourselves comfortable,' he said as though whether they did or not made no odds to him in any case.

'Much of the staff used to work for Ronald's father's household, they were very happy to see him.'

'Is Azrael up to his old tricks yet?'

~

Oblivious to the two, on the other side of the wall to Qattren's left, Ron cowered in a broom cupboard.

'Rooo-ooon,' called Azrael. 'Oh, Rooo-ooon!'

On the other side of the door, the tip of a blade scratched the surface of the wood.

Ron placed his palms together and laced his fingers in prayer, his eyes fluttering shut.

~

Qattren smiled faintly.

'Getting along like a house on fire,' she said. 'I would imagine the little prince is enjoying his new accomplice.'

'I don't doubt it.'

~

'Where's Ron?' Azrael asked theatrically. 'Oh, Rooon-aaald?'

The blade scored another line on the wood, peeling off another strand.

Ron whimpered.

~

A cupbearer of about ten years of age poured them each a goblet of wine.

Emmett took a small sip.

Qattren ignored hers completely.

'So,' Emmett said, lowering his beverage.

~

Azrael flung the door open, knife held horizontally in front of him.

'There he is!' he shrieked in delight.

Ron howled in terror.

~

'How can I help you today?' Emmett said over the screams.

Qattren paused to listen through the wall for sounds of mortal danger.

Ron sobbed prolifically, which was a definite sign of life.

Satisfied that widowdom was at least another day away, she replied to Emmett. 'I wish for a change in your Peace Tax. I wish to contribute to the payment myself, along with the king of Adem.'

He raised an eyebrow. 'You wish to be taxed for the silence on Prince Vladimir's death?' he asked for clarification.

'Yes.'

He shook his head slightly in bemusement. 'Why?'

'I think it unfair that the fee be placed solely on one witness,' Qattren said. 'As preposterous as the concept of us murdering the prince in cold blood is, I do not wish to make a war of it. And I don't trust Seth Crey to keep up his payments regularly, as judged by his spectacle last week.'

'Agreed,' he said. 'But I would have thought, considering your reputation, that getting off scot-free on this one would please you?'

'My conscience precedes my pride in this case,' she said. 'I am as much responsible for not preventing this accident as Seth Crey is. If you insist on laying blame for the incident, it should be laid equally.'

Emmett regarded her thoughtfully. 'Your conscience, you say. As opposed to your need to ensure that Prince Vladimir is thoroughly forgotten about for some reason?'

Qattren said nothing, her expression unreadable.

Her met her gaze. 'As long as my payment comes in, I care not whose pocket supplies it.'

She smiled faintly. 'Then we shall split the bill fifty-fifty and your master of coin will send me a bill quarter-yearly?'

'As long as I don't receive a reply in horse manure again,' he said in distaste.

A knock arrived on the door again and a messenger peered into the doorway.

'Yes?' Emmett said.

'My lord, Queen Felicity has gone missing. She has taken Prince Azrael with her.'

'When?' Emmett demanded, his voice taking a sharp tone. 'I heard Azrael in the next room only a moment ago.'

'She dismissed her guards, leading the prince into the east gardens. She took a horse and fled with the prince before we could see what she was doing.'

'What do you mean, fled?' Emmett asked dangerously.

The messenger produced a note. Emmett snatched it, flicking it upright to frown at the contents.

'It appears your sister has run away, my lord,' Qattren said with just a hint of pleasure.

Emmett inhaled through his nose and stood.

'Find her,' he told the messenger in a growl. 'Now!'

~

Seth awoke in his own bed, in his own palace, with his pregnant wife beside him and his twin children curled into a heart shape between them. His lips pressed together fondly, he smiled at them all and planted a kiss on each head, nearest to farthest: Russell, Ginny, Cienne and one more for the impending arrival.

Emmett's grotesque display of extravagance was now replaced with his own keep's practical sturdiness. Firm concrete blocks patterned the walls behind tapestries and curtains, all coordinating with the deep emerald of the wide gilded rug.

He got up and dressed in plain viridian velvet before waking his wife with a tweak of her nose. 'Are you getting up?'

'No,' she mumbled, rolling over.

He grinned and kissed her hair.

Downstairs, Seth ate his breakfast in peace as his uncle the Duke of Osney shuffled over with a bow.

'We have noted down everything discussed in today's council meeting,' he said, placing a scroll on the table beside Seth's scrambled eggs.

'Thank you, Osney,' Seth said cheerfully. 'I shall read it at my leisure.'

'Very good. May I add you're looking very dapper this morning?'

'Why, thank you!' Seth trilled, smoothing down his leotard.

Osney left as Seth finished his eggs and rose, stretching his arms wide. The sun shone brightly through the stained-glass windows in a pink rainbow. Seth admired it and rose to head for the courtyard, to enjoy it while it lasted.

Alas, just as Jon opened the door for him, rain began to pour.

'Oh, well,' Jon said sadly. 'It was nice while it lasted.'

'No need to think negatively, my friend,' Seth said brightly. He clapped his hands twice.

The rain stopped immediately. Seth even saw the raincloud bow at him before leaving.

'Very good,' he told it cheerfully.

Later that day, leaving his two children in the gardens to enjoy the sun, Seth strolled across the front grounds to the portcullis, where his butler was waiting, along with a coach.

'Have a good day, my liege,' Jimmy said, bowing with a flourish.

'And you,' Seth said, climbing aboard.

He reclined in the cushioned seats as the coach circled the palace. They rattled down the north side of the hill, down a bumpy road, but Seth didn't mind that. He looked forward to his arrival as the market of Buttercup approached and passed beside him, and the houses of the village suddenly came into view.

The coach ground to a halt, their ten-minute journey at an end.

Seth opened the door himself before the driver got the chance to move and leaped from the coach to make a beeline for the house.

Adrienne opened the door, beaming radiantly at him.

Seth grinned at them both. 'Hello, you.'

Their son grinned back from Adrienne's arms, revealing the little gap where his first adult tooth was slowly coming through. 'Hi Dad,' he said, his blond pudding-bowl fringe flopping over his eyes.

Seth brushed his hair aside with a smile. His name was Albert, for some reason. They called him Al for short.

'Hello, little man,' he said softly.

Adrienne gave Seth a kiss. 'I've missed you.' She rested her head on his right shoulder, and Al rested his on the other.

Seth wrapped an arm around each of them, feeling at peace.

'Seth.'

His eyelids flickered closed and he gave his little family a squeeze.

'Seth!'

Seth jolted awake.

The coach jerked to a halt, heralding their return home. Ginny sprawled across her parents' laps, snoring gently through a film of drool collecting on Seth's knee.

Cienne shoved his head from her shoulder and slid her notably un-pregnant body from beneath Ginny's sleeping one. 'You've been asleep since we left,' she said almost icily. 'Make yourself useful and take Ginny up to bed, then go and see Jimmy. The guard says he's looking for you.'

Seth glowered at her.

She leapt from the coach, little Russell in tow.

There was no use trying to talk to her when she was like this. Seth stretched his arms above his head for a moment before turning his attention to his sleeping daughter, silently calculating the best method of lifting her without waking her.

Settling with waking her with a murmur, he exited the coach with Ginny cradled on one shoulder. He glared up at the clouds momentarily as it started to pour, and a nameless manservant placed a cloak over his head and shoulders.

'Thank you,' he said quietly. He pulled the hood of Ginny's cloak up himself and jogged up the path to the keep.

After depositing his daughter into Despina's arms, Seth jogged back downstairs to the courtyard, where he found Jimmy waiting patiently under the shelter of, bizarrely, Ginny's Wendy house.

Seth stooped slightly to enter the short doorway to the little wooden house, painted an alarming shade of pink. He squatted onto a mushroom-shaped stool, his knees about level with his shoulders and his clothes dripping onto the timber floor. 'Jimmy, why are we in the Wendy house?'

'The leotard cost me fifty gold pieces, would you have it ruined in this weather?'

Seth eyed the intricate gold embroidery on the black clothing. 'Yes.'

Jimmy rolled his eyes. He squatted across from Seth in a similar fashion. 'I haven't come out here to talk about clothes.' He shifted uncomfortably. A little wooden tea set littered the tiny table between them, a little pool of water sitting undisturbed beneath an upturned cup.

'Jimmy,' Seth said in a withering tone, 'we're in a courtyard in the middle of a castle. There's a building all around us, you don't need to sit on Ginny's favourite stool.'

'Actually, I do. See, Lyseria… she's eaten another dragon-feeder.'

Seth rolled his eyes. 'And?'

'And…' Jimmy hesitated. 'And his widow is very attractive.'

'Ah,' Seth said in realisation.

'Yes. And the reason I want to speak to you away from the rest of the servants is that I'd like you to give your condolences personally… and bring me with, obviously,' he added, 'but of course everyone else might get arsy that his widow gets the special treatment and no one else's does, so this naturally has to stay between us.'

Seth heaved a sigh. 'You want me to do this now, I suppose?'

'Please. She's a massive royalist, apparently. Might help my chances if you wear your Sunday best?' he added, ever the opportunist.

Seth looked fed-up. 'You want me to *change*?'

'It's not the hardest thing you've had to do for a favour, surely?'

'I don't *do* favours,' Seth seethed. 'I'm the king, favours happen to *me*.' His eyes rose to the ceiling. 'Fine. Where does this woman live?'

'Little village north of here, called Buttercup Village if I remember rightly.'

Seth scowled. 'What a coinky-dink.'

To Jimmy's bemused expression he said, 'Get me a coach, then. I'll find you at the entrance in exactly fifteen minutes.'

~

III

'This is an excellent view of the rear grounds, my lady,' one of the minions of hell said pleasantly, peering over the edge of her balcony. The rain had briefly stopped and the sun beamed down on the keep, leaving the veranda comfortably dry. Unfortunately.

'Indeed it is,' another underling added, impressed. 'It must be lovely to awaken in the morning to this view. It's a wondrously designed piece of garden, too.'

'An ample view of the court's archery yard, also,' piped up a waspish-looking product of the seven deadly sins.

'Because princesses have nothing better to do than stare out of windows all day,' Lilly said wryly. 'Get away from the balcony and sit down. We have business to attend to.'

The three men turned from the veranda and gravitated to the elliptical table in the centre of the drawing room, where Lilly was already seated with Jon acting as Jimmy's representative.

The men's miscellaneous papers – which had very little purpose other than to demonstrate importance, Lilly sneered in her head – already coated the surface of the table, in between goblets and small platters. Jon picked idly at a mixed berry bowl while kippers steamed in the centre – clearly they had Lilly's food preference confused with Cienne's again. Some baby cousin of a cousin – Lilly had too many on her mother's side to bother keeping up with – loitered in the corner of the room burdened with a wine jug as big as she

116

was, awaiting the inevitable beckon.

The Duke of Osney was away on 'council business', leaving the meeting's dealings to be left to three of his minions: Manderly, Hinterton and another man whose name Lilly had forgotten and who she simply referred to as the Jasper.

Manderly and Hinterton were as different in builds as a barge was to an arrow, but both favoured the same kind of hideous embroidery patterns Eleanor insisted on attempting on her handmade articles of clothing, a kind of filigree-attempt. It ended up having the same effect as simply dropping a wad of silver thread on the front and stomping it into place. They also appeared to have curled their hair and oiled it into ringlets. The smell of the oils was cloying as best and revolting at most. Lilly almost preferred the kippers.

The third dressed plainly and hadn't bothered with the pungent oils, but he made her somehow more uneasy. The Jasper became less of a nickname as the minutes waned and more of a personality trait. Lilly felt increasing urges to squish him under the toe of her boot.

'Will the king be joining us?' Manderly asked brightly.

'Where's all the money gone?' Lilly asked, jumping to the point.

'Ummph,' Manderly spluttered in alarm. 'Was the money gone? I hadn't noticed.'

Jon's nose wrinkled. 'You're the master of coin.'

Manderly's eyes widened. 'Well, there, buh, well, er, buh, um.'

Hinterton leapt in at this point. 'The palace has been in debt for quite some time now, since shortly after your brother became king, in fact.' He arched an eyebrow at Jon in distaste. 'Is there a reason for the presence of the servant?' he cut across himself, glaring pointedly at Jon.

'I'm Mortimer Crey, fifth in line to the throne,' Jon said cheerfully. 'Nice to meet you.'

Hinterton gaped at him with his mouth open. 'You're... you're the...'

Jon chortled in satisfaction. 'Shut you up, didn't it?'

Lilly clicked her fingers in front of Hinterton's face, making him blink. 'You said we've been in debt for years. Who do we owe money to?'

'Oh, various people.'

His voice was nonchalant, but the veil of sweat along his hairline told a different story.

Lilly glared at him. 'Such as?'

His gaze shifted guiltily to Manderly, who cowered.

Lilly faced Manderly patiently, waiting.

He cleared his throat daintily. 'Mssrmemmett.'

'Which?'

He coughed into his fist. 'Mister Emmett,' he repeated, emphasising the "T" sheepishly.

Lilly gave him a withering glance. 'Mister Emmett.'

'Yes, your grace,' he mumbled.

'The king's *arch nemesis* Mister Emmett?'

'That's the one, yes.'

Jon simply slammed his head facedown onto the table.

'Why do we owe four years' worth of money to *Mister Emmett*?' Lilly asked in the patient tone of voice reserved for the most loathed of stupid people.

'Well, you're probably aware from the queen's letter earlier this week that the king has ordered the boycott of—' Hinterton began.

'Yes, but that was only the other day!' Lilly said loudly. 'We've paid the tax in full from day one! We raised taxes especially to do that! What have we owed him for that has caused the vault to be empty?'

Manderly and Hinterton gulped in unison and turned to the waspish one for assistance.

As though waiting for his moment, the Jasper smiled.

'The tax has been sent directly from the tax collectors to Stoneguard,' he said. 'That sum has amounted to ninety per cent of the palace income, tax rises included, with the rest having to supply imported foodstuffs, textiles, and that tea the Queen drinks as birth prevention.'

'So that's how she manages it,' Jon said in interest, lifting his head from the table. 'I was beginning to think Seth was impotent.'

Lilly grimaced. 'You aren't the one who walked in on him ejacu—'

'We also have to consider the added special expenditure,' the Jasper cut in sharply, 'which includes but is not limited to weddings, transport to weddings, transport to asylums after the bride's apparent escape from said transport...'

Lilly bristled at this point. Her hackles rose almost like a canine's, and kept rising until he finished.

' …ships to visit foreign relatives, dragon after dragon after *dragon* of which only one seems to have survived—all of which the master of coin has been forced to take out multiple loans for. Which Mister Emmett was all too kind to arrange with us for a reasonable interest rate.'

'What's the interest rate?' Lilly asked.

'Not my problem.'

'How *isn't* that your problem?'

'He gave me some money and a yacht, you see,' he said with a smile.

Jon's jaw hung open. 'So you stick us up to our eyeballs in debt and fly away unscathed,' he said in disgust. 'You big fucking wasp. I ought to swat you.'

'Permission granted,' Lilly said savagely.

Jon snatched a loan contract from the desk, rolled it up and slapped the man's nose with it.

The Jasper blinked twice, then turned back to his budget as if nothing had happened. 'The interest rate is twenty-five per cent of the gross—'

'That's not reasonable at all!' Jon exclaimed, appalled.

'—to be paid quad-yearly over a period of fifteen years commencing from the beginning of this year. That will soon include any outstanding Peace Tax at the same rate, thanks to the king's latest hissy-fit.'

'Insults to the king, is it? Sounds like he needs another swatting, Jon,' Lilly said amiably.

Jon bent the rolled-up parchment over the waspish man's pointy head. 'So what are we talking in real money?'

'Assuming that the boycott goes ahead,' he consulted his budget, 'and that any unpaid bills are not added to the debt, we will be paying it off in quad-yearly instalments of seventy-five thousand pounds each season.'

'How much is that altogether?' Lilly asked, dreading the answer.

'Three hundred grand a year,' Jon said in a gravelly voice. 'For fifteen years. We're skint until the twins come of age.'

Lilly's eyes glazed over desolately. 'So much for my thirtieth birthday party.'

The Jasper met her gaze and simply shrugged.

'Swat him again, Jon,' Lilly said with venom. 'Swat his *face*.'

Jon complied, but his heart wasn't in it. The paper barely made a clap. Manderly furtively cleared his throat and pointed at the budget.

The waspy one squinted down. 'Ah. It appears I miscounted the zeros,' he said, without the barest hint of remorse. 'That is in fact three million a year.'

Jon stared at him in initial incomprehension before swatting the man repeatedly with every ounce of his strength.

'We're gonna have fun explaining this to Seth,' Lilly said glumly, burying her head in her arms.

~

Seth sat sheepishly at the widow's dinner table. The floors consisted of broken pieces of flagstone covered over with rushes, and the entire house seemed crammed into the space of one room, and not a big room at that. Seth reckoned his privy was larger than their house and garden combined. Small children surrounded them, sitting cross-legged in a circle.

'Would you like sugar in your tea?' the widow asked timidly from the sink.

'Oh, we couldn't possibly—' Jimmy began, with his best ladies' man voice.

'Speak for yourself,' Seth said, twirling his hand to continue.

She peered into the sugar bowl, calculating, before finally just pouring the entire contents into Seth's tea. He watched on with a pained expression and wished he hadn't said anything.

He'd never seen such hopeless poverty before. They didn't even have a proper tea set, he spotted: his cup was made of wood, just like Ginny's toy version. *They were lucky to have tea to put in it,* he thought with a faint sense of despair.

Nevertheless, he accepted his wooden cup of weak tea with a smile as the widow sat across from him, Jimmy sidling close surreptitiously.

Seth shifted his gaze back to the five children sitting cross-legged on the floor around his chair. He glanced at each one uneasily as they stared up at him, awe-struck. His gaze fell on a four-year-old beneath the table, with a blond pudding-bowl cut and silver eyes. Just like Adrienne's eyes…

Seth frowned and rubbed his eyes, driving the dream from his thoughts.

Jimmy elbowed him, startling him.

'Tell her, then!' he hissed.

Seth grimaced at him. 'No, you tell her.'

'You have to tell her, you're his employer!'

'I'm not the one who wants to shag her!' He glanced at the widow. 'Sorry.'

She bowed her head politely. She was blond, which ticked all of Jimmy's boxes, but she wasn't quite as pretty as the blond Jimmy was eyeing up in the kitchens last week, Seth thought critically before remembering that this was a widowed mother he was thinking about.

Seth smiled thinly again. 'I'm very sorry to have to tell you that your husband has had an accident,' he said slowly. 'He's… passed away.'

She exhaled heavily, her eyes closed. 'The dragon?'

Seth made another pained expression and nodded, his lips pressed together.

She sobbed, holding a hand over her face.

Jimmy grasped her free hand in his own firmly.

Smarmy git, Seth thought with a scowl. He wouldn't have been surprised if Jimmy had shoved the man directly into Lyseria's maw to clear the way.

Seth licked his lips and snuck another glance at their youngest child, who gazed up at him, oblivious. Seth privately nicknamed him Al.

'I'm so sorry,' he mumbled, meeting her gaze guiltily.

'No,' she said hurriedly, wiping her eyes with the palm of her hand. 'He would have preferred it to happen this way. He didn't want to go like my younger brother…'

Seth raised an inquisitive eyebrow.

She met his gaze, as though afraid to continue. 'He didn't want to get the flux.'

Seth's eyes narrowed. 'What's the flux?'

'Disease,' Jimmy explained shortly. 'Been doing the rounds in Serpus.'

'My little brother had just visited from there,' she continued miserably. 'He said he was lucky to avoid it… and then he got ill…' She wiped her eyes again. 'And then my youngest got it.'

Seth glanced down at Al, this time warily.

Jimmy also retracted his hand from the widow's to wipe on his shirt.

The widow noticed and shook her head. 'Her name was Lily, your highness. After the flower… and your sister…' She dragged in a shuddering breath. 'We buried her eight weeks ago. No one's been ill since, we thought that would be it, that there would be no more funerals this year…'

Seth folded his arms on top of the table, his eyes distant. He looked up at the widow. 'What's your name?'

'Linda, my liege.'

'Linda.' Seth rose to his feet and held out his hand, which she took. 'Let me help you.'

'Your majesty, there's no need—'

'Let me help you,' he insisted.

She trembled slightly. 'We need money,' she admitted. 'I'll have to remarry—'

'And have another five children to feed?' Seth ignored Jimmy's imploring glances. 'I'll sort out your money.'

'Your majesty,' she said in astonishment. 'I, uh, don't—'

'Your husband did nothing but an excellent job on that bloody stupid animal,' he said firmly. 'The least I owe him is food for his children.' He gazed down at all five of them, four boys and an older girl, and ruffled Al's hair before walking to the door.

Jimmy realised what he was doing and repeatedly shook his head. 'Sir…'

'Meet me outside the door,' Seth said to Linda.

Jimmy sawed his throat with the edge of his hand.

'I'll be ten minutes,' he said, rising.

'Sir,' Jimmy growled, following close behind. 'Don't do it, sir.'

Seth ignored him and waved down the treasurer's coach.

'Sir!' Jimmy shouted in alarm.

Ten minutes later, a crowd had formed in the centre of Buttercup Village. It followed Seth Crey and his butler as Seth laboured his way to the widow's cottage under the weight of an entire wheelbarrow's worth of gold coins.

'Seth,' Jimmy gritted through clenched teeth.

'Can't talk,' Seth grunted, driving the wheelbarrow around a corner. 'Philanthropy-ing.'

'You can't afford to be philanthropy-ing!' Jimmy exclaimed. 'That money is for the Peace Tax! You know, to stop Horseface Emmett from letting everyone kill us?'

'Horseface Emmett can whistle for it,' Seth said, struggling on.

'No he can't! Put it back, you've three yards to turn back, it's not too late—'

It *was* too late. Linda's saucer-like eyes had found the wheelbarrow.

Seth parked the gold in front of her and took a deep bow.

'This is for you and your family,' he told her breathlessly, 'no obligation, no interest, no payment back required. This is for all the singed eyebrows, broken bones, back problems and smoke-inhalation illnesses your late husband suffered for me and a meagre wage and never complained about—'

'To you, he didn't,' Jimmy muttered.

Seth stomped on his foot. '—and this is for,' he took a deep breath, holding a hand up, 'your loyalty to me and my family in such a horrible year for you, and for your beautiful daughter, named after my less-than-beautiful sister,' he heard a few laughs, 'who was taken much, much too early from you.' He took another breath and leaned on his knees. 'Just don't let me push wheelbarrows of gold up a hill again.'

The crowd burst into uproar, clapping and whistling. Linda sprinted around the wheelbarrow to throw her arms around his neck, much to his alarm. She was quickly followed by her daughter and, to Seth's silent joy, Al.

'Thank you,' she wept into his ear, kissing his cheek hard. 'Thank you so much.'

'It's fine,' he said hoarsely, rubbing her back.

Linda released Seth for a moment to raise her youngest son onto one shoulder before throwing herself onto Seth again, holding him and her son tightly, her head on his right shoulder, Al's head on his left.

Seth was too shocked to notice himself holding them back so tightly it almost hurt.

Jimmy stood beside this spectacle, his arms crossed disapprovingly.

'She's going to be lynch-mobbed the minute your coach rounds the hill, you know.'

Seth ignored him.

The crowd closed around them – either to pat his back or palm some of the coins, it was difficult to tell through the chaos – but Seth didn't mind. He thought he'd glimpsed Adrienne half a dozen times among the throng of villagers, and he didn't mind that it wasn't her either.

Until suddenly it *was* her, standing on her doorsteps some yards away, only just visible in a tiny gap in the crowd. Adrienne stared at him from her doorstep, Howie behind her, leaning against the doorway sullenly. She caught Seth's eye and grinned. Adrienne was smiling at him. And it wasn't a dream.

And he didn't care who saw him smiling right back.

~

Thankfully, Felicity Emmett was the only one who saw him smile back. *So this is the mistress*, she thought, eyeing Adrienne's figure in interest. *Pretty*. She watched him disentangle himself from the crowd as she waited on her brother's horse, Azrael sitting sleepily in the saddle in front of her.

Seth strolled happily back to his coach in the market.

Jimmy followed, his mouth opening and closing wordlessly.

'I can't believe you just did that,' he said in disbelief. 'I cannot believe you just did that. I had no idea even you could be this stupid! You've just given her all your money! You bloody idiot!'

'I think the term you're looking for is "my liege",' Seth said.

'No,' Jimmy corrected, his index finger pointed at the clouds, 'no, "my liege" is what you call someone you have respect for. "Bloody idiot" sounds a bit more like it. Bloody! Idiot!' he shrilled, punctuating each word with a manic wave with both hands.

'I said it last week and I'll say it again,' Seth said irritably, passing Felicity's horse without a second glance. 'I'm not paying this stupid Peace Tax anymore. I don't owe him anything. She needs that money more than he does anyway.'

'That's not the point!' he exclaimed. 'He's not a nice man!'

'That's funny,' Seth mused. 'When I was a kid, my mum always told me good people got rewards, not the other way around.'

'She *would* tell you that, she's as thick as two short—'

Seth climbed into his coach, ignoring him.

Jimmy sighed and glared up at the sky.

'Seth!'

Seth peered back out and froze.

Adrienne halted two yards away. She smiled tentatively.

Seth hopped out.

Jimmy dropped his head on his hand. He pivoted to make a beeline for the pub in defeat.

Adrienne approached Seth with trepidation. 'That was so kind,' she said softly. 'What you did for Linda.'

Seth shrugged. 'He was a nice bloke.' *Probably*.

She smiled more broadly.

For a moment, Seth deliriously considered making a move while he had the moral high ground. Then he glimpsed Howie and recalled his unborn son with a sudden weight on his chest. He stood fearfully in front of them, his legs like jelly.

'Hello, Howard.'

Howie bowed, as stiffly as Seth had greeted him. 'Your majesty,' he said icily.

Adrienne licked her lips. 'I went to see him while you were away.'

Seth said nothing.

'When can I bury him?'

A dark cloud descended over him. He lowered his head, running a hand through the front of his hair. 'I was just going to do it myself. I can't be sure if he's actually… ours, so… it's more symbolic than anything…' He looked up at her. 'Would you like to be there?'

'Yes,' Howie said for her, linking his fingers with hers. 'We both would.'

Seth scowled at him bitterly.

'We'll need a coach up to you,' Adrienne said in a small voice.

'I'll send one to you tomorrow, first light,' he said.

'Thank you, Seth,' she said meekly.

She remembered, he thought.

'Just Seth,' he'd told her four years ago, in the courtyard. '"Your

125

highness" is a term for people who are below me.' A category that would never include her.

'I'll see you tomorrow, then,' Seth said gently.

Adrienne curtsied. Howie bowed his head, maintaining sullen eye contact.

Seth bowed back to her and gave Howie a last, quick glare as they turned away from each other. So much for not owing her anything.

Seth climbed back into the coach with a heavy heart and closed his eyes. He should have told her to piss off. He should have ignored her and drove the coach away. But he couldn't. The girl had an effect on him.

He opened his eyes and was startled.

Felicity Emmett was trying unsuccessfully to sneak Azrael aboard the coach without Seth noticing.

Felicity swallowed.

Seth frowned at her.

She lifted Azrael up in both hands with an eager, lopsided grin. 'Surprise!'

~

IV

The air was hot and heavy, the wind sluggish and lazy.

Candlelight flickered within the heavily concealed cabin in the trees. Inside, Estiah perched on a stool next to the window, peeking outside whilst keeping a steady momentum with her stitching. The crimson gown flowed like a river from one end of the cabin to the other. Estiah's green eyes bored themselves into the king of Adem's skull as he painstakingly scaled the branches outside her window. His voice fluttered in through the glass in the form of an impressive collection of swear words.

Estiah wondered idly how Crey was getting on with the footholds. She pulled her gown up for inspection. It was different from her usual style, which was short for ease of climbing, but she could afford to upgrade to something more luxurious now that her castle was being built.

A bump against the door marked her visitor's arrival.

Estiah laid her gown aside and rose, brushing her long red hair behind one shoulder.

Crey pushed the door open, revealing a bedraggled set of embroidered attire and a scowl. Flaxen hair hung over his eyes until he brushed it away with an impatient hand, shaking dew from his face. He eyed her from head to toe, his slim build hunched miserably forward. 'An impressive dress,' he commented in a low, smooth drawl. 'Not like your usual attire at all.'

Estiah glanced down at herself. Scraps of thread clung to her fitted linen trousers and shirt. 'One can't climb in a flowing gown, strangely enough.'

Crey frowned at her tone. He leaned against the closed door, his arms folded. 'I hear you have declared yourself Queen Estiah Myrianna of the Forest. *My* forest.'

She looked him up and down. 'You didn't want it.'

'That matters not.'

'It does when there are neglected inhabitants involved,' she said smoothly, almost in indifference. 'They may not have a place at your council table, Seb Crey, but they do matter. In case it slipped your notice.'

Seb Crey arched an eyebrow. 'And you've been appointed the official spokesperson of these "inhabitants", are you?'

Estiah's blood ran warm. 'Typical of you to insinuate that they aren't people.'

'They aren't.' Seb's voice was clipped. 'They're little mutants with a penchant for attacking my people. I have come to give you a warning. This land is, my right of birth, mine. No harlot is taking possession of it, even if it is full of miniature barbarians. I suggest that you tear down your castle and leave quietly before I am forced to start making a lot of noise.'

Estiah gazed at him thoughtfully and approached in slow, calculated steps. 'I am not averted to noise, your majesty.'

Seb glared at her. 'You should be,' he said in a whisper.

Estiah turned with a snort and returned to her seat, the light from the dozens of candles shining on her copper-coloured hair. 'What are you going to do?' she asked testily. 'Stick me with your sword?'

Seb swallowed hard. 'Don't play with fire.'

'I often play with fire,' she said. 'Quite literally, in fact.'

'And you want my forest,' he said, smirking. 'A match made in heaven, isn't it?'

She swung around, her hair billowing in a circle. 'The difference between you and I is that my fires know when to stop burning.'

Seb blinked. 'Explain.'

She smirked at him. 'I don't think I need to. I can see your eyes roving. Most unbecoming for a diplomacy visit, but I've heard discretion isn't your strongpoint.'

He gulped audibly, his eyes wandering down her tight-fitting clothes. He blinked and averted his gaze. 'I don't know what you mean.'

Estiah smiled faintly. In spite of her indignant rage, heat had risen to her cheeks. He *was* quite comely for a neglectful despot…

A bump on the road startled Qattren from her memories.

They arrived in the heart of Serpus. Cobbles rattled the coach wheels in a rhythmic tattoo, bouncing them gently on the cushioned seats of the rented carriage. They slowed to a careful walk, weaving between throngs of city dwellers.

Qattren blinked away the haze misting her thoughts. Queen Estiah Myrianna. It had been a long time since she had taken that name. Her motif the phoenix came from the day after the Battle in the Orchard, the day she changed her name and fled into hiding. She barely had any memories left of her last life: they had been buried away, far out of reach, where they wouldn't hurt as much.

Arthur Stibbons' Street was thick with people as the bright Wednesday afternoon market progressed with vigour. Qattren climbed from the coach and strode forward through the wide cobblestoned main street, her path unobstructed as the residents silently slunk out of her way.

Ron skittered after her nervously, his hands behind his back. 'Are you going to tell me where we're going yet?'

'Nope,' she said shortly, staring ahead, her stride unbroken. 'Just keep your hands firmly behind your back.'

Ron's gaze rose to the heavens. 'It's a pub, then?'

Qattren silenced him with a glance before swerving into the King Seth, formerly (yet still colloquially) known as the King Death.

Several punters looked at Ron with distaste and left as subtly as possible. Everyone knew that while Ronald Horne had the mind of a child, he was also, somehow, a raging alcoholic – and they also knew that once he got drunk, his dialogue suddenly betrayed an underlying streak of intense and distinctly un-childlike erotic humour. Drunk Ron lacked the charming innocence of his sober counterpart utterly. Drunk Ron made Jimmy De Vil look like a saint.

On this occasion, Ron did as Qattren obeyed and kept his hands held tightly to the small of his back. His wife approached the counter and was swiftly ushered behind the bar. A meandering path of corridor between barrels and crates led them to the barman's living quarters, a tiny apartment at the back alley decorated sparsely.

'So,' Qattren said in a friendly tone, brandishing a full bag of silver. 'What have you got?'

The barman held his lone hand out in expectant triumph. He nodded to the small square table in the centre of the bare flagstones, indicating for them to sit.

'Mister Rosethorn does indeed live in Buttercup Village now,' the man said in surprise. 'How did you suss that out? He's been nowhere outside the house since they arrived, by all accounts.'

'I have my ways,' she said modestly. She lowered herself into one plain chair with more grace than the appearance of it warranted.

Ron frowned, joining her to her left. 'Howie's back?'

'What about his girlfriend?' Qattren said.

'Making herself a nice living selling ointments and things there,' the barman replied, 'according to the neighbours. They affectionately call her the Rash Cream Girl.'

'Lovely,' Qattren said with a slight smile.

'May I ask what's so special about her?' the barman said curiously.

'You may, but I don't pay you to know the answer,' she said. 'Has the king visited her at all?'

'Twice,' he answered. 'Once after coming from the market, where the villagers saw him with the little prince, and the second time he visited the widow of a man who worked in the palace, giving her gold for some reason or other, and they had a chat there, though no one heard what it was about. Mister Rosethorn was with her that time.'

Qattren threw the bag of silver at him.

He caught it in his lone hand.

'Thank you,' she said. 'I'll be back in two more weeks, keep an eye on them both until then.'

'I have a question,' Ron said.

'Yes, dear?'

He was looking at the one-armed barman. 'How do you manage to run the bar single-handed with only one arm? Surely that would slow you down, but the place runs at high speed.'

'Trade secret,' he said with a wink.

'Is that the most important question you have right now?' Qattren asked incredulously.

'Oh, yeah, also, what are you spying on Howie for?'

That was better. Qattren breathed a sigh of relief. 'It's not Howie I'm spying on – yet. It's Adrienne I need to keep an eye on. You know why.' She touched the side of her nose.

'Oh, because she's Seth's mistress.'

Qattren dropped her head on her hand. 'I need to teach you what touching the side of your nose means.'

'Thought you had an itch,' he said, hurt.

'So that's what you want her for?' the barman said with a grin. 'Wiping out the competition?'

Qattren gave him a withering glance. 'Give me some credit. I'm out of his league and he knows it. I'm not after *her* for anything. But I do want a word with her lover. Come, Ronald,' she said briskly, rising to stride out to the main bar again.

'You can't fool a barman, my lady,' he said in amusement. 'Looks like you have some competition in King Seth Crey, m'lord.'

'I should be so lucky,' Ron said, following Qattren. 'She'll just be off to lecture him, I suppose. She likes to remind people of her moral standards.' He eyed the barman. 'But when we return in two weeks, I want to know exactly how you manage to do cocktails that fast with one hand.'

The barman smiled slyly.

~

The Bastard sat at the outskirts of Castlefoot on a low stone wall, tail gently swaying.

Geldemar trotted along it towards him and *glowed*, his own much longer tail standing bolt upright. It had been a while since he last employed the Holy Flying Cat persona, he reflected, admiring his gleaming stripy tail. Alas, Serpus paid him no notice. Flying cats weren't quite the novelty they were in Stoneguard, Geldemere thought sourly.

Albie squinted through the beams of white light.

Geldemere gave the Bastard's snout a cursory sniff and lay on his stomach beside him, tucking his paws beneath himself. Together, they watched a crowd gather around a group of priests in cowls in the city square usually reserved for executions and palace announcements. Brown stains marred the cobbles beneath them, remnants of past executions and punishments.

Raphael Emmanuel III clapped his hands for silence.

'Ladies and gentlemen,' he announced grandly, 'we are here today to witness history being made! Today, for the first time ever, the two faiths of Truphoria are finally united to bear witness to one power, and henceforth, our new order shall be known as—' He paused for dramatic effect. '—the Knaves of Salator Crey!'

'Eh?' a voice said from a group of priests in bemusement.

The Prophet frowned and turned around. 'The *Knaves*,' he said in annoyance. 'We agreed earlier in the week that that was what we were calling ourselves!'

'But what about the Seven?'

'They're godly servants,' he corrected. 'They're called the Knaves as well! We discussed this already!'

'I wasn't there for this!'

'Well, where were you, then?' the Prophet demanded irately.

'This is going well,' the Bastard commented.

'This is what happens when you put two directly opposing orders into an unruly cult,' Geldemar said, shaking his head. 'He should have had his head knocked in for suggesting this.'

'You're just getting arsy because he called you common,' the Bastard said.

'I never agreed that the Seven were to be made inferior to Salator

Crey!' the man argued. 'They are all equal entities!'

'I never said—' the Prophet protested.

'You called them slaves!'

'Knaves,' he corrected. 'As voted by the majority of the group!'

'Who are part of the faith of Salator Crey!'

'I think you're lucky to get a concession they even exist,' a priest of Salator Crey piped up, a ring of brown hair circling his shining pate. 'As far as I'm concerned, the Seven are as fictitious as the Maids of Sullenport.'

'Blasphemy!' He launched himself at the Unbeliever of the Seven.

'OI! Stop it!' The Prophet tried feebly to break the rolling priests apart with the toe of one sandal. 'Unhand him, the pair of you! No one is to harm a man of the cloth, even other men of the cloth! This is an abomination unto the gods!'

'How many of them?' demanded the priest of the Seven, holding the priest of Salator Crey in a headlock. 'Because if it's Salator Crey, I couldn't care less!'

The Prophet wrenched the pair of middle-aged men apart and glared at them.

'It doesn't matter what the Seven are!' the Prophet barked. 'We are working on behalf of them and Salator Crey, slaves or not! The catalyst of the prophecy arose in the Seven's diocese, and the Prophet,' he gestured at himself with a flourish, 'arose from the jurisdiction of the Crey god. Fate has bound our two faiths—'

'Fate's a member of the Seven, he wouldn't—'

'Shut it! Fate has bound the two faiths, inferiority notwithstanding, so we must take advantage of this opportunity to bind the people against the Antichrist! Now stop fighting and act your age!'

The two priests breathed heavily.

'Jo's right,' one of them concluded. 'We must work to end the great fight.'

'Yes,' the Prophet agreed, breathing a sigh. 'But my name isn't Jo, it's Raphael Emmanuel III.'

'Who're the first two?' a man asked.

The Prophet made a face. 'First two what?'

'Raphael Emmanuels,' he said. 'If you're the third one, who're the first two?'

The Prophet's face reddened. 'Oh, how should I know? Just call me Raphael Emmanuel III!'

'It's a mouthful, though,' a priest pointed out.

'So what? It's holy! It is the name *all eight* of the gods gave unto me in a dream where they pronounced me the Prophet and Messiah and delivered unto me *Godly Enlightenment*.'

The Bastard winced at the shrill proclamation, him being currently in the form of a dog with sensitive ears.

'Yeah, yeah,' said an onlooker, 'but your mother christened you Joe-without-the-"E", so—'

'That is *not* my name!' he said hotly. 'It is *Raphael Emmanuel III*!!'

'Nothing wrong with the name Joseph—'

'Don't make me declare you a witch,' he threatened.

'Ah, he's finally getting to the point,' Geldemar said, flicking his ears.

'Speaking of witches,' the Prophet said, glowering at the square at large, 'that is another matter I wish to announce. My visions have decreed that much of the suffering of the prophesised end of the world is to be caused by sorcery. Therefore from this day forth, all witches and sorceresses are to be brought to trial with the new faith for grand genocide-to-be.'

'Why not sorcerers and warlocks?' a woman in the crowd demanded. 'Why just women?'

'Because of evil womanly wiles and the dreaded cyclic bloodletting,' he said darkly.

'That's bollocks!'

'That's our verdict!'

'That's suicide,' the Bastard said in disbelief.

'That's Raphael Emmanuel III for you,' Geldemar sighed.

'Why aren't men to be trialled?' the indignant woman wanted to know.

'Sorcerers' ways are honourable, unlike that of their female counterpart—'

'You mean because they're celibate like you lot?' she asked with a snort. 'You're killing women because you're not getting any, is it?'

The Prophet spluttered. 'No! Of course not! They're just, they're... stop arguing the will of the Eight!' he snapped lividly. 'Anyone who is found to be a sorcerous woman, as described in the unabridged version of the *holy prophecy*, is to be trialled and executed as a witch. Including *you*,' he snapped at the woman as her mouth opened, 'if you don't shut your trap!'

'You're on about "grand genocide-to-be"? *This* is genocide!'

'Shut *up*!'

'How many witches do you reckon he'll actually execute?' the Bastard said.

'The last cult managed a grand total of ten actual witches,' Geldemar said.

'That's not so bad.'

'Out of an approximate twelve million candidates.'

'Oh. Not so good.'

The Bastard glimpsed Qattren out of the corner of his eye, watching the monks in interest with Ronald Horne just behind her. Geldemere spotted her too and abruptly ceased his glowing.

'She's cutting it fine, standing so close to the Witch-finder General,' the Bastard commented.

As if hearing him, the woman pointed directly at Qattren. 'Oh, here you go! There's your first witch! Off you go!'

Raphael Emmanuel III stared at her, stricken.

Qattren waited patiently, meeting his gaze with a neutral expression.

The Prophet's Adam's apple bobbed. 'N-no proof she's a witch per se—'

'There you go! It's a publicity stunt to shut up outspoken feminists,' the woman declared, pointing at him.

Qattren observed the argument breaking out and lifted a nonchalant eyebrow, beckoning Ron back to their coach.

~

Jimmy split open the wax sealing the letter from his Uncle Scleestophrak and read it carefully. A smile spread across his face in a wide crescent-shape and he folded the letter again to slide into his jacket's inside pocket.

'You look happy all of a sudden,' Jon said, grumpily.

He still wasn't over the fifteen-times-three-million – forty-five million! – pound debt the council had accrued under Mister Horseface Emmett. They were due to get a new oven in the next budget, he recalled with a sinking heart. He hadn't swatted the waspy-looking man half hard enough, Jon thought irately.

He didn't have the heart to tell Jimmy yet. The butler had been planning his paid vacation since his employment with the Creys commenced. If anyone ever told him, Jon figured, his first response would be to sell Osney's skin to pay for the holiday instead.

Jimmy patted Jon's black curls. The resulting swell of rage nearly made Jon tell him about the bankruptcy out of spite.

'Indeed I am happy,' he said cheerfully. 'I've come into some money.'

I don't suppose you'd mind lending it to the treasury, since you're so flush? Jon thought sarcastically. In his head, at least for now.

He poured some milk into a jug for the Lady Felicity.

'Good,' he said aloud. 'Maybe you can give me back some of that money you very "charitably" took off my hands when I handed in my lordship.'

'Now, Jon,' Jimmy said in a reasonable voice, 'you know footmen don't have money and for good reason. You would only get it stolen. It's in a better place now.'

'You mean the knocking shop?'

Jimmy shushed him and elbowed his arm. 'It's a valuable city resource,' he argued.

'Like you need it when you have Kingie out there to butter up the local widows for you,' Jon said in disgust.

'Shh,' Jimmy hissed.

Felicity passed them. She grabbed her son around the middle and hauled him back out of the kitchens, murmuring apologies.

Jimmy watched her leave. 'What's she doing here, anyway?'

'What I want to know,' Jon said in disgruntlement, 'is why a bastard butler gets all his rich great-uncle's money. The man is *loaded*. Who did you have to kill to get all that?'

Jimmy froze. 'How did you know I was a bastard?'

'I'm a genius,' he said shortly. 'Shouldn't Ronald Horne get it?'

Jimmy shushed him again fervently.

'Not so loudly!' he hissed. 'Not everyone knows that Aaliyaa Horne was my auntie and I'd quite like it to stay that way. At least until my inheritance comes through.'

Jon pondered this in silence for a moment. 'So Aaliyaa Horne was your maternal aunt, then?'

'Half-aunty,' Jimmy corrected. 'My father was illegitimate.'

Jon frowned. 'So you're a bastard *squared*?'

'I'd rather you didn't use the word "bastard",' Jimmy said dully. 'If anything, it should be the father that gets that title, not the child.'

Jon tilted his head to one side in concession.

'Not that it matters, My parents married shortly after I was born and legitimised me as a result, meaning I'm not a bastard anymore.'

'As someone who works for you, I beg to differ.'

Jimmy scowled at him. 'You chose to be here,' he reminded him. 'That means I *can* have you killed just like any other employee, cousin of the king or not.'

'Yeah, you won't, though,' Jon said, flippant.

Jimmy sighed. *Can't risk it*, he reminded himself.

'Your old man was still a bastard, though,' Jon went on.

'So?'

'So how is it you get the money?'

'Last surviving blood relative,' he said abruptly.

'Except for Ron,' he pointed out.

'Oh, he didn't know about Ron and Vladimir,' he said flippantly.

Jon frowned again. 'But,' he said, 'they're *royalty*.'

'Ah. Well.' Jimmy looked sheepish. 'That might be because I told him Aaliyaa miscarried them and died childless.'

Jon gaped at him. 'Give Ron the money, you evil bastard!'

'No,' said Jimmy, shielding his pocket with the letter hidden within. 'It's mine.'

'What's yours?' a voice asked.

Jimmy made a horrible face. 'Nothing, sir, absolutely nothing—'

'Jimmy's got money coming and it's illegal,' Jon babbled at high speed, pointing at him.

'No, it isn't!' Jimmy hissed despairingly.

'It's Ron's money, not yours. Embezzlement, that is, *embezzlement*, take if off him, put it in the vault,' Jon said speedily.

Seth's eyes narrowed and he wrenched Jimmy's jacket open.

'No, don't take it,' Jimmy said feebly, 'it's mine…'

Seth extracted the letter and opened it. 'This is Aaliyaa Horne's maternal uncle, is it not?'

'Yep,' Jimmy said miserably.

'He's loaded.'

'He *was*,' he said glumly.

'You know,' Seth said, smugly, 'you might as well give it to Ron, because if you get it—'

'It automatically belongs to you,' he finished with a horrible scowl. 'Bloody feudal system.'

'Oh, does it now?' Jon asked in interest. 'Does that include all the money you took off me—'

'Shh,' Jimmy hissed, placing a finger across Jon's lips.

'Tell you what,' Seth said with a grin, pocketing Jimmy's letter, to his despair. 'I'll keep your inheritance in a safe place for you,' he patted his trouser pocket, 'and we'll forget all about how you robbed my little cousin, alright?'

Jimmy glowered at them. 'Well, I'd rather you had it than Azrael Horne,' he conceded reluctantly.

'That's the way,' Seth said with another grin. 'Which means Horseface Emmett doesn't get another tower on his shitty castle. Speaking of old Horseface, his sister takes extra sugar in her tea.' He clapped his hands playfully.

'As you command,' Jimmy said tiredly. He topped up the sugar bowl and shoved the tea tray into Jon's chest.

Seth patted Jimmy's head and led the way to the left antechamber from the throne room, where Felicity was trying ineffectively to distract her son with jam pies.

'The cook made then for you,' she said feebly.

'I want the sword,' Azrael said in awe, his gaze fixed to the broadsword on the wall above the fireplace.

'Ah, no,' Seth said, ushering the boy away. 'I want my son to live *past* the age of four, thanks.' He sat beside Felicity at the table as Jon served the teas. 'Jon!' he howled suddenly, 'stop giving him food!'

Russell deflated in disappointment.

Jon flinched upright, the jam pie swinging out of reach. 'But look at him!' Jon wailed, gesturing at the boy. 'He's looking at me with the big eyes!'

'He looks at everyone like that!' Seth exclaimed. 'It isn't exclusive to you! Do you think that expression is reserved solely for you?'

Jon flung a weak glance at Russell and mouthed 'sorry', placing it back on the tray.

Felicity suppressed a smile, perched at Seth's left. He glanced at her uncertainly. 'Are you sure this is a good idea?'

Felicity nodded. 'Definitely. I'm...' Her lower lip began to tremble. She tensed it, a dimple forming above the chin. 'I'm not a good enough mother for him, and my brother... he's, he... he's not a suitable influence.'

Seth hesitated. 'Does your brother know you're here?'

'It's not his business,' she said. 'I'm the queen and Azrael is my son. Azrael is besotted with him, it isn't natural. And he's teaching him things, every day. The wrong things. I want him to be around people that aren't nasty to others for no reason.'

Jon lifted both eyebrows.

Seth avoided his gaze. 'What will you do if he ... becomes nasty to you for this?'

'I don't care, he can't be any worse than Aaliyaa Horne.' She looked despondent. 'He controls everything. I'm supposed to be the one to teach him morals and values and my brother just whisks him away. I don't want him to be like my brother.' She gazed down at Russell affectionately. 'I want him to be like you.'

Seth blinked. 'Me?'

'You're always kind to people—'

'Am I?'

Jon made a non-committal noise and tilted his hand from side to side.

'—and your children, the twins,' she went on, touching the top of Russell's head, 'they're always so happy and sweet, and if that means I won't get to see him very often, then so be it. I want to come back in a few weeks' time and see him like this.'

She gestured at Russell, who grinned up at her through a face covered with jam. The little swine had managed to reach the tray, Seth thought in despair. *He'll be riddled with gout at this rate.*

Seth glanced at Azrael, who was eyeing one of the battle tapestries on the wall above him with awe in his eyes. He *could* do with mellowing a bit, Seth conceded. And he was sort of sweet, if you caught him at the right moment… Russell could do with a real friend. One that didn't consist of butter and flour, for one thing.

He caught Felicity's eye and was alarmed to find a pang of fondness for her. Or was it just the sensation of receiving a compliment? Seth never could tell, if he was honest with himself.

'Well… if you're sure—'

'Felicity?'

Seth groaned internally.

Cienne strode across the room.

Felicity rose and they kissed each other on the cheek briefly.

'Nobody told me you were visiting, it's lovely to see you!' Cienne said brightly. 'What are you two talking about?'

Seth made a face. 'We're fostering the prince,' he announced.

Cienne blinked. 'Prince Azrael?'

Seth nodded. 'Yes.'

Cienne's face stiffened as she realised that he was serious. 'No, Seth.' It was exactly how she said no a week earlier, when Seth had asked her for another child. It had devolved into another argument. A vicious one.

And another one where she got her own way.

Seth's blood boiled. He rose quickly, shoving the chair backwards on the tiles with an ear-splitting shriek.

'Tough,' he snapped. 'It's been sorted. You are now the mother of three. Congratulations.'

He glanced at Felicity, who looked alarmed.

'I'm sorry,' he mumbled. He straightened his back. 'I'm taking the boys for a walk. May as well start with the tour!'

He left before Cienne could open her mouth.

～

V

In the chill autumn breeze outside the keep porch, Felicity began to weep.

'Take him home with you,' Cienne begged, rubbing her shoulder. 'A mother shouldn't be without her child. Look, you're getting all upset.'

Seth grabbed his wife by the side of her neck and pulled her head close to his. 'We're keeping him,' he hissed. 'Get used to it.'

To Felicity he said, 'Do you want to give him a cuddle before you go? There's no hurry.'

She smiled at him before sweeping Azrael up into a hug. He grimaced and squirmed a bit. She hung on tight, kissing him soundly on the cheek five times.

'I love you,' she said into his ear. 'Don't resent me for this. And be good. I'll visit you every holiday and send you letters for the servants to read to you.'

'I want to play,' he complained.

Felicity put him down and he scampered off across the grounds, the morning sun making his brown hair shine. 'He'll be alright, won't he?'

'He'll be fine,' Seth soothed.

She smiled at him and Cienne both and embraced Cienne warmly. She then hugged Seth around the ribs, to his alarm.

'Thank you,' she said into his collar.

He wrapped both arms lightly around her shoulders. 'Don't be a stranger,' he told her with a little squeeze.

'Sister.'

They looked up at the new voice with a frown each.

'He wouldn't take no for an answer,' Elliot said frantically from behind the group of newcomers. 'He just barged in.'

'Come here,' Emmett said.

He stood imperiously before them in purple attire – the colour of royalty, Seth noted irritably. He was flanked at all sides by massive men in full battle regalia. Bodyguards – for now, at least.

At her brother's command, Felicity disentangled herself from Seth's arms to walk to Emmett's side, her head bowed.

Like a scolded dog, Seth thought with hatred.

'What's happening here?' Emmett demanded softly, in his usual monotonous drawl.

'I was just on my way home to tell you...' Felicity trailed off.

Emmett wasn't listening to her. He was staring at Seth.

Who drew himself to his full height and met his gaze. 'Felicity has asked me to foster her son for a few years,' he said amiably. 'And we have accepted. Haven't we, dear?'

'Yes,' Cienne said curtly.

Emmett's expression was stony – stonier than usual, Seth noted.

'I don't think that will be necessary,' he said smoothly. 'Azrael? Come. It's time to come home.'

Azrael lifted his head from the toy soldier collection he and Russell were engrossed in, his face a portrait of confusion.

'No it isn't,' Seth cut in sharply.

'Excuse me?' Emmett said in faint surprise.

'His mummy said he's going to stay here with Russell,' Seth told Emmett slowly, talking through his tongue as though he was speaking to a small child. 'He's not coming home today.'

Azrael grinned toothily and continued with his and Russell's game.

A muscle twitched in Emmett's jaw. 'He's perfectly well looked after at home. He doesn't need to be fostered.'

'Good international relations are paramount to a happy reign, he'll appreciate it when he's older,' Seth said smugly, having drafted this thought out in detail beforehand. 'I think he'll like it here.'

'It's much too sunny. I don't think he will like it here.'

'He likes the sun fine. I think he will like it here.'

'He likes his own castle. I, his blood relative, *don't* think he'll like it here.'

'*I think he will like it here*,' Seth gritted through clenched teeth.

'He's staying here,' Felicity said strongly.

Her brother turned to her with a blink. 'What?'

'We have put together a formal contract,' she said. 'Signed by me: the Queen of Stoneguard. My son is staying here. I have allowed it.'

'Sister,' Emmett argued.

'Your sister has a name,' Seth said coldly. 'Use it. She is called Queen

Felicity Horne, and she says she has allowed it. As she is your superior, I suggest you do as she likes, or that cushy little king regent number might start disappearing.' He raised his eyebrows.

Emmett eyed his sister.

Felicity stared him down, her normally doe-like blue eyes hard and cold. Seth swelled with pride.

'Fine,' Emmett said through the twitchiest jaw muscle Seth had ever seen. 'Azrael will stay here for as long as her majesty decrees. But the queen is required in Stoneguard.' He glowered at Felicity. 'If that's quite alright with you?'

Felicity merely turned and strode in silence to the portcullis, a handful of guards in her wake.

Emmett glared after her and then at Seth, who gave him a friendly smile.

'I expect to see this quarter's instalment of the Peace Tax in my treasury within the week,' he said, following his sister sullenly.

Seth let the friendly smile slither off his face. 'I bet you do.'

'This was not a good idea,' Cienne said.

Seth sighed. 'Well, it's done now.' He stared up at the sun, trying to guess the time.

Where was Adrienne?

~

Emmett took his time walking to the portcullis. Guards gestured him through the opening gate, heads bowed as the gravel path crunched under his feet. His coach lingered on the kings' road only a few yards downhill.

Felicity had just finished chatting to the guards and was climbing aboard. He grasped the neck of her cloak and dragged her down, backhanding her across the face as she pivoted to protest.

'I am your older brother,' he said coolly.

Felicity planted a hand on her reddening cheek, stricken.

'Father sent me here to counsel you. Now why do you think he didn't leave *you* in charge of affairs?'

Felicity didn't answer.

Emmett let the question hang in the air and stepped into the coach ahead of her. 'Get in,' he barked. 'We have a long journey ahead of us.'

Another coach caught his attention and he peered past her.

A girl with auburn hair with a young man Emmett recognised immediately were sitting in a vessel much too luxurious for their social standing. He watched with faint curiosity as the coach horse trotted uphill, into the main gates to halt at the mortuary, where Seth Crey waited.

Emmett wondered who Howard Rosethorn was burying as the girl exited the coach to face Seth uncertainly. He smiled faintly to himself. He could see the romantic tension from a mile away.

Whoever he was burying, he thought as Felicity sat beside him, it looked as though they were about to get a neighbour.

~

Seth paid the coachman and turned to face Howie and Adrienne.

She looks lovely in black, he thought wistfully. Well, everyone did, he reminded himself. But she looked especially—

Seth tore his mind from how lovely Adrienne was and smiled thinly at them. 'Morning.'

'Morning,' Adrienne said softly.

'Shall we get on with it?' Howie asked in a low voice.

Seth scowled at his impatience but held his tongue. 'This way.'

They entered the mortuary solemnly, and Adrienne took a deep breath. 'Daddy.'

Adrienne gasped audibly.

'Christ in a bucket,' Howie exhaled under his breath. He grabbed her hand, the blood draining from his face.

'I want to see the baby,' Ginny said firmly from just behind them.

Seth's pulse hammered through his ribs. He took two deep breaths to regain his bearings and knelt at his daughter's level. 'How did you know there was a baby in there?'

'I heard Mummy say. I want to see,' she whined. She bounced on her heels, her white-blond hair swaying.

'But he's sleeping,' Seth said weakly. 'You'll wake him.'

'I won't,' she whinged.

Seth sighed and glanced at Adrienne.

She mouthed, 'It's okay.'

He looked at Ginny again and picked her up with a sigh. 'Alright. But be very quiet.'

'Okay,' she whispered.

He hoisted her onto one shoulder and glanced at Adrienne once more.

'You can go in first,' she said. 'I can wait.'

He nodded once and, inhaling, he entered the mortuary with Ginny.

The boy lay in his crib. He really did look fast asleep, but Seth knew better. He clutched Ginny tightly and walked to the side of the crib, where a small bench chair had been placed thoughtfully beside it. He sat, standing Ginny up between his knees to see better. The musky smell of neglect consumed the room. If Ginny noticed it, she was unperturbed by it.

'Aw,' she said softly. 'He's cute.'

Seth peered over Ginny's shoulder. 'He is.'

The gashes on his face and arms were little more than faint outlines, stitched and covered by some form of makeup the undertakers had used too thickly. A christening gown covered the rest of him, layers of silk rippling like milk. Seth was struck by how much he looked like Ginny when she was tiny.

Seth swallowed hard and gave Ginny a squeeze, pressing his nose against her temple. She smelled just the same as she did when she was a baby, like milk and... oranges?

'You've been stealing from the pantry, haven't you?' he murmured.

He took her hands in his own. They were freezing.

'Maybe,' she said coyly, snickering.

Seth smiled and blew on her knuckles. 'Are you cold?'

She shook her head. 'You're warm.'

He felt the words move through her, her lungs moving in and out, the air whistling through her blocked nose. Her hands were warming up now. All thoughts of Adrienne were gone at this point.

'So are you,' he said a thought too late.

Ginny looked at him and seemed to register that his thoughts were not entirely with the cold or the stolen oranges. She kissed his cheek and started prodding his jaw, where a shadow of a beard lingered.

'Love you,' she said. 'Your face is spiky.'

He smiled thinly and gave her jaw a poke, making her snicker.

'Ginny?' Cienne said softly by the door.

Ginny gasped and scrambled her way to the floor to run at her mother. 'Shh!' she hissed. 'The baby's sleeping!'

Seth watched her. He didn't want to look at him anymore.

Cienne met his gaze and approached slowly. 'She shouldn't be in here, Seth.'

The rebuke hit the back of his ribs. He turned his gaze to the ground.

Ginny glanced outside at a butterfly and quickly give chase. A wave of affection very nearly overtook the weight of the grief in his chest. He briefly considered explaining everything to her, about death and everything else that came after, just so she could stay at his side. He hurriedly thought better of it. Cienne was right. She was far too small to be burdened with such things.

'Do you want me to stay with you?'

He looked at Cienne. She seemed genuinely concerned – then he remembered how bluntly she had refused another child, back at the Emmettfort, and tried to explain it away by emphasising the pain it had caused her, as though his entire intention had been to cause her harm.

He heaved a sigh. 'No,' he said finally. 'You'd better distract the twins.'

She nodded, peering across at the baby. Pain crossed her features.

'He looks just like them,' she whispered.

Seth frowned down at the floor. 'I know.'

Cienne left after that. It was the first time in three years he was glad to see the back of her.

Adrienne slipped inside as Cienne left. She cowered away from Cienne. Seth noticed, fuming, that Cienne had glared at her on her way out.

He rose as she halted beside him, standing between the table and the little cushioned bench. Her gaze was fixed to the crib. Seth's was fixed to her face.

They stood like this for a moment.

'Does he have a coffin or...'

Seth moved to the edge of the room and brought over a covering. 'It's... it's a lid.' He placed it on top of the crib and fastened it into place.

'Can I see him again before you...' Adrienne faltered.

He obediently lifted it off again.

Adrienne adjusted the boy's gown with light, fleeting movements, her lips pressed together.

Seth pressed a hand against the back of his neck as she did so.

'Daddy.'

He flinched and swung around to face Ginny. 'I thought you were with Mummy?'

'The baby looked cold,' she said meekly. 'I brought him a blanky.'

A light pink woollen blanket trailed at her side, her small fist wrapped around the end.

Seth softened. He dropped to his knees in front of her. 'But that's yours,' he said softly. 'You've had that since you were tiny.'

'But I'm a big girl now, I don't need it.'

He wished he'd never told her that. He'd only said it to stop a tantrum about being parted with it for wash day. He took a breath.

'Do you want me to tuck him in?' Adrienne said softly to Ginny.

He turned to look at her.

Tears glistened on her cheeks.

One thing at a time, he reminded himself.

He led Ginny Adrienne's side. She handed the blanket to Adrienne, almost with reverence, and watched as Adrienne placed it over his gown.

'There,' Ginny said with satisfaction. 'All warmy.'

Adrienne sobbed loudly. She gulped it back down, feigning a cough, and smoothed the blanket, eyes fixed to the surface.

Seth knelt briefly to peck Ginny's cheek. 'Go and play then,' he said thickly. 'I'll be back later on, alright?'

She nodded and ran at the doors. 'Love you!'

'Love you too.'

Adrienne sniffed. 'She's beautiful.'

'Thank you.' Shame crawled under his skin. *Rub it in her face, why don't you.* He watched Adrienne weep some more and placed a hand on her back.

'Go out to him,' he said, referring to Howie. 'I'll get you when he's in the coach.'

She nodded and walked from the room, leaving Seth alone with the dead boy. He eyed him uneasily.

Making sure Adrienne was gone, he very carefully lifted the pink blanket from his body. He couldn't part with it. It was Ginny's.

The shame returned, but he didn't put it back. Instead he folded it into four and tucked it into the inside pocket of his jacket. He lifted the lid soundlessly.

Adrienne stood alone at the coach as the undertakers lifted the litter into the overcast sunlight. Howie was nowhere to be seen.

'Where did he go?' Seth asked, glancing around.

'He'll pick me up from here later on,' she said quietly. 'He didn't want to intrude.'

Seth nodded, glad.

They travelled around the back of the castle, just the two of them and the casket, around the farm where Seth had found him only a few days before. The countryside passed by and Adrienne peered out of the little carriage window.

'I found a place for him,' Seth said, feeling an explanation was needed. 'It's out of the way, you know. Quiet.'

She nodded and swallowed. 'How did he end up there?'

'We don't know if it's even him—'

'But he looks like you! He looks like...' She trailed off helplessly.

Seth inhaled sharply.

She wrung her hands around the material of her skirt. 'I can't wrap my head around it. He hadn't even been born. Did he even die that day? Did he survive somehow and live for months in some dark hole someplace—'

'Try not to think about it,' Seth said in a pained voice.

Her eyes filled. 'I'm sorry, I'm just so confused...'

'I know.' He rubbed circles into her shoulder-blades. 'So am I.'

They slowed next to a rock wall and the two of them got out, Seth carrying the box via a leather handle on either side. He led the way to a gap in the wall, where a small meadow lay amongst some wildflowers and trees. It was pretty, as far as graveyards went. A great view of the surrounding countryside rolled into the horizon, a patchwork quilt of greens.

'This is nice,' she said softly.

He half-smiled, half-heartedly.

They arrived at a little graveside and knelt to either side of it, Adrienne helping with the casket. They lowered him in slowly. A mound of earth sat at the end, freshly dug. Seth slid it back over the casket himself. Adrienne moved to help.

'There's no need…'

She helped anyway.

It didn't take long for the hole to fill. They smoothed down the loose earth. Seth took a small bag of seeds and scattered them over it, pressing them down. *Flowers*, the undertaker had said before they set off, pressing the bag into his palm with a kind smile. *In a month's time, it might help to have somewhere colourful to remember him.*

They rose to their feet. It was tidy, which was better than he had expected. He brushed some crumbs of dirt from his trousers, wiping self-consciously at the stains on his knees. A small penance, he supposed.

Adrienne stood next to him, drinking in the silence. 'I should have held him.'

The Bastard materialised behind them, a ghost in the wind.

'Yes,' he said softly to his mother. 'You should have.'

Seth didn't respond to this. He simply stood there and ignored her comment. He suddenly felt like he wanted her to leave. *If it wasn't for her, you'd still have a son*, he thought to himself with a rush of anger.

'I'll never have another child,' she said dully.

'Good,' Seth blurted.

Adrienne turned to face him. 'Excuse me?'

'You're excused.' He faced her, simmering. The words stuck to his windpipe, clinging a moment on their way out. 'If you hadn't done what you did, he would still be here. You would have been able to hold him whenever you wanted.'

Adrienne's brow furrowed beneath eyes brimming with fresh tears.

'Always quick to judge, aren't you?' she said thickly, trembling. 'I wouldn't have killed our child at all, for your information. I wasn't given a choice. Your uncle and that priest of yours did it. On your orders, I assume. Just goes to show how fast you pin the blame on someone else when it suddenly comes back to bite you.'

Seth stared at her, his mouth ajar. 'What about my uncle and the priest?' he said hoarsely.

'As if you're interested,' she said, facing the hills.

'Tell me,' he said, more softly this time. He stroked her hair. It had

148

that wet stringy texture that indicated she hadn't washed it in a while. 'I'm interested now. Tell me what happened.'

She sniffed. She began, the words coming hard and brittle.

'They told me they could summon their god if I brought them a treasured possession to use in the ritual. They convinced me they could summon him to us and we could implore him to let Howie live and close the Hole. I brought them a box Howie had made for me.'

She paused a moment, the words lodged in her throat. They finally poured out thickly. 'And they fed me a drug that made me miscarry and they held me down while they put the box between my legs and let our child fall into it, and then they put it on their bloody altar and finished their *fucking* ritual and He came and took my baby away.'

The Bastard froze. He hadn't known this.

Neither had Seth. The colour dissipated from his face.

Adrienne sobbed, gasping for breath. 'Are you *fucking* happy now?'

'A-a-a,' Seth stammered, 'Adrienne, I didn't know. I thought you had *chosen* to do it. They *told* me you had chosen to do it. I took what they said to be the truth, I didn't know…'

She just wept helplessly.

His hand brushed her back. He slid it around her ribs and pulled her close. His other hand cupped the back of her neck, tucking her head under his chin.

She quietened then, as if his touch soothed her.

His palm pressed up and down her back, circling to push figure-of-eights into her shoulder blades. 'I wish I could have just been with you,' he found himself whispering.

She didn't reply.

'I should have looked after you, like I said I would.'

She wrung her hands around his elbow, locking his hold on her neck. 'You're here now,' she said hoarsely. 'I'm glad you're here now.'

He kissed the crown of her head, burying his nose in her hair.

Her arms slid around his ribs, warm in the chilly wind.

'Do it,' the Bastard urged. His fingers clicked against his thigh in a steady rhythm.

Seth didn't need urging. His mind was already turning the idea over.

Adrienne lifted her face to his, her eyes wide and glistening.

Seth traced her jaw. His surroundings faded as his attention homed in on her eyes, sad and slightly bloodshot from crying.

'Go ooon,' the Bastard crooned, clicking his fingers faster, 'do it—'

Seth swooped in for a kiss before he could change his mind.

~

The Bastard leapt maniacally on the spot. 'Yes! Yes! Didn't I tell you I could do it? Didn't I? Didn't I?' he said to Geldemar, who had materialised behind a tree.

Geldemar peered around it, lifting a lecherous eyebrow.

Seth pulled his mouth away from hers, wide-eyed.

Adrienne stared at him with disbelief before grabbing him around the back of his neck and kissing him back.

Her breath landed on his left cheek in warm waves. Her lips were dry and cracked, but he didn't mind: he just shut his eyes and bathed in the feel of everything else, her hands on his neck, her torso pressed into his, her—

He shivered and inhaled her scent, all florals and leaves as always, and he ran his palms up her back, tracing every curve. His week-long headache melted away between her fingertips digging into his scalp.

She parted her lips slightly to breathe in and out.

It drove him into knots. He walked her backwards into the tree – to Geldemar's distinct alarm – pressing her body between the trunk and himself and slipping his own hands behind her neck. He kissed her hard and deep, his eyes squeezed shut.

He felt funny. He felt *really* funny.

'You should probably move,' the Bastard advised.

Geldemar hid on the safer side of the tree, his eyes wide.

'Oh God,' Seth said.

Adrienne's mouth moved down the side of his neck.

His breath hitched as she squeezed him against herself, her hands wandering. *It's happening,* he thought in a shrill voice. Waves of heat crept up his ribs, her hands—

'Stop gawking, you pervert,' the Bastard scolded, a hand respectfully averting his eyes.

150

Geldemar watched on, engrossed

—were fiddling with his clothes now, unknotting laces.

Seth squeezed his eyes tightly shut, burying his face in her hair, his arms hugging her and the tree together. He let her get on with it, let her pull his shirt up a bit – her palm brushed his skin and he shuddered, giddy at her touch – and as her touch searched lower, he brought his hands down to assist hers…

A blanket fluttered to the grass. Adrienne's fumbling had somehow dislodged it. An icy wave swept up Seth's spine. He suddenly remembered whose grave they were standing next to.

He jerked himself away from her, stumbling backwards, breathing heavily. Adrienne watched him wide-eyed. Her mouth was pink from his unshaven face.

'Seth?' she said breathlessly, panting slightly.

'I can't do this,' he gasped, his gaze shifting from her to the blanket. 'I can't, not now, not ever.'

He swept past her, snatching up the blanket as he went, and speed-walked past the coach to the vacant field beyond and out of sight. He paused on a hilltop and stared out, breathing heavily and shivering uncontrollably.

'What was that?' he asked himself shrilly. 'What the *hell* was that?'

His lips had gone dry. He licked them. They still tasted like Adrienne.

His fingers stroked the soft little blanket in his hand. He brought it to his face and buried his nose in it. It wasn't Ginny's blanket anymore: it didn't smell like milk and oranges. It smelled like their terrible powder, that lingering scent that polluted a funeral parlour. He should have let him keep it.

'I'm so sorry.' He dropped to his knees. 'So sorry,' he whispered, to his dead son, to Adrienne, to Ginny, to Russell, to *Cienne*…

He dropped the blanket onto his knees and closed his eyes in silence, at anything but peace.

~

Seth's cheeks were flushing again.

Raphael Emmanuel III squinted down at the sleeping king, his hood hanging around his shoulders for a change. He raised a hand and slapped Seth across one reddening cheek.

Seth jerked awake, wide eyes falling on the Prophet. 'What the hell are you doing here?'

'I could ask you the very same question.'

Seth looked around, wondering where 'here' actually was. It turned out to be the field adjacent to their makeshift graveyard – he must have fallen asleep, he figured. He eyed the self-proclaimed Prophet in the midday sun and frowned. 'Did you follow me here?'

'I came looking for you when I couldn't find you at the palace.' Suddenly he slapped him again, harder.

'OW!' Seth roared, clutching his left cheek.

'You did it, didn't you?' he demanded shrilly.

'I didn't!' The answer was automatic. You learned not to confess to anything when your father was King Theo Crey. He paused a moment before adding, 'What am I supposed to have done, anyway?'

'You know!' The Prophet spluttered, waving his arms about. 'The sex! You had the sex, didn't you?'

'I wish,' Seth said sourly. Then he remembered he was the one who had ceased the process and mentally chastised himself. He caught the Prophet's angry glare. 'I didn't, alright? I just kissed her a bit!'

'A bit?! Your lips are bright red!'

Seth licked them self-consciously. 'So?'

'I told you not to do that!' he exclaimed hysterically.

'I don't take orders from the clergy!'

'Well, you should! Now I have to sort out your mess once and for all!' He swung on one heel and flounced off in a flurry of robes.

'Sort out what mess?' Seth demanded crossly.

The Prophet pivoted into the forestry to the left and, thankfully, vanished.

Seth slumped back against the bark of the tree he'd fallen asleep on and yawned. A nudge on his foot made him jump up again.

Lilly's dog stared at him intently.

'Oh, what do you want?' Seth asked hatefully. 'Have you been following me as well?'

The little terrier stepped over his legs and planted his muzzle on Seth's right knee, sunning himself.

Seth scowled at him before deciding he could make worse friends. He scratched behind the dog's ears and stroked his fur, tracing the brown spot on his white back idly. Albie lifted his head to gaze lazily at him. Seth realised with a start that he had a scar running right down one side of his nose.

'You've been through the wars, haven't you?' he murmured, rubbing his neck.

He had scars there too, he found, tracing the rope-like marks between his fur. Upon further inspection, Seth discovered that the dog had scars everywhere.

He frowned, looking at the scar on the dog's face again. It looked achingly familiar. It if was on a human face... a baby's face—

Seth lifted Albie's chin in one hand.

You're like my son, he thought.

Albie gawped up at him. *Albie*, he thought. Short for Albert. Lilly had given her dog the same name Adrienne had given their son in his dream.

Seth put his left hand on top of Albie's head and held it like that, sandwiched between his palms. This dog was exactly like his son. And he'd come looking for him.

Seth frowned and shook this off with a snort. He pushed the dog away. This was stupid. What did he think, that Lilly's pet dog was his son reincarnated?

Albie shook his head rapidly, ears flapping. He stalked off, affronted.

You've got sunstroke again, Seth told himself. He stood slowly and recognised his coach a few yards away. He thought it had left with Adrienne hours ago.

He approached. 'Thank you for coming back for me,' he said to the coachman. 'That was decent of you.'

'It was decent of you to look after that girl's child for her,' he said, bowing his head. 'It's not every day a bereaved mother gets a private burial run by the king himself. You've a good heart, my lord.'

Nice of you to assume the best of me.

Aloud he said, 'Thanks again,' and climbed into the coach in silence.

The horses trotted back to the palace.

~

PART THREE: WITCHHUNT

I

mmett peered around the door to his sister's quarters. 'Felicity!'

Felicity jerked upright in bed, mopping her tearstained face with her sleeves.

Silk sheets consumed her, with identical sheets flanking the wide balcony to her right. The marble walls gleamed after their morning scrub. They looked slimy to Felicity, who curled in the centre of an enormous four-poster bed that made her feel like a dormouse in a plate of cream. A gust of wind threw itself into the room, raising a wave of gooseflesh along her bare arms. That was what she hated about the marble palace, she thought: it was always freezing in there. Not like back home, where the climate suited such a cool building material.

She missed Azrael. They had only been home a couple hours so far, but it felt like much more without Az. She'd never felt this much pain in all her life – a hole gaped inside of her chest, the edges weeping. The late morning sun shone into her room in Emmett's new manor in the district of Squirm, illuminating the ivory masonry covering, well, *everything*.

'FELICITY!'

She jumped violently and slid out from beneath the covers. 'What is it?' she asked, almost in a whisper.

She didn't dare raise her voice to her brother since he had struck her. She knew she had crossed a line by giving Azrael to the Creys. The familiar image of her brother in the flowerbed all those years ago flashed behind her eyes. She quickly buried it.

Her brother in the present day stood in the centre of her drawing room, a length of parchment cradled in both hands. 'I received a letter.' He froze, frowning at her. 'Why is your face wet?'

Felicity wiped her nose. 'I'm missing my son a bit, that's all.'

'Wipe your face. It was your decision to give him up, no one else's. You got rid of him. You ought to be happy, shouldn't you?'

She flushed, her heart beating fast. She most certainly was *not* happy. She *had* to give him up, she told herself. She just couldn't explain why. She didn't have words to match the feeling in the depths of her stomach, and she didn't particularly want to paint a picture for her brother either.

Considering her rebuked, Emmett's frown smoothed out. His gaze returned to the parchment. 'A friend of mine has been in touch.'

'What friend?'

'Lord Tetzel's son-in-law, Henry Meyer,' Emmett said briskly. He opened one side of the folded sheet. 'Tetzel's daughter was taken ill a few years ago, caught the consumption from socialising with the peasants or some such. Meyer inherited the entire estate. You remember Lord Tetzel, I assume? He was poisoned at the Creys' tournament a few years ago.'

'Uncle Tetzel, yes,' she said, her emotions rising. 'He was very kind to me.'

'Worked out well for him, didn't it?' Emmett said flatly. 'I had initially intended to foster Azrael to Meyer, but since that is now *clearly* out of the question, I've had to send him an explanation instead of a child.'

Felicity flushed deeper.

'Luckily, he seems happy enough. He'll be visiting in a few weeks to see you instead.'

A dainty frown furrowed Felicity's brow. 'Me?'

'You. You're to be betrothed.'

The frown ironed itself out in horror. 'To be *married?*'

'That's the general idea of a betrothal, yes.'

Felicity spluttered. 'But… why? I'll have to move, I have to be here, I'm the queen—'

'You're the queen *dowager*,' Emmett said. 'An unnecessary component of the royal court, given it has a regent. In fact, that's the reason I agreed to his suggestion in the first place. You're becoming quite incapable of doing what you're told.'

Felicity gritted her teeth.

He continued. 'You need to be put on a leash. Meyer's proximity to the palace makes him more than suitable for the job. Once you're married to him, you can crawl back to the Creys and beg them for your son back, assuming he's still alive and in possession of all his limbs by that time.'

Felicity flushed once more, but this time the embarrassment came second to something else. Something *hotter*. 'Perhaps when I'm crawling back to the Creys, I can beg them to dismember your limbs instead,' is what Felicity said in reply. In her head.

'Yes, brother,' she said stiffly instead.

He regarded her, as though hearing her thoughts and inspecting her brain for anything else. 'Get dressed and come downstairs,' he said. 'We're getting you fitted for a new wardrobe.'

Felicity glowered at him and did as she was bid.

~

Hope hesitated. 'Are you sure he insinuated exactly that?'

Castlefoot Market bustled with activity. Midday beamed down upon the village and the market was in full swing, but most of the attention had gone on the kindling salesman, who excitedly told everyone around him about the goings-on in the upper square.

The Prophet scowled resentfully at the mistrust in Hope's voice. He polished the stake lovingly, his acolytes piling timber and coal around it. 'He committed an act of adultery and could not recall the event shortly afterward,' he said firmly. 'That is an act... of witchcraft.'

'You just want an excuse to burn her, is all that is,' Hope scoffed.

'No! She did do the sex with him! I saw! He just couldn't remember it!'

'So you were spying on him?'

The Prophet lifted his shoulders around his ears. 'Lil bit,' he conceded, indicating with his thumb and forefinger. 'I may have just happened to behind a hedge near where they were canoodling.'

He waggled his fingers at the word 'canoodling' like most people did at the word 'magic'.

Hope licked his lips, attempting to employ tact as best he could. 'Might there have been a misinterpretation?'

'No, there mightn't!' he snapped. 'Anyway, she *is* a witch. It's obvious.'

'She's only an old quack,' Hope said. 'Feeding people smelly leaves and patching up wounds doesn't make her a sorceress.'

'On the contrary, my dear Father Hope,' the Prophet intoned, 'for I have done my research and have found Miss Hart to be a powerful healer of deadly ailments of all manners!'

Father Hope raised his hands into the air. 'And we're killing a powerful healer of deadly ailments because…'

'She has bewitched the king!' he said shrilly. 'With her horrible womanly wiles!'

'What has that to do with the prophecy?'

'Uh, everything!' he said deliberately. 'Our prince is the Knight of Raining Thorns – not her silly carpenter boyfriend Sir Howard Born-in-a-Hedge-Thorn or whatever he calls himself. We must protect him from them at all costs.'

Hope rolled his eyes. 'Just because you fancy someone doesn't mean you can go setting fire to the competition.'

'I'm not burning the king!' he protested, horrified at the idea.

'I meant the healer to be the competition,' he said in a withering tone.

'What? I—I don't fancy the king!' he squealed. 'That's blasphemy! The gods don't approve of that at all!'

'It's merely a different pairing to the traditions established for child bearing,' Hope said. 'I don't see why the gods would have a problem with that. It's not like it's a dog or anything.'

The Prophet eyed him distastefully. 'Are you accusing me of bestiality?'

'No, I'm only saying that if you *were* to fancy the king, that would be quite alright.'

'I do not fancy the king! Or dogs, for that matter!' the Prophet shrilled. 'Swiftly changing the subject, the woman has been sighted healing the elderly of blindness in addition to various deadly diseases known to be signs of displeasure from the gods themselves.'

'So?'

'*So*,' he said irritably, 'if you had sent someone a message of discontent at something, only to have an interfering woman go and, and *cure* your message in transit, how would you feel about that?'

'I don't know, brother, I've never heard of anyone curing a polite letter of complaint before.'

'That isn't my point,' he said. 'My point is that if a god sees that his punishments are not, well, punishing efficiently, he's going to get mad. And what does a mad god lead to?'

'Piles,' Hope said.

'No, not *piles*, the apocalypse. You know, big explosions and so forth? Tiny bit more extravagant than bloody *piles*?'

'*Bloody* piles is an entirely different matter,' he said.

'Stop talking,' the Prophet said swiftly. His gaze caught something in the near distance. His voice dropped to a low intone. 'Look – evil approacheth.'

Hope rolled his eyes. 'At least refer to her by her own name. We're not in the dark ages.'

The Prophet stared into space with a dull expression.

Adrienne passed them with a basket of shopping.

Drama is lost on these people, he thought in frustration.

$\sim$

After an attempt at mixing inks resulted in more disaster than a painting session with the twins, Jon had wrested control of the writing desk. The fine mahogany was wasted on Seth Crey. Jon ran a hand over the shining polish, marred by the myriad dark shadows of frequent ink spilling and wine sloshing. *Wonder how much this cost new*, he thought with a scowl, comparing a hypothetical bill to their piling debt.

Seth circled the ink-spattered rug with his hands behind his back, his forehead screwed up in concentration. Dark footprints appeared around the blackened rug as Seth strode, to Jon's exasperation.

'Frederick Gertrude,' Seth dictated.

Jon sighed heavily and leaned over the parchment, hoping his bad spelling would go unnoticed.

After much consideration, Seth had decided to drown his sorrows by focussing on his birthday celebrations at last. Thinking about what to do with Adrienne was giving him a headache. Maybe he'd ask Uncle Fred for some advice, he thought, drafting the letter in his head. He wouldn't think badly of him copping off with another woman – his daughter had copped off with half the populace of Portabella, after all.

Speaking of women, he hadn't seen Cienne around lately. *Probably avoiding me lest I impregnate her through the air*, Seth thought sourly. He didn't know what was wrong with her. Yes, the twins had made their entrance to the world a difficult and scary one, but what were the chances of having another set of twins?

Rather than tempt fate to reply, Seth returned to his letter.

'I am writing to invite you to a soiree—is that the right word?'

'Sounds more like a cream cake,' Jon said.

Seth grimaced, scanning his internal thesaurus.

'Summink wrong with the word "party"?' Jon asked wryly.

'He's from Portabella, isn't he?' Seth agonised. 'They're all posh over there – wait, what am I saying? This is Uncle Fred, he's like a homeless person dressed in silver filigree. Write "party", then.'

Jon scribbled obediently. 'How d'you spell that, then?'

Seth frowned. 'What, party?'

'No, filigree.'

Seth flailed his arms. 'No! Don't write that bit!'

'You told me write everything you say out loud.'

'Not those things, the things for the letter.'

'Yeah, what you say out loud goes in the letter.'

'Oh, for God's sake, no, look, alright, when I do quotation marks in the air like this,' he jiggled two fingers of each hand in the air, 'you write what I'm saying. Is that clear enough for you?'

'Alright,' Jon said mildly.

'Alright, then,' Seth said, testy. He lifted his fingers into the air. '"I am writing to invite you"—'

'Shouldn't that be "Jon is writing" since I'm the one doing all of the actual writing?'

'No! Just write what I tell you to write, will you? Don't write that, look, just, just start again…'

Jon rolled his eyes. He screwed up the letter, throwing it at Seth's forehead.

Seth let it bounce off his brow with a scowl. 'Ready? "I am writing to invite you to a party to celebrate my birthday. It's been a long while since we last met, it would be wonderful to catch up with you. How is your leg? Apologies again about the fiasco with the elephant.".'

Jon winced, penning the word 'elefunt' with an increasing feeling of doubt.

'"It will be nothing fancy, just a banquet and some music, so there will be no need to bring my grandmother or my cousin Elyse.".' Seth shuddered. '"Particularly Elyse.".'

'Writing that down in *big* letters,' Jon said.

'Good. "Looking forward to seeing you there, without Elyse, yours affectionately, your nephew, Seth R.".'

'But your surname begins with a "C",' Jon said.

'Yeah, but "R" means "royalty", innit.'

'Innit,' Jon echoed, with emphasis on the "T".

'Yeah!'

'Yeah,' Jon echoed.

'I mean yes!' Seth shouted.

Jon cackled.

'Why am I justifying my dialect to you?' Seth demanded hotly. 'You're a prince of the realm, *technically*, and you use profanity like punctuation.'

'And you're a king of the realm who uses the word "innit",' Jon said.

'Pot, kettle, black,' Seth argued.

'You don't even know what a kettle is.'

'It's a thing,' Seth said haughtily, 'that makes tea!'

'Oh yeah, how?' Jon tested.

'Um. I tell Jimmy to make me some tea, and, um. Tea comes out.' He looked weakly at Jon's expression and decided to stop the argument there.

A knock came to the door. Jimmy stepped into the room, looking antsy.

160

'Sir, your presence is required in the market immediately,' he said. 'The guards are having kittens out there.'

'Why, what is it?'

Jimmy turned to the nearest south-facing window and pointed.

Seth squinted out at the open window. 'A bonfire,' he said blankly. 'What's so special about that?'

Jimmy pointed more specifically at the figures *surrounding* the bonfire.

Seth tried vainly to make out the face beneath the familiar burgundy cowl before realising that he already knew who it was. There was an auburn-haired woman beside him—

Seth made a running leap for the window.

'No!' Jimmy caught him around the armpits. 'The stairs would be a much more advisable route, sir.'

Seth blinked. 'You're right.'

'I try to make a habit of it.' He guided Seth away from the windowsill.

Seth sprinted for the corridor. 'Send that to the rookery!' he called back to Jon.

'Will do,' Jon said. Not before underlining the word Elyse a couple more times.

～

II

A throng had developed as Seth finally arrived at the centre of Castlefoot Market. He'd never known the market to hold so many people on a Thursday – especially with a dirty great smoking pyre in the middle of it.

He skidded to a halt at the back of the crowd, already ten yards ahead of a wheezing Jimmy, and gagged aloud, pressing his sleeve against his nose. The smell of burning meat was palpable even from several yards away.

'Jimmy, who was that?' he asked in panic, hopping to see over the crowd.

'Some blond bird,' he said shortly. 'Adrienne's in that line up there.'

Seth breathed a sigh of relief, which he instantly regretted. Smoke climbed down his windpipe. 'Get me over there,' he said with a cough.

'The king!' Jimmy bellowed, storming between a pair of men carrying little boys on their shoulders. 'Make way for the king!'

People made a path swiftly, which Jimmy hastily directed.

Seth jogged down it, to the bemusement of many.

'King! Make way for the king, now! No, that one died the other year, this is the new one!'

The last of the crowd parted, all of them with their shirts open and sleeves pushed to the elbows amidst the blaze.

Seth stared up at the pyre, breathing through his teeth.

'Your majesty!' the Prophet trilled in excitement. 'What a pleasure to see you here!'

'What is this?' Seth said in simmering fury.

The blond 'heretic' burned steadily on the stake above them, her head lolling to one side. The flames lapped at her bonds, loosening them and causing her to slide to one side. Her heart had already given out from the heat, he surmised, and her legs and lower torso thinned away to bone under the orange—

Seth felt acid rise in his throat and swallowed it down, turning his anger onto the Prophet. 'Well?'

'Oh, you know,' the Prophet said flippantly, waving a hand vaguely at the dead woman, 'the usual weekly purging. Jolly good fun, once you get past the stench. It is such an honour to have you witness the gods' work, your majesty.'

He actually means it, Seth thought in horror. *He really believes that they're evil – and he's having fun burning them*!

Jon was right, he was a lunatic. And when the Phantom Egg Flinger calls someone insane, that makes him *really* insane. Insane to the power of two.

'Take her down!' Seth shouted at him.

'Oh, of course. Oi!' he yelled at some white-faced altar boys. 'I said put it out when they die! Hurry up, we've got four more heretics to purge yet, don't waste the kindling!'

They pelted the fire with wet towels before throwing one over the woman's remains to pull her from the stake and throw her unceremoniously onto a cart to their right.

Seth bent double and threw up at the brutality of it all.

A snort sounded from behind him. 'You sure this is a Crey?' a man asked. 'He looks a bit wussy to me.'

'Maybe he's that bastard son of the queen's my old man keeps banging on about.'

Seth frowned, turning his head to him in outrage. 'My mother never had a bastard!'

The man snorted. 'And the king sent her first child into exile for fun, was it?'

Seth turned fully to face him, waiting for elaboration.

'Of course he's the king!' the Prophet said irately, having heard the entire exchange. 'He just has a gentle stomach. NEXT!'

Another girl was dragged onto the steaming stake, trembling.

Adrienne trembled also, tied at the wrists. Her face stiffened, teeth clenched, the tendons in her jaw standing out. She had been placed at the other end of the queue. *Saved for the end*, Seth thought bitterly. *The grand finale – high treason for conspiring to infidel with the king.* He could see it now.

They stared at each other helplessly.

'Jimmy, what do I do?' he said in a small voice. He looked close to tears.

Jimmy sighed and took matters into his own foot.

Seth let out an animal wail from the back of his throat.

The Prophet jerked around at the sound.

'He's having a vision,' Jimmy announced, pointing at Seth.

Seth kneeled on the ground, his face twisted in agony. His hands hovered over his groin.

'You know, from God…' Jimmy added, as though unclear.

Seth breathed out shrilly, his hands in the gravel in front of him.

The Prophet's eyes widened. He bolted forward, his next victim forgotten. 'Your majesty!' He helped Jimmy lift him out of the throng. 'What do you see?'

'Stars,' Seth squeaked. 'Lots of stars.'

'It really is a vision,' the Prophet whispered.

'Really,' Jimmy said dully.

Seth gurgled, clutching his nether regions.

Jimmy pried Seth's hands away by the wrists, in case anyone sussed the actual cause for Seth's fit. 'What's He saying to you, sir?'

Seth shot him a horrible scowl.

Jimmy twirled one hand repeatedly, mouthing 'Play along.'

The Prophet's eyes were closed, his hands pressed firmly together.

Seth squeezed his eyes shut. 'I dunno, I can't concentrate.'

Jimmy's fist connected with something bruised.

Seth howled.

'Sorry, it's for your own good,' Jimmy murmured without remorse.

Seth bit his lower lip, splitting it down the middle. 'He said... He said to me, erm... oh God Jimmy, why did you have to kick me in the goolies?'

The Prophet's eyes bolted open. 'What? I missed it!'

'He said Salator Crey has declared these women to be innocent,' Jimmy said sharply.

'What? Why—how? What did He say, exactly?' the Prophet demanded.

Seth's eyes watered.

Jimmy flexed his knuckles in front of Seth's face.

Seth gritted his teeth. 'It's the hair,' he said finally.

'Hair?'

'Two of them, they're red-heads,' he said, pointing at the Adrienne and the remaining victim. ' "She who hath hair of... of red... isn't a witch",' he finished lamely.

The Prophet's eyes flicked to the pyre. 'But Miss Hart is more auburn than actual red,' he said, ever the opportunist.

'Auburn's just a red trying to be a brown,' he said, quoting a comment of Lilly's. 'Quote, unquote. Not a witch.'

'But she committed high treason against the royal family!'

'Not a witch!' Seth snapped. 'Quote, unquote!'

'She bewitched you into illicit contact—'

'Ho no she did not,' Seth said in remembrance.

The Prophet hesitated. 'But she was the main attraction!'

'Oh dear,' said Jimmy. 'Might as well cancel the whole show, eh?'

'But,' the Prophet spluttered, 'the purging—'

'Release them!' Seth growled savagely.

'Alright then,' the Prophet squeaked. He flicked a signal to the altar boys.

Seth gathered his bearings and thrust himself to his feet. He sprinted to the pyre as the crowd parted around him.

Adrienne met him halfway and he threw his arms around her neck – only to take in the odd glances from the crowd and hug the other victim as well, just to be fair.

Jimmy dusted his hands off, satisfied with a job well done.

Seth and Adrienne exchanged one last look before turning in opposite directions.

The Bastard clucked in disapproval, tapping his heel on the ground.

'So much for that idea,' Geldemar said.

'The hell it is,' the Bastard muttered. He strode up behind Adrienne.

'What are you doing?' Geldemar said, alarmed.

The Bastard *slid* into her back.

'You can't do that,' Geldemar said in horror.

'Watch me,' the Bastard said before inserting his head into hers.

Adrienne gasped.

Seth spun on the spot.

Adrienne turned to look at him, white-faced. 'Seth,' said the Bastard, through her.

Geldemar ran both hands over his face. 'Oh God.'

Adrienne/the Bastard ran towards him—

And tripped on her own feet, crumbling to the ground.

'Christ!' Seth skidded to a halt alongside her, guiding her to her feet. 'Are you alright? What happened?'

'I, um, I, uh…' Adrienne stammered.

What is wrong with her legs? the Bastard howled internally. *Why won't they move properly?* Her feet floundered beneath her, failing to gain purchase.

'Told you,' Geldemar said smugly. 'You have to learn to crawl before you can walk.'

I thought it was a metaphor!! the Bastard howled into the atmosphere of Sal'plae.

Seth slid an arm around her ribs, holding her in a semi-standing position. 'Are you alright? What's the matter?'

Adrienne/the Bastard clung to Seth's shoulders and hung there. 'I…

feel very faint,' she said.

Geldemar winced.

It came out loud, much louder than her usual breathy tones. The Bastard winced and tried again. 'It's.. the heat. Yes, the heat!' he – through Adrienne – exclaimed before restraining himself. 'I'm quite overcome… with the heat… and nearly being burned at the stake, yes. That's it.' Adrienne/the Bastard looked up into his face, eyes wide and imploring. 'Carry me?'

'I can't watch much more of this,' Geldemar said, dissipating.

Seth complied immediately. He hooked an elbow behind her knees and hoisted her into his arms.

Adrienne/the Bastard wrapped both arms around his neck, looking slightly smug.

'I'll take you to the palace, get you checked over,' Seth said, hastily making for the castle.

The Bastard was about to add another swoon before Seth abruptly halted.

At the worst possible moment, Howie appeared, looking irate.

Seth met his gaze. 'I believe this is yours,' he said, hoisting her into Howie's arms. He hurried away before Howie could open his mouth.

The Bastard looked at him, stricken. His spirit flopped out of Adrienne's body, tumbling onto the ground. Nobody noticed him.

'What was that about?' Howie asked sharply.

'I'm not sure,' Adrienne said uncertainly. 'I think I might have fainted.'

The annoyed look dissipated from Howie's face. 'Oh, are you alright?' She nodded, dazed.

Marbrand strode into the market with a sealed letter in hand. 'What's going on here, then?' he asked, nudging Jimmy's arm.

'Oh, just some nutter trying to kill the king's mistress,' Jimmy said idly. 'Nothing to worry about. Non-requited love rearing its ugly head, I imagine.'

The Prophet bounced on the spot irately. 'I do not have a crush on the king! I don't know why people keep saying that!'

'The raunchy portrait may have had something to do with it,' Jimmy said with a cynical smile. 'Anyway, there's nothing wrong with it. It's not like buggering dogs or something.'

'So?' he said shrilly. 'I don't like it!'

'I've met people like that, you know,' Marbrand said idly. 'They're not inherently bad once you keep them away from animal shelters.'

'How do you get to meet people like that?' Jimmy wondered.

'You get to meet all sorts when your first name's Say—the same as… other men's. Must be off, taking a letter to the rookery.' He shuffled off, red-faced.

Seth had reached the top of the hill when a shout made him pivot.

'Your majesty!' Stanley Carrot, Lilly's manservant, skidded to a halt in front of Seth, propping himself up on his knees. 'Something's wrong with Lilly-Anna, sir.'

Seth followed his finger to a black horse in the market, on top of which his sister was bent double, her face a horrible shade of grey.

'She's been throwing up all morning, sir, my Aunty Petunia threw a fit when she saw what she did to the Crook's deluxe suite,' Stan rattled off. 'She says she has a really bad pain in her side.'

'Let me see,' Adrienne said. She swung free of Howie's arms.

'What is it?' Seth asked worriedly.

She paid no notice of his queries, jogging towards Lilly, her fainting spell forgotten. Adrienne helped Stan pull Lilly from the horse, carefully avoiding her stomach. Stan placed her feet on the ground and they stood her up between them.

Lilly buckled, nearly toppling face-first into the dirt.

Seth caught her around the middle with one arm.

'It's alright, my love—' he said.

His hand had pressed into her swollen abdomen.

Lilly summoned all her strength and thrust her knee into Seth's trousers.

He released her with a yelp.

'Are you trying to kill me?' she screamed into his face.

'There goes the other one,' Seth said, in his own world of agony.

Adrienne held her up by the armpits. 'Help me get her to the town hall,' she told Stan curtly. 'And find a way to keep those gawkers away from the door.'

'I'll get the guards,' Jimmy offered.

Seth made to follow after Lilly when Adrienne stopped him.

'Go away if you aren't going to be any help,' she said bluntly.

'I am!' he protested.

'I'll have to do a rectal examination and might have to cut her open. Are you sure?'

Seth hesitated. He didn't like the sound of anything involving Lilly's rectum.

'Better him than me, I'm squeamish,' Stan said, recoiling.

Seth took over Stan's post at her left armpit and helped Adrienne half drag, half carry her to the deserted town hall. To Seth's disgust, Howie loitered nearby, looking bemused, as always.

'What did I miss, exactly?' he asked, glancing from Lilly to the abandoned pyre. 'What's that awful smell?'

'Burnt human flesh,' Adrienne said. 'Are you going to help me take care of Lilly or are you going to stand there asking questions?'

Howie followed them meekly, giving Seth a horrible look as he passed.

They lowered her onto her back in the middle of the aisle. Adrienne immediately began to unlace her trousers. Seth averted his gaze as the examination commenced. She rattled off questions, which Lilly answered monosyllabically. Seth couldn't keep track of what was said.

She lifted her shirt to prod her gently. Lilly nearly punched her until Seth and Howie held an arm down each.

Adrienne placed a finger lightly where the pain was most prominent. She then extracted a scalpel from the left pocket of her dress.

'Did you really think I would just wait for you to rescue me?' she said wryly to Seth's confused expression. 'This is why I persuaded him to leave me until last. Are you sure you're not squeamish?'

'It's Lilly, I'm staying,' he said strongly. Inside, he whimpered pathetically.

'Hold her down, this is going to hurt,' Adrienne instructed.

He turned his head away as Adrienne cut a slit into Lilly's abdomen.

Lilly shrieked, her voice muffled.

Howie had put a rolled up bandage between her teeth, Seth realised.

As the surgery commenced, Lilly slowly quietened, her breathing shallow. Seth's eyes were locked to her face. It was not turning a pleasant colour.

The next thing Seth heard was a squelch. He spun to face Adrienne – who handed him something that made the blood drain from his face.

'Take this,' she ordered.

Seth paled further. He held a hand out flat to accept an engorged bulb-like abscess. 'That came out of Lilly,' he said shrilly.

'There's also a lot of blood coming out of Lilly,' she said darkly. 'Pass me the syringe in my bag, Howie. Seth, give me your handkerchief.'

'But I've been blowing my nose on it all—'

He earned a terrible look and meekly handed over the handkerchief.

Lilly paled again and was silent and still, which wasn't like her.

Seth stroked her hair with his free hand, holding the swelling at an arm's length away from them.

The cloying scent of blood rolled through the room. Only the sounds of breathing occurred as Adrienne worked, Lilly's rattling, Adrienne's calm and steady, Seth's coming in bursts as he tried not to breathe in the smell of blood.

'Okay,' Adrienne said. 'Thread me a needle?'

Howie poured transparent alcohol onto a tiny needle and handed it over, threaded and all.

Adrienne began to stitch up the wound.

Seth grimaced at the thing in his hand.

'What do I do with this?' he asked, lifting the thing slightly.

Adrienne glanced up in annoyance.

'Put it in a jar and keep it for all I care,' she said shortly.

Seth glared at it fearfully and threw it out of sight. It landed on a back bench somewhere with a wet plop, to Seth's relief. He had half-expected it to explode.

'Done,' Adrienne said after a few moments. 'Help me bandage her up, Howie. You go find a coach,' she told Seth.

'Right,' he muttered in a slight state of shock. 'I will. Thank you.'

'Thanks,' Lilly whispered.

'Don't mention it,' Adrienne said. 'Especially not to the villagers, what with an engorged appendix lying around somewhere.'

Seth made a face and left.

The coach house kindly offered him a carriage free of charge and he sat inside just outside the entrance as Lilly was carried out.

Adrienne rested Lilly's head on Seth's lap and Howie deposited her feet onto the arm of the seat to Seth's right, on Adrienne's instructions.

Seth looked into Lilly's face. 'How you feeling?'

Lilly squeezed her eyes shut. 'Like I've had my guts cut out and thrown around the room.'

Seth looked at Adrienne gratefully. 'Please come back and work for me.'

Adrienne paled.

'The healer we have now is useless. He would have let her die if it meant he could avoid a rectal examination. At least come and look after Lilly.'

She hesitated from just outside the carriage door. 'I'll think about it.'

He smiled at her.

She smiled thinly and stepped away from the coach, closing the door.

Seth scratched lightly on the edge of Lilly's hairline as she drifted to sleep.

The coach rolled up the barbican, which was thankfully a smooth ride up. Back in the village, Jimmy scowled at the receding coach.

'Thanks for the lift,' he scathed.

~

'If she was an evil sorceress, why would she have saved the princess's life like that?' Father Hope asked testily.

The Prophet sat cross-legged on the step of the pyre, his lower lip sticking out. 'She's bewitching her way into the palace.'

'He was offering her a place, which she declined,' Hope said.

'That's because she was playing hard to get,' the Prophet snapped. 'Classic womanly wiles in action!'

'I'm just saying if I were a healer, I would have killed the princess mid-operation and slapped my "womanly wiles" on him when he was grieving,' Hope said mildly. 'Make it look like an accident, like.'

'That would be the obvious thing to do,' he said sullenly. 'The king would never be foolish enough to fall for that.'

Hope raised a sceptical eyebrow. 'He was foolish enough to think a cut on the hand had killed him for two decades.'

'Silence!' the Prophet barked. 'I must think.'

No one said anything for a few moments.

Rainclouds began to loom overhead, and an acolyte began to point that out when the Prophet shushed him harshly, quieting the boy, who flushed.

A few more moments passed.

'Eureka!' he exclaimed, leaping to his feet.

'What did you say I was?' Hope said, affronted.

'No,' he said, waving his hand at him in impatience. 'I have an idea.'

~

III

Seth sat hunched forward in his seat in the drawing room, his face crumpled. Behind him, the fireplace crackled merrily, radiating a pleasant warmth across the trio.

'How's Lilly doing?' Jimmy said, pouring another cup of tea.

Eleanor turned a page in her book from Seth's left. 'Spark out, bless her. She'll be fine in a few weeks. She was lucky to bump into that young lady.'

'Mmm, lucky,' Jimmy said, flinging Seth a sly glance.

Seth simply stuck his tongue out at him.

'Any word from Cienne's dear father?' Eleanor asked.

Seth frowned at her. 'Why would there be?'

'He's been taken ill, apparently,' she said in earnest, ever the gossip. 'Looks as though he might be on his deathbed, so Cienne's handmaiden tells me. We're waiting for a summons to Portabella any day now.'

'He wants me to go all the way over there to watch him die?' Seth scoffed.

'Not you, Cienne. You'll have to stay here, of course, and perhaps without any distractions you might like to attend those dreaded council meetings?'

'Might be an idea to find out why Jon wants to set three of them on fire,' said Jimmy, who still hadn't been told about the forty-five-million-pound debt.

'Don't see the point,' Seth said. 'They've been doing fine the past four years without me.'

'That's all you know,' Eleanor said quietly.

Seth gave her an odd glance.

Eleanor refused to meet his gaze.

'I'm not sure about this visit to the mother country,' Jimmy said uneasily. 'Seth left on his own tends to equal Russell with access to his own shit, if you'll pardon the expression.'

Seth gave him a sharp glance.

'I'm sure he'll fend for himself for a few weeks,' Eleanor scoffed. 'He's not a baby anymore. He's nearly forty now.'

Seth shot her a look of pure outrage. 'Thirty-seven,' he said deliberately, 'is *not* forty!'

'It's not twenty-two either,' Jimmy said.

Seth's mouth twisted. 'As is evident by the *neutering* you delivered me earlier.'

'Neutering?' Eleanor said, looked sceptical.

'Oh, he's fine,' Jimmy said.

'Fine?' Seth exclaimed. 'I'm still out to here!' He held out a hand in front of him, about six inches from his groin.

Brisk knocking erupted from behind the door.

'Hang on, I'll just get that,' Jimmy said, striding to their left.

'Don't overreact, Seth, it's not like you need them anymore anyway,' Eleanor said with uncharacteristic crudeness.

The look of pure outrage was back, this time with comically angry eyebrows. 'Don't encourage her! Don't you want grandchildren?'

'I have grandchildren,' she said. 'Two of your offspring are enough.'

Seth glowered at her.

Jimmy returned with a pained expression. 'Sir...'

Cienne burst past them in a flurry of white petticoats before he could say anything further. 'Come through to the drawing room, there's a lovely little sofa we can use.'

'Praise the lord!' Seth exclaimed, rising.

'Swelling's gone down, then,' Jimmy said to Eleanor.

'Um, not you, Seth,' Cienne said in amusement. 'Come straight through, Mister Emmanuel.'

Jimmy admired the comical eyebrows' return.

Raphael Emmanuel III, aka the Prophet, entered their quarters, easel in hand.

'What the hell is this?' Seth demanded in a shrill whisper.

They ignored him, queen and prophet both, and they simply strolled on to the settee opposite theirs. Seth followed lividly. Cienne draped herself across the settee in an infuriatingly attractive manner.

Seth stood over the right-hand arm, where Cienne's head rested. He folded his arms. 'What's going on?'

The Prophet peered at him over his hands, his fingers formed into a rectangular frame in front of Cienne. 'The queen has commissioned me to do the royal portraits, my liege.'

'You what?'

Cienne shrugged nonchalantly, her chin in her hand.

'You know I despise him!'

The Prophet's face fell.

'Why?' she asked curiously.

Seth splayed his arms into the air.

'Well, he burns people, for a start,' he said, 'makes a general nuisance of himself at the best of times and, oh yes, breaks into our private quarters and paints lewd portraits of us on the walls.'

'Won me the prize, though,' the Prophet said meekly.

The angry eyebrows made a third appearance.

'You wanted to keep the lewd portrait, so I recall,' Cienne said, enjoying herself. 'He's a very skilled artist, he'll do perfectly. Now, Mister Emmanuel. I want you to draw me like one of your Portabellan girls.'

The Prophet frowned. 'You *are* Portabellan.'

She rolled her eyes. 'That was a culture reference, dear.'

'Oh. I didn't get it.'

'You haven't got time to be posing for pretty pictures,' Seth snapped. 'I thought your father was dying?'

'I told you, it's only man flu. They would have sent for me if it was that bad.'

Seth glowered at the Prophet as he unpacked his paper and charcoals.

173

Cienne sighed. 'When he does send for me, I have to go, dying or not. It isn't to spite you, Seth. He'll want to see the twins.'

His eyes widened. 'You can't take the twins!'

'Not both of them, no. Russell will have to stay—'

'Both of them have to stay!'

'Really?' she snapped. 'Looks like we will need those portraits after all. Start sketching.'

The Prophet snapped open the legs of the easel in the one-handed flourish of an expert at work.

Seth threw everyone a horrible glance before meeting Jimmy's gaze. He jerked a thumb at the door. 'Talk her out of it,' Seth hissed as they leaned on either side of the doorframe.

'The portraits? Someone has to do them, and the country's running low on painters thanks to the family tradition of killing them in a strop.'

'No, not the portraits. I quite like the way he does my eyes, as it goes,' Seth said. 'I don't want her dragging my kids to the mother country.'

'It's only fair he gets to meet them. His entire country is going to them in a decade and a half. Anyway, I doubt they'll cart the prince off anywhere. It's customary to present the *princess* to foreign countries. They're often fostered over there for a few years.'

Seth's eyes bolted open. 'They can't take my Ginny Winny!'

'They can't take the next heir, he might get murdered,' Jimmy said. 'That's why you weren't allowed out of the palace until you were thirty.'

'But she's my favourite!'

'Bit unfair to the little boy,' Jimmy said mildly.

'Well, it's true, and I can't let Russell follow me around the place, he's a—' He snapped his mouth shut.

'A tattle-tail?' Jimmy finished.

Seth planted a finger on his lips. 'Yes. I don't want them going.'

'Why not? It's educational. As enlightening as it is watching Corporal Moat excavating his nostrils, the kids need culture.'

'What if they come back with an accent?' he said in distress. 'I'm lucky Cienne trained herself out of it, what if they get it? It gives me nightmares! That was the last accent I heard before I died!'

'But you didn't die,' Jimmy said with emphasis. 'We've discussed this.'

'I know that, but it's traumatic. That and r-ravens,' he said mid-shudder.

'It's no use upsetting your father-in-law because of your traumatic adolescence. There are worse relatives for them to be meeting.' Jimmy jerked his head towards Eleanor.

Seth shuddered again, this time with feeling. 'Elyse.'

'Exactly.'

He glowered at the butler. 'You're saying you're going to disobey me, then?'

'Hard to break the habit of a lifetime, sir.'

Seth rolled his eyes and waved him away, returning to the lounge. 'If you want something doing,' he muttered – and then the solution occurred to him. 'Cienne, you remember Adrienne?'

Cienne bolted upright, earning a wail from the artist. 'What about Adrienne?'

'Oh, didn't you hear about Lilly?' Seth said airily. He leaned an elbow on the Prophet's right shoulder, deliberately obstructing his ability to draw. 'Got a nasty case of the… what do you call it?'

'Appendix infection, she called it,' Jimmy said. His eyes darted at Cienne's expression.

'They used to call it cramp colic in my day,' Eleanor said, seemingly unaware of the tension rising in the room.

'Seems Lilly might need monitoring for the next few days,' Seth said. He met the burning gaze of his wife. 'I reckon she'd be perfect for the job, don't you?'

'Oh, certainly. Her terms seem to have Erik completely baffled,' Eleanor agreed, oblivious.

Cienne reddened, her eyes blazing.

'I'm sure he'll fend for himself,' Jimmy said, trying to remedy the situation.

'Nonsense, he's a pompous little sod anyway,' Eleanor said. 'When are you thinking of bringing her in?'

Jimmy grimaced painfully.

'Why, as soon as possible,' Seth said with relish. His gaze was cemented to Cienne's. 'What do you think, dear?'

Cienne's posture was rigid. 'Whatever you think, dear,' she said through gritted teeth.

Seth grinned toothily at her and strode to the door. 'I'll organise the arrangements for her.'

'You do that,' she gritted again.

The door closed softly behind him.

'Look at the two of you,' Eleanor said fondly. 'Collaborating over even the littlest tasks. Completely unheard of in my day.'

'Never mind him,' the Prophet said, waving frantically at her to lie down. 'Get back in position.'

Cienne gave an irate huff, leaning back on her right elbow.

~

Archie scrubbed at a table edge with some sandpaper.

A crack sounded from behind him. He flinched violently and pivoted. The four chairs he had varnished and left to dry in the sun lay in splinters outside the front door.

Archie slammed his sandpaper on the ground. 'For Christs' sake!'

Howie peered around the doorframe. 'You alright, Archie?'

Archie heaved a beleaguered sigh. 'Fine, fine,' he said. 'Just some teenager trashing my stuff.' He brushed dust from the newly made dining table beside him, which was now short four matching chairs.

Howie helped Archie lift the table to the corner of the workshop. 'I thought you said this was a nice area?'

' "Was" being the operative word,' replied Archie in annoyance. He met his gaze as Howie started sweeping sawdust out onto the street. 'How's the house going?'

Howie grimaced. A mental image emerged of a pile of dismembered timber frames, most bearing angry boot marks – the remains of their front porch.

'I've been getting distracted lately,' he said finally. He met Archie's questioning gaze. 'The Creys have offered to re-hire Adrienne.'

'Oh, that's good, isn't it?'

Howie frowned at him – then remembered. Archie never knew about the baby.

The entire episode regarding Adrienne and her unborn child had been carefully omitted from the account they had given to Archie. The event had been need-to-know information, and Archie simply didn't need to know. As far as he was concerned, Adrienne had been assaulted in the city after dark. Nothing regarding Seth Crey impregnating his niece was ever uttered in his presence.

That said, Howie thought. Archie wasn't exactly Seth Crey's biggest fan. Their last week in Serpus had ended with Archie in hiding after he had shoved him into the Hole. Seth escaped with his life. Archie still half-expected him to hunt him down and kill him for the affront – which explained the relocation of his workshop to the village of Teal about ten miles from Buttercup Village.

'I suppose they gave a good salary,' Howie said in reluctance.

Archie gave him a sidelong glance. 'But?'

Howie shuffled his feet. 'There's a reason she wanted to leave that fast, that's all.'

Archie waved this off. 'She would have refused the job if there was a problem,' he said. 'She's a big girl now, she can look after herself.'

'But...' Howie hesitated, wondering how to word this. '... there was this... bloke,' he said weakly. 'Kept bugging her to... you know. Wouldn't leave her alone.'

Archie blew a nonchalant raspberry. 'She does *medicine*. She could kill him and make it look like complications from the clap. She'll be fine.' Archie shot him a wry glance. 'She owns tiny knives and knows where main arteries are, remember?'

Howie quirked a half-smile.

'Tea?'

Howie bobbed a grateful nod.

Archie climbed the stairs at the back of the workshop. 'You could always angle for a job there yourself,' he added thoughtfully. 'Keep an eye on her, make sure she's alright. If you're that worried.'

Howie considered this in interest.

Another crash sounded, marking the demise of Archie's brand-new table.

'BLOODY HELL!!' Archie roared. He kicked the landing furiously.

A cloaked Despina sprinted up the street at high speed.

~

Father Hope gazed wistfully at the Prophet's work in progress. 'I wish sometimes that God hadn't blessed you with such a talent for human likeness.'

'I beg to differ,' the Prophet said. 'Now I can watch over him in person. See? I told you He had a plan for me.'

'You mean apart from pissing off the king?' Hope said. 'Probably, but the reasonable thing to do would be to honour her highness with a more tasteful image. The altar boys are dribbling.'

He gestured at the altar before them, currently empty of decorations but full of aroused pre-teens staring up at Queen Cienne's portrait – particularly the portion concerning the upper part of her corset.

'That's the idea, obviously,' the Prophet said, rolling his eyes. 'That way, King Seth thinks better of betraying her, and the boys understand the magnitude of sacrifice they're making for the Gods. Anyway, what are they going to do? Break their vows of celibacy with a framed sheet of—GET YOUR HAND OUT OF THERE, YOU LITTLE ANIMAL!!'

The Prophet jerked a pubescent hand out of the depths of its owner's robes, his own hand shielded in his sleeve.

'They're adolescents,' Hope said patiently. 'Look at her! It's human nature to think like that. You need to cut them some slack.'

The Prophet glared at him, rubbing the boy's hand vigorously with a kerchief.

Hope cast his gaze around the room once more. The new leader's current object of worship was Queen Cienne Fleurelle, the prophesised Mother – and so he had flogged all of their chapel's brand-new goblets and furnishings to bribe the court into hiring him as the royal portraitist. Bland timber boards remained of the chapel floor, a faint demarcation illustrating the loss of the aisle carpet. Hope heaved a mournful sigh. He couldn't really blame him, though. The queen was very attractive – and so was the old queen, come to that. Hope wished he could paint.

'Where's she mentioned in this prophecy, anyway?'

The Prophet clicked his fingers. A nun entered the vestry to fetch a book, which she delivered into Father Hope's hands. She glanced at the Prophet coyly.

The Prophet attempted a charming smile – the effect scuppered by him promptly dropping his sketchbook on his foot.

Hope flicked through the pages of the Prophecy. All two hundred pages of it. 'This is very long-winded,' he said. 'I thought you said you wrote the entire thing out on the night of the Vision?'

The Prophet paused. 'I did,' he said. 'And then I later fleshed it out.'

'Is half of this even true? A hole in the world itself? A murdered king every half decade? The "Undead Hero"? You ought to put this out as fiction, you'd make a killing.'

The Prophet scowled at him, rubbing his toes. 'Killing is the right word! Everyone would be dead! Why does everything have to be about money with you?'

'I've been in this priesting lark for too long to take any of it seriously anymore,' he said with a sigh. 'If you ask me, you'd be better off saving up your painting money for a nice cottage in the countryside with young Sarah.'

The Prophet gave a violent flinch. 'Sarah's a nun!' he said, appalled.

'Less chance of catching anything nasty, then. I think you make a fine couple.'

'I think you think too much!' the Prophet snapped. 'I suggest you study the Prophecy like a good little priest and stop annoying the world's saviour, thank you!'

Hope backed away slowly in retaliation, not before giving Sarah a sly glance.

~

IV

Seth was having a wonderful dream about Cienne when he woke with a start. He sat up with a confused grimace. 'How did I get here?'

Foliage obstructed the faint blue light the dusk still allowed. Seth was no longer in the castle. He was at the back, in the small crop of woods surrounding the grounds. He couldn't think of why this particular bit was so familiar until he saw the bonfire.

The flames rose high but were barely distinguishable behind the black smoke emitting from his father's body. Seth frowned at King Theo and turned to look at the axe, lying on its side beside him.

Didn't he take that away before the fire got going? He could scarcely remember. It had been over four years ago, though his vivid memories of the axe sticking out of his father's throat begged to differ.

So why was Seth sitting in that very scene four years after the fact?

Realisation dawned on him. This was one of those bloody dreams again. He rolled his eyes and craned his neck, expecting to see Qattren hiding behind the crackling bonfire. The flames rose a little higher... and King Theo stepped out.

Seth gaped up at his father's burnt face, ravaged until he was barely discernible by the red and black sores. His beard and clothes, while blackened, were, thankfully, still intact.

'Tried to kill me, is it?' he snarled, his voice thick thanks to the smoking, weeping would in the side of his neck.

Seth nodded timidly.

His father observed him for a moment.

'BLAH!' he roared suddenly.

'WAAH!' Seth wailed.

He flinched back, arms flying over his head.

King Theo smiled contentedly.

Leaves crunched behind him. Seth turned his head slowly, not taking his eyes off his father until the last second.

Russell stood behind him, his pudgy hands behind his back. 'Hi.'

Seth blinked at him. 'G-go back inside,' he said, glancing at his father anxiously.

'Why?' the boy asked belligerently.

Seth glared at his son. 'Because I said so!' he snapped, more out of terror of his father than anger at his son.

Russell's face crumpled in fury. 'You can't tell me what to do!'

Seth stared at him in alarm. He'd never seen him so angry – or angry at all, in fact.

'The tables have turned now, son,' King Theo said with glee.

'What are you talking about?' Seth said. 'He's just tired. Go to bed now, Russell.'

Russell snorted audibly, a resounding no.

Seth scowled at him. 'GO!'

'MAKE ME!'

Seth inhaled deeply. 'Fine. Stay here, and let Granddad eat you. I'm sure you'll be particularly tasty after all those apple pies, won't you?'

Russell's mouth quivered, his face reddening.

Seth turned back to his father and wrinkled his nose at the smell, rot and burning. 'What do you want?'

King Theo leaned forward. Seth inhaled the corpse's rancid breath involuntarily. He suppressed a cough.

'A life for a life seems fair,' King Theo gurgled in malevolence.

Seth went cold. He turned to face Russell—

Who swung the bloodied axe around in an arc towards his head.

Seth jolted awake violently and fell off the bed.

~

'So, Daddy,' Ginny said conversationally at the breakfast table. 'Wass my present?'

Seth blinked. 'Sorry?'

The main dining hall was bright in the morning sun, its great table littered with idling nobility. Steam billowed from the platters as servants bustled around them, dishing out portions – fried bacon, salmon, stewed fruit. The scents of boiled egg and freshly baked bread wafted up Jimmy's nostrils, making his stomach grumble. He suppressed a grumble of his own. If the royal family didn't decide what they wanted to eat soon, he might starve to death.

'Her birthday present,' Jimmy supplied in response to Seth. 'She's been blathering on about what she wants for her fourth birthday for about an hour now.'

'Oh.' Seth hadn't noticed. He was too busy gazing uneasily at his son.

Russell chewed his eggy soldier while staring at his father – menacingly, Seth thought.

'What?' Russell asked through a mouthful of yolky bread.

'Nothing,' Seth squeaked, ducking his face down to his bacon.

Beams of early morning light poured through the stained glass flanking the table, bathing Ginny's shining hair in a purple glow.

'I likes the sea,' Ginny said idly. She shredded her buttered bread with little intention of consuming any of it. *Like mother, like daughter*, Jimmy thought sourly. 'Ganny made me a picture of the sea with fishies on. And a big fishy that was bigger than the little fishies.'

'The dolphin?' Jimmy said. He assumed it was a dolphin, anyway. Lady Eleanor's needlework skills infamously left a lot to be desired.

'Yeah!' Ginny said with enthusiasm. 'I like dolphins. I like dolphins a *lots*.' Her gaze penetrated the air and made a valiant attempt to enter Seth's forehead as well.

'I see,' Jimmy said, looking amused. 'You're about as subtle as your father on heat. Are you going to eat any of that bread?'

'No,' she said sweetly, gazing at what used to be a thick slice of wholemeal. 'I like cake. I like cake *lots* too.'

'I want one too!' her brother piped up.

'Of course you do,' Jimmy said tiredly. He waved Jon off in search of cake.

'So, Daddy,' Ginny said.

'Hmm?' Seth said with a distant smile.

'What's my birthday present?'

'Um...' he said, his thoughts still within the world of the lucid dream. '...whatever you want, love.'

'A dolphin?'

'Sure.'

Ginny leaped a foot in the air with a whoop. 'I gettin' a dolphin! I gettin' a dolphin for my birr-day!'

'I want one too!' Russell squealed.

'Oh God,' Jimmy groaned. He aimed a smack to the side of Seth's head.

Seth jerked around. 'What was that for?'

'You are going to buy her,' Jimmy said, in crippling levels of cynicism, 'a dolphin.'

Seth blinked at him. 'I'm buying her a what?'

'Dolphin.'

'What is a "dolphin" when it's at home?'

Jimmy ignored this. 'Where were you planning on putting this,' he inserted another wry pause, 'dolphin?'

'Found a place for the dragon, didn't we?' he said in protest.

'Which one, the one that kills employees or the one that destroyed the mausoleum?'

Seth scowled at him and turned back to his uneaten breakfast.

'So what's Russell done now?' Jimmy asked.

Seth shook his head. 'I don't know what you mean.'

'Nobody else has ever looked upon a child eating breakfast with that level of terror – unless King Theo really was a cannibal.'

'Nothing, he just…' Seth looked sheepish for a moment. '… tried to kill me in a dream.'

Jimmy rolled his eyes. 'Because if *you* dreamed it, it must be real.'

Seth made a face at him and risked a quick glance at Russell. Now that the ludicrousness of the situation had been pointed out, the boy was much less frightening. Which may or may not have had to do with the amount of his own hair he was eating.

He flung him a withering glance, wondering if Cienne would change her mind on his proposed haircut. His baby curls had fallen out a year ago and were always too matted to warrant their preservation anyway.

Seth gazed at the boy's fringe in silence for a moment. 'Bring my boy to my rooms,' he instructed, '… with a knife.'

Jimmy watched him walk to the stairs.

'Sir, it was only a dream!' he said in alarm.

Seth rolled his eyes. 'No, I'm not going to kill him,' he corrected, 'not yet, anyway. I'm going to give him a haircut.' He glanced sideways at Jimmy. 'What?'

Jimmy's face twisted in horror – even more than it did when child murder had seemingly been proposed. 'That's not a good idea. You know how *she* feels about his hair.'

'She can keep it in a little box if that's what she's so bothered about,' Seth said, rolling his eyes. 'He'll start coughing up hairballs if we let this go on.'

'Still not a good idea,' said Jimmy in a pained voice. 'We have a maths idiom in the kitchens, I think it's quite applicable here - Cienne plus incidents she dislikes, minus sex, equals bad things happening with garden implements.'

'That's your argument for everything, isn't it?' Seth said sourly. 'She also triggered a twenty-year-long mental illness, stole my bodily fluids for her shrine and sexually assaulted me as a catatonic teenager, but no, no, you have to make fun of the lazy eye, don't you?'

'It was funny,' Jimmy said.

Seth glowered at him.

He cleared his throat. 'Of course, all that other stuff was definitely *not* funny. But it does reinforce my argument considerably.'

Seth's eyebrows rose critically. 'She's going to beat me for cutting our son's hair?'

'Amongst other things, yes.'

Seth clicked his fingers. 'You're not talking about his hair at all, are you? You're talking about Adrienne.'

Jimmy winced. 'I was hoping you'd think better of that one on your own. We have enough troubles without a rampaging queen on the loose. Plus I don't really fancy being your nurse for the next twenty years again.'

'Oh, I'm sorry you feel that way,' Seth said, suddenly sounding a lot more cheerful. 'Looks like we'll need to employ her here after all if my wife's as volatile as you think she is.'

Jimmy clicked his tongue off the roof of his mouth. 'Your funeral,' he hollered up the stairs after Seth.

~

Mere hours after Jimmy's warning, the medical turret of the Creys' Keep became thronged with rubberneckers.

'You've been replaced,' Seth called crossly. 'You need to leave!'

'NO!' Erik hung out of the top window of the turret. 'She's younger than me! By an entire decade! This is despicable!'

Seth rolled his eyes and placed his hands on his hips.

'I've been training for this job my entire life!' Erik snarled venomously. 'I was bandaging severed arms since she was in swaddling clothes! You can't replace me with a little girl with half as many years' experience! I don't care whose paramour she is!'

'Whatever a paramour is, she isn't one!'

'A paramour, your majesty, is a tart,' he said haughtily. 'Her name even rhymes with it!'

'She's not a tart!' Seth said hotly. 'She's a very capable young woman, and it is merely a coincidence that she happens to have once been... somebody's bit on the side.'

'Tart,' he said.

'Shut it!' Seth snapped. 'You said yourself when you saw Lilly, she performed the most skilful surgery you had ever seen.'

'How do you know I was telling the truth?' he said shrilly. 'I could have lied so I wouldn't have to redo the surgery!' Eric's face fell, the realisation of what he had blurted out abruptly dawning.

'In which case, firing you sounds like an excellent idea,' Seth retorted. 'Get out. I won't say it again.'

Eric slammed a hand onto the windowsill angrily and stormed away.

'He'd better be on his way out,' Seth growled.

'He will be, sir,' Corporal Moat promised, wielding a crowbar with an eager grin.

Ten minutes passed. Adrienne arrived in time to hear the contents of her soon-to-be workshop smash and clatter within.

'Maybe I should just leave the job,' she said, hovering at Seth's side.

'Sod that,' Seth said.

They ducked away from each other. A round bottle whizzed between their heads from the window.

'THIS IS MY HOME!' Erik howled.

'No longer!' Moat yelled.

The door burst from its hinges and landed at Seth and Adrienne's feet. Eric was forced out by Moat and one of his soldiers. Adrienne watched them pass and gave a timid wave. 'Sorry.'

Erik snorted lividly on his way out of the grounds.

Adrienne turned to face Seth, who shrugged.

'He'll get over it.' He gestured to the shelves of ruined bottles and vials with a sheepish expression. 'Make yourself at home.'

Adrienne grinned and slipped into the little room to salvage what she could. Seth watched her with a smile.

Jon sidled up to him and tickled his right nostril with the corner of a letter. Seth flinched away, his nose twitching.

'From Mister Horseface,' Jon said with a smile.

Seth lifted one side of the broken wax seal with a wry expression. 'Have you been reading it?'

Jon looked down at his shoes. 'I was bored,' he said meekly. 'I thought it might be something interesting from your Cousin Elyse.'

'Get lost, you nosy little pervert.' Seth flicked his ear with one fingernail, making him squeal.

Adrienne watched Seth in silence.

Seth leaned on the doorframe, examining the letter with a scowl. 'Asshole.'

'Who's Mister Horseface?' Adrienne asked.

'An asshole,' Seth sighed, folding the letter back into thirds and ripping it into two.

'... and your Cousin Elyse?' she added, quirking an eyebrow.

'You don't want to know and, frankly, I wish I didn't.' He turned his head to give Jon a side-glance. 'Can I help you?'

'No, I'm fine,' he said with a smile.

Seth glared at him and planted a hand on his forehead to push him away. 'Try not to make eye contact, it just encourages him,' he told Adrienne, who smiled thinly.

'It's not him I'm worried about, it's your wife. She's not going to like seeing me around.'

'Don't worry about her either. I'll deal with her if she causes trouble.' He reached into the doorway to pat her shoulder in reassurance.

'Ahem,' he heard his own voice say coldly.

Seth faced Howard Rosethorn. 'Oh, hello,' he said in a flat voice.

'Good morning,' Howie said icily. 'My mentor and I were wondering if you had any work going?'

'How should I know?' Seth snapped.

Adrienne noticed him. 'Hi, love,' she said brightly. 'What are you doing here?'

'Don't mind us, we're just chancing our arm at a bit of work,' Archie said before catching sight of Seth. He froze.

186

Seth gave him an odd glance. 'Do I know you?'

Archie's eyes widened perceptively. 'Oh. No. Probably not. My name's Archie.' He held out a hand, hoping to God he wouldn't recognise it as the one that landed on his back at the cusp of the Hole.

'He's my uncle,' Adrienne said with a smile.

Seth wagged a finger at him. 'Ah. Very nice to meet you.'

He shook Archie's hand, to Archie's extreme surprise. 'Er… likewise!' Archie exclaimed, shaking hands with a manic grin.

Howie glowered at the pair of them, his jaw jutting forward.

'I gather you're a carpenter?' Seth said in interest.

'In Teal, yes,' Archie said brightly, relief seeping from him in waves.

'Lovely area, that side of the castle,' Seth mused.

'Yeah, it was 'til our neighbour's house got robbed,' Howie cut in.

'Oh really?' Archie asked, grimacing in sympathy.

Seth shot Howie a distrustful side-glance. Howie paid it no notice, instead gazing thoughtfully at the ceiling. 'Yeah, recently widowed, too. Linda, I think her name is? Took everything, apparently. Can't think why they targeted her in *particular*.' Howie's gaze swung back to Seth.

Who refused to meet it, instead looking sheepishly at his boots. 'How terrible,' he said in a small voice.

'I thought it was,' Howie said, coolly.

Adrienne shot Howie a scowl.

'Congratulations on the kids, by the way,' Archie added, turning to brighter pastures.

'Oh, thank you!' Seth said, beaming. 'I made them myself.'

Archie laughed.

'You got any work going?' Howie cut in sharply.

Seth stuck his lower lip out and shook his head. 'Don't think so.'

Howie flung an arm out, gesturing at the broken doors and shelving.

'Don't think so,' Seth repeated in the same nonchalant tone of voice.

'Well, you know where we are if you think of anything,' Archie said. He pointedly nodded towards the shelving – or lack thereof.

'Thank you,' Seth said with a smile. 'Be sure to visit us again if you need anything. Archie.' *Only*, he added privately.

'I might do that. Thanks very much!' Archie beamed, waving on his way back to the portcullis.

'What a nice man,' Seth said absently.

Howie gave Seth one last glare and followed Archie.

Seth craned his neck to follow them around the corner and said to Adrienne, once they had left earshot, 'Archie doesn't know about us, does he?'

'It had better stay that way,' Adrienne warned. 'He's very set in his ways.'

'He'd never forgive you?'

'Oh, he'd forgive me, he just wouldn't forgive you,' she corrected, turning back to her sanctuary. 'Kind of like Howie.'

'I'd make an effort to appease Archie, Howard's just a stroppy shit.' Another corner of parchment made its way into Seth's right nostril. 'Jon, do you mind?'

'Sorry,' Jon said, handing over the letter. 'I didn't bother reading this one because it occurred to me that it might be an invasion of your privacy.'

Seth lifted an eyebrow. He patted the top of Jon's head. 'Brownie points for you, then.'

Jon smiled faintly.

Adrienne giggled quietly with a little squeak, which Seth liked. He pulled open the letter as Adrienne sat on the worktable and watched him.

'Oh! It's my Uncle Fred,' Seth said brightly, folding the letter. 'He's arriving at the palace in a couple days for my birthday.' Seth waved Jon inside. 'Jon, inform Jimmy that the party shall commence as soon as my uncle arrives,' he said grandly. 'Will you be there?' he added to Adrienne.

'Course I will,' Jon said easily. 'Thanks for asking!'

Seth scowled at him. 'I wasn't talking to you. Didn't I just give you a task to fulfil?'

Jon sighed and wandered off.

Seth raised his eyebrows at Adrienne, nodding at the keep.

She hesitated.

'It's only over there,' he coaxed, pointing. 'Practically on your doorstep now. It's nothing too formal.'

She licked her lips.

'Come on!' he exclaimed, nudging her shoulder. 'A full feast, all on my coin. I want to make it up to you for assuming the worst all those years ago.'

She smiled shyly. 'Alright, I'll come.'

He pointed at her commandingly. 'Yes, you will.' He winked and swept across the yard.

Adrienne watched him stride back to the keep, his hands in his pockets. She counted the years mentally, totting up his age. Thirty-seven. Or eight. Roughly. He wasn't greying though – he looked practically the same. Unless he was changing the colour somehow. His mother had managed it—

Lilly-Anna's face interrupted her musings by glaring in her direction. Her complexion was still pale from her healing operation wound, but there was no keeping Lilly Crey from her combat training. Adrienne watched Lilly as she hovered outside the armoury with Stanley Carrot and *glared* at her, twirling a small dagger between her fingers.

Adrienne eyed her uneasily before darting her gaze back to the workshop. She wondered if Lilly was as dangerous as she made herself out to be. Then she wondered why she was wondering.

Until Jon sprinted between her and Lilly. Adrienne instead wondered about the sanity of the Creys' staff as the footman entered the keep after Seth at high speed, holding…

… a bleating lamb?

~

V

'Seth, do you trust me?' Jon asked breathlessly.

'No. What a silly question.' Seth faced him on his way to the council chamber and frowned. 'What are you doing with that sheep?' he asked in exasperation.

'Don't let those men in!' Jon squealed. He bolted across the entrance hall to the courtyard, the lamb held out in front of him. It bleated in alarm.

'Why?' Seth demanded.

'Just trust me!' he called over his shoulder as the lamb wriggled frantically.

'But why have you got a sheep?' Seth called in bewilderment.

Jon vanished upstairs.

A knock came to the door. Seth tugged one side of the heavy double doors himself, out of curiosity.

'We'd like to speak with the sheep thief, please.' A man roughly his own age greeted him with a hassled grimace, accompanied by a small teen.

Seth looked them up and down, examining the stained breeches in particular. He wracked his brains for a moment before resolving that trying to find logic in the decisions of Jon-formerly-Mortimer-Crey was like trying to teach Ginny what all the chess pieces did.

'Sorry, you've just missed him,' Seth said in a tired voice, closing the door.

'But he's just run in there with me—' The farmer's voice cut off behind the thick oak.

Seth stormed into the east antechamber. He filed a mental draft of Jon's death warrant for future reference. 'If anyone so much as mentions what Jon's just done there, I'll throttle them.'

'Very good, sir,' said Osney, who tried to avoid talk about his son as much as possible. 'Shall we begin?'

Seth flung him a distrustful glower.

A ring of men greeted him around the edge of the ornate council table, littered with wine goblets and parchment. Seth made a beeline for the head of the table, the largest chair. Osney had placed himself at his right-hand side, he noticed with barely suppressed rage.

Adrienne's words lingered in his head, the images they conjured along with them. His uncle and that horrible priest Giery. Seth levelled his breathing, filling his lungs slowly. *Not yet*, he reminded himself. *Best to address this in private.*

Seth clicked his fingers on his way to his seat.

Russell followed, pork pie in hand. Seth lifted his son onto his lap and accepted a set of clippers from a sceptical Jimmy as Osney began to speak.

'There have been no further developments with the witch-burning crisis,' he said as Seth started work on Russell's hair. 'Since their leader was commissioned here as the portraitist, there have been no reports of any—'

'I can see!' Russell squealed in amazement.

Seth held his fringe aloft, chopping.

'This is how the world looks *without* a curtain of hair in the way,' Seth informed him. He glanced at Osney. 'Carry on.'

Waves of flaxen hair fluttered across the table and onto the boy's front.

'Yes, erm… the witch-burnings, yes,' Osney said, losing his trail of thought. 'Where was I?'

'There were none,' Hinterton said helpfully.

'Yes, erm… there were none.'

An awkward silence ensued.

'And?' Seth said, frowning at his work-in-progress.

'And, erm, Mister Emmett,' Osney continued, 'has sent us his update on the Peace Tax, which has increased by three-fold due to—'

'Three-fold!' Seth exclaimed. He sheared a little too much off the side.

Osney winced at the scissors. 'Yes, due to Queen Qattren Meriangue coming forward to contribute to the fee.'

'So because she offered to help pay it, he'd charging three times as much?' Seth demanded.

'That and an incident regarding Queen Felicity that you're supposed to know about already?' he added, angling for elaboration.

Seth growled. 'Qattren can pay it on her own, then,' he announced. 'Her half is already one and a half times as much as I was giving him – that will do him. Anything else?'

'Queen Felicity has also requested to visit, to see her son,' Osney went on. 'She plans to arrive in the winter to stay for the new year.'

'That sounds good to me,' Seth said easily, putting down the shears.

Osney eyed Russell's haircut with a wince. 'You've hashed that up, haven't you?' he said before he could stop himself.

Seth frowned at him. 'No, I haven't.' He examined his own handiwork critically.

Russell's fringe alone bore a striking resemblance to a staircase viewed from the side. And it was still in his eyes.

'Alright, maybe I have,' he relented, handing the child to Jimmy. 'Anything else I should know?'

'Yes, my liege,' Osney said.

Jimmy stood Russell on one of the chairs and began to put his head to rights.

'Our informants have reported some strange activity from the Hornes over the last couple of weeks.'

Seth rolled his eyes and slouched in his chair, playing with a quill. 'Qattren, I take it?'

'Yes,' he agreed. 'After King Samuel's remains were brought to the Forest to be buried, the pair have been spotted in various locales surrounding Serpus and the palace, vanishing into back rooms with spies to discuss your recent interactions with a young lady near the outskirts of the palace.'

Seth flinched and stabbed his finger with the quill. 'How do you know that's what they were discussing?'

'Because I am one of the spies, my liege,' he said, a tad sheepish. 'She pays very handsomely for a Forest savage, my liege.'

Seth's eyes narrowed. 'I'll have a word with her, then. And you will cease to do so, I trust?'

'As you will, my liege,' he said, scribbling. 'That about wraps it up, I think.'

'Everything alright money-wise?' Jimmy asked, still working on Russell's hair.

Three men froze at the table.

'As far as I am aware,' Osney said evenly. 'What makes you ask?'

'I gather Princess Virginia is after a dolphin for her birthday,' Jimmy said without missing a beat.

'Maybe we could think of something *proper* for their birthday?' Seth said.

'You can't go wrong with a nice manor, my liege,' one of the lords said cheerfully.

Osney hissed at him, sawing his throat with the side of his hand.

'Capital idea,' Jimmy said with a vicious grin.

Seth turned his gaze to Russell. 'Would you like a new house for your birthday?'

Jimmy paused in his work to allow Russell to nod eagerly.

'One for each of them, then,' Seth said to Osney, as though placing an order for a cake. 'They don't like to share.'

Osney winced while Seth doodled on a blank sheet of parchment. 'As you will, my liege,' he said, throwing a meaningful glance at the three worriers.

Jimmy glared at them all, giving Russell's fringe a final *snick*. 'Finished,' he announced, turning Russell's head from side to side. 'He looks almost human now.'

Russell grinned and rubbed his close-cropped hair with both hands.

'That feels better, doesn't it?' Seth said with a grin.

'One last thing privately, my liege,' Osney said in a low voice as the council dispersed.

Seth lifted his eyebrows expectantly.

'It's about Mortimer, my liege.'

'You mean Jon?'

Osney winced. 'Yes. I know he appears to thrive under Jimmy's capable command, but the boy simply isn't well in the head. May I have your permission to have him committed to a sanctuary in Serpus?'

Seth's expression turned stony. 'What?'

Osney blinked. 'Have him committed to an asylum in Serpus?' he asked again. 'I mean, he simply doesn't act in a conservative manner, my liege.'

'A conservative,' Seth echoed, 'manner.' His voice was hollow.

'Well, the stealing, my liege—'

'Oh yes. He thieves farm animals,' Seth said sharply. 'What an irredeemable monster. Let's imprison him.'

Osney flinched as though he'd been struck.

'We have had worse men within these walls. Or have you forgotten about the man who assaulted him in the first place?'

Osney's face twisted. 'My liege, I only meant… the things he says… the boy claims your father knew his whereabouts the entire time. I simply cannot believe that my elder brother would know where my only child was and not tell me anything! The boy must be deluded!'

Seth gave him a withering glance. 'My father rarely spoke to you in anything other than the manner of a servant. He barely acknowledged your existence. If he did know where Jon was the entire time, I find it completely plausible that he kept it from you. If he hadn't, I'll warrant the mass grave would have held an extra skull in it.'

He flinched again.

Seth leaned forward. 'You lock up dangerous people. Jon might be a nuisance, but he's not a threat to anybody. So no, you cannot get rid of him just because you don't want to look at him anymore. *You failed him.* The embarrassment is the least you deserve.'

Osney simmered. 'He's my—'

'Son? Yes, I know. I have one of those. I used to have two, do you recall the first one?'

Osney paled. Seth took that as a resounding 'yes'.

'Because I do,' Seth said in a low intone. 'In spite of your attempts to have him forgotten. You will not be attempting the same to my cousin. If you don't want Jon around you, the door,' he pointed behind Osney's shoulder, 'is right there.'

Osney exhaled and twisted to leave, fuming.

Seth faced Jimmy, who stood by the door, Russell with him.

'And you thought your old man was bad,' Jimmy said, shaking his head. 'At least he never gave up on you outright.'

'No, he just used to drown me into submission,' Seth muttered. He looked Russell in the eye and ruffled his hair, doubling over to brush stray hairs from the shoulders of his little jerkin.

Jimmy opened his mouth and shut it hesitantly before finally opening it again. 'Does it make you glad he's dead? To at least know he isn't around to torture you anymore?'

Seth looked up at Jimmy through a furrowed brow. 'Sometimes.' He got up and left the antechamber with his son in tow.

Jimmy stayed behind in the empty room, thinking. Or more appropriately, remembering.

'How did you know it was Seth that killed the king?' he had asked Jon three years ago.

'Saw him,' he said, as though he'd seen him walk through a door as opposed to kill a man.

Jon had been feeding Lilly's dog apple pie at the time – Jimmy couldn't remember why this was strange. Perhaps there was a repressed memory there somewhere.

'… I saw it in a dream,' Jon had said as Jimmy gaped at the revelation. 'I can see into the future.'

Whether he could really see into the future or not remained to be seen. But Seth did look awfully guilty just there… just for a second or two…

Jimmy weighed up the options. If Jon was as nonsensical that day as he ever was and had lied about Seth killing King Theo, that meant everything was fine. If he was somehow right, either by premonition or pure blind chance, then Jimmy was working for one of the most dangerous men in the world. No one approached King Theo Crey with malice aforethought and *lived to tell the tale*. That meant if Jimmy let on that he knew, he was a dead man.

And here I was, thinking Seth Crey was about as threatening as an orange peel.

Although… Jimmy had an evil thought. It would make an excellent subject for blackmail. And he had been after a paid holiday from work since… well, since he started age fifteen.

And a bonus on his wages would be nice.

And a nice house of his own.

Jimmy paused for barely a second before bolting to the kitchen for more details.

~

Meanwhile, outside:

'Ah,' Seth said, hovering by the open antechamber door. 'Hello, Cienne.'

Cienne halted stiffly in the entrance hall, bathed in the glow of a little rainbow falling from the stained glass. She performed a fleeting smile, which was her attempt at disguising unbridled fury.

'Seth. What are you doing with that little boy, who does he belong—' Her eyes widened in recognition. 'RUSSELL!'

Seth gripped the boy's shoulders.

Russell clutched at his new haircut, in case his mother's anguished wails made it suddenly grow back.

'YOU CUT HIS HAIR!'

~

'Herpes?' Felicity shrieked. 'You want me to marry the Earl of Herpes?'

Emmett reclined behind his desk in his private quarters, Felicity standing before it. Felicity's shrill exclamation rebounded off the marble walls and into Emmett's brain. He squeezed his eyes shut, trying to ward off his hangover.

'That's what I said,' he said, pressing his fingertips into his temples. 'I had a few drinks with the man, he's really quite pleasant.'

Felicity narrowed her eyes. She couldn't quite imagine what her brother looked like drunk. He never indulged in more than the bare minimum of anything. She had heard from somewhere that a person's true self came out when they were drunk – in which case he couldn't have gotten *that* drunk or he would have had Henry Meyer flayed just for fun.

'You never told me he was the lord of Herpes,' she seethed. 'It's nicknamed the Disease District, they named a sexually transmitted disease after it!'

Emmett paused, scrutinising her face. 'What on earth would you know about a sexually transmitted disease? You have the mental age of an eight-year-old.'

Felicity paused also. 'I imagine its some sort of… skin disease,' she said. 'Of the face.'

Emmett arched an eyebrow. 'Indeed.'

Felicity licked her lips.

Emmett tore his gaze back to his paperwork. 'He's arriving in a few weeks to meet you, after wrapping up a few things in his district. You will not mention anything regarding… skin diseases,' he finished, emphasising the pause. 'I don't want you to jeopardise this engagement.'

'Of course,' Felicity said sourly. 'May I leave?'

He bobbed his head.

As she turned, Emmett spoke. 'You interest me, Felicity.'

Felicity frowned, slowly pivoting back on one heel.

Emmett raised his head to meet her gaze. 'I often wonder what it is you're *actually* hiding from me and, while past experience would suggest it to be harmless, I still wonder if it shouldn't concern me slightly.' He lifted an eyebrow. 'Should it?'

Felicity held her breath. 'I have no idea what you mean.'

Emmett's mouth stretched open in what Felicity was horrified to discover was an actual *smile*. 'Of course you don't.'

Felicity sucked in a breath. She knew that tone of voice. Emmett using *that* tone of voice was akin to a tiger baring its teeth.

'I'll be in my quarters,' she said, fleeing the room.

~

Despina ran like hell. Her shoes slapped the concrete flagstones – her soles were flapping far too easily for her taste. The Bastard owed her a fresh pair. His little job was burning through the stitching.

'Oi!' Archie called, sprinting after her. 'Give those back!'

She meandered around startled shoppers, the chisels held tightly to her chest.

'OI!' Archie screamed.

Despina ignored him and tore off down the city thoroughfare. She skidded to a halt at the crossroads and veered right, vanishing around a corner and slipping into Sal'plae.

Archie rounded the corner to find his chisels dumped unceremoniously into the dust.

'What is wrong with that little girl?' Archie said upon his return, chisels in hand. 'If she isn't breaking all my work, she's nicking my equipment!'

'Maybe she's just poor,' Howie said.

Archie counted the chisels in his hands. 'They're all here,' he said, puzzled.

'Stupid, then,' Howie suggested.

Archie rolled his eyes and slumped onto a bench with a sigh. 'Do you know her?' he asked suddenly.

Howie blinked. 'Me? No, why would I?'

'She only seems to come by when you're here,' Archie said.

'Maybe she fancies me,' Howie said, a touch smugly.

Archie shot him a withering glance. 'She *must* be stupid, then.'

Despina crept up behind them while their backs were turned from the door. A sledgehammer landed between them with a deafening crack.

Archie and Howie shrieked. The bench collapsed between them, casting them into each other, head-first.

Despina bolted out of the door.

'Since she likes you so much,' Archie seethed, rubbing a lump in his scalp, 'you can chase her. Go on!'

Howie sighed and rose to give chase, but she was long gone.

PART FOUR: THE PARTY

I

'm sorry I hit him,' Cienne said.

Eleanor threw her a reproachful look.

Throngs of servants hastened across the dining hall in various states of stress. A long row of young girls circled a spot across the table – one of the lords had caused great consternation by allowing his dog to release violent diarrhoea in the middle of the floor, precisely at the moment that soiree preparations reached full swing.

The long table yawned down the length of the dining hall, covered with a velvet cloth in the Crey colour – emerald. One half was set with silver plates and cutlery, ready to be filled. The other end was reserved solely for canapes, which Cienne knew for a fact would probably be there all evening. They looked about as appetising as wet parchment.

'You need to control your temper,' Eleanor scolded. She faffed with the table layout as she spoke, lining the canapes in order of size before changing her mind and rearranging them in order of edibility.

'I know, but it's difficult when he deliberately tries to annoy me,' Cienne said with a sigh, sitting at the centre of the table, her chin in her palm.

'You need to compromise with

him.'

'He's too stubborn. He's worse than Ginny about that bloody dolphin.'

'Hitting him isn't going to make him any better,' Eleanor said. She gave a pink ball an experimental lick before throwing it under the table for Albie. 'There's a saying my mother gave me when I first married your father-in-law. "Kill him with kindness".'

'What did that achieve in your marriage?'

'Nothing with Theo, he used to just ignore me. But Seth isn't like him. He likes being fussed over. You give him your present later on, he'll be putty in your hands.'

'I don't know why I bothered putting so much effort into it,' Cienne said dully. 'He'll never use it.'

'Oh, I don't know,' Eleanor said with a wry smirk. 'If *you* tell him you like it, he'll be bound to change his mind…'

Cienne rolled her eyes. Mostly because she knew Eleanor was right.

∼

'Please be careful,' Jon said fretfully.

Seth's quarters were, for a change, the only serene area in the keep. Both palms planted heavily on the surface of his writing desk, Jimmy examined a map of the world keenly.

'You're a worrier all of a sudden.' He lifted a heel of bread with more butter on it than was seemingly digestible and took a sizable bite. 'I've conned my way up the food chain this high,' he said, thickly, 'I'm not going to lose my head just yet.'

'I don't care about you, I don't want him finding out I can see into the future.'

Jimmy suppressed a derisive snort. He still didn't believe that for a second, but if humouring him kept the nitty-gritty details of the king's homicide coming…

He swallowed his bread. 'I'm just telling him I have a reliable source,' he said to Jon. 'He's going to be more preoccupied with organising my holiday to Mellier, believe you me.'

Jon watched him scrutinise Mellier with a doubtful expression.

Lilly peered in at them from the door to Seth's study. 'What are you doing in here? Seth's screaming bloody murder because you're not down there to direct the preparations.'

Jimmy sighed. 'Since it's bloody murder he's screaming.' He pushed himself away from Seth's desk. 'What preparations are there, besides putting out the booze?'

'He's got a seating plan drawn out because someone told him they spotted Elyse crossing the grounds,' Lilly said with a smirk.

'I'm not terribly surprised,' he said, drawing on the court rumours about the duchess-in-waiting and a large cucumber – neither of which factored into King Seth's ideal evening.

For self-preservation's sake, he followed Lilly downstairs, Jon at his heels.

Three years' worth of dirt were finally being lifted from the tiling – the circle of girls had evidently done too fine a job on the dog's leavings. Seth stood in the middle of the chaos, doing largely nothing and getting in everyone's way, Jimmy noticed.

Jimmy sidled over, glancing around. He grimaced. 'What's wrong with your eye?'

Seth's eyelid glistened, a mess of bluish-grey. He wiped yellow pus from his eyelid. 'Side-effect of angering a queen who wears lots of rings.'

'You ought to have someone look at it,' Jimmy said queasily. 'It looks infected.'

'It's fine.' A small cut hovered just between the eyelid and brow, crusted with brown and yellow scabbing.

'Why don't you go see Adrienne about it?' Jimmy asked. 'You made enough of a fuss to hire her, you might as well put her to use.'

Seth winced. 'I don't want to… anger her.'

Jimmy frowned, tilting his head to one side.

'Cienne,' Seth elaborated.

Jimmy lifted an eyebrow.

'Don't look at me like that!' Seth snapped. 'She can be quite frightening when she wants to be.'

'Sir,' he said, 'is there something you're concerned about?'

Seth shifted on his feet. 'Don't want to talk about it.'

'Are you sure?'

Seth heaved a sigh, turning his gaze to the ceiling. 'It's emasculating, isn't it?' he exploded finally.

'Sir,' Jimmy said patiently, 'I had to host one of Ginny's little tea parties with her toys the other day. It can't be more emasculating than that.'

Seth huffed. 'It's… she's been… hitting me a lot.'

'Why?'

'Any reason!' he hissed at him. 'Any little thing at all, she just… hits first and asks questions later. And, she, ever since, whenever I instigate, you know… she just gets violent, as if I was forcing myself on her.' His shoulders sagged, defeated. 'I'm frightened of her, Jimmy.'

'Have you spoken to your mother about it?'

'I did,' Seth said sullenly. 'She just said she's "spirited".'

'I've had "spirited", sir,' Jimmy said wryly, 'none of them have given me anything resembling *that*.' He pointed at the glistening mess of bruising.

Seth jerked a handkerchief out of his pocket, dabbing away another blob of pus.

'Hi-ah,' Lilly said, arriving at his side.

Seth flinched violently, jerking the wound open.

'Ew,' Lilly said, wrinkling her nose. 'Please get that looked at.'

'He can't, he's frightened Cienne will hunt him down and kill him if he goes near the medical turret,' Jimmy said.

'I told you that in confidence!' Seth snarled, dabbing.

Lilly peered at it, pursing her lips in distaste. 'At least put an eyepatch on, it looks unsightly.'

Seth scowled at her.

Jimmy's eye caught a round-faced blond by the dowager queen that seemed annoyingly familiar. He quickly cycled through his internal directory of prior conquests.

Lilly followed his gaze. She clutched Seth's arm in sudden alarm. 'Seth, hide.'

'Why, what?' he asked, pivoting. 'Who is it? Please don't tell me Fred brought the grandmother with him? I can't have both of them in the same place at once, it'll be carnage!'

'No, it's Elyse.'

Seth swore and bolted for the double doors. 'I am going to have *words* with Uncle Fred! Where is Fred?' He reached the courtyard. 'FREDERICK!' he howled towards the fountain.

'Oh, she can't be that bad,' Jimmy said.

Lilly nudged him silent.

He turned to face the pretty blond he'd spotted earlier. The tightly fastened corset and abundance in petticoats revealed her to hail from Portabella – hopefully one of the areas inhabited by Truphorian nobility. Jimmy's Portabellan was on the bad side of rusty: one of the Cienne's handmaidens once described his diction as 'akin to that of a carnally frustrated toad'.

'My lady,' Jimmy said with a bow.

Lilly suppressed a snigger.

'My lord,' the woman said with a slight curtsy. 'It's a fabulous turn out, isn't it?'

Upper-class Truphorian, Jimmy recognised, born and bred. *Excellent.*

'Are you new at court?' she asked, openly curious. 'I've not seen you before.'

'That'd be because he's usually wiping Seth's shit off the floor upstairs,' Lilly said. 'He's the butler. Jimmy, this—'

'Lady Gertrude,' she introduced herself, holding out a hand.

He pecked it dutifully. 'You've lost weight,' said Jimmy in surprise. 'And around seventy years of aging.'

She giggled. 'Gertrude is my last name,' she said in amusement. 'I don't give my first name out to just anybody.'

'Ah, I see.' He was beginning to like Lady Gertrude the Younger. He reckoned he'd have more than just her first name out by the end of the evening. 'You must be a relative of the queen dowager.'

Queen Eleanor had relatives all over the south of Portabella, families that had bought land during the country's economic boom, when castles in the region could be bought for the price of a pork pie in Serpus. Jimmy straightened his shoulders in anticipation. He'd never had anyone from Portabella before.

Lady Gertrude smiled indulgently at him. She then cast Lilly a dismissive side-eye. 'And you are?'

Lilly blinked. 'Lilly,' she said simply.

She gave Lilly a withering glance. 'Lilly what?'

'Of Adem?' Lilly answered cynically.

'Princess Lilly-Anna Crey, my lady,' Jimmy said. 'Contrary to looks and smell, this is King Seth's sister.'

Realisation finally broke through the barrier of snobbery. She curtsied, almost reluctantly. 'I recall you now. You were only about ten last time we met. You've gotten big since then.'

'So have you,' Lilly retorted.

Lady Gertrude eyeballed her in a way Jimmy once again found inexplicably familiar. She turned her gaze to the dining table. 'I must speak with my aunt,' she said, giving Jimmy a smile. 'I'm sure we'll meet again later, Mister...'

'De Vil,' Jimmy finished with a bow. 'As in "handsome".'

Lilly made a face as her ladyship flounced away.

'No wonder you're single,' she said. '"As in 'handsome'"?'

'Yeah,' he said mildly, gesturing at himself. 'Haven't you heard the phrase "handsome devil" before?'

'Yeah – by people who are single,' said Lilly.

Jimmy let her have that one because of Orl, but made a mental note to make light of her smell more often.

'Lady Gertrude,' he said instead to himself, watching her converse with Eleanor.

Lilly followed his gaze. 'You're not her type, mate.'

He smoothed his hair back. 'I can make myself her type.'

'Doubt it. Unless you change your hair blond and become a close relative.' She caught Jimmy's bemused gaze and grinned. 'You've just met Lady Elyse Gertrude.'

Jimmy froze in horror. '*That's* Coffin-Jumper Elyse?'

'The very same,' Lilly said with a giggle.

'But she seems so nice,' Jimmy said despairingly.

He watched Lilly leave for the courtyard.

'Why does he get all the nice ones?' he wailed after her.

∽

As if on cue, Adrienne peered around the doorframe.

Establishing that Lilly wasn't in the vicinity, she shuffled into the hall, waving Archie behind her.

Archie watched her duck behind a couple as a woman very similar in looks to Seth made a beeline past. 'I thought you said we were invited?'

'By Seth, yes,' Adrienne said. 'Not Cienne.'

'Who?' Archie asked, forgetting who Cienne was completely.

'Oh God,' Adrienne said in disgust. She hid behind Archie as a young man passed her. 'They invited the old medic? Why would they invite both of us? That makes no sense at all!'

'Maybe this Cienne invited him?' Archie said.

'Probably,' Adrienne said bitterly. She was about to say something further when she was quickly cut off.

Archie didn't notice. 'Pity Howie's stuck guarding the workshop from that vandal,' he said. 'Think they'd let me have my birthday here? You know, family of the staff and all that? Fifty-five's a big year, isn't it?' He turned. 'Adrienne?' he said into thin air.

Her back met the wall around the corner of the building. The chill evening air hit her face once again, the steadily-filling courtyard thrumming with life.

Lilly-Anna Crey's frown came into view.

Adrienne suddenly realised how much smaller Lilly was up close. She seemed much taller than her actual five foot five and was just over a couple inches shorter than Adrienne.

'What's your game?' Lilly demanded.

Adrienne hesitated. 'I'm not playing any games.'

Lilly's eyes flitted up and down the length of her, her skirt in particular.

'Stay away from my brother,' she snarled, 'or you'll regret it. We're expecting this do to wrap up around midnight. I trust you can keep your hands off him for that long?'

Adrienne glared at her and looked her up and down — well, *down* and down. 'I'm seeing someone else,' she said coldly. 'I'm not like that.'

'And Seth's the bleeding archpriest of Adem,' Lilly said wryly. 'Go and pray on someone else. He's been through enough.' With that she turned and rounded the corner.

Adrienne glowered in her wake, seething.

~

II

On the gatehouse, Seth squinted out at the distant mountains – insofar as he could through a film of pus. He groaned loudly and rubbed his left eye vigorously.

It squelched and dribbled. He smacked a hand over it irately, pulling his eye patch from his trouser pocket. The band clung to a mysterious button on the inside, stretching slightly.

Corporal Moat released it with a flick.

'Thanks,' Seth grunted. He attached it with his left eye firmly shut. 'Are you sure you don't mind me loitering up here?'

'No, not at all,' Moat said. He picked his nose in his inimitable style – little finger inside to the knuckle and palm turned towards the heavens. 'Nice having someone to chat to.'

He twitched his nose and held one nostril closed to blow a specimen over the portcullis.

'Must be,' said Seth.

Footsteps landed on the stairs to Seth's right. With a stabbing panic, Seth briefly entertained the notion of jumping off the battlements before hearing a THUNK from his uncle's walking stick.

He pivoted, his face breaking out in a grin. 'Uncle Fred!'

Another grin rather similar to his appeared on a much more weathered face. Frederick Gertrude laboured his way to the top of the gatehouse.

'How are you, Seth?' he said in his faintly country drawl.

Seth gave his uncle's clothes the once-over. The style for males in the Truphorian-inhabited regions of Portabella was lace and metallic thread, and lots of it. His current attire was a deep pink creation Seth's mother would fall in love with, coated with silver embroidery and lace at the collar and cuffs.

The style was in sharp contrast with his accent, which echoed that of the sailors in the docks of Sullenport. He talked like a fishmonger – he even looked like one, Seth added internally. His face was weathered from his various outdoor hobbies, albeit drawn and gaunt of late. There was nobody in the higher classes quite like Uncle Fred. He was like a greyhound dressed in a leotard.

'Your wardrobe is getting worse, you know,' Seth told him.

'That's what happens when you put women like my daughter in charge of ordering it,' Fred said with a half-smile. He combed back his silver-threaded mousy hair and clapped his free hand onto Seth's shoulder, his left wrapped around the top of his walking stick.

'How is your daughter, by the way?' Seth asked queasily.

'See for yourself,' he said, rolling his eyes downwards.

A blond head bobbed back and forth across the grounds beneath them. Looking for the blond head of her cousin to torment, Seth thought with a shudder.

Lilly was the most notorious of Seth's relatives, but that was only because Elyse was kept a closely guarded secret. The entire Gertrude family were mostly kept a closely guarded secret, in fact. Eleanor had had a pre-marital relationship with who would later be engaged to her daughter, but at least she didn't leap onto her mentally-ill cousin in the night and lick him.

Many people said Seth was the image of his paternal grandfather, Seb Crey, but Seth's facial features derived from his mother's younger brother Frederick. Unfortunately, so did Elyse's. Whenever Seth met her, he often felt he was looking at reflection of himself with a wig on and a pair of sizable breasts.

Elyse's face turned upwards.

Seth quickly ducked out of sight.

Frederick waved down at her, a smile plastered onto his face. 'She caught up with us at the docks. Leapt on the first horse she found after the coach left. Wouldn't take no for an answer. Even your grandmother couldn't distract her.'

'Mind you, Granny could repel an audience faster than a skunk's backside,' Seth said.

'Very true,' Fred laughed. He grasped Seth's shoulder again.

Seth realised it was less to show familial affection and more to lever himself onto the seat beside him. 'Your leg no better since the accident?'

'Having an elephant fall on your leg tends to have some long-lasting side effects,' Fred said.

Seth winced. 'Sorry.'

'Whatever happened to that elephant?'

'The dragon found the jackpot and dived for it before we realised what was happening.'

'Ah.' He rubbed his calf, his expression decidedly unsympathetic. 'Can't say I'll miss the big bugger.'

Seth scowled. He loved that elephant.

'How are the kids?' Uncle Fred asked, massaging his knee.

'Great,' Seth beamed. 'I'll take you to meet them as soon as Elyse is out of sight.'

'How horrible are your children?'

'They're not horrible at all! What are you trying to—oh…'

Realisation dawned.

'I could convince them to be *quite* horrible,' Seth said. 'Just as Elyse comes around the corner…'

Frederick grinned.

~

Archie had given up his search for Adrienne and had veered into the dining hall, making for the drinks table. He reached for a cup and was beaten to it by another hand - Despina.

They locked eyes for a full twenty seconds.

'You,' Archie said.

'Shit,' Despina said. She turned and legged it, cup still in hand.

'Oi!' Archie yelled, hurtling after her.

The wine sloshed from side to side, spilling out as the goblet made its swinging descent down the length of the hall.

'I didn't need a drink that badly,' Marbrand said idly.

'Can't talk, fleeing.' Despina thrust the cup into his chest and bolted through the door to his left.

Marbrand peered into the half-empty cup in annoyance.

Archie leapt past, gasping for breath.

~

Ginny lifted a silver saucer in front of her face and huffed rapidly onto the surface. She wiped it with her sleeve until it gleamed and gazed into it, lovingly.

'I so pretty,' she sighed, admiring her reflection.

Uncle Frederick smiled. *Seth's the father, alright.* 'You must be Ginny,' he said, sitting at the dining table in front of her.

Ginny squinted at him. 'Who are you?'

'I'm your Uncle Fred,' he said.

She squinted further. She had a faint notion that 'uncle' meant 'present giver'. 'I like dolphins, you know.'

At the end of the table, Jon spotted the Crey siblings by the canapes. He elbowed his way through the gentry. 'Hel…lo?'

Lilly peered behind Seth's eyepatch. It had soaked through.

'Do you need a hand?' Jon offered.

'No, I got it,' Lilly said, jabbing his eye with a handkerchief.

'OW!' Seth shrieked, slapping her hand away. 'You nearly took out my eye!'

'You can't wear an eyepatch all day, people are sniggering.'

'You were the one who said it was unsightly. I'll have Adrienne look at it later, stop fiddling with my eyelid!'

'I'm only trying to help,' Lilly said in that mild voice she employed when she was highly amused by Seth's distress.

'Well, don't, it's stinging. What do you want?' he said sharply to Jon.

'Nuffin,' Jon said in a small voice. 'Just came to say thanks for not putting me in the nut house.'

Seth's gaze softened. 'No need. I'm sending your father away tomorrow. He's outstayed his welcome anyway, if you ask me—'

'Seth.'

Seth pivoted. 'Adrienne,' he said.

That name sounded familiar. Jon frowned at her, trying to remember.

'I brought my uncle with me,' she said meekly. She glanced at Lilly and stepped slightly to the left.

Lilly had a face like thunder. Jon cowered a bit himself. Lilly with a face like thunder didn't bode well.

'I hope you don't mind,' Adrienne continued to Seth.

'Not at all, no,' Seth said, smiling.

'Is your eye alright?' she asked, squinting at it.

Lilly grunted in disgust and pivoted, making for the wine table.

Jon eyed Seth. Whoever this was, he was certainly very pleased to see her. Maybe it was a good thing. Seth Crey had far too many enemies as it is.

She flushed a light pink as she grew closer to examine his eyelid. Maybe she fancies him, Jon thought. She cleaned his eye with her own handkerchief, considerably more gently than Lilly did.

Jon watched this in amiable silence. Then his expression froze.

Adrienne.

'Seth's tart,' Jimmy had said.

Jon looked Adrienne up and down.

She only looked about sixteen!

And she left court four years ago… which would have made her about twelve years old! Seth was five years older than Jon, who was thirty-two, which means back then Seth would have been—

Jon's jaw dropped in horror.

Seth, oblivious, smiled at Adrienne's tedious small talk.

A crash sounded at the other end of the table. A drunken brawl had broken out. Adrienne rolled her eyes. 'I'd better see if they're alright. Pop down to me later and I'll clean this properly. Have a good night.' She gave him a coy glance.

Seth winked at her. It made Jon's skin crawl.

Adrienne didn't seem to mind. She smiled fondly at him as she turned to leave.

Jon's eyebrows met in distress.

Seth tore his gaze from her retreating form. 'What's with you?'

'How could you?' Jon asked in disbelief. 'After all I've been through?'

Seth blinked. 'You've lost me.'

'You're a… a bloody… kiddy-fiddler!'

Seth spluttered in nonsensical bemusement. 'No I'm not, where did you – what are you talking about?'

Jon jabbed a finger in Adrienne's direction.

Seth shook his head. 'No, no! Your calculations are off. See—'

'She's a little girl!'

'She's twenty-two! She was eighteen when we met! That's… fully grown human age!'

'Kiddy-fiddler,' Jon said in disgust. 'I'm ashamed of you.' He eyeballed Seth before stalking to the courtyard.

'No! Eighteen's allowed!' Seth bellowed after him. 'I was a prince! It was my duty to, to bugger the social minority! It's fairy-tale stuff!'

The term 'kiddy-fiddler' factored into Jon's muttered reply.

'She's twenty-two!' Seth roared.

A yard behind him, Lilly suppressed a snigger. 'The eyeball's probably karma.'

'Shut up,' he snapped. 'She's older than you, so it's allowed.'

'I'm twenty-seven.'

Seth flexed his hands on either side of his sister's head. 'I'm fond of you,' he gritted. 'Don't make me murder you.'

Lilly kissed his forehead and skipped to the dinner table.

Seth grimaced in her wake and sighed heavily, his hands still throttling the air. A finger tapped his shoulder. He pivoted.

'I would like to apply for annual leave, sir,' Jimmy said amiably.

Seth rolled his mouth. 'No.'

'But—'

'Ffft!' He hissed through his teeth and waved Jimmy away.

'Annual leave untaken for twenty years amounts to an owed total leave of—' Jimmy said valiantly.

'I said "ffft"!' Seth snapped, spinning on one heel.

Jimmy watched him hurry off and, after a few false starts, broke out of his etiquette training for long enough to shout, 'I know what you did!'

Seth froze. His heel turned slowly, the other foot dangling a fraction off the floor. 'What do you know?' he said in a low voice.

Jimmy approached. His ankles swayed with each step. 'You can't *fathom* how much I know.'

Seth's eyes narrowed. 'Are you trying to blackmail me?'

'Trying? I think I'm succeeding.'

Seth licked his lips, calculating his next move.

'Excuse me.'

Seth pivoted again. 'What?'

Archie stepped back a bit, Despina's elbow gripped in one hand. 'This girl's been smashing up all my work for the past few days!'

'Bully for her,' Seth snapped.

A finger tapped his shoulder. 'As I was saying about the annual leave,' Jimmy said.

Everyone seemed oblivious to the murderous rage in Seth's eyes.

'My clients are at my throat because of her!' Archie continued, giving Despina's arm a shake.

'I reckon about a year, year and a half,' said Jimmy.

'Two of them came at me with pitchforks the other day!' Archie wailed.

'Somewhere sunny, you know, like Mellier or something. All expenses paid would be nice—'

'—I've never seen anyone so angry about a sock drawer—'

'—one of those big racist hats too, you know the ones, so I don't burn or anything. Expensive, mind, but I s'pect you can afford it—'

A poke landed on his shoulder. 'Happy birthday,' Raphael Emmanuel III said adoringly. 'I brought you a present.' He displayed a miniature portrait of Cienne, looking extremely appealing beneath an elaborate bow tied to the frame.

Seth's eyes flicked around the dining hall. There was no sign of the real-life Cienne anywhere.

Seth glared horribly at the Prophet and screamed into his face.

The Prophet stumbled away and landed on the floor, bringing a cup bearer down with him. He held the painting up, like a make-shift shield.

Seth glowered down at him.

The entire hall watched him in silence.

He stepped over the Prophet and into the courtyard, directly into the path of Adrienne.

'Are you alright?' she asked in concern. 'I heard screaming.'

He softened, remembering how easily his problems had faded away when they were under that tree. 'Come upstairs with me,' he said softly. 'We need to talk, properly, we need to—'

Adrienne blinked. 'I can't. Lilly warned me to leave you alone—'

'Lilly isn't here.'

'Um,' Lilly piped up from between them, 'yes I am.'

Seth planted a palm over her forehead and shoved her away. 'Darling,' he said to Adrienne, brushing her jawline with his fingertips.

She flushed a light pink.

'I'm sorry I pushed you away,' he said.

She touched his hand and he held hers.

'I want to be with you.'

Her eyes flicked upward to meet his. She slid away. 'I shouldn't be here… Cienne will be here somewhere, I can't… she'll…' She hurried off mid-sentence.

'Where are you going?' he breathed out in exhaustion.

Lilly peered around his shoulder to watch Adrienne flee into the entrance hall. 'I'm guessing not *upstairs*.'

Seth faced her irately. 'You've been threatening her.' He advanced on her as she backed towards the wall. 'You threatened her, you threatened *her*, you bloody—' He shoved her collarbone.

Lilly's back collided with the doorframe.

'You are a colossal waste of space!' he barked in her face. 'The father should have shipped you off north years ago like he wanted to!'

Lilly froze, stricken. She met his gaze with a hurt expression.

He held it stiffly before storming into the entrance hall. Everyone wisely decided to part around him. He glimpsed Adrienne dragging Archie away. Archie still had his hand wrapped around Despina's elbow until Adrienne swatted it away.

'She owes me money!' Archie hissed.

'Leave her alone!'

And she was gone.

A finger tapped Seth's shoulder. Corporal Moat stood greasy-faced in front of him, smelling faintly of roast boar.

'Got any more of that pig?' he asked with his mouth full. 'It's lovely.'

Seth eyed the table laden with meat and bread and cheese. There was something distinctly insulting about it. He approached it and, with a mammoth effort and assistance from a helpful Jon, he tipped the table over with a deafening crash.

Cutlery shattered against the flagstones. The noise scored deep lines across Seth's brain, but what was another noise on top of the endless queue of idiots haranguing him? What was another chaos on top of the endless cacophony of light and noise—

'Seth!'

He swung around. Eleanor gawked at him, her brow furrowed.

'What?' he snapped, spreading his arms wide.

She shook her head. 'What's the matter?'

Seth kicked half a bowl across the hall savagely. 'It doesn't matter.' He strode to the front door.

Elyse made to follow.

'You stay the *hell* away from me,' he hissed, unable to manage any more shouting.

She backed off quickly, taking the hint for a change.

Seth vanished out into the darkness.

A moment of stunned silence was suddenly broken by a door opening to the east. 'Surprise!' Cienne exclaimed. She exited the antechamber, laden with a long, wrapped box with a bow on top. She observed the destruction of the buffet. 'Have I missed something?'

~

A knock arrived at the door one bell after midnight. Petunia opened it.

'You look like you walked the entire way here,' she observed. 'Haven't you got horses up there?'

Seth glowered at her, elbowing his way past.

'Your majesty,' Keith said with a very extravagant bow. 'Lilly dead or something? Haven't seen her in a week, that's not like her.'

'Recovering from surgery,' Seth grunted. 'I'm not here about Lilly. I want auburn hair.'

Keith waited patiently for further details. He didn't receive any. 'Just the hair or the lady to go with it?'

'All of them.'

Keith and Petunia exchanged glances.

'I'll see how many I can find,' Petunia said brightly.

~

III

'Don't listen to him, darling,' Eleanor soothed. 'He didn't mean it, he was just upset.'

'The look of pleasure he had when he said it begs to differ,' Lilly growled.

They strolled the grounds early the next morning. The sun beat down on the two as they loitered outside the portcullis, hoping to head Seth off before Cienne caught up with him first.

They watched Adrienne enter her turret absently. Lilly smiled a bit at the sight.

'Spoke to Marbrand earlier,' Lilly said, eyes trained to the turret for the drama to come. 'Apparently Seth had asked him on his way out for directions to the nearest brothel. He sent him to Serpus on foot. Thought it was hilarious.'

'Why didn't he just ride a horse?'

A passing merchant gave the queen dowager an odd glance.

Lilly sighed with the pained expression reserved for her infinitely embarrassing mother. 'Mum, you need to work on the concept of context.'

'You know what I mean,' Eleanor snapped. 'They don't all try to kick him to death. I don't know what he's so frightened of. Even Ginny can canter her little pony.'

'He says it's because their gums show when they grin.'

'Half the girls of Serpus look like that,' Eleanor pointed out, rolling her eyes. 'Anyway, I hope he likes the present Cienne had made for him. It was very expensive.'

'Does it have auburn hair?' Lilly asked.

'Well, no, it's a—'

'He probably won't have time for it until next Sunday, then.'

'Lilly,' she scolded. 'He had a bad day, that's all. He'll snap out of it by teatime.'

'He's been having a bad day since he was thirteen,' Lilly scoffed. 'He needs a slap, king or not king. And I'm inclined to give it to him.' She made a beeline for the keep.

'Why do people having a midlife crisis always have to make a big mess everywhere?' Jon asked in annoyance.

Lilly entered as he swept stray shards of glass shrapnel into a small bucket.

Jimmy stood nearby, setting the newly righted table. 'You wouldn't have a big mess at all if you hadn't helped him tip over the table.'

'I didn't.'

'Of course you didn't,' Jimmy said tiredly. 'How silly of me.'

Lilly eavesdropped on this exchange with a confused expression before deciding she had better things to do than psycho-analyse Mortimer 'Jon' Crey.

'I thought about it,' Jon explained, 'but I decided instead to leave him struggle with it on his own and give up in embarrassment.' He paused. 'No. No, wait, actually, I think I did help. I'm not sure.'

'Is this a "being able to see into the future" thing?' Jimmy asked wryly.

'Yep. I see two of everything that might happen, until I do something that makes one of them happen,' Jon said brightly. 'Like just there when I saw Corporal Moat walk into the pantry – well, until I started chin-wagging with you and forgot about my cleaning. Now he's going to skid on that bit of broken crockery and land on his ass instead.'

Sssleereek!

Moat squealed, his feet flying out from under him.

Jimmy flinched as Moat landed on the flagstones with a dull thud. 'Your delirium is starting to get frightening.'

'So's yours,' Jon retorted. 'Come on, back to it. Seth's on his way through the market as we speak.'

Jimmy rolled his eyes. 'If you say so.'

~

As it happened, Jon was right.

The coach rattled past a row of wooden houses close to the main road through Castlefoot. Sunlight beamed into the carriage window, directly into Seth's eyeline – his hand had become permanently fixed to his brow. He glanced out through watery eyes.

A topless woman leaned out of a low window, waggling her fingers at him.

'Is that a brothel?' Seth asked in a monotone.

Marbrand followed his gaze, oozing innocence. 'Well, would you look at that?'

Seth glared at him. 'On my doorstep.'

'After all those miles,' Marbrand said almost mournfully.

Seth's eyes thinned.

They carried on uphill and into the palace grounds. The portcullis shut after them with a bang. Seth hopped out just as Lilly was entering the armoury. He stared after her for a moment before heading to Adrienne's turret first. 'You're leaving again.'

Adrienne turned, a bag of belongings in her hand. 'Lilly rehired the old medic,' she said flatly. 'He's returning this afternoon. They want me out.'

'She can't do that,' Seth said angrily.

'She already has,' she snapped back. 'And I imagine she had royal permission from the queen.'

Seth watched her helplessly. 'I'll send him away again—'

'There's no point!' Adrienne exploded.

Seth swallowed carefully.

'They'll just fight back another way, you know they will!' She dropped her bag onto the worktable.

'But I *want* you here,' Seth said.

Adrienne arched an eyebrow, her eyes fixed to her bag. 'We all know why that is, I get reminded of it by every member of court.'

Seth heaved a sigh, running his hands through his hair.

'This love story is getting boring,' Geldemar said, hovering invisibly against the sink.

The Bastard glowered at him from the door. 'The three-act structure doesn't *have* to have three sexual acts in each one. Bugger off if you're that bored.'

Geldemar yawned. 'Not a chance. Howie's bound to wander in any minute now. It's his way.'

'I've got someone keeping him occupied already, he's distracted for the meantime.'

'Despina's thievery, yes.' Geldemar paused thoughtfully. 'She's very pretty, Despina, isn't she?'

The Bastard glanced at him. 'And?'

'Just an observation,' he said mildly.

'What are you getting at?'

As their argument progressed, Seth and Adrienne hovered in sullen silence, oblivious.

'You know that isn't why I hired you,' Seth said in a low voice.

'It helps though, doesn't it?' She looked at him. 'I can't do it, Seth. It feels wrong.'

'And being with him feels right?' Seth said. 'Is that why I never see you with him anymore? Or why he wasn't at the party last night?'

'I didn't think you'd want him there—'

'You would still have brought him! But you didn't! Because he's not the same, is he?'

Adrienne made a disgusted noise and sidled past him.

He stepped in front of her. 'I'm—bloody—' He dropped to his knees on top of her toes. 'I'm throwing myself at your feet here, and you're pushing me away!'

Adrienne pulled her feet from under him, seething. 'What I did… I didn't do that for fun, alright? I didn't give your uncle and that priest the benefit of the doubt for nothing. That sacrifice was for him, whether I planned to give the child or not. I'm not going to give up on Howie just because you've decided you want to be with me! He's worth more to me than that!'

'You weren't saying that at the funeral.'

Adrienne stared at him, stricken.

Seth grimaced, his cheeks reddening.

'You started that, so I recall,' she said coldly, her voice thick with tears. 'And you ended it quickly enough as well, once you realised you were too good for me.'

'That's not why I stopped at all,' he said just as coolly.

'I don't care why you stopped,' she said. 'Get this into your thick head. You're more pain than you're worth. I want *nothing* to do with you.'

Seth trembled on the spot. The Bastard didn't think it was anger.

Adrienne eyed him in alarm as tears formed in his eyes.

Seth wiped them away in annoyance. 'Fine,' he said, struggling to speak. 'Your loss.'

Adrienne's expression twisted from anger to pity. 'I'm sorry.'

Seth shook his head slightly, an eyebrow arching. 'It's fine. You're right anyway.' He rose to his feet, brushing his knees off.

Adrienne looked at the ground in remorse.

'He handled that surprisingly well,' Geldemar noted. 'Any of his predecessors would have forced himself on her by now. He took it like a champ.'

'The hell he did,' the Bastard seethed, striding toward them.

Geldemar watched in distaste. 'This isn't going to end well. You'll give her concussion if you keep doing that!'

The Bastard ignored him

'I do love you, you know,' was the last thing Adrienne said of her own volition before a purple light consumed her vision.

The Bastard blinked her eyes into focus.

Seth met her gaze – or what he thought was her gaze, which was actually the Bastard's. 'You do?'

The Bastard lifted Adrienne's face to his.

'To the moon and back,' he said, his voice echoed by Adrienne's.

He kissed Seth hard.

Geldemar grimaced. 'That's just wrong.'

Seth released a breath he didn't know he had been holding. He sandwiched her between himself and edge of the worktable.

Uh-oh, the Bastard thought as his—no, Adrienne's pelvis met the table edge.

Suddenly their lips parted and Seth's tongue started getting *very* friendly.

Not good, the Bastard thought in a panic.

'I told you that was a bad idea,' Geldemar scolded. 'Day one, I told you: never helm the body of a mortal being. It causes all sorts of problems, especially with your poor experience.'

Noted. I won't do it again, I've learned my lesson, the Bastard squeaked internally. He squeaked aloud.

Seth started rooting for the end of Adrienne's skirt.

Make him stop, make him stop, alright, I didn't give him permission to start exploring!

'I can't help you,' Geldemar lied. 'Push him off and run for it!'

No! That's exactly the opposite to the plan! Oh God, what's going on now? What's he doing? What am I doing?

'Creaming, I believe they call it,' Geldemar supplied, with a grin. 'She must be somewhat aware. Come on, time to leave, I think, give them a bit of privacy.'

Hang on, I have to figure out how.

'Hurry, then, Seth won't hold out for much longer,' Geldemar said, thoroughly enjoying himself.

Seth lifted Adrienne onto the worktable on her back.

You know what would help? Getting me out of here instead of throwing out unhelpful comments!

Seth ripped the buttons of her blouse open.

Now what are you doing? the Bastard thought desperately. He lifted Adrienne's head to glare at him in bemusement. *Those aren't for you, what are you—why? Why do people do this?*

'Don't knock it 'til you've tried it, he's in the thralls of—' Geldemar's head jerked to the right mid-sentence. 'You'd want to leave very fast. Someone's coming.'

Please say it's the Prophet, that'll put him right off—

'Worse. Qattren.'

The Bastard swore and finally threw himself from Adrienne's body.

Qattren paused outside the apothecary door.

A translucent Seth Crey sprinted for the nearest well and leapt inside.

Eyes narrowed to slits, Qattren threw open the door.

'Seth Crey!'

Seth bolted upright and peered over his shoulder.

'What were you *doing* to those?' Ron asked in distaste from behind Qattren.

~

Geldemar hovered unseen by the well in the centre of the castle grounds, his arms folded. He called over the splashing within, 'You've been in there for an hour, surely you're clean by now?'

The Bastard scrubbed his chest vigorously with a handkerchief. God alone knew the point of the undead demi-god possessing a handkerchief, Geldemar thought, unless his spirit form was susceptible to colds.

'You deserve it, you know,' Geldemar said, his voice ringing with condescendence. 'It was you who tricked him into it, not the other way around.'

'I'll never be clean!' the Bastard exploded. His voice rattled out of the well, followed by deep echoes.

'If you insist on abusing your power like that, I suggest possessing someone who doesn't have a chance of being molested mid conversation.'

'I didn't deserve it!' the Bastard whimpered, still half a conversation behind.

Geldemar paused, giving him a moment to catch up.

Finally, the Bastard's eyes lit up. 'You're right,' he said. 'We need to work on someone else. Someone male... or little...'

'And preferably related to him, just in case,' Geldemar added.

The Bastard leapt to his feet.

'Russell.'

~

Seth sat crouched on the edge of his throne, looking sulky. The polished mahogany gleamed around him and under his elbows, spiralling ropes of faux snakeskin.

This isn't right, he thought to himself. The Creys were the continent's longest reigning authority. Sitting on the throne informed everyone that you were one of the most revered powers in the entire world while they stood in front of you as your lowly worshipper. Right now, he felt like he was perched on the naughty step in front of his mum instead.

'What were you doing?' Qattren said.

Seth glowered at her through his eyelashes.

She tapped her foot on the ground.

'Making love,' he said.

'Were you now?'

He eyeballed her stormily. 'Actually, you interrupted at the crucial moment, but the intention was plain.'

'Blatantly.'

Ron sat against the wall, nursing what Jimmy called a special cup of tea. *No wonder his liver's shot*, Seth thought nastily.

'This won't do, you know,' Qattren said.

'What business is it of yours?'

'My husband is friends with your sister. It would be nice for him to roam the grounds unmolested.'

'It's not him I intend to molest.'

'No, Ron's fully grown,' Jon said from the kitchens.

'SHUT YOUR TRAP!' Seth howled.

Qattren giggled. 'Oh, dear,' she said with a smile. 'Jon does have a point. You've been married for longer than she's been alive.'

Seth seethed. 'Just because you look twenty-five doesn't mean you are. Remind me: how much older than my dear old granddad are you?'

'Mmm, good point,' she said. 'Having said that, he wasn't in a relationship at the time.'

'Yes, he was,' Seth said, 'he was married to my grandmother.'

'Yes, but their marriage was purely political,' Qattren said. 'Ask your grandmother, we got on like a house on fire. She was thankful to have the man away from her, they couldn't stand each other. You and Cienne, on the other hand, are quite different.'

'A marriage is a marriage,' Seth said stubbornly. 'If he can cop off with another woman, so can I.'

'Fair enough. So long as Cienne feels the same way,' Qattren said. 'I presume you have discussed this with her? As opposed to creeping about behind her back?'

Seth flushed. 'I don't want to hurt her.'

'I'll take that as a no,' Qattren drawled.

'You don't understand, if I tell her I'm in love with someone else, she'll—'

'She might be a bit of a hothead, but she has the capacity to be reasonable,' Qattren said. 'She knows what she signed up for. She's been taught by everyone she knows to expect to share you. She birthed two of your children. Give her the respect she deserves and tell her the truth. She can retire into the countryside away from the two of you with her dignity intact.'

'I don't want to. I want to be with Cienne as well.'

Qattren lifted an eyebrow. 'Ah. I hadn't realised you were building a *collection.*'

Seth gritted his teeth. 'I want her to be happy. I want to make *both* of them happy.'

'So do I,' Qattren said. 'I like Cienne *and* Adrienne. Which is why I think you should be honest with them. But since you don't want to do that, I warn you not to go near Adrienne or there will be consequences. She has her own boyfriend. Let him make her happy.'

'Ah,' Seth said, dripping with sarcasm, 'so it's "do as I say, not as I do", is it?'

'Yes,' she said breezily. 'Or I'll set your bed on fire.'

He flung her a withering glance. 'What if Cienne's *in* it?'

'Oh, I don't care who's in it, it's to be done out of principle.'

'And I'm supposed to believe you'll follow through on that threat like you have the other twenty dozen times?'

She merely pointed at a tapestry running down the wall between two windows. It was the one where the colour blue was used much in abundance. Seth got the point. Fire was not something she was afraid of employing.

'You can't force me to choose between the women I love,' Seth argued. 'I love Cienne obviously, but I love Adrienne too.'

Qattren rolled her eyes.

'She found me in my hour of need. It was *fate.*'

'Really.' Her voice was flat.

'Haven't you read a romance novel in your entire life?'

'I have. They bore me.'

Seth made a face at her. 'You're just bitter and alone, aren't you?'

'The world's much clearer that way. Have a nice day—but not *too* nice.'

Seth scowled at her as she strolled to the entrance.

Ron, still cradling his cup, rose to follow her.

'That's quite enough of that for you.' She removed the cup from Ron's hands.

Ron's face fell. He thought he and Jimmy had been discreet.

'I believe I saw Lilly enter the armoury a short while ago,' Qattren said.

'Instead of disintegrating your liver *again*, you might join her for a catch-up?'

Ron glared at her and did as she bid.

~

IV

In the armoury, Lilly poured through her father's personal collection. King Theo had fancied himself a connoisseur: in his sixty years of life, he had amassed an article of every type of hand weapon imaginable, from tiny throwing daggers to ornate swords to his own favourite, the execution axe. These she took the task of maintaining, despite their lack of use – lifting each item from its display hooks, testing the sharpness and giving them a polish with a soft cloth.

Lilly lifted a blade and slid it from the sheath to gaze at it – a fine damask steel. No. This one was coming inside. She closed the sheath with reverence and, carefully, placed it on the counter beside her.

Ron entered and placed both hands over her eyes.

'There's only one person stupid enough to blind me in a room full of weapons,' she said with a smile. She faced him, exchanging a brief hug. 'I didn't see you last night. Were you at the party?'

'We arrived just as the table was knocked over. Qattren decided we should keep our heads down, in case we were next.' He hesitated. 'I was going to go see if you were alright, but you looked angry, so…'

'It's okay,' Lilly said with a brief smile. 'I'm always angry.'

Someone cleared his throat at the door.

'I should leave you two to talk,' Ron said quietly, backing out of the armoury. 'I'll catch you in a few…'

Lilly turned her back on Seth and avidly examined her father's favourite sword again.

Seth leaned his back on the doorframe. 'Are you alright?'

She ignored this, running a hand down the sheath. 'Have fun at the brothel earlier?'

'No,' he said sourly. 'They all had the pox.'

Lilly pointed outside. Seth followed her finger to Adrienne's turret.

'I meant that one,' she drawled.

Seth frowned at her. 'That's not fair.'

She snorted. 'A little boy died by her hand and me *calling her names* isn't fair.'

'That wasn't her fault. She explained that to me.'

'Oh, good. Since you're in the mood for explanations, you might have a conversation with Cienne about what you've been doing sneaking around.'

Seth bristled. 'What business is that of yours?'

Lilly swivelled around.

'Cienne's the closest I have to a sister,' she snarled. 'D'you think I like pretending I don't know what's going on whenever you disappear? She tries really hard to please you, Seth, and you go and—'

Seth snorted. 'Yeah, punching me in the face and making my eyelid swell up with pus really shows how hard she tries.'

'Then tell her not to! Talk to her, for God's sake! She's not that bad! If you sat her down and *told* her it was upsetting you, she'd stop. But no, you go and cop off with a child murderer who'd probably have killed you long ago if she was in Cienne's shoes and told everyone you'd had a nasty case of gonorrhoea.'

'She's not a monster,' Seth snarled.

'Neither is Cienne. You're just painting her that way to explain away your wandering knob-end.'

'This coming from the tart who went "pirating" with three blokes the other year,' Seth blurted.

Lilly shot him a hard glance. 'Tart?'

'Yeah,' he said, nodding. 'That's what you are. A tart, pretending to be one of the lads. Poor old Orl never stood a chance.'

Her upper lip twitched. Before Seth could blink, Lilly had drawn King Theo's sword.

Seth just about had the presence of mind to grasp the nearest blade to hand. The hilt wobbled in his grasp, causing the still-sheathed blade to sway.

She launched herself at him, her blade level to his throat. He ducked and deflected. Lilly's edge cut into the leather sheath, leaving a gash. Lilly staggered back half a step and approached again. Her sword twirled in her right hand, her left hand gripping the sheath. Seth retreated out of the armoury with his hands wrapped tightly around the heavy sword. He staggered to the right.

Lilly struck again, missing his head by a hand's breadth.

He planted one knee into the ground to steady himself. He didn't have a chance, he realised, holding the sword horizontally above his head with trembling arms. He'd opened an old wound in mentioning the dead and it was bleeding pure fury. And fury just made her blows more accurate.

Lilly glowered at him, her upper lip raised. 'Do you even know what you're doing with that thing?'

'Lilly, stop,' Seth said feebly.

Lilly laughed briefly. 'No!' She sprinted at him, arching her sword down. He blocked her blow with a squeal. 'You've had your way with no arguments for far too long,' she snarled, swinging her sword over her shoulder again.

He deflected her strike and held her sword back. He rose slowly, both hands straining on the sheath. People stopped to stare at them, including Stan and Ron.

'Lilly—' Seth began.

Lilly raised her right leg and kicked his chest, knocking the breath from his lungs with a dull *snap*. He crumpled to the ground, the sword – which he still hadn't had a chance to unsheathe – skidding across the gravel.

'You're right about him being a rubbish father to you,' she said. 'He didn't beat you half enough.'

He stumbled to his feet, gasping. She swung at him again. The steel blurred and sliced his forearm open, making him cry out. She sheathed her sword as he stepped away from her, cradling his bloody arm. She advanced, holding the covered weapon in both hands, and butted his nose with the hilt.

Seth toppled into the dust.

Lilly beckoned at the side-lines with one finger. Stan stepped forward obediently. She thrust her sword into Stan's hands and stood over Seth.

Seth knelt on the ground, clutching his nose.

She dropped behind his back and squeezed his ribs, making him hiss. 'I don't like seeing you suffer,' she murmured into his ear. 'But you brought this on yourself. Break off whatever's going on with Adrienne or I'm telling Cienne everything. Do you understand?'

Seth choked on the blood from his nose.

She gave him another squeeze, making him yelp.

'Fine!' he gargled.

'And I want an apology for what you said about Orl,' she snarled.

It came in a faint, shrill whisper. ''Mmzzorry. Bleeze virgive me.'

She kissed his temple and left him to it, waving the spectators away.

'I was going to ask if you wanted to visit Howie with me,' Ron said, 'but I'm scared you'll do something horrible to him.'

Lilly laughed. Her laugh turned into a wince as her gait gave way to a slight limp.

'Easy on the swording from now on, eh?' Stan said. 'You're still recovering from that hole in your gut, remember?'

'Hard to forget that, mate.'

Ron glanced from one to the other, nonplussed.

She slowed to a halt, leaning on her knees, and quickly relayed the story of the stomach surgery. 'I would like to see Howie, though,' Lilly said. 'I am technically his sister and he's the one relative I have who's never given me cause to hit him.'

'I like him, too,' Stan said. 'He's a really nice bloke.'

'I like Seth too, mind,' Ron said.

'Why? I don't. No offence, Lilly.'

'You're alright,' she said to Stan. 'Only reason I didn't gut him back there is because I don't like to bear a grudge. It's weird, though. There's something about the two of them, I think Ron's the only person who likes them both the same. Everyone always loves one and hates the other.'

'Except for Vladimir,' Ron said. 'He hated them both equally.'

'Must be a Horne thing,' Stan mused.

'He wasn't a Horne,' Ron said in a thorny tone.

Lilly and Stan froze for a moment.

'Except instead of hating Howie, most people just forget about him,' Lilly said, opting to skip that entire exchange completely.

'I'll confess I did, the last couple of years or so,' Ron agreed.

Lilly gazed into the horizon pensively. 'Me too.' She paused, touching her abdomen carefully. 'Maybe we can forget about him for one more day,' she said, leaning on Stan's shoulder.

~

Cienne was stitching a painstaking embroidery of some flowers as Seth passed through the drawing room. His face was bright crimson, and not because he was embarrassed.

'Seth Crey, what the hell have you done to your face?' She bolted after him, into the bedchamber to the ewer.

'It broke,' Seth grunted, dabbing his nose with a wet cloth.

Cienne snatched his face in both hands.

Seth screamed.

'Something your father taught me the first time I broke your nose,' she said by way of explanation, releasing him.

Blood poured down his chin. Seth hastily scooped it up with the cloth. 'The first time?'

'Don't ask.'

Seth released a shrill breath, his hands wrapped around the newly righted cartilage.

Cienne guided him to the settee by one hand. 'Tell me what happened.'

'Lilly happened.' He dabbed blood from his upper lip.

'Hmm, I should have guessed,' she said dully.

Seth sighed through his mouth. 'Why didn'd my fawdder teach me how doo use a sword?'

'He started to,' Cienne said, perching on the chair and pulling him down beside her. 'And then you got ill. I suppose you can blame me for that one.'

Seth slumped into the soft two-seater, flattening Cienne's embroidery.

She tugged it free to finish a long stitch, colouring a pink petal. 'This seems the opportune moment for you to open your birthday present.'

Seth frowned. 'My birrday was weeks ago, wad took you so long?'

'Our children are very talented at hide and seek,' Cienne said cynically. 'It took me a quarter of a year just to keep the bow on.' She gestured to the present, on the top shelf of a bookcase, where Ginny and Russell couldn't reach it.

Clutching his broken rib, Seth gingerly lifted himself to his feet. After deciding that the shelf was too high for him in this state, Cienne rose to assist him.

Together, they lowered the present onto the dining table. Seth pulled the cloth covering open. He lifted the lid on an ornate mahogany box and gaped inside in awe. 'It's a broadsword.'

Snakeskin covered the hilt of the steel blade. The guard had been crafted into a serpent's yawning jaws. It reminded him of the sword his father had given to Howard Rose-Prick, the one Qattren had shattered into a million pieces.

He lifted it out and slid the blade from its sheath. All that was different was that the glass blade was replaced with ordinary steel. It was no less fine for all that – as far as Seth's lack of expertise could tell. He slipped the sheath closed and gazed at Cienne. 'Thank you.'

Cienne grinned and lifted her shoulders. 'Do you like it?'

'I love it,' he whispered, stroking the lines and edges. 'I'll have to learn how to use it.'

'I have just the man for the job,' she beamed.

~

'They claim the debt is entirely our own,' Lilly said, 'but there's no record of what exactly this loan has been paying for.'

A sea of green gardens surrounded them. The archery field lay to their left, a yawning expanse of green stripes, abandoned in favour of the weekly hunt. To their right, the now-dubbed Guardhouse stood tall at the bottom of the spiral gardens – the elaborate circles of flowerbeds and gravel paths that, until three years ago, had decorated the front of the Keep Chapel.

They sat in the gazebo, in plain sight of everyone. They had established early on that meeting in private attracted all experimentation of eavesdropping, so they pretended to have tea round the back of the palace instead. This was an unusual sight in itself. The nearest Lilly ever came to having tea was throwing a teapot at someone's face during combat.

'And they're still pinning the blame on everything that happened in the Dead Lands,' Lilly continued. 'Funny thing is, they never wrote any of these transactions down, not in any substantial detail.'

'That's because our treasury didn't pay for any of those things,' Eleanor said crossly. 'The dragons were gifts from the Dead Lands, and the wedding was organised by Karnak. He paid for everything. The council must think we have the memory of a gnat! What does Seth think of this?'

'Er… we haven't told him yet,' Lilly said. 'He's very fragile, isn't he? We don't want him getting upset.'

'You don't want him getting upset?' said Eleanor wryly. 'You beat him with a sword as little as two hours ago.'

'Yeah, and now I'm over it,' Lilly said, examining her nails. 'He's learned his lesson. Doesn't mean we have to feud over it. Anyway, broken noses heal. Crippling debt doesn't.'

'He's the king! We can't molly-coddle him forever!'

'What can he do about it anyway?' Lilly asked with a shrug. 'We can hang the perpetrators, but the debt's still gonna be there. We're skint, Mum. They've fleeced us completely.'

Jimmy arrived with a tea tray, looking uncertain. 'Jon told me to come here straight away,' he said, glancing back at him. 'Any idea why?'

'Didn't he tell you?' Lilly asked.

'He said something along the lines of "if I tell you, you'll hit me",' he said, setting the tray on a garden table between the three of them. 'What's this all about?'

Lilly took a breath, thinking back on his desired annual leave. 'You'd better sit down.'

Jimmy frowned, lowering himself on a seat beside Lilly.

Lilly exhaled in one breath. 'We're in debt by about forty-five million pounds.'

Jimmy blinked rapidly. 'We're in debt by…'

'… forty-five…'

'… *million* pounds?'

Lilly nodded. 'We'll have to tighten our belts a bit.'

Jimmy squinted at her, trying to process this information. 'Forty-five… million pounds,' he managed after a lengthy pause between the words. 'But… what about my annual leave?'

Lilly patted his shoulder.

'How did this happen?' Jimmy whispered, distraught.

'That's what we want to find out,' Eleanor said. 'Can you draft a new budget for the household?'

'I suppose so,' Jimmy said with a heavy sigh. 'Can I at least put a public hanging on the budget? I could make a day of that, bring in a fortune. We could sell souvenirs.'

'Actually, we, can't,' Lilly said.

Jimmy and Eleanor pivoted to face her.

'I've been keeping an eye on them while everyone was busy with Seth's party,' Lilly said, 'but I lost them three days ago. It looks like they've done a runner.'

Jimmy's face twisted.

'As soon as we find them,' Lilly soothed, 'you can be the first to destroy them.'

He picked up an empty teacup and threw it at the doorframe. It shattered on impact and the pieces flew across the gravel.

'You know you'll be the one clearing that up, don't you?' Lilly said after a moment.

Jimmy made an exasperated sound and threw his gaze to the heavens.

~

V

Having cleaned as much evidence of his thrashing from his face as he could and with a fresh change of clothes, Seth descended to the courtyard.

After the drama at the armoury, most of the castle residents hovered at that end of the grounds in the event of a repeat performance. The courtyard around them was serene, the only signs of life being the distant motion of butterflies spiralling around the flowerbeds and the gentle sound of water flowing from the fountain's serpent head. Marbrand waited by the fountain, brandishing a broadsword of his own.

'I thought you were night staff?' Seth asked. He followed the path to the ring of gravel where the fountain, a concrete snake with its head rearing, sat in the centre, cheerfully spurting water skyward.

'So did I,' Marbrand said cynically. 'Yet, here we are. Show us your sword, then.'

Seth grasped the hilt in his left hand and pulled it from the scabbard. His rib gave out at the weight, and he dropped it to the ground with a gasp,

230

clutching his side with both hands. Marbrand stepped forward to peer down at it.

'It's a fine sword,' he said evenly.

'It's too heavy,' Seth complained.

'You're injured,' Marbrand said. 'Maybe we should leave you some time to get over the thrashing your baby sister dealt you. Sword-work isn't for the feeble.'

Seth scowled. 'Feeble,' he muttered. 'If you're going to be so condescending, I'll take my business elsewhere.' He turned back to the main hall.

'Oh, alright then,' Marbrand said, sheathing his sword and lifting a dagger from his belt to pick his nails. 'But having your ass kicked by Theo Crey's daughter is one thing. Having it kicked by the enemy, however...'

Seth paused, one foot poised in the air.

'... you won't be able to dismiss him when he's being condescending. And if you thought *that* was a public beating—'

'Oh, alright,' Seth said, 'let's get on with it, then.' He returned to his sword to lift the hilt. He hissed through his teeth, a hand pressed to his side.

'Best start with footwork, shall we?' Marbrand said.

Seth exhaled and nodded. He took a few paces away from the sword and faced Marbrand, nodding for him to continue.

Cienne perched on a bench on the other side of the fountain, watching with a smile.

Marbrand guided him patiently through the desired stance, pointing at his knees and heels. Seth followed along as best he could. Marbrand appeared to approve.

'... same principle with retreating, only reversed: slide your front foot back, out of the way of your opponent's sword: that's it, and reset your stance: perfect. This is advance and retreat: that's why you do when you have time to be careful, but since you have a grating personality, this will seldom be the case. Lunging is what you'll need: same principle, only instead of sliding and stepping forward, you're going to jump for—'

Something belted the back of Seth's head with a *poing*.

'Look what the lads made!' Elliot said brightly. He snatched up the ball, which had rebounded from Seth's head and bounced in his direction.

Seth pivoted angrily.

A roughly spherical ball of leather sat on the palm of Elliot's right hand. Judging by the way it had left the king's head intact, Marbrand deduced that it was full of air.

'It's a ball,' Elliot said superfluously.

'So I see,' Marbrand said slowly.

'The lads have been playing this game they've invented with it. It's great fun.'

'How do you play?' Seth asked, his footwork lessons forgotten.

'You kick it at people's heads as hard as you can, from what I gather,' Marbrand said flatly. 'They're not great at the concept of an objective. Come on, let's keep going.'

'But we're just about to start a game,' Elliot said. 'We need two more players, if you want a go, your majesty.'

'Alright, then,' Seth said, following Elliot.

'I thought you wanted training?' Marbrand bellowed after him.

'I'm taking a short break,' Seth called over his shoulder. 'Stretching my legs.'

'You aren't, I'm off to bed!' Marbrand snapped irately. 'It's not my job to wait around after you, not in the daytime!'

Seth ignored him, scooping the ball from Elliot's arm and turning it over in his hands. 'So how do you play?'

It turned out that the great minds who had created this ball game didn't actually know how to play it either. Seth stood at the foot of an empty dog cage and was told to guard it from the ball as everyone else attempted to kick it past him. Then they stopped five seconds later to decide whether points were to be awarded to each player or two designated teams before fighting over who was going to be the second cagekeeper and commencing a fist fight on whether touching the ball with hands was allowed.

On the other side of the keep, Russell happily paraded a custard slice his grandmother had given him. A man approached him and, making sure no one else was watching, transformed into his father. Russell gawked up at him and briefly wondered whether a story like this would warrant another cake from his grandmother.

'Don't you tell her anything!' the Bastard hissed at him.

232

Russell simply stared wide-eyed at him.

The Bastard sat cross-legged on the ground in front of his brother, adjusting his black leotard self-consciously.

'I know this will sound completely unbelievable, right,' he began, 'but I'm not your father.'

Russell's mouth hung open slightly. 'Is Dimmy my father?'

The Bastard blinked. 'Jimmy?'

'The cook heard it from one of his sauces. I think the cheese one.'

'Sources, you mean. No, Jimmy isn't your father. If he was, you'd be a lot better-looking.'

Russell blinked.

'No, what I mean is,' the Bastard continued, 'your dad is your father, but I'm not him, I'm someone else.'

The boy blinked again. His expression had somehow become even *more* blank.

The Bastard blinked too, trying to explain. 'I... he... the king,' he raised his eyebrows.

'Daddy,' Russell prompted.

'Yes, him... I'm not him, he's over there, playing ball.' He waved in the vague direction of the archery field, where a continued attempt at football was being held.

Russell looked confused. 'But you look like Daddy.'

'But I'm not though, I'm someone else,' the Bastard said fervently.

'But you look like him!' Russell whined, bouncing on his heels.

'I'm not him, though, I just look—' he said feebly.

'You're trying to twick me!'

'I'm not trying to trick you, no, don't cry,' the Bastard whined, patting the boy's shoulders, 'don't, look, come here, look, see this?' He traced the scar down the side of his nose. 'Daddy doesn't have this, does he? So I can't be Daddy, can I?'

Russell looked balefully at him. 'But you look just like him!' He put his arms around the Bastard's neck, distressed.

'I know, I'm distraught about it,' the Bastard said dryly. 'Look, look at me. What colour are his eyes?'

'Boo, like mine,' Russell said immediately, looking into the Bastard's

233

eyes. 'Oh.' He squinted. 'They're gay.'

'Grey,' he corrected.

'Oh.' He hesitated. 'Why do you look like Daddy?'

'Well,' he began.

Russell dropped himself into the Bastard's lap.

The Bastard eyed him in awkward silence. 'Right. You know how you're Ginny's brother?'

'Yah. We have different bedrooms now.'

'Great for you. I'll just clarify, Jimmy isn't your father, alright?'

'Okay,' Russell said dutifully.

'Alright? So you and Ginny have the same Daddy, right?'

He nodded.

'Well, he's my father too.'

The child looked at him as if he'd claimed he was a rabbit. 'Huh?'

'I'm your big brother.'

He face crumpled. 'But I'm the brother.'

'Yes, but you have one of your own,' the Bastard said patiently.

'I don't have to share with Ginny?'

'N—well—no mate, I'm all yours,' he relented to shorten the discussion.

He hugged the Bastard again, much to his discomfort. 'Have we got the same mummy too?' he asked in the Bastard's ear.

'No, I had a different one,' he muttered. 'She… threw me away… when I was small.'

Russell pulled away in horror. 'She put you in the bin?'

'Kinda. I'm a ghost.'

'But you're real.' He poked him in the eye to verify.

'Ow! I'm a clever ghost,' he said, rubbing his left eye.

'Okay.' A pause. 'Ginny's scared of ghosts. Can we scare her?'

'In a while,' the Bastard sighed, noting the sibling animosity for future reference.

This seemed to satisfy him. He wrapped his arms around the Bastard's neck again and gave him a dribbly kiss on the cheek, to his distaste. 'I won't put you in the bin.'

'Oh, good,' the Bastard said painfully.

'And Mummy won't either—'

'No! You can't tell Mummy about me!'

'Why not?' Russell squeaked.

'Because... well, she'd tell Daddy, wouldn't she?'

'Why can't we tell Daddy?'

'Because... because he let my mummy put me in the... bin.'

Anger crossed the toddler's features. 'What a bastard.'

'Don't use that word!' the Bastard scolded, harsher than he intended. 'It's a very nasty word.'

'Sorry.' His eyes brimmed again.

The Bastard softened a bit. 'Well, it's alright, he is one.'

Russell gave him a small smile. 'What's your name?'

'The B... oh. I, er, never got one.'

'You can share mine,' he said kindly. 'And my cake.' And he split his custard slice in half, pressed the bigger bit into the Bastard's hand and left happily.

The Bastard stared after him blankly, then looked at the slice in the palm of his hand.

'What a sweet little boy,' Geldemar said fondly from behind him.

'Who'd have thought he came out of Seth Crey's willy,' the Bastard agreed. He scrutinised the cake with something of a smile.

'Yeah.' Geldemar paused for dramatic effect. 'Except you've forgotten something, haven't you?'

'What's that?'

'You forgot to ask him to spy on Seth,' he hissed.

The Bastard froze. 'Ah, shit!'

They vanished into Sal'plae.

Corporal Moat sat dizzily in the spot the Bastard left him in, rubbing his head as the hair atop it turned from blond back to dark brown. He glanced down at half a custard slice in his hand, nonplussed, before pressing it into his mouth with a shrug.

~

Lilly sat at what was undoubtedly the world's shoddiest table. It listed to one side, sending a dribble of tea from the rim of Lilly's cup into a slow roll across the surface. She lifted the cup to take a sip. The table wobbled, two of the legs rattling.

Lilly frowned at it, distrustfully. 'You made this yourself, you say?'

Howie grinned and nodded in the same way Seth did when he was congratulated on the twins – as though it was talent and hard work that resulted in any success achieved as opposed to pure, blind luck.

'I'm a full-time carpenter now,' he said brightly. 'I get a lot of business out here.'

'Different client every day, I imagine,' Stan said.

Lilly leaned her elbows on the tabletop. It creaked dangerously. She wisely removed them with haste.

'No two the same,' Howie said, oblivious.

The table was one of many artefacts in the cottage that Howie had crafted himself – and he had evidently developed a unique style. Haphazard upholstery and wobbly chairs surrounded them in the cramped living area. Lilly knew from previous comparison that in terms of personality, Howie was Seth's – mostly – polar opposite. She wondered what Seth was so talented at that made Howie so awful at carpentry. Alienating people, probably.

'How's Adrienne settling in?' Howie said.

Lilly winced. 'We had to... dole out redundancies,' she lied. 'Sorry.'

A sullen expression fell over Howie's face. 'Oh. I s'pose you have your reasons.'

They sat in silence for a moment.

Howie's expression went vacant. 'Would anyone like a beer?'

Lilly's gaze darted from Stan's to Ron's momentarily.

'Yes please,' Stan said uncertainly.

Howie smiled brightly and rose.

Lilly, Stan and Ron leaned towards each other.

'Does he seem slightly more... dead around the eyes than usual?' Lilly asked them.

'Definitely,' Ron agreed.

'Dead as a doornail,' Stan concurred.

'The old Howie would never offer the woman who sacked Adrienne a drink,' said Ron.

'Well, he probably would have,' Stan said, 'but he would have had a funny look to give her first.'

'Yeah, but, you know, politely,' said Lilly.

Howie returned with four mugs. 'I'll just put these here while I run and get—'

The table legs collapsed under the weight of the mugs. They tilted completely sideways, depositing the tabletop onto the flagstones with a clatter.

The trio winced, lifting their hands out of the way.

'Oh,' said Howie.

Lilly patted his arm. 'It's alright. You want a hand fixing it?' *It might have a chance of staying upright then*, she thought treacherously.

'Yes, please,' he said with a grateful smile.

They upturned the table together. Howie watched with a blank expression as Lilly waited for instructions. Establishing that they weren't going to get any, Stan said slowly, 'Shall we get the glue, then?'

'Yes, I'll get it,' said Howie. He crossed the room to the shed outside, passing a glue pot sitting on the kitchen counter as he went.

'Now I'm worried,' Ron said.

Lilly went to fetch the glue.

Someone cleared their throat behind them. 'Can I help you?'

Lilly made a face.

Howie poked his head in the back door with a grin. 'Hello, you. How was your morning?'

'I was sacked, so. You know. Not great,' Adrienne said sharply. 'What have you done to the table now?'

'It just needs gluing, I just need to find where I put the—OI!'

A girl's form blurred through the sitting room, carrying several of Howie's tools.

'You again,' Adrienne snarled. She stuck her foot out.

The girl squealed and tilted face-down into the dust, tools flying.

Adrienne snatched the back of her cloak and jerked her upright.

Lilly squinted. 'Despina?'

Despina's eyes widened. 'Bollocks.'

∼

'Jon?' Jimmy said. 'You haven't turned to bestiality, have you?'

Jon glared at him. The lamb craned its neck upwards as far as it possibly could, eyes bulging. Jon put the bottle in its mouth absently.

'No,' he said. 'I'm just looking after him, that's all.'

Jimmy made a face.

Rays of sunlight lanced in from the open balcony doors of the top floor's guest apartment. The sparsely decorated drawing room had been converted into a makeshift paddock. The smell of sheep shit assaulted him from the rushes underfoot – it staggered into his nostrils and plummeted into his lungs with each breath, so potent it was practically tangible. Jimmy's only guarantee that he wasn't in fact eating the shit was the hand he had pressed against his lower face.

Jimmy watched the lamb drink, its long neck undulating. 'But… why? Why did you… why… just, just why?'

'I had a vision saying that I'd need a small animal at some point in the near future,' Jon said patiently. 'So I saw him and I thought, might as well get it now and have it ready for when I need it.'

'Need it for what?'

'Dunno,' Jon said brightly. 'He's cute though, innee?' He rubbed the lamb's head with his free hand.

Jimmy spluttered for another moment before deciding, wisely, to ignore it. 'Right.' He glowered out at the sunlight. 'Honestly,' he said in disgust. 'The sun's splitting the stones out there and I'm going to be stuck in here all day, drafting this stupid budget. I've had to give everyone a pay cut, including myself, and we're still only just scraping by. I'm poorer than a church mouse.'

'I'm getting by just fine,' Jon said. 'If you didn't spend it all on fancy clothes, you'd be loaded.'

Jimmy lifted an eyebrow. 'Doubt it.' He spotted a copper tin on the writing desk beside him and peered inside.

'Seth copped on to them yet?' Jon asked, feeding the lamb with a look of serenity.

Jimmy spotted a pile of coins inside and, surreptitiously, palmed all of them. 'Nope. He's too busy off chasing skirt. Suits me, if I'm honest. If he had a say, he'd have me work for free, the bastard.' Jimmy grimaced at him.

Jon cooed at the creature as if it was an infant.

'You're cleaning this up yourself, I hope you realise that,' Jimmy said with disdain.

'Fine by me,' said Jon. He beamed at the little sheep and stroked its ears back.

~

VI

'So you were sword-fighting again, then,' Lilly said with a grin.

Seth scowled at her from the middle of the kitchen, a bag of ice from the pantry pressed against his temple. 'Actually, Corporal Moat kicked me in the head playing football,' he grunted. 'At least he didn't break my ribs and dislocate my nose, like someone I could mention.'

Lilly snorted, decidedly un-remorseful.

Seth leaned his free hand on his right knee and crouched at Despina's feet. She sat meekly on a stool in the middle of the kitchens, her hands folded between her knees.

Adrienne stood behind her, looking irate.

'What are you up to?' he asked, more out of curiosity than suspicion.

'I fancy him,' she said, her expression impassive. 'A lot. He's very handsome.'

'Now, I don't believe that for a second,' Seth said, 'because you're quite intelligent, and intelligent people don't fancy men with conversation as stimulating as a dry peanut.'

'I'm sorry?' Adrienne said.

Seth swallowed. 'Usually,' he amended.

Adrienne's left eyebrow rose in disgust.

'So what are you doing, stealing from him?' said Seth.

'And vandalising our property,' Adrienne piped up. 'And my uncle's.'

'Why, do you fancy the uncle as well?' Seth asked playfully.

Despina suppressed a snigger. 'No, I don't fancy anyone. We need the money.'

'But you don't take anything!' Adrienne shouted. 'You just smash up our stock and hide his tools everywhere! And you and your father are both in the employ of the king, what could you possibly need money for?'

'We fancy getting a conservatory done,' Despina said, cool as a breeze.

'You're lucky the king doesn't confiscate your home to reimburse us,' Adrienne said haughtily.

'That's excessive esteem for someone he sacked this morning,' Despina said.

'Oh! One-nil to Marbrand,' Lilly intoned.

'Shut up,' Seth snapped, pointing at Lilly.

Lilly held her hands up in surrender.

'Your father never mentioned anything about money,' Seth said to Despina. 'Usually he'd be pestering for a pay rise.'

'He has a gambling problem, my liege,' she lied easily. 'He would rather this issue not be brought to light either, if it please you.'

My liege. If it please you. Seth noted the use of etiquette in silence.

'She needs to be punished,' Adrienne said angrily.

'Oh, shut up, you're not the Queen of Adem yet,' Lilly said in disgust. 'They're good people. She's just looking out for her old man.'

Seth frowned at Despina.

Despina met his searching gaze with a gulp.

'Adrienne, can you wait outside?'

'I won't leave until I see that she's being punished—'

'You were told to piss off,' Lilly said coldly. 'You can either leave via the door behind you or the window behind me, your choice.'

Adrienne glowered at her, slamming the main door shut behind her.

Lilly met Seth's gaze and shook her head. 'Gammy eye notwithstanding, even you can do better.'

Seth shot her a foul look and grabbed a stool. It screeched against the flagstones to a halt and he sat, forearms braced against his knees and gaze trained to Despina's. 'Why are you really distracting him?'

Despina stared at him in a daze. She could see now why the Bastard had taken his appearance. Seth didn't strike much of a figure by himself, but put some scars across his face and a dark edge in his eyes and he'd look quite dangerous. His eyes were different, she noticed. Seth's were close-set and blue while the Bastard's were grey and cold. The variance gave their faces completely different contexts.

She was told Seth had a wandering eye, but it appeared to have developed a severe case of pinkeye of late. It crisped up around the eyelid and glistened hideously. It wasn't wandering now, she saw – both eyes were fixed firmly on her own. She wondered if the Bastard was watching her too, from somewhere.

She wondered if he was looking at her now.

She realised with a start that Seth's expression had grown cold.

'When you're quite finished staring at my crusty eye?'

'Sorry,' she said hastily. 'What was the question again?'

Lilly grinned at her from the sink. 'It's gross, innit?'

Seth flung his sister a nasty hand gesture, his gaze locked to Despina. 'Why are you distracting Howard Rosethorn?'

She was staring at his eye again.

'You're still looking at it!' he exploded.

'I'm sorry, I can't help it!' Despina exclaimed, reddening.

Seth sighed irately and pulled his eyepatch on. 'Better?'

'Yes.' She giggled treacherously.

Seth glared at her with his good eye. 'Is someone paying you to keep him away? Is that what you meant by needing the money?'

'I don't need the money, I lied about my old man's gambling problem,' she admitted. 'But I am being paid to distract him.'

'Who's paying you?' Lilly asked.

She considered telling them about the Bastard, but only for a moment. With their lineage, they had enough to contend with without the nanny claiming that a doppelgänger of the king was whispering in her head.

'Some lord,' she said. 'I don't know his name.' Which was true, she didn't know the Bastard's name. He didn't appear to have one.

Seth sensed her thoughts drift away again. 'Do you fancy this lord?'

She hesitated. 'Yes.' She felt the Bastard's presence around her, grinning maniacally, though she couldn't explain how she felt this. She definitely resented it, however.

'Oh,' Seth said slyly.

She smiled thinly.

'What does he look like?' Seth asked, leaning forward. 'Black hair? Thin? Kind of horsey faced?' He gestured at his nose, suggesting an elongation.

'No,' she said with a frown. 'That's Wotsit Emmett, I wouldn't spit on his shoes for silver.'

'Well, that's a relief.' Seth sighed in content. 'So who is he?'

'He dressed in very fancy clothes,' she lied, weaving an image swiftly in her mind. 'He had tanned skin and his hair was brown and wavy, he had it tied behind his head. He was pretty too, big brown eyes and dimples and straight, white teeth.'

Seth had crooked teeth, her mind digressed unhelpfully. Sort of turned inward at the canines. The Bastard didn't. His were very straight. Marbrand had once told her that the royal family had a tradition of correcting their children's teeth in adolescence by bashing them into line with a hammer and holding them in place with steel rods for two years. Looks like it was an exaggeration after all.

Instead she added, 'He had a bit of an accent, too.'

Seth shifted forward a bit.

'Can you tell which accent?' Lilly asked before he got the chance.

'Not at all, I'm rubbish at accents,' she said. 'He spoke Truphorian fluently.'

Seth ran a hand through his hair. 'Did he say why he wanted Rosethorn distracted?'

'No, just that he wanted him away from you,' she said honestly again.

Seth sighed, thinking.

'Do you want me to keep following his orders?'

'Definitely. For one thing, I don't much want Howard Rosethorn near me anyway and for another, I don't want this lord to know I know about him yet.' He faced Lilly. 'Orl never had any relatives, did he?'

'None that were nobility,' Lilly said, frowning. 'He had a lot of half-siblings. They were never acknowledged by the Ambassador, though.'

'Huh.' He turned his attention back to Despina. 'Thank you for telling me this.'

'Well, you'd sack me if you didn't,' she said.

Seth smiled and ruffled her hair. He had a dimple on one side of his face, she noticed, just like—

She diverted her thoughts with difficulty.

'Don't hesitate to throw something heavy at Howard's head if the need requires,' Seth said, opening the kitchen doors.

'He didn't say anything about killing him,' she said in amusement.

'He didn't say anything about *not* killing him, either,' he added, leaving with a wink.

Despina grinned, flushing a light pink.

Lilly frowned at her, her mouth turning up in amusement. 'Low birth notwithstanding,' she said, 'even *you* can do better.'

The light pink darkened to bright red as Lilly entered the courtyard. Despina turned away from the door, her face hot. What was the matter with her? Staring at Seth Crey like that? If she didn't know any better, she would have thought she *did* fancy him.

Seth wasn't going to know that, though. She felt confident her lies about the foreign man could withstand any input Lilly had on the situation.

'They will,' Seth said in her ear, his voice a low whisper. 'I'm impressed. You have a vivid imagination.'

Despina felt a stab of panic before she turned and noticed the scar. A jolt of a different kind ran through her chest and down her spine.

The same face she'd just been speaking to smiled in front of hers, the same jawline, the same hair, the same dimple on one side – entirely identical to Seth Crey but for the set and colour of his eyes and the scar running from one eyebrow down the length of his nose, nearly reaching the corner of his mouth. But where Seth's presence made her feel no different to any other noble in the palace, the Bastard made her flesh tingle.

'Hi,' she said in a squeak.

His smile broadened. 'You like me.'

Despina frowned. 'No I don't. Shut up.'

'Yes you do. You *liiike* me,' he sang, grinning. His teeth were perfect. Seth's weren't even that bad, but it made a hell of a difference.

She blinked the thought away. 'Shut up!'

'I don't mind,' he said, smirking. 'It could be worse, you could fancy the real Seth Crey – he's afraid of birds.' He licked his lips. 'If you're lucky, I might pay you for your services in something more, you know… fun.'

'Oh my God, please go away,' Despina groaned.

The Bastard grinned toothily – his teeth were whiter than Seth's – and tucked a strand of hair behind her ear. 'See you around.' He dissipated in a flurry of mist.

Despina stared into space in a trance, trembling from his touch. She turned to gawk out the open double doors at Seth. He didn't compare. He was being attacked by pigeons, for one thing. It was as if the Bastard was the real king and Seth was a comic caricature.

Did she really have a crush on him? She was pretty sure she didn't.

Despina watched Lilly-Anna Crey weep with mirth at her brother's misfortune.

~

Jimmy trembled with silent laughter.

Seth's arms flailed comically as no less than five pigeons accosted him from all sides.

The Bastard – as Albie – flung Geldemar a wry glance.

Geldemar sprawled against the fountain in cat form – minus the glowing, for a change. 'What? I get bored when you go off conspiring, you know.' He whistled, which was a feat for an avatar whose lips weren't designed for whistling.

They flew off momentarily before returning. They seemed to have a taste for Seth's clothes.

This is just typical, Seth thought in between attacks. It couldn't happen at a time when he needed someone like Elyse or Vladimir's creepy son to leave him alone, no. It had to happen when he was about to chat up a woman.

Adrienne exited the courtyard and tried to pretend he wasn't there.

Seth battled the maelstrom of feathers and yellow faeces raining down upon him. 'I HATE BIRDS!!' He threw himself to the gravel, his head in his hands.

Lilly finally contained herself long enough to ward the pigeons off with some seeds. 'You make taking the piss out of you real easy.'

A honk erupted from beside the kitchen doors, loud and alien in the empty garden. Lilly and Seth looked at Jimmy. Who pressed a fist into his mouth, trying to stem it.

'We've warned you about your laugh before,' Lilly scolded. 'It frightens the children.'

Jimmy cleared his throat and regained posture. 'Sorry.'

Lilly giggled and strolled across the courtyard.

Seth kept on staring at Jimmy, a memory surfacing. *'I know what you did!'* Seth faced Jimmy, his jaw set. 'I believe we have something to discuss about yesterday.'

The mirth fell from Jimmy's face.

'About something you know?'

Jimmy's eyes flicked towards the kitchen doors. Within a moment, his entire body had vanished inside.

'No, you bloody don't!' Seth snarled, rising in pursuit.

Lilly glanced at them and shrugged, feeding the pigeons in peace.

~

Jimmy rounded a corner and fled for a secluded corner of the kitchens. He threw himself through a skinny door there.

The servants' staircase coiled upwards in tall, steep steps. Jimmy struggled his way up the crooked, sloping steps, more used to indulging in the sleek marble stairs of the upper classes than stumbling up the claustrophobic darkness to the servants' level two floors up.

A terrible smog drifted out of the servants' floors and collided with his face at force. He retched and devolved into a fit of violent coughing. He slowed to clear his lungs, glancing over his shoulder.

There was no sign of Seth behind him.

Jimmy slowed to a comfortable stroll down the narrow corridor to a miniscule bedroom at the end. It was warm despite the bare stone and distinct lack of curtain and carpet. A waft of foul odour assaulted him on the way. He ignored it as always.

He opened the door to Seth's stormy gaze and gave a small scream. 'What the hell are you doing in there?'

'The fireplaces in the dining hall have secret tunnels behind them,' Seth said with a smile. 'One of them is conveniently situated in your room. So.' He lifted his eyebrows. 'You know what I did,' he said evenly. 'You yelled that at me two days ago.'

Jimmy gulped, meeting his gaze.

'What did you mean by that?' Seth asked casually.

'Jon's penny box,' he blurted, the first thing to come to mind. 'You stole his money. From his room. You just blamed Raphael Emmanuel III because you knew Jon didn't like him.'

Seth frowned. 'That was you.'

Jimmy froze.

'Oh, so it was,' he said, feigning surprise. 'I must have been mistaken. And drunk. Drunk and mistaken. Never mind. Must be off.' He turned to flee.

'No,' Seth barked, grabbing his elbow.

Jimmy squealed. 'Don't do me in,' he blurted before he could stop himself.

Seth's eyes widened.

'I'm too good-looking to be a corpse,' Jimmy said. 'I'll be good, I promise.'

'You saw,' Seth whispered.

They stared at each other in equal measures of terror.

'Hello,' Jon said.

The two wailed in unison.

Jon stood in the doorframe between them, looking as ever like he was vaguely pleased with himself about something nobody in the world knew about. 'I seem to have misplaced my money,' he announced.

Jimmy's gaze flitted to Seth for a nanosecond.

Having made his monetary issues clear, Jon turned to his cousin. 'Funny seeing you here,' he mused. 'Nobody in the royal family seems to come in here unless a crime has been committed.' He faced Jimmy. 'Has a crime been committed?'

Seth shifted his eyes from Jon to Jimmy. 'You're in it together,' he said, pointing from one to the other. 'He knows, doesn't he?'

Jimmy gulped.

Jon just smiled vaguely into space.

Seth thought carefully about his next move.

As he did so, Jimmy thought feverishly that it was about time for the king to have another religious vision.

'HAW-OCK!!' Seth howled.

Jimmy climbed over his doubled body and ran for his life.

Jon peered down at Seth as he rolled on the floor in the thralls of agony. He chortled. 'Still funny the second time you see it.'

~

Russell slept soundly, snoring gently. Despina breathed a very silent sigh of relief, gently closing his favourite storybook. The boy had been steadily pushing up his nightly story limit. Tonight's seven battle stories was a new record. It had to be at least halfway through third turn by now.

She exited the children's darkened rooms quietly as the night nanny took her place. Her feet led her through the empty palace on default. A yawn burst out of her and her stomach gnawed at itself: a bite to eat before bed was in order.

She reached the bottom of the stairs and swerved into the kitchens. Every utensil had been put away for the night, the braziers tapering to a red glow and naught but a faint whiff of smoke and meat lingering behind.

Despina sighed, making a beeline for the pantry for some fruit.

The Bastard leaned on the edge of the counter, smiling at her.

She jolted to a halt and swallowed. 'Hi.'

His smile turned inward into a smirk. 'Hi.'

Despina hesitated. 'Can I help you?'

'Nope,' the Bastard said lightly. 'I just came to tell you your services are no longer required. Thank you for your help.'

'No problem.' She wrung her hands inside her pockets. 'Can I ask you something?'

The Bastard arched his eyebrows.

'Why do you look like Seth Crey?'

He licked his lips. 'You don't choose questions that are easy to answer, do you?'

'It's just…' Despina shrugged. 'It's a strange choice, is all.'

The Bastard straightened his jerkin, brushed it off. 'It's probably easier if I show you.' He nodded her toward him.

Despina approached slowly. He took her hand in his own, linked their fingers together.

Images flicked behind Despina's eyes.

A church altar. A long, lush burgundy carpet underfoot. A woman, with auburn hair. The one who had dragged her to the palace, she realised. What was her name again?

'Adrienne,' the Bastard said softly, a narrator beyond the vision.

Adrienne raised a cup to her lips.

Blood poured from her, a vast wave, too vast to come from one human being. It pooled on the surface of the carpet before sinking in to it, a dark shadow on the matching fabric, spreading into a lake. Despina was in the middle of it, she realised with horror, caught in a tidal wave of thick red blood, carried helplessly to that dark sea below. A wooden box interrupted her fall and she vanished into oblivion—

Pain. Barbs gorged her skin, leaving deep marks on her face and torso. She had no limbs, she realised with horror – she hadn't had time to develop them yet. She was merely a ball of brains and organs, being attacked by some spiked weapon, many of them: branches, she realised. Trees and branches. The smell of blood remained, tinged with the scent of pine. Her wounds stung, new strikes opening across the existing, over and over. A blinding white sting shot across her face, down the length of her nose to the corner of her lip. The scar, she realised. *His* scar.

Whiteness consumed her vision.

'RISE,' three voices rasped at her as one. 'BE CALM. YOU ARE MINE NOW. COME TO ME.'

She recognised one of those voices. *Theo Crey's ghost.*

'No,' the Bastard said in the present. 'Close, but no.'

Hands cradled her form with delicate care, holding her in as her sense of self wavered. He held her close, enveloping her in a warm light. She pulled herself inward, grew stronger. The light built her up, gave her limbs, helped her grow. But not to heal.

'COME TO ME,' the tri-vocal entity intoned.

She obeyed. The white was total, abating only faintly at the edges surrounding the entity. She slid toward the blinding light, crawling through the ether.

Power swelled inside her chest. Heat poured through her lungs and windpipe, almost choking her with its intensity. Fury. Pure, utter fury.

'GOOD,' the entity said. 'USE IT. EMBRACE IT. IT IS YOUR POWER. SHOW THEM WHAT YOU HAVE MADE OF YOURSELF.'

She found herself standing on hard ground. She rose to her full height. Black clothing folded around her, silver thread popping into place. Heat flowed through each limb, flowing out from the pit of her stomach.

Another scene flitted in and out of her awareness. An older man in extravagant clothing, approaching Adrienne. 'From the king,' he said.

A bag of coins dropped into her hand.

Pain shot through her chest. She knew it was not her own.

'She gave me up for coins,' the Bastard said, a wisp of breath on the air.

A scream threatened to erupt from her. It swelled to bursting in her chest, her ribs creaking with the pressure, like a door straining against the latch.

Another image, a basket. Seth Crey leaned over it, lifting an infant from within. He cradled the child, smiling weakly into the tiny face within the blanket. The scream whistled out of her in a shrill exhale, steam whistling out of the kettle.

'YOUR REPLACEMENTS,' the voices said in disgust.

Despina choked on the Bastard's anger. 'THEY'LL PAY FOR THIS,' she said in a strangled voice. Three strangled voices, in fact: one faint and barbed as thistle, one harsh and guttural, and one the voice she'd known as the Bastard for three years now. 'THEY'LL RUE THE DAY THEY GAVE ME TO THE HOLE.'

Despina collapsed onto the flagstones of the kitchens. The heat abated now, her own natural body temperature replacing it. Apart from her face, now pressed against the icy flagstones.

The Bastard took both her hands and gently helped her to her feet.

She trembled. 'I'm so sorry.' It felt an inadequate sentiment.

The Bastard smiled weakly at her. 'Why on earth should *you* be sorry?'

Tears rolled down her face. She buried her nose in his chest. 'How… how do you live with this? How do you bear to look at them after what they did?'

The Bastard set his chin on top of her head. 'I have my ways of coping with these things,' he said very quietly.

The anger had left a void in her chest. She felt vacant. 'Do you feel that all the time?'

'Yes.'

She stared into space, her left temple pressed to his collarbone. 'Now I know why you insist on being so annoying.'

The Bastard laughed quietly. 'Now you know.'

They stood in silence for a moment. The braziers fizzled out, leaving them in increasing levels of darkness.

'I know my company can be intolerable at times,' the Bastard said, 'but d'you think it would be alright if we could be friends?'

Despina lifted her face to his. 'I think that would be fine,' she said faintly.

He smiled at her, tucking a strand of hair behind her ear.

She shivered. 'I'll probably feel more comfortable if we *stay* friends, though, given that you're actually about five years old. The whole idea does scream "child grooming", just a bit.'

He quirked a half-smile. 'I think that would be fine.'

~

Jimmy's latest violation of Seth's marital equipment had knocked him fully unconscious for ten minutes. Adrienne sat by his side in sullen silence as he lay in the dull light of the medical examination room – having been deposited there by an excited Prophet who had to be poked sharply in the back with a number of surgical devices before he would leave the turret again.

She sighed heavily. Of course Erik was nowhere to be seen – he had gotten sniffy the second time he saw Adrienne since his reinstatement, deciding that since she insisted on loitering, she could make herself useful. Which left her looking after Seth, as usual.

The Bastard watched her simmer with resentment and waved a hand over her face, dismissing it. A moment later, he slipped into her left side and turned his attention to Seth.

Seth awoke in relative darkness, his lower torso throbbing periodically. He scowled at the ceiling. Jimmy was going to get it this time, make no mistake. He closed his eyes and tried to will away his headache so he could go back to sleep.

A curtain of flowery-smelling hair flopped onto his face. He tried to blow it away until its owner brushed it off, revealing her face. 'Are you alright?'

'Will I ever make love again?' Seth asked weakly.

Adrienne smiled faintly and brushed her knuckles down his jaw. 'Why don't we find out?'

The Bastard fled, having mastered the knack at last.

They went ahead and kissed as he left, without demi-godly intervention and without cessation – until Seth's loins let out a scream and reminded him that romance was going to be a family friendly affair for at least a few more weeks.

~

PART FIVE: THE SECRECY OF THE COACHMAN

I

he late dawn slid through the half-open burgundy curtains. Six weeks had passed.

'I appreciate you letting me stay, by the way,' Jimmy said, tidying his bunk.

'Not a problem,' the Prophet said brightly. He touched up a curtain in his portrait of Russell Crey, a project he had been working on for the past couple of weeks.

A chill wind harkened the beginning of winter, but the large window still let a wide beam of sunlight in to greet them. Jimmy stretched. The mahogany wood panelling lent Jimmy an air of opulence that put the palace slums to shame as he watched the Prophet paint.

He'd crept into Jimmy's room at dawn to take advantage of the quality of light, but Jimmy hadn't heard him come in. The young man worked in complete silence – and with exquisite detail, Jimmy thought, thinking back on Queen Cienne's portrait with an air of wistfulness he'd never felt for the woman in person.

'It's nice to get the opportunity to prove wrong all those child abuse rumours you helped to spread. I wonder if your scepticism has eased slightly in your stay?'

'Nope. Not at all,' Jimmy said in equal degrees of cheer. 'But since the bunks are warm and I don't have any children I'm aware of, I'm willing to give you the benefit of the doubt.'

Creepy tendencies aside, Jimmy found the Prophet to be quite pleasant, now he got to know him. The only thing he couldn't stick was his habit of feeding him little bits of bread, like he was doing now.

'Would you care for some breakfast before you leave?' he asked, holding out a piece of bread. 'I could bless you while I'm at it, kill two birds with one stone.'

Jimmy gave the bread a sceptical glance. 'I've been feeding myself for about forty years now,' he said, plucking the bread from his hand, 'I'm a bit of an expert.'

He popped it into his mouth and grimaced. Disgusting – dry and sticky, like eating parchment. Not to worry. He'd nick something off Seth's lunch tray when he went to collect his wages. He hadn't done any work this week to warrant the payment, but the royal family didn't need to know that.

He smoothed his linen and gave a large cobweb on the rafters an irritable swipe as a green-clad teen entered the room. 'Message for Jimmy de Vil.'

Jimmy froze.

The Prophet frowned slightly. 'As in "devil"?'

Jimmy gave an unconvincing giggle. 'Funny coincidence, eh?' He snatched the note, hoping it wasn't a death warrant from Seth Crey.

Lilly wanted to see him.

'Tell her I'm on my way,' he instructed the adolescent, who nodded.

The Prophet shook out one of his robes for loan.

Jimmy counted out money for the coach.

'I hope you manage to patch things up with the king.'

Jimmy snorted audibly. Apart from tidying his own bed, he hadn't cleaned or otherwise served anyone since he'd kicked Seth's fundamentals – he was in particular enjoying the copious helpings of wine he was given and not having to make anyone a cup of tea. He was staying in hiding as long as he could get away with it.

He accepted the robe with a genial nod and swung it around himself. He also feigned a hunchback so he couldn't be recognised from a distance –

though he needn't have bothered.

Seth was much too distracted with 'political business' that was so 'delicate' that entry into his quarters was banned on pain of death and anyone following the king on his 'external meetings' would be 'interrupting important state matters' and would be 'dealt with accordingly'. Seth had had a lot of time to think up this story while he was 'ill' or, as the Prophet kept telling everyone, recovering from his latest 'vision'.

Jimmy wondered how his life had come to be so full of inverted commas as he left the Prophet's diocese and headed to work.

Lilly's quarters were as they always were when she inhabited them – a pigsty, Jimmy thought. Bottles and bedsheets covered the rug in her bed-quarters, and miscellaneous weaponry littered the floor surrounding the display cabinet she was in the middle of re-organising. Lilly paced in circles around her drawing room, trying to clear her head. The exercise didn't stop her from striding back to the window out of irate habit.

'Look at him,' Lilly hissed, nodding down. 'Loitering while he waits for her to clock off. You can practically smell the desperation.'

Jimmy peered over her shoulder.

Seth strolled idly through the rear gardens, his hands in his pockets. He gave the keep a cursory glance and spotted Lilly inside her window.

Lilly's eyes narrowed.

He raised a hand over his head, waving his fingers up and down.

'Filthy bastard,' she seethed, waving back the same way.

Seth smiled up at her fondly.

She smiled back.

Jimmy wondered if Seth could see the vain throbbing in her left temple from all the way down there.

'We need to do something about them,' Lilly said icily.

'Why don't we just tell Cienne?' Jimmy asked.

'And let her kill him?'

'It's better than her killing all of us once she finds out we never told her,' he pointed out. 'She'll cop on to him any day now.'

'That's not soon enough,' Lilly said angrily. 'We're going broke here, and he's swanning off to the village in a big fuck-off coach with a fistful of jewellery for her. She's bleeding him dry. Lovers shouldn't treat men like that.'

She shot him a wry side-glance. 'That's what little *sisters* are for.'

Jimmy quirked a half-smile.

She looked at him imploringly. 'Can't you… covet her or something? You know, for your country?'

He grimaced. 'Really? Yeah, I'll covet you and the twins while I'm at it, and, sod it, I'll covet Jon as well, why not?'

'Randy dogs would hesitate to covet Jon's ankle, that's why.'

'Maybe they'd like to covet your breakfast instead,' Jon said coldly by the door, pivoting.

Lilly dropped her head in remorse. 'We shouldn't bully him. He's been through a lot.'

'Down in the kitchens, we call it character building,' Jimmy said. 'The bullying,' he clarified, 'not the… we're not monsters down there.'

'I dunno, your girlfriends are getting younger,' she said.

'Women your age are my limit,' he said haughtily. 'I'll not be seen with anyone any younger than you. That would be obscene.'

'I'll take your word for it, since you can count further than twenty-five.'

Eleanor knocked and entered the drawing room, frowning. 'Cienne's just got a letter from her father,' she said, beckoning to the two of them to follow her.

Lilly and Jimmy exchanged baffled glances.

~

Seth whined, his knuckles whitening around the curtain pole Howie had created.

'Why are you watching this?' Geldemar asked in a pained voice.

'For more productive reasons than you are,' the Bastard retorted.

Seth's eyes rolled upward.

The Bastard was fixated to them, as though he was examining melee techniques. That was because Seth had lost the ability to stand up properly roughly two minutes ago and was hanging onto the curtain pole for dear life. The Bastard crossed his fingers and prayed for it to dislodge and crack his head on the way down, but alas Seth climaxed before the Bastard's idyllic slapstick fantasy could be fulfilled.

'Give it time,' Geldemar advised, reading his thoughts. 'Howard's shoddy carpentry is legendary, it's bound to happen sooner or later.'

'Usually when I'm not around,' the Bastard grumbled.

Adrienne's head popped up from under the windowsill. She rose to her full height to face Seth, wiping her chin on her sleeve. 'Your turn.'

Seth smirked. They turned on the spot, facing each other. 'How long until he gets back?' Seth asked in a low murmur.

'Not for hours, I shouldn't think,' she said offhandedly, looking him up and down in earnest. 'She can run to the Far Isles for all I care. He'll chase her that far for that colander, he hasn't got the wits to do anything else.'

Seth grinned and ran his gaze down the length of her. 'You ready?'

She giggled in reply and laughed out loud as he dropped to the ground, her skirts billowing over his head.

'That's quite enough of that,' Geldemar said, stepping in front of the window as Adrienne's face began to flush. 'I thought you had relieved Despina from her duties? Why is she still running around distracting Howard Rosethorn?'

'Seth's paying her to do it now,' the Bastard said dismissively. 'Nothing to do with me.'

'No, you're just brainwashing your mother and watching them fornicate instead,' he said, folding his arms. 'That's much more enterprising.'

'There's nothing else to do,' the Bastard said. 'Our work is done. All there is left is to wait for Russell to find out and tattle to Mummy.'

'Just you be careful Seth doesn't find out about you.'

'He won't,' the Bastard assured him, patting his shoulder. 'I have a grand entrance to make. Nothing's getting in the way of that.'

Adrienne leaned her elbows on the windowsill, her eyes squeezed shut.

Geldemar flung her a disapproving glance – which was the pot calling the kettle black, the Bastard thought wryly. 'So where is your little friend?'

'With *his* little friend.' The Bastard grimaced at the thought of Azrael. 'He really is a creep, that child.'

'Yes, well, you've seen his maternal family,' Geldemar agreed. 'Poor Vladdy pales in comparison.'

Adrienne squeaked, leaning heavily on the sill with her head dangling outside.

'Don't the neighbours wonder about this carry-on?' Geldemar asked.

'He's common-looking as muck,' the Bastard said. 'They don't bat an eyelid at his visits. I did have a hand in masking the lewdness from the gate. They have eyes, after all.'

They turned back to the window.

Seth and Adrienne stood upright again, taking turns to smooth down her dress.

'When will you be back?' Adrienne said.

Seth reached up to grip the curtain pole again. 'Why don't you come to me?'

'What about next week?'

'What about sooner?'

The Bastard yelled in exasperation.

'Argh, just pick a day!' he shouted at them as they murmured in each other's ear. 'Every conversation is "what about this? What about that? What about up there? What about on the window? What about this orifice? What about circular?"!'

'He is good at his circular,' Geldemar commented.

'Why not tomorrow?' Adrienne breathed.

'Why not today?'

The curtain pole cracked free and clapped both of them over the head on the way down. The Bastard smirked in satisfaction.

'Ow,' Adrienne said, a hand to her head.

'Oops,' Seth said.

'About time,' the Bastard said with relish.

~

'Why,' Cienne said icily, 'was I not told?'

Lilly, Eleanor and Jimmy stood in a line in the middle of the east antechamber, looking sheepish. Cienne glared at them, sitting in her husband's seat at the head of the council table. She turned her attention to the letter in her hands.

'My father has written about Philip Manderly: the master of coin. According to one of my father's advisors, Manderly has been purchasing millions of pounds' worth of textiles from Portabella's capital over the past two years. Some statues from a prominent sculptor were commissioned from there as well. They've totted up the figures and it's added up to around thirty million pounds – twice as much money as we had in the treasury in the first place.' Cienne dropped the letter onto the desk, looking irate. 'How much is the debt exactly?'

Jimmy cleared his throat. 'Fuddyfivemillionpunds,' he mumbled.

'Forty-five million pounds,' Cienne said flatly.

'Yep,' Lilly said shortly.

'Whose orders are they?'

'We don't know,' Eleanor said in a quiet voice. 'We've been trying to find out.'

'Does Seth have something to do with this? Someone mentioned a manor was being built for the twins…?'

'We've ruled him out on the grounds that even he isn't stupid enough to cause this much trouble for a four-year-old,' Jimmy said.

'It would have to be a massive manor to cost thirty million pounds in furnishing alone,' Lilly said.

'If it is a manor, we can only assume that the rest of the money has gone to building it,' Jimmy said. 'Question is, who does it belong to? Is it Manderly's or was he just instructed to pay for it by someone else?'

'You know who vanished not long after the master of coin?' Lilly said.

Jimmy knew immediately. 'Osney.'

~

Water fountained over Seth's head, arcing in delicate plumes. It bathed him in a faint shower of droplets. Marbrand planted a foot on the ground to either side of Seth's head, his stern face obstructing it.

'It's a first for me to say this to someone at your level,' he said down to Seth, 'but I think you're actually improving.'

Seth scowled at him through a bloody nose, the latest of many.

'Go pug yourself,' he said thickly.

'A pug is a breed of dog, my liege. You must have it mistaken for something else entirely. Get up.'

Seth hauled himself into a sitting position, spitting blood.

Marbrand kicked his sword back in his direction. 'How old is Russell now, my liege?'

Seth scowled. 'Is this a jab at my aptitude with a sword?'

'I'm merely enquiring.'

Seth eyeballed him. 'Nearly four.'

'Indeed.' Marbrand planted his feet one in front of the other, the rear foot facing sideways.

Seth spread his feet sideways to steady himself, his legs straight and stiff. He frowned at Marbrand's disapproving gaze but didn't rectify his stance.

'I glimpsed him and Prince Azrael sparring with sticks yesterday afternoon,' Marbrand continued. 'He'll be a fine swordsman one day.'

'Unlike me, you mean. Don't insult my intelligence by masking your insults in casual conversation—ah!' His legs flew out from under him.

'Don't insult your own intelligence by taking notice of insults,' Marbrand said. He suddenly appeared behind where Seth had stood, which was now where the back of his head sat in the gravel. 'Your paranoia has better uses. Concentrate on what you're doing.'

Seth growled loudly and thrust his torso upright.

'And for God's sake fix your footing,' Marbrand said in annoyance. 'It was the first lesson I taught you for a reason. Bend your knees, make yourself flexible.'

'Let me stand up first,' Seth scolded, rising to his feet. A foot landed in the small of his back. He fell to his knees. 'What did I say?' Seth yelled, slamming his blade against the gravel.

'Nothing I have to listen to,' Marbrand said. 'Don't assume all of your opponents will obey your every command. You're only king to those who respect you, and that number is currently a very little one. Get up.'

Seth ground his teeth and stamped a foot into the ground.

'You're not a prince anymore, Seth Crey,' Marbrand informed him. 'You're responsible for your own decisions now, and if they're all as abysmal as your melee tactics, you'll need some semblance of swordsmanship just to survive them.'

Seth's knuckles whitened on both hands around the hilt.

'Your father isn't around to clean up after you anymore,' he added spitefully. 'And I'm not intending on being his replacement.'

Seth brought his sword around in a horizontal arc, turning into a standing position to face Marbrand. Marbrand deflected easily, bringing his sword up to deliver a blow from above. Seth batted this away with ease and made to stab Marbrand –

Only to receive a clap around the ear from the flat of Marbrand's blade.

'So you were going to gut me, is it?' Marbrand asked in amusement.

Seth flopped onto his side, dust lifting to fill his good ear.

'A nice idea, but you should have disarmed me first. A few more heavy blows with your sword would have done the trick: my sword is lighter and weaker than yours, plus my right index finger was trapped in the door by Elliot this morning.' He flung the offender a reproachful glower.

On a bench by the wall, Elliot mouthed an exaggerated 'sor-*ry*', rolling his eyes.

Marbrand's attention returned to the king. 'If you hadn't been so hasty, I could be lying dead on the ground as we speak. Similarly, I could have opened your throat from ear to ear, but I felt that would somewhat hinder your education.'

'You love to talk, don't you?' Seth said, trying to mask the fact that he couldn't hear.

'No need to yell, we haven't all been deafened by a sword blow,' Marbrand said breezily. 'Get up.'

'My ear hurts,' Seth complained.

'So do mine, your whining can be quite piercing,' Marbrand said, getting impatient. 'Up. Quickly now.'

Seth moaned, rising unsteadily to his feet. The ground spun between his hands and knees. 'Hasn't it been an hour yet?'

'Nope,' Jon said brightly from the side-lines. He sat on a memorial bench erected on King Theo's anniversary, a bowl of porridge sitting on the flat of his palm. 'Time drags when you're shit at something, doesn't it?'

'And you can do better, can you?' Seth scathed.

'Yes, I can.'

'Liar!'

'Gimme the sword, then,' Jon said airily.

'You won't be able to lift this,' Seth said as Jon approached, 'it's as big as you are.'

'*You* couldn't lift it six weeks ago,' Marbrand said. 'Let him have a go. You can rest your head before I batter it some more.'

Seth rolled his mouth from side to side and thrust the blade hilt-first in Jon's direction. He then sat in Jon's place and proceeded to eat his oatmeal.

Jon and Marbrand circled each other. Sure enough, the blade was almost as long as Jon was tall, but he seemed unperturbed by the weight. Examining his stance with approval, Marbrand commenced his opening tactic.

Which was to talk him to death, Seth thought wryly.

'So, Jon,' he began in a drawl, 'how much have you learned from your time in the kitchen—'

Jon launched himself at Marbrand mid-sentence. Their blades met with a clang. What happened next was so quick their movements blurred. The next thing Seth registered was Marbrand's sword flopping into the fountain beside him with a splash.

Jon circled Marbrand, his calves swaying with nonchalance. He tucked Seth's blade under his armpit, giving the pommel a gentle pat.

Marbrand remained in battle stance, hands still wielding the air where the hilt of his sword used to be.

Seth gawked at them.

Jon smiled faintly.

'How the hell did you…' Seth trailed off.

Jon just smiled and inclined his head with a tilt to the left.

'That,' Marbrand said in astonishment, 'was excellent.' He retreated to the fountain to retrieve his sword. 'You're a model student of Theo Crey if I ever saw one.'

'Yeah, that's what happens when you show up for practise,' Jon said.

Seth flicked a glob of porridge at him from his spoon. 'When did you get sparring lessons from my father?'

'Once a week until I was twenty. Started when I was about…' He tilted his head from side to side, calculating. 'Nine-ish? Oh, and he taught me archery when I was eight, but I was shit at that. What about you? You good at anything, or…?'

'Very funny,' Seth seethed.

'Right, you next,' Marbrand ordered, sword in hand once more.

Seth groaned and rose. He and Jon switched places.

'My breakfast!' Jon protested shrilly from behind him. 'It's nearly gone, you git!'

Seth ignored him and copied Marbrand's stance, holding his sword bolt upright.

'Right,' Marbrand said, poising himself. 'Now do what he did.'

'Alright,' Seth said in determination, stretching his neck from side to side.

He ran at Marbrand, his sword held over his shoulder.

Marbrand raised his sword in an identical fashion to parry. His blade swished through thin air. Marbrand frowned and looked down a second too late.

The flat of Seth's broadsword slammed into the back of Marbrand's knees. Marbrand flew onto his back. Seth planted his feet on either side of his head and grinned down at him.

Marbrand wheezed, completely winded.

'How was that?' Seth asked smugly.

Marbrand nodded. 'Fine,' he managed.

~

II

The coach halted at the top of the hill. Jimmy got out and craned his neck, a hand over his brow in defence of the setting sun. 'Well, shit.'

Some investigation from the governor of Breaker's Hold led them to the southern outskirts of Osney, Duke Richard Crey's district. From the top of the hill, they had an exquisite view of the Duke's new palace, 'awarded to him by the king for services to the crown'. Jimmy wondered what services this was or whether Seth knew about it.

Jon exited the coach under the afternoon sun to stand beside him, glowering downward. 'Why don't we have a hedge maze?' he complained. 'Those things are cool.'

'I'll try to fit one into the new budget,' Jimmy grumbled.

The hedge maze in question filled most of the grounds. Tiny figures moved between the spiralling rows of foliage, lined with brightly coloured flowers and dotted with courtyards. Two of these courtyards were set with a gazebo, with a third being constructed at the far end of the maze, near the mansion itself.

Jimmy had visited Portabella briefly with King Theo back in the day, but their palaces had nothing on this masterpiece. It was the architectural equivalent to one of the cook's elaborate pink birthday cakes – except the frills and angels were detailed in expensive stonework instead of icing and hard sugar. There wasn't a square foot of the outside walls that wasn't decorated. Judging by the price of the furnishings, there probably wasn't a square foot inside that wasn't decorated either.

'On the bright side, that seems to be the twins' birthday present sorted,' Jimmy said.

'Hmm,' Jon said. 'Let's have a look-see.'

They climbed into the coach and, with a tap to the roof, rolled downhill.

The gates opened for them surprisingly quickly. It appeared even the Duke of Osney's staff were being deceived: some of them even asked Jimmy with open curiosity what it was Osney did to warrant such a large reward.

'Tidied up the coin vault,' was Jimmy's sour reply as they rolled past.

They bypassed the maze holding a score of gardeners trimming the foliage, and trundled down a wide gravel path down to the mansion, where a large cart was being unloaded by a group of men. They were please to discover the Duke among them, barking orders.

The coach stopped in his line of sight.

'Take the chandeliers into the great hall,' he instructed before noticing it.

He gaped at Jimmy as he climbed out, with Jon at his heels.

'Good morning,' he said in surprise. He inclined his head at Jimmy before shooting his son an uneasy glance.

'Hello, Dad,' Jon said with a smile.

'Hello, Mortimer,' he said, earning a grimace from Jon. 'What can I do for you?'

'We're placing you under arrest,' Jimmy said. He flicked the coach a signal.

Elliot and Moat exited the coach, armed with short swords.

Osney blinked. 'What for? What's this about?'

'The treasury,' Jon said. 'Or lack thereof.'

Elliot and Moat grabbed an arm each.

'We also want the whereabouts of Philip Manderly and his two friends,' said Jimmy, his voice ringing with seldom-used authority. 'Are they with you?'

'No, I haven't seen them for nigh on—'

'Have those damned carpets arrived yet? I'll have to get on to those bloody incompetent Portabellans...' Manderly froze on his way out of the mansion's entrance. Everyone glared at him. 'Is everything alright?'

Jimmy clicked his fingers.

Two more guards poured out of the coach.

'We'll just have a quick look around,' Jimmy said brightly. He strolled through the throng of staff with Jon in tow.

A three-tiered indoor fountain greeted them in the entrance hall, over twice the height of the Creys'. A young woman with a vague resemblance to Jon perched on the top tier, gazing into a book cradled in her forearms. Water overflowed out into the pool and splashed Jon as they walked past, to his disgust. Beyond the fountain, statues of various literary figures lined the walls in between monuments of another, much uglier woman in the great hall.

The three watched the staff install three brand new chandeliers to the vaulted ceiling above.

'Any chance of getting a refund on any of this tat?' Jon asked.

Jimmy cast a speculative glance around the hall. 'Not likely,' he said. 'It's all bespoke. Who's going to pay money for that ugly tart?'

'Leave my dead mum alone, she was a lovely lady,' Jon said, hurt.

'No, not her, the new wife.' Jimmy pointed at the ugly statues. 'You can see why this one never had kids.'

They gazed up at her in varying degrees of disgust.

'So what now?' Jon said.

'We could try to sell the house,' Jimmy said half-heartedly.

'Good luck. It's a remote area, isn't it?' Jon said. 'No one wants to live here, that's why he had enough land to build it. The monastery is based here, for a start. We all know what happens when you live near those bastards. And anyway, we'd need Seth's permission.'

Jimmy heaved a sigh.

The guards brought their prisoners inside in chains. Osney blubbered through a face coated in tears, Jon was disgusted to see, and Manderly's two friends had been gathered up as well, the three of them looking impassive.

'It was their idea,' Osney spluttered, choking on his own phlegm. 'They told me I deserved a reward. They told me I'd done a great job on the country all these years. They told me they had plenty of money, they told me—'

'Nobody's going to care what they told you once we've paid the executioner,' Jimmy snarled. 'You ordered the loans from Horseface Emmett and now you have to pay for them. We're confiscating all your lands and placing you under arrest, in the name of the king. Put him in the Tower,' he finished, with relish. He'd always wanted to say that.

Osney was dragged away, sobbing.

The man Jon recognised as the Jasper shrugged out of his guards' grip. 'You realise you'll need us to recover the crown's resources?'

'I don't think so,' Jimmy said with a snort. 'Someone has to be interested in a pink princess castle, even if it is next to a paedophile factory.'

'The king doesn't know about the current financial situation, does he?'

Jimmy glared at him. 'What he doesn't know won't hurt him.'

'It might if you can't sell the mansion,' the Jasper said with triumph. 'Confiscated lands belong to the king, you need his permission if you want to sell it. That includes not just his property, but the contents of said property as well. Statues of ugly wives notwithstanding, you have no chance of getting back any money spent on this project. Unless you want to tell King Seth that he's in debt by about forty-five million pounds?'

Jimmy clenched his teeth in hatred.

Jon nudged his elbow. 'I find hitting him with this helps.' He handed Jimmy a rolled-up sheet of parchment.

Jimmy snatched it, twisting the paper so hard it almost tore.

~

Adrienne stormed across the entrance hall. The stained glass threw garish colours over the flagstones in her path, a sharp contrast to her own dark mood.

She hated doing this. *Hated* it. She thought about Howie and felt a pang of sadness. She hated what she was doing to him – even if he was too oblivious to notice.

He had been so vacant lately, throwing himself into attempts to keep Despina Marbrand away from their property, setting booby traps around the perimeter of their house and *glaring* out of any open door or window, in case her cloaked form might appear outside.

She should have told him long ago. But every time she toyed with the idea, something wafted over her mind and cleared it of any thoughts of him whatsoever, replacing him with… Seth, for some reason.

She had never had a preference to Seth, far from it. Howie was better suited to her. He was also broader in the shoulders, younger and more pleasing to the eye than Seth, and more importantly, he was attentive, in every department. It wasn't as if experience made it better either, as was agonizingly evident in the slimy kisses Seth produced and the tendency to huff and puff into her ear. Encounters with Seth Crey were about as erotic as looking at a horse.

Which was what baffled her. Most of the time she left more in frustration than infatuation, but somehow, a thought of him edged its way into the forefront of her mind and made her swell with anticipation. Before she knew what had happened, she had arranged another meeting.

It was like she was under some kind of spell.

Her reverie was broken by the sound of swearing up ahead.

'Have at it, you curd!' Corporal Moat shouted. His sword twirled around him in an inelegant manner.

Seth simply stared at him, his sword hanging limply at his side.

'Have at it, you… wank-stain! You scum, you bastard, you, you curd!' Moat panted. His words grew indistinguishable from the intermittent grunting and huffing of exertion.

Seth turned questioningly to Marbrand. 'Why can't I just fight you anymore?'

Marbrand stood with one foot against the low fountain wall, facing away from them. 'Because you know my attacks.' He ran a whetstone down the length of his own blade, braced aloft on his knee.

'Oh, he's going to attack me, is it?'

'Apparently. Keep your eyes on him.'

Seth faced Moat, but he needn't have bothered. Moat ranted away with his blade swinging in all directions – this time only the word 'curd' was discernible. Seth shook his head in annoyance and circled him.

Moat rambled away, oblivious. 'You filthy—' His sword dropped to his side. 'Where'd he go?'

Seth rammed the end of the pommel into the back of Moat's head.

Moat grunted and tilted to the ground, unconscious.

'Oh, hello,' Seth said brightly to Adrienne. 'Here to see me?'

Adrienne gave him a coy smile. 'If you're not too busy, your majesty.'

'Not at all. I'll take you in the next room,' he said with a wink.

Adrienne reddened profusely.

Marbrand's eyes turned to the heavens. He kicked himself away from the fountain edge, making a beeline for the kitchens.

'Is that the mistress?' Eleanor demanded.

'Yep,' Lilly sighed.

They sat on the memorial bench by the fountain, watching them retreat indoors.

'The servant?' Eleanor squeaked. 'She's not making herself very subtle, is she? Strolling around like she owns the place.'

'It's her way. I tried threatening her, if it helps,' said Lilly.

Eleanor shook her head, disgusted. 'How Cienne remains oblivious, I have no idea. Where is she, anyway?'

'Off to the harbour to meet Half-Prince Frilly-Ass from the Land of the Petticoat,' Lilly said. 'He's come to see his half-niece and -nephew for their birthday. She took Ginny with her. Seth nearly threw a fit. Lord knows what he'll do when she has to get married in fifteen years.'

'Shouldn't you have gone to meet him?' Eleanor asked. 'Being his beloved wife?'

Lilly snorted. 'He knows where he stands. Or he will once those "rumours" about my own mistress reach him. I imagine that's why Cienne hasn't copped it yet – she must think they're talking about me.'

'Isn't the mistress seeing Howard?' Eleanor asked, baffled.

'Yep,' Lilly said dryly. 'She did the whole "replacing for a younger model" bit completely the wrong way around.' She frowned into the entrance hall. 'Speak of the devil.'

Howie stood in the centre of the main hall, looking about himself.

'Hi!' Lilly said shrilly, springing towards him.

He swung around. 'Hullo, Lilly.' He glanced around. 'Is Adrienne here? I thought I could hear her voice a minute ago.'

Just as he said it, Lilly *did* hear her voice. It was emanating from somewhere to the east and sounding increasingly urgent.

'No, haven't seen her,' Lilly lied. She faced her mother. 'Howie, you've met my mother?'

'I have,' he said, giving her a low bow. 'It's nice to see you, your highness.'

Eleanor smiled fondly and flicked some dust from his jerkin. 'Likewise.'

'I'm glad I bumped into you, actually. I wanted to ask about Adrienne's job.'

'Oh, yeah?' Lilly frowned slightly at her mother.

Who stared wide-eyed at the east antechamber over Howie's shoulder.

Lilly followed her gaze and her jaw dropped, pulse racing. 'Go on,' she prompted Howie.

Seth pinned Adrienne against the doorframe and rummaged frantically in her blouse. Her mouth was plastered over his in what was decidedly the *opposite* of the kiss of life.

Lilly delicately handled Howie's shoulders and turned him fully away from them. 'How can I help?'

'Well, I was hoping she could have her job back—'

Eleanor bolted for the doorway in a flurry of petticoats, her slippers skittering across the flagstones.

Lilly held him firmly in place and nodded frantically for him to continue.

Eleanor shoved Seth and Adrienne into the antechamber.

'She's getting very irritable lately and she—'

The antechamber door slammed.

Howie paused and turned to glance at a flustered Eleanor. She leaned her back firmly against the door and waggled her fingers at him.

'—she's sort of taking it out on me a bit,' he finished. 'Are you alright, your highness?'

'Fine, fine,' Eleanor squeaked faintly. 'Just a, a draft from the antechamber, you know…'

'Oh, okay.' Howie turned back to Lilly, unperturbed. 'So yeah, I was hoping you could have a word? I know Seth has it in for us, but he can't just sack people whenever he feels like it, it's not fair on her.' He frowned slightly, the most aggressive facial expression Lilly had ever seen on his face.

'… I'll see what I can do,' Lilly said, relaxing slightly. 'What d'you mean, taking it out on you? Is everything alright at home?'

Howie made a face. 'Not really…'

Seth moaned from inside the antechamber.

Eleanor slammed the side of her fist on the door to shut him up.

'… she's just… angry at me, all the time.' He paused in frustration, struggling to find the words. 'Everything's always my fault. All I'm trying to do is keep our things safe from that vandal, and she just keeps, you know, snapping at me to get out of the way and leave her alone…'

'Be quiet, Seth,' Eleanor snapped under her breath, reddening with humiliation.

'… I just thought if I got her job back for her, she might cheer up a bit.'

Lilly turned her brows upward in the middle in sympathy. 'Aw. Well, look.' She placed a hand on his shoulder, more to hold him away from the doorway than to show a feeling of friendship. 'You still love her, don't you?'

'Of course,' Howie said, rubbing his scalp.

'And how long have you been together?'

'Four years,' he said.

'… maybe,' said Lilly, in a fit of innovation, 'you should take your relationship up a notch.'

Howie frowned. 'What d'you mean?'

Lilly simply held her left hand in front of them and prodded her wedding ring.

'… oh.' Howie's eyes widened slightly. 'Oh, I hadn't thought of that. That's a really good idea. I think, yeah, yeah, I think it's time, isn't it? We should get married.'

Eleanor nodded in rapid enthusiasm. 'That's a wonderful idea!'

'Yeah!' Lilly agreed emphatically. 'Ask her to marry you! And you can have it here as well, if you like, since churches are a bit of a sore spot for her…'

'Yeah,' Howie said, lost in his own imagination.

'… and we'll have a big party, no expenses spared, and then you can, you can… take her on holiday,' she added for good measure. 'A nice long holiday, just the two of you. Somewhere sunny, and… very far away.'

'And we'll keep Seth *very far away* from the two of you on your special day,' Eleanor added.

'Yep, exactly,' Lilly said. 'Don't want him making an arse of himself in the middle of the—'

'Nngh, Seth, Seth!' Adrienne called, her voice muffled through the wall.

Eleanor and Lilly froze in unison.

A steely silence ensued, broken only by the soft squeak of shifting furniture next door.

Howie glared at the door. 'I take it that's Cienne?'

Lilly paused, scanning for signs of sarcasm. She couldn't find any. 'Probably,' she hazarded.

Howie arched an eyebrow. 'Poor woman. Let's just say Adrienne didn't give him a glowing reference.' He smirked with a hint of relish.

'She must have settled for you for a reason,' Lilly said in relief.

Howie grinned, looking distinctly happier. 'Thank you! I'd better go shopping for a ring!'

'Tell you what,' Lilly said, linking her elbow in his, 'I've a shitload upstairs from my arranged-marriage-husband that I don't want, you can have first dibs before I flog 'em. Call it an early wedding present…'

Howie beamed into space as Lilly walked him to the stairs.

Eleanor waited for them to leave earshot before sighing in relief. 'That was too close,' she whispered to herself.

Seth cackled behind the door.

'Oh, shut up, Seth!' she screeched at the door.

~

III

In the dowager queen's private quarters, Eleanor sat at a long table with Lilly and Jimmy around her, her arms folded in front of her. 'So you found him?'

'Yes,' Jimmy said. 'There's no doubt they are extremely intelligent, resourceful men that would have had a lot to offer the palace council were they not such *evil greedy frigging bastards.*'

'It's a big house, then?' Lilly said with dread.

'Pretty big, yeah,' Jimmy said with a pained expression.

'I figured as much,' she said. 'D'you arrest them?'

'Yes, but there's a problem,' Jimmy said with a wince.

'Why?'

Jimmy pulled out a weathered roll of parchment. 'I've done some more investigating on the master of coin.' He unrolled the parchment for the two to see. 'Philip Manderly is closely related to the Emmetts, and he's on excellent terms with nearly all of the major families in Truphoria. If we kill him, everybody we know is going to want blood.'

'Excellent,' Eleanor drawled. 'And I was so looking forward to his trial. We haven't had a good one since Theo was first crowned.'

'So basically, we're stuck with him,' Jimmy said, folding his arms on the tabletop.

'Unless we appoint someone else,' Eleanor said. 'We're well entitled to do that.'

'Yeah, but Emmett will get arsy and up our tax,' Lilly said.

'He's going to up our tax no matter what we do,' Eleanor sighed. 'We will not pussy foot around this fool any longer. If we can't trust Seth to look after affairs, then it's up to us to pick up the slack. We are Creys, not, bloody…' She flung a hand at Jimmy for lack of better example. '… de Vils.'

'Oi,' Jimmy said, affronted. 'The Gertrudes aren't all that either.'

She narrowed her eyes at him.

'Who do we appoint as master of coin, then?' Lilly asked.

'As a loyal member of the royal household and scion of a long-standing ally to the Crey cause—'

'Forget it,' Lilly said abruptly.

Jimmy's face fell. 'Fine,' he said grumpily. 'Good luck getting volunteers to deal with the forty-five-million-pound debt.'

'There's an obvious candidate, really,' Eleanor said breezily with a smile.

'Is there?' Lilly said.

'And luckily for us, he's on his way to us as we speak. *And* has great incentive to stick around in the job.' She reached out and patted Lilly's wedding ring.

'Oh,' Lilly said dully, glaring at it. 'Him.'

~

The Bastard perched on a bench in the inner grounds, beside Russell. He had discarded the dog outfit for the moment – it had confused the boy greatly a day ago when his aunty's dog toddled over and said hello in his father's voice. Better to borrow Moat's frame for the moment. He tapped the little boy's shoulder.

Russell looked up at him fondly, a toy soldier in each hand.

'How's Daddy doing?' the Bastard asked idly.

'He's god a girlfriend now,' Russell babbled. 'She got red hair, I saw'd her in the bedroom when Mummy went to get Uncle Alan. She's preddy.'

'She sure is,' the Bastard agreed.

'I follow him like you said to,' Russell said, proudly.

'Perfect.' The Bastard ruffled his hair, making him grin. 'Where's your little friend?' the Bastard said, glancing around. 'I haven't seen him for a while.'

'He went to look at the crown,' Russell said.

The Bastard frowned. 'Why?'

'He says it's his now.' Russell made a face. 'Daddy said it would be mine when I was older.'

'It will be,' the Bastard said. 'Just… don't go in there anymore, alright?'

'Why not?'

'Because it's dangerous,' the Bastard said. 'There's sharp things in there, you might get hurt.'

'Oh.' Russell nodded obediently. 'I stay away from there, then.'

'Good boy.' The Bastard gave him a wink.

He threw himself into the Bastard's arms, to his immense discomfort.

I'm going to have to train him out of that, he thought nauseously.

~

'I think we should go on holiday,' Howie said.

Adrienne sighed, straightening her back. *What fresh nonsense is this?* She shifted on her knees in front of the flowerbed. 'Go where?'

'I don't know,' he said, staring into the sky. He sat in the grass behind her, bathing in the sun and not deigning to help Adrienne with the weeding one little bit. 'Somewhere sunny,' he said in a dreamy voice.

'It's sunny here,' she said with a frown, shifting herself into a kneeling position.

'I know, but you know... somewhere exotic. And remote. Where it will just be the two of us.' He stroked her ponytail in one hand.

'Maybe next year,' she said, her attention rooted to a stubborn dandelion hidden in the shrubs.

Howie looked dejected. 'Maybe next year.'

The village fell into silence broken only by trotting hooves from the market.

'Adrienne?' he asked in a small voice.

'What?' she said impatiently.

'Will you marry me?'

Adrienne froze solid.

Howie waited.

She said nothing for a few moments. 'Um... no.'

Howie stared into space. 'No?'

'... no.'

His jaw gaped open. 'Oh.'

Adrienne looked at him, stricken. '... maybe next year,' she offered.

Resignation settled into his features. 'Maybe next year,' Howie said dully.

Adrienne held her breath, waiting for an argument. It didn't appear she was going to get one.

'I'm going to see if I can get my job back,' she said after a moment.

'Okay,' Howie said distantly.

'Are you alright?'

'Yeah, fine.' His light voice did not match the bleak look on his face.

Guilt crept up the back of her neck. 'I'll see you later.' She rose to her feet and left quickly.

Howie sat where he was, processing his thoughts. He took the ring from his pocket and let it slip from his fingers to land in the gravel.

~

Back before the clergy was evicted from the Serpent's Knot, all the regalia of the king's coronation used to be kept in the castle chapel. In the vestry, as a matter of fact: Jon became well acquainted with the crown and sceptre during the worst years of his life as he stared at the gold and amethyst inlay gleaming softly in the candlelight, night after night. Father Giery took great pride in maintaining them. Almost as much pride as Seth had in executing him.

Nowadays, the official crown and its accompanying ornament were kept in a small room behind the throne room. The tiny chamber was previously kept for storage, but since it had become the home of the crown jewels, it had been renovated into a place of worship.

Old tapestries covered the walls and flush carpeting had been put down. A coronation was a religion in and of itself – people hesitated to touch the crown outside of coronation preparations.

No one gave much of a crap about Seth's silver knock-off – which sat in Russell's toy chest, unbeknownst to the rest of the keep – but the original crown, the one King Theo had worn, and King Seb before him, and King Rubeous before that, the one reserved for coronations and then not touched until the next king was crowned, was to the people of Adem what Salator Crey's remains were to the clergy: irreplaceable, invaluable, and more priceless than even the King of Adem himself.

Night fell on the Serpent's Knot as the two small princes crept into this back room.

'I don't like this place,' Russell said quietly. 'It's dark.'

'Baby,' Azrael scolded. 'I wanna see the crown.'

Russell followed him down the green carpet, his face pulled into distressed creases. They tiptoed over the carpet to the other side of the dark room. A glass cabinet reflected the candlelight from the throne room outside.

'I'm scared,' Russell whispered.

'Shush!' Azrael snapped in a low voice, approaching the glass cabinet. 'I wanna put it on. Hold this.' He handed Russell a toy soldier. Azrael had cut its head off with a sharp kitchen knife sometime previously.

Azrael halted in front of the cabinet, squinting inside.

Each artefact had a shelf of its own: the crown on top, the sceptre below. Each was cradled by an emerald-coloured cushion.

Azrael snatched the tiny brass handle and gave the cabinet door a sharp tug. It opened with ease.

'Come on!' he hissed at Russell, who skulked in the background.

'I don't like it here,' he said, backing away. 'I'm going to find my daddy.'

'Your daddy's busy,' Azrael sneered. 'Come on!'

Russell clutched the mutilated toy and did as he was told.

Azrael pulled the crown from its shelf and turned it in his hands. 'It's pretty,' he said, admiring it. 'It's not made of rock.'

'Put it back,' Russell said, close to tears. He didn't like Azrael when he got like this. He didn't get like this often: most of the time Russell was glad to have someone to play with, even if he kept breaking his toys. Some of the time, however, he was just a little too sinister for him. He didn't know the word 'sinister' himself, but he could recognise the vibes. He could only describe it as 'bad'.

'No,' Azrael said, raising it to place on his head. 'It's mine now.'

'Put it BACK!' Russell shrieked, suddenly furious.

Azrael stared at him in alarm but placed it on his head regardless. 'Ouch!' he shouted, jerking it away from his scalp. 'It bit me!'

'Where?' Russell asked in alarm.

Azrael threw the crown to the ground irately. It bounced once before rolling diagonally away from him, to Russell's left. 'On my ear.' He started to cry.

He rubbed his hand behind his left ear and his fingers came away bloody. Azrael screamed and bolted out of the room, sobbing loudly.

'Wait!' Russell called, his heart thumping. He wasn't supposed to be in there. The Bastard had warned him: he didn't know why, but that wasn't the point. He wasn't supposed to be in there.

He lunged for the discarded crown and picked it up around the rim.

He felt a stab of pain and dropped it to find a drop of blood dangling from his index finger.

Russell let out a little wail and wrapped his free hand around the right index finger. Biting down his tears, he diverted his mind from the wound and picked up the crown again, returning it to the cabinet. Small blobs of blood dotted the cabinet door, but he didn't notice.

Having returned everything to how it should be, he fled the room after Azrael, his legs pumping.

~

'You said what?' Seth said, laughing.

'I said no,' Adrienne said. 'Stop laughing, it isn't nice.'

'You just said "no",' Seth said, cackling.

'What else was I supposed to say?' Adrienne said. 'Stop laughing, he was really upset.'

'So upset, you decided to mend things by coming to my bed?'

She slammed an elbow into his ribs.

They lay back on his four-poster, the entrance to his quarters firmly bolted from inside. Adrienne flopped her head back on the inside of Seth's elbow as he dangled his hand in mid-air, twirling a lock of her hair in his fingers.

'Why do you come here?' he said.

She linked her fingers in his free hand. 'I don't know. Something just takes me over whenever I think of you, like a pink fog.'

He kissed the back of her hand. 'Me too.'

They lay in silence for a while, staring at the curtains hanging down on Seth's left.

'I'm thinking of breaking things off with him,' Adrienne said.

Seth frowned. 'Why?'

Adrienne frowned back at him. 'Because I'm seeing you now?'

Seth made a face. 'Don't do that.'

'What do you mean? Why not? I don't have feelings for him anymore, it's cruel to just string him along like this—'

'I don't want people to suss us out,' Seth said stiffly. 'It will look suspicious. Just stay as you are.'

Adrienne stiffened. 'I thought you would be pleased that I didn't want to be with him anymore.'

'I am,' he said. 'I'm just thinking of your reputation.'

'I don't care about that,' she said. 'I love you.'

Seth didn't say anything for a moment.

'Don't you feel the same?'

'I do,' he said in a whisper. 'But…'

Adrienne deflated. 'Cienne.'

Seth turned his eyes upward. 'Yes.'

Pain shot through her chest. 'Are you going to tell her about us?'

Seth shook his head firmly. 'I don't want her getting upset.'

'Don't you think she should know?'

'She isn't finding out,' Seth said. 'Neither of them are. She's the mother of my children, I'm not upsetting—' He realised what he had implied a moment too late.

Adrienne sat upright.

'You're never going to forgive me for that, are you?' she said in a soft voice. 'You know it wasn't my decision or my fault and you're still holding it against me.'

'That's not what I meant, I'm sorry I said that.'

Adrienne stared into space. Her throat grew tight.

'You had better head home,' Seth said. 'Cienne's due back sometime today.'

She didn't move.

He lifted himself upright, stroking her back. 'I'm sorry I upset you. I'll come to you soon, alright?'

She nodded twice.

He held her close from behind and kissed her cheek, tucking his chin in the crook of her neck.

Her stomach fluttered, in spite of her emotions.

'I'll see you soon,' he murmured.

'Alright,' she whispered.

He released her and lay back down again, rubbing his eyes.

Adrienne rose without a word and left.

IV

'Have you noticed anything odd about Adrienne?' Archie asked.

Howie stuck out his lower lip and shook his head. 'Not at all.'

Archie sighed and drank deep from his flagon of beer.

The King Death bustled around them. The usual midday rush slid past them, brushing their table: they made the most of it while King Seth was still oblivious to the pun on his name. They needn't have bothered: it had been four years since Seth had recovered from his Ghost of Adem illness. If he was going to notice them, he would have done so by now.

'I haven't seen her for ages,' Archie commented.

Howie sipped his own beer as if on default, as though he was deep in thought. The only thing that contradicted that statement was that Howie didn't appear to think at all these days. It was like his brain was almost completely empty.

'Neither have I,' Howie said distantly. He circled the rim of his cup with one index finger. 'When I come in the door, she's either out or in bed already.'

'Aren't you worried?' Archie asked in exasperation. 'What happened? Did you have an argument recently or something?'

'I asked her to marry me the other day,' he said vaguely.

Archie deflated in relief. That was it. She was shopping for wedding dresses. Thank God. A grin crept over his face. 'That's incredible!' he exclaimed. 'Why didn't you say that in the first place? That explains everything.'

'She said no.'

Archie's elation dissipated rapidly. 'Oh.'

Howie shrugged, sipping his beer.

Archie grimaced at him. 'Aren't you upset?'

'No. I'll try again next year.'

Archie spluttered. 'Did she say *why* she said no? Is she leaving you? Why are you not worried? She's worshipped you from the minute your foot stepped in my door. Why did she say no?'

'Dunno,' Howie said. 'I might take her on holiday.'

'But,' Archie said.

'Holiday's a really good idea,' Howie said to himself. 'Somewhere hot. And sunny.'

'Howie,' Archie said severely.

'Holiday.'

Archie slapped him across the face.

Some men from the neighbouring table turned in anticipation of a fight but were quickly disappointed. Howie just sat there like a vase.

'Is there anybody home?' Archie asked, waving a hand across Howie's face.

Howie blinked once in response.

Archie sighed again. 'I'm gonna head to the castle tomorrow and see if I can find her.'

'Alright,' Howie said blankly.

Archie watched him in concern. *He's heartbroken*, he thought in distress. *What's going on with her?* He got up a moment later and left him there.

Howie showed no intention of following him out. He just sat there, nursing his cup of beer. He remained like this for a while until a woman sat down beside him.

'Hello, Howie.'

He faced her, breaking from his reverie – or lack of. 'Oh, long time no see,' he said pleasantly. 'How have you been?'

'Fine,' she said. 'Are you alright?'

Howie paused. 'I don't know.'

Anna leaned forward. 'Want me to help you find out?'

~

Midday saw the arrival of the Fleurelle party on the horizon. Jon watched Adrienne slip out to hurry down the path to Castlefoot, his brow furrowed in disapproval.

Jimmy busied himself in the kitchens, fulfilling Seth's desires of a massive banquet. Fellow staff tried excruciatingly hard not to notice the massive fake beard he was wearing to disguise himself from the king.

Russell meandered around the legs of the kitchen staff, begging for pastries and chatting to himself. Jimmy kept a close eye on him. He seemed to be developing a fever lately, no doubt from roaming the grounds with his little friend Azrael. His one-sided conversation – apparently to Albie – was occasionally interrupted by a fit of shivers. It wouldn't do for Jimmy's little wingman to get ill before the arrival of Cienne's new handmaidens. Jimmy hoped he was okay.

'Seth's tart's done a runner,' Jon observed, entering the kitchen with a yawn. 'I take that to mean the queen's returning?'

'Yep,' Jimmy said, his voice muffled by the black mass covering his face. He finished loading a trolley with food to bring to the dining hall. 'You wouldn't load that other trolley over there, would you? Moat says she's only about fifteen minutes away and I've only got two hands.'

Jon did as he was bid and headed for the large table in the centre of the kitchen, covered with delicacies of every description. 'Anyone tell her about Seth's mistress yet?' he asked, hefting a huge boar onto the trolley with a huff.

'No. I think the Prophet's biding his time,' Jimmy said. He hesitated a moment and, in lieu of entering the hall and exposing himself, rolled his full trolley to one of the porters.

It hit the porter in the stomach and lifted him off his feet and out of the door into the hall.

'I wonder what happened to him?' Jon said of the Prophet.

The kitchen porter landed at the dining table with a clatter.

'I haven't seen him in ages.'

~

—The Prophet sat in his own private chamber on the third floor, painting a portrait Seth commissioned of himself. He muttered to himself as he worked.

'You think I've forgotten about you,' he murmured, 'but I haven't. I'm watching you. I'm watching you very closely… eek!'

He lost his grip on the paint palate.

It flopped face-down on the carpet. He lifted it up gingerly, took note of the oil paint sinking into the lush cream carpeting and plonked his box of tools on top of the evidence.

He returned to the painting, dipping his brush into the remaining paint. 'I'm waiting,' he muttered again, as if nothing had happened. 'You will conform.'

~

—'Oh, he's probably chucking paint around somewhere,' Jimmy said, throwing some loaves of bread on the bottom shelf of the trolley. 'You know, in between erotic daydreams about the king.'

'Any news about my old man?'

'None,' Jimmy said with a sigh. 'He's in the Tower, but we need to meet with Seth and explain everything before doing anything with him. Since he's royalty, we'll probably just exile him or something.'

'What about the master of coin?'

'Nothing we can do about him,' he sighed. 'We had to let him go, we can't touch him. Maybe Cienne and her brother will have a solution, but until we speak to them, we'll have to let things lie.'

'The waspy one got what was coming to him, though?'

'Oh yes,' Jimmy said with relish. 'He'll be shitting parchment for the next week.'

Jon grinned.

~

'So what's he coming over for?' Seth asked his mother.

'Ah... about that.'

They hovered outside the front portcullis in wait for Cienne and Alain, Cienne's half-brother. Eleanor had Russell on her lap as they sat on a bench by the wall, getting ready to show him off. The three-year-old was the sole heir to the throne of Portabella, despite having a living maternal uncle. Issue from a second wife didn't count in the Portabellan line of succession – and Seth didn't like to leave a good gloat go to waste.

'His mother is on to us.'

Seth gulped. 'She wants a grandchild, doesn't she?'

'Several,' Eleanor winced. 'Apparent Alain was told not to return to Portabella until he has conceived an heir. Lilly is not happy.'

'I wouldn't be either if I had to push a small human out of my—'

Russell shook violently, his limbs juddering.

'Oh dear, are you cold?' Eleanor asked in concern, rubbing his back.

'Yes,' Russell squeaked, his teeth chattering.

Seth flung a glance at the sky. The wind bore the beginnings of a winter chill, but nothing the boy's fine velvet clothing couldn't ward off. The sun still bathed the grounds in light and warmth.

'We'd better bring you straight inside,' Eleanor said firmly, turning to the double doors.

Seth watched them go, giving Russell a worried glance.

His concern was interrupted by the clatter of coach wheels. He swung his gaze around to see the barbican filled to the brim with horses and litters. It appeared the Half-Prince of Portabella had brought half the Fleurelles' court with him.

Seth rolled his eyes and rose, straightening his jerkin.

A huge magenta carriage trundled up to the gate. Seth flinched away from the horses, two large black stallions, and sidled around them, giving them a wide berth as the carriage door opened and—

Seth's jaw dropped open.

Cienne's legs yawned out of the carriage, one after another: both free of the usual constraints of petticoats.

'Um, hello, darling, how, are, you…' Seth trailed off.

Cienne smirked, straightening. A glittering gown of magenta, two shades lighter than the coach, poured down the length of her slim frame. Two ridges accentuated her narrow shoulders, circled in silver thread rendering floral patterns. Seth followed the patterns as they twirled down her arms to the wrists. Identical patterns flanked the ribbons fastening the gown over a white under-dress. Seth's eyes ran down the underdress in particular as it circled her cleavage and ran down her torso behind the ribbons, until just short of her knees, whereupon it split in the middle to reveal—

Seth tore his gaze away with difficulty.

'I'm well,' Cienne said airily. 'How are you?'

Seth swallowed repeatedly. 'Good.' He flicked a hand in the vague direction of her legs. 'You look, look lovely in that, that outfit, it, it's very… nice.'

Cienne smirked again. 'A gift from my father. Fashioned in our signature colour, with rose detailing. Do you like it?'

'V-v-very much, yes. Out of interest, how does it come off?'

Cienne cackled and clapped a hand over her mouth, gesturing for Seth to be silent.

Her brother, the small effeminate Alain, followed her from the carriage to bow down before Seth with a flourish.

Seth glanced at him, making a face. He waved his hand up and down. 'You can get up now. Thanks.'

Alain rose, his chestnut hair gleaming in the sun. He wore the masculine equivalent of Cienne's attire: minus the exposure of lower limb. He began a torrent of cordial sounding Portabellan.

Seth nodded along with a faint smile, a staple in his arsenal of automated facial expressions.

'His highness is very pleased to arrive at your wondrous home, your majesty,' translated a young man of around twenty, lingering behind Alain with his curly head bowed.

'Great. Glad to have you here.'

The translator paused before registering that there would be no more to come. He arched an eyebrow and rattled off a rendition to Alain, albeit embroidered with proper court etiquette.

Alain grinned in response and grasped Seth's hand in both of his own before entering the castle.

Seth gave him an odd side-glance before turning back to Cienne. 'It's lovely to see you.'

Cienne beamed at him. 'Likewise.' She slid her arms around his neck and kissed him deeply.

Seth spotted a few retainers giving her alarmed looks before his eyes fluttered shut. 'Are they alright?' he asked when they broke away. 'They look as if we had just done something scandalous.'

'We did,' Cienne said with a laugh. 'They're very prim and proper where I come from.'

'Are you sure that's where you came from, then?'

She giggled, linking her arm into his elbow.

'Hey!' a small voice trilled. 'Wait for me!'

Seth untangled himself from Cienne and bolted back to the carriage to sweep Ginny into his arms.

'Hello!' he trilled. 'Did you have a nice time!'

'Ya!' she shouted at him, elated. 'They ga'me bikkits with pretty icing!

And they brought a big cake, look!'

An elaborate three-tiered cake covering in intricate filigree-like icing teetered between three servants. The magenta theme made for a garishly unappetising appearance.

'OH, oh, and! And I got a new dress!'

She flapped her magenta skirts into the air in demonstration, a miniature child-version of her mother's gown.

'So I see,' Seth said in amusement. He smacked a loud kiss on her cheek. 'Come! Let's see if this cake is any good!'

Ginny squealed with delight.

Seth's chest swelled. He hoisted her onto one shoulder, brushing magenta skirts out of his face.

~

'Jimmy!' Eleanor barked into the kitchens. 'Come here!'

His voice gravitated out faintly from deep within the kitchens. 'I can't! I have to stay in here!'

Eleanor heaved a sigh and stormed into the kitchen. She bounded up to Jimmy, heels clacking on the flagstones, and yanked his fake beard off.

'Half of the canapes are covering in little bits of black wool! What on earth is the need for this?'

'Shush, he can't know I'm back here,' Jimmy hissed, eyeing the open door.

'Why? What did you do exactly?'

'Nothing!'

'Then go out there and pick all the wool out of the buffet! And give Seth something to eat, he's already sloshed and it isn't even third turn yet.'

'I can't!' Jimmy wailed. 'We aren't getting along very well at the moment!'

Eleanor pulled his apron off and shoved him out of the kitchen.

~

Lilly and Alain were seated side by side at the dinner table, the former looking increasingly annoyed at the physical contact with the latter.

'It is a pleasure to meet you once again, my dear lady,' the interpreter said in a dull voice as Alain prattled in a similar fashion.

Lilly tried vainly to shrug Alain's ringed fingers off her own. 'Listen,' she said over the two voices, 'your mum ain't here, and mine don't give a crap. You can lay off the touchy-feely bollocks, alright? If you want me pregnant so badly, there's plenty of good-looking men in the local brothel, along with equally good-looking women to assist them! You don't need to lift a finger—let go of my hand!'

The interpreter said something about the retainers being spies for Lady Elsabet.

'Oh God,' Lilly groaned.

Seth sniggered at her from the head of the table, his shoulders shaking. She caught Seth's eye and flicked him the bird.

The evening's celebrations swelled as the court – minus Lilly – welcomed Alain with open arms.

Russell hadn't made a reappearance. Not even word of the massive Fleurelle-themed cake had stirred him from his bed. Seth glanced at the stairs, his brow furrowed in concern. No illness had kept him away from a cake-filled party before. Seth resolved to send Erik straight up to him in the morning.

Heralded by a bombastic drum trio, the castle musicians swung into action. Ginny danced with Cienne as a rousing jig commenced.

Lilly swerved around them, trying to shake off her unwanted husband. 'Go away!' She flung him the most universal gesture she knew – the two-handed 'shoo' motion.

The interpreter hovered behind Alain, muttering.

Alain responded in what Lilly shortly learned with horror to be the Portabellan for 'Let's just get this over with and make a child.'

'NO! PISS OFF! Don't make me fight you, I'm trained in all forms of armed combat! GO AWAY!'

Alain ignored the worried interpreter and made to follow her.

Lilly bolted out of the double doors to the courtyard.

Jimmy stacked some empty plates. Eleanor's tapping foot diverted his attention to his left. 'Yes, your highness?'

Eleanor snatched the bandanna wrapped around the lower half of his face. 'I've had enough of this,' she snarled. 'Seth!'

Seth jogged over.

Cold steel went through Jimmy's digestive tract – metaphorically. He hoped it wasn't a premonition into a more literal future.

'I don't know what's happened between the two of you,' Eleanor said tartly, 'but I want it sorted out now. Talk!'

Jimmy lifted his shoulders around his ears.

Seth scowled at him, squinting through five tankards of beer. 'They say,' he said, 'that my left testicle was ruptured, you know.'

Eleanor pinched her eyes between her thumb and forefinger.

'I'm sorry for what happened?' Jimmy proffered.

Seth shrugged his shoulders.

'You know what? I have a belly full of beer and my wife and daughter are home – I don't care what you did.' He held out his arms. 'Come on. Let's hug it out, come on.'

Jimmy very hesitantly let Seth envelope him in his arms.

Eleanor dusted her hands off and left, a job well done.

'Don't blackmail me again,' Seth hissed into Jimmy's ear. 'What happened to my father stays between me and you, understand?'

Jimmy nodded feverishly.

'And don't touch my ball-sack again or I'll hobble you!'

'Understood, sir.'

Seth smacked a beer-scented kiss on his cheek, making him grimace. 'Move back in tomorrow,' he ordered, serving himself more food.

'I'd like to stay with the clergy, actually,' Jimmy piped up eagerly.

Seth frowned. 'With the clergy?'

Jimmy mopped Seth's kiss off his face with the bandanna. 'You know, free food, no rent, wine on tap…'

'… and those nuns won't deflower themselves,' Seth finished with a grin. 'Whatever, it's your coach fare. My mother wants you up here early tomorrow for some council meeting, mind.'

Philip Manderly would be attending, Jimmy remembered. 'Oh, I'll be there,' he said in earnest.

Seth eyed Jimmy's hands rubbing together and furrowed his brow.

Cienne deposited her daughter with Ronald Horne and pinched Seth in the ribs, nodding for him to follow her to the throne room.

'Tell me,' Cienne said. 'How are your lessons coming along?'

Seth grinned. 'Great. I have muscle definition for the first time in my entire life.'

'I look forward to seeing that,' Cienne said with a sly smirk. 'I'll have to watch your next lesson, see how good you're getting.'

'I'm getting *quite* good, as it goes,' Seth said smugly.

They passed the courtyard on the way. Seth glimpsed Lilly's head between two rose bushes. 'What's she doing in there?'

'Hiding from my brother,' Cienne said. 'He's taking his orders from my stepmother very seriously.'

'That doesn't bode well for him.' Seth grinned.

'It'll bode worse if he disregards the queen consort's wishes,' Cienne said with a smile. 'Elsabet is formidable, even in comparison.'

Lilly felt breathing on the back of her neck.

She shrieked, startling Seth and Cienne.

'Seth!' Lilly called, sprinting away from Alain. 'Wanna spar?'

'No,' Seth said. He frowned at his sister.

She circled the two in an attempt to lose him.

'Why don't you just tell him you're not in the mood?' Seth asked.

Lilly cowered behind him. 'He doesn't understand!' She covered her eyes, as though not being able to see *him* would result in the vice versa. 'If he doesn't know what "shoo" means, he won't understand anything!'

Seth put an arm around Lilly's shoulders. 'D'you want your big brother to beat him up for you?'

'Yes,' she whimpered. 'Him or me, whichever will get him to leave.'

'You it is,' Seth grinned. He made a sweeping gesture at Alain. 'Back off, we're fighting, you know,' he wielded an imaginary sword and swung it back and forth, 'you know, Cienne, tell him.'

Cienne giggled and translated.

The next twenty minutes were spent displaying Seth's aptitude with a sword. The fact that he lasted twenty minutes before being disarmed and managed not to injure himself proved Seth's point to be correct. He *was* getting quite good, as it goes.

Cienne had turned bright red at this spectacle and it wasn't long before Seth was quickly ushered inside by his waistband.

Lilly panted with exertion, beginning to sheath her sword.

Alain appeared behind her and covered her eyes.

Ron got lucky in the armoury the day he had attempted the same. Then again, Ron wasn't stupid enough to cover Lilly's eyes when there was a sword in her actual *hand*.

Fump!

~

V

'I take it you like what you see—'

Cienne interrupted him by pressing her mouth over his.

Seth made a muffled squeak.

She pressed him backwards into the throne and mounted him, her knees pressing into his hips.

Seth broke away to draw breath. 'This is nice.'

She threw her skirts backward out of the way. *The slit in the front came in very useful*, Seth thought.

He jolted slightly and slouched in his throne, swallowing. 'Shouldn't we take this upstairs?' he asked as Cienne buried her face in his neck. 'There's the, the children, they'll walk in, and, and the guests, and, ah…'

'I told my ladies-in-waiting to guard the doors,' she said in his ear. 'I've been looking forward to this *all day…*'

Seth squeaked unintelligibly. He let her lead the way, his hands locked to the small of her back.

Meanwhile, outside, Cienne's chief lady-in-waiting deposited Jon at the back door of the entrance hall and snuck off for a drink. She warbled something in Portabellan. Jon nodded blankly, watched her go with a shrug and folded his hands at the small of his back.

Qattren waited patiently in a similar fashion.

Jon paused. 'You waiting to be let in?'

'Yes,' she said brightly. 'I thought I would be polite today and actually be welcomed in for a change. Since the king has company and all. May I come in?'

Jon shrugged. 'Since you asked nicely.' He pivoted, swinging the doors forward.

The two froze.

'Ah,' said Qattren.

Jon tilted his head to one side and sighed. 'You're making a *mess.*'

'AAH!'

~

After clothing had been readjusted and the throne had been thoroughly scrubbed, Seth sat on it in a more dignified manner flanked on either side by Cienne and Jimmy.

Qattren cleared her throat. 'There's someone you need to keep an eye on,' she said. 'You know, when you find the time.'

Seth rolled his eyes. *You don't want me with Adrienne, you don't want me with my own wife…*

'Who are you referring to?' Cienne asked, her arms folded.

'You remember your old chambermaid, Anna?'

Seth's eyes glazed over. 'Vividly.'

Cienne scowled at him. 'Well, don't.'

Seth bowed his head.

'I spotted her in Arthur Stibbons' Street this afternoon,' Qattren said. 'She was with Howard Rosethorn. They looked too cosy for my liking.'

'Looks like Adrienne's been left high and dry,' Jimmy commented.

'Couldn't have happened to a nicer person,' Cienne said.

Seth stiffened, stung by the remark. 'What's she up to?'

'Nothing good,' Qattren said. 'You had her coached off to Mellier, as I recall.'

'Is that where she ended up?' Seth asked in interest. 'I always wondered.'

'You mean you didn't know?' Jimmy asked in amusement.

'I told him to take her far away. I didn't think he'd take her *that* far.'

'No wonder she's pissed,' Jimmy said. 'You gave a weirdo in a coach free reign on the palace jockey. God knows what he's done to her.'

'Again,' Cienne said, 'couldn't have happened to a nicer person.'

'In any case,' Qattren said, 'you may want to find her before she gets any closer to Howie.'

'Why, what's the worst she can do?' Seth asked. 'Give him herpes?'

'Just keep an eye on her, that's all,' Qattren said coldly, turning to leave.

Seth eyeballed her. 'Wait for me upstairs,' he told Cienne, giving her a kiss. 'And don't take that dress off without me!'

Cienne watched him dart out of the front entrance in bemusement.

'What's the matter with you?' Seth asked Qattren. He jogged after her as she meandered around the gentry.

She waited until they reached the vacant portcullis before swinging toward him to reply. 'Anna is not what she seems.'

Seth frowned. 'Explain.'

She sighed, wondering how to explain this. 'There's… someone else. A man… sort of.'

Seth made a face.

'Listen,' Qattren pressed. 'There's a… person… out there somewhere who would do you harm. And I don't like how she's appeared out of nowhere. You need to keep an eye out.'

Seth's eyes narrowed. 'You mean the man Despina was working for?'

Qattren blinked. 'Yes. How did you know?'

'She told me,' he said. 'Who is he?'

'I don't entirely know,' she said. 'He just calls himself the Bastard.'

Seth shot her a sceptical glance. 'He calls himself the Bastard,' he drawled.

'This isn't a joke,' Qattren snapped. 'He's coming after you. And your family.'

She turned to leave again.

'Is that it?' Seth asked incredulously. 'You've come all this way for that? "The Bastard is coming after you"? Tell him to get in line! There are about six illegitimate people with a grudge against me, and guess how many have a dragon and a castle? None. That's not going to frighten me away from Adrienne, if that's what you were hoping!'

'That's exactly what I'm worried about,' Qattren said. 'Be careful.'

She dissipated, a separating dust cloud replacing her slight form. Seth gagged. Frequency in number never made her departures any less nauseating.

Seth flapped dust away from him and pivoted, deciding he didn't care. *Let him come*, he thought to himself. *I have an appointment with my wife tonight,*

290

Bastard or no Bastard.

~

Despite his late night with Cienne, Seth rose with the dawn, rousing his manservant with a nudge from his toe. The serving man twitched awake, rolling over on the drawing room hearth with a yawn. *Maybe it was time to build him a room of his own*, Seth mused – before forgetting about him and focussing on his morning's task.

The cool morning air swept through the courtyard, lifting leaves and petals into a twirling dance around the flagstones. Marbrand resumed his place at the fountain as Seth arrived. He yawned widely, his back turned.

Seth took the opportunity to lamp him with the flat of his sword.

Marbrand stumbled, clutching his ribs. 'BASTARD!'

Seth grinned. 'Is that any way to speak to your king?'

Marbrand drew his sword and threw himself at him, but it was no use.

Seth darted back and forth with ease, deflecting and dodging his blows and delivering a few nice ones in return. He was getting good at this, Marbrand reflected. Just as well: he'd need these skills for what Marbrand had planned for him.

'Alright, alright, I yield,' Marbrand gasped, struggling to catch his breath. 'I have a few new recruits here – they can swing a sword, so watch out. Aiden! George! Sam!'

Three bulky teens rounded the fountain edge, armed with short swords.

'Right, off you go,' Marbrand said, waving them forward.

'Which one am I fighting?' Seth asked.

'All of them.'

The boys charged on him at once. Seth screamed.

Cienne watched the scene from the balcony in her and Seth's private study, leaning her elbows on its low concrete wall. She decided she liked this sword-fighting idea very much.

Seth hopped backward over and over, trying to gain distance using the footwork technique Marbrand had taught him. The boys ran at him, disregarding the footwork, he noticed.

'Come on, is that the best you can do?' Seth hollered, deflecting with ease.

One boy gained enough confidence to leap forward, his sword raised.

Seth batted it away and kicked the kid in the stomach, sending him flying backwards into the other two. One went down with him in a heap. The other stumbled and righted himself, resuming his stance.

Seth inclined his head in approval and came at him, swinging and dodging. The boy, largest of the two by Seth's reckoning, panted steadily. Seth rushed him and tripped him up, leaving him in a cloud of dust.

Seth turned to his balcony and bowed at Cienne, who giggled.

'This victory is for you, my love,' he crooned.

One of the smaller teens jumped on his back and knocked him on his face.

'That's what happens when you get distracted chasing skirt,' Marbrand said. 'No offense, your highness,' he amended loudly for Cienne's benefit.

Cienne curtsied, no offense taken.

'Alright, off him,' Marbrand ordered the teen. 'We have things to cover.'

'I'd better leave you boys to it, lest you get more distracted,' Cienne said with a smile. She blew Seth a kiss.

He caught it in one hand with a wink.

Cienne vanished inside.

He turned to the boys to smooth down his hair. 'Lovely, isn't she?' he said smugly, making them laugh.

'She's a ride,' one of them said with enthusiasm.

'What did you call her?' Seth asked dangerously.

'Nuh-nothing, my liege—nyah!'

Seth chased him, sword raised.

Cienne smirked to herself and left the balcony, turning left at the corridor to her son's quarters. She entered the room silently and froze, her gaze locked on her son.

Despina was the first to hear her scream.

~

Jimmy hovered outside the council chamber and was shocked to see Seth approaching. 'Sir,' he said in surprise.

Seth raised his eyebrows at him, opening the door.

'You're at a council meeting,' Jimmy said in astonishment. 'Of your *own* volition. Have I inadvertently entered a parallel universe?'

'Not to my knowledge,' Seth said. He seated himself at the head of the table, bracing his feet on the edge. 'I just wanted to see why you were so eager to be at this meeting.'

'Ah, well,' he said, sitting at Seth's left, 'that's a long story that would be infinitely more entertaining watching the master of coin—'

'Sir!' Despina gasped, bursting through the open door.

'Is everything alright?' Jimmy asked in concern.

'It's the prince,' Despina said through laboured breaths. 'I've sent the medic up to his rooms, he's not well—'

Seth threw his feet to the flagstones. 'What's wrong with him?'

~

'He had a fit,' Cienne said through tears.

Erik pushed past her. His knuckle touched Russell's forehead and burned. 'How long has he had this fever?'

'Only last night. Despina called you during the party, why didn't you come?'

'Ask your mongrel master of war and his latest foe,' Erik muttered.

Russell lay flat in the middle of his bed, coated in sweat. His sheets were a crumpled heap at the end of his bed.

Cienne knelt on them, gulping back tears.

Erik placed his head close to the boy's chest.

'Is he alive?'

'He's breathing,' Erik said. 'That's as much as I can say without knowing exactly what happened. To be honest, there isn't going to be much I can do—'

'Well, what bloody use are you, then?' Cienne snapped.

Footsteps hammered in the corridor. 'What happened?'

Cienne faced Seth with a shuddering breath. 'He had a shaking fit.'

Seth paced forward, pushing Erik out of the way. He put a hand on Russell's brow. It burned under his fingers.

'There isn't much I can do,' Erik said weakly.

Seth ignored him and bolted out of the room.

'Where are you going?' Cienne howled after him.

'I'm getting a real medic.' Seth leapt down the stairs three at a time and tore off through the castle. He barged past Jon at the opening doors and sprinted straight for the stables.

Mounting a horse and sliding to one side in inexperience, he jerked the horse forward and sent it galloping north.

~

'I think we should go on holiday,' Howie said.

Adrienne sighed. 'You've asked me this already.'

They sat at the rickety kitchen table in front of a meagre breakfast of bread and cheese. It was the first time they had been in the same room together since the proposal.

'Oh yeah,' Howie said dully.

Silence ensued, broken only by the faint galloping of hooves in the village.

'I met Anna in town the other day,' he said distantly.

'Who?' Adrienne said irritably.

'You know. The Creys' old chambermaid.'

Adrienne froze. 'And?'

Howie shrugged nonchalantly. 'Just had a chat. She was in Mellier for a couple years. She's looking well.'

'Good for her,' Adrienne seethed, realising what she was implying as soon as she'd implied it. *Do as I say, not as I do, is it?* she scolded herself.

'She might try and get her job back at the palace,' he said as the hoof-steps skidded to a halt.

'Look, why are you telling me this—'

Their front door burst open.

'Please help me,' Seth said, his voice thick with tears.

~

Adrienne knelt by Russell's side and placed a fingertip under his left jaw.

'Seth, no,' Cienne wept, clutching his shoulder.

'It's alright, he'll be fine,' Seth soothed, holding her hand in both of his own. 'He's in good hands.'

'What was he doing yesterday and the day before?' Adrienne asked Despina.

'He was just playing around the castle,' she replied, wringing her hands. 'He started getting a fever yesterday, so I put him to bed during the festivities. He slept most of the evening.'

'Was he playing anywhere in particular around the castle?'

'I spotted him running out of one of the storerooms off the entrance hall,' Despina said, wracking her brains. 'I can't think of anything else.'

'I hurted my finger,' Russell said hoarsely.

Adrienne moved her head close to his. 'What was that, sweetheart?'

'I hurted my finger.' He held it up to demonstrate, but weakness overcame him. It quickly fell onto the sheets again.

Adrienne inspected his hand. 'Aha.'

His right index finger was swollen.

'Do snakes ever appear in the gardens?'

Everyone frowned.

'Snakes?' Despina asked, bemused. 'In the woods, maybe, but not in the grounds. Not that I've ever seen, anyway.'

'It looks like an adder bite. I can fix this.' She took a needle from her pack and a slim metal tube.

'No,' Cienne whined.

'He'll be fine, don't worry,' Adrienne said, but Cienne wasn't talking to her.

Her nails dug into Seth's left hand. 'She'll kill him.'

Seth shot Cienne a barbed glance. 'No she won't.'

'Seth—'

'No she won't,' he said, his voice slow and firm.

Adrienne inserted the pipe to the inside of his elbow. Seth had never seen instruments like that. Where did she even get them from? She pulled the stopper from a small vial with her teeth. Slowly, she dripped the liquid within into the pipe, one drop at a time.

'I'll need to stay here and administer this every few minutes,' she said. 'He should be fine in about a day or so.'

'What is it?' Seth asked. He eyed the tube protruding from his arm with discomfort.

'Anti-venom. He was bitten by a snake, I think.'

'You think?' Erik snarled. 'And how can you be so sure?'

'I've seen it before. I study these things, which is what you should have done. Not that it would have helped, your skills and equipment date back to the dark ages.'

Erik flushed, turning his eyes away.

'I'll keep an eye on him, make sure it's working.' She turned her gaze onto Russell. 'You must keep this in your arm, alright? I know it hurts, but you must be brave.'

'Okay,' he whispered, trying not to look at it.

Seth found it difficult to look at himself.

'Daddy,' a small voice said by his foot.

'Ginny,' Seth said in a pained voice, 'he's fine, look, you can't be in here—'

'It's alright, as long as she keeps away from the tube,' Adrienne soothed.

Ginny stepped around the adults and peered at him from Adrienne's side. 'You alright?' she asked, stroking his hair.

He was still sweaty and pale, but he nodded valiantly.

'He might still have convulsions every so often while the anti-venom kicks in,' she warned.

Erik took over vigil, holding the pipe vertical with care.

'Every two minutes,' she reminded him. 'Send for me around third turn and we'll take shifts.'

Erik nodded, his attention on the drips coming from the vial.

'Alright,' Ginny said in reply. She gave Adrienne a hug.

Adrienne hesitated a moment before gently patting her back.

Seth met Adrienne's gaze and mouthed, 'Thank you.'

Adrienne smiled thinly. 'Can I speak with you outside?'

Seth followed her out to the corridor, Cienne at their heels.

'Will he be alright?' Seth asked, wringing his hands.

'He'll be fine. Me and my tutor have been fine-tuning things like this for many years. He's the one who had my tools made for me. What I wanted to talk to you about is the servant's quarters.'

Seth and Cienne frowned.

'What about them?' asked Cienne.

'I passed them on the way up. They smell appalling. When was the last time you were in there?'

Seth shrugged. 'No idea.' Except that he did – he'd been in there the day after the fiasco at the party. The place was a pigsty. 'Obviously they don't have any leaks or anything.'

'But are they cleaned regularly?'

Seth shook his head and shrugged again. 'I don't know. That's the housekeeper's job to know these things.'

Adrienne gave him a withering glance. 'You need to do an inspection,' she said. 'You need to clean the entire castle and check the windows in the servants' quarters. Leaks don't just come through ceilings. You can't use all your resources keeping yourselves comfortable if you're going to let your servants languish in destitution.'

'Who do you think you are?' Cienne snapped, her voice thick with tears. 'Giving orders to the king and queen—'

'I've just saved your son's life,' Adrienne said hotly. 'Snakes are the least of his problems if you're leaving half the castle rot and spread disease. If you want him to live past the age of four, you need to take my advice—'

'I don't need to take any advice from a woman who thought her carnal needs were worth more than her own child,' Cienne said bluntly.

Adrienne froze, her face taut.

'Cienne!' Seth hissed.

'No, I'm sorry, but it's true, alright?' Cienne said. 'It was a choice between her child and her boyfriend, and she chose the boyfriend. If you had a glimpse of real motherhood,' she snapped at Adrienne, 'you wouldn't take that tone with me. We give the world to our little boy, whereas you couldn't even let yours keep his life.'

Cienne snatched the extra vial of anti-venom from Adrienne's hand. 'I'll have Erik replenish his stores of this potion and we'll investigate the servants' quarters. The butler will escort you out, Miss Hart. Erik can pick up where you left off.'

Adrienne trembled. 'As you wish, your highness,' she said stiffly.

Jimmy gestured to the stairs.

Cienne was about to enter her son's room when Seth jerked her around. 'You can't talk to her like that.'

'I can talk to her however I like,' she said coldly, opening the door.

Seth closed it, turning her around by her shoulders. 'I know you're upset about what happened,' he said quietly, 'but she did nothing but help him—'

'She was trying to tell me—'

'Don't interrupt me,' Seth said firmly.

Cienne closed her mouth.

'I brought her up here to help us, not to be abused by you,' he said. 'I told you what had actually happened to the baby: you just decided to ignore that and spout false information to hurt her. I don't know why you're so bothered about it anyway. It wasn't anything to do with you in the first place.'

Cienne stepped back, stung. 'It was your child, of course I—'

'But he wasn't yours,' Seth cut in. 'He is,' he pointed at the door behind her, 'and you've just driven off the only person who could help him. What if the same thing happens to Ginny? What if she gets ill and we don't find her until it's too late?'

'Seth—' Cienne said, fresh tears emerging.

'I don't want to hear it,' he said curtly, elbowing her aside.

Russell was fast asleep when Seth opened the door.

Despina pried Ginny's hands from Erik's elbow.

'I can do it!' Ginny insisted. 'I be the nurse and help—'

'Yee-noooo,' Seth said quickly. He scooped his little girl into his arms.

Ginny eyed her weeping mother over his shoulder.

Seth noticed. 'She's just worried about your brother,' he murmured. 'He'll be fine soon. Let's go outside and let him rest, alright?'

Ginny nodded.

Seth carried her out to the stairs, avoiding Cienne's baleful gaze.

~

VI

Archie strode up to the portcullis in time to see Adrienne exit in tears.

'What on earth's happened?' he said in alarm, jogging up to put an arm around her elbows.

She was too choked up to answer.

Archie steered her back to his coach and paid for a lift to Serpus. Soon they rolled downhill, the thatched buildings of Castlefoot sliding past.

'Adrienne,' he said as they rounded into Castlefoot Market.

She looked up at him through watery eyes.

'Tell me what's going on,' he said firmly.

She didn't reply. She seemed unable to get the words out.

Archie observed her. 'Is he seeing someone else?'

Her head shot up. 'Who?'

Archie shook his head in wonder.

'Howie!' he exclaimed. 'Who else have you been living with for the past four years?'

Her eyes welled up. 'It isn't him. It's me.'

'I don't understand. What's you?'

'Being unfaithful.' She met his gaze, her brow furrowed upward. 'I'm… I'm the king's mistress.' It sounded strange saying it out loud.

Archie looked bemused. 'Since when?'

The coach jerked to a halt. Archie stuck his head out to see that a felled tree had blocked the road. He returned his attention to Adrienne. 'How long has this been going on?'

'A few weeks.' She choked up, her expression wretched.

Archie shifted forward in his seat, his elbows against his knees. 'Has he hurt you?' he asked in a low voice. 'Has the king forced himself on you?'

'No,' Adrienne whined.

'Because if he has,' Archie said savagely, gripping an imaginary object in his hands, 'I will make a barbed stool and fold it up his skinny ass—'

'No, he hasn't hurt me,' she wept.

Archie dropped his hands, along with the imaginary stool.

'Then what's upset you?' he asked gently.

Her eyes rose to meet his. Archie had the distinct feeling that there was something hiding behind the tears, some piece of information she was struggling to conceal from him. 'I'm in love with him,' she whispered.

'And he doesn't feel the same way about you.'

She nodded, tears rolling down her cheeks.

Archie gazed at his niece in empathy. 'I know how you feel.'

Adrienne gazed at him.

'About having feelings for someone who belongs to someone else.' He heaved a theatrical sigh. 'Believe it or not, even your grumpy old uncle once harboured feelings for a woman.'

'Who?' she said hoarsely.

Archie quirked a rueful half-smile. 'Your mother.'

Adrienne lifted her eyes incredulously. 'You were in love with my mother?'

'Unfortunately.' He laughed shortly. 'I remember telling you this when we first met, actually.'

'Really?'

'You were a week old, you wouldn't remember.' His rueful smile faded slightly. 'I was in shock. I was prattling away to you about your parents, as though you might remember and I wouldn't have to explain it again. I felt much the same way you're feeling now.' His smile faded completely. 'I hated your father after they started seeing each other. Secretly, anyway. Now I wish they were still here, rubbing it in my face while I was pining after your mother. At least she'd be alive to appreciate it.'

She wiped her eyes dry. 'Did my father know?'

'God no,' Archie said with a laugh. 'He was a foot taller than me, I would have been mincemeat. Anyway, she was his. He looked after her. He earned their life together more than I ever would.' He met her gaze. 'You have one thing I never had when I loved your mum.'

'What's that?'

'Another man.' He paused. 'Not that I wanted a man, I was after a wife, but you know what I mean. A partner.'

She sniffed. 'It doesn't feel like that most of the time. It feels like he's barely there.'

'He's just upset. If you just sat down with him—'

'I can't tell him. I can't, he'll do something stupid. Or he'll tell the queen. Seth said she can't know, he doesn't want to break her heart.' Her voice broke.

'But he's perfectly fine breaking yours.'

Adrienne gazed out of the window at the stationary countryside. She seemed fixated to a tiny sapling outside, but her expression betrayed that her thoughts were elsewhere, in another time. 'Have you ever looked at me as a child and imagined I was yours?'

Archie was taken aback. 'All the time, actually,' he admitted. 'I had dreams about it where she was still here, helping me look after you. I always felt guilty about it. It was like imagining my brother—'

'Never existed,' she finished with him.

'Yes.' He shuffled backwards uncomfortably. 'You know it would never have been possible in real life? Me being your father?'

Adrienne nodded. 'I know. She loved Jacob.'

'Deeply.' He looked downcast. 'He was the pretty one, you see,' he added, circling his own face.

Adrienne gave him a half-smile. 'What was her name?'

Archie frowned. 'Didn't I ever tell you?'

'No.' She laughed a little. 'This is the first time I ever heard you speak of her. I used to think you had forgotten it.'

Archie snorted. 'Never forgotten.' His eyes glazed over.

'It must be awful. Wanting something so much and seeing it so far out of reach.'

Archie shook his head. 'Not anymore. There's something that makes me feel better about her.'

'What's that?'

Archie grinned broadly. 'That you have four aunties with three children apiece and she chose *me* to adopt you out of all of us.'

Adrienne grinned back. 'Guess she loved you after all.'

'Maybe a little.'

They paused for a moment in the silence of the countryside, listening to the coachman outside straining to move the felled tree.

Archie realised with a start that he still hadn't answered Adrienne's question. He did so, his voice softer than his usual sarcastic tone. 'Her name was Rihanna.'

Adrienne looked up. 'Rihanna Hart,' she said, trying the words out together.

Archie met her gaze.

'I'm glad Rihanna chose you to be my father,' Adrienne whispered.

She looked so much like her — and Jake. *The best of both*, he thought. The old pain jabbed him at the thought of his brother's name. He still missed the little sod – more than he missed Ri. Archie cracked a bit inside. Outside, he cracked a smile. 'Me too.'

~

The Bastard waited for Cienne to head to the council meeting before crouching at his brother's bedside. 'Can you see me?' he whispered, ever so softly.

Russell's gaze fell on his and his face lit up. 'Hello.'

Thank God, he thought, deflating. Seeing Moat morph into King Seth might have looked amiss to the other guards in the playroom adjacent. 'Hello, mate,' he said with a thin smile.

Russell smiled bravely.

The Bastard ruffled his hair. 'How's your finger?'

He pointed it at him, showing the Bastard the healing spot on the tip. The swelling had abated, now that he had consumed an hour's worth of medication, and his face had lost a fraction of that grey pallor.

'All better,' he explained.

The Bastard shot him a half-smile. 'You didn't put the crown on, did you?'

'No,' he said. 'It bit my finger, and Azal's head.'

The Bastard frowned. 'It bit Azrael's head?'

'On his ear.'

The Bastard sat back on his haunches, his face taut. 'Oh God.'

The brothers' eyes met.

'Will he get sick too?' Russell whispered.

'Maybe,' the Bastard whispered back. A wave of anxiety hit him, making his arms tingle. Metaphorically.

'I got medicine,' Russell said, full of optimism. 'I be better soon.'

'You will.' The Bastard hesitated. 'He might not, though.'

Russell frowned a bit too, then decided he was too tired to be anxious right now.

The Bastard tried a reassuring smile, but it came out crooked. 'Get some sleep,' he said, before vanishing.

He reappeared before Jon at the main doors. 'Jon.'

Jon lifted his eyebrows at him. If he was surprised to see a spectral edition of Seth Crey standing before him, he didn't show it.

'It's... Albie,' said the Bastard with reluctance. 'I need your help. Discreetly.'

~

'They're seeing each other, aren't they?'

Eleanor froze. 'Who are, dear?'

The two queens, past and present, descended the spiral staircase arm in arm, Cienne's eyes still pink from crying.

'Seth and that girl,' Cienne said.

Eleanor laughed unconvincingly. 'What? That commoner?' She snorted theatrically. 'If he turned his nose up at Elizabeth del Loux de Hae, what on earth would he be interested in her for?'

Cienne gave her a wry glance. She held her tongue on what she thought about Elizabeth del Loux de Hae.

They were met at the foot of the stairs by Philip Manderly, to Eleanor's disgust. 'Yes?' she said coldly.

'Just came to wish you a good morning before our council meeting,' he simpered. 'How is the dear little prince?'

They looked him up and down with varying degrees of distaste.

'He's fine,' Cienne said in gruff tones. 'Shall we?'

They entered the council chamber. Manderly froze.

Seth sat at the head of the table, his feet propped on top of his council papers. Jimmy flanked his right side, looking smug.

Ginny perched cross-legged on the tiles nearby, painting a piece of parchment. Along with the floor around it.

'Y-your highness!' Manderly shrilled, grinning broadly. 'What a pleasant surprise!'

'Sit,' he said.

The three of them obeyed.

Cienne placed herself on Jimmy's other side, avoiding Seth's gaze.

'Any sign of Alain yet?' Eleanor asked keenly from Seth's right.

Just as she'd said it, Alain Fleurelle came flying through the door and

303

slammed into the edge of the table.

'Sorry we're late,' Lilly announced, strolling in after him.

They parked themselves at opposite ends of the table, Alain beside Cienne, Lilly with her mother. He'd gotten the hint, Cienne judged by his blackened eyelid.

'Right,' Jimmy announced, clapping his hands together. 'Now that we're all here, let's get down to business.' He paused, peering out of the door. 'She's calmed down now, it's safe to come in,' he called cheerfully.

Alain's translator shuffled to Alain's side, giving Lilly a wide berth.

Seth frowned around the table, mouthing a head count. 'Is this everyone? I could have sworn there were more of you.'

'That is one of the main issues to be discussed, sir, on which Philip Manderly here will fill you in,' Jimmy said, with relish.

Manderly looked alarmed. 'Eh?'

'Oh yes,' Jimmy said with glee. 'You have a lot to fill the king in on, don't you, Mister Manderly, sir?'

Manderly spluttered. 'Um, er, um, I couldn't possibly know where to start, sir, your majesty.'

'You're in charge of money, aren't you?' Seth said.

'… yes.'

'Well, let's start with that, then.'

'Um.'

Seth stared at him in the silence that followed, the only sound being the muttering of the translator.

'All good, sir,' he said, bottling it.

'*Really?*' Jimmy said in a pained voice, screwing his face up.

'Yes, money's coming in, and going out, in the usual fashion…' He trailed off lamely.

Seth rolled his eyes, already bored.

'Just tell him the truth, Manderly,' Eleanor sighed.

'It's empty, sir,' he said swiftly.

Seth swung his legs to the floor, sitting upright. 'Empty?'

'Vacant,' Jimmy supplied. 'Bare. Devoid of any money whatsoever.'

'How?' Seth demanded.

Jimmy turned to Manderly, smiling faintly.

'The Duke of Osney wished to surprise Princess Ginny with a new estate for her birthday, sir,' he said, finding a scapegoat.

'*Really*?' Jimmy said again in the exact same tone of voice.

'And costs ran up,' he said, ignoring Jimmy, 'leaving us with no alternative but to apply for a small loan—'

'Really?' Lilly joined in with him this time.

'—which the Duke was having a bit of trouble paying off—'

'Real—'

'Is someone going to get on with it sometime today?' Seth said impatiently, his eyes locked to the ceiling.

Manderly heaved a sigh and rattled off, 'The Duke erected a house for himself and ran up a debt of forty-five million pounds.'

'Took you long enough,' Jimmy said irritably.

'Forty-five—' Seth's chest heaved, his face twisting with rage. He shifted in his seat. 'Is this why Osney's vanished?'

'He's in the Tower, awaiting your mercy, sir,' Jimmy said, smug.

'Good,' Seth said, breathing heavily. 'I will have my fun with him in a moment. Tell me more about this loan, Mister Manderly.'

Manderly gulped repeatedly.

Jimmy shot him an impatient nod. 'The loan was borrowed from Mister…' he prompted, turning his hand in circles.

Manderly gave him an imploring look.

Jimmy smiled at it, thoroughly enjoying himself.

'… Mister Emmett,' Manderly finished lamely.

Seth peaked his fingers, his eyes fixed to the chandelier. 'Mister Emmett?'

Manderly whimpered in reply.

'Mister *Horseface* Emmett?'

'The very same,' Jimmy said, shaking his head in mock disappointment.

Seth licked his top teeth, his lips pursed together. 'Get out,' he whispered.

'But sir—'

'Your position will be filled by Lord Fleurelle going forward, Mister Manderly,' Eleanor said sweetly.

Alain blinked when this was translated, evidently alarmed. 'But—'

'You are dismissed,' Seth said firmly. 'Don't let me find you in court again.'

'My lord, what's going to happen to me?' Manderly wailed. 'My wife, my children… how will they survive without me?'

'Oh, we won't be killing you,' Seth said. 'Not yet, anyway. We will be confiscating your titles and seizing your lands to replenish the vaults, until such time as the arrangements for the rest of your short life have been finalised.'

'As for your wife, I'm sure she'll have an annulment and subsequent replacement established, courtesy of her father,' Jimmy said spitefully.

'Supposing this week's sexually transmitted disease doesn't kill her,' Lilly mused.

Manderly was escorted out by Corporal Moat.

'What are we going to do about him, then?' Jimmy said, suddenly sombre. The high from the beginning of the meeting swiftly dissipated.

Seth blinked. 'Is hanging people not good enough anymore?'

'We hung his accomplices,' Jimmy said in wistful reminiscence. 'I feel we ought to pull something special out of the hat for him and Osney.'

'Why don't we dump them in the middle of the Dead Lands?' Lilly said. 'I can say with authority that the place is not pleasant, much less without supplies.'

'Not dramatic enough,' Seth said, leaning back and placing his feet on the table again, ankles crossed. 'I'll think of something.'

Jimmy smirked, one of the few times he felt excited about the classic Crey sadism.

Alain whimpered something in Portabellan.

'What are we supposed to do about the forty-five-million-pound debt?' the translator supplied.

'I'm sure you'll think of something, provided Lilly doesn't distract you too much.' Seth grinned, giving Lilly a wink.

She favoured him with a grimace in return.

'I'll write to my father,' Cienne said. 'He'll have some ideas.'

Seth ignored her. Pointedly. 'That everything, then?'

'There are some nuns being burned at the stake in Serpus,' Jimmy said.

'I'm sure they deserved it,' Seth said, rising with indifference.

'What are you up to today?' Eleanor said, trying to sound flippant.

'Just things in town,' Seth said, stepping over his daughter, who was busy painting his chair purple. 'I'll be back before third turn.' He left the room with some haste.

Cienne looked around the room and saw everyone, apart from her brother and his interpreter, refusing to meet her gaze. She felt a flush of anger and rose, her chair shrieking backwards. She fled the room, brushing Ginny's side and swerving to avoid her.

'Sorry,' Ginny said absently, crawling under the table.

Eleanor, Lilly and Jimmy exchanged glances.

'She knows, doesn't she?' Lilly said with a grimace.

Eleanor simply winced in reply.

Jimmy shoved his chair back and paused, frowning down at his feet. 'Have anyone else's shoes just turned purple?'

Everyone's gaze turned to the floor.

Ginny cackled.

～

Cienne strode in pursuit of Seth, her skirts in her hands. She spied Seth far ahead, exiting the entrance hall with haste.

She fled after him, her skirts flapping.

By the time she had arrived at the inner gate, his coach was rattling downhill, the portcullis winching down behind him.

'Where's he going?' she called up to the gatehouse.

The guard above shrugged. 'Didn't hear, sorry. D'you want me to fetch you a coach, your highness?'

Cienne shook her head. She gawked out of the gaps in the portcullis, her shoulders drooping. *He's going to her*, she thought. She was sure of it.

～

Jon looked mournfully into Tim's eyes. His small lamb gaped up at him, a picture of innocence. Jon sucked in a breath and exhaled through pursed lips, shuddering.

It would have been nice, he thought bitterly, *if the visions had been just a little more specific for a change.*

His grip tightened on Tim's soft, woolly chest. The lamb was unperturbed. He trusted him.

Jon took him to the edge of the balcony, glancing down. A wide concrete path lay ten feet across, from the keep walls to the edge of the archery field. The field was completely empty – for now. If he didn't hurry, someone would see him and his whole plan would go up in smoke.

Jon trembled. Tim trembled with him as a result. Jon's mouth hung open, the words struggling to come. 'I didn't want it to end like this.'

Tim rubbed his nose against Jon's chin, which didn't help.

Tears began to form around the edges of Jon's eyes. 'Sorry, little man,' he said, holding back tears. 'It's you or us.'

Tim gawked out at the countryside, paying his words no notice. Jon squeezed his eyes shut.

And dashed Tim's head against the edge of the balcony.

Blood spattered across the stonework and into Jon's face, a steady fall of red pouring down the inner side. Jon threw him over the edge swiftly. A small thud sounded far below. His eyes still squeezed shut, Jon wiped away tears, smearing the droplets of blood across his cheeks.

Taking a moment to gather himself, he raced out to the stairs to retrieve the body.

~

PART SIX: A CONVENING

I

Adrienne lay beside Seth, who snored audibly.

After hiding in the hedges for two hours, waiting for Archie to leave, Seth had finally apologised to Adrienne in his own inimitable style. The next morning, it took Adrienne twenty minutes of over-analysing the event to realise that Howie hadn't come home.

Adrienne lifted the quilt with care and slid closer to Seth, trying not to wake him. He slept on, oblivious.

A few miles downhill in Teal, Archie polished a set of drawers on automatic, his thoughts on Adrienne. A shadow lurking in the doorframe alerted him to the presence of Despina.

He turned to meet her gaze, scowling. 'You want me to smash this for you, save you the trouble?'

Despina rubbed the back of her neck. 'Actually, I wanted to apologise.'

Archie blinked. 'Oh, right.' He gestured to a soft chair in the corner, one of three he had made for himself. 'Fancy a cuppa?'

Despina eyed him warily before accepting a seat.

Archie lit a stove in the corner and filled the kettle from the tap. He was cranking the rusty lever with difficulty when Despina murmured, shyly.

'I'm sorry for all the bother I

caused you. Is your son here? I kind of gave him the run-around, didn't I?'

Archie laughed. 'He's my foster son. I haven't seen him for a couple days, actually.'

Despina frowned as Archie set the kettle over the fire to boil. 'That's odd,' she said. 'I saw him around the village a minute ago with his girlfriend. I assumed they were on their way here.'

'His girlfriend?' Archie said with a frown. 'Reddy-brown hair, tall…'

'That's her.'

'Yeah, she's my niece. She's at home, I dropped her off yesterday. They were going to have a talk this morning. I wasn't expecting them at all today.'

Despina leaned back in the armchair, bemused.

Archie licked his lips. 'Did he seem… upset to you at all?'

Despina shook her head. 'No, he sort of seemed… blank? He was a bit…' She waved a hand in front of her eyes.

'He's been like that for a while,' Archie said darkly.

They sat in silence.

'Is he not usually like that?' Despina asked.

'No… well, not to that extent. Usually he's able to have a coherent conversation without forgetting his own name.'

Despina stared into space. 'The Bastard,' she murmured to herself.

Archie's eyes thinned. 'What did you call him?'

'No, not him.' Despina met Archie's gaze. 'I think we should bring him back here. He might be in trouble.'

Archie shook his head. 'What kind of trouble?'

'I… can't be sure.'

Archie paused a moment before taking the kettle off the heat and leading the way outside.

~

Russell was looking much better. Cienne sat by his bedside the following morning, holding his hand.

Erik removed the intravenous needle from his arm. A miniscule dot marked the place where the anti-venom had been injected. Erik patted it clean with a cloth damped with spirits and wrapped a small bandage around his elbow.

'Finished?' Russell asked pleasantly.

'All done,' Erik said brightly. 'Just some rest for a day or two and you'll be right as rain.'

Sure enough, his fever had abated completely. He hadn't had a seizure since. Her faults aside, Adrienne knew what she was doing.

Cienne heaved a sigh and peered out of the open door. There had been no sign of Seth since the council meeting. She resolved to stay out of his way: bothering him would only make things worse.

She had avoided Lilly and Eleanor as well. Why wouldn't they admit it? Why not tell her? Was she not as much a part of their family as Seth now? Why leave her completely in the dark? She harboured a desperate hope that she was mistaken, that Seth was organising a surprise gift for her or something. Their faces in the council chamber yesterday still nibbled at her anxieties, though.

Unbeknownst to Cienne, the Bastard materialised across the bed from her.

'Hi,' Russell smiled at him, waving.

Cienne shot him a half-smirk. 'Have you made an imaginary friend?'

Russell glanced from her to the Bastard. The Bastard twirled his finger next to his temple, pulling a silly face. Russell giggled. 'Yes, Mummy.'

The Bastard tapped Russell's elbow. 'You should tell her about Daddy's girlfriend,' he told him.

Russell said, 'Woss a girlfriend?'

Cienne frowned. 'A girlfriend.'

Russell turned back to her. 'Daddy's got a girlfriend. My friend said.'

Cienne's stomach turned. 'Has he?'

'It's my friend's mummy,' he said. 'The one who put him in the bin.'

Her insides whirled, her mind spinning. 'What do you mean?'

Russell looked confused and turned to the Bastard for help.

'Whose mummy?' Cienne insisted.

'*His* mummy.' He pointed at the Bastard.

Cienne stared at the blank space of air where Russell was indicating. Her eyes met the Bastard's by accident – the coincidence was frightening.

'The lady with the reddy-brown hair,' the Bastard supplied, holding her gaze.

Russell relayed this information to his mother.

Cienne stared at the Bastard, unknowing. She could feel a presence of some sort. She didn't know what.

'Adrienne,' she said softly.

'Aidee-en,' Russell echoed.

Cienne's gaze flitted to Russell. 'How do you know this?'

'I saw'd him go to her house. In the coach.'

'Tell her where she lives,' the Bastard said.

'She lives in the place where the cake lady is.'

That's helpful. The Bastard face-palmed. 'Buttercup Village. Tell her.'

'Buttercup,' he said vaguely.

'Buttercup?' she said, frowning. That sounded familiar.

Russell flopped his head to face the Bastard. 'Can I go sleep now?'

'Buttercup Village?' Cienne hazarded.

Correct, the Bastard willed to her. Conviction settled on her face.

'Can I?' Russell pestered.

The Bastard nodded. 'You can go to sleep now.'

'Yes, of course you can,' Cienne also replied to him, lost in her own thoughts. Buttercup Village. That wasn't far from here.

The Bastard watched her sit there. He waved his arms impatiently. 'Off you go, then.'

She got up obediently and left the room.

The Bastard ruffled Russell's hair and got up to follow her.

Part of her didn't know why she was bothering. It would never change anything. He was king, after all, he could do what he liked. Only thing was, ordinary husbands had the decency to tell their wives who they were sleeping with. They didn't invent four years of exclusivity.

We aren't ordinary, she told herself. She and Seth actually loved one another, for a start.

Unless he doesn't, the Bastard pushed into her head. *Unless he was faking it.*

She rolled the idea around as she reached the ground floor. He might have been seeing her all along, she realised, crossing the throne room and then the entrance hall yonder. He might have put it all on to get a handful of kids out of her. It made sense, she discovered. He'd started acting off as soon as she'd rejected a third child.

She slowed down on her exit and halted at the doors. They were shut tight. 'Jon?' she called. Perhaps he was outside.

It appeared that he wasn't. No answering shout greeted her from outside.

She sighed and pushed the doors open herself. They swung open reluctantly, heaving and creaking. She made a note to commend Jon on his job at some point – it was harder than it looked.

Leaving them gaping open behind her, she jogged downhill to the gatehouse.

~

They arrived outside the village pub to see Howie sitting in the sun, accompanied by an auburn-haired woman. Archie strode up and gave her hair a playful tug before realising with a start that the hair did not belong to Adrienne.

'Oh God, I'm so sorry,' he stammered.

The stranger massaged her scalp, glaring at him.

'Sorry, thought you were my niece,' Archie said with a nervous grin.

Anna glared at him and turned her eyes to the heavens.

'This is Archie,' Howie said, ignoring the awkward tension. 'He's my uncle.'

'… actually, I was your foster father last I looked,' Archie said uncertainly.

'Archie, this is Anna,' he continued blithely.

'Hello, Anna,' Archie said with an absent wave. 'Howie, we need a word. You remember Despina, don't you?' He held a hand towards Despina, who glared at Anna distrustfully.

'Nice to meet you, Despina,' Howie said as though he hadn't just spent the past three weeks chasing her across the countryside for various stolen objects.

Despina frowned at him. She leaned over the table between them. 'Do you know someone who calls himself the Bastard?'

Howie gazed at her. 'No, sorry.'

'Someone called the Bastard hired me to annoy you these last few weeks,' Despina said. 'Do you know any reason someone might want you distracted?'

He shook his head, his lower lip sticking out.

He isn't concentrating on you, she realised, irritated. 'Think,' she said sharply. 'Is there someone who would do you harm?'

'No, I get along with everyone.'

Archie splayed his hands out in exasperation. 'What about Seth Crey? You never liked him, did you?'

'I know about him already, he's only out to distract him so he can sleep with—' She cut herself off.

Howie blinked his eyes into focus. 'Finish that sentence.'

Archie winced.

Despina stammered. 'U-u-u-uh, um… he… paid me to distract you while he had it off with your girlfriend.'

Howie's eyes glazed over. His face was blank as before, but this was different. They could sense the shock radiating from him. 'He did what?' he asked in the faintest of whispers.

'He… h-he…' She trailed off helplessly, clearing her throat.

Archie looked on, helpless as she was.

Howie met his gaze. 'So *you* knew, then.'

'Only since yesterday. I told her to talk with you last night, tell you everything. But you never came home, did you?'

Howie's expression turned cold. 'I wasn't out doing *that* if that's what you're implying.'

Archie's eyes widened. 'No, that's not what I meant, I'm just, I'm worried about you, mate.'

Howie's face adopted a withering look, his eyelids heavy. 'Where's Adrienne now?'

'At home. She's waiting for you.'

'Take me home,' he said, monotonous.

~

The Bastard met Geldemar by the side of Adrienne's bed.

Cienne's coach rattled up the village.

'I need a word,' the Bastard said, urgent.

'In a while, I want to watch this,' Geldemar said in earnest.

'This is urgent! I need to know if Theo Crey actually—'

He was interrupted by a horse's whinny outside. Cienne had arrived.

So had Seth, to be judged by his facial expression.

'Oh, Christ,' the Bastard groaned, stifling a retch.

'Athletic for someone who can scarcely hold a sword over his head, isn't he?' Geldemar said, enjoying himself.

'Oh, get out, you depraved goon,' the Bastard spat.

Downstairs, Cienne leaned on the door experimentally. It swung off the latch easily. Peering around, she crossed the main living area to the stairs against the back wall.

The cottage walls were bare cement blocks, rough to the touch. Dishevelled furniture crowded the small room, cheap timber assembled poorly. Cienne ascended the stairs step after cautious step, being careful not to make a sound.

Where's Howie? It was definitely the right house: a helpful old lady knew the 'rash cream girl' very well and pointed her in the right direction. She apparently hadn't attended a royal parade in the last few decades – she soon regretted being so helpful when she learned that no, Cienne was not selling the ointment cheaper than her.

She reached the landing to the sound of quiet giggling. She froze. This was trespassing.

She inhaled, trying to ease the tightness in her chest. What if it was a huge mistake? The old lady never mentioned him – surely the presence of royalty was cause for gossip?

Unless he came here often, a treacherous part of her mind whispered.

But what if I'm being paranoid? What if it isn't him up there with her? What if I'm about to barge in on Howie and his girlfriend having some alone time?

She briefly entertained the notion of bumping into Howie having alone time with someone else. The treacherous part hummed contentedly at the childish fantasy. She drew herself upright and followed the giggling, her ribcage thundering.

The two were, thankfully, more or less dressed by the time Cienne had drawn the courage to push the door a bit wider. He was tickling her: they had attempted to get dressed and leave but were distracted by each other before they could finish. Cienne knew this. It used to be her getting the tickling.

There was a wistful moment where Cienne deluded herself into mistaking him for Howie. Then he turned his head while kissing her ear and the delusion was broken.

Adrienne threw her head to one side with a laugh and, finally, saw Cienne. 'Seth!' she gasped, jerking him back.

His head turned to the door. The smile slid from his face.

'Cienne,' he said under his breath.

A familiar creature grabbed onto her arteries and held on tight. Cienne recognised it. She had a feeling it would be hanging there for a while.

'Cienne?' he repeated, pushing himself upright.

As though sleepwalking, she turned, expressionless, and walked down the landing.

'Cienne!' Seth scrambled for his boots and stumbled from the room.

Feeling slightly outside of her own body, Cienne descended the stairs and exited the cottage.

Seth ran to catch up. 'Wait!' he called out of the front door as she crossed the road. He ran to her, hopping halfway to pull his other boot on. 'Cienne!' He sprinted to the coach as Cienne got in and jumped in after her. 'Are you alright?'

He placed a hand on her shoulder-blades.

His touch sent a shiver down her, as always, only this time it revolted her. She stared straight ahead, ignoring him.

'Cienne,' Seth said softly, searching her face. 'Cienne, I'm sorry.'

Her gaze wandered to the coach window and caught Howie's. Her stomach lurched.

Howie stared into the coach, past Cienne to scrutinise Seth's bedraggled appearance. He looked as stunned as she felt.

She drew breath shakily and a tear fell, just for him.

A hand gathered her hair behind her ear. The loose curls caught on it before flopping back over it again.

'Cienne,' Seth whispered.

She met his gaze for the first time.

'I have to explain,' he said, his face taut with worry. 'I love you. Please let me explain.'

The claws on her heart grew cold.

'You don't love me,' she said. 'You never did.'

~

Despina waited respectfully at the side of the road.

Archie barged into the cottage. 'Adrienne!' he roared. 'Get down here now!' He glanced back out of the wide-open door.

Howie stood in the middle of the road, staring after the departing coach. Despina was attempting to gently guide him back to the house, but he wouldn't move. Archie imagined he'd lost the ability to.

'Adrienne!' Archie bellowed again.

She appeared at the top of the stairs, her face streaked with tears.

He glowered at her. 'Got caught in a spot of rain, did he?'

She choked on a sob. 'Archie—'

'I asked you,' Archie said, a hand held irately in her direction, 'to just tell him the truth. That's all I asked of you, and you didn't do it.'

'Archie, I, he just, I—'

He pivoted, paying her excuse no notice.

Despina had managed to persuade Howie to the edge of the road. He leaned on the wall outside the door, staring into space.

Archie walked out to meet him. 'Mate.'

Howie slid to the gravel.

Archie crouched in front of him. 'Do you want to stay at mine for a bit?'

'Yes, please,' he whispered.

'Come on, then,' said Archie with a thin smile.

He slipped an arm under Howie's armpits. Archie and Despina managed to pull him upright between them. They released him as he walked on his own, lost in his thoughts.

Adrienne didn't come out of the cottage.

~

II

'Right,' Geldemar said brightly. 'That's our job done.'

The Bastard grabbed his arm as he made to disintegrate.

'What?'

'I want to talk to Him,' the Bastard said.

'Who, dear?' Geldemar said pleasantly.

The Bastard pulled Geldemar forward by his shirt until their noses touched. 'Him,' he said, inflecting the capital 'H'.

Realisation dawned. 'Oh, Him. I'm sure He's quite busy, I haven't spoken to Him in nigh on—'

'Make it your business,' the Bastard snapped, 'to speak to Him now. I want to see Him *now*.'

'You look angry,' Geldemar observed. He gestured at Adrienne weeping on the edge of her bed. 'Aren't you pleased with our handiwork?'

'I am pleased,' the Bastard growled. 'But I'm pissed off about something else. Something between me and Him. Tell me how to find Him.'

'You should know, dear, you did spend an entire induction year with Him back in the Dead Lands—'

'JUST BLOODY TELL ME!' the Bastard howled in Geldemar's face.

Geldemar jerked away from him, his jaw clenched. 'I don't know how to find Him,' he snapped. 'He told me to find you and keep an eye on you, because He would be too busy to do so Himself. And then He vanished from the usual place. I haven't been able to get hold of Him since.' He eyeballed the Bastard, who glowered back with equal intensity. 'Why?'

'None of your business,' the Bastard said, turning to leave.

'Oh, it's a secret, is it?' Geldemar asked sourly.

'From you,' the Bastard said, 'it is. But I may reconsider if you choose to help me.'

Geldemar ground his teeth. His curiosity was his own worst enemy sometimes. 'Fine,' he spat. I will try to find Him and get back to you. And then you will tell me everything. Alright?'

~

Cienne watched the scenery waft past as she was engulfed in a tidal wave of excuses. Seth prattled on and on, touching her neck and her hair repeatedly in profound distress. She wasn't really listening. Her rejection of a child was a factor, she was vaguely aware. Other pieces of information floated in and out of her ears: their arguments over the years and recent weeks, Seth's feelings about his bastard son, something that happened at his son's burial – he'd kissed her at the graveside, that was it. He'd kissed Adrienne next to his son's grave, passionately. It had spiralled from that point, he said.

She didn't really care anymore. Her thoughts drifted back to her son and decided to stay there, on her own son, who was poorly. Who was getting much better, actually, all thanks to Adrienne.

Her thoughts touched on Russell's imaginary friend – his imaginary friend was Adrienne's dead son. Small children picked up more than people could comprehend. Russell knew everything. She wondered how much Ginny had picked up. Would she have mentioned if she knew? If Daddy had a secret, Ginny would keep it for him. She always loved Seth best.

The rumble of the coach smoothed out as they entered the grounds of the palace.

'Cienne,' Seth said. 'Please say something.' She could hear the pleading in his voice. His hand was still on her back, rubbing in reassuring circles. It was starting to make her feel sick.

She waited in silence for the coach to stop and slid out.

Seth stroked a lock of her hair dejectedly as she went. He didn't trouble himself to follow.

Cienne stormed into the keep and made a beeline for the stairs, lost in a thoughtless daze. She climbed all the way to the top floor and peered into her son's room, much in the same way she had peeked into Adrienne's earlier.

Russell was deeply asleep, his chest rising and falling silently. The pallid complexion of his illness had thankfully abated, letting colour flood his little face again. His illness was gone, it seemed.

Cienne perched on the chair next to his bed and examined him.

He'd been bathed before she left: his fair hair was dry now, combed to the side and shining. She examined the shape of his eyes, his forehead, every line of his mouth. It was all Seth. Cienne had never felt anything but happiness at the fact. She'd paraded her tiny Seth around the castle when he was first born, him and Ginny, Seth's tiny copies. There was so much of him in them, and so little of her.

Cienne spluttered and her cheeks grew warm with tears.

~

Howie's tea began to stagnate. Archie eyed him across the kitchen table, his fingers knitted together.

Despina hovered by the stove, having placed herself on refill duty.

'Feeling up to some dinner?' Archie asked him.

'No,' he said, his first syllable of the evening.

'You sure? It's my special pork mush. You like my special pork mush, don't you?'

He simply blinked, still staring into space.

Archie eyed him in concern.

Howie's face was drawn, his jaw jutting forward. His eyes were pink around the edges: he had been crying on the way home. Archie's stomach sank. He'd been so quiet, Archie and Despina hadn't noticed.

'D'you want something stronger?' Archie asked finally.

Howie's head bobbed.

Archie got up to hunt out the gin, thankful for the opportunity to help.

Despina approached to sit beside Howie.

'Who's the Bastard?' he asked her in a whisper.

Despina met his gaze.

'You said you were working for someone called the Bastard,' he elaborated. 'Who is he?'

Despina told him all she knew.

~

A messenger thrust a letter into the coach.

Stuck in his seat, too reluctant to enter the keep and the carnage waiting for him there, Seth took it absently and opened it, his mind on Cienne.

> *Seth Crey,*
> *I write to you to remind you of the next quarterly bill of the Peace Tax, which is overdue. I urge you to pay this fee promptly, in addition to the next instalment of your kingdom's current loan agreement.*
> *In light of the capture and undecided fate of my cousin Lord Philip*

Manderly, I have come to the conclusion that my nephew is no longer safe in your custody. Please send a response to this missive along with the payments outlined above and we can organise transport for the prince.

On the subject of Lord Manderly, I would heartily suggest that you release him without charge. Relations between Adem and Stoneguard are on thin ice. Let us not break that ice quite so rashly.

My kindest regards to you and your kinfolk,

G. Emmett PR.

PR. Prince Regent. He had labelled himself *royalty* now.

Seth simmered at it in silence before screwing it up and throwing it out onto the gravel.

~

George Toffer stood at the bar of the King Death and caught the attention of the barman. The barman barked a dry retch, tugging his collar over his nose.

Toffer didn't notice. 'Where can I find the—' He checked the back of his left hand. '—knaves of Salator Crey?'

'Ah,' the barman said. He held his breath before releasing his collar in order to point with his only hand. His voice became strained. 'Down the left arm to the next right turn. Bloody big spire. Can't miss it.'

'Thank you very much.' Toffer smiled, turning to exit.

The barman kept his mouth and nostrils tightly closed until the brown mist trail of faeces and body odour dissipated. He exhaled audibly.

Toffer followed the barman's directions. If he was aware of the exclamations of disgust from passing pedestrians, he made no indication of it.

'Eurgh!'

'Ugh!'

'Have a bath, mate!'

He turned left and then right at the end of the road, scratching irritably at his salt-and-pepper beard, which was currently the home of several species of lice.

Meanwhile, at the end of the road, the Prophet joined Father Hope at the front step of the monastery and dealt their visitor a magnificent bow. 'Your Eminence.'

Abraham Furlong – or 'His Eminence' as he preferred to be known – nodded amiably.

He had always been old, Hope remembered. Even when he was first anointed, he was old – and now he was even older. And uglier, Hope thought nastily. Boils popped up unfortunately down the sides of his bulbous nose, and frown lines criss-crossed over his brow in an intricate tapestry of disdain. His jowls sagged below a wispy goatee and his eyes could scarcely be seen between the bags surrounding them.

Liver spots coated the hand he held out to Hope and the Prophet – not to shake, Hope noted with a cynical eye. His palm was turned down, an immense diamond shining up at them from one knuckle.

The Prophet kissed it.

Hope tried not to think about it.

'My sons,' His Eminence droned, ascending the front porch steps. 'How is our agenda coming along?'

'Very well, Your Eminence, very well,' the Prophet smarmed. He turned, swinging the doors inward with a flourish. 'The clergymen have all been admirably—oh, for goodness' sake!'

The dining hall was packed with writhing limbs. The priests were fighting again.

The Prophet erupted. 'WHAT ON EARTH ARE YOU FIGHTING ABOUT NOW?!'

The men erupted in kind, shouting over one another to be heard.

'He denied the three Christs!' a black-robed man howled.

'*He* denied the existence of the Twins!' another bellowed in a dark red that revealed him to be a clergyman of the Seven.

'He piddled on our Cross!'

'He was trespassing on Salator Crey's burial ground!'

'He wiped his nose on the Cloth Used at the Deadening!'

'He took the last roast potato!'

'SHUT! UP!' the Prophet roared.

'Some teething problems with the merger,' Hope muttered to His Eminence.

His Eminence clapped his hands until there was relative silence. 'Gentlemen, gentlemen,' he called as the crowd eyes his bright red robes with an air of wariness. 'We are all in this together! Let's all take a moment, shall we?'

A knock on the front door behind them interrupted their moment.

'Excuse me,' Toffer said hesitantly.

The entire populace of the monastery of the Knaves reeled back in united disgust.

Toffer, to put it mildly, looked the worse for wear. His dark red robes stank and were stained with mud – or an equivalent in colour to mud, at any rate. His scratching dislodged several tiny ants and fleas from his overgrown goatee and his hair stuck out in several different directions. His feet were bare and had been for some time – the soles and sides of his feet were black beneath the threadbare robe brushing his toes. His body odour was tangible to the unfortunate few who stood directly in front of him – namely, Hope, the Prophet and His Eminence, all lingering half a yard away from him.

'Father Toffer!' exclaimed one of the monks of the Seven.

'Who?' asked His Eminence.

'The priest of the capital of Stoneguard,' one of the Seven's monks supplied. 'He's been dead for over three years!'

'Not dead, brother,' Toffer said. He brushed down his robe, though dust was the least of its problems. He spotted the bright red robes of His Eminence and, sensing superiority, entered simper mode. 'Hello, my name is George Toffer, lovely to meet you.'

He held out a hand. It was crawling with earwigs.

His Eminence declined with a polite recoil.

'How can we help you?' the Prophet asked. 'Besides running you a hot bath, I mean.'

'I've come to see the leader of the Seven's faith,' said Toffer, glancing around. 'Is there a leader here?'

'That would be me,' His Eminence intoned. He stepped forward, inhaled some of the translucent brown smog and quickly stepped back again.

Toffer frowned at him. 'No, you misunderstand,' he said. 'I wish to see the leader of the *Seven's* faith.'

'Yes,' said His Eminence. 'Which would be me.'

Toffer continued to frown. 'But you're the faith of Salator Crey.'

'Yes,' said His Eminence.

Toffer blinked. 'We're *enemies*.'

'Not any longer. The faiths have now joined, Father Toffer. The Crey God and the Seven Gods have been acknowledged in unity.'

Toffer's eyes widened. 'Oh, I see.' He barked a laugh. 'Good one. Didn't think you Crey blokes had a sense of humour. Very well done. Now, where's the real leader?'

'Real leader?' said His Eminence. 'I *am* the real leader. This is no joke, Mister Toffer. I'm very sorry to hear that you think we of the Crey God are jesters by nature.'

'Right,' said Toffer in tones of derision. 'Right, so you're telling me that the faith of the Seven, who you think are devils, have joined forces with the faith of Salator Crey, who is a proved devil in the Testament's 36th Article in the Book of Anthrax, against what? Swearing? Fornication?'

'Neither,' said His Eminence icily. 'The Creys are our target. We propose to peacefully enforce an abdication in favour of the ruling members of our united clergy.'

'Well, that doesn't surprise me,' Toffer said with a sniff. 'I suppose Aaliyaa Horne put you up to this? I know she's a devout follower of the Seven, but even we know she's a loon.'

'Aaliyaa Horne is dead,' His Eminence snarled. 'She was killed by the sister of Seth Crey.'

Toffer gulped. 'Killed?'

'Indeed.'

'Oh.' Toffer looked queasy. 'That's bad.'

'So you will join us, then?' His Eminence asked.

Toffer blinked. 'And do what?'

'What else do armies do?'

'Armies?' the Prophet echoed, looking bemused. 'I thought we were bringing them to our point of view through peaceful means?'

'Ah, well,' said His Eminence, walking to the back of the canteen. 'Bring me the floor plan and a pin, Brother Andrew.'

A monk shuffled off as the Prophet watched him, frowning.

'I've been having a think about it for the past few weeks,' he said, pacing up and down the width of the hall, 'and I've decided it's about time for another holy war.'

'Oh, God,' Hope groaned.

'*Gods*, Father Hope,' His Eminence corrected, halting in his pacing as the monk returned, a large scroll in hand. 'Salator Crey and the Seven have all led us to one purpose, and one purpose only.'

His Eminence unfurled it and pinned it to the back wall, holding down the bottom of the curling parchment with one hand.

'We will storm the castle and purge it of the Creys,' he announced. 'Then we will take over the continent as one faith, led by the new King of Truphoria, His Eminence—'

'—the Archpriest Abraham Furlong,' Hope echoed in a hollow voice.

'Oh dear God,' the Prophet said in similar tones.

Toffer looked outraged. 'Holy war?'

His Eminence glanced at him. 'Yes, Father?'

'You want me to fight in a holy war?' Toffer exclaimed loudly, drawing stares. 'After three years of hiding in pig shit and deprivation from the wrath of the Creys, you want me to fight in a holy war in the name of the tyrant who gave Father Giery free reign on the country's under-twelves populace? Sod off!'

'Are you neglecting your duty to your new faith, Mister Toffer?' His Eminence's voice became dangerously soft.

'Yes! Yes, I am!' he shouted. 'And so should all of you!' He pointed around at the collective of monks, Seven and Salator Crey alike. 'Alright, those of the faith of the Propaganda God I understand, you lot have always been corrupt,' he said to the black robes, 'but the rest of you! *Our* religion is pure, it always has been! *We've* never committed child abuse or embezzlement, so why would you want to follow a faith that has? He's not out to join the faiths, he's just out to recruit an army! Our gods would want nothing to do with this farce, you know they wouldn't!'

'These men know what's good for their faith,' His Eminence cut in.

'Oh yeah? Step forward anyone who thinks this man's a despot!'

The black robes all took a step back, but the vast majority of burgundy robes muttered conspiratorially. The men made a decision and unanimously stepped forward.

'See!' Toffer gloated. 'See, I was right! Sod your holy war, we're off! We have real gods to appease! Come on, let's get back to Stoneguard!' He turned to the doors.

Which slammed shut in his face.

'I don't think so,' His Eminence said serenely.

Black robes surrounded Toffer and his men, forming a ring around them.

Hope squeezed the Prophet's arm, firmly. 'I think it's time to leave.'

'But—'

'I'm sure you'll reconsider your position on the matter when you hear my terms,' said His Eminence.

Some of the black-robed monks pulled blades from their pockets.

Hope pulled the Prophet towards the back door by his elbow.

'What, you gonna top us now, is it?' Toffer sneered.

'Well… yes. We are.'

A gesture sent one of the knives plunging into Toffer's stomach. Toffer's eyes bulged. The colour drained from his face.

'One by one,' His Eminence continued.

Another knife entered a monk to his left, who yelled.

'Until you join our cause,' His Eminence finished.

Three more men yelped as blades squelched behind him.

'It was you who inspired it, you know,' His Eminence explained. 'The attempt on the prince and princess's lives was a step in the right direction. It's just a pity you bottled it before we could get there to help you.'

Toffer coughed, blood dribbling down his lower lip.

'You've made your feelings perfectly clear. How about your accomplices?'

More knives impaled the burgundy robes. More screams pierced the air.

The Prophet clamped a hand over his mouth. Hope tugged on his shoulder. 'We need to leave,' he said fiercely.

'No,' the Prophet said, his eyes glued to the scene. 'We'll be fine. He won't hurt me, I'm his nephew. We can talk him out of this war, look, they're surrendering, see… those ones will be fine, it's just a flesh wound, he's not really killing, killing them—'

The amount of blood pooling the floor begged to differ.

Hope hissed in the Prophet's ear. 'We need to get to the Creys. We need to warn them.'

The Prophet pressed his lips together.

The two burst out of the back door.

~

III

Felicity folded her hands in her lap.

The entire staff of the Emmettfort flanked the two siblings in two rows, yawning the length of the great hall. Portraits of their parents were hidden behind maids and serving men, all awaiting the arrival of Henry Meyer. Emmett himself sat at her left in the Stonethrone as she sat in the flanking, duller mahogany counterpart, her gaze fixed to the entrance.

The reddish-brown doors opened, letting a burst of sunlight hit the violet carpet. 'Felicity!'

Felicity leapt to her feet. 'Uncle!'

Zephyr Emmett grinned broadly and jogged up to meet her. He looked no older than she was, despite the ten-year age gap – his boyish haircut was a similar shade to the double doors and his face bore no lines of age. She threw herself into his arms in the centre of the hall, squealing.

Her brother surreptitiously rolled his eyes to the ceiling.

'You should have written to me! You should have told me you were coming!'

A silhouette in the doorframe cleared his throat. 'I had the impression it was me you were entertaining today.'

Felicity jerked her head to one side.

A new face appeared under a short crop of black hair, though unfortunately for him, a few lines around the eyes betrayed his middling years. Which wasn't to say he wasn't handsome – quite the opposite. If it weren't for his questionable choice in friends, Felicity would be quite taken with him. His clothing laced with gold thread, his smug grin boasted of plenty more wealth besides.

Emmett rose from his seat. 'Henry.'

Henry Meyer strode down the long violet carpet to meet them in the centre, Emmett following suit from the other end of the hall. Meyer clapped hands with each of the Emmett men in turn before turning to Felicity with a low bow.

Felicity spotted Emmett nod impatiently at her in her peripheral vision. She gave Meyer a curtsy.

'My lady,' Meyer said grandly. 'You are more beautiful in person than I could possibly imagine.'

Felicity smiled faintly, rising to meet his gaze in silence.

'It appears she's come over quite shy all of a sudden,' Zephyr remarked.

Meyer tilted his head to one side in amusement. 'What think you of me, Lady Felicity?' he asked with a playful gesture at his slim torso.

'You're a little older than I imagined,' Felicity blurted, before amending, 'My lord.'

Emmett's hand rose to his eyes with an exasperated groan.

Lord Meyer, on the other hand, laughed aloud. 'Your brother was right,' he said. 'There is more to you than meets the eye.'

She smiled thinly, bending her knees once more.

Meyer smiled in return and offered her his elbow. 'Shall we stroll the grounds?'

'Let's,' Emmett agreed.

They walked out of the open entrance, Emmett giving Felicity a meaningful glance on the way.

'When shall we set out for Serpus?' Zephyr asked.

Felicity blinked. 'Serpus?'

'As soon as possible,' Meyer said, his hand placed on top of Felicity's in his elbow. 'I can't wait to meet my stepson. Any word on him since the Creys fostered him?'

'Our cousin claims he is well,' Emmett said.

'Cienne has written to you?' Felicity asked, perplexed.

'Of course,' Emmett said, his face impassive. 'She's been writing more and more frequently, particularly these last couple of weeks, in fact. Perhaps she is hinting at something. I hear she wasn't too keen on having the prince as part of her household.'

Felicity shot him an icy stare.

'I hear he's a handful,' Meyer said, as fondly as if Azrael was his own son. 'I look forward to bringing him to visit Thintower. I have lands that stretch as far as the eye can see,' he boasted to Felicity, who nodded with little interest, 'plenty of room for horse-riding. Do you ride, my lady?'

'Occasionally,' she said. Her gaze turned slowly to Emmett. 'When my brother allows.'

Emmett flicked her a side-glance. 'Perhaps you should start the journey today?' he said to Meyer. 'I have some paperwork to do before I go, but I won't be far behind. You could try your charms on the young prince,' he shot his sister a smug look, 'persuade him to leave for Thintower ahead of the wedding. I'm sure he would be enamoured by his new home.'

'Agreed,' Meyer said. 'Then I will make the arrangements.' He lifted Felicity's hand to his lips and left with another flourishing bow.

'Quite the charmer, eh?' Zephyr said to Felicity.

She was too busy glaring at her brother to listen.

Emmett met her gaze and raised an eyebrow. 'What?' He dabbed the side of his fleshy mouth with one sleeve. 'Something around my mouth?'

'There will be if you keep on,' she muttered. She turned on her heel to follow Henry Meyer.

Zephyr turned inquisitively towards Emmett, who shrugged.

~

Seth ascended to the archery field dejectedly as a game of football progressed. Light poured down upon it from the east, blinding him. He flung an arm over his eyes with impatience. 'Hi, Lilly,' he said, in the tones of someone looking for an excuse to rant.

Lilly paid him no attention, her gaze locked onto the field.

'Cienne never came to bed last night,' he said. 'Have you spoken to her at all?'

'Nope,' said Lilly, squinting. 'Go stand by that other cage, will you?'

'I need to talk about this, this is serious!' Seth whined.

Lilly sighed, adjusting her stance. 'You can talk to someone about it at the cage, alright?'

'She's never been like this before, you didn't see her face,' Seth

329

agonised. He stepped in front of Lilly's view.

She shoved him out of the way. 'I don't care! Go guard the cage, Seth!'

'Lilly! Please speak to her, tell her I never meant to hurt her!'

'No!' Lilly shrilled, appalled. 'You've made your bed, now lie in it! She's pissed off at me and Mum as it is!'

'But my marriage is in tatters!'

'And the cage post is *still* empty!'

Seth groaned loudly. 'I don't know what I'm supposed to do! She hates me!'

Lilly rolled her mouth irately. 'Fine, *I'll* take the cage post!' she announced loudly, pivoting.

'No!' her team-mates yelled in alarm. 'Not Lilly!'

Seth sighed and turned back to the keep.

'ANYONE BUT LILLY!!'

~

Seth threw himself into his throne and stared up at the vaulted ceiling, deep in thought.

Jon peered into the door. 'Oi.'

Seth glanced at him.

'Visitor for you.'

Seth waved him through.

Raphael Emmanuel III tiptoed into the throne room, wheeling a trolley full of wrapped parcels. 'I finished the portraits, your majesty.'

Seth surprised the Prophet with a rare smile for him. 'Excellent! Can I see them?'

The Prophet unwrapped each parcel and laid them out on the flagstones before the dais.

Seth rose to his feet and descended the steps, pacing at the foot of the frames to peer at each one. He grinned down at his own in particular before coming to Cienne's portrait with a sombre stare.

'Your majesty,' the Prophet said uncertainly.

Seth pulled himself away from Cienne's likeness, his expression vacant.

'There's something I need to warn you about.' The Prophet grimaced. 'It's the Archpriest, my liege.'

'Mm-hmm?' said Seth.

'He's… well, he's… he's launching a holy war and trying to take over the kingdom and he's just stabbed a load of monks of the Seven!' he exploded with a sigh of relief.

Seth's face was impassive.

The Prophet peered at him worriedly. 'Sir? What should we do?'

Seth blinked at the floor rapidly. 'Do you think a bouquet of flowers would make up for Cienne finding out about my mistress?'

The Prophet blinked. 'Sorry?'

'She likes flowers. And I can't think of anything else. She's devastated.' He turned his gaze to the Prophet. 'What do you think?'

'I… don't really have the experience to give an informed opinion,' the Prophet said weakly. 'Anyway, about the holy war—'

'I'll ask Jimmy, he's good with women,' said Seth fervently, striding to the kitchens.

'But the holy war—'

'I'll pay you next week. Thanks!'

'But the war!' the Prophet wailed.

The kitchen door slammed behind him.

The Prophet shifted from foot to foot, his expression pained.

Jon poked his head around the door. 'I'd talk to Lilly if I were you.'

~

Seth loitered in the dining hall, leaning against the table. Jimmy had been evasive, to his immense exasperation. Servants bustled in and out on various errands, paying him no notice. One of them was adjusting the new portraits placed along the east wall until a person entered the room.

'May we have a moment?' asked Qattren softly.

The manservant bowed and exited the hall.

Seth faced her. Her attention was on the east wall.

Rich reds and purples contrasted the royal family's pale complexions. Each painting bore the porcelain quality of the very best Truphorian portraiture – with the very worst examples usually bearing the two-dimensional gawkiness of an artist who only saw a real person once, from afar, possibly through a thick bout of cataracts.

The portraits had been hung in order of first-born: the twins were placed in the far-right corner, then came Lilly (with creative licence taken on her attire), Cienne beside her, looking radiant, Seth after that, a pale space where the Duke of Osney had been recently removed, Eleanor and Theo followed next, regal as ever, and, on the far left, Seth's grandfather.

Qattren stared pensively at that last painting.

'You still love him,' said Seth, watching her.

'Yes,' said Qattren. 'Looking at his portrait, I often wonder why.'

Seth inspected King Seb's portrait properly for the first time. He was everything Seth would be if all of Seth's dreams had come true – or at least, his portrait was. His biceps were defined beneath the white linen he wore as he lounged on a reclining settee, his arms crossed behind his head. His fair hair was twice as long as Seth's and hung lazily over his eyes, unlike Seth's which stuck bolt upright in the air at odd angles. Surrounding him were folds and folds of large red curtain and, lying around him with gazes of devotion, three half-naked and *extremely* attractive young women.

'What a poser,' said Seth.

He walked past his own portrait, on which he stood in coronation regalia, holding a solid gold elephant above his head with one hand.

'Yes,' Qattren agreed, grinning at Seth's likeness in passing.

Seth returned to the dining table and leaned the small of his back against it. 'To what do I owe the pleasure?'

Qattren folded her arms over her chest. 'You recall one of our previous conversations?'

'I recall both of them,' Seth said, squirming. 'You'd interrupted me making love both times.'

'To two different women,' she agreed. 'I gather Cienne is no longer on speaking terms with you.'

Seth scowled at her. 'Yes, that's right.'

She smiled brightly at him.

Seth squirmed some more. She'd never smiled brightly at him before. This didn't bode well.

'I recall telling you not to sleep with Adrienne again,' she paused, smiling broadly, 'or I would set your bed on fire.'

Seth cracked up laughing.

Qattren's head tilted to one side in amusement. 'Something funny?'

'Where've you been for the past God knows how long? I've been sleeping with her for weeks!' He spread his arms wide.

'That would make the appointment much overdue, then.'

A scream broke out from the archery grounds.

'Now what?' Seth groaned.

Outside, the Prophet hovered at the side-lines of the football match, his hands covering his eyes. On either side of him were Jon and Jimmy, the latter looking increasingly distressed while the former was enjoying the spectacle, along with an apple bake-well.

Seth halted beside Jimmy. 'What's going on—'

'Sir, duck!' Jimmy shouted.

Seth bolted to the ground. Something metal whistled through the air where his head used to be. An axe smashed through a carriage behind him, reducing it to splinters. '*What the hell is going on?*'

'Some idiot's gone and put Lilly in the cage post,' Jimmy said.

Seth turned his gaze to the pitch.

Corporal Moat's victory dance for his latest goal had been harshly interrupted by Lilly snatching him by the ears. She slammed his head against the bars of the cage in rapid repetition.

'I *knew* this wouldn't end well,' Marbrand muttered two yards behind them.

Jon dusted crumbs off his hands and sidled to the cage. He held out both hands in front of him, as though approaching an angry lion. 'Lilly,' he said gently.

Sweat dripped down her temple. She swung Moat's head into a particularly jagged part of the cage.

'Lilly,' Jon said. He pried her fingers from Moat's ears, reaching over from a short distance. 'Look at me, Lilly.' He guided her away by the shoulders, placing himself between them.

Moat crawled to the edge of the lawn, gagging on his own blood.

Lilly met Jon's gaze with a blank expression.

'It's just a game,' Jon said softly.

Seth gawped at him. 'Has he lost his mind?'

'She's going to throw him over the wall,' said Jimmy with conviction.

He tilted his head to the garrison and raised his voice. 'Someone get a sheet and catch him!'

Seth gawked on in horror.

'Take a deep breath,' Jon went on. He released her slowly.

She inhaled deeply, exhaling the words. 'It's just a game.'

'That's right.' He breathed in with her.

'It's just a game,' they exhaled in unison.

Lilly took deep breaths.

Moat spat in her direction.

She shrieked at him.

Seth darted forward, jerking Jon out of the line of fire.

Lilly charged at Moat, tackling him into the grass.

Seth carried him to the sidelines by his armpits. He set his feet delicately onto the grass.

'Well, it nearly worked,' Jon said.

Lilly lifted a lump of limestone into the air.

Elliot wrenched it from her grasp from behind. 'No!' he shouted, throwing the rock away. 'If you kill him, it's a penalty shot! We can't risk it!'

Lilly panted with fury. 'You're right.' She shrugged her arm from Elliot's grasp and backed off. 'You're safe for now,' she seethed at Moat.

Moat gathered up the remains of his nose in both hands and squirmed off the pitch.

The game restarted with Lilly, for some reason, still in cage post. The Prophet, with his unfortunate affliction of being unable to say no to people, was put in the opposite cage in Moat's place. Seth had given him a large shield, just in case.

An immense clatter of leather-on-metal and an irate screech heralded the first goal against Lilly.

'We need to have this game banned,' Jimmy stated. 'We won't have any staff left at this rate.'

'We would if they just let Lilly win,' Jon said. 'It's their own fault. Watch your head.'

Jimmy ducked, but he wasn't talking to Jimmy.

The ball *poinged* off Seth's head, sending him flying back into a pack of onlookers.

'Sorry,' a voice gravitated from the throng of players.

Hope cowered behind a cage, in front of which stood a shield, apparently of its own accord.

'How did I get roped into this?' the shield asked in despair. 'There's a bloody holy war about to happen and I'm stuck here, about to be murdered by the king's sister! And potentially hit on the head with a ball!'

'You're alright at the minute, it seems to be attracted to King Seth's head.'

Seth took a knife from his belt. 'I'll pop it!!' he shrieked. 'I've done it before and I'll do it again!'

'NO!!' the teams roared.

'KICK IT AT SOMEONE ELSE'S HEAD, THEN!!'

'Our team's rubbish without Corporal Moat,' Hope commented.

'Oh, I don't care about the team!' the Prophet howled, his voice echoing off the back of the shield. 'I just want Lilly-Anna to make my evil uncle go away!'

The ball rebounded from his shield. He screamed piercingly.

'You can see into the future, can't you?' Hope asked. 'It must come out alright in the end, otherwise what's the point?'

The Prophet sprinted out of the way of the ball. It hit the back of the cage with a chorus of groans and cheers.

'Wait here, I'll get help,' Hope said, jogging away.

'No, don't leave me!' the Prophet squeaked. 'I don't want to die alone!'

The ball bounced off the shield. Another scream erupted.

'And stop squeaking like a sissy, it's only a ball full of air,' said Hope.

'That last one wasn't me,' said the Prophet.

They glanced at each other and then at the 'ball'.

Lilly-Anna Crey was suddenly wielding a newly blood-stained broadsword.

'That's it! I'm off!' The Prophet dropped the shield on top of his late team-mate's head and pegged it, Hope at his heels.

Across the pitch, three more shields had materialised since the broadsword's inclusion to the game.

'Lilly,' Seth said slowly. 'Give us the sword.'

Her upper lip twitched beside the blade, making him wince.

'We can cancel the penalty shot if you *just put down the sword*,' said Jimmy.

Her opponent trembled violently in front of her.

Lilly's eyes narrowed. She levelled the blade vertically.

His red hair dripped with sweat, eyes flickering down to the ball at his feet – but only for a second.

'No,' Lilly said in reply to Jimmy. She locked eyes with the penalty shooter. 'Come on, then.'

The boy's eyes rolled inwards. He crumpled to the grass.

'You need to put down the sword!' Seth exclaimed. 'You're running out of opponents!'

Lilly sighed heavily. To everyone's relief, she placed the sword aside. It rested on the ground just inside the confines of the cage for later.

And the game continued. Despite the loss of the penalty shooter and the Prophet, Lilly's cage rattled three more times in quick succession. Moat's replacement as team captain, a lanky middle-aged man with hair loss, kicked the ball and cackled with triumph as it soared for the goal.

The cage clanged deafeningly.

That was the last straw for Lilly. The broadsword wheeled straight for the captain's head.

It was here that Ginny arrived, dolly in hand. A prudent Marbrand pivoted her around as a thunk sounded.

'Right! That's it!' Seth screamed over the chaos that followed. 'ARREST HER!!'

'What for?' Lilly howled, irate. 'I didn't do anything!'

Blood sprayed across the pitch, spattering half of the players.

'Put her in her rooms!' Seth called, propping himself up against his knees.

She bolted down the length of the pitch and leapt on top of the opposition's cage, bouncing off in the direction of the portcullis. The soldiers leapt in pursuit.

'Your majesty!' panted a new arrival. A teenaged messenger with a letter. 'I come directly from Osney, your majesty,' he said with a bow. 'The Queen Felicity of Stoneguard is arriving on the morrow to collect Prince Azrael. She will be accompanied by the Earl of Herpes—'

A honk erupted behind one of the freestanding shields. Jimmy.

'Pardon?' Jon said from behind his own shield adjacent.

'Herpes, sir,' the messenger said. 'It's a district in the Ary Islands. Best known for their beautiful women, I believe.'

Another honk sounded, despite Jimmy's best efforts to contain it.

'Go on,' Seth said, shoving an elbow into Jimmy's side.

'—Lord Henry Meyer, Lady Felicity's betrothed.'

'What time are they expecting to arrive?' said Seth.

The messenger didn't reply. His attention was diverted to Lilly, who had climbed onto the battlements to throw rocks at her oppressors.

'Don't mind her, this is normal for her,' Seth said, tapping his shoulder. 'When are they expecting to arrive?'

'Late morning,' the messenger replied before turning his full attention to the battle at the gatehouse.

Seth left him to it and sighed heavily, pivoting to enter the keep.

Jimmy and Jon judged it to be safe to discard the shields, letting them fall to the ground.

'Lady Felicity's had it, then,' Jon commented.

'You never know,' said Jimmy. 'Manderly's missus has lasted for years, and herpes is the least of her problems.'

'Whether she gets a disease or not isn't my concern at present,' Seth said sourly. 'Guess who will have to tell the child he's getting a new father?'

'Looks like he found out already,' Jimmy said, pointing at the keep.

Seth followed his finger with a squint.

Plumes of flame and smoke leapt from the window of Seth's bedchamber. A silhouette could be seen amongst the smog, giving a cheery wave.

Seth sighed heavily. 'No, I know exactly who that is.'

He fancied he could see Qattren's smile from all the way down there.

～

IV

Lilly managed to resist arrest for long enough to sprint to the top of the keep. Using the billowing smoke from Seth's rooms to lose her pursuers, she fled past the door to her nephew's quarters before hearing faint sobbing and doubling back.

Cienne was weeping.

Casting a wary eye up and down the corridor, Lilly stepped into the room, closing the door behind her.

Quite oblivious to his mother's misery, Russell chattered away in the corner of the playroom, tossing toy soldiers into the air in an apparent re-enactment of Lilly's escape.

'Lilly, no!' he whispered dramatically, his back to his illustrious aunt. 'Don't hurt him! Not the sword! Quick, get her! Aah!' A tin soldier hit the ceiling with a click.

Lilly suppressed a grin, turning her attention to the window.

Cienne sat facing it, hiding her tears from her son.

Lilly crossed the room and placed a gentle hand on her sister-in-law's shoulder. Cienne broke from her reverie, wiping her eyes.

'The little man's better, then,' said Lilly.

'Lilly, no, AAH!' came the dramatic whispers of the doomed soldiers.

'Hopefully he stays that way,' Cienne mumbled.

'He will,' Lilly said confidently. 'He's not as soft as he looks, this one.'

Cienne's eyes remained cemented to the window. Soldiers – the real-life edition – wandered the grounds outside, searching for their escaped prisoner. Seth remained at the sidelines of the football pitch, hands on his hips and head shaking in exasperation.

'He really wants you to talk to him, you know.'

Cienne rubbed her eyes, which were pink and swollen. 'No, he doesn't. He wants another attempt to talk his way out of it.' She faced Lilly sharply. 'Why didn't you tell me?'

Lilly flushed.

'I thought we were sisters.'

'We are!' Lilly exclaimed. 'I didn't want you to get hurt! I was trying to talk him out of it, or threaten her away, or, or *something*. I didn't just leave it happen because I didn't care!'

'Nobody,' said Cienne, 'bothered to tell me.'

'We didn't want you to… flip out. And hurt him. You were doing that a lot lately.'

'Seth mentioned that,' Cienne said bitterly. 'It's funny how much of the blame here lies with me when *he* was the one being unfaithful.'

Lilly's voice dropped, stung. 'I'm not blaming you. I'm just explaining why I didn't tell you.'

Cienne met her gaze fleetingly and put a hand on her knee. 'Sorry for taking it out on you.' Her tone of voice was more resignation of defeat than apology.

Lilly deflated. 'I'm sorry I didn't say anything. It was a mistake.' She lifted her voice again. 'But in my defence, I thought there were more important things for you to worry about. Like the debt. And your son.' She flung a hand towards Russell in demonstration.

Cienne gazed at him, her expression pained. 'You wouldn't understand,' she said. 'My whole world revolves around that man. I'm not like you. I don't have anything else. I just have him. I put everything I had into this family. And no one could show me the decency of simple honesty.' She stared blankly at the grounds. 'I've never been good enough for him.'

Lilly looked at her piteously. 'It's not your fault you were married off to an idiot.'

'I should have been able to make it work, everyone else does.'

'You're not everyone else. You're better than them.'

Cienne snorted, turning her face away.

'So what are you going to do about it?'

Cienne met her gaze, her eyes shimmering. 'What do you mean?'

'You're not gonna let him get away with it, are you?'

'What else can I do? Beat him to death? You said it yourself, that was what got me into this mess in the first place.'

'I'm not blaming you. I said that as well,' Lilly said in a barbed tone.

Cienne heaved a sigh. 'I just have to get on with it.'

'No, you don't.' Lilly tilted her head down until Cienne met her gaze again. 'Creys don't get their own back by crying about it. They get *medieval*.'

'I don't have the temperament to get *medieval*. I'm not a Crey.'

'You've been my sister for twenty-four years. You *are* a Crey.'

Cienne smiled thinly.

Lilly grinned back. 'Now, back to Seth. There's a visitor coming to the palace in, oh,' she examined the position of the setting sun, 'two hours from now, who might be able to help you with Seth's comeuppance.'

'Who?'

Lilly peered down. 'Oh, actually,' she said with glee, 'she's arrived ahead of schedule.'

Cienne followed her gaze to the portcullis, where a coach entered, slowing to a halt.

'Hide me for a few hours until all the fuss has died down,' said Lilly, 'and I'll tell you exactly what we're going to do.'

~

A different coach decorated with the arms of the Emmetts rolled to a halt outside an inn on the north outskirts of Serpus. The throng of pedestrians dissipated at the sight of the black spider and violet backdrop.

'We'll spend the night here,' Emmett announced.

Felicity gazed out at the cobblestoned street and wood-panelled homes lined up beside them like soldiers. Her eyes stared into space, her thoughts on her son.

Lord Meyer placed a hand on her wrist. 'Are you alright?'

She met his gaze and nodded with a smile that hurt. She'd been forcing a smile all the way through Truphoria, mostly at his bland jokes and incessant bragging. She found herself almost wishing the Wastelands really *were* as dangerous as the rumours – it might have shut him up for a couple of days. Despite never visiting the place, she could quite possibly describe every inch of Henry Meyer's lands from hearsay alone, from the moat circling Thintower to the meadows flanking the twenty-mile-wide lake in the centre of it all. She didn't have the slightest idea how she was going to spend the rest of eternity with this bastard. She was sick of the sound of his voice already.

'I'm fine, my lord,' she said. 'I'm just a little worried about Azrael. He may think I abandoned him.'

Emmett raised a perceptive eyebrow. It was like a retort in itself.

'Not at all,' Meyer said with conviction. 'I was fostered as a child, for a much longer time than the prince. The weeks will have flown past.'

'That's assuming he's as well as the Creys make out,' Emmett said.

Zephyr glared at him and spoke for the first time that journey. 'If Cienne Fleurelle told you the child was well,' he said, 'than you can take it

340

that the child is well. My sister did not bring up a liar.'

The eyebrow simply lifted again.

'Of course, if you'd rather stay in Serpus tomorrow, I'm sure Felicity and I are in safe hands with Zephyr,' Meyer said coolly. 'I'd rather we didn't cause animosity on my first visit – if that's quite alright with you?'

Emmett observed him. 'As you wish.'

Felicity looked at her betrothed in a new light.

His blue eyes glared into her brother's. They were like chips of ice. *The enemy of my enemy*, she thought.

Zephyr changed the subject. 'We appear to be low on funds after the last inn,' he said. 'Perhaps Felicity could share a room with Lord Meyer for tonight?'

'Could she?' Emmett said sharply. 'I feel that would be improper considering they aren't wed yet. Perhaps she should stay with me.'

'She could, my lord,' Meyer snapped, 'but I feel *that* would be improper considering that you aren't currently wed to her either.'

Emmett licked his lips, planning his next retort.

'I'm certain the inn keep will own a room with two beds,' Meyer added. 'Perhaps the Lady Felicity would be comfortable with her uncle? What do you think?'

Felicity started. She wasn't used to being asked for an opinion. 'Yes, I would be happy to share with Zephyr,' she said falteringly.

'Excellent,' Zephyr said, opening the coach door before Emmett could get a word in. 'Come, let's see if we can negotiate a small bit.'

They exited the coach, leaving Emmett simmering.

~

Seth peered into Lilly's bedroom. 'AHA!'

The actual room itself couldn't be seen under the mountains of miscellaneous junk surrounding the curtain-less four-poster. It was curtain-less on the behest of the chambermaids, who had enough bodily fluids to clean from the royal sheets without the contents of Lilly's nose.

Amongst the filth, Lilly flailed in mid-air for a moment, her eyes wide. 'Whassup?' she slurred from beneath the covers.

Seth didn't reply. Instead, he stepped outside and slammed the door

341

in front of him, pulling a key from his pocket.

'What are you doing?' she asked from inside.

'Placing you,' he said, twisting the key, 'under house arrest.'

'Oh, what?' she wailed. 'I didn't do that much damage!'

'No,' Seth said sarcastically, 'you just cut a man's head off, shattered another man's sternum and ran pretty much my entire day staff into the woods where nobody can find them.'

'I'll be good, just let me out!'

'Not a chance.' He threw the key to the far end of her drawing room. 'Your meals will be delivered to your room. Have a good evening.'

'Oh, come ooonn-uh!'

Seth strolled out of the room, ignoring Lilly's indignant cries. He entered the corridor to find his nearly-four-year-old daughter at his feet, almost immediately.

'Tuck me in,' Ginny commanded. 'Now!'

'As you command, your supreme majesty,' Seth intoned with a low bow.

Ginny giggled and tried to pull him along by his ears.

'Seth.'

He disentangled himself and pivoted.

Cienne stood in the doorway of their drawing room, smiling faintly at him.

'Cienne!' He jogged forward to meet her. 'Are you alright? How are you? How's the little man?'

'Good. He's sleeping, I think he's fine now.' She licked her lips. 'They have finally cleared up the mess Qattren made of the bedchamber – a new bed has been set up and dressed. Are you coming in?'

'Now? The sun only set a few minutes…' He trailed off. Her meaning had suddenly occurred to him.

Cienne smiled, confirming his thoughts.

Seth made a pained expression. He turned from his wife to his daughter and back again.

'Come on!' Ginny insisted, tugging on his arm.

He was in turmoil. Ginny. Cienne. Ginny. Cienne. Dizziness overcame him. 'I'll be right back!' he said to Cienne, who grinned in reply.

342

He snatched Ginny up by her armpits and sprinted for her room. Once she was tucked in, Seth rattled off a fairy tale from the book on the bedside table as fast as he possibly could and ran away from an immensely confused Ginny to leap into the darkened bedroom and throw the door shut behind him.

His wish for Cienne to talk to him was not granted, but he didn't mind that. He had other wishes to fulfil that were slightly more urgent anyway.

~

V

Morning dawned on the palace of the Creys, cool and pale. Two Emmetts and a Meyer rolled through Castlefoot Market in the soft light of dawn, heading for the barbican. Felicity pulled her cloak around herself. Winter was setting in like steel against her bones.

Seth awoke in blissful silence, the amber light of the rising sun settling on him and his wife.

'Last night,' she said, 'was amazing.'

Cienne sounds different, he thought vaguely. Perhaps she had a cold.

He rolled over to face her, his arm curled around her with a satisfied grunt. He squinted at her with one eye. Then both eyes snapped wide open.

Elyse grinned toothily at him. 'Hello gorgeous.'

Seth's eyes bulged. He howled.

An entire murder of crows burst out from the foliage beside the keep.

Cienne smiled sleepily from the soft chair in Russell's playroom as her husband's screams reverberated across the grounds.

~

The aforementioned murder of crows soared over and around the portcullis. Some of them hit the wall in their haste and landed on the roof of a coach passing underneath.

Felicity startled at the sound from within.

Zephyr and Meyer flanked her on either side, each man gazing out of the window adjacent. Meyer scrutinised the entrance of the keep with a frown of confusion. 'I thought we had sent a messenger?'

'Yes, he arrived a few hours before we stopped in Serpus.'

'Where's the household?' he demanded, glancing around. 'The entire household should be waiting outside for our arrival, where are they?'

Felicity rolled her eyes.

Zephyr noticed and squeezed her shoulder, his expression sympathetic.

At the keep's entrance, Jon observed the coach with a concerned squint as the coaches cantered uphill.

Ginny appeared at the open door to his right. Jon eyed her squinty face with sympathy. 'Did the screams wake you up as well?'

'Yes,' she said, yawning. She soon got over her fatigue to launch herself across the grounds.

Jon smiled at her in amusement.

The coach halted a couple yards away and the three visitors climbed out.

'Good morning,' Zephyr greeted Jon, who inclined his head. 'May we have audience with the king? I am Zephyr Emmett, accompanying Lord Henry Meyer and Lady Felicity Horne.'

Ginny's voice turned Jon from the introductions.

'Hi, Daddy!' she called into the well, her voice reverberating.

'Hang on, I'll just fish him out of the well,' Jon said, strolling off.

Zephyr watched him in bemusement.

Jon halted at Ginny's side and peered down. 'D'you want me to fetch some soap?'

'I'll never be clean!' Seth exclaimed. He scrubbed his crotch rapidly with a handkerchief, the water clapping at the underside of his jaw.

Jon squinted. 'Probably not, but you have visitors. Will you be receiving them here or what?'

Seth snapped to attention. 'Who is it? The Emmetts?'

'Two of 'em. And some bloke called Meyer.'

Seth scrambled to his feet, his bedclothes sloshing. His foot landed on something barbed and he swore loudly, reaching under the surface. The attacker turned out to be an ornate toy soldier, presumably belonging to Russell.

'I'll put 'em in the throne room,' said Jon. He carefully pried Ginny away from the edge, where she precariously dangled.

Seth waited until he heard the double doors slam. 'Will someone help me out?' he called, with no response. 'Hello?'

~

Meyer inspected the masonry around the doorframes with interest, wandering around the hall with his hands behind his back. The carved limestone snarled back at him, numerous serpentine jaws yawning in an eternal sneer.

Felicity held Zephyr's proffered arm and leaned towards him. 'I wonder where Azrael sleeps.'

'He'll be on the third floor,' Zephyr said. 'That's where the nobility sleeps, it's an indicator of class.'

'The foster child?' Meyer said from behind them, fondling a statue of a python to the left of the entrance. 'Sleeping next door to the royal family? I doubt it. Ah, your majesty.'

Felicity turned to face Seth, who dripped from head to toe.

Seth raised the toy soldier into the air. 'My little boy,' he explained, lifting his shoulders. 'Distraught without it, you know how it is. Give me one moment.' He fled for the stairs, his bare feet plopping beneath him.

Meyer laughed shortly. 'They do things quite differently here, don't they?'

'They're very... down to earth,' Zephyr said. 'The procedures of court seem to be quite lost on them since the passing of King Theo.'

'Indeed.'

Meyer met Felicity's gaze and lifted his eyes to the ceiling, as though lamenting the barbarian rulers. She lifted an eyebrow in return.

Once his sopping clothes had been exchanged for proper court attire, Seth emerged from his rooms.

Elyse rounded the corner.

Seth darted back into the drawing room.

She passed him obliviously, looking dreamily into space.

Certain that her heels had clicked out of earshot, he skittered out and knocked on the door to Azrael's quarters, bouncing on his heels. There was no answer. Frowning, he opened the door slowly. 'Hello?'

His drawing room, aka soldier battlefield, was empty. A quick glance into his bedroom told him that was empty too. Seth wracked his brains in confusion. He wondered where a four-year-old went at the crack of dawn. Nowhere good, he knew from experience. 'Despina?'

She exited the quarters next door. 'Yes?' she called from the corridor.

'Where's Azrael?'

She lifted her shoulders. 'Haven't seen him for the last two days.'

Seth frowned. 'Aren't you his nanny?'

'No, Mister Emmett forwarded his nanny from Stoneguard,' said Despina. 'She's been looking after him for the past few weeks. You know, grey hair, short? Has a dirty great boil in the middle of her forehead?'

'Oh, her.' He wrinkled his nose in remembrance. 'She'll be in the servant's floor, will she?'

'I'll go and find her as soon as I've wiped Russell's breakfast off the ceiling,' Despina promised.

Seth nodded with a smile and descended the stairs.

~

'You'd have thought they'd be a bit more organised,' Meyer scoffed, getting impatient. 'This is a royal visit, after all.'

Felicity stopped herself from sighing. She wondered what the implications would be for poisoning her husband and brother and burying the bodies in the bog around the back of Emmettfort. Being hanged by the neck until dead couldn't be worse than listening to Meyer's ego swell.

She faced the doorway as little feet pattered through. She was disappointed to find that it was Seth's son instead of hers.

'Your highness,' she said gently, striding forward to crouch at his feet. 'Where's Azrael?'

'I don't know,' he said with a shrug, peering at his feet.

He's shy, she realised. She'd never seen Azrael become shy in front of a stranger. This was a new experience.

She gave him a reassuring smile. He simply stared at her through his lashes, wide-eyed.

Seth thundered down the stairs, halting in front of the thrones to bow at his guests. 'Sorry for the delay,' he said. 'He's just woken up, his nanny is seeing to him now.'

'Good, good,' Meyer said, with a reluctant bow. 'Thank you, your majesty.'

Felicity eyed Seth. His forehead was wreathed in a thin veil of sweat. She wondered if he was frightened of Meyer. Seth sat carefully in his throne, adjusting his leotard. His eyes scanned the guests, as though deciding who was the least threatening. They settled on Felicity.

'How is he?' she asked him.

Seth's eyes widened ever so slightly. 'Fine,' he managed. 'He's fine.'

He hasn't seen him, she realised. 'He wasn't upset or anything?' she said. 'About me leaving him here?'

'No, not at all,' Seth said, wringing his hands. 'He hasn't had a chance, my children have been running rings around him.'

Or running away from him. Russell still stood behind her, examining his feet. Azrael was too headstrong. Russell was timid as a mouse, and Azrael had never gotten along with girls his age. They were probably terrified of him.

A door slammed behind him. A servant girl in the dull green dress of servitude skittered across the hall to whisper into Seth's ear.

The colour drained from Seth's face. 'I'll be right back, there's an issue in the servants' quarters,' he rattled off before hurrying after Despina, his hands shaking.

Felicity watched him go with dread.

Meyer sidled to her. 'Something's wrong.'

She nodded once. 'He looked like someone had died.'

~

Seth held a handkerchief to his mouth and nose.

'The flux,' Despina said, her voice muffled behind the hem of her apron. 'We didn't know she had it. We thought it was a winter bug.'

The woman had been gruesome enough before, but her appearance in death outdid that by spades. Blood and faeces covered the sheets beneath her and her white shift was brown with filth and stains. Her hair was drenched in sweat – almost as drenched as Seth's was with water from the well. Dysentery had ravaged her face: she was gaunt and drawn near the end, her eyes sunken.

'Why didn't anyone notice the smell?' Seth said in revulsion.

'They said it always smells like this,' said Despina. 'I've never been in here. I live with my father behind the keep, I've only ever been in the children's quarters.'

'Surely it would seep out? We'd notice it on the ground floor. Something that bad can't just stay in one place.'

'It doesn't. There are secret tunnels hidden between the ceiling of the ground floor and the floor up here.' She tapped the wood panelling beneath them with her foot. 'My father told me ages ago. That's why the keep is so tall. There are two or three feet of empty space beneath us, it must get ventilated out.'

Seth ran his free hand through his hair. 'Where the hell is he?'

'Could he have found the tunnels?' Despina asked fearfully. 'Maybe he's trapped in there.'

A stab of fear hit Seth in the stomach.

She met his gaze. 'I'll round up the servants.' She jogged out of the room. 'I'll start a search party, then I'll bring the twins to the playroom.'

'I'll check the upper floors myself. Don't let on to the Emmetts that he's missing, will you?'

'I'll be discreet.' She dissipated into Sal'plae. It was faster.

Seth turned his back on the dead woman and rubbed his eyes, heading for the stairs.

Lilly appeared outside the window as he passed it. He paused, doubling back. 'Lilly?'

She hung outside the first story window, her hands gripping the outside frame. Her face creased in dismay. 'I was climbing down,' she said, her voice quiet through the fogged glass. 'From my balcony. From my room.' She hung her head. 'I'll come quietly.'

Seth sighed and shook his head, reaching for the clasp. She leaned to one side as the window swung outward.

'Get in. I need you to cover for me downstairs. Azrael's gone missing.'

~

A torrent of servants bolted through the throne room past a bemused Meyer.

'I'm beginning to think they've lost him,' he said.

'He's probably fine,' Felicity said, her face taut.

348

'Let's just sit down over here,' Zephyr said, beckoning to the soft chairs against the wall. 'I'll find the kitchens and see if someone can't get us some wine.'

'This is intolerable,' Meyer seethed. He dropped into a chair with his arms crossed. Felicity perched delicately in the seat beside him. 'If something has happened to Azrael—'

'Don't,' she said, her voice thick. 'I can't bear to think of it.'

He watched her trembling in her seat and deflated. He lifted a hand to brush a lock of her hair behind her ear. She flinched violently.

'Sorry!' he exclaimed, jerking his hand back. 'I'm so sorry, I forgot. Your ordeal… it completely slipped my mind. I didn't mean to make you uncomfortable.'

She watched him out of the corner of her eye. He faced her with his brow furrowed in dismay. His hand hovered a few inches away from her. His earlier confidence had fled, to be replaced with an awkward hesitancy.

'It's fine,' she said, not facing him fully.

He licked his lips, lapsing into silence.

~

Seth scanned the entire third floor except for Azrael's empty quarters. He peered into wardrobes, crawled under beds, glanced out of the windows on the off-chance he might appear in the grounds. He found a pair of small boots under Russell's bed and pulled them out for inspection.

Russell's feet were still in them. 'I found my soldier!' he squeaked, brandishing the toy in triumph. 'Azal kicked it under the bed, but I got it back!'

'Great,' said Seth, on his knees in front of him.

'Where's my 'magin'ry friend?'

'I dunno, in your head I suppose,' he said with a yawn. 'Have you seen Azrael anywhere?'

'No. I'm gon' find my friend,' he said, climbing back under the bed. 'I think he hiding here somewhere.'

'Well, fine, but stay in here, alright?'

'Okay,' he said, flinging a sock out into the open.

Seth rubbed the back of his ankle fondly and rose to continue the search downstairs. He entered the second servants' floor a few moments later.

A waft of sour air washed over his face. He retched and pressed his handkerchief over his face again. The skinny corridor smelled foul. It smelled like something had died. Trying not to think of who had already perished within these walls, Seth strode down the corridor, poking his head into doors as he went.

Most of the rooms were used for storage and held miscellaneous furniture, but further west, the sour odour became more potent. Seth peeked into the four-by-four-foot rooms and grimaced as the air became warmer around him. How hadn't he noticed this before? Smells travelled. It was impossible that something this tangible could be contained in two floors.

The corridor curved right as he reached the far end.

Seth rounded the corner, peering into more doors. There were no servants to be seen – all out searching for Azrael, he guessed. The rooms were all empty, but still bearing that strong odour of something off, something—

He opened another door and retched aloud. He'd just found a servant – or what used to be a servant, he saw, before death had taken their soul and left its body to rot. It was black and almost skeletal – *almost*. He hadn't seen something this horrible since his father's body – and even then, he had at least been burned before he had a chance to go bad.

He slammed the door shut and kept looking, his handkerchief pressed tightly to his face.

~

'Hello,' said Lilly.

Meyer's eyes ran up and down the length of her. 'You're Lilly-Anna Crey?'

'Yep,' she said. She gestured to Jimmy, feeling his authority was needed. 'This is Jimmy.'

'Are you King Seth's aide?'

Jimmy hesitated. 'Um… kind of,' he said. 'I aid him with pulling on his trousers, among other things.'

Meyer scanned the two several more times. 'I see.' He turned to

Zephyr. 'He loses our child, vanishes into thin air and thinks it perfectly acceptable to present a street urchin and a manservant?'

'This *manservant* is the last scion of the fortune of Cientra,' Jimmy said coldly. 'And I'll have you know the street urchin is bloody good with a sword.'

'You're the scion of Cientra?' Meyer said wryly. 'You're Lady de Vil?'

'Lady who?' Jimmy said, alarmed. 'Who is she? Why don't I know who that is?'

'Look,' Lilly diverted, 'he hasn't lost any child, there's just been an accident among the servants and he's sorting it out, he'll bring Azrael down from his rooms as soon as the stairs are clear.'

'Clear from who?' Meyer demanded. 'A torrent of servants fled out of the front doors only a few moments ago! Who else could possibly be up there?'

Felicity watched the argument from the soft seats between two busts of the Creys' ancestors. She was completely silent.

'There's no need to panic, there's really nothing wrong at all,' Lilly assured him in her distinctly out-of-place East Serpus drawl. 'Just have a seat, we'll get you another drink while we wait—'

'We're going to wait some more?' Meyer said, throwing his hands into the air. 'Oh wonderful, because it was so much fun waiting around for the past two hours already!'

'Just… bear with me, I'll go upstairs now and find out what's going on—'

'You *have* lost him, haven't you?' Meyer said. 'You're trying to bide time so that your staff can search for him.'

'No, it's not like that at all, see—'

'I found him!' cried a voice.

Lilly swung around. 'What? You found Azrael?'

Meyer arched his eyebrows with a snort at Zephyr, who inhaled deeply.

Ginny stood in the doorway, holding up a toy soldier. 'No,' she said, the soldier drooping sideways. 'I found Russell's soldier.'

'Oh,' said Lilly tiredly. She walked over to kneel at her feet. 'We're not looking for that, we're looking for Azrael, have you seen him?'

'Pathological liars!' Meyer exclaimed, throwing his arms into the air.

'No,' Ginny said in reply to Lilly. 'I go look for him.' She jogged out before Lilly could get another word in.

'Does anybody,' Meyer said coolly, 'want to tell me what's going on now?'

Lilly rose and turned to Jimmy, who made a face.

'I'll find out,' Jimmy said, pivoting.

∼

Seth fled from the rot-infested second floor and bumped into Jimmy. 'Jimmy, I've just been in the servants' quarters—'

'You were in the first and second floor?' Jimmy asked in horror.

'Yes, I've just found—'

'You were in there *personally*?'

'Yes,' Seth repeated irritably, 'and there's a dead body in—'

'Are you mad?'

'What's wrong with you?' said Seth irately.

'The place is diseased!' he exclaimed. 'That's most of the reason I still live with the clergy!'

'Why the *hell*,' Seth shrieked, '*didn't you tell me this earlier*?! There are *dead bodies* in there!'

Jimmy paused. 'Are there?'

'Yes!'

'Oh.' Jimmy jerked one corner of his mouth downward. 'Wasn't that bad a few weeks ago.'

'Yeah, it *would look* as if they were there a few weeks, yes,' Seth snapped.

'Oh.' Jimmy gulped. 'You didn't find an Azrael-shaped one in there, did you?'

'No, that's why I was in there. I can't find him anywhere.' He sighed heavily. 'Is Lilly alright down there with Felicity?'

'It's Felicity's new bloke you need to worry about,' said Jimmy. 'The man is *pissed*. Ginny just let slip he was missing.'

'Shit. I'll check his room again. Go help with the search party.'

'No chance, I'm running you a hot bath and hunting out some rubbing alcohol,' Jimmy insisted, descending the stairs to the kitchens. 'Breathing the air alone will give you a permanent case of the runs.'

Seth left him to it and hastened upstairs.

He gave Azrael's drawing room a more thorough examination, rooting through wardrobes and closets and hoping against hope that the whole fiasco was merely an extended game of hide-and-seek the twins had forgotten about. He checked behind curtains and furniture and finally turned towards the bedchamber, peering around the doorframe at the bed, tucked into one side of the large room to make space for all his toys.

To his relief, he spied the balcony doors hanging slightly ajar. A shadow lingered in the narrow crack between them.

'Oh, there you are,' Seth exhaled, opening the door.

The dark shadow turned out to be a jerkin. A barb-like branch from the oak tree outside the balcony clung to one button-hole, leaving it dangle in the wind. Another dark shadow on the edge of the balcony wall sent a chill through him.

Seth scrambled backwards with a gasp.

~

'He's not in there, then?' Jimmy asked in dismay.

'No sign,' she said, dejected.

He reached for Despina's elbows, hauling her out of the slim gap in the staircase wall. Together, they slid the blocks into position until they clicked back into place. Jimmy hadn't been aware of this one. The entire staff knew of the chutes hidden behind the fireplace, but he'd assumed this entrance was simply bad masonry. Turning his back from the protruding white blocks, he faced Despina. 'Are there any more hiding spots being checked?'

'Only the tunnel under the floor beneath us, we're not aware of anything else. Maybe we should check his rooms. He could have found an entrance we don't know about.'

Jimmy clicked his fingers. 'I'll get on that.' He pivoted and ascended to the top floor.

He entered Azrael's rooms and spent a good ten minutes scanning for open trapdoors before he noticed Seth sitting on the edge of the boy's bed, trembling. 'Sir?'

Seth flinched. 'Jim?'

Jimmy frowned and entered the room. As soon as he saw the gaping balcony door, he stepped back in alarm. 'Is that blood?'

Seth nodded, his eyes vacant.

Jimmy bolted to the balcony wall. He carefully avoided the congealed pool of blood running down the middle of the wall in a small waterfall of thick red.

The grounds were still, apart from a smattering of servants along the outskirts, searching the flowerbeds for Azrael. Jimmy looked closer at the gravel. A pink bruise blossomed directly underneath him, very faint.

Jimmy's spine grew cold. 'What the hell happened to him?'

'I don't know, I never found him,' Seth said, in little more than a breath.

The pinkness trailed along the gravel for a yard before tapering off.

Jimmy raised a hand to the back of his neck. He trembled, all over.

'I think he's dead,' Seth said in a hollow voice.

$\sim$

VI

Felicity sat at the edge of the throne room, her hands folded in her lap. She locked her gaze to the space in the centre of the room. She knew. She knew as soon as she'd entered the castle. Her instincts were confirmed with the arrival of Jimmy, who slowly descended the stairs and, his gaze distant, calmly said in a soft voice:

'He's had an accident.'

Meyer stared at him in complete incomprehension before shoving past him and leaping up the stairs.

Jimmy didn't stop him. He instead turned his attention to Felicity. He crossed the room to kneel at her feet, meeting her gaze with wide, helpless eyes. He didn't bother with an explanation. Felicity could see the resignation in his eyes – an explanation wasn't going to cut it and he knew it.

'Is there anything I can do?' he asked weakly.

Felicity shook uncontrollably.

Her uncle edged around him to sit at her side, an arm around her shoulders. 'If you could hunt out a drink for her?' he suggested. 'Something strong?'

Jimmy rose without a word and made a beeline for the pantry. Alcohol was an area he was comfortable with. When he returned, Felicity was on her feet, adjusting the folds of her skirts. She still trembled, but her face was determined. 'May I s-see my son?'

~

Meyer examined the congealed pool of blood, a hand pressed to his face.

Seth leaned against the windowsill, his hands pressed together against his mouth, his thumbs tucked under his chin. He felt cold all over. The image of the blood stain below was trapped behind his eyelids – except in his mind, it was his own boy, Russell, lying in the gravel below, dead.

Seth pinched his mouth shut and took a deep breath, his eyes lifted to the ceiling.

Meyer ran his gaze over Seth, scrutinising him.

'We didn't know he was missing,' Seth said, his face screwed up. 'We didn't know his nanny was sick, she died two days ago, we didn't know. I just assumed he was fine—'

'I understand,' Meyer said softly.

Soft padding behind him heralded Felicity's arrival. They all watched her enter. She stood in the centre of the doorway, Jimmy a step behind. She was still trembling.

Meyer watched Seth stare at the balcony behind him. As though sensing the images floating behind his eyelids, he said, 'Find your boy, and your little girl. We should be on our own.'

Seth hesitated before finally giving him a nod. He sidled out of the room, avoiding Felicity's searching gaze. His hand brushed her shoulder before he left.

Seth rounded the corner and froze to the sound of Felicity's soft cries.

'He fell,' he heard Meyer whisper. 'They haven't found his… do you need me to search for him?'

'I can't… I don't… I don't know…' She squeaked out each word, barely able to get them out.

Seth squeezed his eyes shut and leaned against the wall, his heart thudding. He didn't know what to do, he couldn't think. All he could see in his mind's eye was the little boy, lying on the gravel in a pool of his own blood.

'Sir?' a soft voice whispered behind him.

His head turned.

Despina touched his elbow. 'The twins are in their quarters,' she said. 'How do I explain?'

'Don't,' he said. He squirmed at the thought. 'They're too young. They shouldn't have to think about these things.'

Despina bowed her head.

Seth pressed his forehead to the wall. He shook visibly. 'They're in the playroom?'

Despina nodded.

He strode the length of the hall. He entered the door in silence and gently closed it behind him.

His children laughed softly beside Ginny's dollhouse. They sat at a dinky round table, Ginny with her teddy, Russell with his soldiers.

'Would you like some tea?' Ginny said in a strange accent that was a cross between Portabellan and the exaggerated aristocracy of the Duke of Osney.

'No, I'm gonna kill him, blah!' Russell said in his dramatic whispering.

Seth smiled. It used to be shouting, until Cienne put a stop to it during a nasty hangover with some sharp words.

Russell stuck a sword into the teddy's stomach.

'Stop! You have to play nicely!' Ginny shouted, wresting the soldier away.

Seth watched this exchange and sidled forward, stopping a foot away and crossing his legs beneath him. Ginny caught his gaze and beamed at him.

'Hello,' he whispered to them.

'Hello!' said Ginny fondly.

She scrambled to her feet to throw herself into his arms. Seth buried his nose in her shoulder. Milk and oranges. She always smelled of milk and oranges. He hoped that never changed.

He held an arm out for Russell and clutched them both as they fought for room. He tried to clear his mind completely, but he couldn't stop thinking of how they smelled. She smelled of oranges. He smelled of sugar and some description of melted cheese. And his first son... he'd smelled of death. He'd never know what he would have smelled like alive.

Or Azrael, now.

Seth buried his head between the twins' and tried not think of the dead boys, of anything at all.

~

Dawn had waned long ago, turning the amber sky to grey. Despina stared down at the coach in which Felicity Horne and her future husband had climbed into, without their son. Despina still felt cold thinking about him.

A soft footstep landed behind her and a warm hand planted itself on her shoulder-blades. 'Everything alright?'

Despina gave her father a thin smile. 'As much as it can be.'

Marbrand gave her shoulder a pat and gazed out from the playroom's third floor balcony. A tall gate had been erected behind them, just beyond the balcony doors. An extra precaution, created too late.

'What happened to the king's melee practise?'

'He cancelled,' said Marbrand in reply. 'He's co-ordinating a scour of the first and second floors, to clean out all the dead and disease. There's going to be a ruckus for the next few days.'

Despina nodded. They watched the coach roll away. 'Should I have done something?' she said. 'I should have prevented it. I should have done something.'

Marbrand squeezed her shoulder. 'You said it yourself, Emmett had sent a nanny to him. She would have prevented this. It isn't your fault she was ill. How were you to know?'

She didn't answer.

He rubbed the top of her head. 'You've done a wonderful job, raising those twins,' he told her firmly. 'And their parents know it.'

She wondered if that was true. Cienne had whisked the children off as soon as she heard about Azrael. She hadn't seen hide nor hair of the Creys since. She pictured the twins tumbling from the balcony. She quickly jerked herself out of that line of thought. There was no use in thinking of all children being dead. One dead boy was terrible enough.

A familiar head of reddish-brown hair appeared in her peripheral vision. Despina focussed down on Anna, Howie's friend, watching her stride up the path to the keep entrance in Crey staff attire.

Despina stared at her with narrowed eyes. 'Do you know that woman, by any chance?'

Marbrand squinted below. 'Think she worked at the palace years ago,' he said. 'Used to hang around Seth Crey a lot.'

'Seth Crey?'

'Around the time King Theo died,' Marbrand recalled. 'She had a shifty look to her. Then she disappeared one day. Must have started a family or something.'

'Or something,' Despina muttered. She turned back to resume tidying the children's toys away.

Anna strolled through the entrance hall below, a smirk creeping across her face.

~

It took ten repetitions of the words, 'Bath, *now*', but Jimmy had finally wrested Seth from the clean-up downstairs – and not before time, either. He'd thrown himself into the work like a madman to forget the events of that morning – and he wasn't going to throw himself back out until the entire two floors were completely bare. Jimmy had to wrestle him away from a wall he was about to knock down with his bare hands.

Now that he was safely in his rooms, Jimmy returned to his post in the kitchens as lunch preparations progressed. He soon wished he hadn't.

'What the hell is *she* doing here?'

Despina turned her gaze from the twins' breakfast tray. 'Working, by the looks of it.'

Donning a thick pair of oven gloves, Anna hefted a tray of loaves to the large table in the centre of the kitchens with ease. Accepting a list from the cook, she sauntered to the door to Jimmy's right with the scroll tucked under one arm. She threw the butler a wink as she passed.

He threw her a dubious squint in return.

'Who is she, anyway?' Despina asked.

Jimmy shook his head. 'Flaming nutter, is who she is. Had it off with Seth Crey around the time King Theo died and then tried to get Queen Cienne executed. She used to go around the kitchens proclaiming herself the

358

Queen of Adem and naming their future children. Bloody oddball.'

'Isn't she seeing Howard Rosethorn?'

Jimmy snorted. 'No, but I imagine that's her next target. She's been hanging around him lately, by all accounts. Must have a thing for blonds.'

'She's not the medic girl, then?'

'No, you're thinking of Adrienne – that's another kettle of fish right there.' He rolled his eyes and turned his attention to the loaves, a subject matter more to his ease.

Despina rolled the subject of Anna around her head on her way upstairs.

~

The Prophet paced back and forth in front of the keep entrance, emitting a nervous noise every now and again.

Jon leaned on the closed doors and watched him, his arms wrapped around himself.

Snow had appeared at last. It blanketed everything, including the two men, and floated delicately onto the grass and concrete, tiny dots slowly lightening the ground to white.

Jon grimaced at it and pulled his cloak around his head. 'Are you coming inside or what?' he called over the cutting wind.

The Prophet ignored him, deep in his own thoughts.

Jon threw his gaze to the heavens. He knelt to pick up a lump of ice.

'OW!' the Prophet howled, clutching his temple. 'What's wrong with you?'

'You're making me dizzy, dancing around in circles like that!'

'So?' The Prophet rubbed the side of his head, where a lump was developing. 'What's going on in there, exactly?'

Jon shrugged, tugging his cloak around his knuckles. 'I dunno. I'm cold.'

'Aw, you're *cold*?' the Prophet mocked, his lower lip protruding. 'Poor doorman, he's cold – I mean, there's a madman in charge of the church and a holy war about to break out in the city of Serpus, but never mind about that, the poor little doorman needs a hot water bottle!'

'I told them you were a nutter. Not my fault they didn't listen.'

The Prophet flapped his sleeves. 'I'm not talking about me! I'm talking about my uncle, the Archpriest! He's just killed several members of the Faith of the Seven, and the king doesn't even care that he's trying to usurp his throne! He's more concerned with his bloody carnal relationships!'

'Yeah, he's like that.'

A tiny knock landed on the other side of the door. 'I wanna come out,' a tiny voice called from inside.

Jon opened the door.

Ginny slipped out, barely distinguishable underneath several layers of pink wool. Her voice was muffled by the thick scarf wrapped over her mouth. 'Where's Azal?'

'What's an Azal?' Jon asked before grimacing. 'Dare I ask.'

'He's lost,' she announced. She noticed the presence of the Prophet and jogged over to face him, her head turned upward to gawk at him.

He grimaced down at her in distaste.

Lilly's head popped out from between the doors. She shivered. 'It's snowing,' she complained, rubbing her arms. 'Bloody hell.' Her gaze found the Prophet. 'Can I help you?'

'*Yes.*' He circled Ginny warily, making a beeline for the entrance.

Jon watched Ginny pound her way down the frozen path. 'Be careful!'

'I will!' she called, her voice snatched away with the wind.

Jon cradling himself in silence for a moment before following her, just in case.

~

Seth sat on the edge of the privy, his elbows braced on top of his knees. The bath sat before him, water stagnating in the elliptical copper bowl. The heat had dwindled out of it long ago. He thought about a quick wash and a change of clothes for Jimmy's peace of mind, but he couldn't bring himself to move.

He dropped his head in his hands and tried to wipe the images from his eyes.

Lilly poked her head around the door. 'Seth, you need to hear this.'

Seth's eyes fluttered closed. 'Give me a minute.'

He rose as Lilly left and made to follow her. His knees gave out and he dropped into a crouch, his palms over his eyes. His throat tightened. The images of the pool of blood flashed over his vision, over and over from different angles. This was his fault.

He tried to suck in a breath and lifted himself to the windowsill. A tiny figure sprinting around on the snow revealed itself to be Ginny.

Lilly's head appeared in the doorway again. 'Seth, are you coming?'

He stared at Ginny for a long time before following Lilly downstairs.

~

Flecks of ice blinded Jon. He squinted after the princess. 'Where are you going?' he shouted in her wake.

'This way!' she called back. She leapt ecstatically through the slush.

Jon whined, running in pursuit.

Carts and horses clogged the front portcullis – the weekly food delivery for the keep. Jon meandered through the throng, craning his neck to keep an eye on Ginny.

She sprinted a few yards ahead, unperturbed by the hoard of merchants.

Jon's shoulder jarred. He collided with a vegetable cart, which emptied its contents onto the ground.

'Oi, watch yourself!' the impatient seller snapped, cuffing his ear.

The side of his head smarted. 'Sor-*ry*!' Jon yelped, affronted. He bolted into a clearer part of the market, clutching his ear.

Ginny fired herself ahead, giggling at the chase.

'Come ba-ha-hack!' Jon yelled in exasperation. He gripped his left side, where a stitch was forming.

Another laugh responded ahead. A small crowd of women parted to let her through.

Jon surged after her, panting. They were getting close to the palace entrance. True to form, Ginny ran straight for it at high speed. The usual loiterers lingered around them, watching her with interest. Jon didn't like the look of any of them.

'GINNY!' Jon howled, sprinting faster. 'GET AWAY FROM THERE!'

Ginny giggled again, stopping briefly to lob a snowball at him.

He dodged just in time and left the keep at high speed. Another throng of people greeted them at the market down the hill, to Jon's dread. Ginny bolted straight into the centre and vanished from view.

'Christs' sake!' Jon spat, elbowing through the throng.

More vegetables were spilled as Jon burst through carts and groups of people, getting increasingly frantic. Ginny was nowhere to be seen.

'Shit,' he gasped, elbowing people out of his way. 'Shit, shit, shit, shit!'

He tripped on a protruding cobble and sailed to the ground. He grabbed the sleeve of an alarmed mother of three and heaved himself up, stumbling on.

He caught a glimpse of shocking pink between an embracing couple. Jon barged between them. One of them went flying, but Jon paid little notice. He locked his sights on the pink blob of wool.

The blob halted abruptly at a coach. Ginny beamed at the person inside, hidden from view. She obviously knew them from somewhere.

Jon's stomach lurched. He threw himself forward.

A horseman sped in front of him. Jon leapt back, heart pounding.

An arm, clothed in a large black sleeve, appeared from within the coach, held out to Ginny. She took the hand. It began to pull her inside.

Jon punched and barged his way through the crowd enveloping him. There was another seven yards between them. He wouldn't make it.

Ginny pulled back suddenly, stepping away. Her expression was confused. Perhaps this person wasn't someone she knew after all.

He surged forward, hope guiding him. And, abruptly, froze.

Ginny stood outside of the coach, her face frozen in a delicate frown. The hand flexed, beckoning her inside.

Jon willed himself to move, but he couldn't. Visions were starting to arise. 'No,' he told his mind angrily. 'Not now. Go away, I don't need this right now.'

Passers-by paused to give him a side-glance, but Jon paid no notice. The snowy marketplace was beginning to waver...

Blood.

Jon jolted back into the present, his heart pounding. He was still in the market. Snow still surrounded him, falling in gentle tufts. Ginny still stood beside the carriage, looking uncertain.

The vision began again, unravelling slowly. *Ginny entered the coach. The*

*coach rolled away, auburn hair fluttering out from the side. Jon stood still, watching them
vanish out of the market and behind a crop of woods.*

People ran after it…

…and those same people began to scream.

*The sounds of Castlefoot Market were engulfed in howls of agony. A battlefield
emerged around him, horses stamping past and around men in arms, bearing green banners.
Bodies littered the cobbles and the sky turned black with smoke, and blood, lots of it, filled
the cracks in the cobblestone, tracing red squares and angles—*

Jon threw himself from the battle, stumbling backwards into a bakery
cart.

Ginny hesitated by the coach, talking to the man within. Jon couldn't
hear the conversation. He raked his nails through his hair. What could he do?

A couple moments later, the market melted away.

And then nothing.

He jolted out of the nothingness, his heart pounding. *What?* He groped
within himself, wracked his brains, straining to fetch a vision, *any* vision.
There was *nothing.*

He threw his head into his hands, squeezing his eyes shut for some
sort of vision, any kind of vision, to tell him how to save her. And it came.
*He thrust himself across the market and hoisted Ginny away, shouting for help – and a
knife appeared in his throat, silencing that shout.*

He jerked back to the present, clutching his mouth for blood that was
not yet there.

Ginny hesitated a moment longer before smiling beatifically at the
stranger and taking his hand.

'No,' Jon whined. He stepped forward.

A horse interrupted him by tramping him and stamping his face into the dirt.

Jon jerked backwards into the baker's cart again. The foreseen horse
sped past, right where he had been about to step.

'Piss off, will you?' the baker said irritably. 'Stupid git.' He shoved Jon
away.

Jon landed in the gravel on one knee, his gaze locked on the coach.

Ginny stepped inside, the stranger guiding her with two hands. Once
she was inside, the hand lifted up to tap the roof of the coach three times.
The horses trotted off.

Jon kneaded his eyes with his palms, warding off images of his own demise. Hideous accidents occurred behind his eyelids. Falling roof slates smashed into his skull, a patch of ice sent him skidding forward onto his head, armoury fell from the blacksmith's cart to carve through his arteries. Every frantic idea to evade them led him to another demise, each caused by a simple step towards her. Jon died a hundred times trying to save Ginny.

The coach rolled through the market, further and further away from him. Jon watched helplessly, his pulse pounding in his throat.

A hand landed on his shoulder, startling him. 'Jon?' Marbrand asked in concern.

'Ginny,' Jon said in a weak voice.

Marbrand frowned at him.

Jon met his gaze and rose.

'Jon, what about Ginny?' Marbrand demanded.

Jon ignored him. He fled to the keep.

The coach rounded the corner behind him. Long auburn hair fluttered out briefly as the two travellers, plus Ginny, vanished behind a crop of forest.

~

PART SEVEN: A FLASH OF PINK

I

awning already, Seth slouched in his throne. Lilly stood before him, accompanied by Raphael Emmanuel III. The Prophet wrung his hands and gave him a faltering smile.

Seth gave him a withering glance in return.

'Hello, your majesty,' the Prophet said, trembling. 'I… hate to annoy you and everything, but, erm, see, it's my uncle… the Archpriest of Salator Crey.'

'What about him?' Seth said, rubbing his eyes.

'He's… well, he's gone bonkers, your majesty,' the Prophet said in dismay.

'And that's normal from any other priest because…'

''Cause he's gone and killed a bunch of other priests this time,' said Lilly.

'Brutally,' the Prophet added. 'He's launching a holy war and coveted your birth right, your majesty. He hopes to take over Adem.'

Seth snorted. 'Wow, how terrifying. What's he going to do, bless me to death?'

'If by bless, you mean stab,' said Lilly, 'then yes. He's already impaled the entire clergy of Stoneguard simply for saying, "I don't really fancy having a holy war".'

'He's going to lead all his men to the keep any day now,' the Prophet said,

365

twisting his sleeves.

Seth rolled his eyes. 'Organise for more guards to be posted around the perimeter, then.'

Lilly frowned at him. 'Is *that all*?'

'Yes, *that's all*,' Seth said testily. 'Marbrand wiped out the last crowd that came to the palace, he'll make quick work of them. I'm not sending out an army for those bloated wine sacks. We're going to have enough problems with Emmett once he finds out about—'

'Erck!' Lilly cut across him, nodding at the Prophet.

'… stuff,' he finished lamely.

The Prophet deflated. 'Right.'

'I'll see you out,' Lilly offered. She walked the Prophet to the double doors. 'I'll have the men ready,' she said, once the doors were shut.

'But the king said—'

'The king… has a lot on his mind at the moment,' she said finally. 'Don't mind him. I'll tell Marbrand to post men around the market while we figure out what to do on a permanent basis.'

The Prophet's eyes rolled upward in blissful relief. He placed his hands together, as though in reverence. 'Thank you.'

Lilly twirled her wrist in mid-air in a satirical royal wave. 'You're most welcome. I'll take you to Marbrand and we'll start making arrange—'

Jon skidded to a halt behind her and barged between them. 'Ginny's been kidnapped,' he said breathlessly.

The Prophet's eyes widened.

Steel dropped down Lilly's chest. 'What do you mean, kidnapped? By who?'

'I don't know, someone in a coach,' he said quickly.

'When?'

'A minute ago.'

'Why didn't you go after them?' Lilly said shrilly.

'I couldn't, I…' Jon trailed off, his brow furrowed in distress.

Lilly bolted to the portcullis, sprinting as fast as she could.

The Prophet swallowed. 'It wasn't a man in a red cowl, was it?'

'I don't know,' Jon moaned. He buried his hands in his hair again. Something occurred to him. He grabbed the Prophet's sleeve tightly, making him flinch. 'People are coming. Lots of—there's gonna be fighting, I just saw it—'

'Breathe,' the Prophet said. 'What people? Robed people?'

'I dunno, all I saw was blood.'

The Prophet's eyes bulged in their sockets. 'They're here *now*?'

'No, not now, but soon, I saw them, they're *coming*.' He made a pained expression. 'They'll be here any day now. We have to *go*.'

The Prophet frowned. 'You *saw* them? How did you see them if they aren't there yet?'

Jon bared his teeth. 'I've told you about a dozen times now,' he said through gritted teeth, 'I can *see* into the *future*.'

The Prophet's eyes widened. 'You can see into the future,' he said in a hollow voice. He squinted at Jon. 'Are you *Mortimer*?'

The double doors opened again.

'What's Lilly screaming about?' Seth asked, poking his head out. 'Where's she gone?'

Jon sucked in a breath and exhaled, pivoting. 'Someone took Ginny.'

Seth's eyes widened. He sprinted after Lilly, barging past the two on his way.

'Why didn't you stop her?' the Prophet asked, his heart thudding.

Jon swallowed, staring after Seth. 'I don't know.'

The Prophet glanced at Seth. He clapped a hand on Jon's shoulder. 'I have a horse,' he said. 'If you go after them very fast, you might just head them off.'

Jon met his gaze, his brow wrinkled.

'It's worth a try,' said the Prophet with a shrug.

Jon gave him a nod. Together, they ran in search of the Prophet's horse.

~

'Sir, take my horse!' Marbrand shouted.

Seth accepted the reins, scanning Castlefoot Market for a flash of pink. 'Why wasn't anyone with her?' he demanded, furious. 'Why wasn't anyone watching her? There are guards everywhere! How did this happen?'

'They said Jon was with her,' Marbrand said. 'I found him in the market, but Ginny was nowhere to be seen. He was running up here when one of the men said he couldn't find her.'

'Why didn't he stop her?' Seth fumed, fumbling with the horse's livery.

'I don't know, he was just standing there, staring at a coach. I didn't think anything was wrong until someone told me they saw her *in* the coach.'

'Who else was in that coach?'

'No idea, but the woman I spoke to might have more information.'

'Find her,' Seth ordered, swinging himself into the saddle, 'and don't let her out of your sight until I've spoken to her myself.' With that he kicked into a gallop.

Snow darted into his eyes like a thousand pinpricks. He sped through the market. The icy wind tore through his thin jerkin, but he barely felt it. The throngs hastily parted, which was just as well. Seth knew only the bare basics of horse-riding, and he could tell by the horse's gait it was not going to suffice.

Nevertheless, he sped through Castlefoot Market, the horse trying clumsily to dodge the obstacles ahead. The main road opened up, empty and white. No coaches were evident ahead.

Seth sped on, the horse more at ease as the carts and people vanished behind them.

A coach appeared on the slope of the hill. Seth kicked his horse onward. It galloped at full speed, Seth clinging to the reins for dear life. The road rushed underneath as he gained on the coach. He could pick out details, the patterns in a purple so dark it was almost black, a motif carved into the back and lined with silver – a black spider, Seth saw with a squint – and on the left side of the coach, a stray lock of hair… blond hair—

Ginny! Sticking her face out of the coach window to catch the wind.

'Ginny!' he called.

He heard a little gasp over the sound of hooves. 'Daddy?' Ginny called over the wind.

A grin spread across Seth's face. She's alive. 'Ginny! I'm coming!'

Her head peered around the frame. He saw her face, beatific beneath a woolly pink hat.

'Daddy!' she called with glee.

'Gin—'

The horse stumbled beneath him. Seth yanked on the reins to keep his balance.

The horse bucked, throwing him to the left. His right foot dragged the stirrup over the horse's back. Seth soared into the grass and landed in a heap on the edge of the road.

The horse galloped on without him, overtaking the coach. It fled past her window, saddle empty.

'Huh?' Ginny said.

The coach's speed increased. It surged on.

Seth stumbled to his feet, his left ankle smarting. With a wince, he began to sprint for the purple coach. His left foot folded beneath his weight, sending him into the ground once more.

The coach horses galloped down the dirt road, the carriage wheels leaving dust in their wake. Seth caught one last glimpse of Ginny's head before it vanished into the coach.

'GINNY!' he bellowed on his hands and knees.

The last sounds he heard were the rumbling wheels and the horses' hooves thundering into the distance.

~

'This *bastard* country!' the Prophet swore uncharacteristically.

The reins hung from the stable wall, right about where the Prophet's roan had been tied. The Prophet pondered what to do next.

Jon didn't wait for his next plan. He bolted from the stables, already on a plan of his own.

'Wait, you'll never catch up to them on foot, let me get you another horse!' the Prophet wailed.

Jon had exited the castle entrance by then. He sprinted through the market and swerved into the crop of forest he'd seen earlier, hoping the road meandered enough to give him time to head them off. The low-hanging branches swallowed him up as the Creys' entire force trampled the marketplace, on the orders of Marbrand.

Marbrand himself stood at the crossroads, stopping coachmen for questioning. It was he who saw Seth limp up from the north road, his face drawn and his jaw tight.

'What news?' Marbrand asked, jogging to meet him.

Seth began to teeter. Marbrand caught him and slid an arm under Seth's left armpit. Seth collapsed against him. 'Emmett,' he gasped, panting.

As he feared. Marbrand tightened his jaw. 'You saw him in the coach?'

'I didn't see who took her, I just saw her. Her little head, poking out of the coach window.' He met Marbrand's gaze. 'It was painted in his colours.'

Marbrand exhaled. 'Some travellers coming from that way saw a coach matching that description,' he confirmed. 'We need to find out if he's had any coaches stolen before we throw about accusations—'

'His nephew just died in my castle,' Seth said, his voice deadpan. 'Of course it was him.' He let Marbrand lead him to the market.

'Is she alive?'

Seth looked defeated. 'For now.'

'None of that,' Marbrand ordered. 'They're headed up the north road, right? It curves around a small crop of forest. The men can cut through the woods and head them off. They can't ride faster than a charger, not lugging a coach with at least two people after them.'

'It only takes a second, Marbrand,' Seth said flatly.

You'd know, Marbrand realised. *It took only a second for your father to die.* 'I'm aware of that,' he said aloud. 'But she's worth more to them alive than dead.'

Seth didn't respond to that. He simply used Marbrand's shoulder as a crutch as they hobbled through the market.

Pounding footsteps heralded the arrival of Corporal Moat. 'I've sent men up the north road, sir,' he said. 'An innkeeper came down from the city and got a good look at the coach. It sounds like Emmett, sir.'

'We've established this, Moat,' Marbrand said testily. 'Anything else? Did he see who was inside?'

'There was a woman, sir, and someone else wearing a cowl. The woman had long auburn hair, sir.'

'Auburn?' Seth said sharply. 'Not red?'

'Definitely said auburn, sir. Dunno what colour *that's* supposed to be, mind.'

'Reddish-brown,' Marbrand supplied. 'Lead more men through the forest there,' he pointed, 'and see if they can head them off. Keep north and stop any coach bearing the Emmetts' colours.'

'Right away, sir.' He saluted sharply and bolted for the keep.

'Where's my sister?' Seth said.

Marbrand frowned. 'Is she missing as well?'

'Better not be. She came tearing down here when we heard Ginny was taken. If you find her, bring her to the top floor of the keep and confine her there. That goes for my wife and son as well, and my mother.'

'Right away, sir.' Marbrand handed Seth over to a fellow guardsman and jogged to the market in search for Lilly.

~

The Bastard waited in the small crop of forest on the outskirts of the Creys' Keep.

'Ah, you're here,' Geldemar said in relief. He appeared in front of him in physical, Vladdy form, glancing around.

The Bastard swore through his teeth. 'What are you doing?'

Geldemar jerked his gaze forward. 'He wants to meet us in this form. I assume you have a material form differing from the little dog costume?'

The Bastard rolled his eyes. 'Alas, no.'

'Oh dear. Well, there's a woodsman working nearby,' said Geldemar. 'Catch him like you did with Moat before and come back here. It should suffice for Him.'

'Why can't we meet in the usual way?'

'He has work here.' Geldemar looked despondent: very out of character for him, the Bastard mused.

'What is it?' said the Bastard. He folded his arms. 'Spit it out.'

Geldemar heaved a sigh. 'He has an escaped prisoner. And He's *very* pissed off about it.'

The Bastard frowned in bemusement. 'What prisoner?'

II

Jon heard the pounding of hoof-steps and leapt out of the way. A torrent of Crey guards fled down the overgrown path, swerving trees and foliage. Jon hid behind an oak tree as they passed and exhaled in relief. They'd have a better chance of catching them than he would.

Letting them know about the battle about to break out would be a nice idea, he thought to himself.

He sprinted in their wake, following the trampled undergrowth.

Another vision sent white flashes across his eyesight. He forced himself to focus. He could feel it getting more imminent by the second. There was only so long he could shove them out, but he needed that time to catch up to the guards. He still had to warn them of the battle.

He squeezed his eyes shut as the white flashes persisted.

A shout jolted him alert. 'MOVE!'

A horseman ran straight into him from behind.

Jon flew, spinning, down a slope to his right. He toppled headlong over shrubs and into tree trunks. As he did so, his premonition saw its chance and took over his consciousness.

Three men stood in a meadow, two of them vaguely familiar to him. The third was Seth Crey, but with a scar running down one side of his face. The Bastard.

Time jumped forward a bit. The Bastard swung his gaze directly onto Jon.

Jon was thrown against a tree, his head exploding with agony.

He jolted to the present. He was face down on the ground. He gingerly felt his temple, which throbbed. The pain was a lesser degree than in the vision. He wondered if he had actually been hurt or whether it was an echo of that pain.

He lifted himself to his feet anyway. The image of the Bastard staring him straight in the face lingered behind his eyelids, as though in warning.

'I don't care,' he announced to the world at large. He stood up straight and cast a look around himself. 'Bollocks.' He'd tumbled farther than he'd thought. He squinted through trees and shrubs, but he couldn't find the guards' trail anywhere. He was lost.

Jon sighed heavily and groaned a little. Then he strode forward.

He made a mental note to brush up on his tracking skills. He meandered and struggled through forestry that all looked the same to him, brown and green, shapeless and meaningless to him. He strained his gaze ahead, trying to catch a glimpse of a road, a coach, horsemen, anything to give him a clue as to where he was. Or even better, where Ginny was.

The cluster of trees became less dense. A beam of sunlight broke through, blinding him. Jon covered his eyes.

'East,' he said aloud. 'Shit.' He had been wandering in the wrong direction.

He continued on regardless, chastising himself for not noticing earlier. A path of sorts opened up in front of him, turning him south a bit. Feeling more on track, Jon followed it, brushing branches out of his way. The path opened up into a meadow. Jon's stomach dropped.

Three men conversed two yards away.

Jon braced himself for the Bastard's wrath and tucked himself down among the tree roots.

The Bastard stood side by side with a younger-looking man. The stranger wore his shoulder-length silver hair in a half-tail above a leotard that would make Jimmy green with envy. But Jon was more interested in the third man.

This one looked a few years older, dressed in plain brown breeches and a grey shift, though he held himself like a nobleman. His hair was a mousy blond and hung over his eyes, but Jon had a vague memory of it once being a bright gold. Had he seen a portrait of this man somewhere? Was that why he was so familiar? The man stood in front of the two, as though scolding a couple of ten-year-olds.

'... NEARLY HAD HIM UNTIL GELDEMAR THREW HIMSELF IN, CLAIMING THE BASTARD DEMANDED MY PRESENCE,' the stranger said in a soft, yet irate voice. Jon noted a kind of echo around his vocal tones: as though some beast spoke each word in tandem. 'HE WAS GONE BY THE TIME YOU HAD LEFT. MERCY ALONE KNOWS WHERE HE IS NOW.'

'I apologise, sir,' the silver-haired man, presumably Geldemar, muttered, his gaze lowered to the ground. 'He claims to have an urgent matter with you.' He swung his gaze to the Bastard, as though in accusation.

The Bastard shot him a sour side-glance.

The older man arched his eyebrows. 'WELL?'

'King Theo,' the Bastard said. 'He tried to kill my father, didn't he?'

Jon frowned. His father? *Seth*?

'MULTIPLE TIMES, YES,' the man said impatiently. 'I CAN'T IMAGINE HIM TRYING TO DROWN HIM PURELY FOR FUN.'

'But more recently,' the Bastard pressed.

The man nodded. 'YES. HE DID.'

Jon's frown deepened. *He's dead, though*, he thought, puzzled.

'How?'

The man sighed heavily, impatient with the entire conversation. 'HE HID AN EMBALMED SNAKE INSIDE THE RIM OF THE CROWN,' he said. 'IN POSTHUMOUS REVENGE FOR HIS OWN MURDER: BECAUSE IF IT WASN'T SETH THAT DID THE DEED, IT WAS NO DOUBT HIS FAULT THAT IT OCCURRED.'

That old bastard, Jon thought. The man had remarkable foresight, though. Jon almost admired it.

'THE TEETH PROTRUDED FROM THE BASE SLIGHTLY, STILL FILLED WITH VENOM. SETH WOULD BE NICKED BEHIND THE EAR DURING HIS CORONATION AND DIE A FEW DAYS LATER,' the man finished.

'I imagine King Theo intended to remove the poison in the event that a death by natural causes was imminent?' the Bastard said idly.

'PROBABLY NOT, ACTUALLY,' the man said, a thoughtful gaze to the heavens. 'HE DIDN'T LIKE SETH VERY MUCH.'

Wonder where he drew that conclusion, Jon thought wryly.

'ALAS, SETH CREY TURNED OUT TO BE ALLERGIC TO GOLD AND HAD A NEW CROWN MADE ESPECIALLY FOR HIM. A PITY, REALLY. IT WOULD HAVE MADE OUR JOB MUCH EASIER. NOT THAT IT MATTERS. IT'S ALL LITTLE MORE THAN OBSCURE COURT HISTORY NOW.'

'"Not that it matters",' the Bastard echoed. 'Not that it matters that Seth's three-year-old son was about to receive his father's death sentence.'

'HE LIVED, DIDN'T HE?' the man said nonchalantly.

The Bastard aimed a punch at him.

He caught the Bastard's wrist with little effort. 'PLEASE. MY REFLEXES HAVEN'T FALLEN THAT FAR BY THE WAYSIDE.' He jerked the Bastard's arm.

The Bastard pivoted, his arm pinned to his back. He gasped and bit back a scream as the man leaned in to growl in his ear.

'FUNNY HOW ATTACHED YOU'VE GOTTEN TO THE CHILD WHO HAS EVERYTHING YOU NEVER COULD HAVE. A CHILDHOOD. A HOME. PARENTS WHO LOVED HIM.'

The Bastard snarled, teeth bared. 'You sat by and let an innocent child die!'

'AZRAEL HORNE IS NO LOSS,' the man said blithely. 'JUST AS WELL HE TOPPLED FROM THE BALCONY BEFORE THE FEVER COULD KILL HIM. SAVE EVERYONE A LOT OF BOTHER. HE WOULD HAVE GROWN UP TO BE A COPY OF HIS UNCLE. DOES THE WORLD REALLY NEED ANOTHER MAN LIKE GOMEZ EMMETT THE YOUNGER IN IT?'

'You have no right to decide these things!'

'DON'T I?' He shoved the Bastard against Geldemar, who caught him in silence. 'I WAS UNDER THE IMPRESSION THAT I HAD *EVERY* RIGHT.'

A ruckus sounded behind them. The group's leader craned his neck to see.

Jon heard a coach's wheels rattling on the south road a mere few yards away, shortly followed by galloping horses. 'STOP! IN THE NAME OF THE KING!'

'I ALWAYS HATED WHEN THEY SAID THAT,' the stranger said in disdain. He clicked his fingers.

Horses screamed deafeningly and collapsed, making Jon flinch. Silence shortly followed.

'THERE, THAT'S BETTER,' said the nameless man in satisfaction.

The rattling wheels faded as the coach rolled on, unperturbed. Jon's heart sank. That was their only chance of saving Ginny.

He just about stopped himself from launching through the meadow. He couldn't risk angering the nameless stranger. He didn't like the thought of anyone overpowering the Bastard. The man was a part-time *demi-god*, after all – even if he hadn't mastered all the tricks yet.

Jon crouched back in the rushes, waiting for them to leave.

'WAS THAT ALL YOU WANTED?' the man asked, picking his nails.

'I wanted you about a week ago!' the Bastard fumed. He stepped away from Geldemar. 'You know, when there was a chance of me being able to save the child! What kind of god are you, letting innocent children die? His uncle's shortcomings are not applicable to Azrael! What was so important that he had to be left to die?'

The man arched an eyebrow. 'THE DEATHS OF THOSE CHILDREN PALE IN COMPARISON TO WHAT WAS SO IMPORTANT.'

Jon furrowed his brow, leaning forward to hear better.

'MY SON IS LOOSE,' the man snapped at the Bastard. 'AND YOUR POOR TIMING HAS MADE ME LOSE HIM FOREVER.'

Jon froze. His son. He glanced from the stranger to the Bastard, the resemblance crystal clear. Suddenly he knew exactly who this man was. He knew the portrait, one he had seen regularly since he was a little child.

Which meant his son... his son was...

Geldemar stepped forward from behind the Bastard.

'He escaped?' he said in a squeak.

The man opened his mouth to retort.

They froze, turning their gaze to the rushes.

A small cry had escaped from Jon's lips.

He *escaped*? Escaped *from where*?

The Bastard gaped at Jon, his expression of horror.

'WHO IS THAT?' the man said dangerously.

'Some servant of the Creys,' the Bastard said quickly. 'He must have been dispatched with the soldiers.'

The stranger lifted an eyebrow and flung Jon an idle wave. 'DISPOSE OF HIM.'

Geldemar made to obey, but the Bastard beat him to it. He launched himself at Jon through the air, soaring like a bird. The next thing Jon felt was an explosion of agony, just as foreseen.

He collapsed as oblivion washed over him.

~

Cienne sat in the ornate rocking chair in her son's playroom. Her heart hammered a rapid tattoo, aching with a yearning intensity. Ginny had been taken. That was all she knew as of yet. She held her breath for Seth's appearance.

Russell sat in front of a miniature toy castle, playing in silence. Despina perched on a step nearby, her head in her hands. A passing cloud dimmed the morning light from the high windows, leaving the yellow-carpeted room momentarily in shadow.

The latch clattered. The three pivoted to face Lilly.

'Seth's on his way up,' she said hoarsely, dropping onto the step beside Despina.

'Is she alive?' Cienne said hoarsely.

Lilly shook her head. 'I have no idea.'

The latch clattered again. 'Cienne,' Eleanor said.

Cienne rose and fled into her arms.

'The men have been sent after the coach,' Eleanor assured her. 'They'll bring her back. She'll be just fine, you'll see.'

'Who took her?' Cienne whimpered, her eyes brimming. 'Why? Why would someone take her? She's so small.'

'Sir Marbrand told me the coach belonged to the Emmetts,' said Eleanor. 'There was something about a woman as well with long hair. That's all anyone knows yet.'

Lilly spun. 'Long hair? What colour?'

'I didn't catch that part,' Eleanor admitted.

Cienne's thoughts landed on Adrienne. 'Long auburn hair, perhaps?'

Eleanor and Lilly exchanged glances.

'She doesn't have it in her,' Lilly said.

Eleanor planted a hand on each of Cienne's shoulders. 'Sit down. Seth will be able to shed some light on this when he arrives.'

Cienne let her steer her back to her rocking chair.

'The Emmetts have taken her, then,' Lilly said.

'They wouldn't,' Cienne said firmly. 'We're family. They would never—'

'Even after Azrael?'

Toys clattered softly in Russell's castle. Everyone eyed him wordlessly, the same half-formed image on the back of their minds.

Cienne tore her gaze from her son and stared at Despina. 'How did you let that happen to him?'

Despina flushed. 'I don't know. I wasn't in charge of his care—'

'You're the nanny,' Cienne said.

Despina flushed deeper. 'Emmett had sent Azrael's nanny from Stoneguard. She told me I wasn't to care for him anymore. Then she died of the flux, yesterday, I think. We didn't know—'

'You had one less child to look after,' Cienne said evenly, 'and you still let one of them go missing.'

'Cienne, this isn't her fault,' Lilly said.

'She was playing outside, guards surrounded her at every—' began Eleanor.

'But she's *still gone*.'

Despina's eyes filled with tears.

Cienne's eyes were cold. 'I think you should leave.'

Despina rose in silence and left. The latch closed softly behind her.

'Don't speak to her like that,' Lilly said quietly. 'She loves those two just as we do.'

The latch opened before Cienne could reply.

'Is everyone here?' Seth said. He descended the shallow stairs entering the playroom. He jabbed Lilly's shoulder. 'Lilly, did you see anything?'

Lilly's head jerked upright. 'No, they were gone by the time I got to the market.'

'Where's Jon?'

'I don't know, I left him by the keep entrance. I haven't seen him since.'

Seth started towards the door again.

Lilly rose, stepping in front of him. 'What can I do to help?'

'You can stay here,' Seth said firmly, pushing past her. He entered the corridor.

Lilly darted at his heels. 'Let me ride after her,' she said in earnest. 'I'll take Lyseria. We can head them off—'

'It takes one well-aimed spear to take her down, and then I'll have a dead sister to contend with as well. I don't think so. Get back in there.'

'I'm not some stupid little girl,' Lilly pressed, trailing him to the stairs.

'Get back in the playroom,' Seth said.

'I'm fully trained in armed combat,' she insisted. 'This is what Dad trained me for. Let me go after her.'

'*Go back to the playroom*,' Seth said through clenched teeth.

'Why won't you let me help you?' Lilly shouted.

Seth spun around, his cheeks flushed. 'You were kidnapped by pirates three years ago!' he barked. 'You've never been in a battle in your entire life, and the only man you've swung a sword at with malice aforethought is me. You froze when a boy you hardly knew got killed. What's going to run through your mind if you see your three-year-old niece lying dead in the back of that coach?'

Lilly paled, but she stepped forward, her nose an inch from his. 'What's running through *your* mind right now that's so helpful? Your only daughter is missing and you're cowering in your castle! Very useful!'

Clap!

Her face swung towards the wall. The right side of her jaw smarted. Shock swept through her arms and legs, a cold fizz in her veins.

Seth rubbed his left palm.

'Why did you do that?' Lilly said quietly, trembling.

He grabbed her shoulder, swinging her around to face him. 'I told you to stay in the playroom,' he snarled. 'I expect you to do as I say.'

Lilly slammed both hands against his chest. Seth staggered back a step. 'I could kill you with a teaspoon from a distance of twelve yards!' she snapped. 'Do *not* hit me again.'

Seth exhaled through clenched teeth.

And snatched Lilly by her hair.

Cienne clutched Russell as the playroom door crashed open. Lilly soared through the door and her stomach slammed into the table, her hair sprawled across the surface.

'Seth!' Eleanor shrieked.

Seth charged in after her and pulled her upright by her jerkin.

'I told you to stay in here!!' he howled, his face pressed against hers. 'That is the last time you talk back to me, you little cunt!! If you leave this room again, I will kill you myself!!'

He shoved her back against the table and stormed out. The door slammed behind him, rattling.

Lilly slid to the floor, gasping shallow breaths.

Russell trembled in Cienne's arms.

Eleanor swept to Lilly's side. 'Darling, are you alright?' She folded Lilly into her arms.

Lilly cried loudly, sobs wracking her chest.

'What's going on?' Russell whimpered.

Cienne lifted him into her lap. 'It's okay, baby.' Her heartbeat skipped erratically. He clutched her dress in both hands, his head buried in the crook of her neck.

'Mum,' Lilly choked, her head bent.

Eleanor lifted Lilly's jerkin to her ribs. Blood soaked her shirt.

'He's re-opened the wound,' said Eleanor in dismay. 'We need Erik.'

'We can't leave the room,' Cienne said in a whisper.

Eleanor rose to her feet.

'Mum, no,' Lilly whined. 'What if he hurts you?'

Eleanor turned as she swung the door open, scoffing. 'Let him try.' She swept out.

~

III

A modest army trudged through the snow dunes to Castlefoot Market. Led by a large figure in crimson robes, they climbed the hill in ragged formation, bowing every so often at the various statues of Salator Crey scattered around the marketplace.

Marbrand eyed them distrustfully. The animate black robes dismounted, filing into the local inn one by one. 'What are they up to?'

Elliot shrugged. 'Who knows? What I'm concerned about is the rescue party. Someone ought to have returned by now.'

Marbrand rolled his eyes. He knew this ragtag pack of morons they called a royal guard would put him on the gallows one way or another. 'We'd better head up there and have a look.'

They headed for the stable yard.

Twenty minutes later, they returned. Marbrand was swearing loudly and colourfully.

'Get the frigging king,' he barked at a lingering guard.

He jerked his horse to a halt beside the nearest boozer.

~

It was a corridor, drafty and frightening. Jon squinted into the darkness.

Steady breathing sounded below him.

Jon strode down the corridor, his face set.

Walking down a level concrete floor, he treaded carefully, his eyes slowly focussing in the gloom. He had no single idea how he came to be in this corridor. His hands flailing in front of him, he tried to manoeuvre his way down the hall.

One sole found the edge of a step. He descended carefully down the set of stairs ahead, his right hand planted firmly on the wall.

He wondered how long he had been wandering around in this place. Was it an hour? An evening? A day? Weeks? Months? It felt like forever. He entertained the idea that his entire life had been spent in this darkness, before remembering Father Giery with a shiver. *Yeah, you wish.*

He froze and opened his ears, listening for heavy breathing.

It was only as he stalked to the other end of the room in search for a door that he heard the heavy breathing resume, back from the direction he had come.

Jon turned slowly, blinking repeatedly, searching the gloom vainly for an outline of a person who was not there. He slowly approached the stairs, listening to his own footsteps clicking on the tiles.

The breathing… It came closer and closer with each step before, abruptly, stopping.

Hot breath landed on the back of his neck. Jon gasped involuntarily. He swung around, eyes wide.

King Theo Crey stood before him, his clothes charred and his face burnt, his eyes bloodshot and angry. 'You're in for it now, boy.'

Jon frowned. 'Why am *I* in for it?'

Theo Crey frowned back at him. 'What?'

'You always liked me,' said Jon.

Theo Crey blinked, then shook off his bemused expression.

'No point screaming, boy,' he intoned. 'No one but you and I will be able to hear it.'

'Alright, I won't bother, then,' said Jon.

King Theo blinked again. He decided to lunge at him.

'So you back from the dead then, or what?'

Theo abruptly stopped what he was doing. 'No,' he said in annoyance.

'No? Only a minute ago, I could have sworn I heard summink abo—'

'Silence!'

'Alright, then,' Jon said mildly. 'I was only asking a question.'

'Well, don't then! Git-head.'

'"Git-head",' Jon said pensively. 'That doesn't sound like something King Theo Crey would say.'

'Well… death changes a man, innit?'

'Innit,' said Jon wryly.

'Yeah!' King Theo exclaimed.

'Yeah,' Jon echoed.

'Yeah,' King Theo said, satisfied.

Jon's eyes narrowed. 'This is the shittiest impression of the king I've ever seen.'

'What's so shit about it?' King Theo demanded.

'You look like King Theo,' Jon said, 'but you sound like the Bastard.'

'How?'

'It's distinctly Seth-Crey-esque.'

'That's bullshit,' Theo said defiantly. 'You're bullshit. Shut up.'

'Yep,' Jon said. 'The *worst* impression of King Theo I've ever seen. Almost as if it was Seth Crey trying to do the impersonation—or someone exactly like him.'

'I—that is, the Bastard, to whom you're no doubt referring—is nothing like Seth Bloody Crey!' he roared hotly.

'Naw, the Bastard's slightly uglier.'

'What?!' King Theo shrieked, offended.

'Dirty great hole right down his face. Not in the least bit appealing to look at—'

'I'll have you know, I—that is, the Bastard, who you no doubt mistake me for—has a mysterious aura that compensates for physical—oh, what gave it away?' he relented dully.

'You've still got the scar,' Jon said.

The Bastard raised a burnt hand to his face. 'I keep forgetting about that sodding scar,' he groaned, his voice softening from King Theo's growl to Seth's lazy drawl.

Jon watched the king's bulk melt away, slimming down to Seth's slight build. Seth Crey's face now scowled at Jon. Jon smiled brightly back.

'Don't I even scare you a little bit?' the Bastard asked in annoyance.

'Ginny Crey frightens me more than you do.' Jon's eyes widened. He remembered. 'Ginny! Shit!'

The Bastard blinked. 'What about Ginny?'

Jon searched his face. The Bastard knew nothing.

'Take me back,' he said.

'Why, what's wrong with Ginny?' the Bastard demanded.

'She's been kidnapped. I have to go back now.'

'By who?' The Bastard's face suddenly slackened. 'Oh Christ no.'

'Who is it?' Jon asked, anxious.

He shook his head. 'I can't say.'

'Tell me!' Jon exclaimed. 'You have to tell me so we can get her back.'

'I can't,' the Bastard said, looking uncomfortable.

'Why?' said Jon with a frown. 'She's your sister.'

The Bastard threw his head back, gazing at the ceiling. 'I know that.'

'Help me get her back, then,' Jon pressed. 'You're a god, it's a two-second job for you! You just click your fingers and poof, she'll be home again.'

'I *can't*,' the Bastard said in a pained voice.

'You can't click your fingers? Clapping your hands would probably do it.'

'No. I mean I can't do anything to help her.'

'Why?'

The Bastard drew a shaky breath.

Jon saw fear behind his eyes and felt a stab of the same.

'Because Salator Crey,' the Bastard said, looking into Jon's eyes in remorse, 'wants all of you dead. And I'm being instructed to help him. Ginny is part of it.' He heaved a sigh. 'I have to make sure you all die.'

Jon's jaw hung slightly open. 'You can't,' he managed. 'We're family.'

The Bastard dropped his gaze. 'So is He.'

Jon searched the Bastard's morose expression.

'This to do with the end of the world?' Jon asked quietly. 'Is that why Salator Crey is getting involved personally? He's fed up of the whole god lark and decided to pack it in?'

The Bastard exhaled tremulously.

Jon inhaled. He released an explosive sigh of resignation. 'You know what, fine,' he said, squeezing his eyes shut. 'Get on with it.'

He heard the Bastard whine. A foot stamped on the ground as though in exasperation.

'Come on, we haven't got all day,' Jon said, to lighten the mood. 'Make with the killing. Preferably painlessly.'

A weight landed on his forehead, bringing him to the ground. Everything went black for a while. Jon felt as if he was gently slipping into a nice nap.

A beat later, he blearily lifted his head. All memory of that morning disintegrated like vapour.

'Why am I here?' he asked himself in bemusement.

He tried to lift himself upright, but his head screamed in protest. He slumped to the grass in agony. Birds twittered in the white light. It was too blinding for him to open his eyes to. With a frown, Jon summoned all his strength and jerked his eyes open.

The light assaulted his brain, boring in through the eye sockets. He winced and glanced around in a squint. He was in the woods. And he was alone.

Until a man leaned over him.

Jon blinked rapidly. His vision blurred. He could just make out a crop of black hair and a golden-embroidered leotard rather like the hideous kind of clothing Eleanor Crey would make. His face was oddly familiar.

The man tutted. 'Done it now, haven't you?' he said in a nasally voice.

Jon tried vainly to control his wavering vision.

The man gave him a wide smile with dimples in it. Jon suddenly recognised him. His heart sank to his stomach. 'This… isn't good.'

Mortimer Crey beamed down at Jon with the smug smile someone who could see into the future might have.

~

'You can't perform this,' Myles informed him.

Rhys rolled his eyes.

An impromptu performance was about to take place in the centre of

Castlefoot Market. It happened more and more after his triumphant debut – fanatics accosted him at every turn, traders bearing gifts, women offering him… other gifts, children relaying his best jokes with a grin. They each had one thing in common: a burning desire for an encore.

They'd never get the food shop done at this rate.

Rhys Hewitt – also known as King Howard – threw a passing glance at his son. The nine-year-old had gotten bored after the third impromptu Seth Crey impression. Sammy had climbed to the top of a tree outside the castle barbican entrance – an indication that Rhys's act probably needed freshening up.

Apparently, his partner thought otherwise.

Rhys splayed his hands. 'What's wrong with it?'

'Are you serious?' Myles exclaimed. 'What's wrong with it?' His black hair, speckled with silver at the temples, stuck up at odd angles – which was due to the amount of times he'd pulled it in exasperation while reading the script. He slapped the offending manuscript with the back of his hand. 'What's right with it?' Myles squealed. 'The entire premise is a bloody disgrace!'

'If we're going to do current affairs,' Rhys said calmly, 'we need to touch on events that are, uh, you know… current?'

'You *can't,*' Myles said deliberately, 'make *fun* of a *child's disappearance*!'

'Oh, it's not that bad,' Rhys scoffed, his gaze to the heavens. 'Kids run away all the time. Sammy does a runner once a week, it's relatable, isn't it? She'll be back when she's hungry.'

'That isn't the point! She didn't just *run away,* she was abduced! This is someone's little girl you're writing jokes about! How would you feel if it was your kid snatched away like that?'

They glanced at the boy in question.

Sammy launched himself from a high branch with a battle cry. A passer-by slammed face-first into the gravel, Sammy straddling his back. He brandished his victim's money with a triumphant howl.

'Frankly, relieved,' said Rhys.

Behind them came the thundering of horses. The crowds scattered, Rhys and Myles along with them.

Black-robed riders littered the marketplace. A crimson-robed horseman dismounted onto Rhys's abandoned stage, trampling his timber backdrop underfoot.

'King Seth Crey!' he bellowed.

Rhys grinned broadly. 'I am he!' he intoned with a flamboyant bow.

Myles buried his head in his hands.

'Do not jest with me, your majesty,' the man growled, his jowls quivering. 'The Faith of Salator Crey have deemed your crimes unredeemable. Relinquish your castle to the Faith!'

'Looks like I have,' said Rhys, 'you've just trod on it.'

'You can't help yourself, can you?' Myles shrieked at him. 'Don't you know who he is?'

'No,' said Rhys, irked. 'He looks like a senile old granddad in a dressing gown.'

'He's the Archpriest of the Faith of Salator Crey!'

'So? He's just busted up my set! It took ages to paint that!'

'I know,' Myles seethed. '*I* was the one who *painted* it.'

'Relinquish your castle!' the Archpriest bellowed.

Rhys clapped a hand on his ear, waving the other irritably. 'Keep your voice down, will you? I'm not him, he's that way – honking great castle. Can't miss it.'

'You just said you were!' shrilled a black robe in the throng.

'I was joking!' Rhys exclaimed. He flicked the end of his greying woollen cloak into the air. 'You think I'd wear this dog blanket if I could afford gold embroidery?'

The red robe heaved a sigh. 'Are you Seth Crey or not?'

'Not. I just take the piss out of him. I told you, honking great castle yonder. He'll be inside looking for his kid.'

The Archpriest snorted impatiently and kicked his mount onwards. Rhys flinched back from his men and their dust clouds. The robed horsemen flocked the barbican entrance.

'Let's get off the market,' Myles said. 'I don't like this.'

Observing the ruins of his set, Rhys followed him to the inn, grumbling. No chance of a performance now. He caught a glimpse of Sammy about to launch himself onto one of the horsemen.

'Oi!' Rhys bellowed at him. 'Get in here!'

The boy worked his way down the branches, disheartened.

Candlelight shone already inside the inn's common room, to counter the weak sunlight of the snowy afternoon. Tucked into a corner table by the window, Rhys carved into a lump of roast ham, Sammy and Myles looking on in anticipation.

Trumpeting drove his attention outside.

'Oh look, it's my muse,' Rhys said with a grin.

Sammy pivoted completely around, his knees sinking into the soft seat of the bench. Myles peered out from the edge, trying to hide himself from the irate priests.

The castle garrison surrounded the horsemen in a ring, each with the flat of his broadsword sitting idly on one shoulder. In the middle of Rhys's ruined stage, dressed in green embroidered wool, was King Seth Crey, his arms folded and his gaze fixed to the Archpriest.

'Open the window,' Rhys told Sammy.

He complied, opening the hinge of the lower pane a tad.

'A holy war?' Seth said, his voice lifting in scepticism. 'What for?'

'For your crimes of adultery, heresy, murder, unlawful eviction of the castle chapel—'

'The one run by a child molester, is it?'

'Father Giery was ours to reprimand,' the Archpriest said. 'It was nothing to do with you.'

'Where my family are concerned,' Seth snarled, 'it is everything to do with…' His voice tapered off, carried away by a passing wind.

Rhys clucked in disapproval. 'Can't hear him.' He pushed the window out further. That was better. He stuck an ear out.

Seth stepped forward, the toes of his boots jutting over the edge of the top step.

'Why are you here now?' he asked, lifting his eyebrows. 'Why now, in the middle of all this?'

The red-robed priest shook his head. 'Of which do you speak?'

'You know what.' Seth's arms unfolded, dropping to his side, fists clenched. 'If you know where my child is, you'd better tell me now before I get angry.'

The priest trotted closer, drawing his horse right up to the bottom step. 'We're already angry, your majesty. And with one word from me, I can demonstrate just how angry that is.'

Seth licked his overbite. 'I have a word, too,' he said. '*Lyseria.*'

A loud *whock* sounded in the distance.

Hot air poured into the crack, washing through Rhys's fair hair. He and Sammy jerked their heads away from the window – just in time for a red wing to slap it and send it spinning out of sight.

The Creys' dragon spun with it, high into the air before swirling around the priests in a flurry of smoke.

'Archpriest, meet Lyseria. Lyseria, the Archpriest of Serpus,' Seth sang, gesturing from Lyseria to the Archpriest with a flourish.

Lyseria threw herself to a halt behind Seth – right on top of Rhys's coach.

Rhys watched, wide-eyed, his arms wrapped tightly around Sammy. Their coach, plus all his belongings and performance equipment, crumpled into splinters.

'Our stuff,' Sammy said, little more than a whisper.

'My costumes,' Myles whined.

'My *money,*' Rhys said in a low moan.

Lyseria shifted her footing. As if on cue, a small chest tumbled out from the wreckage, jingling to a halt a yard behind her tail.

Rhys's eyes were glued to it.

Seth's eyes were similarly glued to the Archpriest of Serpus.

'I have no idea where your child has got to,' the Archpriest said in a sneer. 'Flaunting your hell-beast won't force an answer out of me. Perhaps who really took her might return her once you've atoned for your crimes. The Faith can put a good word in for you… once you've relinquished your castle.'

Seth spread his arms wide, fluttering his hands to each of his garrison. 'Can't you count? I have more men than you. And this doesn't even touch the surface: I have twice as many inside the keep – oh, not to mention the hell-beast over here. I think that means the castle remains mine.'

The Archpriest stuck his fingers between his withered lips and whistled.

Horsemen – ten, twenty, thirty, Rhys lost count within seconds – flooded into the market from the surrounding woodland. The Creys' garrison cowered as horsemen totalling to twice their number and more formed a ring around their own.

Rhys sat transfixed to the scene. A hand gripped his shoulder.

'We should leave,' Myles implored. 'If that dragon starts flinging fire everywhere—'

'And do what?' Rhys hissed at him. 'That thing just flattened our coach! And where the hell is the horse? I can't see it anywhere!'

'I think that's its leg under the dragon's bum,' Sammy said, pointing.

Rhys threw a gesture at his son. 'There we go. We're stuck here until we can get out there and get my money.'

'You're not seriously considering going out there, are you?' Myles exclaimed in a frantic whisper. 'This isn't something that's just going to blow over!'

'Oh, nothing's even happening out there! I could go out and grab it now if I wanted to!'

'Oh, shut up Rhys, you're hardly going to…'

Rhys's face lit up.

Myles's darkened. 'No.'

Rhys slid out from behind the table.

'Rhys, sit down, for Christs' sake!' Myles shouted, heedless of the staring punters.

'No, I'm getting my money,' he said. He slipped his cloak around his shoulders and fastened it. 'I'll just sneak around them while they're talking, they won't even notice a thing.'

'Rhys, is it really worth it?' Myles moaned.

'That's my life's savings out there!' Rhys exclaimed, gesturing. 'It took twenty years of my life to earn that!'

'You didn't earn it! You nicked it from the monk that won the talent show!'

'*Liberated*,' Rhys corrected. 'And there was no proof he really painted that porno anyway, so I call it disqualification. Make sure my kid doesn't rob anyone, I won't be long.'

'What? Rhys, no, think of little Sammy, d'you want him to be an orphan?'

Rhys frowned at him, arching an eyebrow.

'He has a mother, you know,' he said in a withering tone. 'I didn't just find him under the bed one day. Be back in a minute.'

Myles protested unintelligibly.

Rhys, flinging a glance around in case of thwarters to his plan, slipped outside.

Oblivious to the newcomer, Seth scrutinised the horsemen. 'Hijacked a pilgrimage, it is?'

'More recruited from said pilgrimage,' the Archpriest said in satisfaction. 'These are minor noblemen from across the continent, numbering at fifteen families, complete with their own troops. All here to serve the Faith.' The Archpriest thrust a hand into the air.

Steel flashed in the dull afternoon sun.

Panic flashed over Seth's features. 'Run!'

His man scattered, making for the barbican. The horsemen pressed in around them, drawing them together like cattle.

'I hope you aren't thinking of employing the dragon,' the Archpriest said amiably. 'Your men will cook just as well as mine, as I'm sure you're aware.'

Lyseria growled a challenge.

Seth held a handout to her, making comforting noises. His eyes remained locked to the priest. 'Name your terms.'

On the curb by the inn, Corporal Moat stumbled.

'Sorry, pardon me,' Rhys said, squeezing past.

Moat jumped slightly, startled. 'Are you mental?'

One of Moat's superiors hushed him into silence, his gaze locked on the king. He and the others seemed oblivious to the royal doppelgänger making for the chest of gold.

'Bearing in mind,' Seth cut across the Archpriest, 'that the castle is out of the question.'

'My terms are clear,' said the Archpriest. 'The kingdom, in exchange for the good men you took from us and rendered homeless.'

Inside the gap where the inn's window used to be, Myles tugged on his hair.

Rhys tiptoed across the wide expanse behind the dragon, in plain sight of just about everyone.

'Should have asked for his will, shouldn't I?' Sammy said.

Myles shushed him harshly.

'I assume you intend to negotiate?' said the Archpriest. His eyes fell on Rhys with a start.

'I have no obligation to negotiate with the likes of you!' Seth barked.

Lyseria growled, in agreement, Seth reckoned.

Rhys froze, totally aware that it was him she was in fact growling at. 'Good dragon,' he whispered, his hands raised.

Lyseria flicked her tail, turning back to the more pressing adversary.

Rhys exhaled through puffed cheeks, his eyelids flickering. He returned his attention to the chest, reaching an arm under Lyseria's quivering tail. The chest sat millimetres from his fingertips.

'If it weren't for the welfare of my own men, I would burn the lot of you to the ground,' Seth snarled. He seemed totally oblivious that the Archpriest's attention was locked to Rhys's antics. 'I still might, in fact. Now, I'd forget about this siege, if I were you, because I'm not in a good mood and arguing with you lot isn't making it any better.'

He frowned at the Archpriest.

The old man craned his neck to the left to see Rhys better. Rhys bared his teeth in a grotesque grimace, both hands twitching closer to the chest.

Myles and Sammy hid their faces in their hands.

The unthinkable happened.

Seth, brow furrowed, pivoted to face Rhys.

Rhys batted at the chest with the tips of his fingers and gained purchase. 'Ha-HA!' He lifted himself to his full height and froze, eyes bulging. 'Ah.'

Seth's eyes bored a hole in the centre of his forehead, eyes half-lidded.

'Hi-ah,' Rhys said, with a wobbly grin.

Seth ran his tongue along the inside of his cheek, irate. It protruded in a lump behind the skin – menacingly, Rhys thought. 'It's King Howard, isn't it?'

The grin dropped from Rhys's face. The bump in Seth's cheek frightened him beyond all logic. Rhys held up the chest in both hands. 'Just came to grab this. I'll leave you to it.'

'No,' Seth barked.

Rhys flinched.

'You stay right there.' The harsh tone softened but was no less deadly. Rhys obeyed, cradling the chest in his elbows.

Seth tilted his gaze downwards, scuffing a boot on the wooden panels. 'Interrupted a show, have we?'

An unintelligible squeak preluded Rhys's frightened, 'Yes.' A lump rose in his throat. He swallowed it down hard.

Seth paid no attention to the pleas. Instead, he turned to the Archpriest.

'Have you seen King Howard?' he asked genially. 'Very popular in the market. Perhaps you've seen his show?' A grin spread across Seth's face. Rhys couldn't tell the intentions behind it. 'In fact,' Seth went on, 'he has a very amusing segment featuring a sketch about my dragon. Fancy that, eh?' He gestured at Lyseria, who was rooting through the wreckage beneath her. 'An acclaimed comedy star featuring *you* in his show! You're practically a celebrity!'

Lyseria snorted through a mound of rubble, uninterested.

Seth whirled back to the priest. 'Actually, that gives me a wonderful idea.' He hopped off the stage, skipping to a halt before the priest. 'Since your pilgrims here have forbidden me from killing you, I see I'm going to have to persuade them to see my point of view. And what better form of persuasion than a little show? HOWARD!!' he roared, making Rhys jump. 'I have an excellent part written just for you.'

A glance at Seth, then the priest, then the dragon, and Rhys quickly put two and two together. 'No,' he said.

Seth's tongue poked the inside of his cheek again. 'Pardon?'

Rhys trembled. 'I said... no.' His eyes darted about.

Armoured men, seasoned battle veterans and young men alike, looked at him as though he was mad. But what was mad about standing up to Seth Crey? He was no King Theo. He was just a wimp with a dragon.

Rhys drew himself to his full height. 'I have a wife,' he went on, his voice wavering. 'And a child. You don't own me. I'm not taking part in a charade to scare this man.'

'I don't recall giving you a choice, Howard.' His volume levels were extremely low.

'*That isn't my name,*' Rhys snarled loudly. 'Whatever you have against that poor Howard Wosshisface, it has nothing to do with me.' Rhys splayed one arm wide, the other still wrapped around the chest of gold. 'It's just a stage name! I tell jokes for a living! Big deal! I did the Earl of Herpes the other day, he laughed his hole off! He didn't point a fire-breathing dragon at me and flatten my horse! You don't treat people like rubbish just because you own a red gecko that breathes fire and a big fuck-off castle! You need to get over yourself!'

A line appeared in the centre of Seth's brow. 'What you need to do,' Seth said flatly, 'is what you're told. Because you're beginning to annoy me.'

'Oh yeah? What are you gonna do about it?'

Seth folded his arms across his chest and lifted his chin. 'What's your name, sir? Your *actual* name?'

Rhys blinked. 'Rhys Hewitt.'

Seth nodded. 'Rhys Hewitt.' He clicked his fingers. 'Lyseria, kill Rhys Hewitt.'

'What?' said Rhys.

Lyseria rose on her forelegs and levelled her nose with his.

'Wait now, hang on,' Rhys squeaked, his pulse racing.

Flames poured through him and tore into the gravel beneath his feet.

~

VI

Emmett placed aside the letters he was writing and laced his fingers together, his expression distant. The innkeeper had left moments ago after relaying the bad news about Princess Virginia Crey, thinking – correctly – that he would probably want to know.

He hadn't guessed however that the reason Emmett wanted to know was because a coach bearing his family insignia had been stolen from his estate in Squirm late that morning.

Emmett brushed his long fingers across the dozens of letters he'd just finished, one addressed to each noble family of Stoneguard, all containing the same three paragraphs. He supposed he ought to write one to Seth Crey containing condolences and offers of men to assist in the search. It was common courtesy.

There was no question that it was his own coach that carried the princess off. The question was who was driving it. It interested Emmett, without a doubt. He would have to make some enquiries.

He rose from the desk as his door opened. The midday sun lanced across the largest room of the inn via the balcony window, interrupted only by his passing frame. He stood in the centre of the room to meet his sister's party.

Meyer entered alone, slipping inside and closing the door carefully behind him.

Emmett lifted an eyebrow. 'Where are my sister and nephew?'

'I've sent Felicity on to your manor in Squirm, my lord,' Meyer said, lowering his head in a bow. 'Your uncle and my guards are escorting them. They should arrive by this evening—'

'Why are they not returning here?' Emmett asked in mild interest.

Meyer met his cold gaze. 'Her majesty is deeply distressed, my lord.'

Emmett's brow creased ever so slightly.

Meyer's brow furrowed in a more pronounced fashion. 'Has no one told you, my lord?'

'Told me what, Henry?' Emmett asked coolly, his patience waning.

'About Azrael. I sent a messenger as soon as we—'

'What about Azrael?' His tone was sharp.

Meyer ran a hand through his hair. 'He's dead, my lord,' he said, his voice breaking.

Meyer had expected some kind of reaction. He didn't get one. Emmett's face was colourless, his eyes like chips of flint – but then he always looked that way. He imagined he could see Emmett's facial muscles slacken in dismay, but it was too faint for him to be sure.

'Felicity is heading to Squirm?' he said finally, impassive as ever.

'Yes.' Meyer wrung his hands. 'My lord, as a father and uncle myself, you have my deepest and most sincere—'

'Let's go to Squirm,' Emmett cut across him. His voice was light.

He turned to tidy some papers away into a satchel. He placed the strap across his torso, gave the satchel at his hip a pat and walked past Meyer to exit the room.

Meyer made to follow when a messenger barged into him, panting. He eyed Meyer's cloth of gold jerkin and dropped a hasty bow. 'Palace staff, m'lord. I was sent to give Mister Emmett a message—'

'You're just missed him,' Meyer said. 'I'm betrothed to his sister, what's the message?'

The boy panted some more, wheezing. His green breeches and jerkin confirmed him to be in the employment of the Creys. 'His majesty King Seth requests your audience immediately—Mister Emmett's audience, I mean. It's in relation to the princess.'

Meyer gave him a slow nod. 'I'll pass it on.'

The boy bowed again and hurried off.

Meyer was alone. He stared into space as the sunlight waned under a passing cloud.

Seth Crey requests Mister Emmett's audience immediately. Meyer didn't think it was to give his condolences – he'd witnessed the chaos first-hand as their coach struggled to Serpus, through roads clogged with hordes of Adem nobility scouring the city for sign of Princess Virginia. He'd have thought King Seth had more pressing matters.

Unless Mister Emmett…

Meyer turned to the desk at the back of the room.

Despite Emmett's efforts to gather his paperwork, a letter still lingered on the tabletop, the ink smeared. Meyer picked up the sheet and scanned it. His hands had folded it into quarters and slipped it into the pocket of his jerkin before his mind had processed the contents.

Oh, he thought finally, turning to follow Emmett's wake. *This does not bode well.*

~

Erik sat back on his haunches, wiping his bloody hands on his apron. 'Good as new.'

'Doesn't feel like it,' Lilly grunted, trying to sit up.

Erik pressed down on her shoulders, lying her flat on the flagstones.

'You might take this as incentive to actually take my advice this time,' he said. '*Rest*. No lifting heavy melee weapons. No fighting. No haring off after kidnappers.'

'None of that opened the wound,' Lilly seethed at the ceiling. More to Seth than Erik.

'None of it helped either.' He turned to Eleanor. 'She really ought to be in a bed rather than the floor.'

'The biggest bed we have in here is about four feet long,' Eleanor said. 'Lilly's small, but she's not that small. We're confined here until my son says so. There's nothing we can do about it.'

'Let me at least request to have you confined somewhere that's of use to me.'

Eleanor sighed. 'I suppose you could ask.'

Erik rose from his knees and gave Eleanor a hand up, bowing his farewell.

Eleanor pointed at Lilly as he left. 'Sleep.'

Lilly rolled her eyes, but closed them in compliance.

Cienne's eyes bore into the brick wall behind Russell's toy castle. Eleanor perched on the rocking chair behind them.

Russell had parked himself on his mother's lap as she sat cross-legged in front of the little castle, a grey miniature of the massive Portabellan fortresses she had grown up in. Russell seemed to have forgotten about the tension surging through the air and was contentedly waging war on his sister's dollies.

Cienne's face was drawn and grey. She probably hadn't eaten today, Eleanor reflected – before realising none of them had. 'Shall I call for someone to bring some food?'

Cienne didn't meet her gaze. 'We're not to leave the room until my husband says so. Considering what he just did to Lilly, I think we ought to obey him for a change.'

'Seth wouldn't hurt you,' Eleanor assured her.

'Seth wouldn't,' she agreed. 'But he isn't Seth right now, is he?'

Eleanor agreed in silence. She didn't know who it was that shoved Lilly into that table, but it wasn't her son in there, not really. His eyes were too hard, too angry. What happened to the funny little boy she knew and loved?

'It's her that's done this.'

Eleanor pulled herself back out of her own thoughts. 'Who, dear?'

'Adrienne.' Cienne stared unblinking at the wall, likely seeing her rival's face imprinted upon it. 'She shouldn't have been let into the castle.'

Eleanor's gaze lost focus, her thoughts on Seth's lover. 'If it wasn't her, it would have been someone else. Someone more dangerous than her.'

Cienne swung her gaze to her mother-in-law. The sadness in it tugged on Eleanor's heartstrings. 'Who could be more dangerous,' said Cienne, 'than a woman who snatches a baby from her home after killing her own?'

Eleanor sat in silence.

~

The flames waned. The ground where Rhys Hewitt once stood now smouldered. A blackened mark was all that remained of him. The chest, its timbers aflame, had toppled onto the blackened cobbles and burst open, sending coins spilling across the square.

The clergy's horses shied away, shrieking. Seth's men closed in, lances raised.

'Going somewhere, are we?' Seth said, his voice light. 'I don't think so. Moat?'

Moat took aim with one eye closed and thrust his spear into the throng. A guttural shriek gurgled out of the priest in place of a scream.

Chaos erupted around Seth, the market a flurry of black robes and blood. Seth turned his face as the latter sprayed him in passing, dotting his left cheek. The lanced darted in and out, cries and grunts tainting the silence. A deafening one, in spite of the pain being inflicted.

Funny, thought Seth, watching Lyseria hurl herself to the clouds. *I'd always thought there would be more screaming.* The most popular tales of the Battle of the Orchards always included a tremendous amount of screaming. No one seemed to get a chance to gasp in real life, much less howl. They bled just fine, though – Seth could smell it in the air.

And they crapped just fine as well, he realised. A different stench altogether wafted over him, thicker and sharper.

A part of him wondered vaguely why he wasn't horrified. Ordinarily he would have run for the hills by now, in search for his mother. That was the old Seth, he thought, the mummy's boy, who had faked a mental illness for twenty years to avoid having children and daydreamed about teaching his father a lesson. Who crept out in the dead of night to meet whores. Who broke his wife's heart without batting an eyelid. That Seth had vanished the moment he walked into that chapel.

His chest clenched. He felt as though a lump of metal had slammed its way inside. He wasn't that man anymore – hadn't been for a long time. He was a better man now – ever since the twins.

The metal inside him grew hot. His children.

Furlong had slipped out – luck on the priests' side had taken down a number of lancers, forming a passage out. Most of the surviving horsemen were following suit, except for one foolhardy example. He galloped at Seth, timber spear aimed point-first at Seth's face.

A ball of flame from above made short work of him. A flaming, blackened husk collapsed into the gravel, man and horse melted into one.

I changed, Seth thought, once the smoke had abated somewhat. As soon as he had clapped eyes on Russell, as soon as he had held Ginny in his arms, he had melted. The selfishness, the greed, the insufferable belligerence – all of that vanished. Seth hadn't known importance until that day. *They* were important. He had finally found people he loved more than himself. He needed them to love him back. He needed to be *worth* loving.

And he was… Almost.

Lyseria razed the ground around him. Crey soldiers darted out of the way. The priests fled for the inn, hoping the building would offer some protection.

Seth watched the Emerald Inn crumble into dust with a faint satisfaction. Not satisfaction. Release. That was it. The metal in his chest smouldered on. This was like smoke pouring from a kettle. The poison abated somewhat, but the heat remained.

Lyseria's wings pounded up and down in a steady rhythm. She hovered over the remains of the inn, gouging through the rubble with her tongue of flame, hunting down every survivor.

There were innocents in that inn. The blow of this revelation lacked impact. The anger burned on, all sense of horror or terror extinct. The innocents were insignificant. There were only three people whose lives he wanted to preserve, and one of them was already dead.

Possibly two.

The selfishness, the greed, the insufferable belligerence. They had gone nowhere, he saw now. The old Seth was still there, the new edition little more than a new set of clothes. Those clothes grew too tight. The old Seth was bursting through the seams.

He'd tried to be better. And this was how everyone repaid him.

Darkness congealed inside his ribs. This heat in his chest wasn't the agony Lyseria wreaked on the people around him. It was a blade like the one at his hip, newly tempered, ready to be quenched. This was power. Seth welcomed it to the world with open arms.

Fire and smoke and horseflesh writhed and polluted the clean air of Castlefoot Market. Seth stood at the head of it, feet planted wide upon the stage, and soaked it all in.

~

All was black on the horizon. Cienne peered down from the gaping shutters.

Eleanor's begs for her to close them had long since tapered off. Erik had managed to have their confines changed to Seth and Cienne's quarters. Lilly slept in their room with Russell curled into a ball at her side. Cienne and Eleanor remained in the drawing room adjacent.

The window faced south: the front gardens yawned out below to the inner portcullis, all snowy and serene and silent. Beyond that, the stable yard bustled with hundreds of men, all sprinting for the outer portcullis.

Beyond that, black smog coated the view. The stunning view of Castlefoot and its surrounding forestry hid behind a charcoal veil. It was as if the Prophet had presented a delicate painting of a panorama, only to pour a bottle of grey ink over it. Judging by the crashing and crumbling in the distance, Cienne didn't want to know what all of it looked like anyway.

A cloud of smoke wafted off momentarily.

Cienne caught a glimpse of a pile of rubble sitting in the centre of what used to be the market square. A figure dressed in green stood in the centre, untouched by the violence, surveying everything. By the tilt of his head, Cienne recognised her husband immediately.

Bemusement overcame the horror gripping her chest.

Seth, who squirmed at the sight of vomit, much less blood, watched the entire spectacle with the fascination of a child watching their first play. No – a child watching a play usually had a smile. He was far from happy. But he revelled in it.

'Cienne,' Eleanor said. 'Come away now.'

Cienne ignored her. She gazed into the smoke, picturing what Seth must be seeing. The gap in the smoke closed. Shadows moved within, but that was all.

Seth was in the middle of that. She wondered how it would feel, to be in the epicentre of a chaos she had created, witnessing someone she hated burn. The thought made her stomach tingle.

She pivoted. 'Eleanor,' she said. 'Tell the guards to fetch me Elliot Maynard.'

Eleanor frowned slightly. 'What on earth for?'

'I need someone who will take orders without question. He's the only one I can recognise outside who isn't trapped in the centre of the market.'

'What orders?'

Cienne smiled. 'Just something small,' she lied.

~

Jon knitted his fingers together in an attempt to prevent him punching his own face. He'd always been cracked in the head. You didn't experience over two decades of temporal fracture without some nasty side-effects. But seeing a copy of himself through the snowy forest alongside him, in the noble attire he ought to have worn himself, was bad even for him. Very bad.

'Even worse than the time you spent three days picking bits of chicken feed from the shed floor until you had a whole bucketful?' Mort asked with a smile.

'Yep,' Jon said through clenched teeth, his temples throbbing. 'Even worse than that.'

He shuffled on up the forest path, Mortimer Crey at his heels. He tried to remember where he had last been. Was it the kitchens? He had a vague recollection of huddling in the snow on the front step of the castle, on doorman duty. Yeah, that was probably it.

So how did he get here? What wasn't he remembering?

Mortimer chuckled under his breath, mumbling something condescending to himself.

Jon swung around. 'What?'

'What?' Mortimer asked, a picture of innocence.

Jon ground his teeth together. He'd been hearing snide comments about himself ever since he woke up. It was turning his headache into a migraine. He wondered if he was as annoying as this bloke in real life before remembering that Seth had strung him upside down once by his ankle. He made a mental note to apologise thoroughly to Seth – and Jimmy while he was at it.

'You're muttering again,' he told Mort in a low, threatening tone.

'Am I?' Mort asked innocently. 'Sorry, Morty.'

Jon gritted his jaw even tighter. It sent a shot of pain through the back of his head.

'Jon,' he hissed. 'My name is Jon.'

'If you say so.' Mortimer sighed, clasping his hands behind his back.

Jon shot him a murderous glance.

He stomped after Mort along the frosty path. Apart from a few hoof-prints half-buried in the snow, the two appeared to be alone. Jon heard an ongoing rumble raging just outside of the woods, but his head hurt too badly for him to pay enough attention to it.

'Where are we, anyway? Why aren't we at the castle?'

'Yeah, we're gonna be avoiding the castle for a bit,' said Mort.

'Why, what's going on there?'

'Usual.' Mort brushed a hanging branch out of his way.

Jon scowled at him. 'What's "usual"?'

'Meh,' Mort said. 'People killing people, you know. Usual. Not our problem, is it?'

Jon glowered at him and picked up a sharp rock.

'Ow!' Mort shrieked, clutching the back of his head. 'What was that for?'

'Annoying me!' Jon snapped. 'Keep at it and I'll find a bigger one. Where are we?'

'I'm not telling you,' Mort said haughtily, 'because you threw a rock at me.' He folded his arms.

Jon lifted his eyes to the heavens. 'How old are you, eight—nyah!' His foot skidded in something soft. His right knee slammed into the ground. On further inspection, he found it to have slammed into a pile of shit. *Human* shit, by the smell of it.

Mort started giggling. 'You've got poop on you.'

Jon glared up at him. *Maybe he is eight*, he thought, exhaling. Perhaps because he stopped being Mort when he was eight, this Mort just stayed that way. Jon was about to snap at him when faint screams from the distance interrupted him. 'Where's that coming from?'

'Castle,' Mort said in disinterest. 'I s'pose we'd better have a nose, is it?'

'At what?'

Mort just strolled in the direction of the screams.

Jon held a hand in front of him in exasperation, willing some form of logic to land in it. 'That's a good idea,' he said wryly, throwing both hands into the air, 'let's follow the screams and get ourselves killed. Brilliant idea.'

'Oh, we'll be fine,' said Mort, 'you can see into the future, can't you? What's the worst that could happen?'

Jon decided to find out.

Anxiety's a trigger, he reminded himself. *If anything's going to make you anxious, it's talking to a doppelganger wearing the contents of Aunty Eleanor's reject pile.* He screwed his brow together in concentration and carefully dismantled his coping mechanisms, getting ready for his vision to waver.

It didn't. His precognition appeared to be broken.

Jon wavered. Anxiety, now unbridled, swept through his arms, sending them tingling for nothing. 'That's not good.'

The ground thundered beneath them.

Mort quickly stepped aside. Jon followed suit.

A horse and rider galloped between them. Jon was alarmed to find both of them to be *skeletal.*

'That's definitely not good,' he said loudly, his voice snatched away in the passing gust of wind.

The horse screamed into the distance.

'Yeah, he's the least of our problems,' Mort said, nodding ahead.

Jon turned back to their destination. The woods opened up to reveal Castlefoot Market – except now, debris lay scattered along the road where food stalls had once stood, the inn now a flaming pile of rubble.

Jon stared at it in horror.

Robed men – priests, he realised with a start – tore through the market, armed to the teeth. They swung at every Crey guard in proximity and plenty of civilians to boot. Steel flashed in the weak sunlight. Heavy footfalls alerted him to the impending arrival of another horseman.

'More men are coming from the castle, surround them immediately!' the horseman barked, his bright red robes billowing around him. He steered his horse around to face the woods. His eyes locked onto Jon, who gawked at him, wide-eyed.

The Archpriest jerked the reins. His charger galloped into the woods, heading straight for Jon.

'Crap,' said Jon.

A blade glinted. It slid from its sheath to catch the midday sun.

'*Crap*,' he emphasised. He glanced at Mort for help.

'I'm just in your head, mate,' Mort said with a shrug. 'You're on your own.'

Jon whined.

The horseman descended upon him.

A figure in a burgundy robe barrelled into Jon's left shoulder. The two tumbled down the hill, head over tail.

The horse halted, its rider glancing around in bewilderment.

Jon's face landed into a tree root. He sank into oblivion once more.

~

V

Eight miles away in Teal, Archie worked an intricate design onto the edge of an ornate bookshelf in relative serenity. Or as much serenity as the village centre allowed on an early Saturday evening. A man's voice in the distance repeatedly yelled, 'What the HELL are YOU LOOKING AT?!' while the odd window smashed, but that was nothing unordinary.

Despina leaned on the edge of the counter, cradling a cup of tea. Howie had retreated to his room upstairs and hadn't come out since the first night. Archie fretted about him. He didn't want to irritate him by continually checking up on him, but he hoped he was okay.

A knock interrupted their friendly silence. Elliot Maynard stood in the door. His expression was frozen.

'Can I help you?' Archie asked, tilting his head up. He smiled and gave him a nod.

Elliot wrung his hands.

Despina read his expression. 'Elliot, are you okay?'

Elliot licked his lips and swallowed. He extracted a folded letter from behind his breastplate and handed it to Archie.

He unfolded it, his eyes darting across the words. His face became a delicate shade of grey.

Six more guards piled into the workshop.

'I am really, really sorry,' Elliot said, with a helpless shrug.

~

Castlefoot was a tapestry of congealed blood and scorched earth. Dusk painted the sky a grey-purple as the inn burned on, forgotten. The evenly spread winter blanket had been reduced to pools of water, littering the ruined market at random. What little snow that remained around the edges had turned pink in the violence.

Lilly's palfrey toed around the pink puddles, her ears twitching nervously. Drawing her cloak around her neck, Lilly led her on, heading for the main road south. If in doubt, head for the King Death.

Many black robes lay burning in the square, but slushy trails into the woods in every direction marked the survivors of the massacre. Lilly doubted they would be back. She hoped the Prophet got away okay, though. He was an alright sort of bloke once you got past the weirdness.

A breeze bit into her face, like a shard of ice. She winced and kicked into a trot, following the blotchy road to Serpus with a relief she hadn't felt since teenage years spent sneaking out behind her father's back.

'Where are you going?'

Lilly flinched so violently she nearly slid from the saddle. She tugged the reins around.

Seth stood in the centre of the stage, right where he had orchestrated the massacre. Something jabbed her in the ribs at the sight of him. Fear.

Why? she scolded herself. *It's only Seth.* The wound on her abdomen gave a yelp, reminding her why.

Seth's eyes narrowed. '*Where* are you *going*?' he repeated, with emphasis.

She drew herself upright in the saddle, eyeing him stoically. 'Pub,' she said shortly. She steered her palfrey back around.

Seth snorted. 'I don't think so.'

She flung him a withering glance. If he thought slamming her into a table was going to frighten her, he had another thing coming. 'I don't really care what you think.'

'Don't your eyes work?' Seth asked lightly. He gestured around them.

Smoke clung to the back of her throat. The air, though clear, was tainted with it.

Lilly snorted. 'You're going to set Lyseria on me, is it? Your little sister?'

'Stranger things have happened.'

'Suppose so,' she agreed. 'You've never called me anything beginning with "C" before.'

Seth hopped from the stage.

In spite of her retort, Lilly felt that stabbing feeling again. The smells of blood and excrement floated past her nose. Her eyes fell on the burning inn, then on another scorch mark in the centre of the market square. His first victim.

She nodded at the scorch-stain. 'Did *he* leave his room without permission as well?'

Seth said nothing.

Lilly waited. 'Lost your tongue or summat?'

She swivelled around. Her palfrey stepped into a pink puddle and shied away, clearly unhappy with the situation. Lilly couldn't blame her. However, she had a point to make, so she pressed on. 'You tore a hole in my gut, you know that? When you threw me across the room in a fit? Enjoy that bullshit now, do you?'

Seth said nothing.

'I looked up to you when I was small,' she went on, unheeded. 'Not for any particular reason, but I s'pose that's just what you do, innit? But now.' She barked a mirthless laugh. 'I dunno what little thing it was I admired in you, mate, but it's gone now, isn't it? And you're too far up your own backside to care.'

Seth lifted an eyebrow at that, but again said nothing.

'Haven't you got anything to say?' Lilly exploded. 'What, you trying to scare me with your silence, is it? You're pathetic! What could you possibly do to scare me? You just hit and scream at people when you don't get your way! You're just a stupid little boy!'

'Am I?' he snarled. 'Just a stupid little boy?' He hopped off the stage and stepped forward. 'You think a stupid little boy is capable of killing our father?'

Lilly frowned. 'What?'

Seth took another three steps. He halted a foot away from her, his head craning up at her. 'Our father,' he repeated. 'Big man with a beard. Used to live here.'

'I'm aware of who he is,' Lilly snarled. 'What are you trying to tell me? You were the one who…'

Seth gave her one last silent glance. He turned to retreat to the stage.

Lilly flung his back a withering glance. 'Oh, piss off,' she spat. 'Whatever game this is, I'm not playing it. You couldn't kill a caterpillar if it crawled under your boot for you.'

Seth turned to grin at her. 'Didn't think you would believe me. Please yourself. I know what I'm capable of. Just you brace yourself when you finally find out, that's all.'

Lilly lifted her eyes to the clouds. 'Whatever.' She jerked her horse around.

He lifted his eyebrows.

'SIR!'

The siblings jerked to the west.

'I've got her!' Moat howled. 'The girl from the coach, I found her!' An auburn-haired girl writhed in his grasp.

Seth froze solid.

'Saw her wandering around the village north, like butter wouldn't melt,' Moat said proudly.

'I haven't done anything! I keep telling you this!'

Moat threw Adrienne to the ground. She landed on her hands and knees, cursing. 'What should I do with her, your majesty?'

Lilly eyed her brother.

Seth's expression grew dark. He didn't reply to Moat's question. Instead, he pulled his sword free. The sword Cienne had given him.

'Put her in the Tower,' Lilly said quickly.

'No,' Seth began.

'Put her in the Tower,' she insisted, 'so that we can question her.'

Seth clenched his teeth. He rammed his sword back into its sheath. 'Put her in the Tower,' he echoed.

Adrienne was dragged upright again. She locked her eyes onto his, wide and frantic. 'What's happened, Seth? Seth, what's this about a coach? I don't understand! Will you please tell me what I'm supposed to have done?'

Seth just glared at her. Lilly watched the dark look in his eye intensify.

'I'll speak to her later,' he said.

Adrienne vanished into the gate.

'Get inside, Lilly, before I tear a new hole in your gut.'

Lilly saw the dark looks, the clenched teeth, the knuckles white around the hilt of his sword. All directed at his *lover*.

Lilly huffed a laugh. '*Fuck* no.'

'LILLY!'

She swung around and galloped south, Seth's screech ringing behind her.

~

Jimmy hadn't noticed the carnage outside until he cracked open a window to let the steam out. He coughed. A cloud of smoke filled his windpipe. 'Who's been feeding the dragon coal again?'

Then he saw the inn. '… oh shit.'

It took a further five minutes for the rest of the kitchen to catch up on current events. Scullery maids hung their heads from windows, craning their necks to catch a glimpse of the carnage.

Jimmy had spent these five minutes being updated by the cook. The spud peeling had sent him daydreaming into another world, one with beautiful women and a nice house in Mellier without any sign of a forty-five-million-pound debt to deal with. The real world he'd landed back into was considerably less pleasant.

'That's the end of Seth Crey, then,' he said.

'Maybe, but not today,' the cook said by the oven. 'He has the dragon, hasn't he?'

'She isn't trained, though,' Jimmy pointed out. 'You can't just point and shoot like a crossbow. She'd turn him into a pork pie along with everyone else.'

'That's not what I heard,' the cook said. 'The bloke that run up from the market said he told the dragon to kill a man *specifically*. Gave the man's full name and everything. And all of the palace militia? Not a mark on them.'

'Oh, please,' Jimmy scoffed. 'He tells her what to do all the time and she just head-butts him. He has as much control over her as he has over Lilly.'

The cook shrugged apathetically. 'Believe what you like. That's just what I heard.'

Jimmy shook his head. *The dragon taking orders*, he scoffed to himself. *What next?*

Despina crashed into him from behind, practically bowling him over.

'Oi! What on earth—'

'He's killed them!' Despina gasped, close to tears.

'What?' he said, wrinkling his nose. 'Who? Who's killed who? Slow down.'

Despina gasped and stammered. 'Seth Crey. He had Elliot come to the… He had orders. He's burned their house down, he killed that bloke, the medic's uncle… I can't remember his name, I met him yesterday, the carpenter…' She thrust a length of parchment at him.

Jimmy slid it from her fingers and skimmed it. His eyes glazed over. 'Shit. The uncle.'

~

A gasp turned him around. 'Your majesty!'

Seth pivoted.

A boy, little more than fourteen, struggled to catch his breath as he approached the makeshift dais. He threw himself into a low bow, holding a package out with both hands.

'I was told to bring this directly to you, your majesty,' he said, gulping a breath.

Seth's brow furrowed. He stepped down from the shattered stage, dodging scraps of timber.

The boy bowed his head upon relinquishing the parcel, turning swiftly to leave.

The package was wrapped in brown linen, tied with a bootlace, by the looks of it. He squeezed it, feeling it give in his hands. Some sort of clothing, Seth surmised. He tugged on a corner of the brown linen and a thread of wool slipped out. Seth's heart contracted at the colour of it.

Shocking pink. Ginny's signature colour.

'Wait!' he called, stopping the boy in his tracks. 'Who gave you this?'

The boy stumbled around to face him, his torso slightly bowed.

'A young man, your majesty, sir, with a red-haired lady. I met them at the crossroads, sir.'

'Did they have a little girl with them?'

'In the coach, yes. Very small, sir, maybe a couple years old, sir.'

Rage threatened to strangle him. 'Why didn't you stop—' Then it occurred to him. This child likely didn't know Princess Virginia Crey from a baker's daughter.

He took a breath and swallowed down the reproach. 'Never mind. Go to the barbican right now, ask for a man called Marbrand and send him to me immediately. Tell him you have news of the king's daughter.'

'Yes, sir, right away, sir!'

Seth gripped the package in his hands and felt something crinkle. A letter was nestled in the centre of the package somewhere.

Seth unwrapped the scarf tenderly. There was a sticky purple stain that looked to be jam, but no sign of blood, to his relief. Another crinkle within the folds reminded Seth of the letter and he shook the scarf out fully, leaving the parchment flutter to the floor.

Seth stared at the note. The messy scrawl burned into his retinas.

Go to Mellier, alone, no guards. The Bastard has your daughter.

Seth collapsed, his knees dropping into the dirt.

The Bastard. The auburn-haired lady. It all made sense now. Qattren had reminded him of what he already knew and his crippling arrogance had shrouded it as usual.

The pink puddles swept across the landscape, drawing him back to another massacre, this time not of his making. This one of his brother's making. His half-brother.

Silas Beult.

The Bastard.

Seth stared into space for a moment. *Long auburn hair*, he thought dully. Anna Beult. Not Adrienne. Anna took Ginny. Adrienne had nothing to do with this.

And he would have had her throat opened for her trouble were it not for Lilly.

Seth slammed the brown linen wrapping into the mud.

~

The tale of the Castlefoot Massacre rolled across the villages the next day like a thick blanket. The tension from passers-by seemed almost palpable around Seth and Adrienne. Neither of them paid any notice.

Archibald Hart's Carpentry Shop lay in ruins. Along the main thoroughfare of Teal, blackened walls and collapsed ruins marked where the blaze tore through the terraced houses. A total of eight people had lost their lives – three shopkeepers, a barber, an elderly couple, and the family of the name on Elliot Maynard's execution warrant.

Elliot was in Marbrand's custody in the Tower. Seth waited for Marbrand's return, his eyes locked to his lover.

Adrienne's eyes roved across the entirety of the shop. Every so often she lifted a foot as if to enter before returning it, trembling, back to its place.

'Are you sure they were in there?' she asked, for third time.

'I'm sure,' Seth said softly. 'The men recovered their remains. I saw them myself.'

She exhaled tremulously. Seth slid an arm around her, but she shook it off. 'What is taking him so long?' she muttered.

As if in response, a horseman thundered down the cobbles. 'The orders were from the royal family, your majesty.'

Seth glared at Marbrand as he dismounted. 'Who in the royal family? Because it sure as hell wasn't me.'

'Despina managed to grab the warrant.' Marbrand untied a roll of parchment from his belt. 'It has your stamp, that's why he followed the order so readily. Elliot isn't known for his literacy, your majesty – he appears to have misread the warrant.' He unrolled the parchment to show him.

'Adrienne Hart' glared at him in thick black cursive.

Seth lowered his gaze to the signature at the bottom. Of course. He crumpled it in half before Adrienne could get a good look at it.

'This is a mistake.' He pulled Adrienne into one elbow. 'Come with me. I'll try to repair this.'

'How? He's gone.' Tears spilled down each side of her nose.

Seth pulled her close.

'I'm not letting this go unpunished,' he said, his forehead pressed to her temple. 'People are going to think twice about hurting you again.'

She burrowed her forehead under his ear to weep.

Seth met Marbrand's gaze. 'Summon the navy and military captains to my chambers for as soon as they can arrive.'

'Yes, sir?' His voice lilted in polite enquiry.

'I have a missing child to account for, haven't I?'

Seth sucked in a breath. The image of Ginny's little head peeking out of the coach made his stomach twist. He scanned the burned-out houses. Six innocents had died today. Six families bereaved now – seven including Adrienne. Adrienne didn't have anybody left now except for him.

Her knuckles whitened around the front of his shirt, her sobs more prolific.

Seth rubbed her shoulder-blades, thinking of Archie. He must have been terrified for her. He had brought Adrienne up alone, she was practically his daughter. She could have been dead, for all he knew. He'd never find out, either. He'd died upstairs, Seth had learned – Archie had fled upstairs after setting his furniture alight, to block Elliot's path, to save his adopted son.

Surprisingly, Seth didn't feel anything in particular about the death of Howard Rosethorn. Nothing at all.

~

Jimmy had been back on spud duty for ten minutes before something else occurred to him. 'Where's Jon?'

No one else took much notice. Most of the staff hovered by the door, peering out and commentating in hushed voices.

Despina sat on a stool just outside the door, with her father. She was in tears again. 'I ran for the castle when the flames went up,' she finished. 'I don't know if Elliot got out.'

'Alright, alright,' Marbrand soothed, rubbing her shoulder. 'He's fine, we took him into custody not long ago. He's perfectly fine.'

'Is he in trouble?'

'Of course not, he was only following orders.'

'Whose orders, though?'

He gave her shoulder a squeeze. 'That's the king's problem, not ours.'

The group inside the doorway rippled. A black-clad elbow emerged from the crowd. Jimmy managed to shove himself through, gasping. 'Anyone seen Jon since yesterday?'

'No,' said Marbrand. His brow furrowed. 'Seth didn't imprison him or anything stupid, did he?'

'I hope not,' Jimmy said, his nose wrinkling. 'Jon's a clean-freak. It's filthy in there. That might just tip him over the edge.'

'I'd make sure, if I were you,' Marbrand said. He put a hand on Despina's head. 'Don't forget, Jon was the last person to see Ginny before she was snatched.'

'Oh God, was he?' Jimmy groaned, his gaze to the ceiling. 'Honestly, you try to keep your head down in this job and the lackey goes and gets himself in trouble. Where's the king now, then? I ought to let Jon out now before he gets his head lopped off.'

Marbrand swiped two fingers across his own throat. 'In the throne room. I'd leave it a while, if I were you. He's with the queen.'

Jimmy lifted his upper lip. 'Better get the cleaning fluid, you mean.'

'No, you won't need that – not unless their argument progresses to physical violence.'

'Argument?'

'I'm not getting into it. I'm trying to keep my head down in *my* job as well.'

Jimmy's head jerked from Marbrand to the door and back again. He hesitated a moment before his overwhelming curiosity drove him to the throne room door.

VI

Seth stood in the centre of the hall. 'Tell me about the death warrant, Cienne.'

'What's to tell, dear?'

Seth gritted his teeth.

Cienne reclined in his throne, her back tucked in a corner between the arm and back. Her right leg was crossed over the left, swinging up and down in idle indifference. She laced her fingers together and wrapped them around her knee, smiling radiantly at him.

'She kidnapped our daughter. There were witnesses to the fact,' Cienne said, blithely. 'You were occupied, so I took care of the matter.'

'Without stopping to confirm first?'

'You didn't feel the need to stop and confirm Lilly's motives when you threw her into the dining table yesterday,' Cienne said. Still blithely, albeit with a stare that could cut through glass.

Seth set his jaw outward. 'Get out of my chair.'

Cienne uncrossed her legs and elbowed herself to her feet. 'According to rumour,' she said, 'you had her sent to the Tower yourself. We're clearly of a similar mind.'

'I sent *her* to the Tower for *questioning*,' Seth sneered. 'I didn't burn her family's home to the ground with them in it! Her uncle did nothing wrong!'

'He brought up a child abductor, I think something went a bit wrong along the way,' Cienne said wryly. She descended the steps, halting in front of him with her ankles crossed. She was wearing her magenta dress with the slit down the centre, Seth couldn't help but notice with exasperation.

'You're wrong there for reasons I'll get into in a moment,' Seth snarled. 'Are you aware your son was in the middle of that fire?'

Cienne tilted her head to one side. 'My son is asleep upstairs, you'll find. Which can't be said for his sister, thanks to her.'

'Oh, your memory's bad all of a sudden,' he said with venom. 'I should rephrase: the son you *abandoned* was in the middle of that fire. Did you know that?'

'Oh, the "freak of nature"?' Cienne said with a laugh. 'Your delusional nature is getting the better of you. You're mistaken. He no longer has anything to do with your little trollop after what you did. If he did live in the

413

house, I would have given orders for him to be removed from the premises. He is still your blood, after all. See what I did there?' She giggled abrasively.

Seth frowned at her, his eyes narrowing. 'You've finally lost your mind, haven't you?'

In fact, she hadn't. Cienne's heart hammered against her ribs, her windpipe filled with ice. She clenched every muscle in her body to keep from trembling. But she wasn't showing Seth that.

Instead, she grinned maniacally at him. 'I suppose you would know best, having just razed the entire market to the ground. How many innocents were in that inn, Seth? Or is it perfectly above board to burn buildings to the ground as long as King Seth Crey's mistress isn't affected?'

Seth laughed. 'Ah, I see. This has nothing to do with our child, has it? You're jealous of her. That I love her more than I love you.'

A barbed ring twisted around Cienne's stomach.

'She's grieving upstairs,' Seth went on. 'She's just lost the closest she had to a parent. Do you remember how that feels? Have you forgotten how it felt to lose your mother? Or does she suddenly deserve that now because she had the gall to shag your husband?'

'She *deserves it for tearing a three-year-old away from her mother*!!' Cienne howled.

Seth's face remained impassive at her outburst. 'Cast your mind back,' he said, calm as still waters. 'Do you remember Anna?'

Cienne made a face. 'Another of your conquests, as I recall. What has she to do with anything? You sent her away years ago.'

'To please you,' Seth agreed. 'Because you wanted me all to yourself. You couldn't stand to share. Since I was fond of you at the time, I got rid of her. A matter of days ago, Qattren flagged sightings of her to us. Do you remember now? You might recall that she bore quite a resemblance to Adrienne, didn't she?'

Cienne froze. 'Oh.'

'Oh,' he said, sarcastic. '*She* took Ginny. Her and her husband: my bastard brother. Not Adrienne, or either of the men you've just had killed in the middle of Serpus.' Seth snarled at her, his teeth bared. 'I think I was right earlier, you have lost your mind. You never stopped to think about it, did you? Ginny was taken in a coach belonging to Emmett: who it appears you've been sending correspondence to behind my back. Why would someone who writes to you on a weekly basis want to help my mistress steal our child from us?'

Cienne's mouth gaped open a moment. 'I didn't know you knew about those letters.'

'I had your desk searched. Marbrand found quite a few illuminating documents inside.' Seth lifted an eyebrow with a snort. 'Why did you hide them from me?' he asked, his voice airy, as though in polite enquiry. 'What else have you been hiding from me? Apart from the thinly veiled *begging* to Emmett to take your cousin's child away?'

'If I want to write to my family,' Cienne said in a barbed tone, 'I will. I am not your property.'

'We *are* your family,' Seth hissed. 'Twenty-four years, we have looked after you—'

Cienne cackled again. 'Family? Your mother and sister made it very clear whose *family* they were when they kept your betrayal from me. And as for you looking after me, I hasten to remind you how backward your account is—'

'I'm bored of this conversation,' Seth said, flinging a hand at her. 'Go upstairs while I figure out what I'm going to do with you.'

'No!' Her voice shook: the tremors came unbidden now. 'You are *not* shutting me away anymore, I forbid it.'

Seth's face flushed. 'You are in NO position to forbid me anything!' he roared. 'Get upstairs before I do something we both regret!'

Cienne grinned widely. She stepped forward. 'No,' she said firmly. 'What are you going to do about it?'

Seth pulled his fist back.

~

'Oh, shit,' Jimmy hissed under his breath.

Cienne lay sprawled on the flagstones, her skirts tangled around her legs.

'What's happened?' Marbrand asked sharply. He nudged past Jimmy.

Jimmy held him back. 'We're staying out of this.'

They peeked out of a slim crack in the doors.

Seth grabbed the back of Cienne's dress and hauled her upright.

Cienne spat blood. 'Seth.' Red drops fell from her lips.

He threw her at the throne. She hurtled into the back and grabbed an arm. The throne tilted back a moment before slamming back on all four legs.

'What am I going to do about it?' Seth said loudly. He paced to the steps.

Cienne's breath came in fast bursts through her teeth, her lip split.

'I'll show you what I'm going to do about it.'

Marbrand launched himself at the door. Jimmy shoved him back.

'I'm not having this!' Marbrand shouted at him, struggling.

'You can forget it!' Jimmy spat. 'We're staying out of this!'

'She's the daughter of the king of Portabella!' Marbrand hissed in his face. 'He'll catch wind of the princess's disappearance any day now! Do you really think he'll be impressed when he turns up to find his only daughter covered in bruises?'

A sickening *thunk* sounded. Cienne cried out. A thud. Seth grunted.

Marbrand and Jimmy refused to look at them.

Despina hovered behind them, a chill going down her spine. 'He's going to rape her.'

Marbrand's face held a similar conviction.

Jimmy pointed at him. 'I'm not having him set us on fire!'

'Being set on fire will be the least of your problems!' Marbrand hissed. 'He's going to cause a bloody world war!'

'Get—*off*!' Cienne shrieked. '*Get off me*!!'

'For goodness' sake!' Despina exploded.

Jimmy and Marbrand flinched. They'd forgotten she was there.

'Are you going to stand there and let him beat her to a pulp and worse?' Despina snapped at the two of them. 'What kind of men are you?'

Jimmy shushed her, waving an arm up and down. 'Keep your voice down.'

'He'll hear us,' Marbrand whispered.

Despina arched an eyebrow and shook her head. 'Unbelievable. You want to help the queen? Go to the Tower and let one of the prisoners out.'

Jimmy frowned at her. 'Why?'

'So that I can interrupt them and tell Seth one of the prisoners has escaped?' she explained as though this was obvious. She pointed at Jimmy. 'You will let one out, and you,' she jabbed a finger at Marbrand, 'will tackle him to the ground and hold him there. He can't set you on fire for detaining an escaped prisoner, can he?'

Jimmy and Marbrand hesitated.

'Or would you rather explain to King Fleurelle why his daughter has been beaten half to death?'

A shrill sob interrupted them. Cienne wept loudly over the sound of soft. rhythmic thudding.

Jimmy heaved a sigh, fidgeting. 'Oh, fine!' He gave Marbrand a shove. 'Run!'

'Give us ten minutes of a head start and then run in there,' Marbrand said to Despina, who nodded.

The two men bolted back through the kitchens.

Despina sidled to the door and peered in, her heart hammering. And was taken aback.

Seth lay curled on the flagstones, at the foot of the throne, soundless.

Cienne, holding her skirts back, kicked him furiously in the stomach, over and over.

'How *dare* you!' she shrieked, her voice thick with tears. 'How dare you do this to me, you *bastard*! This was your fault, *all your fault*, you should have been faithful, you should have looked after us, it was your job, your job to look after me and the twins, you failure, *you utter, utter failure*!! *I HATE YOU*!!'

She kicked him three more times in quick succession.

Seth wheezed.

Cienne collapsed in a heap by his side. She clutched his face, her nails digging into his jaw like claws. She leaned in to snarl one last thing into his blood-coated face. Her free hand groped the throne for a cushion.

She's gonna kill him, Despina realised. As surprising as the outcome was, Despina was relieved. It would be easier to stop Cienne than a rampaging, lust-ridden rapist. Cienne could be reasoned with.

Her nails gained purchase on a green cushion. In spite of her brief relief, Despina's heart stopped.

'Where's your friendly poltergeist when you need him?' she muttered to herself. She craned her neck, ensuring Marbrand and Jimmy were gone.

Seth gave a strangled cry. It was muffled to obscurity.

'Oh, bollocks to your ten minutes!' she spat.

She threw herself through the door.

~

'I don't understand!' the Duke of Osney wept.

Marbrand straddled the small of his back, to his immense discomfort.

The Tower froze solid at this time of year. Slits too thin for a thumb to fit through let in a tiny amount of sunlight, allowing them a sparse amount of grey light. The depressing conditions of the Tower were the least of Marbrand's problems. He was having trouble keeping a hold on the Duke of Osney. The man lay completely still with terror: Marbrand's problems concerned the ice beneath his feet. It was like detaining a giant slug.

'I haven't done anything wrong!' Osney wailed, his stomach sliding on the flagstones. 'I never tried to escape, I swear on my son's life! Jimmy let me out! He did! Ask him!'

'He doesn't care,' Jimmy said, offhanded. 'Though you could have put *more* than a half-hearted swear on poor Jon's life. Speaking of Jon, you haven't seen him lately, by any chance?' he added as an afterthought. 'He went AWOL yesterday morning. He didn't come visit you beforehand, did he?'

'Why would he? He hates me,' Osney wept bitterly. His grubby prison shift slid further up his back. 'He has every right to. I was a terrible father. He was raped and abused because of me, violated in places no child should ever—'

'Alright, a simple "no" will suffice,' Jimmy said, grimacing.

Footsteps landed heavily on the staircase.

'That's him,' Marbrand said in a strained voice, wobbling. 'Try to look a bit more like you've just run a mile.'

'Oh, yes.' Jimmy leaned on his knees, panting audibly.

Marbrand gave him a withering glance. 'Yes, that looks *entirely* convincing.'

Seth halted before them, glaring at everyone. 'What happened?'

'No idea, sir,' Jimmy said between laboured breaths.

Overdoing it a bit, observed Marbrand with a sigh. He'd clearly never run so much as a yard in his life.

'Found him legging it down the corridor, we managed to corner him here.'

'They're lying, your majesty! They let me out, it's some sort of game.'

Seth's eyes narrowed. They were both blue and swollen.

Marbrand noticed. 'Everything alright with you, your majesty?'

Seth pulled himself to his full height. His hand hovered momentarily over his ribs. 'I'm fine,' he said stiffly. 'Where are the guards?'

'He dismissed them!' Osney shrilled, pointing at Jimmy.

'He'd thrown them down the stairs, sir, they weren't fit for work,' Jimmy said.

'He's lying! He dismissed them *before* I got out—'

Seth ignored Osney. 'And where's his cellmate?'

'Elliot's right where we left him, your majesty,' Marbrand said. 'He raised the alarm, sir. He hollered down to us from his cell as we were crossing the grounds.'

Seth craned his neck.

Elliot peered out of his cell door at the end of the corridor. His feet, per Marbrand's orders, remained firmly *within* the doorframe.

'I think he's learned his lesson now, your majesty,' Marbrand piped up, before he could change his mind. 'Perhaps we should put him back on duty. It appears we're short on Tower guards again.'

Seth nodded, albeit reluctantly. 'Do so. And remind him to only answer to me from now on, not my stupid wife or anyone else.'

'No problem,' Marbrand said.

Seth nodded in dismissal.

Marbrand shoved himself to his feet, making a beeline for Elliot's cell.

Osney lifted himself into a sitting position.

'Let me help you up, Uncle,' Seth said gently. He gestured at Jimmy for assistance.

Jimmy acquiesced, albeit reluctantly.

'It's a trick,' Osney gasped. He picked at his palms with a wince. Blood wept from the scrapes within.

'I'm sorry,' Seth said. They led him outside, to the gazebo. 'I had no idea you had been locked in these conditions.'

Osney squeezed himself into the garden furniture.

'I was under the impression you were put into house arrest,' Seth explained, brow furrowed in dismay.

'I'm quite alright, your majesty, thank you,' Osney said, patting his elbow.

'We'll escort you back to your quarters as soon as you've had time to rest,' said Seth, a hand planted firmly on Osney's shoulder. 'This should never have happened.'

'No harm done, your majesty,' Osney gulped. 'It appears my cellmate isn't the only one who has learned his lesson. I am deeply sorry for my part in the debt.'

Seth shook his head. 'Think nothing of it.'

'I'll figure something out, your majesty,' he continued in earnest.

'Don't worry about it. I have a plan of action to deal with that myself. I have a more pressing matter at present that needs your attention.' He leaned closer. 'It's your son.'

'Mortimer? Is he alright?' he asked in concern.

'That's the thing, nobody knows,' said Seth. 'He went missing shortly after my daughter – he was looking after her, I think, saw the abduction. No one has seen him since. I need you to trace his last movements so we can start a search – I need to speak with him about what happened.'

'Naturally, of course, of course,' Osney said, nodding rapidly. 'I shall do everything I can, your majesty.'

'Needless to say, your arrest has been suspended.'

Osney breathed a sigh of relief. 'Thank you, your majesty.'

Seth clapped his shoulder. 'Return to your rooms and rest today. I'll meet you in Arthur Stibbons' Head this time next week. Hopefully we'll have news of him by then.'

'Yes, your majesty. Hopefully we will.' Osney left before Seth could change his mind.

'What are you up to, sir?' Jimmy asked carefully.

Seth met his gaze and lifted an eyebrow. 'You'll just have to wait to find out.'

~

Qattren read a letter from Gomez Emmett Jr and, swiftly, tore it in half.

'Seth Crey, you will be the death of me one day,' she said aloud with a sigh. She rose from her dining table to enter Sal'plae. The white marble drawing room melted to lilac, the dark wood panelling turning from ebony to blue, as if bruising.

The Bastard appeared in front of her.

Qattren favoured him with a soft smile. 'Hello. What brings you here?'

'He's prequel to a higher power, of course,' Geldemar said with a grin.

Qattren watched him materialise, her soft smile dissipating. 'What do you want?'

'Oh,' Geldemar said, hurt. 'He gets a smile and I get a telling off! Me, your oldest friend!'

Qattren rolled her eyes. 'You only find me when you want something. Go on, what is it? Bear in mind, if you've come to claim my Ronald again, I will hurt you.'

'Oh no, it's not him I've come for, though the full set of Horne brothers wouldn't be unwelcome,' Geldemar said. He cast a cursory examination over Qattren's quarters as he spoke. 'You have another visitor on the way over, I've just been sent to update you on current events. Long and short of the matter, Seth Crey's just started a world war.'

'So I gather,' Qattren said wryly, waving the parchment into the air.

'Yes, he's killed the majority of Abraham Furlong's following, and seriously injured the man in person while he was at it,' Geldemar said. 'Something about Furlong wanting his castle and Seth's daughter going missing. Set the dragon on them, burned down an inn outside the keep. He's very angry.'

'You don't aim a dragon at someone unless you're angry, Gelde—' Qattren froze mid-quip. 'Go back a bit. What was that about Seth's daughter?'

'Come, now,' another voice quipped. 'You're usually quicker than this.'

Ice slid down her middle, freezing her in her tracks. Qattren's jaw fell ajar.

A man strolled down the centre of her dining room and halted, Geldemar and the Bastard flanking him on either side. Seth's resemblance to him had often been remarked upon, but in his presence once more, the resemblance faltered. Slim, six-foot, blond, blue-eyed – though they shared these traits, Seth didn't carry them as well as he had. He was much younger than the last time she saw him. He was an age with Seth now, his fair hair the way she remembered it, swept sideways at an angle, a few strands hanging over his forehead. But his face... Qattren had tried for so many years to commit it to memory, so very hard...

She'd almost forgotten how breath-taking he was.

'Hello, Qat,' Seb said with a smile.

~

Eleanor read the letter from Lilly before folding it in half, her expression distant.

'Ginny's been taken to Mellier,' she said. 'Apparently Seth received a letter from the abductor, though he never bothered to mention it to us.'

Jimmy sat at the other end of the dining table, stricken. 'And who took her?'

Eleanor hesitated before answering. 'He just calls himself the Bastard.' She stared into space for a few moments before continuing. 'The navy are heading for Mellier on Lilly's orders. Seth's furious, but at least it isn't aimed at any of us for a change.'

Eleanor exhaled through pursed lips. She craned her neck to glance behind her at Cienne, who sat at the writing desk in the corner, trembling. Eleanor had persuaded her into a bath and a change of clothes, but she shook, nevertheless.

Anchoring her elbows into the dining table, Eleanor pressed her knuckles into her eyes. 'How did Lilly get out?'

'Climbed out of the window,' Jimmy said. 'We really ought to get rid of the ropes of ivy.'

'No point ruining my aesthetic, is there? She'll only escape another way.' Eleanor heaved a sigh. 'She's gone after Ginny, hasn't she?'

'No idea. She just told the guard she was going to the pub. There were a couple of sightings in Serpus earlier today, though. She may have just sent them ahead.'

'The entire navy? Who in God's name thought it was a good idea to take her orders without writing here for confirmation?' Eleanor buried her head in her hands. 'Where is Seth, by the way? He isn't chasing after his sister with that bloody dragon, is he?'

'Not at present, your highness. He's writing to the King of Portabella.'

'At last, a sensible idea.' She eyed Cienne over her shoulder again. 'Fetch her something hot to drink, will you?'

Jimmy turned to the door out of habit to relay the order to Jon. He remembered his disappearance with a start, and deflated. 'Right away, your highness.' He left the room in silence.

Eleanor gazed at the letter in her hands, her eyes glazed over.

Cienne took note of her expression. 'You really did have a bastard son.'

Eleanor opened her mouth and closed it a few times. The words seemed to be stuck.

'Yes,' she finally managed. 'Silas Beult is my son.'

~

PART EIGHT: WAR

I

attren trembled. 'This isn't possible.' She stared at Geldemar, wide-eyed. 'It isn't him, is it? It's Gale, or Theo, or… one of them has changed his face, it can't, it can't be…'

'Not this time,' Geldemar said softly.

Seb Crey smirked. 'My apologies,' he said, 'where are my manners?' He swept forward and scooped her hand into his own. Before she knew it her knuckle was pressed to his mouth.

She felt faint. And abruptly hated herself for it.

'Some may call this hypocrisy,' he said, 'but it appears I need your services again.'

Qattren backed away.

'My grandchildren have gotten themselves into a heap of trouble,' he went on, as though nothing of great importance was amiss. 'Two of them, anyway. Jon's in a bit of a bad way, but it's Seth I'm here about, of course. Wonderful name, Seth, isn't it?' he digressed, quirking a half-smile. 'Reminds you of someone, doesn't it?'

'It's a trick,' she whispered. But it wasn't. She knew: by the way he breathed, his posture. His voice smooth as warm butter where it had been as dry as the

424

rustle of parchment the very last time they had met. The quirk of his mouth. That sodding smirk of his…

Seb met her gaze, her fingers wrapped in one hand.

'Not this time,' he said softly.

Qattren fell into his eyes, entranced. The hard exterior she had forged over herself melted and sloughed from her skin. She was vulnerable again. She felt a need for him to hold her upright, to take her in his arms and hold each other upright as they once had, so many years before…

'Earth to Qattren,' Geldemar sang in a high falsetto.

Qattren blinked into focus.

The Bastard snorted.

Qattren shut her eyes again tightly and re-opened them. 'What do you need me to do?'

Seb half-smiled. He ran a finger under her chin – something else she hadn't felt in fifty years. 'Ginny's been taken,' he said. 'Seth's little girl.'

A jab jolted Qattren back into reality.

'The chances of getting her back…' He heaved a sigh. 'They're slim, Qat.'

Behind him, the Bastard pressed his lips together.

'Seth can't take it, it's… he isn't strong enough to do what needs to be done. He doesn't know it yet, but he needs you. All of them do.'

Qattren's mouth went dry.

'They need us,' Seb said quietly. 'You and I. The Emmetts have taken one of my kin – *our* kin. They need to learn not to cross us.'

'What do you need me to do?' she asked again.

Seb smiled. 'You already know.'

The Bastard spoke up, reluctantly. 'It's my baby sister, Qat. She's a tiny child. She didn't deserve this.'

Geldemar just looked at her imploringly.

Qattren glanced at Seb's eyes again – momentarily. She didn't dare lose herself in them again.

'I'll meet Seth at his palace.' She paused. 'Are you sure you want me to do this? After last time?'

Seb simply smiled. 'We have no choice.'

~

Lilly met Ron in the outskirts of the Forest under the gaze of twilight. The Forest's reputation often came in handy for clandestine meetings: only the faint sounds of wildlife and rustling leaves could be heard, their silhouettes muffled in the gloom.

'How is he?' She spoke quietly, just in case anyone was listening.

Ron, mournfully, held up a toy soldier in reply. It was totally mangled: chewed in places, beaten in others, the head squashed beyond recognition. Lilly recognised it with a pang of sympathy. Ron had owned that toy since he was a toddler.

'He's fine,' said Ron levelly.

Lilly quirked a half-smile.

Odd shadows consumed them, thanks to the soft candlelight from Ron's cabin a couple yards away. It looked cosy in there, Lilly thought, shivering. She wished she was in there as opposed to standing out in the frozen woods. Alas, there was no room in the tiny cabin for more than two people. 'Has Qattren clocked onto us yet?'

'I told her I was coming to visit him,' he said. 'She hasn't asked any questions since, so I presume she doesn't know yet.'

'Ron?' Lilly asked. 'Did Jon say *why* he had to smuggle him away?'

'He didn't, not specifically.' Ron hesitated. 'He said something about a plot to kill him. He didn't know whose plot or anything.'

Lilly nodded slowly. 'I've been trying to find Jon all day,' she said with a frown. 'He isn't in Serpus or anywhere near it, he's just vanished. Why didn't he tell any of us? He could have told me. I would have helped him.'

She craned her neck, peering into the window of the one-room cabin.

Azrael slept peacefully inside it, on one of the two beds crammed inside. Toys surrounded him, all belonging to Ron and most in the same condition as the soldier in Ron's hand.

'He couldn't talk about it, Lilly,' Ron said in a whisper. 'Whatever it was Jon knew, it was bad. He could barely say anything when he brought Azrael here. He just kept saying "mind him, mind him, if he has a fever get the medic girl straight away". I don't know what he was so frightened of. Azrael's been fine.'

Lilly closed her eyes briefly.

'Have you told Seth yet?'

Lilly shook her head fervently. 'I ain't telling him nothing now.' Her gaze swung to the castle a few miles away, merely a yellow blob of light on the hill behind them. 'I've been writing to my mum since I met that messenger from the Bastard. She said he hit Cienne.'

Ron paled. 'Would he have…' He jerked his head to the cabin. 'If we hadn't…'

Lilly didn't respond. She rubbed her healing abdomen wound.

The wind whistled through the foliage above them.

'I don't know what's wrong with him,' Lilly whispered. 'He should be out finding Ginny, not rampaging around the castle like this…' Her voice failed.

Ron sighed and wrapped an arm around her shoulders. Never usually one for receiving comfort, Lilly dropped her chin on his shoulder.

'Makes Vladdy pale in comparison, doesn't he?'

Lilly coughed a laugh. 'Vladdy was small fry. I'd be able to handle a brother like Vladdy.'

Ron rubbed her arm in agreement and stepped back. 'What will you do now? I'd let you stay the night, but…' He held his hands into a square, roughly sizing up the amount of free space in the cabin. 'I don't think you'd fit.'

Lilly snorted. 'Nah, you're alright. I have free reign on the local whorehouse. I'll be fine.' She eyed her palfrey as she spoke, as though her travel plans were written on her flanks. 'The ships should be on their way now. One of the trade ships is due back to Wake's Port sometime next week. I'll follow them on that.'

'Wish I could come with you,' Ron said glumly. 'I've come to hate babysitting.'

Lilly gave him a sympathetic glance. 'Sooner you can palm him off on his mother again, the better.'

Ron's face darkened in anxiety. 'She's another person I'm worried about. I can't help but think about this conspiracy Jon is going on about. Is she okay? Is she caught up in it? It's hard to know.'

Lilly eyed the castle again, with a pang. She was homesick already, she realised.

'I've a bad feeling we'll find out any day now.'

~

Joseth Fleurelle eased himself into his throne, wincing.

'The pain?' Elsabet asked in concern.

'Always,' he said, barely a whisper.

His queen planted a kiss on his temple, passing him the cushions from her own seat.

Magenta banners fluttered gently in the breeze, adorned with silver-thread roses. The cool limestone blocks gleamed in the sunlight – it cast large squares of white light from the broad windows, each littered with Lady Elsabet's pet cats, bathing in the warmth. The heat poured onto them in waves, despite the gaping main doors. Where it gave Elsabet's pale complexion a gentle warmth, all the sun gifted King Joseth these days was pain and discomfort. He pried his shirt from the sores on his back, wincing. The shirt was too tight. He would need another size up.

Retainers filed into the throne room, lining up against the side walls. Their embroidered finery glinted off the marble flooring below, passing glimpses of light on the blueish-silver flagstones.

The nobles stared at him, aghast.

Where the nobility and Queen Elsabet wore heavy garments and corsets and oiled wigs, King Joseth had dispensed with them in his convalescence. A light, loose white shirt clothed him now, with simple beige leggings. His hair, long and grey and now thin from stress and pain, hung in a low tail under his ear, to keep it away from his back. His feet were bare: he had redistributed his servants once his illness had become physically apparent, in order to maintain some level of calm in the palace. Rumours of his illness had already leeched into the public. There was no use in exasperating that concern.

Elsabet was an image of radiance, as always. Her long, thick black hair hung from an intricate braid circling the crown of her head, cascading down her left shoulder in loose waves. Her tightly corseted blue gown shimmered, a tasteful parting in her skirts revealing a leg from the knee downwards, in the current style. A full twenty years his junior, she was a stark contrast from the sickly, frail old man at her side. If she felt the same as he did, she didn't show it.

He had hoped to keep his illness from his daughter. She had gained a joyfulness to her these last four years, ever since the twins had been conceived – would that it could have lasted, that her daughter – his granddaughter – could have remained safe.

It shamed Joseth to have to reveal his illness to her in this way, but it couldn't be helped. The situation had grown too vast for such things.

Soldiers entered the main doors ahead of them, two in front bearing Crey banners. They parted to reveal Seth Crey, his attire a simple emerald green.

Joseth glanced around. He couldn't see Cienne anywhere. A red-haired woman of an age with Seth stood at his side in a feathered white gown. The rest of their retinue were soldiers.

'Your majesty,' Joseth said graciously. 'My wife and I are pleased to receive you.'

Seth bowed deeply. 'I am as pleased to be received.'

'Be welcome in our palace as a close friend in these troubling times. Our servants are preparing a banquet as we speak, in your honour.'

'I thank you, your majesty, but we do not intend to stay long.'

Joseth lifted an eyebrow.

Seth approached the dais. He kneeled at the foot of the steps, his head bowed.

'Please rise,' Joseth interrupted him as he opened his mouth to speak. 'Let us speak as friends. Where is my daughter?'

Seth straightened up. He swallowed. 'Cienne has elected to stay in Adem, your majesty. The distress of the current situation had taken its toll on her.'

'Of course,' Elsabet said softly. Her Truphorian accent was a contrast to Joseth's lilting one. 'I ask that you pass our love to her on your return. Her family will provide whatever need she requires, always.'

'I was hoping you would say that, your highness.' Seth met Joseth's gaze. 'My apologies for my abrupt arrival and lack of notice, but we require troops as a matter of urgency. As my letter explains, we believe the Emmetts are involved in my daughter's disappearance. I intend to storm his palace and trace where she has been taken.'

'Is that wise?' Joseth said, his voice soft as ever. 'The Emmetts are a powerful family. Your letter states that a bastard brother of yours took her, I believe. I feel it would be more prudent to send out an enquiry to all the docks and trace them from there. I can organise this from my end as soon as this meeting adjourns.'

'Ordinarily, I would agree with you,' the red-haired woman said. 'But I believe matters have escalated past that point.' She approached the dais and halted at Seth's side in a deep curtsy. 'Qattren Meriangue of the Truphorian Forest, your majesty.'

Joseth's eyes widened perceptively. 'Ah.'

Qattren smiled faintly. 'My reputation precedes me, I see.'

'Indeed. Nevertheless, I welcome you to our palace. Could you elaborate?'

Qattren produced a letter, rolled and tied with purple ribbon.

Elsabet rose to accept it, passing it wordlessly to her husband. Joseth pulled the ribbon free and unrolled it.

'He intends to band all Truphorian nobility against the Creys,' Qattren said. 'My husband Ronald Horne has also received one, in addition to the Lords of the Ary Islands. One of the earls there is also betrothed to Felicity Emmett. Our only option is to destroy him before he gets the chance.'

'He claims you have murdered his nephew,' Joseth said softly.

'That is a lie,' Seth said vehemently. 'It was a tragic accident.'

'It does not surprise me that he would twist an accident to his advantage,' Qattren said. 'He has also fabricated a murder plot against the late Vladimir Horne, the boy's father. He has been extorting money from the Creys for the past four years and has manipulated Adem's council into accruing a substantial debt. Emmett has blackmailed and bankrupted the Creys, and now he wants to overthrow them.'

'We had no wish to cause the Emmett family harm until now,' Seth said firmly. 'My wife is close with the two siblings. We fostered Azrael on Felicity's request. We have paid his lamentable "peace tax" for the last four years, excluding the latest quarter due to a disagreement on the motives of my bastard brother, who is known to work for him.'

'I agree,' Qattren said, 'that it is the bastard brother at fault here. But he was seen taking the princess in a coach bearing the Emmett's colours. As Seth says, they have had no reason to harm Emmett until now. Silas Beult was either given the coach by Emmett or had knowledge of the Emmetts' discontent towards the Creys and pinned it on them. And if the latter is the truth of it, then Emmett clearly conspired to harm the Creys before any dispute concerning the children had arisen.'

Joseth examined the letter intently.

'He's been planning this the entire time,' Seth said. His voice wavered.

Joseth met his gaze.

'He organised my daughter's murder to exert some form of power over us,' Seth went on.

'There's no account of her death—' Qattren said softly.

'It's been a week,' Seth said, his voice breaking. 'If she was alive, we would have recovered her by now.' Tears poured down his cheeks. He brushed them away harshly.

Joseth's eyes bore into his. 'How many men?'

Seth rubbed both palms over his face and regained posture. 'As many as you can spare.'

Joseth's back smarted. He clenched his face, ignoring it.

'We will need to strike fast,' he said, through gritted teeth. 'I can only spare half of our forces. Once Emmett Sr hears of the storming of the Emmettfort, he will raze Portabella to the ground. We will need to hang on to as many men as we can for that eventuality.'

'There's no need to worry,' Qattren assured him. 'I expect for the entire strike to take no less than ten minutes total. If we leave this morning, your entire force will be back here by midday at the latest.'

Joseth frowned. 'How?'

Qattren smiled faintly. 'Spare me five minutes of your time and I will explain exactly what we are going to do.'

~

II

The Bastard lounged in Geldemar's settee, gaze locked upwards. He clasped his hands between his knees, picking at the edges of his nails.

Vladimir loitered behind him, tea set clasped in both hands as always. He frowned at the visitor as the Bastard glowered at the peak of the vaulted ceiling.

Vladimir cast a quick glance at Geldemar. Geldemar sat at the head of the elliptical table in his usual position – well, his usual position outside of the prisoners' daily violations, Vladimir thought with a shiver.

Ensuring he wasn't watching, Vladimir sidled around the settee. 'Question.'

The Bastard's gaze met his with an idle swing of his head. It had that lazy, Seth-Crey-esque-ness about it. Vladimir eyed this with nonchalance. He wondered when he had stopped hating Seth Crey. *That first night with Geldemar probably did it.* He only had the energy these days to hate one person with all his might. Seth Crey was no longer worthy.

'Now that all the pieces are set,' he said, returning to his query, 'what exactly are you going to do with yourself?'

The Bastard's face pivoted back skyward. 'Sit here, I suppose.'

Vladimir frowned slightly. 'Sounds awfully dull.'

'I could take Geldy up on his offer to join *his* extracurricular activities, of course.' He met Vladimir's horrified glance. 'It's still a firm *no*, by the way. You're not *that* pretty.'

Vladimir heaved a furtive sigh of relief.

The Bastard's gaze lingered on him. 'What makes you ask?'

'Well,' Vladimir said. 'Eternity is a long time. Geldemar has his meddling. *He* has… whatever it is he does. And Qattren has her little forest. What do *you* have?'

The Bastard paused. 'Nothing.' He went back to his skin picking. 'I could watch it all unfurl, I suppose.'

Vladimir shot him a cynical side-eye. 'You sound as if you don't enjoy the prospect.'

'I don't.' The Bastard ran a hand up the back of his neck and over his close-cropped hair. 'It seems unfair now.'

'How so?'

A beleaguered sigh emerged, his chest sinking with its release. 'They made it seem like it was purposeful. What they did to me. But they don't act like people who do these things on purpose. They act as if… as if they loved me somehow.'

'Your parents?'

The Bastard nodded once.

'Perhaps they did,' Vladimir suggested. 'Have you checked for yourself?'

The Bastard frowned. 'Checked?'

'Their memories.' Vladimir's shoulder swivelled against the upholstery towards him. 'I would have thought that would be the first thing you did. To see what possessed them to sacrifice their own child. It's what I would have done.'

The Bastard met his gaze again. He muttered to himself for a moment. 'I hadn't… I thought it might, but now, maybe…' He threw himself to his feet. 'Geldy?'

Geldemar's head shot upright. 'Yes, dear?'

'Is Vladimir busy?'

Vladimir stiffened.

'No, but he will be at seven,' Geldemar said, smiling to himself.

Icy horror dribbled down Vladimir's spine. It would never get easier, he thought in despair. Never.

'I have a task for him, it won't take long.'

'Do as you wish with him, as long as I get him back in one piece,' Geldemar said, uninterested.

'You shall.' The Bastard's gaze lingered on Geldemar's back. It looked distinctly unfriendly. He flicked his eyes back to Vladimir. 'Come with me.'

Vladimir followed him to the door, wary.

'And relax,' the Bastard added in a withering tone. 'I told you, you're not that pretty.'

Vladimir halted on the outside porch as the Bastard pulled the double doors closed. Sal'plae's purple tinge engulfed the scenery far below, the green fields now blue in the strange atmosphere. They weren't over Stoneguard at the moment, Vladimir observed – he knew the curvature of its rivers like the creases of his own palm, its peaks and valleys imprinted on his mind from his years of perusing his future kingdom. *Not yours anymore*, he reminded himself, deflating. It wasn't even Ronald's anymore, thanks to him.

Vladimir pulled his attention back to the porch.

The Bastard approached the cistern beside them, filled with holy water or whatever substance the Seven had filled it with to torture otherworldly petitioners. He dipped two fingers inside and flicked the water into the empty space across from the door, wiping the digits on his jerkin after in distaste.

The water dispersed before them, circling to form an entrance of sorts. Vladimir recognised it from the Bastard and Geldemar's prior voyage into the mind of Seth Crey.

'His or hers?' he asked distantly.

The Bastard grimaced. 'I'm sick of looking at his one. Let's go with hers.'

They stepped forward as one.

~

Felicity had spent her first week back at Emmettfort confined to her rooms. Her brother had sent her there, as though punishing her for throwing her dinner at him.

She lay curled up on the bed, her arms wrapped around her knees and her thoughts wrapped around her son.

Meyer had visited her three times during the week, bearing small gifts and kind condolences. The playful and smug qualities in him had vanished, for the meantime anyway. He was particularly careful around her. As much as she still didn't trust him, Felicity appreciated the gesture. Perhaps he wasn't so bad after all.

Her brother hadn't given her a second glance since they had returned. Felicity was rather glad of that too. If he hadn't been sending her meals to her rooms and confining her there, she would have avoided him anyway. The sooner she left for the Ary Islands, the better.

A servant entered in the usual manner: scuttle in wordlessly, leave the tray on the table, scuttle back out again.

Felicity drew a breath through her nose and pushed herself upright. She had no intention of eating the half-cold meal in front of her, but she was parched. She hovered over the tray, her nightgown swishing around her ankles.

A letter lay on the tray beside a cup of water. The grey seal bore an illustration of three stones stacked into a triangle. The Hornes.

Frowning, Felicity lifted the letter and broke the seal. It was Ron's handwriting. She could recognise the deliberate lines anywhere. She scanned the contents. He wanted her to meet him at the Forest as a matter of urgency.

Discarding her meal, she made a beeline for the wardrobe. The first items to come to hand were a garish pink fleece-lined dress and jacket ensemble, but she took no notice. She threw off her nightgown, leaving it flutter to the ground.

The cold bit her throat and face as she finally left the tower.

The staircase had seemed much shorter when she ascended them a week ago. Her impatience to finally leave the Emmettfort increased the length of the tower by thrice, it seemed to Felicity. She hoped she could get to the gates without being intercepted by her nosy brother.

Her heart hammered against her ribs. He would stop her. She knew he would. He had to have total control over every situation. There would be no talking her way out of this one.

'Good afternoon, my lady,' said the stable master with a low bow.

She halted inside the stables, casting a glance around.

'You'll be wanting Rummy, is it?'

'Er, yes,' she said, wondering what Rummy was.

It turned out to be an auburn-coloured palfrey, a gentle horse given to her by Meyer a day ago. She hadn't even noticed. The horse bowed her head as Felicity caressed her ears. She didn't have the slightest idea how she was going to get herself to Adem through all this snow, but that was an issue for another day. For now, she needed to get out of the Emmettfort.

The stable master readied and saddled Rummy himself and led them to the yard afterwards. 'Take care on the ice, my lady.'

'Thank you,' she said, mounting. She and the horse tore off across the yard before the stableman could utter another word.

The insanely huge upper grounds lay almost entirely devoid of human activity. A scattering of servants in cream-coloured clothes loitered at various intervals, litter picking. The patio tiling yawned ahead of Felicity as she steadily closed the gap between herself and the inner portcullis. She urged the horse forward, a weight within her dissipating. Nearly there. If she could just talk her way out of the inner portcullis—

A hand closed around her left ankle.

No— was all she had time to think before being pulled backwards from the saddle.

Concrete rose to meet her. Her face slammed into a patterned tile with force. Skidding to a miserable halt, she tremulously slid both palms beneath herself. Blood poured from her nose.

She was swivelled around before she had a chance to pull herself upright. White clouds blinded her.

'And where are you going?'

Her brother wore cream today. She groaned. She'd been keeping a lookout for his signature violet. She glowered at him without favouring him with a reply. Emmett (she wouldn't refer to him by her father's given name, she decided – this man was nothing like their father, in fact he was barely human) reached a hand towards her throat.

Felicity flinched, but he only clutched a handful of her jacket and pulled her into a sitting position.

'I hear you received a letter this morning,' he said in his usual monotone. 'Care to share your news with your dear brother?'

An old image came sharply into focus. A young Zephyr pulled her away from the flowerbed, as he had done in every flashback for the past fifteen years.

'Do not speak of this to anyone, understand?' he said in an undertone, her chin gripped firmly in the palm of his hand. 'He will know if you do. Your innocence is all that protects you, little niece. Hold onto it. And never let it go.'

'I don't know what the letter said,' she replied. 'I knocked it into the fireplace by mistake.' She lifted herself to her feet and brushed dust from her clothes, pointedly.

Emmett lifted an eyebrow. 'You knocked it into the fireplace?'

She nodded, locking her eyes to the ground ruefully.

'Who was it from?'

'Ronald,' she said, opting for a kernel of truth.

Emmett inspected her face for a moment. 'If you knocked it into the fireplace,' he said slowly, 'where were you going in such a hurry?'

'The rookery,' she said immediately. 'To send him a letter back and explain. I thought he might send the message again.'

'You did.'

She tried to stare him down. Her heart pounded, treacherously loud.

The pounding of hooves beyond the barbican tore their attention from one another. Men in copper armour galloped into the courtyard.

Meyer, Felicity thought, relieved.

Emmett's eyes rolled upward, an apparent show of dislike. 'How can I help you?' he drawled, intending his voice to carry.

To the contrary, it merged into the cacophony. The horses and clatter of armour tore through the early morning quiet like a knife through a wedding veil.

'Hello?' Emmett repeated loudly, exasperated.

A bellow from behind the crowd forced them to part. Meyer himself tore through at a gallop, his grey stallion heaving.

'Where is everyone?' he demanded, pivoting.

Emmett furrowed one eyebrow. 'Who is everyone?'

Meyer spun around, clockwise, anti-clockwise and back again. 'The men!' he exclaimed, dropping the reins to splay his arms. 'The cavalry, the infantry, the bloody archers, even!'

'They're off duty,' said Emmett, irked. 'They tend to do that in a time of peace.'

'A time of peace!' Meyer shrieked.

Emmett half-frowned again.

'A time of peace,' Meyer repeated, as if his previous scream had gone unnoticed. 'Have you not seen what's going on out there?' He spotted their bemused expressions. 'Nobody told you.'

'Nice to see you're keeping with the current trend,' Emmett said irritably. 'Would you mind enlightening me as to why your men are traipsing around my courtyard?'

'The Creys!' His voice plummeted from a shout to a whisper. 'They've… that… her, they've hired that woman, from the Forest…' He gestured up and down along his shoulders, indicating a hair length.

'Qattren Meriangue?' Emmett interrupted.

'Yes!' he exhaled in relief. 'She's working for him, she's…' He huffed a harsh breath. 'Magic. There's magic, just… pulsing all around the castle. She's summoning something, all over the hill, everywhere! We need to

437

prepare for attack!'

Emmett stared at him, uncomprehending. 'She's summoning something?'

'Is that not what I've said?'

Emmett's eyes narrowed, ever so slightly. 'Show me.'

Meyer bolted for the portcullis. He seemed to have forgotten he was the only of the three currently riding a horse.

Emmett's irises rolled upwards, almost completely out of sight. He reined in a passer-by, dressed in the copper breastplate of the Meyer household guard atop a magnificent war horse. The soldier, refusing to relinquish the horse, was unceremoniously shoved off.

'What does he mean by magic?' Felicity asked.

Emmett froze in the act of stepping into the stirrup. Rumbling sounded to the south. 'Looks like we're about to find out,' he said, almost blithely. He mounted and galloped for the battlements.

Felicity huffed. Her eyes fell on her horse standing a yard away, rejected by her brother, for some reason. *Has to make an impression*, she thought cynically, eyeing the back of the warhorse. She bolted for it, swiftly pursuing him downhill.

Having laboured up the steep flight of steps, she stood at her brother's side, breathing heavily. The city of Stoneguard sprawled below, a collection of browns and greys. The green hills beyond were wreathed in mist. She narrowed her eyes. 'What is that in the distance?'

Meyer and Emmett said nothing.

Felicity pulled her gaze from the anomaly before them. Looking at her brother, she felt a stab of fear. What little colour he ever had in his face completely fell away. His jaw fell slack. For perhaps the first time in his life, he was afraid.

'That,' he said, 'is oblivion.'

~

Six minutes was all it would take.

The air around Emmettfort rippled. Violet tinges appeared in fleeting traces, coming and going, coming and going. Men on the battlements took aim with arrows and crossbows, each with an air of uncertainty, for there was nothing to aim at. Only ripples.

The hills pulsed on for a few moments. And then they appeared.

Thousands of men bearing bright pink banners charged at the gate.

Cavalry poured out, horses screaming and steel flashing. Violet banners met magenta before crumpling into the throngs of armoured man and horse. A quarter of a century after the death of Persephone Fleurelle, her husband and birth family were finally at war.

Abruptly, the Fleurelle force evaporated in puffs of grey ash.

The Emmett palace guard glanced around, confused.

Blue flame shot out like an arrow and consumed them all.

Qattren stood at the bottom of the hill, lowering her hand. Cobalt flames licked at the bones of the guardsmen, licked them away until they were gone. The gravel path turned to ash and hollowed into a blackened trench. The stench of ash obliterated the winter air. It was familiar, all too familiar.

Magenta banners reappeared in flurries of dust. Her allies poured into the gate, giving the blazing trench a wide berth.

Qattren's eyes fixed to the trench, the flickering white and blue. Her signature move. The old panic began to set in, and then she remembered their purpose here. Ginny.

Her heart burned with a heat equal to the blaze before her. Her blood ran black in her veins. It was a side of her she never hoped to see again. She strode forward, snarling.

One minute had passed.

~

Raw heat rose from beneath their feet. The mortar glowed between the bricks, an eerie turquoise.

Emmett bolted from the battlements and sprinted for the stairs. Meyer followed, not before grasping Felicity by the hand on the way.

The blocks forming the battlements trembled underfoot.

Meyer leapt the stairs two at a time. Felicity stumbled along with him, her skirts gathered in her hands.

A flame cracked its way through the flagstones, a striking blue. Felicity shrieked, leaping to one side. The edge of the staircase struck her left ankle. She pitched sideways, her stomach dropping.

Meyer jerked her upright by an elbow and they carried on.

Her breath caught in her throat. The ground wavered twelve feet below her. She tore her gaze from it, her heart pounding.

Meyer threw an arm out just as they reached the bottom, halting Felicity in her tracks. Copper-clad soldiers fell into rank at the foot of the stairs.

Felicity's pulse hammered again.

The monstrously huge forecourt brimmed with steel and banners. Swords flashed in the air at regular intervals, but the screams – one over another in layers, each so loud and guttering Felicity couldn't make out man from horse.

'Surround her!' Meyer barked.

He guided Felicity down the remaining three steps. The soldiers formed a tight ring around the two. Feeling stifled, Felicity stumbled along as best she could, the wall of steel and amber cloaks rendering the forecourt a mystery.

She had a barely a millisecond to wonder why a complete stranger's retinue was protecting her instead of her brother's.

~

One and a half minutes had passed. Emerald banners, finally, flooded the hillside. Everything was according to plan.

They surged uphill in droves, spears forward. Stragglers from Emmett's household guard were swept up by the swarm, every lone soul cut down and trampled into the dust.

All except Qattren, standing in the forecourt, biding her time.

As the swarm converged into the entrance, a lone horseman pounded uphill. Crey soldiers parted in the courtyard to let him in. His armour gleamed, despite the weak sunlight of the winter morning – the emerald enamelling across the breastplate identified him as an expensive arrival.

'The king,' whispered a few Crey militants.

I doubt it, thought Qattren privately.

Reaching behind his back, the newcomer tugged a flail free. Still galloping to the keep entrance, he swung it in slow revolutions at his side.

The Crey militia wisely stood back. Some halted to watch as the mace's head, roughly the size of a child's, wreaked havoc on the unlucky skulls of the Emmett household guard. One group that was not spared from the horseman was Henry Meyer's guard, making their torturous ascend into the keep's entrance hall.

The throng had dwindled to a handful of wounded yet resourceful men. Meyer and Felicity remained unharmed. Now that most of the guard had dissipated, Felicity could see the carnage surrounding her – and she soon wished she couldn't.

Crey cloaks and banners littered the room, despite many of the fallen bearing the coat and arms of the Emmett's. Every face that was even vaguely familiar to her lay dead at her feet – all except for Meyer, who searched feverishly about for something, perhaps some kind of refuge.

Casting quick glances over the blood and shit, her mind unable to comprehend the horror of it yet, Felicity ignored the fighting and searched for her brother. No sign.

'My lady!' Meyer barked.

A horse had materialised out of the chaos, bloodied and terrified but unhurt. Meyer pulled himself into the saddle and beckoned to his men, who hoisted Felicity up behind him.

The horseman trampled a man into the marble tiles and skidded to a halt by the back wall. Felicity gaped at him as he pivoted, his horse snorting, and launched himself at them.

She almost slid back down as the guards fumbled. Men in unfamiliar armour swarmed into the hall. They surrounded Meyer and Felicity.

'Hurry!' Meyer snapped.

Felicity swatted the guard away and flung herself up behind Meyer.

He sped for the back-right corner as the crowd closed in. Trampling men into the tiles, he surged under an arch Felicity was unfamiliar with and plummeted down a wide set of stairs to the cellars.

The horseman galloped around the soldiers and into the arch in pursuit.

Darkness fell on them. Pinpricks of torchlight outlined their route and the horse followed them, eager to escape the bedlam above. Felicity clung to the back of Meyer's coat. He stared straight ahead, apparently oblivious.

Hooves pounded behind them.

Meyer kicked their palfrey wildly. They surged and meandered down tunnel after tunnel. Felicity had no idea where they were.

'Out of the way, out!' screeched Emmett. His borrowed warhorse collided with them as he emerged, white-faced, from a dark corner.

The main tunnel opened up ahead. They galloped on.

~

Qattren gazed through the smoke, standing still in the middle of the castle thoroughfare. 'Now.'

A lingering cavalryman nodded and galloped inside, his emerald cloak flapping. Moments later the entire Crey/Fleurelle force erupted from the remains of the castle gates. They didn't need telling twice.

The horseman led the charge, halting at Qattren's side to give her a nod. She gave him a nod back. Marbrand fled, discarding the wieldy flail.

Qattren stormed across the forecourt. Throngs of steel and leather pounded out of the premises, a mass of bodies and pounding feet. Every single body gave Qattren a berth of at least three feet. Within seconds the entire palace was empty.

Qattren continued into the keep, pristine apart from a spatter of blood glaring out from a white marble pillar. She ascended a spiral staircase to the south tower, mounted the top floor and began to shove doors open, peering.

Every room of Emmett's chambers had been ransacked. Every bookshelf lay empty, each drawer cleaned out. Every document, she saw with satisfaction, had been taken away.

She marched into the centre of the drawing room. A few stragglers from Emmett's household guard cowered by the walls, along with men in noble raiment. His council, Qattren surmised. They must have interrupted a meeting.

Dust rose from the flagstones to meet her. Qattren lifted an eyebrow. 'I thought you had changed your mind?'

Seth materialised in front of her. If he still had discomfort at the procedure, he didn't show it. 'Not at all,' he said, almost brightly. 'Let's get started, shall we?'

They stood side by side facing the main entrance, and watched.

Lyseria burst into the double doors and screamed.

The group by the wall bolted. The guards wielded their swords, but neither were fast enough. Flames poured over them all, melting blade and setting clothes alight.

Seth watched steely-eyed, his hands folded behind his back.

Howls erupted. Lyseria threw herself at the men and tore them apart. Hideous squelching noises erupted from the walls, silencing the screams. Blood pooled in the cracks between the flagstones, a red gridwork.

Once the men had become a mere pool of flesh, Seth clicked his fingers, drawing a circle with one finger pointed to the ceiling.

Lyseria raised her shoulder-blades and thrust herself through the ceiling.

It came down in a shower of bricks and dust. Roof tiles tumbled through the gap above, landing a bare foot away from the two. Flame soon followed, briefly flashing overhead.

'We should leave,' Qattren announced.

'Stay,' Seth said mildly. He stared up at the gaping hole in the ceiling, lined in flaking mortar and dangling pieces of wood. 'She won't hurt us.'

Crashes from the rest of the palace begged to differ. Shrieks erupted every so often, ethereal in the distance, as though imagined.

'Watch it crumble with me,' Seth whispered.

Qattren stared at him.

The wall behind them slid down in a cloud of dust. More bricks followed, tapestries and portraits littered in between, crunching and snapping.

With sufficient damage complete, Lyseria returned down the ceiling she had burst through. She landed before them, sitting demurely in the centre of the rubble. A pained expression took her. Qattren recognised it immediately.

Lyseria lifted off again. A faint glow emitted from where she had previously sat.

Qattren placed a hand on Seth's shoulder. The two dissipated as the glow intensified.

~

Meyer and Felicity emerged from the tunnel into glaring sunlight.

Snow surrounded them thickly, over every tree. They were on the mountain edge, Felicity realised. A narrow, deep valley separated them from the south side of the palace, a view she seldom saw of her home. The Emmettfort was now wreathed in smoke, its broad hill overrun with fleeing soldiers.

Two doors hung open on either side of them, the drainpipe floor ridged. Their horse toed the snow tentatively. They had lost the horseman halfway through the tunnel, shortly after running into Emmett. He appeared to have swerved into another side tunnel, to Felicity's understanding.

Emmett himself halted at the edge of a steep drop overlooking the Emmettfort. He sat upright in the saddle, his charcoal warhorse breathing heavily beneath him.

'The tunnel,' Meyer said, in between heavily exhales, 'would have been a nice thing to know about when they *first* came over the horizon.'

Emmett ignored him. The only sound around them was faint noise from the palace, distant and indistinguishable.

Meyer dismounted to approach the edge, following his gaze.

A black smear flashed into the clouds briefly. Within seconds of this, the castle erupted.

Red clouds exploded through the turret roofs. Windows smashed, the shards glittering in the weak winter light. Burst after burst after burst blew towers and walls into dust and debris. Bricks flew in their direction, bouncing off the trees and cliff edges ahead of them. Luckily, they were just far enough away to evade collision.

With an earth-rumbling roar, the foundations of the palace broke. The keep crumbled in on itself, sliding down like a melting candle. One by one the turrets followed in the same way, molten slush residing where firm stone had once stood.

Emmett remained fixated to it, his expression glassy.

'Now what?' Meyer said, pale.

Emmett blinked rapidly, looking more lost than he had ever looked before.

'War,' he said simply.

~

III

Jon blearily opened his eyes. Wood-panelled walls greeted him where grass and moss had been before. He lifted his head and whined. His brain was throbbing.

'Easy,' hissed a voice to his left. 'You have concussion, be careful.'

Jon hissed through his teeth. 'What——?'

'You fell in the forest and hit your head,' the voice said. 'I'm Raphael Emmanuel III, it's the first week of winter, we're in a kindly old lady's cottage, you've been here for three days and the king's on a murderous rampage, so we're keeping you away from him at all costs, at least until he's calmed down a bit.'

He paused as Jon tried to process this.

'Sorry if that's a bit much all in one go,' he said. 'It's just that you've been waking up every three hours and asking those same few questions over and over, so. Thought I'd cut to the chase.'

Jon picked at something scratchy at the base of his neck.

'Oh, and the old lady gave you her cardigan,' Raphael added with a shrug.

It was a garish shade of pink. Jon grimaced and decided he had bigger problems at present. 'Where's Jimmy?'

Raphael shrugged. 'Where he usually is, I suppose.'

Bracing himself for pain, Jon sat up with a squeak. 'Bring me to Jimmy,' he gritted through clenched teeth.

～

'Find anything?' Vladimir rifled through a high shelf, examining bottles in disinterest.

'Nothing but cough remedies over here,' the Bastard said in a dull monotone.

Adrienne Hart's mind resembled an elongated version of the Creys' medical turret. Shelves of bottles lined the walls from floor to ceiling, all containing some kind of medicine recipe – each stopper slid open to reveal an image of a specific illness, mostly of the hideous skin variety, and the name of the remedy to cure it. It stopped being interesting about fifty bottles ago, the Bastard thought in annoyance, sliding another bottle into a group of others with a small bong.

'It can't all be just medicines in here,' Vladimir said in disbelief, searching. 'She's not a filing cabinet.'

The Bastard straightened up, his hands on his hips. 'There's more. She's hiding it. This is a distraction for her.' A glint in the corner of his left eye caught his attention.

A lock shone in the candlelight, tucked in a gap in the shelving.

'Aha,' the Bastard murmured.

They discarded the bottles and surrounded the door. The key remained in the padlock, the Bastard spotted with a frown. Upon turning it, the lock sprung open, sliding easily from the latch.

The reek of death seeped out.

'Explains the distraction,' Vladimir said through his hands, pressed tightly around his mouth and nose.

The Bastard slipped through.

Two long rows of beds greeted him. The dead seemed strangers to him – who were all these people? All manner of human greeted him here: children, elderly women, wounded soldiers. The beds yawned down the length of the hall. An endless hall, paved in dull flagstone and stretching to eternity. How could one person possibly...

She could. It was her job to know them. They had died on her watch.

The Bastard paced the length of the aisle, slowly. A hand trailed the posts at the end of their beds, plain beds with white linen, each person laid out neatly in grey bedclothes. Each faint touch elicited an image: a procedure. One that would have saved them, or at least removed the pain. He watched a hypothetical Adrienne brush a woman's cheek gently on administering a liquid and felt his mother's pain, a stab of regret. He soon tucked his hands under his armpits instead.

'Look.' Vladimir's voice drifted over the eerie silence.

Other cabinets punctuated the rows of beds along the walls, books littering the shelves this time. Vladimir had approached one, a book open in his hands.

'What?' the Bastard said, grimacing. 'It isn't a love story about my bloody father, is it? Because the last thing I need is an image of the two of them—'

'Don't you have enough of those?' Vladimir asked sharply, the comment cutting into the air. 'You've spent the last few months assaulting them by forcing them into this twisted love affair, what's another scene on top of those?'

The Bastard made a face. 'Assaulting them? They enjoyed it, it was nothing like—'

'Like what Geldy does to me?' Vladimir said in a low voice. His upper lip curled as he stared at the Bastard in hatred. 'It is *exactly* like that. They didn't want this, you did. Do you remember how it felt when you took over her body and couldn't get out, how it felt when his mouth was on you and there was *nothing* you could do about it?'

The Bastard froze. 'It… it felt hideous.' The words slipped out in a whisper, barely audible.

'Precisely.' Vladimir turned a page, almost tenderly. 'There are whole pages missing from this "love story", you know. Just blank. She can't remember half of it. Don't you think she would have savoured this if it had been something she had wanted with every fibre of her being?'

'I wouldn't know, would I?' the Bastard said, quietly. 'I've never known any of these feelings.'

Vladimir met his gaze, his expression more gentle this time. 'I know.' He eased the book closed and placed it back in its slot.

They continued on. The endless rows of beds soon gave way to a wide hearth, decorated with portraits. Two large portraits, to be exact. The hearth, he noticed, despite its crackling fire, was devoid of the warmth of flame.

The Bastard was stunned to see himself in one of the paintings before realising that it wasn't him, it was a similar face. Howie.

Archie hung beside him, wearing a wry half-smile.

'What happened to them?' Vladimir asked in a hushed voice.

'They died,' said the Bastard. His gaze dropped to the mantle.

A nondescript box lay beneath the frames, roughly the size of his palm.

'This is it,' he said to Vladimir. 'This is me.'

Crookedly-aligned timber confirmed his thoughts, along with the clumsy letter A. He reached out and touched the carved letter, tracing its rough surface.

Vladimir vanished. The room, with its fireplace, vanished. The box vanished, all in a wide beam of pink light. The chapel filled his peripheral vision. Panic consumed him at the sight of the altar. He couldn't tell if it was Adrienne's or his own.

The Bastard paced the length of the thick carpet. He couldn't quite tell what colour it was – only the pink of the stained glass could be discerned of his surroundings. The recollection must be vague, he thought.

Adrienne knelt at the dais, her head bowed. Her attire had maintained itself in this memory: a long skirt, coloured a washed-out green, with a pale grey blouse tucked into the high waist. A soft swell under the waistband revealed the child within her. *Me.*

Wispy figures drifted around her, indistinct.

The Bastard circled her prone form. Her eyes were closed. That explained the hazy surroundings. Her thoughts at the time permeated the thick atmosphere. The Bastard had to strain his ear to hear them.

This will work instead. It has to. Father Giery believes in it, he seems so nice…

She sounded so young. The Bastard felt a sharp ache in his stomach – no, *her* stomach. He had kicked her, or rolled or something. Another ache occurred in his chest now, a lingering, longing ache. She cradled the swell with one hand, breathing slowly. Reassuringly.

How could I have ever thought of giving him away?

The Bastard's breath caught in his throat.

Her imagination wove a brief image of an infant, vague in structure, at least at this point in time. A pang in her chest emerged as she felt his little form press the inside of her abdomen. She was thinking of him, of her life with him in it. Not a sacrifice. A son. The Bastard recognised this feeling – he had felt it when speaking to Despina. She loved him.

A pain struck the Bastard's chest and he knew it this time to be his.

The box reappeared, sitting inside an ornate gold case, pressed between her knees. A cup found its way into her hand. One of the wraiths had pressed it into her fingers. It was beginning.

'No,' said the Bastard.

Agony ripped through his centre, forcing him to double over. He couldn't tell her pain from his anymore, it was synonymous. He forced his head upright, forcing his gaze back onto his mother.

The wraiths shoved the interlaying boxes beneath her. Adrienne grappled for it. One figure grasped her elbows, holding her arms back. Hands wrenched her skirts out of the way, and the blood, the blood...

It poured down the length of the aisle. He couldn't tell metaphor from reality anymore. It swelled into a crimson river, meandering through his boots and across the width of the chapel, a grotesque flood.

A wraith lifted the boxes to the altar. They brimmed with blood, her blood. And his.

'You lied,' the Bastard said in a hollow wail. He collapsed, his knees splashing in the blood of his mother. 'You *lied*!' he howled at the beams of white bearing down on his mortal form.

Adrienne howled with him. She thrashed in their grip, spasms curling her torso forward. Her chest strained for air between each sob until the blood loss became too much. She succumbed, her arms dropping limply into her bloodied lap.

He could stomach no more. The Bastard pivoted back into the dim hospital room.

Vladimir's eyes widened on the flagstones beneath them. Blood poured down these as well. 'I take it that answered your question.'

The Bastard clutched his stomach, nails poking into the fabric of his jerkin. 'They violated her,' he said, choking on his tears. 'And I came along and did it all over again...'

Vladimir didn't approach. He simply gazed at him with a sigh. 'How were you to know what you were doing? You were just following your teacher's lead.'

The Bastard wept.

~

Eleanor accepted the letter from Jimmy with a smile. 'Thank you,' she said with a sigh. 'It's nice to have something... well, nice to think about.'

'Friend of yours, your highness?' Jimmy asked idly. He stood with his back to the enormous fireplace in Eleanor's quarters, the blazing flames illuminating him in an amber glow.

'A very good one,' she said brightly. She broke the coral seal on the back, in the shape of a starfish. 'She used to be one of my ladies-in-waiting when I married Theo. Tried to seduce him, for some reason. Didn't work, of course, he had her sent to Stoneguard to get rid of her.'

'Wasn't axe-shaped enough, I imagine,' he commented.

Eleanor smiled faintly at the jest. She unfolded the letter and read it, her back turned away from the window and the charred remains of Castlefoot beyond. 'Any word back on what Seth's doing?'

'Not a thing. He went missing yesterday, nobody's seen him since.'

Eleanor's face slackened.

Jimmy frowned slightly. 'What is it?'

'I've just read the answer to my own question,' she said, her voice flat. 'The Emmettfort has just exploded. The Crey banners were seen descending from the top of the hill shortly before it happened.'

'Oh, not again,' Jimmy said painfully.

Eleanor's complexion turned almost as white as the sheet in her hand. 'I thought it was a once-off,' she whispered. 'What's happening to him? The Castlefoot Massacre, it was just trauma, and the Stonekeep was a mistake, but this… this was on purpose, wasn't it? What else is he going to do? What else has he *done*?'

Jimmy didn't respond to this. 'At least tell me Mister Emmett was inside?'

She shook her head. 'Unknown.'

Jimmy craned his neck to glance at the flames behind him. *Looks like the paid vacation is off*, he thought with a shiver. He turned to the window. 'Any sign of him on the horizon?'

Eleanor squinted out of the window, but she needn't have bothered.

The door clicked open. Seth poked his head inside, looking rueful. 'I've come to apologise,' he said in a small voice. 'About the other day.'

Eleanor's eyes widened. 'The other day? What about this morning?'

Seth's eyes dropped to the floor. 'You heard about Emmett, then?'

'How? I take it Qattren Meriangue took you to the Emmettfort, unless you and our entire cavalry *flew* there? Have you no shame? Going to the likes of *her* to start a war—'

'She came to me, actually,' Seth said levelly. 'She agreed with me that Emmett's actions were an act of war and he needed to be exterminated. The taxation and the debt were one thing. A *child* is quite another.'

'What on earth did you think you were going to achieve?'

'I got what I needed out of it,' he said firmly.

'Did you get Ginny back?'

He didn't respond to this.

'That's what I thought,' she said, her arms folded, the letter dangling from two fingers. 'And now any hope of him persuading the abductor into giving her back has gone up in smoke. Are you pleased with yourself? Are you?'

'You know what, *yes*,' Seth sneered, 'I *am* pleased with myself. And I'll be even more pleased with myself when I find the bastard who took her on his behalf – *your* bastard, if I'm not mistaken.'

The blood drained from her face. 'I'm not responsible for the actions of my children,' she said in a quiet voice. 'Not him, not Lilly, and certainly not you.'

'Why didn't you tell me?' Seth demanded, crossing his arms. 'You let us assume he was our father's, the day Lilly told us who he said he was. Why didn't you tell us? Or aren't you responsible for *that* either?'

'I have my reasons, which are none of your business.'

'Then my reasons for the Emmettfort are none of your business either.' He turned and left, the door slamming behind him.

Eleanor crumpled the letter in one fist and let it drop to the floor.

'Shall I put the kettle on?' Jimmy said after a moment.

$\sim$

Rhys cried out. 'Easy with the arm! That *hurts*!'

'Good,' Myles said testily. 'That'll learn you for riling up a dragon-toting murderer.'

Sammy sat with his legs dangling off the edge of the cliff.

The Forest gleamed in white, highlighting the red sores on Rhys's forearms. The cliff edge they had been deposited on two days earlier sported magnificent views of the horizon, which Myles would have enjoyed had he not a temperamental patient with second-degree burns to cream up.

Around them, tents littered the woodlands along the cliff edge. A diverse group of Castlefoot survivors lingered around campfires, talking quietly amongst themselves. No doubt about the demise they had all been magicked away from a mere week ago.

Myles slapped another scoopful of aloe vera oil on Rhys's other arm, making him wince. 'I honestly think,' Myles snarled, kneading his arm with more force than was required, 'I made a terrible mistake teaching you comedy. You realise this will mean divorce for me, right? Actual divorce. I may never see my son again!'

'You never see your son anyway,' Rhys pointed out.

'And whose fault is that?'

Sammy stared thoughtfully at the ocean as the two bickered. 'I like that lady,' he said, out of nowhere.

Rhys shoved Myles away. 'What lady?'

'The one who rescued us.' He pivoted, his legs crossed beneath him. 'The redhaired lady.'

'Oh, her,' Myles said reproachfully.

'What's wrong with her?' Rhys snapped. 'Everything's a problem with you, isn't it?'

Myles squeaked unintelligible indignation, his hands flailing. 'She set half the continent aflame! I think that's a bit of a problem, don't you?'

'That wasn't her, that was her mum,' Rhys said.

'Her mum, my eye,' Myles snarled. 'She's a maniac.'

'Yes, but she's a *friendly* maniac,' Rhys said, 'who's rescued all these people and is looking for a place for us to live, so be nice.'

'She's really pretty,' Sammy said. 'She wears amazing clothes.'

Rhys paused. 'She does, doesn't she?'

Myles punched his arm. The sore part.

Rhys howled. 'What was that for?'

'You're married,' he barked. 'Try to remember that next time you ogle a flame-throwing maniac and get us into even *more* trouble!'

'I didn't mean it like that, I was just—stop hitting me! Stop it!'

Sammy turned back to the cliff edge, smiling into the sunrise. He pictured the shimmering silver-green gown again. *I wonder what I'd look like in one of those...*

~

Despina peered into the queen's drawing room. A chest lay open in the middle of the rug. Cienne threw clothes and books into it haphazardly, peering around for anything else.

'Can I help, your highness?' Despina asked tremulously.

Cienne rose and turned, giving her a sour glance. 'I think you've done enough.'

Despina stepped back, stung. 'I haven't done anything.'

'Oh, you haven't done anything!' Cienne exploded, splaying her arms. 'You've only let the king's daughter run off and be kidnapped and started a war with Stoneguard, but you're right, how silly of me. *You* didn't do anything, did you?'

Despina dropped her eyes to the floor.

Cienne turned back to her packing.

'Where are you going, may I ask?' Despina said carefully.

'Home,' she said, impatient. 'I'm taking my son to meet his grandfather. And demand a reason for why said grandfather helped his son-in-law to murder my cousin.'

Despina paused. 'But you're not allowed to take him out of the country without the king's permission.'

Cienne straightened up. Her blue eyes became chips of ice. 'He's the next heir to the throne of Portabella. I can take him wherever I want.' She swung the trunk closed. 'If you tell anyone you saw this, Mister Emmett won't be the only one having a funeral this week. Take that as your dismissal. Get out of my sight.'

Tears flooded her vision. Without a word, she left.

Marbrand caught up with her on the way home. He stopped her arm, gently. 'What's happened? What are the tears about?'

Despina wiped her nose. 'I've just been sacked.'

He put an arm around her shoulders and guided her the rest of the way home, muttering about noble liberties and tea. Ten minutes later, Despina had a cup of tea in her hands and Marbrand had the full story.

'I'm never going to see that little boy again,' she said weepily.

Marbrand gave her shoulder a squeeze. 'You will,' he assured her. 'You just need a clean slate with the woman.'

'How?'

'Subterfuge.'

453

~

Jimmy parked himself on the kitchen counter with a sigh.

'I never thought I'd say this,' he said to the kitchen at large. 'But I actually miss Jon.'

'He'll be pleased to hear that,' said Isla. Brushing a lock of red hair from her eyes in impatience, she placed a hand on her unborn child, now just two weeks from full term. 'You'll never live it down when he gets here.'

'If he gets back alive,' Jimmy said, morose.

'He looks pretty alive to me,' she said, pointing at the window.

Jimmy frowned, hopping off the counter to see.

Sure enough, stumbling up the hill from the hunter's gate with an arm slung across the Prophet's shoulders, was Jon, looking disorientated.

'My God, he's kicked the shit out of him!' He raced to the side door to let them in.

Isla brought a stool over immediately. She shoved it under Jon as he was about to collapse.

'Jon?' Jimmy said gently. He crouched in front of Jon and planted a hand on his elbow to steady him. 'Jon, mate? You alright?'

Jon stared at Jimmy's ear in apparent horror. 'You can piss *right off*!'

Jimmy recoiled. 'Charming. I was about to bring you a custard slice. I shan't bother now.'

'Not you,' Jon said impatiently. 'Him.'

Jimmy followed his finger.

A colander hung innocently from a hook above the drain, dripping softly.

'Right,' he said slowly. 'And what did he do exactly?'

'He's been a git ever since I woke up,' Jon snarled.

'This may be a shock to you,' Jimmy said, 'but that is in fact a colander—'

'And the same to you, mate!' Jon hollered over him, at the colander.

Jimmy glanced back at the offending article. As before, it hung unassumingly in its place. 'Isla,' said Jimmy, 'go get Erik, will you?'

The redhead hurried off.

'Jon—' Jimmy began.

'Listen, you prick,' Jon ranted at the colander, 'you might have the same face as me, but we are nothing alike! I'm a normal bloke that contributes to society, you're just an entitled little piss-fart! You heard! Piss-fart!' Foam dribbled down Jon's lower lip.

Jimmy recoiled, looking at the Prophet. 'What *have* you lot done to him now?'

'Nothing!' the Prophet squealed. 'He was like this when I found him.'

'Jon, do you remember what happened?' Jimmy asked carefully.

'No idea,' he said. Then he froze, his eyes blazing. 'Not you again! You can piss *right off*!'

He pointed a finger at Jimmy's face.

'… who?' Jimmy ventured.

'*Him*,' he spat. He was glowering at the colander again. 'He's been a git ever since I woke up.'

'Yes,' said Jimmy, 'you've just said that—'

'And the same to you, mate!'

'I see,' Jimmy said. He turned to the Prophet again. 'So what happened as far as we know?'

The Prophet relayed the story as Erik entered the kitchens with a big bag.

'I think he hit his head on a tree root on the way down,' he finished, directing the comment to Erik.

'Okay,' Erik said curtly, kneeling at Jon's side. 'Does he have any long-term medical conditions?'

'Just the precognition, I think,' said Jimmy.

Erik frowned. 'The which?'

'He can see into the future.'

Erik sat in silence for a moment. 'Looks like we're going with that, then,' he said finally. 'Keep his head still and try to get him to shut up a minute, will you?'

Jimmy stood back with his arms crossed as the Prophet complied.

Erik peered into Jon's eyes. 'Is there any pain at the moment?'

'There's a pain in my arse standing at the counter behind Jimmy,' Jon spat, pointing. 'He's been a git ever since I woke up.'

'And where did he come from?'

'Dunno. What happened? I was in the forest a minute ago.' Jon looked puzzled.

'You hit your head. What were you doing in the forest?'

'Dunno. Oh, not you again,' he groaned. He glared at the colander once again. 'You can piss *right off*!'

'That's about as much as we're gonna get from him, I think,' Jimmy said.

Jon's face blanked. 'I was in the forest a minute ago. What happened?'

'We're trying to figure that out,' Erik said, tilting Jon's head to one side to examine a cut along his hairline. 'Looks like you're concussed.'

'And the imaginary friend?' Jimmy prompted.

'No idea what the story is there. But I'll find out. Give me a minute while I stitch up the gash on his head and we'll take him to his quarters.'

'Ah,' Jimmy said, paling. 'He… doesn't have quarters here anymore.'

'Why not?'

'Well, we reckon the king… kind of wants him dead.'

Erik rolled his eyes and buried his face in his hands.

There was a tense silence for a moment.

'What happened? I was in the forest a minute ago,' Jon said, puzzled.

~

Seth sat in his quarters an hour after Qattren had deposited him home. His limbs throbbed with fatigue. Travelling to and from Magicland so much in one day made his body ache.

Though no more than the ache lingering in his chest ever since Ginny had vanished from sight.

The black fog within him returned, descending. His mother was right. Destroying the Emmettfort didn't make anything better. Ginny was still missing, likely dead. And the pain was still there, the aching emptiness. It would always be there.

Sitting in a cushioned chair by the window, Seth pressed his temple against the glass. Thick smog blanketed the remains of the marketplace. Seth was surprised to realise he didn't feel a thing. He wondered at that. Shouldn't he feel guilty or something? The loss of Ginny seemed to eclipse everything else. Everything ended when that little face vanished into the coach.

Exhaling heavily, Seth closed his eyes, willing the pain to ease just a little. He opened them again to see Adrienne standing before him.

'Hello,' he said weakly.

She smiled thinly. 'Hello.' She paused. 'You look like you could do with a hug.'

His arms went out immediately.

She collapsed into them with a sigh, perched on his lap. He buried his forehead into the crook of her neck.

'I probably wouldn't have caused all this mess,' Seth said, 'if someone had just done this earlier.'

Adrienne laughed, albeit half-heartedly.

They deflated slightly. Her arms tightened around his neck.

'How are you?' he asked.

'Tired. Always tired.'

'Me too.'

She traced his collar. 'Is he gone?'

'I don't know. There were so many people. I didn't see him when I went in, but he could have been hiding, or fled. I hope he's dead now.' He hesitated. 'I'm a monster, aren't I?'

She pulled away slightly to meet his gaze. 'I think you have every right to be after what he's done.'

He tugged on a lock of her hair. 'I'm sorry about Archie.'

Her expression darkened. 'It was supposed to be me.'

'It was supposed to be nobody,' he said in a growl. 'She had no right to do that.'

'Yes she did,' Adrienne said. 'Something like this was bound to happen the moment I came back to you, but I did it anyway.'

'It was my fault. You told me to piss off and I pushed you anyway.'

'It was never a hard no.' Adrienne turned to the window. 'I keep thinking about that day. The day they gave him to… you know,' she finished weakly.

Seth gave her a squeeze. 'I know.'

'Our lives would have been so much easier if...' She frowned down at the forecourt, cutting across herself. 'What's he doing down there? He's running in circles like a headless chicken.'

Seth followed her gaze.

Erik jogged to the front turret, stopped halfway to shout something unintelligible at the keep before returning in exasperation.

'I'm going to find out,' Seth said, sliding out from beneath her.

~

IV

Isla hurried back to the kitchen, washing basket still in hand. 'The king's coming!' she said. 'He spotted Erik, he's coming downstairs.'

'For Christs' sake!' Jimmy exclaimed. 'What are we going to do with him now?'

Jon sat on the stool, both hands aimed at the colander in an everchanging array of distasteful hand gestures.

Mort stood there, arms crossed with a look of amusement. 'You realise how much of a berk you look to them right now?'

'It makes me feel better,' Jon seethed.

'Look, just shove him in the pantry,' Isla said.

'No, he'll make too much noise effing and blinding at the cutlery,' Jimmy said, hands behind his head. 'We need somewhere to hide him.'

Mort tutted. 'See the fuss you've made? We wouldn't have this problem if you had a manor in the countryside like you were s'posed to—'

Jon screeched at him.

Jimmy cut him off via a hand over his face.

Seth and Erik reached the kitchen entrance together, from opposite ends. Erik froze. Seth frowned at him. 'What *is* the matter with you?'

Erik's mouth hung open, grasping for words. Finding none, he instead bolted inside.

Seth frowned and followed him.

A blanket of silence fell on the noisy kitchen. The usual bustle ground to a halt, the entire workforce still. Seth hovered in the centre of the room, his hands on his hips.

'Where's Jimmy?' Seth asked in a low voice.

A crash and a curse floated out from the pantry. Jimmy emerged, looking slightly bedraggled. 'Afternoon, sir,' he said, faltering.

Erik appeared at Jimmy's heels, looking frightened.

Seth's eyes darted around the kitchen.

Every eye he met was wide with fear. The limbs accompanying them twitched.

'What's everyone in a fluff about?'

They flinched, as though he had shouted instead of asking in a calm, soft voice.

His eyes met Jimmy's. 'Is someone unwell?'

'Er, yes, sir.' He wrung his hands and glanced at Erik. 'Nothing to worry about, just someone's time of the month.' He laughed shortly.

Seth's eyes darted about again. Every female in the kitchen was over the age of fifty – apart from Isla, who was pregnant. 'Who?'

Jimmy froze. '… me.'

Seth's brow furrowed.

Jimmy swallowed.

'You're,' Seth said, slowly, 'having a menstrual period?'

'Bloody stool, sir,' he corrected, reddening. 'I… was being humorous.'

Seth narrowed his eyes.

'My timing's off because I'm worried, sir,' Jimmy said. He twisted the edge of his jerkin between his fists.

Seth eyed this tic with a quizzical expression. 'Are you hiding something from me?'

Every feature of Jimmy's face widened. 'No,' he trilled. 'Unless you mean the stool—'

'Jon hasn't appeared suddenly, has he?'

The blood drained from Jimmy's face. 'Nope. Haven't seen him. Been pre-occupied with Erik and the, erm… rest of it.' He pointed at his trousers, hoping to evade probing questions.

Seth lifted an eyebrow. 'Fine.' He made to leave and turned back. 'I don't judge, you know,' he said nonchalantly. 'You can sleep with whoever you want, male *or* female. It's not a criminal offence.'

Jimmy glanced at Erik and squeaked. Both of them turned purple.

'Thank you, sir,' said Jimmy, his voice breaking. 'That's reassuring to hear.'

Seth nodded. 'As you were. Preferably *away* from the food, though.'

'Right you are, sir,' Jimmy said weakly.

Seth pivoted and swept out. Quickly.

'Never,' Jimmy hissed at Erik, 'speak of this!'

'Oh, don't worry, I'm speechless after that performance,' Erik said, fuming.

~

The Bastard materialised with a flourish. 'You called?' He recoiled at the sight of Marbrand's glower. 'Well, that's a fine welcome, isn't it?'

The Marbrands' sitting room bathed in an amber glow. The fire roaring beside them, they and the Bastard congregated in the lounge as dusk fell outside.

'We're here on business,' Marbrand said curtly. 'So don't get comfortable there.'

This he said as the Bastard reclined on his favourite armchair.

The Bastard sighed, hopping off. 'If you insist,' he said, grouchily. 'What do you want, then?'

'I've done enough favours for you,' said Despina. 'Now it's your turn to do one for me.' She told him what she needed him to do.

The Bastard shrugged. 'Can do.'

She blinked. 'Really? Just like that? No coercion, no cajoling, nothing?'

'We're friends, remember?' he said. 'I am capable of being nice to people, you know. That and it serves my purposes. So long as you allow me one boon in return.'

'Oh God, here we go,' Marbrand said, rolling his eyes.

'I want to visit my brother. At least once a week.'

Despina blinked. 'Why?'

'Because he's… small and cute and he gave me a cake once, alright?' he ranted speedily. 'It's none of your business why, I just want to be able to see him regularly. Is that quite alright with you?'

'Quite,' Despina said mildly.

'Good! Let's get on with it then.' And he punched her in the face.

She found herself lying on her back. Her father and the Bastard stared down at her from either side.

'Impressive,' Marbrand said. 'She looks nothing like herself.'

'That was the idea,' the Bastard said wryly. He swung his gaze back to Despina. 'Your name is Isla now. You were until very recently working as a scullery maid in the kitchens: she'll know the face, she's been here donkey's years. You,' he pointed at Marbrand, 'will be taking in the real Isla when she starts getting contractions this evening.'

'And how can you time that so accurately?'

The Bastard gestured down at himself. 'Demi-god?'

Marbrand swung his head from side to side in concession.

The Bastard's gaze returned down to Despina. 'You're looking for a new start in life after recently losing your new-born son. Remember the child, because she *will* check with her servants. And don't forget to tell Russell to call you by the new name: he'll recognise you just fine. He'll play along without any fuss, he isn't very inquisitive.'

'Thank you,' Despina said, prodding her eyelid. 'But was the punch in the eye necessary?'

'No, I just had some frustration to release,' the Bastard said, wringing his fist in one hand.

~

Cienne sat in the darkening throne room, on Seth's seat.

Servants hid now. The braziers sat empty along the walls, dead ash where flames would usually blaze at this time of the evening. The stained glass, usually bright shades of purple and red, bathed the hall in the only remaining light, a dull grey mist. She recalled a bright summer day as Ginny played here, her hair turning blond to pink to blond as she ran in and out of the rays from the windows. It hit her then. She would never see that little girl again.

Cienne felt like she ought to be crying, but she was just too exhausted.

Thumping from her left alerted her to the servants hauling her luggage down the stairs. Planting both palms on the arms, she heaved herself from the throne, lethargic. Her coach would be waiting outside the hunter's gate as arranged. It was about time she got there before Russell's new nanny lost her nerve and deserted her new position.

Smoothing her fur coat – her father had sent it over with Qattren, presumably because Seth was still too angry to give it to her himself – over a thick woollen gown, Cienne strode out of the hall, boots clicking on the flagstones.

Snow fell softly again. It crunched beneath her feet as she alighted from the porch. She halted by the gate with a faint smile.

A girl with red hair held Russell by the hand.

'Hi!' he exclaimed, with a grin.

'Hello, sweetie.' Cienne threaded her fingertips through his hair, running them back and forth over his scalp. 'Are you ready to go?'

He nodded enthusiastically.

She turned to the new nanny. 'I'm so sorry, what's your name again, my love?'

'Isla, your highness,' Despina lied.

Cienne smiled and entered the coach.

Despina – or Isla, now – crouched to meet Russell's eyes. 'Remember.'

'Always use the new name,' he repeated. 'And don't tell Mummy.'

Despina touched his nose affectionately.

He grinned at her, her face familiar to him as always.

They followed her into the coach and rolled into the night.

~

Jon's eyes fluttered open. 'What happened? I was in the forest a minute ago.'

'I'm gonna kill him in a minute,' Jimmy exclaimed.

Jon shot him a bemused glance and looked around. He was in a small bedroom with wood-panelled walls, similar to his own but furnished with an extravagancy Mort approved of. Burgundy curtains cast the room into dim red light, which was fine by Jon. His head felt as if it was splitting down one side.

Knowing that sitting upright was likely to cause more damage, Jon stayed lying down, the duck-down pillows and mattress reminding him vaguely of his childhood, for some reason.

'Where am I?' he asked, feeling relaxed.

Jimmy winced. 'You've hit your head. Erik reckons you had concussion.'

'That sounds lovely.' Jon wracked his brains. 'Still can't remember what happened, though.' He scratched the back of his neck and was bemused to find he was suddenly wearing a pink woollen cardigan. 'Where am I exactly?'

'You seem a lot better now,' said Raphael Emmanuel III, standing behind Jimmy. He turned to Jimmy in earnest. 'Doesn't he look better?'

'Much less confused,' Jimmy agreed.

'Well, good,' Jon said, 'but you never said where it is we—'

'You've missed a *lot*,' the Prophet continued.

'An awful lot,' Jimmy added.

'Yes, but where—'

'Yeah, you'll never guess what Seth's done now,' Jimmy added, a tad too enthusiastically.

'Jimmy, where am I?' Jon said sharply.

Jimmy gulped. And told him.

Seconds later, the front door burst open. Jon leapt out. Jimmy and Raphael grabbed an arm each, leaving him dangling over the porch. 'LEMME OUT!!'

'No!'

'I'll die in here!'

'No you won't, you're an adult now,' Jimmy said from his left.

'I'm still small,' Jon said weakly.

The two pulled him inside. Jon's heels squeaked against the laminate flooring.

'I can't be in here,' Jon said desperately, writhing in their grasp.

'Are you serious?' Jimmy exclaimed, twisting him around. 'Have you *seen* the carnage in Castlefoot Market? You're staying here, where he can't find you.'

'I am not staying here,' Jon declared.

'Yes, you are,' Jimmy said firmly. 'You don't seem to realise how bad things have gotten.' A bead of sweat plummeted from Jimmy's brow. 'I'm *scared* of him, Jon. Do you know how ridiculous that sounds? I'm *frightened* of *Seth Crey*. I never thought I'd say that sentence with sincerity.'

'What were you thinking?' Jon shrilled. 'Bringing me to a monastery! You know what happened to me at the church, you *know* I can't stand it here!'

'It's the only place Seth would never think to look,' Jimmy explained. 'That and we had basically five minutes to find somewhere to put you, unless you'd prefer the chopping block.'

Jon shrugged violently from their grasp. 'Who lives here? I want names, details—'

'Just me and Father Hope,' Raphael said.

'He leaves immediately,' Jon said directly.

'Oh, he's fine, we had a drink last night while you were asleep,' Jimmy said flippantly. 'I doubt he has any interest in buggering anything, much less *you.*'

'He leaves immediately,' Jon said forcefully.

Jimmy scoffed. 'He's harmless. He wouldn't hurt a fly.'

'He *leaves immediately*,' Jon said through clenched teeth.

'But—'

'You wouldn't want me to stab someone, now would you, Jimmy?'

Jimmy exhaled. 'Fine,' he adhered, with no intention of adhering to anything.

Jon glowered at the two of them. 'I'm going to bed,' he announced, pivoting. 'And if anyone thinks of following me there—'

'You overestimate the sex appeal of a shrill chicken farmer on the average human,' Jimmy said with a grimace. 'You'll be fine, we'll stay in the kitchen if you wish.'

'Good. Do that, then.' He returned to bed – or at least got halfway before turning back to ask Raphael for directions.

Lying awake as the afternoon waned to evening, Jon wished his knife could be put to good use as Mort micro-examined every inch of the bedroom in disdain.

'Talk about ratty,' he commented, prodding a curtain with his sleeve pulled over his index finger.

'Speaking of rats,' Jon muttered.

Mort squinted at him. 'What's with you?'

'Oh, nothing,' Jon said wryly, 'just a bit miffed at having me head caved in and being shoved into a paedophile factory.'

Mort shrugged, turning back to his examination.

Jon laid back and tried to relax. *All church places look the same*, he thought hatefully, glaring at the riveted ceiling and each curtain. His headache pounded on, and not just on account of his surroundings.

'Why are you here?'

Mort shrugged again. 'I've always been here. On the inside. Usually screaming at you to move back into the castle and have a proper bath.'

'Yes, but why are you being more... vocal?'

'Because you've buggered everything up, haven't you?'

Jon frowned. 'This isn't my fault.'

'Yes, it is,' he said, almost cheerfully. 'You go to all the trouble of changing your name and depriving yourself of your birth right to stop getting into trouble, and by the end of it, you're on the run, your cousin's kid is missing because of you, and the entire world's about to end. You didn't half fluff that up, did you?'

'How is being a nobleman going to make any difference?'

'It isn't. It would have before, but not now. If you'd been a nobleman, you could have stopped all of this a long time ago.'

'How?' Jon exclaimed.

'By stopping King Theo from going outside with Seth Crey.'

Jon made a face. 'That's not my job.'

'Then whose is it?'

'*Not mine*,' he emphasised. 'I'm not following some silly plot of the church, not after what they did. Let some other mug be the Knight of Wotsit.'

'Why?' Mort pestered. He leaned over Jon's bed with his hands on his hips. 'I'm fed up of you forcing us into destitution.'

'Really,' Jon said, bored.

'We're royalty!' he exclaimed, throwing his arms into the air. 'We are the nephew of King Theo Crey! Is the nephew of King Theo Crey going to sit in a ratty cottage feeding stupid chickens his entire life? No! He's going to go back to his castle, tell Seth Crey where to stick his murdering backside and take our life back!'

Jon nodded. 'Seems reasonable so far.'

'Exactly! Get your clothes on, we're going straight to the castle and we're gonna take back our throne.'

'And *there's* the catch,' Jon drawled. He folded his arms over the edge of his blanket.

'Come on, get dressed, there's a good lad. We have a kingdom to rule!'

'Nope,' Jon said, shimmying deeper into the covers. 'I'm not going down that route, you can forget it.'

'Why not?' Mort demanded. 'Honestly, you can see why they call you mad, can't you? You're really going to stand by and let *Seth Crey* rule Adem for the next four decades?'

'Yeah, he's not so bad,' Jon said lightly. 'He's just having a hard time of it lately.'

'Yeah, and who isn't?' Mort said spitefully. 'You can tell him to get over it before we chop his head off. He thinks he's got problems? Was he violated from age five to eight? Did he have to fend for himself in the forest for three weeks as a little kid? Does he work in the kitchens now because he's too scared of something horrific happening to him in his own home? Nope, he didn't. So why should we have pity for him?'

'Just because bad shit happened to you,' Jon said calmly, 'doesn't mean the shit that's happening to other people is less important.'

'Maybe if he dealt with it better,' Mort said in defiance, 'people might have more sympathy for him. As it is, he'll have to go.'

'Because killing anyone not having as hard a time of it as you is the best way to deal with trauma.' Jon froze. Trauma. Of course.

'It makes me feel better,' Mort said, echoing Jon's earlier sentiment. Though Jon felt putting rude hand gestures at someone was a far less dangerous form of catharsis. 'Puts things into perspective for them. Now, let's get going before Jimmy comes in and changes your mind.'

Jon huffed. 'Fine, if it'll shut you up.' He flung himself out of bed.

The place was dark and deserted. Jimmy and Raphael had gone to bed ages ago. The two crept into the main chapel, where the front entrance was situated.

'I say we strike now, while he's asleep,' Mort whispered, despite lacking the capacity to be heard by anyone but Jon anyway. 'He'll be spark out after his busy week. We'll have his head off and out of the building before anyone realises anything's amiss.'

'Good idea,' Jon said. 'D'you know, I vaguely recall there being some kind of ceremonial sword, actually.'

'Ceremonial sword?' Mort said with a frown.

'Yeah, for knighting templars or some such. They'll have one in every church, won't they? In the vestry, probably.'

'Would have been nice to know about this when Father Giery was on the warpath,' Mort said irritably, leading the way.

'Well, I didn't know about it then, did I?' Jon whispered hotly.

Mort opened the vestry door and poked his head inside. 'Whereabouts is it, then?' he said. 'I can't see any—'

Jon shoved him inside.

'Wait!' Mort yelled.

Jon slammed the door and locked it.

Mort threw himself against the other side.

'LET ME OUT!! YOU CAN'T LOCK ME IN HERE, NOT HERE, ANYWHERE BUT HERE—'

Jon leaned himself against the door by one shoulder. 'I can and I have!' he said to the door. 'And you can bloody well stay there!'

Fists hammered on the door.

'You can knock that off for a start,' Jon said, calmly. 'When I'm ready to be angry about what happened, I'll decide how to deal with it. Conquering the world isn't for me. And you know that.'

The commotion slowly subsided. Jon lifted himself from the door gingerly.

Silence resumed in the vestry.

Jon dusted his hands off. 'That's the end of that.' He turned and went back to bed.

Happily, Mortimer Crey didn't bother Jon again.

~

V

Jimmy knocked gently on Seth's open door. 'You sent for me, your majesty?'

Seth waved him in.

The morning following the destruction of the Emmettfort dawned bright and sunny. A weak warmth came through Seth's window. He bathed in it, seated in his settee beside the window, his mind elsewhere.

Jimmy licked his lips and stepped aside. Raphael entered the room behind him. 'I've taken the liberty of replacing Jon, sir,' Jimmy said carefully. 'I hope that's alright? He's decided to take your side over religion's, for obvious reasons. Also he has decades of experience cleaning stained glass, so.'

Seth gave Raphael an uneasy glance. 'He won't... follow me to my rooms or anything, will he?'

'No, no, I've drawn up a contract,' Jimmy said, handing him a sheet of parchment. 'He's legally forbidden to come within twenty feet of you without express permission from you personally.'

'Oh. Good.' Seth scanned the contents. 'That's fine, then. Er, what did you say your name was?'

'It's just Raph now,' the man who was formerly the Prophet said. 'It's... less of a mouthful.'

'Right. Good.' Seth folded the parchment in half. 'Since I have you both here, I'll get this over with. I'm promoting you to head of council, Jimmy.'

Jimmy's eyes widened. 'Me?'

'I can't trust anyone else not to syphon the palace funds,' Seth said wryly. 'At least if you do it, it will be obvious by your extravagant taste in clothes.'

'Oh. Um... thanks. I appreciate it.'

Seth inclined his head and swung his gaze to Raph. 'So there's a butler position going. If you're interested.'

Raph curtsied. 'Certainly, your majesty. Thank you!'

Seth nodded, turning his gaze back to the window.

Raph beamed ecstatically.

Jimmy, on the other hand, looked slightly worried. 'So I take it the debt is... dealt with?'

Seth smirked slightly. 'Turns out he had a mountain of gold pieces in the bowels of the palace that would have turned Lyseria's ears green with envy. Let's just say I commandeered it in the name of war.'

Jimmy nodded.

Raph bounced on his toes, grinning. 'Do I get to wear clothes like his from now on?' He jabbed at Jimmy with the index finger of both hands.

Seth hesitated. 'Well, the dog blanket would give off the wrong kind of look, wouldn't it?'

'Indeed. Indeed. Thank you, your majesty!'

Jimmy gave Raph a sidelong glance. 'Give him a week. He'll be sick of it by then.'

Seth quirked a half-smile. 'Can I speak with Jimmy alone, please?'

Raph bowed and left.

Seth pointed at the chair tucked into the desk beside Jimmy. He sat obediently.

'Osney has agreed to meet me at Arthur Stibbons' Head again in two weeks,' Seth said. 'He's tracing Jon for me. I take it there's been no news of him in the kitchens or anything?'

'Not a word,' Jimmy lied.

Seth nodded. 'Make sure he comes straight to me if he ever shows up. I want words with him about Ginny, whether he likes it or not.'

'I'll bring him here myself if he does, sir,' Jimmy lied.

'Good.' Seth sat upright. 'Before we deal with them, I suppose we should do something about my wife.' He clicked his fingers at his manservant by the door. 'Would you send for her, please?'

Jimmy halted him with a raised hand before he could take a step. He stared at Seth, frozen. 'You... weren't informed?'

Seth frowned. 'Informed of what?'

Jimmy licked his lips again. 'She,' he said, 'left the palace last night with a number of retainers. Heading for Portabella, apparently. I thought you knew, I thought he'd sent for her or something...'

Seth simply stared at him. 'Where's Russell?'

Jimmy froze. 'I haven't seen him.'

Ice climbed up Seth's back. 'No.' He threw himself to his feet. '*No.*'

He launched himself past Jimmy and out of the door. Stumbling and sliding on the flagstones, Seth burst into Cienne's rooms, the door swinging and bouncing off the opposite wall. Empty.

He continued on to his mother's quarters. Empty.

Finally, he arrived at the children's quarters. Toys lay littered across the surface. The room hadn't been touched since Ginny's disappearance. Russell's toy castle was set up in the corner, a vast collection of wooden turrets on a little hill. Russell himself was nowhere to be seen.

Eleanor sat in front of it, on her knees, tear tracks glinting in the sunlight. Alone.

Seth collapsed onto the floor and wept.

The afternoon yawned on. It occurred to Seth, as he sat on the floor, that he owed everyone an apology. He met his mother's gaze. 'I'm sorry.'

She made no effort to move. 'You'll have to do better than that.'

Seth swallowed with difficulty. His mouth and throat were dry. He hadn't had a drink of anything all day. He slid his hands beneath him and pushed himself to his feet.

Lilly's quarters resided at the far east of the keep, the door tucked into a corner of the corridor.

Seth knocked before entering. A sure sign of a special occasion.

'Lilly?' he said gently. 'Are you here?'

These rooms were empty too.

Seth stared into space. Gone. He suddenly remembered: she had taken the navy to Mellier. She was long gone by now.

'I wish I was dead,' he said quietly.

'So do I, sometimes.'

He faced Qattren, lingering behind him.

'Where are they?' he pleaded. 'Please tell me you know.'

'Lilly's at Wakesport, waiting on the navy to collect her,' said Qattren in a soft tone. 'She'll come around. She isn't one to bear a grudge. Cienne's going home. I fear she won't be so forgiving.'

'Home?'

'To her father. Russell is with her.'

Seth swallowed. 'What about Ginny?'

Qattren looked mournful. 'I don't know.'

Tears dripped down his face again. He was too exhausted to wipe them away.

'But I'll find out,' Qattren said firmly. 'I will find who took that little girl and I will kill him myself. And I will have no remorse for it.'

Seth met her gaze. 'Do you have remorse for this?'

She paused. 'No,' she said. 'Not yet.'

'I do,' he rasped.

A distinct expression of relief passed across Qattren's face. She nodded. 'Good.' She seemed vulnerable for a moment. 'You're so much like Seb that it hurts me sometimes.'

470

Seth snorted. 'He doesn't seem the type to blub like this after a battle.'

'Oh, he did,' Qattren said with a weak smile. 'Often. Particularly during the war. He's a delicate soul, in truth.'

Seth stared at the floor behind her, vacantly.

Qattren held his elbow, squeezed it. 'Find Adrienne,' she advised. 'You've gone to enough trouble to have her. You might as well be with her.'

Seth smiled weakly. 'That's a good idea.'

~

Lilly sat at the dock, waiting. The snow had all but melted, four weeks after the Castlefoot Massacre. The usual bustle of activity flowed around her. Docks were rarely affected by court affairs. A bitter wind cut into the back of her neck. Lilly tugged her collar upright and wrapped her arms around her thick coat, her eyes on the horizon.

A fist bumped against her shoulder-blades, in a friendly way.

Lilly deflated, relieved. 'I didn't think you'd come.'

Tully hopped onto his palms and dropped onto the ledge beside her. 'Never say I passed on the chance to kick my brother's head in.'

Lilly smiled, for what seemed like the first time in years.

He eyed her, his brow slightly furrowed. 'Heard about your brother.'

'What about him?'

'That's he's gone a bit…' He twirled a finger beside his temple.

Lilly heaved a sigh. 'I suppose he has every right to,' she relented. 'I just feel like there are better ways of dealing with this.'

'He won't have to deal with it soon,' Tully said. 'We'll have her back by summer, I guarantee it.'

Lilly nodded.

They lingered in a companionable silence for a moment. It reminded her of the ship, she realised with a pang. They often bathed in the sunlight together, leaning against the rail to gaze at the empty horizon. She had missed these moments. Even the ones she's had with Si.

Si.

'Why would he take her?' she exclaimed suddenly. 'I knew he was insane, after what he did to Orl, but… a little girl? I thought he was better than this.'

'So did I,' Tully said morosely. 'Him *and* my sister.'

Anna, Lilly realised. She was Tully's sister – the tale of Si's courtship and marriage with his own adopted sister had been bandied around *the Devourer* for weeks when she was first told it. Lilly tried to pull Anna's face to mind. She hadn't been very familiar with her during her time in the keep. 'They wouldn't…?'

'Hurt her?' Tully said, rather sharply. 'Doubt it. Anna ain't like that.'

Lilly said no more on the matter, though she wasn't convinced. Another harsh wind blew from the water, carrying with it the smell of sand and seaweed. Lilly missed that smell. It smelled of home.

'What's that coming?' Tully asked.

She followed his gaze to the sea. Silhouettes appeared in the distance, specks against the west side of the horizon. Lots of them.

Lilly smiled. 'It's our lift to Mellier.'

'Looks like your brother's navy.'

Her smile turned to a smirk. 'My navy now. I liberated it.'

They watched the specks grow in size.

'I wouldn't want to be Si when that lot land on his doorstep,' Tully said, amused.

'Neither would I,' said Lilly. 'That'll learn him for crossing a Crey.'

~

Jon slipped slightly on the cobbles in his haste to reach Arthur Stibbons' Head.

'I *really* don't think this is a good idea,' Jimmy said in a pained voice. 'At least wait until this blows over.'

'The longer I hide from him,' Jon said, 'the guiltier I look. And I'm not guilty. I'll explain myself, we'll hug it out, all will be forgiven. Now calm down. You're getting funny looks, trembling like that.'

Jimmy scowled at him, following closely behind.

Osney, standing in the centre of Arthur Stibbons' Head, sweated profusely.

The cobbles were slick with ice, despite the return of the sunshine. Many of the shops surrounding him were closed, market stalls abandoned, bars locked, their doors boarded up. The blackened remains of the market on the hill nearby wrought an instant halt in customer footfall.

Despite this, a crowd was gathering. That was never a good sign.

Osney shifted on his feet, his patent leather high-heeled clogs clacking on the cobbles. The growing throng began to part at the back. Crey household guards reached the head of the street, green banners fluttering.

Osney's eyes involuntarily began to widen.

The guards parted a foot away from Osney, revealing Seth Crey.

'Good morning, your majesty,' Osney said in a whisper. His voice could go no louder than that. 'Alas, I have no word of Mortimer, despite my best efforts. I will return to the investigation as soon as we adjourn here.'

'That's going to be a problem.'

A dozen spear-tips emerged, halting a mere foot from Osney's face, in all directions.

Osney swallowed. 'S-sir?'

'You have some crimes to atone for,' Seth said. He clicked his fingers.

A chopping block was deposited between them. Osney's eyes traced the curvature of the top and followed the black dribbles falling down the—

Osney slammed his eyes closed.

'Crime number one,' Seth announced. 'Syphoning huge amounts of money from the royal coffers to put towards an extravagant manor without prior permission. That was strike one.'

Osney trembled violently. Pins and needles swept across his arms and legs.

'Crime number two – attacking the king's mistress in 1365 and resulting in the miscarriage of her child.' Seth's eyes burned at this one. 'Strike two. I've been biding my time with this one.'

Moisture streamed down his legs, to Osney's humiliation.

'Crime number three.' Seth leaned on his knees, looking up into Osney's downturned face. 'Harbouring and/or failing to disclaim the whereabouts of his son from the authorities and hindering questioning on the abduction of my daughter.'

'I don't know where Mortimer is,' Osney wept. Until suddenly he did.

Mort—*Jon's* face appeared in the throng, at the back. He seemed confused.

'M—Juh—suh—' Osney stuttered.

'That,' Seth went on, 'would be strike three. Unless you've changed your mind?'

Osney flapped his mouth for a moment, unable to slot his words into order.

Seth stepped forward. 'Tell me where Jon is,' he said. His soft voice carried across the empty square. 'And both strikes will be cleared permanently. You will walk away from this square an absolved man, your station and titles intact. Do not tell me where Jon is…'

A man appeared, heavy execution axe in hand.

Seth's gaze flicked from the axe back to Osney. '… and we proceed with the execution.'

Osney urinated again. The smell permeated the air now. He was sure Seth could even smell it.

Jon gaped up at them, his mouth ajar.

Osney met his gaze. Every wrong he had dealt that boy ran through his mind at high speed. Shame laid heavy punches every step of the way. Osney's eyes fluttered shut. 'I'm sorry, Jon,' he mouthed to Jon.

Pain spread across Jon's face.

Osney opened his eyes, a decision made. This time, his voice carried over the square. 'I don't know where Jon is.'

Jon frowned up at him.

So did Seth. 'Right.'

The executioner planted a hand on Osney's shoulder-blades. Fear shivered out from that point, like spiders crawling across his skin. He collapsed to his knees and was pushed face-down into position.

He saw nothing but the cobbles under his face. He thought he heard Jon's voice cry out distantly, but he couldn't be sure. His blood ran too fast through his ears for him to make it out.

A cool line appeared on the back of his neck. Lining up his swing.

Hot breath crept into his ear. Seth. 'Last chance.'

Osney caught a whiff of bonfire on him, a smoky musk. He had a feeling that would be a permanent element of Seth's being from now on. A new trademark.

The duke's decision resolved. 'I don't know.'

The smell left as abruptly as it had arrived. He had stalked off.

474

The end came quick and hard.

Jon watched his father's blood run thickly down the cobbles, pouring between each brick and pooling in each tiny pothole. It seemed an endless amount of blood for one human being.

A white coldness seeped into his veins. He recognised this, Jon realised. It had happened twice before: once when his mother died and again, much later, when King Theo had. His eyes travelled, of their own accord, back up to his father's neck.

Jon turned on one heel and walked away. 'Let's get back to the monastery.' Jon never thought he'd say that phrase willingly.

Jimmy scuttled at his heels. 'I am so sorry,' he said helplessly.

Jon didn't say anything for a moment. 'Did he tell you he was going to do that?'

'No! I would have told you, honestly, he—'

'You've nothing to be sorry for, then.' A monotone.

They walked down the length of Arthur Stibbons' Torso together, side by side.

'D'you,' Jimmy faltered, 'do you wanna talk about it?'

'Not really.' Monotone again. 'Think I need to just… sit with it on my own for a bit.'

'Of course.' A pause. 'You know where I am. When you're ready.'

Jon met his gaze. 'Thanks,' he said, almost brightly.

Jimmy simply nodded and followed him back to the monastery.

~

VI

Seth strolled down the road where Archie Hart died.

Adrienne sat cross-legged outside the door, in the black stain that had spread from the four houses to the roadside. She stared vacantly into the doorway. The door itself had crumbled into splinters in the blaze.

Seth watched her from afar from a moment before approaching and dropping himself beside her. He took her hand in his own, laced their fingers together. She put her head against his shoulder and sniffed. Tears seeped through his shirt.

The air felt stained. Ash and smoke still lingered faintly on the breeze, as if the flame were still alight somewhere, kindling quietly. Adrienne looked into the top window, where her family had died together.

'I'll arrange for him to be buried, with our son,' Seth said quietly.

Adrienne sucked in a breath. 'And Howie?'

Seth paused for a moment. 'Him as well. They should be together. Where you can grieve in peace.'

She sandwiched his hand in both of her own. 'You wouldn't mind?'

'No,' he whispered. 'Of course not. They're your family. And you're *my* family now.'

A whine escaped in between two sobs. 'What am I going to do?' The timbre of her voice left a crack in his chest.

'You're coming home with me,' Seth said firmly. 'Cienne is gone. Lilly is gone. My mother's sulking, but can get on with it. I'm recognising you as my new partner. I'm looking after you – for real this time. I'm making up for the four years they stole from us.'

The Bastard's spirit lingered on the other side of the road, his hands in his pockets. He gazed at his mother in silence – particularly her expression. It betrayed a distinct lack of confidence.

'Enjoy it while it lasts,' he said softly.

～

Qattren returned to her quarters.

The tranquillity of her palace was startling after the taut atmosphere of Adem in general. Faeries bustled to and fro on various duties, content and unperturbed. A servant lingered, running a cloth down the ornate furniture in her study until Qattren dismissed her with a wave.

Brightly coloured birds greeted her, writhing for space above the marble panelling spanning the bottom half of each wall. Kicking off her shoes, she stalked down the lush amber carpet, running a hand across the painted plaster.

She might as well enjoy her home now. After this latest atrocity, she may well never see the light of day again. She traced the brush strokes travelling from each feather to another with a sigh. She dropped herself into a nook built into the wall, to a cushioned chair set between three bookcases.

Her fingertips brushed the chain around her neck, automatic. She pulled the jewel free, traced each facet. She summoned a blue flame, which caressed it.

Geldemar materialised.

'Are you alright?' he asked in concern. 'You only ever summon me in an emergency. What is it?'

Qattren met his gaze. 'I would like to see Seb again. To hear why he wanted me to do this.'

Geldemar frowned slightly. 'To do what?'

A similar frown marred Qattren's brow. 'What?'

'I don't know what you're talking about. What do you mean, you want to see Seb? His tomb?'

Qattren blinked firmly. 'I want to see Seb. He came by the other day, to make me help Seth.'

Geldemar's face softened. 'Qat, he didn't.'

Her frown deepened. 'What do you mean, he didn't?'

'He's dead, Qat. He's been dead for over twenty years.'

Shock trickled down her limbs in waves. 'He isn't dead. We spoke to him, you were there. You and the Bastard.'

'The which?'

For all his concerned glances, Qattren wanted to punch him in the face. 'The Bastard,' she emphasised. 'Seth's undead bastard son.'

Geldemar shook his head, his brow turned upward in the middle. 'Qat, are you alright?'

'I'm alright!' she exclaimed. 'I'm currently wondering if you're alright, since you don't seem to recall two extremely familiar people!'

'Qat, I do recall those people,' he said patiently. 'They're both dead. I think there's some misunderstanding.'

Qattren's eyes narrowed. 'Why are you lying to me?'

Geldemar shook his head. 'I'm not. Qat, you're not well. Come with me to our domain, we'll look after you and try to figure out what's happening.'

'You're lying. You were there, you and the Bastard and Seb. You all told me to help Seth destroy Emmett and his palace.'

Geldemar's eyes widened. 'You did what? How? How did I not know

477

about this? When? When was this?'

'Two weeks ago!'

Geldemar stared at her, stricken. 'Qat, what have you done?'

Qattren's vision started to waver. Fear spiralled over her body. It never happened? She imagined him. He never existed. The Bastard never existed.

It was all in her head.

'Get out,' she said briskly.

Geldemar hesitated. 'I don't want to leave you on your—'

'GO!' she howled.

Geldemar backed away, hands raised. 'I'm coming back in an hour to check on you,' he said. 'Please don't do anything silly.' He dissipated into Sal'plae.

Qattren stared despairingly into space.

Geldemere watched her normally firm sense of self crumble. 'Sorry, Qat,' he whispered, fading into the other realm, the realm of Salator Crey. 'It's you or us.'

~

Father Hope strode up the path to Creys' Keep before halting to adjust his crotch. Trousers, he decided, were the bane of human existence.

Darkness fell over the keep in a wave of blue, the frost glowing on the grassy plains. Father Hope followed Jimmy's instructions to the rear of the keep, stopping occasionally to tug on various elements of his jerkin and breeches, bought in a hurry and poorly measured.

He rounded the corner to find a young man facing the back wall with a young woman pinned against it. Hope collided with them and squealed.

'Sorry! Sorry, don't mind me, just heading to the—' Another, familiar squeal stopped him in his tracks. 'Is that Raphael?'

'Avert your eyes this very instant!' Raphael Emmanuel III shrieked.

Father Hope complied, covering his face with his hands. 'Averted, averted!' he assured Raph. 'I hardly recognised you under all that gold thread.'

'What are you even doing here?' Raph howled.

Hope peeked at them.

Raph's arms were wrapped around the waist of a young woman with amber hair—

'Is that Sister Sarah?' Hope asked in interest.

'Do not speak of this to anyone!' Slight rustling sounded as the two adjusted their attire. 'It is very early days,' Raph continued, 'and we still need to break it to our parents that we aren't people of the cloth anymore, and our vow of celibacy is void now on orders from the king, so it's fine now, so, so... there.'

Sarah hid her face in Raph's collar.

'But you're the Prophet,' Hope said mildly. 'What happened to saving the world? You were quite obsessed with it once upon a time.'

Raph yanked his trouser strings up and knotted them over his jerkin. 'Yes, well, I, was... mistaken, it seems. You may leave now.'

'Mistaken? Just like that? What about your calling?'

'I never had a calling, alright? It was, I, see—' Raph huffed. 'I made it up,' he relented. 'Jon the Doorman was the Prophet all along. I just... followed his lead. With his prophecy. Which I stole. And... added to. From my imagination.'

Hope glowered at him. 'You caused a holy war for nothing?'

'No! My uncle told me to! His Eminence, he got it into his head that it was me who wrote it, and he made me write the whole thing out more coherently and had it made into a lovely illustrated manuscript and since it meant I wouldn't be left alone with Father Giery like the others, I went along with it. I was going to be next, you know,' he said miserably. 'I had to protect myself. By pretending I was the Prophet.'

Hope gave him a wry side-glance. 'Were the amateur theatrics necessary?' He put his arms in the air in a 'V' shape in demonstration. 'You know – "Godly Enlightenment!!" and all that?'

'It wasn't amateur,' Raph said haughtily. 'It fooled the Archpriest, what more do you need?'

Hope tutted audibly. 'The dishonesty,' he said, sighing theatrically. 'Unbelievable. From a man of the cloth. Absolutely disgraceful.'

Raph glared at him. 'You never answered my question. Why are you here?'

'Jimmy sent me to the palace to fetch some cream cakes from the pantry,' Hope said. 'For poor Jon, after his bereavement this morning. There are some nice custard ones he likes, that ought to make up for being put into hiding because of this thieving imposter here—'

'Fine,' Raph said with a pained expression, 'I'll bring them home later, just leave. It's getting awkward.'

'Much obliged. Have a good evening!' Hope beamed at them and gave them a nod before leaving.

Truth be told, he was glad Raph had given up the priesting lark. His mental health was coming leaps and bounds and besides, witch-burning lost its charm after the first four goes.

~

Elliot's gaze fell on the chest of drawers beside his bed. Leaves and branches flowed smoothly across the top and sides, carved in high relief into the thick oak. The front of each drawer bore motifs of Elliot's childhood – buns and apples and buttercups, each rendered in breath-taking detail. Elliot's entire savings had gone on it – i.e., the chest of gold Seth Crey had gifted him three years prior for saving his family's lives. And it was worth it. Elliot had sworn fealty to Archibald Hart from that day on, vowing to buy only handcrafted Hart furniture from now on. He hadn't had a chance to buy another piece.

Elliot's eyes roved over it. He gave the top of the chest a loving pat.

'Mind how you go, mate,' he said to Archie quietly.

The rest of his room was quite plain. A cot in the corner of the room was the only other furniture in his quarters – 'I'm not shelling out for any other furniture,' Marbrand had told him and the other night staff sternly when they moved in. Not that they needed it. Marbrand had declared his living room to be a common area for all night staff, provided all drinking occurred outside of the premises.

Elliot lifted himself from his cot and made for said common area.

Marbrand reclined in an armchair in front of the blazing fireplace, a letter open in his hands.

'How's she getting on?'

Marbrand looked up. 'She's arrived safe. Queen doesn't suspect a thing.'

'Good.'

Marbrand folded it carefully and set it onto the table.

'Russ,' Elliot said with a hesitant pause. 'You know Archie, the bloke in the fire? There's something I should probably...'

Pain crossed Marbrand's features. He paled significantly.

'You alright?' Elliot said in concern.

'Fine, fine,' he said distantly. He ran his palm up and down his left side. 'Heartburn, that's all. What were you saying?'

Elliot simply watched him in concerned silence.

Marbrand's hands rifled across the table for his pipe. He filled it with trembling hands and lit it, holding it close. His face was grey.

Elliot watched tendrils of smoke trickle into the air between them and picked up the distinct smell of cooked liver. His funny weed from the Dead Lands smelled like that.

Marbrand instantly relaxed.

A tense silence ensued for a moment longer before Elliot gathered the presence of mind to reply.

'Nothing,' he said. 'Doesn't matter.'

~

EPILOGUE

weat poured down Si's back. Humidity pounded onto him, the gaping doors and windows in futile wait for a breeze. Amber light bathed the Bastard's Bed & Board in hot waves. He paused for a moment to gaze at the piles of plates and cups left to go. *That's the afternoon by the looks of it*, he thought with a sigh.

Small footsteps sounded from behind the bar at his back. He pivoted. 'You're a bit young for a punter, aren't you?'

The little girl grinned. A flowery dress in shades of lilac swung around her ankles. 'What's a punkle?'

Si cracked a smile, placing aside the glass he had been polishing. She was about three or four, tiny, blond and cheerful. She hopped to the bar on one leg, panting.

'I'm on holiday,' she announced.

'So I see.'

A pink sheen on her forehead revealed her to hail from cooler temperatures, along with a well-off Truphorian accent.

Si leaned over the bar, his arms crossed beneath him. 'Where's your mum and dad, then?'

'They at home,' she said. 'They too busy to be on holiday, because of being king and queen.'

'That's a shame,' he said, humouring her. *Kids get funny ideas*, he thought to himself. 'So if your mum and dad are king and queen, you must be a princess.'

She grinned widely. 'Yeah, I am! How did you know?'

'Educated guess,' Si said with a grin, lifting himself upright. 'You want a drink, then?'

'Yes! An orange one!'

He winked and turned to fetch her drink. 'Who are you on holiday with, then? Your big brother?'

'He my uncle,' she said. She bounded up to the bar and climbed onto a stool. 'He outside with the horseys and his girlfriend.'

'Is he a prince?' he asked idly, reaching into the cold store for a bottle of orange juice.

'No,' she said, almost sadly. 'He's just a man.'

Si shook his head in amusement. 'Doesn't he have any money?'

The girl giggled. 'We don't need money,' she said, her inflection implying the silent addition of the word 'silly'. 'I'm a princess!'

'And where are you the princess of?'

'Adem,' she said without hesitation.

'Oh yeah?' he said playfully, turning to face her. 'So how come I've never heard of you?'

'Because you never asked my name, silly!'

'So what is it?'

'Virginia Amelia Gertrude Crey of the kingdom of Adem. In Truphoria,' she rattled off speedily.

Si tilted his head to one side. 'That's… a long name.'

She grinned. 'Yep. My daddy calls me Ginny.'

Si hesitated. 'And what's his name?'

'Seth Crey.'

His eyes widened. He gulped.

That was it. There was no way a normal kid would know his name. Or be able to fabricate a name for herself that long with such conviction.

Except that there was one problem. Her only uncle was in Portabella and was known to travel only in twinkling groups of twenty. The only other man who could possibly fit that description was Si himself.

His expression became sombre. 'Who brought you here, Ginny?'

'Me.'

He tore his gaze from Ginny's.

Anna stood by the door with a young man behind her. Si's heart dropped to his stomach.

'Ginny,' she said in a kindly voice, albeit an unconvincing one. 'This is your other uncle!'

Ginny swung towards Si, her face beatific. 'Really?'

Si's mouth went dry. 'This isn't good.'

The young man behind Anna bore a remarkable resemblance to Seth Crey.

'You don't need to tell me,' said Howie.

~

Dramatis Personae, for your reading convenience

The Harts (and family friends):

Howard Rosethorn, an orphan born on the Night of Raining Thorns (see Historical Notes)

Archibald (Archie) Hart, his foster father who took him in as his carpentry apprentice

Adrienne Hart, Archie's niece and Howie's biggest admirer, training to be a surgeon and apothecary specialist

Keith Large, a friend of Archie's who runs a chain of brothels

The Faith of the Seven (who think Salator Crey is the devil):

Father George Toffer, head of the church of Stoneguard and current fugitive

The Seven Gods… or Devils, depending on your point of view:

- Geldemar, God of Greed – sometimes known as the Holy Flying Cat
- Gale, god of nature
- Theo, god of war
- Rubena, goddess of rebellion
- Fortune and Misfortune, conjoined twins of fate
- Liana, goddess of desire

The Faith of Salator Crey (who thinks the Seven are devils):

His Eminence Father Abraham Furlong, Archpriest of the Faith of Salator Crey

Father Giery, head of the chapel of Creys' Keep.

Father Hope, head of the church of Serpus

Raphael Emmanuel III, also known as the Prophet, also known as Joe-without-the-e, also known as a bit of a weirdo

Salator Crey, the world's creator

The three Christs, his demi-godly children come down onto earth to get everyone drunk or something

The Household of the Hornes

Felicity Horne (nee Emmett), Queen Dowager of Stoneguard, wife of the late Vladimir and mother to his child

Azrael Horne, King of Stoneguard upon his majority, son of Felicity and the late Vladimir

Gomez Emmett II, Felicity's brother and King Regent on Azrael's behalf

Ronald Horne, the second heir to Stoneguard and Azrael's un-nefarious uncle

Qattren Meriangue, Queen of the Forest and Ron's wife

Vladimir Horne, Ron's elder brother (deceased)

Samuel Horne, Ron's father (deceased)

Aaliyaa Horne, King Samuel's wife and mother of his sons (deceased)

The Household of the Creys:

Seth Crey, King of Adem

Cienne Fleurelle, Queen of Adem, sole heir to the throne of Portabella and

Seth's wife

Theo Crey, King of Adem and Seth's father (deceased)

Eleanor Crey, Queen Dowager of Adem and Seth's mother

Lilly-Anna (Lilly) Crey, Seth's younger sister

Stanley Carrot, Lilly's dogsbody and fellow mischief-maker

Lyseria, the family dragon

James 'Jimmy' de Vil, the family butler

Jon, previously known as Prince Mortimer Crey of the kingdom of Adem, son of the Duke of Osney and nephew of King Theo Crey

Richard Crey, Duke of Osney and King Theo's younger brother

Father Giery, the palace priest (deceased)

Sir Marbrand, head of the palace guard

Sir Elliot Maynard, second-in-command to Marbrand

Corporal Moat, the nose-picking portcullis guard

The Beults

Silas Beult, bastard brother of Seth and Lilly Crey

Tully Beult, his adopted brother

Anna Beult, Si's wife and Tully's biological sister

… and the Bastard, the undead natural son of Seth Crey and Adrienne Hart

Historical Events of Note:

The Night of Raining Thorns
1345 YM (Year of Mortality) – twenty years prior to the events of *Rosethorn*

The night the Queen of the Forest's castle was exploded by a dragon, starting a series of detonations across the Forest to the outskirts of Serpus. The name derives from the residents of Serpus, who spotted a flash in the distance and a shower of rose thorns from the foliage of the Forest, which had been blown in their direction.

It was also the night Prince Seth Crey was attacked by an assassin during the festivities for his upcoming wedding to Princess Cienne Fleurelle. Around the same time as this attack, Queen Persephone Fleurelle, Cienne's mother, was found murdered in the woods surrounding the Creys' Keep.

These events sparked a brief conflict between the Queen of the Forest and King Theo Crey, the supposed instigator of her palace's destruction, wherein she employed demonic beasts to attack his men. The conflict ended suddenly but uneasily, with both parties avoiding each other's territory and ensuring their subjects do the same.

~

The War for the Orchard
1315-1325 YM

A series of conflicts between King Seb Crey and Lord Janus Horne of Stoneguard for a series of provinces in Truphoria.

Truphoria once contained a series of provinces including Stoneguard and Adem, all ruled by the Creys – except for the forestry to the east, which had been conquered by the Queen of the Forest early in King Seb's reign. Lord Janus and a number of like-minded contemporaries decided to partition the rest of the continent into five independent countries – only for King Seb Crey to veto the decision in so flippant a fashion that it started a war – along with the then Prince Theo (aged 10) stealing an apple from King Janus's prized orchard.

One of these conflicts resulted in the involvement of the reclusive Queen of the Forest. In 1320 YM, she razed three of the six provinces in a fit of rage, consuming half of Truphoria in blue flames lasting several years afterwards. Everything from cities to countryside was completely destroyed in the blaze, including all wildlife, natural resources and people.

To hastily make amends for this catastrophe, King Seb reluctantly agreed to the partition, declaring Janus Horne King of Stoneguard, Truphoria's sole remaining province beside Adem and the Forest.

~

The Bloodthirsty Reign of King Rubeous Crey
1280-1295 YM

King Rubeous Crey came to the throne in 1280 upon the sudden disappearance of his father during Rubeous's coming of age ceremony. Following his coronation, he married thrice: to two women who lasted barely a year into the marriage before taking their own lives, and to his final wife Lilith, who bore him five children.

Only two of these lived past infancy. Using lack of dowry funds as an excuse for his actions, King Rubeous would murder and eat all children of his born female. Seb was the only child not subjected to this horror by lieu of being a viable heir.

When his younger sister was born, Lilith had a psychotic break shortly after labour. She dragged herself from the birthing bed seconds after bearing the child, hobbled to King Rubeous's chambers and bludgeoned King Rubeous to death before he had a chance to touch this newest victim.

His brother, the mild-mannered Gideon, was named King Regent until Seb, then two, came of age. He pardoned her immediately for the crime, given the tyranny of his brother's reign, and she would stand as King Seb's advisor during his reign in years to come.

Thanks for reading!

This book is self-published by Donna Shannon under the imprint DS Books. To help support the author, please leave a review on Goodreads, social media (@donnashandwich) or any online book retail outlet.

You can follow Donna Shannon on Wordpress, Goodreads, Facebook, Instagram, and Threads for all things books, art and general nonsense.

Many thanks for supporting an indie author in their journey!

www.ingramcontent.com/pod-product-compliance
Ingram Content Group UK Ltd.
Pitfield, Milton Keynes, MK11 3LW, UK
UKHW041948110325
456102UK00014B/98/J

Contents

What to Do 2

Riding a Roller Coaster 4

The First Roller Coaster 6

More Roller Coaster Ideas 8

Tall, Fast, Scary 10

Chasing Roller Coasters 12

A Taste of Terror 14

Something to Think About 16

Do You Need to Find an Answer? 18

Do You Want to Find Out More? 19

Word Help 20

Location Help 23

Index 24

What to Do

Choose a face

Remember the colour you have chosen.

When you see your face on the page, you are the LEADER.

The LEADER reads the text in the speech bubbles.

There are extra words and questions to help you on the teacher's whiteboard. The LEADER reads these aloud.

When you see this stop sign, the LEADER reads it aloud.

STOP
My predictions were right/wrong because . . .

You might need:

- to look at the WORD HELP on pages 20–22;
- to look at the LOCATION HELP on page 23;
- an atlas.

If you are the **LEADER**, follow these steps:

1 PREDICT

Think about what is on the page.

- Say to your group:

"I am looking at this page and I think it is going to be about…"

- Tell your group:

"Read the page to yourselves."

2 CLARIFY

Talk about words and their meaning.

- Say to your group:

"Are there any words you don't know?"

"Is there anything else on the page you didn't understand?"

- Talk about the words and their meanings with your group.
- Read the whiteboard.

- Ask your group to find the LET'S CHECK word in the WORD HELP on pages 20–22. Ask them to read the meaning of the word aloud.

3 ASK QUESTIONS

Talk about how to find out more.

- Say to your group:

"Who has a question about what we have read?"

- Question starters are: how…, why…, when…, where…, what…, who…
- Read the question on the whiteboard and talk about it with your group.

4 SUMMARISE

Think about who and what the story was mainly about.

When you get to pages 16–17, you can talk to a partner or write and draw on your own.

 or

Riding a Roller Coaster

I am looking at this page and I think it is going to be about… because…

Some people love to ride roller coasters. They love to be thrown from side to side, and be shaken and jerked around. They love fast roller coasters that climb up high and then suddenly drop. Their stomach **tingles** and their heart feels like it is going to jump right out of their chest. They scream, but they love the ride. And when it is over, they want to ride again.

Some people just love a taste of **terror**.

Are there any words you don't know?

Let's check: tingles

Who has a question about what we have read?

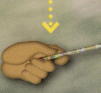

Why do you think some people like to ride roller coasters even when they are scared?

The First Roller Coaster

Many years ago in Russia, people **carved toboggans** out of ice. They sat on blankets on the cold seats and slid down mountains. The only problem was, if they wanted to ride again, the riders had to climb back up the mountain.

Then people came up with the idea of building ice slides. These were tall wooden tracks covered in sheets of ice. People climbed up steps to get to the top then rode down on toboggans.

I am looking at this page and I think it is going to be about… because…

Are there any words you don't know?

Let's check: carved

Who has a question about what we have read?

What do you think the problems might have been with ice slides?

More Roller Coaster Ideas

I am looking at this page and I think it is going to be about… because…

After the ice toboggans came wooden sleds. These were made out of **hollowed**-out tree trunks. They had runners and so they went faster.

Later on in the United States, small carts were made to carry coal on the railway lines. They were **gravity**-powered carts. They had hand brakes to make them stop. These wheeled carts started an idea. People could use them to ride down tracks. This is when the first true roller coaster was born.

Are there any words you don't know?

Let's check: hollowed

Who has a question about what we have read?

Why do you think people wanted to ride in a cart like this?

Tall, Fast, Scary

I am looking at this page and I think it is going to be about… because…

Roller coasters today get bigger and **scarier** all the time. People always want to make the fastest, the tallest or the scariest one. They want to break the **record** for the roller coaster with the most drops and **loops**.

One of the tallest and fastest rides is the Kingda Ka. It cost millions of dollars to make. People are **strapped** into trains and they must hold on tight. The ride, however, is over in just 28 seconds.

Are there any words you don't know?

Let's check: strapped

Who has a question about what we have read?

Why do you think people want to make the scariest and fastest roller coasters?

Chasing Roller Coasters

I am looking at this page and I think it is going to be about... because...

Some people like Colin McWilliam travel all over the world to ride roller coasters. Colin has ridden more than 500 different rides. He says that when you ride a roller coaster, you should look down. That way, you can feel the most speed.

Colin was one of the first people to ride a roller coaster called Thirteen. This ride is so **terrifying**, people can't ride it if they are too young or too old!

Are there any words you don't know?

Let's check:
terrifying

Who has a question about what we have read?

Why do you think people can't ride Thirteen if they're too young or too old?

A Taste of Terror

I am looking at this page and I think it is going to be about… because…

The roller coaster called Thirteen spins through a **pitch-black** forest. All of a sudden, the ground between the tracks **crumbles** and gives way.

Nicola Pickford has ridden Thirteen. "We drop like screaming stones," she said. "We fell from the top. I screamed." Nicola thinks that screaming helps.

When the ride is over, people climb out. Their legs are **wobbly**, but they feel good.

This is a taste of terror.

Are there any words you don't know?

Who has a question about what we have read?

Let's check: pitch-black

What do you think Nicola means by, "We drop like screaming stones"?

Colin McWilliam takes the first ride on Thirteen.

This page was mainly about fact fact

STOP
My predictions were right/wrong because . . .

Something to Think About

 or

A Taste of Terror

loop

dip

corkscrew

top hat

camel back

boomerang

tunnel

batwing

banked curve

something new

Imagine that you've been asked to design a scary roller coaster. What would you include in your design? Talk about your ideas with a partner, or draw them.

Do You Need to Find an Answer?

You could go to . . .

Library >

Expert >

Internet >

Do You Want to Find Out More?

You could look in books or on the internet using these key words to help you:

Kingda Ka

roller coasters

Russian ice slides

Switchback Railway

Thirteen roller coaster

Word Help

Dictionary

carved	made a shape by cutting from something
crumbles	falls apart
gravity	the force that pulls everything towards the Earth
hollowed	with the middle taken out
loops	shapes that go upside down
pitch-black	very dark
record	the best that has been
scarier	more frightening
strapped	fastened with straps

terrifying	something that is very scary
terror	very great fear
tingles	a stinging kind of feeling
toboggans	long narrow sleds without runners
wobbly	shaky

Word Help

Thesaurus

jerked	jolted, pulled, tugged
scream	yell, shriek
shaken	jiggled, trembled
strapped	buckled, fastened, fixed
taste	sample

Location Help

Where the Roller Coaster Started

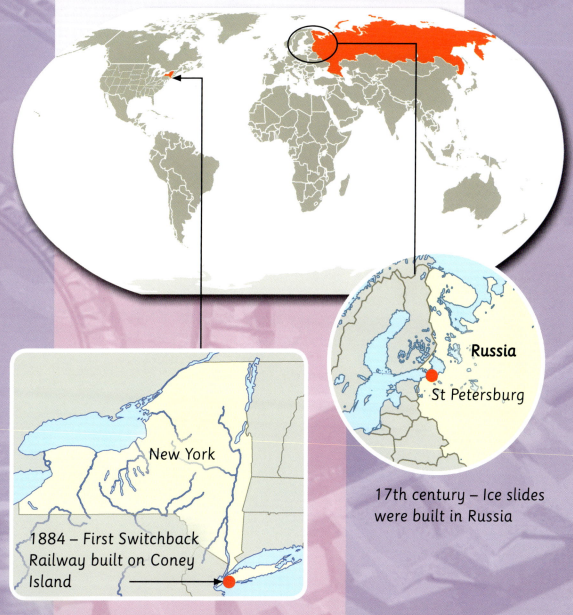

17th century – Ice slides were built in Russia

1884 – First Switchback Railway built on Coney Island

Index

Colin McWilliam..12–13, 15

drops.. 10

gravity-powered cart 8

ice slides 6–7

Kingda Ka 10–11

loops 10

Nicola Pickford.. 14

Switchback Railways....................................8–9

Thirteen roller coaster.................................. 12, 14